Do Unto Others

E.J. Blair

Published by Cross Cultural Publications, Inc.
Post Office Box 506
Notre Dame, Indiana, 46556

All of the characters in this book are fictitious, and any resemblance to actual persons, living or dead, is purely coincidental.

Cover illustration by Dorothy Blair
Cover design by Joan Addison

No part of this book may be reproduced or used, stored in any information retrieval system or transmitted in any form or by any means, electronic, mechanical, photo copying, recording or otherwise without prior written permission of E.J. Blair except in case of brief quotations embodied in critical articles and reviews.

Copyright© 2002 by E.J. Blair
All Rights Reserved
ISBN: 0-940121-75-1
Library Of Congress: 2001098370

*To Students of Medicine
Wherever They Are*

APPRECIATION

Many thanks to the staff of Cross Cultural Publications
for their help in the creation of this book.

AUTHOR'S NOTE

'Do Unto Others' is a novel and to be read in any other context would be a mistake.

The title is an inaccurate abridgement of the Golden Rule, familiar to students of both the Old and New Testaments, the Law of the Prophets, according to Matthew 7. The story attempts to deal with the practical strengths and weaknesses derived from this principle, particularly in the pursuit of one aspect of medicine, namely orthopaedic surgery, where - as with all forms of human inter-relations - it is of paramount importance to 'Do No Harm'.

All of the characters are fictitious, as are their individual parts in the incidents described. They have never existed but are real as they are composites of many people, portrayed through their passion and apathy, hopes, dreams, aspirations, good and evil, all traits common to men and women, varying only in degree.

Nor to my knowledge, is there a city called Shipton, anywhere in Canada. Of course, for reader orientation, geographical locations are reasonably correct.

As for the characters, I have tried to write about Canadians with the affection and affinity that I feel for them but without sentimentality. These feelings are also extended to Afghanistan where three times I've had the opportunity of visiting and working in a professional capacity. I have written about them as I have known them, as I have read about them, met, laughed and talked with them.

As for the national and international events, they are historically correct and are treated over a span of thirteen years, commencing in 1959. The development of orthopaedics as a sub-specialty began in earnest after World War II and is still forging ahead with technological advances. Associated changes include the introduction of a government sponsored medical payment plan and how the national control over the qualification of specialists has had to be revised.

Finally there is an moral to be drawn from the story. It is more difficult to prove a doctor with an innate personality quirk guilty of professional misconduct than one involved in social impropriety which in our permissive society is rather silly.

Prologue

1959 - Id-i-Qurban

Mahmud & Dr. Best

Mid 1959

"Loosen the tourniquet, Lil."

Dr. Best was ready to close; only a few minor bleeders to tie.

"Just a sec," his wife replied, "I must suck out his throat."

Delayed by an anaesthetic routine Best backed away from his patient and the green sheets where a pale leg emerged like a branch of driftwood. He called to the shadowy figure beyond the foot of his table, "Gimme a wipe."

Roxane moved into light shed by a portable lamp. Capped, masked and gowned in cotton she noticed his glistening brow, dampened a wash cloth in a basin of water and began to blot. A frown, shirring her forehead from the moment the operation began, faded to free a pair of dark relucent eyes. When finished she tightened his mask and stepped aside.

During this interlude two others, aseptically dressed like the surgeon, busied themselves tidying the wound. Anisa handed Sayyid a bulbous syringe loaded with sterile saline. Raking open an incision on the outside of the foot, he squirted it into the wound, flushing out foam and bits of fleshy debris easily trapped in a gauze swab. When he was satisfied the returning fluid was clear Sayyid withdrew his retractor and returned the empty syringe to Anisa. She laid it on her instrument table and discarded the gauze in a stainless steel bowl.

Beecher observed their activity. He knew little of the three young Afghans assisting other than they had advanced remarkably in the time he and Lillian had been working within the mud-brick walls of an ancient caravanserai. He knew even less of his fifteen year old patient except the youth was a distant relative, a brader-jan of the present company who periodically attended classes at the Christian school. It was more important to sort himself out medically and improve his surgical skills. Lillian being well versed in Farsi and Pashto became familiar with them.

Smiling behind his mask Best felt his coaching had produced an efficient team and he exulted in his work. Granted most of the procedures were trivial rated by Western standards nevertheless his efforts had been worth it. This very case made him particularly proud; it was his first elective operation. The other procedures: the appendectomies, the cleansing and suturing of lacerations, setting of fractures, incision and drainage of abscesses, even the two Caesarian sections were absolutely necessary. But the case before him, the white withered leg with the misshapen foot, was on his operating table by choice alone. A dazzling height! A magnificent ending to three years of material sacrifice! Whoever replaced him ought to value this gift. Tomorrow meant home to North America and the beginning of a new career.

His surveillance continued, waiting for Lil to signal clearance of the respiratory passage. The slanted eyes of Sayyid and Anisa returned his gaze. They were Hazara that much he knew, oriental seeds of Genghis Khan, while Roxane was of Persian descent. He studied her profile when she tilted her face toward the head of the table. It was as tanned as her companions but raised in relief contrasted sharply with their flatness. Except for her black eyes and obvious sexual differences her likeness to the patient was remarkable.

How the young man came by his blondness was intriguing. Having discussed the oddity, as most Afghans were dark, the Bests decided in a country where a multitude of races mingled at the crossroads of humanity the accumulation of a vast genetic pool made it possible. There was no point in hunting any further. Consequently in not delving into ancestry they didn't know their dormant case was the favoured son of a rich and powerful man, owner of an enterprising trading company and Governor of Parwan Province. It wouldn't have mattered. To them rich men, poor men, beggar men and thieves deserved the same treatment and they professed to render unto others treatment fancied for themselves.

The fully corrected foot lay bathed in a cone of light. Pleased with the apparent result, Best chuckled and bent to examine his handiwork. Hours of concentration were exacting their toll in spite of the euphoria he presently felt. His thighs, pressed against the table, ached and a cramp gathered the muscles between his shoulders. He shifted uncomfortably from one foot to the other, and to relax his stiffening knees maintained a part of his body weight through fisted knuckles on the edge of a door slab he used as an operating table. Thinking how well this improvisation had held up, Best tested its strength by bouncing his weight on it. "Good wood is scarce in Afghanistan, in fact any kind of wood. Hard to believe I won't need it again. How's it going Lil?"

"He has lots of mucus," she answered without looking up. Lillian had removed the face mask; its connecting tubes, bellows and canister were resting on a chair behind her. Her chin was pressed against the patient's forehead and she was peering down a laryngoscope. A tug upward on the handle lifted the patient's tongue and jaw. Simultaneously she directed the free end of a suction tube into the back of the throat. Glancing at a glass bottle on the floor as the spluttering intensified she was convinced more air than mucus was being drawn through the system. "You can turn off the pump Roxane," she ordered. "We must save our electricity."

Lil raised her head. Strands of mousey hair scurried off her glasses as she puffed upwards. Minimized by thick myopic lenses her pale green orbs were barely visible. Through a film of splattered mucus she eyed the surgeon. "What were you saying?"

"Release the tourniquet," Best repeated. "I'm finished except for checking the bleeders."

Lil readdressed Roxane who was crouched on the floor about to empty the suction bottle. "Hold his head," she ordered, "and keep it tilted backward, like I am."

The young woman caught on and Lillian knelt beside the table. Partly raising the darkening drape, she crawled under but could only feel around. The patient was naked save for a bicycle tube encircling his thigh and wound so tight she couldn't free a loose end.

While she struggled Beecher hollered, "For crying out loud, leave his pecker alone and get on with it. We haven't got all day!" If he presumed to be funny his voice was not in accord.

Unruffled she drew a pair of scissors from a pocket and began to snip, her small hands tugging at the rubber till it let go, thankfully before her husband came up with another crude remark. The constricting band had caused a dent in the flesh beneath. She kneaded it until there was no longer a hollow and resumed her primary duties.

Roxane was supporting the head in its extended position but disregarding Lillian's instructions was coddling it on her breast. The damp cloth used to wipe Dr. Best lay across the eyes and she was caressing the patient's hair with the tips of her fingers.

Lil sighed, slowly shook her head and said nothing. Quickly she took over, sucking out more sputum until pleased the airway was clear she lifted the washcloth and re-strapped the respirator.

Handing the laryngoscope to her assistant, she demanded, "Shine it at his eyes."

Roxane did as she was told while the anaesthetist observed the pupils more closely. They were smaller than normal and constricted further when the light was aimed at them. Touching the cornea with her coat sleeve she set off a blink reflex. Assessing the two reactions, Lil concluded the anaesthesia had diminished and proceeded to pump more gas into the lungs. After repeating this manoeuvre a few times the pupils were found to be smaller, surrounded by a circle of emerald blue, brighter than the waters of Band-i-Amir.

The eyes affected Lillian. Ether had decorticated them, turned them upward and inward, but she remembered their inquiring directness and warmth. She thought of the patient as a human being, a bronze paladin, perfectly formed in other ways. Compassion resurged and she prayed silently as she had the night before and during breakfast for success in curing the youth's affliction. She closed his eyes protectively, thinking how hardened eye specialists must become in the course of their work -

"For God's sake, Lil! Re-wrap the tourniquet!"

Her fantasy was disrupted so abruptly Lillian jumped. She cocked her head to get a better view of the patient's foot and saw blood gushing from the wound. The heel was half embedded in a heap of currant jelly. Below the table a dark wet swath soaked the sheets. Stalactites of clotting blood dripped from the dependent edge and a mound of stickiness rose from the floor.

Panic pitched his voice as Best insisted, "The tourniquet! The tourniquet! Come on Lil, get with it!"

"I can't," she replied.

"Why not?"

"I cut it."

"You cut it!" Best was dumbfounded.

"Yes, and we don't have another."

"Then grab some rope and tie it around the thigh."

Beecher glanced about the dull confining room as if the walls were caving in. There was no substitute available.

"I'll take your belt," she suggested, "It'll do."

With no alternative Beecher backed away from the table while his wife felt for the rope. Under his operating gown he wore a light blue baggy suit. She flipped up the back of the tunic, and hugging from behind found a knot in front of his voluminous trousers. Undoing it, she whipped the rope through copious pleats.

His pants fell, mopping the sticky floor as Best trampled savagely to free his feet.

"How's that?" Lillian asked, when she had fastened the rope securely to the patient's thigh.

"It's not tight enough!" Beecher complained, and passed her the wooden handle of a chisel, "Slide this under the rope and twist it."

"Okay now?" she asked after a suspenseful moment.

As if anything louder than a whisper would produce more bleeding Beecher murmured, "I think so."

"Why the blood?" Lillian queried, reappearing from under the drape.

"I'm not sure. Much more than I expected; too much for cut bone. If it's coming from a vessel I can't tell. The toes didn't turn as pink as I'd like when you removed the tourniquet and they're still pale. As the collateral circulation seems intact, I think I'll close the wound."

The bleeding slowed and stopped. The rope was removed and the incision sutured. Best, happy with the position of the foot, applied a cast.

"Sayyid," he ordered, "Get Hayabillah and take this guy to the private room. Make sure the foot of the bed is elevated and put him on intravenous chloramphenicol. I'll check him later."

Hayabillah acted as an orderly when not herding the villager's goats. He had been squatting outside and appeared, upon hearing his name.

The boys placed a saw horse adjacent to each end of the table and spanned the gap with a canvas stretcher. After transferring the patient they each hoisted an end and with Lil bent on keeping Mahmud from choking on his tongue made their way through the front entrance.

When they had gone Beecher removed his operating garb, but for the shirt, and ducked out the back. It was a keyhole opening, facing south with a foot high threshold. Often he either struck his head or tripped to fall inside or out depending on his momentum. Lil had teased. 'I bet you dance well,' she giggled while helping him up after he'd crashed the first time; but he couldn't take it and became angry. Thoroughly shaken by a blast of profanity she withdrew into her protective shell of silence and decided not to kid him again. This time he made it like a pro.

Despite the tiring operation he felt good. Lately events had been moving at an accelerated pace. Losing his pants tickled him. The incident would make an interesting anecdote. He smiled at his bloodied legs and trudged across the sandy courtyard looking like Wee Willie Winkie minus a cap and candle.

It was mid-day. A brilliant sun reflected oppressively from the dry earth and clay plastered buildings. At the far side of the courtyard an arch crested the entrance to a narrow street, its narrowness being exaggerated by its high walls.

Best turned west along this corridor and maintained his clumsy stride - each scuff of a sandal raising a puff of dust to waft in the stifling air - passed random heaps of soil, possibly the ruins of a stable entrance or a bazaar. If these mounds had been rooms at one time there was little proof for their roofs were long gone and the jagged partitions, eroded by the elements, were reduced to Lilliputian heights.

The wall to his left gradually lowered, allowing a view of the southern rampart, more crumbling walls and open rooms. Four, shingled like the hospital, sheltered a classroom and three houses. On the wide common between Beecher and the buildings, children were pestering a flock of sheep. "Not a place where sheep may safely graze," he grunted, seeing a number of animals being mauled and hauled about on leashes, their bleating blending with the joyous shouts of their captors. Heedless of the fuss insatiable goats nibbled patches of grass.

Farther along the wall allowed access to a diagonal path and the living quarters. Best vaulted the depression to land on the back of a mongrel dog. Equally surprised the animal yelped and retreated a few yards, leaving a mutton hock between Beecher's feet; head and tail lowered it growled menacingly. He stooped to pick up the joint and toss it back but it soon turned black with countless flies. Sickened by the sight he changed his mind and started along the path.

Before a series of crude dwellings Tom Bereskin was pumping gas into a ten gallon can. By the time Best came within hailing distance he had replaced the container in a jeep.

"The generator tank ran out, so has our depot," the Mission Chief said, trying to clean a pair of podgy hands by scraping them on the back of his jeans. "It's the third time this morning; you must have used a lot of fuel."

Beecher feigned surprised. "Huh, that much?"

Tom removed his baseball cap and unconsciously slicked his pate with what remained of the oil on his palm. Toying with the cap momentarily he spied Beecher's streaky legs and wheezed. "Looks like you lost something."

Best's expression did not change. "My pants got a bit messy."

Tom tossed his cap in the air and burst out laughing. "Inside or out?" He could barely ask.

"Very funny," Beecher retorted in a dull monotone. Deciding not to let the Mission Chief's wit get the best of him, he turned his attention to the jeep. His eyes hadn't adjusted to the brightness of the day. Squinting he regarded the vehicle and announced, "I'm going to the bazaar this afternoon and will need transportation."

"Fine," said Tom, "I'll go with you. It'll give me a chance to fill up at the petrol station."

Beecher looked put out. He wanted to get a few souvenirs and would barter on his own, not with Lil and their son, Bereskin or anyone. Rather than speak his mind he hinted that the Mission Chief had more important things to do. "What about school? Don't you have classes?"

A grin broadened Bereskin's face. "There isn't any," he declared. "You've forgotten today is the tenth of Dhu'l Hijra, the beginning of Id-i-Qurban. Tomorrow those sheep on the common will be slaughtered."

"Yes," Beecher nodded, "and while everyone in Afghanistan is enjoying the feast we'll be heading home."

"You're having supper with us tonight. Ruth has it arranged. With your gear packed away, it's the least we can do." Bereskin paused, listening to the soft drone of a 'superconstellation'. He searched the heavens and found the shiny metal speck as it flew south-eastward over the Koh-i-Baba.

"I wonder if the Barbers are on that plane, Beech."

"Who?"

"The Barbers, your replacements."

"Yeah," Beecher answered, his mind ten thousand miles away.

The following day Darius Abdullah Mahmud was still recovering from the effects of the anaesthetic. Plagued with nausea and vertigo he felt faint whenever he tried to sit. Though the smell of ether was not as strong as the previous night, injections of morphine had caused further retching. He was lying on a steel cot in a dingy room. Midmorning sunlight attempted to break through two small dirty windows above him. Roxane, Anisa and Sayyid sat on the floor at the foot of his cot. When he began to stir they grouped around it and Sayyid spoke. "How goes it brader-jan?"

"I'm sick to my stomach," Dari complained, struggling to see his elevated cast. "Who split it?"

"Dr. Best earlier; he was worried about the circulation in your toes." While answering Roxane noticed there was no change in their dusky colour nor in wound seepage compared to a line she'd drawn on the plaster post operatively. Her brows arched. "You must remember, you were talking to him."

Dari observed his foot was in a normal position, almost ninety degrees to the leg. A smile brightened his face. "I remember! I told him my toes point in the right direction; before the operation it looked like I was walking backwards."

He tried to move his toes but couldn't, nor could he feel them. "Touch the big one," he insisted, having difficulty reaching it himself.

Roxane pinched them all. "They're so cold!" She began to massage, wondering what else could be done to improve the feeling. "Any better?" she asked.

"What are you doing? Are you touching my toes?"

"I'm rubbing them." She stopped, startled by a premonition something was wrong. She rubbed harder but the deathly cyanosis remained. What else could she do? Her agile mind couldn't come up with an immediate answer other than get a qualified opinion.

The Bereskins had taken the Bests to the airport and wouldn't be back for a week. She didn't trust the village Shaman; besides him there was no one with medical experience in Bamiyan. For all she knew there were no doctors north of Kabul. Waiting for Best's replacement to arrive might be too late. Her voice trembled. "We must find someone who knows what to do."

Weak from blood loss, pain and vomiting, Dari leaned back on the pillow. His eyes closed and a sinking feeling overcame him as he recalled Dr. Best's words. "I have received a call to return to North America and study orthopaedics. I pray God will look after you."

So far the unaccountable surgeon's prayers fell on a God who was either deaf or not impressed with the supplicant. Dari winced. Best had gone, leaving him in trouble. He began to perspire.

Abandonment he could handle. His mother left before he was old enough to reckon and was soon forgotten. By a strange coincidence she had also gone to North America to some place in Canada where her father re-established his furrier business - so Malikar had told him. Any subconscious resentment vanished with her and if Dari ever thought of his mother it was not for lack of emotional sustenance. Whenever Nicole's name was raised she remained an object of curiosity. It felt unnatural to be thinking of her under the present circumstances. He had a few friends in the zunana; or for comfort and reassurance there was Ghubar and his father when Malikar wasn't away on business.

His early years were tough. As the indulged son he was harassed by jealous siblings bent on giving him a greater handicap than he had, and the smouldering dislike of his conspiring step-mothers thrust him into potentially dangerous situations. Still with substance, perspicacity and a buoyant wit he had survived, untainted by self-pity. Malikar, attracted by these manly traits, overlooked the deformity and offered his son love and respect.

Yet it was the tall slim Panjsheri-Tadjik, Ghubar, whom Dari found most reliable. Fourteen years Malikar's senior the warrior had served three generations of Mahmuds.

Compulsively he felt for the taw'iz, a misshapen medal on a chain dangling from his neck. It had been his grandfather's; Ghubar had given it to Dari upon Zulfikar's death. The good luck charm, warped by an unpolished slug from a Safi rifle, had almost killed the old man. When Dari was only a few feet high Ghubar had taught him to shoot a similar weapon, so long it couldn't be balanced without a stand. The smooth black-walnut stock inlaid with mother-of-pearl was a consoling breast against his boyish cheek. For targets the Tadjik would set out pieces of broken pottery on the bank of the Panjsher River. One day a large hawk glided by, its eyes fixed on a frantic bobec. In that instant Ghubar snatched the rifle, leading the bird as it folded its wings. Feet from the ground with feathery brakes extended it clutched and veered over the languid water. Ghubar fired and a thunderous report echoed among the surrounding boulders, muting the splash of the hawk, the bobec squashed in its thorny claws.

Presently Dari felt his leg was in the grip of a giant predator. The narcotic was wearing off, but he couldn't tolerate another dose. The nauseous side-effects were as unbearable as the pain.

How would Ghubar and Malikar react to his predicament? There had been shame caused by the deformity and Dari vainly wanted it fixed. Dr. Best said he could do it. Now the doctor had gone and Dari was worse off than ever. He could blame Best but he himself had opted for the surgery. Upset with a decision of his own ending badly, he might have kicked something, and with his bad foot. But there was more to it; the doctor had promised a cure and he'd believed him - in fact, Dari was presented with no alternative. Now he regretted his choice, perhaps too late; and it wasn't the first time he'd received unsuccessful treatment.

Soon after birth, before Dari's mother had gone, his foot had been manipulated by a French speaking Consultant at the University. Ghuber had driven them to have Dari's correction casts changed. Later the consultant operated but the deformity recurred.

Malikar was disappointed after a second and third operation failed. He rationalized his son's problem was the will of Allah, best left alone, particularly after receiving advice from another specialist while on vacation in Srinagar. The doctor, an English surgeon, told him to wait until the foot had stopped growing when the bones could be reshaped and fused in a normal weight bearing position.

Dari remembered the holiday in Kashmir. It was after grandfather Zulfikar had been killed in the Safi Revolt of '47 and Malikar took him and his grieving grandmother, Tahmina, to a rented houseboat moored on peaceful Lake Nagin. The setting was paradise and Zulfikar's spirit was felt all around. With little mental effort Dari could recall the magic sounds of early morning: the shrillness of many birds, harmonized chanting from a Hindu monastery across the lake and water lapping at the teakwood hull.

Deciding to down-play the boy's disability, Malikar let him be, and was pleasantly surprised to see him progress in other ways. Dari became an excellent swimmer and riding was not beyond him. He was encouraged to lift weights and as he matured his father relished the results: an exceptionally strong back, powerful shoulders, laudable upper extremities and bigger than average thighs. Though the right calf remained withered, the affliction was allotted no more importance than a cosmetic defect.

Dari fell asleep and when he opened his eyes sunlight no longer bathed the dirty windows above him.

Roxane was stroking his clammy forehead. "Uncle Rishtya will take you to Kabul tomorrow." Her face was inches from his as she spoke in a reassuring tone. "It's almost two o'clock. I've brought you something to eat."

Mahmud looked about the room.

Sayyid was in the same place, sitting in the same position; he beamed, contouring his flat features. "The Sahib says I can drive the Bentley." The Hazara sounded a shade less than ecstatic. "There will be room for you to lie down in back. If we start early we should be there by late afternoon."

Roxane was less enthusiastic. "Anisa volunteered to come tonight. But it won't be necessary; I intend to stay. Besides," she smiled, "I'm going to Kabul too."

She moved to a chair near the door where she had draped her chadri. On a low table next to it was a tray containing food and drink. She poured a cup of green tea, adding a large portion of sugar and a cardamon stick. "You would rather have something to drink first?" she asked and passed him the vessel.

He accepted and while he drank in large gulps she soaked a sample of nan in the stew and held it ready to pop into his mouth. "Here," she coaxed, "You need something more nourishing."

"No," Dari sighed, "I'll bring it up." Through tired eyes he watched her return the food to the table. Before they closed completely he saw she had changed from her nursing uniform and was wearing a blue silk dress gathered at the waist by a sash of the same material. Below the hem, baggy white pantaloons flowed to her ankles.

They'd been friends since they were young, closer since the death of her father, Mir Ghulum, and her mother's second marriage to Roxane's uncle Rishtya.

Roxane, Soroya's eldest, was barely ten when Dari first became aware of her. It was in Bamiyan at the wedding feast. He was one and a half years older. She was playing hop-scotch with her sisters in the courtyard of her grandfather's qala. He had hobbled up, pulled one of her braids and declared, 'You're it.'

Soon the playing squares, scratched in the bare earth, were obliterated by the marks of children's dashing feet. Even with his handicap, try as she could Roxane was unable to catch him, much to the delight of grandfather Zor, grinning so widely the waxed ends of his moustache stuck out like the horns of a Marco Polo ram. One point glanced off Dari's forehead when he accidentally ran into the old man. After awhile she gave up and tagged someone else.

The festivities lasted a week. Roxane's former cousins became brothers and sisters, her uncle Rishtya, her father, although she never referred to him as such.

When the traditional sugar loaf was broken over Soroya's head it shattered into many pieces, a good omen, interrupted by Dari's stealing the cone; he relinquished it upon Ghubar's insistence. The event ended with the throwing of candy-coated almonds and walnuts, Dari and Roxane competing for the delectable ammunition from the front row of well-wishers.

The next day the Mahmuds left Bamiyan in Malikar's Daimler. While Dari waved wildly through the rear window Roxane ran behind as far as the gate. Dejected she watched the dust settle where the road turned and disappeared.

From then on, whenever their extended families met, Malikar and Soroya became increasingly aware of their offsprings' affinity. Before long Dari was invited to Rishtya's for no special reason. In return Malikar arranged outings to include Roxane; one adventure the following year was a visit to his mother's native village in Nuristan. Forever after, there was no doubt in his mind of the girl's devotion to his son.

High on an eastern mountain the village was inaccessible except by a narrow trail through forests of pine and prickly wild holly. Forced to leave the car with Ghubar to guard it, they traversed grass and grey rock, sticking to a steep slope above a roaring river, climbing higher and higher until they reached a series of log houses built one on top of the other.

A red-bearded giant, Dari's barefoot granduncle Lysander, greeted them at the bottom of a split log staircase and took them to a cool upper level ventilated by large windows. Tahmina came from the kitchen to greet them. Dari had not seen his grandmother since her spiritual search in Kashmir. Her skin, wrinkled as tanned doe, stretched translucently over her frail bones. Pinning a whorl of silver hair to a few reddish strands, she fixed him with luminous eyes and embraced him saying, 'My how you look like Zulfikar and you'll be as tall as he was.' She smiled, and fondling his blond curls sadly added, 'but your grandfather's hair was so black.'

After lunch Malikar retired to a backroom to play cards, smoke and swap yarns with cousins he hadn't seen in a long time, leaving Dari and Roxane free to join the other children in 'Blind

Man's Bluff', a dangerous game when played on the level but possibly fatal on a rocky mountain slope.

To avoid the blindfolded player the cousins tumbled and rolled, projecting their bodies beyond the edge of the roof, becoming more daring as the game progressed, moving closer to the edge, so close the sightless stalker could easily take a step too far and fall. When it was his turn to be bandaged Dari nearly did. The stiff joints of his right foot misled him and he plunged into space. As he clung to the roof by his fingers, only his strong arms and Roxane's tugging pulled him to safety.

Dari's reverie ended in terror. Before he realized where he was he'd grasped the frame of the hospital cot and shot into a sitting position. The two small windows above him were black. A single flickering candle sat on the table where earlier Roxane had placed the food tray. Now she huddled in a corner half asleep.

In the faint light he stared at her outline. "Are you all right?" she asked.

"I don't know."

"What do you mean?"

"The pain has lessened but I still can't move or feel my toes."

"You'll be fine," Roxane reassured. "Dr. Best said so."

"He talked a lot this morning," Dari recalled. "Said something if I'd known before I'm not sure I'd have let him operate."

"Like what?"

"It was the first time he'd done this type of surgery."

Roxane thought back to the doctor's gay demeanour while he explained the procedure, and indeed he'd made such a statement. "But he's a good surgeon," she insisted. "He saved Baba's life."

"True," Dari agreed. Bowel obstruction had almost killed Zor Mahmud and Dr. Best had relieved it. "It was a matter of life or death, Roxane. My case is different. 'Either your foot points backwards or I straighten it,' he said, focusing on my deformity whenever he saw me."

Dari sighed in desperation. Why had he not been informed of the risks? Because he'd never asked; Dr. Best's self-confidence precluded any doubt. Dari felt used. A few hours ago Best boasted how the operation was a success. It seemed the doctor was unaware of his mistake or had been lying. Dari began to hate him.

Roxane sensed his enmity and offered encouragement. "Don't worry brader-jan. Everything will be better when we get to Kabul."

"No", he muttered, "I'm going to lose my foot...Somewhere! Somehow!...I'll get even."

Part One

Sunday, November 10, 1963
to
Friday, November 22, 1963

Dr. Best & Dr. Lindsay

CHAPTER ONE

Dr. James Lindsay, twice depressed, slouched over his oak desk. A tall man, he rested both elbows on its leather top, absently plying a colourful brochure.

Following surgery Ella Klassen died of a massive pulmonary embolus, a tragedy which likely wouldn't have happened if he hadn't operated. During convalescence she lay on a Stryker bed, afraid to move or be moved when the nurses turned her face up or down on its rotary frame. To include her in any activity, limited by the narrow cot and the doctor's order she was not to sit, were desperately resisted; and her attitude worried him.

Intractable pain due to a defect in the lower spine, allowing vertebral slippage to occur, inhibited her - so she insisted - to the point where coping with household chores was no longer possible. Obliged to believe her as there was clinical evidence to support her symptoms, Dr. Lindsay tried every conservative measure: bed rest, traction, flexion exercises, heat and drugs but nothing lasted except a plaster body cast. Consequently he decided to restrict her instability permanently by a fusion. The operation went well. Bone taken from her ilium was placed across the spondylolisthesis. In order for the graft to take, movement of the lower spine had to be limited; to further insure immobility a wire loop was fixed around the vertebrae. 'Instrumental surgery,' he winced, for instrumental he'd been.

A few years earlier Jim performed a similar operation on her sister, Opal, with good results. Opal's problem was also instability but for a different reason. She'd had a previous operation for herniated discs elsewhere. Though this surgery eliminated her leg pain she was left with an extremely sore back. Jim's graft consolidated within nine months, binding the last three lumbar segments to the sacral portion of her pelvis.

Why the first operator had chosen to remove so many discs when probably only one was causing her leg pain and do nothing about the instability he'd created was never explained.

In turn Jim was remiss when it came to answering Opal's questions. She couldn't understand why the first surgery had increased her back pain. Irritated by the operator's silence she sought her lawyer's advice. In time - and the surgeon was never informed of the discretion exercised on his behalf - Opal's satisfaction with the result of her second operation lessened her wish to press charges and she settled down to count her blessings.

At the funeral home while he was paying his respects to the Klassens, Opal reminded him in front of the family, 'at least my operation was a success.'

What a perplexing remark! Did her audience mistake the attempt to draw attention on herself as a hint something had gone wrong? If not, Jim should have expected it; Opal, as colourful and translucent as the gem, was just as dull.

He said nothing, nodded amicably and forced his composure. How could Jim explain to a group of mourners he was not to be held responsible for an embolus? His notable presence among them was to convey his sympathy not to cover up. Or was it? He felt grossly inadequate.

A blood clot - undetectable as it clung to the lining of Ella's deep veins - had been sucked upwards by the heart to the lungs and dammed the vital transfer of oxygen and carbon dioxide. Ella suffocated and died instantly. Maybe she could've been saved by an emergency operation but there was barely time to diagnose, let alone explore. Such heroic embolectomies were reported in literature dealing with advances in thoracic surgery but their result was rarely successful. The anticoagulant drugs he'd prescribed to thin her blood and prevent the incident had not helped. The probability of saving her was extremely low. On the brighter side, few patients undergoing major surgery developed this complication and not all of them died. Death related directly to the size of the wayward clot. Thank God smaller emboli were more frequent. His batting average for elective operations was exceptionally good. So why could he not shake his self-blame?

Chances were Ella would have improved in time on the conservative regime prescribed before the operation or on no treatment at all, though it might have taken ages. But her mind was fixed on surgery.

Suppose she'd discharged him and gone to another surgeon. The blow to his ego would have been transient and cause no great loss of self-confidence. Rationalization might've prompted him to comment. 'Oh well, that's the way the ball bounces.'

"But the ball did bounce my way," he murmured. "I should have let it pass."

Meriel, his wife, was the same age as Ella. Losing Merri, his companion of almost twenty years, would be an insufferable blow. Comparing the two women he knew Merri would not have had the operation; stoically she would've persevered the months of misery - though not in total silence - and adjusted her activities accordingly. Slowly the truth surfaced. He would have reacted the same way and rejected surgery. He confronted himself accusingly. "You, Jim Lindsay, have performed an operation you would not have had yourself."

None of the doctors had criticized him. No one accused him of indiscretion. The only comments he heard: tough Jim, forget it, nothing you could do, better luck next time, were mundane cover-up for his associates' true feelings, 'there, for the grace of God, go I'.

The cliche 'better luck next time' had also been extended in a letter from Geoffrey Robb, examiner for The Royal College of Surgeons. The P.S. was galling. 'If you wish to know the reasons why we decided to have you repeat your 'oral' exam I will be happy to discuss them with you on Nov. 13th should you appear in Toronto to assist on the Forsey case.'

It was an offer he would've been foolish to refuse. Still he wondered. Whether he passed or failed did not affect his hospital privileges or economic status. He'd already been accepted on the strength of his specialist certificate obtained by passing a previous examination. Nor did it alter his ability as an orthopaedist. The Fellowship was a recognition of academic excellence; pride drove him to try. Failing it was degrading. As it involved his self-appraisal deeper than the Klassen case, his anxiety was more acute.

He had slipped off to London early in September to sit the 'writtens'. Six weeks later a telegram arrived announcing his success with an invitation to attend the 'orals'. In between the two sets of exams he practised and as fate would have it, one of his patients, an adolescent with lateral curvature of the spine, required surgical correction. The scoliosis was too advanced to respond to bracing so he had sent her to Dr. Robb for another opinion. By chance Robb turned out to be one of three men assigned to appraise him during the 'orals'. To Dr. Lindsay's embarrassment Robb, in the presence of the other two examiners and before Jim had received a question from any of them, remarked, 'The girl you referred with the scoliosis has been booked for surgery.' Jim had been completely unnerved. Was it Robb's way of asserting his professional superiority? Or was it to make the other examiners aware Dr. Lindsay might be trying to bribe his way through the examinations? The inferences jammed his brain. Consequently he did not perform well.

Light flickering from a crystal tumbler arrested his thoughts. Across the room an open hearth half full of maple logs blazed warmly. It was a rough fireplace built with a variety of split granite rocks and sandstone. The mantle, a thick slice of walnut, held a few trophies. Tinkling ice, melting in the crystal tumbler, stirred him. Condensation on the outside of the glass had dampened a brochure which he'd carelessly used as a coaster. Wiping the modestly decorated pamphlet on the sleeve of his cardigan, Jim studied it along with the accompanying letter. On the letterhead to the right of Aesculapius' staff he read, MEDICARE - a program of S.E.R.V.E., with an italicized phrase - Send Enlightened Relief Volunteers Everywhere. A list of executors graced the left-hand margin. The text was brief but informative.

Washington, D.C.
Wed., Nov. 4, 1963

Dear Dr. Lindsay

Thank you for your inquiry of Oct. 19th./63. The enclosed material will give you an idea of our program and the countries we serve.

As we have no volunteers to Afghanistan during March and April of next year we will be happy to make a reservation for you. This is a popular tour with our visiting orthopaedists and we give the month of choice to the first individual who makes a firm commitment.

MEDICARE is a voluntary service and the cost of financing your transportation to and from the participating country will have to be borne by yourself but the costs are income tax deductible in the form of a contribution to S.E.R.V.E. Of course this arrangement may not be possible in Canada and you should contact our Ottawa office for verification.

We shall be glad to answer any further questions not covered by the enclosed pamphlet.

We do hope you will decide in our favour.

The letter was signed by a retired Rear Admiral, one of the names appearing in the margin. Jim tossed the letter aside and turned to the brochure. It was entitled 'Light A Medical Path' and was well illustrated with photographs of white-coated medical and paramedical people, adequate operating and classroom facilities and crippled, starving, waiting humanity. There was an introductory message from the chairman of the Advisory Board, quoting Einstein, 'The concern for man and his destiny must always be the chief reason for every technical effort. Never forget it among your diagrams and equations. Only a life lived for others is worthwhile.'

Other sections of the pamphlet explained the challenges, accomplishments and present projects of the organization. The final paragraph ended with - Education procreates - Jim never finished reading for his den door suddenly opened.

"Dad, someone's coming up the drive. Mum's busy in the kitchen and I just washed my hair so you'll have to answer it."

Jenny, the Lindsay's second child disappeared as quickly as she had entered. 'Jumping Jenny', Jim mused and swivelled to look out the front window. The base of a large Colorado spruce obscured the driver and most of the bat-winged rear end of a '59 Chev., parked out front. He heard a car door slam and musical chimes herald the unknown force pressing the button on the porch pillar. Within seconds he crossed the parlour to the foyer and pulled open one half of the double front door.

A sturdy young man with dark curly hair stood beyond the threshold. He was slightly shorter than Jim but heavier. An indoor complexion accentuated his eyes and his lower jaw receded into a layer of jowl. It receded further when the corners of the stranger's mouth raised an enigmatic grin.

Succinctly measuring the stranger, Dr. Lindsay acknowledged him in a cool inquisitive tone, "Yes?"

The young man spoke with intimidating intimacy. "Corny, I'm Beecher Best."

Astounded, Jim dropped his extended right hand. No one had ever called him 'Corny'. He was christened Cornell James Lindsay, Cornell being his mother's maiden name. Other than his birth certificate over which he had no control, the only place 'Cornell' ever appeared was on his diplomas. He had gone by his middle name since birth. No one, not even people who had known him from childhood, ever called him that. To friends and colleagues he was Jimmie or Jim, or behind his back, so he had learned through the hospital grapevine, C. J., but Corny! Of all the cheek!

Jim stiffened, defiantly resolved to find out if the young stranger had knocked on the wrong door. Before he could ask Best passed him and strode into the parlour. Fighting off the urge to demand where in hell this presumptive intruder thought he was going, Jim discreetly closed the door to his study. There was no way he was going to allow this tactless fellow the hospitality of his private hearth. Certainly not after such a soul-shaking introduction. "Won't you sit down?" he urged.

Best eased himself into a parlour chair. Pointing toward the study he demanded, "What's in there?"

Jim was about to tell him it was none of his business; civilly he parried with a question of his own. "You have obviously come to see me about something important Mr. Best. What's on your mind?"

"It's Dr. Best," Beecher smiled, "and I'm going to set up in Shipton. Presently I'm free but will start practising orthopaedics in January. Friday I was notified I'd got my exams."

"You passed the Certificate?"

"No the Fellowship," Beecher beamed proudly and carried on, "It was a piece of cake."

Floored by a mixture of awe and resentment Jim shook his head. That someone so young, probably lacking surgical experience, not to mention the common social graces, could convince a panel of examiners he deserved a chance to join the teaching staff of a University Hospital was absolutely incredible. Who the devil was setting the standards?

"Congratulations," he offered flatly. "May I ask who your examiners were?"

"McFayden, Blythe and Robb, the same men who examined you."

In spite of himself Dr. Lindsay's jaw dropped. How on earth did this upstart know about his trying the Fellowship. He hesitated to ask but need not have for Best supplied the answer.

"Robb told me you'd had a go at it." Beecher smirked. "Admires your guts, taking it on after being out of academics for so long. He's a personal friend of mine. He's active in the Christian Medical Association. I've known him since med-school. He looks after my son. Our oldest boy Robbie - we named him after Dr. Robb -

has a mild degree of cerebral palsy and is to have his heel cords lengthened soon."

For a moment Jim stared. Had this relationship any influence on the outcome of Best's examination? Finding it difficult to think otherwise, through clenched teeth he asked, "Why Shipton? Why do you wish to practice?"

"I grew up on Spruceridge. My mother still lives there. So did my wife, Lil. We have friends here particularly at St. Matthew's church. Why not?"

Jim shrugged. "If any of your friends are doctors they must have advised you we don't need another orthopaedic surgeon."

"On the contrary," Beecher argued. "Three of my classmates practising near the General assure me of their support. According to them there are plenty of orthopaedic problems. In fact they are doing so well they have built their own clinic. They're dissatisfied with the service they get from the surgeons."

Dr. Lindsay cleared the bitterness gathering in his throat. Superficially Dr. Best had a point. The group of G.P.'s to whom he alluded were a new breed cutting their eye-teeth on a restive populace turning to socialized medicine. Most of the patients they saw had little wrong with them. It seemed people no longer respected advice found in their granny's book of home remedies. Instead they were being rushed off to larger centres for a second opinion or treatment whether or not it was available locally. All of which undermined confidence in Shipton specialists. Trying to remain impartial, he continued. "A third orthopod joined us last year. Fortier, the new man, gets a fair number of cases from the French-speaking sector but he's not as busy as he'd like to be. I dare say there are plenty of reasons but none of them are Fortier's fault. Most of Shipton's general surgeons were trained on the job during the war or by a preceptor right after. They were operating on broken bones before I arrived and still do. Even the older G.P.s continue to set fractures."

"They haven't had modern training," Beecher interjected. "Their poor results will only make me look better."

Dr. Lindsay shrugged. "You're discounting experience!"

"Yeah," Best admitted though he did not sound convinced. "It makes no difference. We live in a free country and I intend to offer the best. According to the latest figures Shipton has a population of just over a hundred thousand and is increasing at the rate of four families a day. If you include the surrounding rural area the medical services cover over a quarter of a million." Best paused. "What do you think of my doing all the hip operations?"

"Which side?" Jim asked facetiously.

"I'm serious. I would like to sub-specialize. Advancements are taking place in hip surgery to open a new field."

Dr. Lindsay was aware experiments were being conducted on joint replacement and different materials had been inserted between the component parts of the weight-bearing joints with some success but he felt it was too early to evaluate the results. He changed the subject. "What about backs, Dr. Best, have you done many discs?"

"Actually no. At the centre where I've been training only the neurosurgeons are taking out discs. The orthopaedic service sees the patients before and after surgery."

"Where 'bouts?"

"Deaconess, one of the larger private hospitals in Detroit."

"What about bunions, knee cartilages?" Jim pursued.

"Well, Dr Lindsay," - it was the first time in their conversation Beecher had paid Jim the cordial respect to which he was entitled - "they're done by the attending docs; as residents we do a lot of hips."

"You mean fractured hips."

"Well mostly."

"What about polio and the interesting operations on residual paralytics?"

"There was the odd case, usually one who'd contacted the disease years ago. I saw a few withered extremities and spinal deformities probably caused by polio but most of them did not return for treatment. Just as well for there was nothing I could do for them."

While Beecher was talking Jim recalled his days as a resident and the large number of post-polio paralytics who came for reconstructive procedures: the muscle and tendon transfers, stabilization of joints, bracing, crutches and wheelchairs. Almost the whole gamut of orthopaedic training was obtainable from one disease. In Dr. Lindsay's opinion polio deserved a monument for it had given birth to a profession. Even the word orthopaedics coined by Nicholas Andry was derived from straightening the crooked spine of a child supposedly afflicted with it. A pity Beecher and other young men did not have the advantage of such a valuable experience. But for the good of mankind the dreaded disease had to be eradicated. Deciding

Do Unto Others

not to push the conversation any further, Jim offered some practical advice.

"Frankly Dr. Best if you wish to set up a practice in Shipton you should learn as much as you can about the whole field. Bunions and knee cartilages are your bread and butter operations; if you don't do a proper job your patients will go elsewhere. Financially this is a good town. Most people have insurance coverage, perhaps sixty percent of them, paying eighty to ninety percent of the scheduled fees set by the Ontario Medical Association. Their hospitalization is paid by the government. Free ward patients who can't pay for a doctor get the same treatment. Their unpaid bills are just written off. There's a lot of good will among our colleagues."

In the past Dr. Lindsay had to cancel debts many times. Not one of them had been a hardship. In the end the patients were grateful and a constant source of referrals. He enjoyed playing the philanthropist. Some people teasingly accused him of playing the Almighty and Jim would reply quite seriously, paraphrasing Ambrose Pare, 'I dressed the wound, God healed it.' However for Dr. Best's interest he elaborated on a more recent case, perhaps more dramatic and details were fresh in his mind. "I billed a man for suturing his median nerves and flexor tendons. He had slashed his wrists in a fit of depression; his wife was running around with another man. That wasn't all. He was a German S.S. officer during the war, responsible for God knows what atrocities. Certainly Aaron Nash couldn't get anything out of him and he devoted a lot of time."

"Who's Aaron Nash?" Beecher asked.

"One of our psychiatrists."

"Sounds Jewish."

"I believe he is."

"No wonder he couldn't. The guy probably knew it and was scared of him."

"Regardless," Jim continued, failing to grasp the significance of Beecher's glib remark, "neither of us has been paid for looking after him and likely never will. In the end he was transferred to Woodholme Sanatorium. Lucky for him we now have O.H.S.I.P."

"What's that?"

"The Ontario Hospital Services Insurance Plan. It pays for a room, lab tests, X-rays, any in-hospital services but not the doctor's fees. Thank goodness P. S. I. pays the rest."

"Well you've certainly done all right in spite of some non-paying patients," Beecher observed. "Probably making a hundred thousand a year. This house is a mansion. Passed it many times and have always wanted to see through."

Jim noted the hint but set himself against showing Best around. Hoping to conclude the conversation, he replied. "Though I doubt if you have anything special to offer the community and doubt if you are really needed here, if you do decide to come you probably won't starve. It will just take a little longer to get started."

Beecher was not paying any attention to these comments. His vision was circumscribing the contents of the room.

Jim glanced at his watch, quite obviously and stood up, implying he might have other things to do. When Beecher remained seated he was forced to make an excuse. "If you'll pardon me Dr. Best I must get back to my study. Perhaps we can continue our talk another time."

Beecher gathered himself together reluctantly and so slowly Jim felt obliged to break the silence. "Where did you take your medical training?"

"Toronto."

"How did you end up in the States?"

Settling back into the easy chair Beecher ventured, "It's a long story. After interning at the Toronto General I went to Afghanistan as a medical missionary."

"Afghanistan!"

Dr. Lindsay suddenly became more interested. Though he had been annoyed with the unexpected visit the mention of Afghanistan intensified his curiosity. Some benefit might be derived from this intrusion after all. "When were you there?" he asked.

"From fifty-six till fifty-nine when I left to begin my residency."

"Were you in Kabul?" Jim asked, pronouncing the capital city 'Ka'bool'.

"It's 'Cobble'," Beecher corrected. As Dr. Lindsay nodded his acceptance the younger man proceeded. "We were there for a short time, upon arrival and departure."

"We?"

"My wife went with me. She's a nurse-anaesthetist. For three years we ran a clinic in the Bamiyan valley."

How a Christian church could go about setting up a mission in a Muslim country was beyond Jim's comprehension. Rather than pose the question, he asked another directly related to his concern. "What kind of medical facilities did you have?"

"There weren't any. We had to set up in a caravanserai, a large area about the size of two football fields, enclosed by a mud wall ten feet high. The Mission also had a school and a church. The main purpose was to improve the general health of the local population. Those interested in learning English were welcome; there were plenty of young people attending. We had no serious objections from the authorities except we weren't allowed to erect a cross."

"What sort of patients did you treat?"

"Almost every disease occurring in a temperate zone: typhoid, dysentery and cholera are prevalent, also your favourite polio. I did not deliver many babies. Most of the women were cloistered in the compounds. The Muslims are polygamists and very jealous of anyone treating their wives, especially foreigners. There is a high degree of deformed pelvi due to adult rickets which gives the midwives a hard time. I encountered several cases of ruptured uteri. Also they've a high incidence of kidney and bladder stones."

Jim was fascinated by the amount of pathology Beecher had seen. "How did you manage all this stuff?" he asked. "Did you have decent equipment?"

Beecher grinned. "Little but useful. I was able to perform most minor procedures: incisions and drainage and the odd appendectomy."

"You did abdominal surgery?"

"Yes, an appendectomy is not a difficult operation."

Jim nodded agreement, however Beecher's next swaggering statement was incredible.

"I did a triple arthrodesis before I left."

"You what!"

"A triple arthrodesis," Beecher reiterated and expanded. "On a young Afghan who had a foot deformity. I fused the bones of his right foot."

Dr. Lindsay was flabbergasted. "How did he do?"

"Well I don't know and I've never heard. We left for home the following morning. It will be five years next June."

Jim had difficulty coming to grips with Dr. Best's latest disclosure. What nerve! A triple arthrodesis, particularly to correct deformity and provide stability of the foot and ankle, was an exacting procedure. He had always considered it an operation that separated men from boys. He stared at Dr. Best, loathe to understand. It was unbelievable. With no formal training this man had tackled a difficult operation under adverse conditions and apparently pulled it off with no supervision.

Jim's speechlessness persisted and during the lull Beecher arose and stretched. "It's time I got home," he said. "Usually we attend evening services and have supper early on Sunday."

"You must tell me more about Afghanistan, I'm intrigued. As a matter of fact I'm thinking of going there as a volunteer."

"Why don't you come to our church next week. I'm giving the morning sermon and intend to speak on the Christian mission at Bamiyan."

Jim stared across the lake, unaware of the Toronto skyline and a wedge of Canada Geese undulating toward him. What manner of man was this? Unlimited confidence; aggressiveness greater than any surgeon he'd come across in sixteen years of practice; a professed Christian who seemed to lack humility and consideration. He was not likeable and if he had any redeeming qualities Jim Lindsay was going to find out, for Beecher Best was determined to set up in Shipton.

CHAPTER TWO

"Bed-time Robbie!"

The youngster struggled pitifully to his feet and tip-toed to his mother, his legs scissoring stiffly. Toy blocks, he was attempting to balance, toppled and spun. One lodged beneath a heel and threw him forward; the rest disseminated in his wake. Lil caught her son before he struck his face on the carpet and gathered him in her arms.

"Why isn't he wearing his helmet?" Jessie demanded.

The clattering had startled Jessie Best and she dropped her newspaper. Glaring at Lil she chastised. "You know he's not to be without it."

True, when she was last at the Crippled Children's Centre Lillian had been given such advice. The doctor had shown her a skull x-ray of another child. There was a linear crack across the frontal bone and he said it was the result of a fall from a playroom chair.

Lil kissed her boy on the brow and hugged him tenderly. "Sorry Robbie, I should be more attentive."

Jessie's grating reproach was typical of the criticism the younger Mrs. Best had been receiving since they'd been staying with her. Though she tried not to give her mother-in-law an opening the old girl managed to find fault whenever the chance arose. This time there was no need. After bathing the boy Lil placed him on the floor within easy reach while she sat on folded legs preparing a sermon for Beecher to deliver at St. Matthew's. She stared wide-eyed at the older woman.

How many foster parents were there before the Bests adopted her? Lillian was never sure. During infancy she was turned over to the Children's Aid when her natural mother, a single parent, died. Passing from one family to another, the only permanent absolute in her life was a protective shell of indifference. It was always around when needed.

As her mother-in-law's menacing face disappeared behind the Shipton Shield Lil shifted the boy onto her hip and escaped through the panelled glass door, leading to a tiny foyer and the foot of a narrow staircase.

Gaining the landing she turned left up the last few steps and proceeded along the short hall to the first door. It opened into the smaller of two rooms facing the street. She refused to switch on the light for fear of waking her other child and quietly crossed to the near wall where she placed Robbie on his side in the single bed - the same allotted to her years ago - tucked the covers around his chin, pulled a tissue from her bra and stooped to wipe the slobber from his cheek. Michael, her youngest, was fast asleep in the adjacent crib, a diadem of tangled limbs and bars. Two and one half years younger he was almost as big as Robbie. He will not fit it much longer she thought, casting an admiring glance at the chubby round figure so full of promise, remorsefully accepting with each passing day his starring activities dwarfed the expectations of her older son.

    Lil crossed her arms and leaned beside the window. It was her own fault. She should have requested flying out to a specialist a week before term. Then the baby's position could've been lastingly converted. If not there'd have been ample time to prepare her for a Caesarean section. Beecher's experience in obstetrics was a laugh; two deliveries as a student, and a straight medical internship added nothing. In Afghanistan he was not even allowed to examine pregnant women. Granted he had removed a dead baby or two but the operations had been done to save the mother after the fetal heartbeat was no longer detectable. He was so cocksure, telling her he could right the position when she went into labour and bring the head down. Why had she trusted him? No doubt because she loved him. The more she thought of it the stronger she felt he cared less for her. "Oh Beecher what's to become of us."

    Afterward they had prayed together, as many times as their Shi'ite neighbours, believing God wouldn't forsake them. But He had and she was being punished for some no good reason as she had been so many times throughout her years of fosterage. What happened during the delivery was not entirely explained. She had been induced by Beecher, given a general anaesthetic and told one of his assistants monitored the level while he caught the baby. In spite of all his efforts the presenting part could not be altered and Robbie was born upside-down. There had been difficulty extracting the head but Beecher did not consider the delay long enough to cause brain damage; if there was, just how much would show up during growth and development. In any case there was no treatment and all they could do was wait and hope and pray. Now Lil was tired of waiting and looked to Dr. Robb for miracles. She sighed softly, "Soon you'll be walking better my dear," and reached for the window blind.

    While it descended, blocking out the street lamp and the crisscrossing shadows of threadbare branches checkering the room, her momentary elation gave way to a chilling sense of imprisonment with oblivion as the only means of escape. It was similar to her feelings so long ago; she was little more than a child herself as the giant form of Jessie Best towered over her like a jailor, spelling out her almost non-existent rights. Awkwardly she groped for the door.

When Lil entered the kitchen her mother-in-law had almost finished drying a stack of dishes. "Forgive me," she said, "I meant to take care of them."

"I suppose you did. Like the pile of laundry I washed this morning," Jessie commented tersely.

" Please believe me mother. I would have if Beecher had not insisted I finish his speech."

"What's that got to do with it? You have the rest of the evening."

There was no use explaining; it would only lead to further misunderstanding. Writing a text was one thing, researching the documentary Beecher intended to deliver was another. The truth would doubtlessly be misconstrued as overstepping her bounds because Beecher's mother was determined she alone was the driving force in her son's life. Lillian's graduation in anthropology from McGill cut no ice with Jessie. She said nothing and returned to the living room to pick up her scattered notes. Arranged in proper sequence they were laid on the dining room table beside a small portable Olivetti. After removing the case Lil rolled in a sheet of paper and adjusted the tabs. Soon the little machine began to chatter noisily, its sound broken briefly with the need to refer to her handwriting.

Two hours later when Beecher appeared she was combing the finished script for typographical errors. He'd entered by the side door and was standing in the kitchen, brushing large flakes of wet snow from his overcoat. His mother heard him come in. Blocking the low archway leading into the dining-room she gushed toward him, her large face full of admiration.

"Squaw winter!" He blew into his reddened hands.

"There's some leftover chicken and veggies warming on the stove," Jessie offered, helping him off with his coat and folding it over her broad forearm. "You sit yourself down and I'll fix it for you."

As Beecher moved in the direction of the dining room she ordered. "No! Here at the kitchen table. Lillian's busy and doesn't need to be disturbed. Much snow out?" she added, purposely retaining him in conversation while she temporarily sat his coat on the counter and set out dishes.

"An inch of the stuff. Not much. First fall of the season. Most of it melts on landing, particularly on the road. Must have started an hour ago. Be gone by morning, unless the temperature drops."

"Any problems driving?"

Beecher's eyes narrowed as he regarded his mother's blank expression. "I told you Mother the streets are bare. You weren't listening."

Arguing that wet pavement could also be dangerous was on the tip of Jessie's tongue but she refrained. Beecher was not in a reasonable mood. "How did your meeting go?" She asked.

"Which one? I've had several."

"You were going to see the General's Administrator when you left this afternoon."

Beecher scowled, "That one."

"Who else have you been talking to?"

"Duggan, Byers and Clayton, classmates of mine. After office hours they invited me to an Academy meeting in the cafeteria at the General. Very poor turn out. Mostly G.P.'s. There were a couple of general surgeons. A guy called Paolone did most of the talking. Seems the Physician's Services Insurance doesn't pay enough for an appendectomy to satisfy Dr. Paolone. According to my friends, his fees are already exorbitant and he won't give any kick-backs for referrals.

"Why should he?" Jessie sounded indignant. "Surely he's entitled to the whole surgical fee with all the responsibility he has."

"The G.P.s want more than fifteen percent for the initial patient work-up."

"Don't they get paid for the office call at the time they make the referral and don't they get paid for hospital visits on their patients following surgery?"

"Yes and no. Some of the referrals result from a patient's phone call and no charges are incurred."

"Anyway, isn't that enough?"

Beecher answered with a mouth full of food. "The bottom line is the gap between incomes."

"Why shouldn't there be? After all Beecher, you've sacrificed four years on a salary next to nothing. Don't tell me once you start these classmates of yours should get one cent of what you'll be able to charge."

The situation wasn't as cut and dried as his mother imagined. Ten years earlier when St. Mary's opened, G.P.'s allowed on staff were not granted surgical privileges other than for very minor operations. Consequently most of them who had been doing their own appendectomies and gall bladders for years at the General boycotted the new hospital. Their patients weren't given a choice when it came to being admitted. Either they went to the General or they got a new doctor and most of the sick went along with their family physician, whom they'd known for years. Paradoxically these same men whose training had been obtained from a preceptor outside of a recognized institution voted in favour of withholding full surgical privileges from a newcomer until the applicant could produce a certificate from The Royal College of Surgeons. As a result new doctors such as Beecher's classmates were curtailed. Bribing a surgeon into fee-splitting by means of a steady stream of referrals could lessen the gap. Duggan, Byers and Clayton were not above it as Beecher had found out. He was still annoyed by their overtures.

"It's not easy Mother. I can't operate without patients."

"You'll have lots of them. You grew up here. Almost everyone knows you, if not by your high-school record certainly from the missionary work you did in Afghanistan."

"Thanks to you." Beecher smiled as he patted his mother's hand.

There wasn't one event in her son's life of any consequence Jessie Best didn't broadcast, usually through the social page of the Shipton Shield. The letters from Afghanistan had run as a weekly series.

"You deserve it my boy. Your success is all I want. Long before your father died I'd planned on your being a doctor and now you've gone beyond. You're a specialist in a gainful branch of the profession. George would be so proud of you."

At the mention of her step-father Lil paused in the act of packing up her typewriter. George Best had always treated her kindly. He was the most benevolent person she'd ever known. A practising Christian, he'd devoted his life to being good to people. How he ever got hooked up with Jessie was beyond her. Where consideration, understanding and patience synthesized his essence, his wife was totally opposite except when it came to her attitude toward their son. The only reason she'd agreed to foster Lil was for Beecher's sake.

That was before the war when the Best's residence and their corner store occupied the ground floor of a big house. The property had been bought with their savings and while George served customers - the Sabbath being reserved for church - Jessie minded the till, her wary eyes roving between her hyperactive offspring and a stack of change. Once her son had enroled in the Spruceridge kindergarten she demanded that George buy a smaller place for themselves nearby. He did but was forced to employ a student evenings and when school was out. Nevertheless there was some benefit as Marvin had a bicycle which relieved George of the deliveries. This arrangement concluded when the young man enlisted. Rather than hire another, Jessie calculated it would be cheaper to take in a foster child; a live-in baby-sitter would free her to work evenings. She did not trust George in money matters. He was too soft.

Lil filled the bill nicely. Beecher was nine at the time and she was almost five years older. The day the Bests came to fetch her at the agency Jessie had been quite curt and not only to Lil. 'George you fool!' she hollered at the slim humped man who reached to take up the battered suitcase. 'She's old enough to carry her own.'

George had let go obediently and stood silently appraising his wife. But as Lil struggled to lift the weight he returned to help her. Angrily Jessie looked on, barely able to keep from physically interfering, while the unselfish pair, each with a grip on the handle, walked toward the car. Thereupon their spiritual unanimity was forged and grew in strength until George's big rheumatic heart could take no more.

Sure George would have been happy with Beecher's accomplishments, Lil thought, but pleased for Beecher's sake, not proud, for George was a humble man. "Your final draft is finished," she called into the kitchen. "If you don't mind I'm going to bed."

Beecher, half risen from the table, was about to follow his wife upstairs when Jessie held him back. "Have another cup of coffee and tell me more about your meeting." Her grip was firm. "Was Dr. Lindsay there?"

Beecher looked protestingly at his mother but sat down. "He was at St. Mary's pinning a hip. So Fortier told me."

"Who's he?"

"Another orthopod."

"I've never heard of him."

It was incredible. Of all the gossip to which his mother was exposed and her concern over every potential obstacle to his career, she had not heard of the latest orthopaedic incumbent! "He's only been here for a year," Beecher sarcastically replied.

"Strange! No one has mentioned him."

"Probably because he's not very busy. Most of his patients are French-speaking from out of town."

"What about that Indian?"

"Ramamurti?"

Jessie shook her head and frowned. "I never can pronounce their names. Why on earth they don't stay in their own country I'll never know. For any God-fearing white man to allow himself to be treated by one of those heathens is sinful."

Beecher considered asking his mother how she thought the Afghans felt about their mission in Bamiyan but thought better of it. Instead he answered directly. "He was tied up in the emergency."

"Who would ever ask for him?"

"He has his following. As a matter of fact some people from our church."

"I know," Jessie shrugged. "It sure beats me."

"He's a novelty, Mother. People are intrigued by his accent. There's an aura of mystery about him. Because they don't understand him they think he has clairvoyant powers. But from what my friends tell me he's slow in the operating room and nowhere near as dexterous as Lindsay."

"But Lindsay's not perfect either. He really made a mess of Beatrice Jones. Operated on her knee and now she's got a horrible scar." When she saw her remark did not impress her son Jessie added, "Dr. Lindsay does have a good reputation and perhaps it would be better to link up with him. He's busy and might welcome your help."

Beecher disagreed. "I'm not so sure. Besides I'd rather be on my own," then paused thoughtfully. "But maybe I'll tag along with him for awhile. It won't do any harm though I'll be darned if I'm going to give away any trade secrets."

The idea of being back-up to another surgeon did not excite him. He yawned and rose from the table.

"It's late Mother," he said, heading toward the door leading into the narrow front hall, "I think I'll turn in."

From the bath Lil heard his heavy foot-steps on the stairs. She was soaking herself when he opened the door.

It was a cramped room with the toilet against the back wall beside the tub. Beecher raised the lid, unzipped his fly and directed a stream of urine into the bowl. Lil's head was less than three feet away. She could feel fine droplets splash against her cheek as he asked, "you going to be much longer?"

She felt like telling him to check his aim as he was hitting the rim but let her remark slide. It was not the first time she absorbed his urine. Once he had wet the bed with her in it. That was years ago when she used to read him to sleep. He complained of being cold and she cuddled up next to him until they both dozed off. When she awoke an hour later her flannel nightgown was saturated.

Finished relieving himself he grabbed a toothbrush from a rack beside the mirror and leaned over the basin, his back to his wife.

Lillian could hardly discern his garbled words through the surge of his brush. But one of them might have been 'thanks'.

"I'd like to soak awhile longer Beecher", she said. "Your speech is on the dresser if you wish to look it over. Give me ten minutes."

When he had gone she re-sponged her face and neck and slid down till the water reached her chin. Although Lil was only five feet two it was a small tub and she had to flex her hips and knees. Lifting one foot she toed the hot water tap. Soon we'll have our own place with gold-plated bathroom fixtures, and a place to get away from Jessie's barbed comments - if it were possible. When George was alive some compromise existed, for Jessie was reluctant to tackle them together. Thankfully the situation lasted till she won the scholarship to McGill.

Jessie had maintained the girl stay home and take her place at the store but George would not hear of it. Much to his wife's chagrin he drew from his savings. Taking Lil by the arms, he smiled. 'You'll need a little extra for clothes and what-not, especially the fare to come home now and again.' Beyond the young woman's shoulder he met Jessie's disapproving frown. Whether he was seething with disgust or full of pity for his wife he covered his feelings with the same calculated air of tolerance that Lil so frequently adopted herself. From then on the poor man was on his own. How sorry Lil had felt for him the day she left; how much more bowed and whiter he appeared when she returned at Christmas.

"George was a saint compared to Beecher but I've made my bed," Lil murmured, "and it's waiting down the hall."

CHAPTER THREE

In the past when she was sure Beecher had finished his homework they would go to the basement for a half-hour session with his electric train. Except for his childish pranks she had not minded as it was a relaxing interlude between her own studies. Once when she was adjusting a derailed caboose he brought his fist down on an open tube of glue and the contents shot all over her blouse. Then there was the incident of pea-shooting her with tapioca. What he needed was a sharp cuff and she was relatively big enough to administer it but she did not have the courage for a simple reprimand. Instead Lil went to her room and locked the door until he tired of drilling her through the keyhole.

At Christmas two years later when Lillian came home from McGill Beecher was in grade ten and had begun to notice girls. Never a shy child, the familiarity with which he greeted her was far more sexual than the younger brother-to-sister relationship she expected; it was amazing how much taller he had grown. She had left a podgy adolescent keenly into building model rail roads. Now he was stronger and his voice had broken. His invitation to the basement had lecherous overtones although it took her another term at university to recognize them. His incessant pawing and patting of her backside while she bent over the tracks was interpreted as nothing more than playfulness. Until he wrestled her to the floor. Once again she ended up with a ruined blouse and not from errant cement. The front was torn and she had difficulty covering her bosom with the remnants as she beat a hasty retreat up the stairs. Afterward he had come to her room and lain beside her. 'Don't tell Mum,' he begged. 'I didn't mean any harm.' She had pitied him and held him close stroking his curly hair.

The following spring Jessie's gallbladder acted up, resulting in an emergency cholecystectomy. Lillian, home from university, took her place at the store. No one was more surprised than George, although he showed nothing but pleasure when Beecher began to drop by late in the evenings to help out. In fact the boy's intention was more to impress Lil than please customers.

How she had enjoyed it. In her entire life Lil never had so much attention. He would fetch things from shelves she couldn't reach, sweep the floor, package groceries and help her with the inventory. Near closing time he would ask if Lil could be released to help with his homework to which George would nod and smile, 'I don't know what we'd do without you, Lillian. Go ahead! Seems his needs are greater than mine.' As long as Beecher was making good marks George would support him. He asked nothing more than effort. No other responsibilities took precedent: cutting the grass, taking out ashes, sifting the clinkers, shovelling snow and generally looking after the house. What George could not manage himself a neighbour's boy was hired to do. 'You two run along,' he'd say. 'Nothing left I can't handle myself.'

They skipped home to Beecher's room and plodded over Latin translations or an English composition, subjects in which Lil excelled. When it came to math and science Beecher had no problems. He had usually finished these assignments before going to the store. Lil would sit with her heels under her on the floor, her ankle length skirt tucked tightly beneath her calves, while Beecher read aloud from the textbook on his desk. Eventually he'd groan, 'I hate this stuff!' or slam the book shut and complain miserably about his inability to understand. 'The problem is your lack of concentration, Beecher,' Lil ventured one night after a week of tutoring. 'It's late. You're tired! Tomorrow why don't you do the subjects you find tough first when your mind is fresh?' This sound advice went by the board. The main purpose in asking for help was to lure her to his room. Having accomplished this he hadn't figured out his next move. Now he was being told what to do and he disliked criticism, constructive or otherwise. In frustration Beecher pushed his chair away from the desk. The leg of it struck Lil on a knee and she cried out in pain. She was rubbing it vigorously when he leaned over to see what had happened. The hem of her skirt lay above the top of her stocking. Daringly he massaged the exposed flesh. 'Not there! It's my knee!' she prompted. 'Oh!' He laughed nervously, 'I'll kiss it better.' But Lil pushed aside his hand and struggled to her feet. 'No you won't,' she cried and faltered. Beecher caught and held her full weight until she could straighten her leg again and with an apology kissed her on the lips. It had been just a peck but combined with the verbal reparation, the first time she had ever heard him ask forgiveness for anything, moved her to return it as she clasped him tightly around the waist. His second kiss was interrupted by the sound of the side door being unlocked. Befuddled they scampered to their own beds. For the next two weeks when old George, weary from work, approached the house the second floor would be in darkness, or if he did notice light emanating from either of their rooms there was never any shining through the crack beneath the doors when he reached the top of the stairs.

Nothing more erogenous than healthy petting ensued. Both were in their own beds before the old man had finished his ablutions and retired into the back bedroom. There was no corridor creeping in the middle of the night. If Beecher wasn't under his own covers with Lil sitting on the edge reading to him he was in her room teasing, tickling or generally cutting up. Undressing in front of her seemed natural; she had been putting him to bed for years. But when it came to removing her own clothes Lil was reserved. 'Some day Beecher, maybe I'll let you do that,' she said reattaching her garter-snaps. 'But not just now.' Between bouts and the books Beecher's knowledge of languages improved.

The scene changed when Jessie came home from the hospital. Opportunities of their being alone in the house became non-existent. Chiefly because Jessie spied her son coming out of the wrong room clad in his undershorts. He should've been sound asleep in his bed. From then on they had a chaperon and before either found a way around this insufferable bundling board it was September and time for Lil to leave. At the train station Beecher gave her a big hug and she promised to write. Shortly thereafter she did but he never answered. Beecher had transferred his fumbling curiosity down the street to a rather dull more permissive girl closer to his age and the lass knew how to handle him. Instinctively she broke him as she did
other colts in the neighbourhood. Afterward he was ashamed and afraid mainly due to a concurrent lecture on sex and the facts of life delivered to the upper school by a Public Health doctor. These feelings sublimated with the building of a soap-box racer and his prospects of winning the spring derby.

Lillian lost her virginity to an air force veteran whom she encountered while associating with a society of Christian students. She had not wanted it to happen. At least not in the manner it did at three in the morning on the landlady's living room floor, but loneliness and contriteness overcame her. John, a bombardier, honourably discharged from the R.C.A.F. entered university at the government's expense. It did not take him long to realize he was wasting his time. Sales were more his line, not academia. To boot, he could see no practical use for the atomic physics course he had chosen. Right answers on test papers were a rarity. When she came to her senses a week later it was too late. The man had needed solace for as long as he used her body - one night. Her enchantment ended at the next meeting of the society when she saw him strolling about with another girl. So a lesson had been taught, but without bitterness. If Lillian learned anything from the affair other than never let a strange man touch her private parts when she was emotionally aroused, it was intercourse did not necessarily result in the dire consequences her foster mother predicted, nor had it been as painful.

During the following Christmas holidays Lil remained in Montreal having landed a job in a department store. When she did get back to Shipton it was only for a short visit before leaving for summer work in St. Andrew's-by-the-Sea. Beecher was close to six feet tall and finished grade eleven. He and George were at the train station to greet her. Driving back to the house in a second-hand Chev she sat between them as comfortable as a chick in a feathered nest, chirping away about university, her course and the few friends she had made. She had remained in this gay mood in spite of Jessie's coolness, keeping Beecher at arm's length until she left. 'Well how's the happy anthropologist or is it philanthropist,' was the old girl's caustic greeting and sent her off a few days later with an equally cruel, 'you've been spending George's money long enough. 'Bout time you paid for yourself,' while Beecher gallantly tossed her suitcase in the trunk.

Seven months later Jessie's attitude was surprisingly better. This time when Lillian returned for Christmas, Beecher himself had been on hand to meet her. Poor George was home in bed with an acute attack of passive congestion, so bloated he was almost unrecognizable.

'Isn't there anything to cure him?' Jessie had asked when Dr. Morrisey appeared to assess the inadequate effect of the digitalis he'd been administering.

'Nothing short of cardiac surgery, possibly a mitral commissurotomy,' the doctor explained. 'That's an operation to widen a narrowed valve in his heart. He's old and besides there's no one in Shipton trained to do it. If he's agreeable, I'll arrangement for him to go to Toronto.'

Jessie thought the G. P. was exaggerating but George pathetically went along with his suggestion and consented to be transferred three days before Yuletide. The eve of the operation Jessie, Beecher and Lil were at his bedside. What he said influenced their lives more infinitely than the Christian example he had tried so hard to set. His words were interrupted with paroxysms of coughing and shortness of breath. 'You all know there is a high risk involved because of my general condition. The doc told me he was talking to you. Consequently, in case there's never another opportunity, you should be aware I've made some provisions, meagre though they are. I've prayed to God - He knows how much I love you - in the hope they will be adequate. There's a few thousand dollars stashed in the Imperial Bank on James Street, enough to complete Beecher's education. Jess, you know exactly how much; you've counted every penny. But it's only to go toward his tuition and board.' His swollen eyes held Beecher steadily. 'No frills! You've had plenty of them in the past. The rest is Lil's. A small insurance policy I've carried for years, and rent from the apartments should see your mother through until you're established and can provide a little more. Although I don't intend to saddle you with this responsibility it does fall under one of the Ten Commandments. Furthermore there are other things I must get off my chest - if it will allow me. May the Lord forgive me for pointing a finger at anyone, Beecher, but you are my son and I feel responsible for your behaviour.'

At this point the old man had to be propped higher on his pillows before continuing, 'There's nothing wrong with your sanguineous temperament. It was a gift of God and none of us had any choice in the matter. Being a gift of God you must put your faith in Him to help identify your faults and pray He'll show you the way to curb them. Bare your soul to Him. Put your trust in Him, and your strengths will outweigh your weaknesses. Up till now you've been a restless self-centred child and I'm afraid I've not been much help. As they say one has to be cruel to be kind; because I can't stand the pain of being cruel to anyone I backed off in the hope some day with the help of the Lord you would come to recognize your shortcomings. My son, you have the potential of becoming a leader. I've seen how generous you can be, how responsive to your surroundings and the moods and feelings of others. You're adventuresome, talkative, personable and friendly as evidenced by your being elected to the senate. You won hands down after you led the whole student body down to City Hall protesting the School Board's ban on intercollegiate football. The Mayor's idea to cut costs and help the postwar effort was the reason reported in the Shield. A ridiculous demoralizing proposal, I agreed, but you had to be the first to throw rotten tomatoes at him - a bit much - and if you hadn't apologized the next day you'd have been expelled. Why you did it, I don't know - you never even tried out for the team.'

    A faint smile crossed George's lips. 'Your compassion will be best served son when you fill yourself with the Holy Spirit. Like Simon Peter who denied Christ three times before the cock crowed you too will undergo a transformation. Your basic temperament won't change but your traits will. Follow Christ, Beecher. Find yourself a profession where you can be of greater service than I've been. But don't look for any reward.' George burst into another coughing spell and it was a few minutes before he could go on. 'Please take this in good spirit. I'm trying to be helpful.' Then he shifted to Lil and his words still echoed in her brain. 'Look after him. He needs you.'

George was spared the agony of an operation; the night before surgery he died in his sleep. At the funeral New Year's eve Lil was amazed at how many people turned out, most of the congregation. Everyone had nothing but praise for him. 'He was a most devoted people's warden, a practising Christian, the salt of the earth,' Reverend Trussell commented in the eulogy, 'a quiet man with an unfathomable depth of meekness, mercy and cheer. He has touched us all with his bountiful spirit. We pray God grant us the will to live up to his courage and faith.'

    Lil had shuddered at these remarks. George had asked her to take care of Beecher. To fulfil this request she was going to need plenty of both; and courage and faith were not her fortes. The old man had mistaken her calm easygoing nature for one who had undergone salvation. Phlegmatically she had tagged along with him. To Lil he had been a comfortable like-minded cinch, more empathic than anyone she ever knew. For the same reason she had associated with professed Christian students at university. Yet true belief escaped her. She could not get entirely involved and the association did not help her introversion.

    It hadn't mattered anyhow. Lil was denied the onerous task. Jessie the busybody took over Beecher's rearing with gusto. The old girl certainly had the right. She must have made it her major resolution for at breakfast New Year's day phase one of her master plan was unveiled. Perversely Lil was included. 'Beecher, you have a year and a half to buckle down and get some decent marks. If you don't you'll never get into medical school. You're marching up to your room as soon as this meal is over. Lillian, you're not due to leave until Sunday. I expect you to spend the rest of your holidays helping him.' Jessie's smile came as a complete surprise. 'Knock some knowledge into him.' It faded fast as Lil retorted, 'You think it's possible?'

In the evening Lil let Beecher mess around with her. Weary from two days of weeping and receiving commiserative friends Jessie retired early; from Beecher's room they heard her door shut. He was half under the covers supporting himself on his elbows while Lil, on the outside, was lying across his legs quizzing him on a passage of Latin. 'Give me the conjugation of the verb rapio,' she asked. 'That's what I'm going to do to you,' he leered and slowly ran his hand up her leg to the crotch. Her curliness under the silken material aroused him. Flinging off the blankets, he began to tug at her drawers. Lil did not move, but put the book aside when his probing fingers began to excite her. 'The garter-belt first,' she urged, and hoisting her heavy flannel skirt and slip ordered, 'Undo my stockings.' He leapt from the bed and with trembling anticipation watched as she raised her hips to release the catch at the small of her back. 'Go ahead, undo them,' she repeated.

The unfastened belt recoiled to her thighs. Paying no heed, he slid it to the floor, taking both stockings with it and returned to his original goal. Lil thrust herself up again, placed her thumbs inside the elastic band of her panties and pushed them down over her hips. In a shake Beecher dropped them beside her other delicate things, and pulled himself on top. Breathlessly, more from the weight of him, Lil sighed, 'do it. Do it now Beecher', then spreading as wide as she could, guided his initial thrust into her wetness. It felt good and better with each successive nudge but to her disappointment just when she quickened with his rhythm, he stopped and backed away.

Curiously she lifted her head. Beecher, kneeling by the edge of the bed, had taken himself in hand. Spellbound Lil watched the tip of his organ swell with each upward stroke until a spurt of semen landed close to her waist. The rest oozed over his knuckles and dripped into her pubic hair. 'A miss!' She smiled at the sticky spot close to her bellybutton. Realizing Beecher was not in tune with her humour, she chastised quietly. 'You shouldn't masturbate. It's selfish.' Quite seriously, he frowned, 'I don't want to get you pregnant.'

Saturday, Beecher dropped by the variety store. The shop was empty and Marvin Husselman, back from war, stood behind the counter. 'What's your mum going to do now?' He asked, after overzealously greeting the youth - in the back of Marvin's mind was the hope Jessie would sell the business. 'Don't know,' Beecher replied, not wanting to lengthen the conversation; he was more interested in the non-prescription pharmaceutical shelves. 'How much are these?' He asked, fingering a small box of contraceptives. Marvin pursed his small mouth, making a clucking noise. He was about to answer with a coarse remark but discretion intervened when he thought of the opportunity presenting itself. Befriending Beecher could be useful. 'Tell you what,' he offered, rolling his big head, 'I've got some army surplus condoms you can have for free. If you want to drop by my apartment later?'

Beecher did and in addition to instructions on how to use one he was introduced to an exciting assortment of girlie magazines. Before Lil left the following day he had worn it three times. Monday after school he was back to Husselman's for more.

Throughout the next eighteen months they saw very little of each other. If Beecher wasn't impressing his chums in one way he would find another such as supplying the uninitiated with pornographic literature and instant 'rubbers' while Lillian went on to graduate with an honours degree. Avoiding athletics like the bane, his energy was poured into public speaking and drama where he excelled, taking the lead role in the annual school play, and being elected by the student body for a 'service above self' award. At Commencement his marks were just above average but good enough to allow him entrance to university. His mother insisted he go to Toronto where George's sister would put him up - free.

'Lil, you'd better become a nurse.' Jessie sternly rationalized, adding, 'There's no earthly use for the diploma you have.' Her actual reason was the beneficial effect her adopted daughter had on Beecher's scholastics. Without Lillian's help she felt her son would never make it into Medicine. 'Get an application to the Paediatric Hospital. I'll lend you the money. I've plenty now Beecher's friend, Marvin, has bought the business. I also hold his mortgage on the building.'

So Lillian became first her brother's keeper and then his wife. Her salary became their major source of income over the next five years. With Jessie's blessing they were married the day after she received her nursing diploma and Beecher had successfully completed his anatomy year. Standing before the chancel at St. Matthew's while Reverend Trussell directed their vows she had no illusions. The going would be tough. Beecher was never sexually faithful to her so why should a piece of paper change him. Still he had always come back with his tail between his legs, lying between his teeth and sorry afterward. To make amends he would take her to a movie, never to a dance or medical school function to proudly display her in front of his friends. Although this was annoying Lil put up with it, thankful Church was the only place he did not mind being seen with her. After they were married she began to attend regularly, dragging him protestingly to the young couple's club. Until one night the guest speaker happened to be a surgeon recently returned from missionary work in Africa.

The tales of medical heroics carried out in such primitive surroundings although told in subdued tones stimulated Beecher to ask so many questions the minister, F.P. Butterworth D.D., had to cut him off with an apology. 'Dr. Robb is a very busy man. He has generously given us one of his rare evenings off and we mustn't detain him. Sorry to conclude this very stimulating talk. However,' he singled out Beecher, 'If you're interested in becoming a missionary I'd be very pleased to discuss the prospects with you anytime.' Very flattering, Lil had thought, but not a suitable role for her swaggering husband unless he changed considerably. Beecher was hooked when he learned the same Dr. Robb was doing post-graduate work in orthopaedics and was to be one of his clinical instructors. During his senior year he followed the surgeon on rounds like a dependent lamb. From then on he had but one ambition.

'Dr. Schweitzer Best,' his fellow classmates would tease. The chance to pooh-pooh them was not long in coming. Six months into an internship he learned of the need for an M.D. at the Afghan Mission. His application was accepted and the year of '56 became one of great expectations.

A noble undertaking but was it for the right reason? Lil wondered at the time and she was still wondering. Now they were back and Afghanistan seemed so far away. Hopefully her husband would shed his fantasies and buckle down to become a good provider.

She stepped out of the bath, wrapped her dressing gown around her and shivered down the short hall to the small bedroom where her relationship with Beecher began.

CHAPTER FOUR

"Come on wake up!"

"Go away and leave me alone." Jason protested, rolling over and pulling the covers about his ears.

"Time to rise and shine." His dad nagged.

"What for?"

"You asked that I help with your boat. Remember?"

Lindsay's son propped himself on an elbow, kneading his tousled hair. "Be with you in a minute." Yawning, he asked. "What time is it?"

"Six-thirty. We must be quiet; the rest are still sleeping. Your breakfast is ready downstairs."

Jim's biological clock awakened him at five. Sunday morning was no exception. Dressed as the weather dictated he would be back from a three-mile run, shaved, showered and finished breakfast before the rest of the family stirred. Jogging was a habit recently acquired and he adhered to it as religiously as cleaning his teeth. Since reading a paper on aerobics, Jim had become a compulsive exerciser and advised his patients righteously. 'Saturate your bodies with oxygen. It's great for connective tissue, tendons, muscles and ligaments, not to mention lung capacity and cardiac reserve.' The scheme seemed to work for him. Although his dark brown hair, greying at the temples, betrayed middle age his body was trim and he felt better, convinced it had increased his stamina, acuity and tolerance toward patients - some of whom could drive a psychiatrist around the bend.

'A poor example' his good friend and colleague Ed Atwater, commented entertainingly. 'Most of the shrinks I know can make it on their own. So much for your high, Jimmie. I'll take a beer anytime.'

The children were reluctant to get involved. There was no fun in it; and Merri had been quite negative. 'I get enough exercise looking after this house. If you have to blow off steam, Jim Lindsay, better do it some place else.' Though their attitudes were disappointing there was no cause for concern. Jason's activities were strenuous enough, being on the swim team and playing basketball regularly while the girls figure-skated all winter and summer. So Jim kept jogging alone, presently enjoying the brisk air.

He was squatting in front of the oven grilling bread when his stocking-footed son slid into the kitchen. "Terrific day!" Jim smiled, "'bout time you came around."

There was no reply from Jason. With his hands full of clothing he was busy trying to keep his balance on the slippery floor. To right himself he flung his arms in the air and toppled backwards. A step ladder chair caught his seat like a hod while the pullover and sneakers shot across the room.

Rising from the stove with a plateful of hot toast, Jim intercepted the flying objects with the impact of a ground to air missile. One shoe ricochetted off an ear, narrowly missing a pitcher of milk; his shoulder deflected the other into the open oven; and the jersey entwined about his head.

Speechless he unwound the cotton sweater to spot Jason sprawled on the stool. The boy's startled expression amused him. "Well, you're awake!"

Jason apologized lightheartedly, "Geez I'm sorry. Lucky I didn't hit that jug of milk."

"You said it!" Jim's smile widened when he noticed the other running shoe in the oven. "You want some of this toast or shall I heat up your sneaker?"

The suggestion promoted more merriment and together they laughed, heedless of the slumbering souls upstairs.

Jim was still beaming after Jason retrieved his clothing and finished dressing. "Here, take your toast. There's coffee if you want some. I'll get things started."

The garage held two cars and a tractor. Rather than tear down the old implement shed Jim and Merri had it restored in keeping with the 'Tudor' appearance of their house. The loft with three tall dormer windows projecting from its steep northern roof remained. The central window was blocked by a basketball rebound board and the area beneath, paved with asphalt, connected the garage and driveway. To please Merri the back of the loft had been converted into an art studio by adding a large skylight to the less steep southern roof, perfect lighting during winter when the sun's rays lengthened.

An ideal place to build a boat, Jim thought, reaching the loft through a trapdoor. The level wooden floor eased placement and bracing of the uprights. Constructed to support the keel and ribs, their height diminished fore and aft to a low point toward the bow where the centreboard slot had been cut. He examined the centreboard well and marvelled at the workmanship. Between the stem and transom five ribs were notched and strung by pairs of battens and chines. Appraising it Jim realized the framework was evenly balanced and ready for planking. He was still leisurely admiring the carpentry when Jason popped through the floor.

"What do you think Dad?"

"Masterful job, everything fits. With your skill someday you'll be the envy of every bone-setter around."

The boy was running his hand over the smooth surface of the transom. Shyly he avoided his father's eyes. "Nah," he replied.

Interpreting the remark as youthful humility, Jim smiled. "You're too modest son. I mean it. An orthopod must be a good carpenter."

Jason looked up sharply. "Thanks for the compliment, but that's not what I meant."

The likelihood of having to deal with a problematic answer to his next question caused Jim to hesitate. Cautiously he asked, "What did you mean 'nah'?"

Jason regarded his father apologetically. "Well, and please don't misunderstand me Dad, I think your work is very interesting and worthwhile but I'm not cut out for doctoring. I'd rather be an architect or an inventor. Maybe a naval architect."

"Fair enough Jase! Your talent and brains will allow you to be anything you wish and I'm sure you'll be darn good at it. However don't toss out medicine yet. It's the greatest profession of them all. A doctor can go anywhere in the world and find meaningful work."

"I suppose you're right. But a doctor has too many headaches. I've heard you complain plenty about being a slave to people, awakened in the middle of the night to order a sedative for somebody troubled by an inability to count - sheep that is - or getting dragged out of bed in the wee small hours to treat a drunk who's fallen and broken something, of being bugged by people everywhere unable to wait for advice until they get to your office. No sir, I want a job dealing with abstract or inanimate objects, ones that won't interfere with my personal life."

And leave something worthwhile behind, Jim thought. In the past whenever the opportunity arose he'd expressed his opinion, more a desire, Jason should follow in his footsteps. There'd been no adverse comment until recently when Merri reminded him he also had

Do Unto Others 53

four daughters. 'Women enter medicine too,' she exclaimed, 'You chauvinist!' Against which he had no argument. Yet traditionally he felt his branch of surgery was a man's field. Up till now he hadn't included the girls. Perhaps he should.

The boy was just drawing conclusions from his own observations and they were accurate. Perhaps Jim had played up the bad side too often? - no doubt when he was tired and in need of a change or rest. So who could blame Jason? He decided not to press the argument, not only because of the possibility of stiffening his son's resistance by repetitively citing the advantages but also lately he had his own misgivings.

Once, Jim was convinced there was nothing more interesting and challenging than the practice of medicine. This motivation increased during his learning years. When it peaked he wasn't sure, likely after starting private practice. Till then he didn't have to scrounge for interesting cases. Choosing medicine hadn't been easy, having had a traumatic experience with doctors when he was young. A tonsillectomy under open drop ether on the kitchen table is not a child's idea of playing games. Also the sights, smells and sounds associated with the in-hospital death of his mother seared his mind. In the end it had been the objective approach of Merri's father which lured him into the fold.

Burl Cunningham was a veterinarian and quite jolly. 'A real nice guy am I,' he'd joke. 'Only loved by animals, kids and little old ladies.' He proved it not long after Jim had begun to walk Merri home from school. One day in spring they'd dropped into the Lindsays' to pick up Jim's dog. On the way to Merri's the terrier ran onto the road and was hit by a car. 'Just lay Bowser on the table and hold his head,' the Doc ordered. 'I'll put him to sleep for a spell.' A metal syringe mysteriously appeared and its contents emptied into the dog's abdomen. Jim was on the verge of throwing up. 'Now we can examine him,' the vet continued. 'There you go. Didn't feel a thing, did you Bowser?' 'His name's Skipper,' Jim almost retched. 'No matter son, he's got a broken bone. He's asleep now, you want to feel it?' Jim was backing off but the doc placed his hand on the exact spot. There was a grating sensation. 'That's his femur moving where it shouldn't. Maybe it will take a pin. Keep your fingers crossed.' Skipper was placed under the fluoroscope. 'There it is, sure enough and he's lucky. Stick around if you want to watch.'

Jim did while Dr. Cunningham shaved the fur from the dog's hip and painted it with iodine. 'Kills the bugs,' he grinned, then scrubbed his hands, donned a pair of sterile rubber gloves and made a small nick over the upper end of the bone. A stainless steel rod, the diameter of the marrow cavity, was inserted through the upper fragment. In awe Jim watched on the fluoroscope as it traversed the break to enter the distal half of the bone. Short of the knee joint the drilling stopped. 'There you go Bowser. Now we'll just nip off the excess.' A couple of stitches closed the cut. In no time, Skipper was standing, all four paws on the floor. From then on, whether or not Merri was home, Jim found himself out back to see what the doc was doing and if there was anything he could watch. There usually was and eventually the doc had let him assist on some operations. The sequel would have been a veterinary career if Merri's influence hadn't prevailed. 'People's problems are more challenging than animals' Jimmie. Don't sell yourself short,' she argued and her father agreed. Although Burl had to chuckle. 'But they pay me for treating their pets long before they'll pay you.'

    The second world war began after Jim had enroled in the premedical course at Western. It was not a large institution and everyone knew each other. In between classes they would gather in the cafeteria on the second floor of the science building and listen to the news. Great celebration occurred December 13th when three British cruisers engaged the pocket-battleship, Graf Spee, off the coast of Uruguay and forced her into Montevideo for repairs. Four days later she was scuttled by her captain. 'Come on Jimmie, hit the deck,' his room mate shouted the following morning. 'I'm off to join the navy. You comin' along?' 'No way my friend. Go get yourself killed if you must. I came here to study medicine. I'm not leaving without a degree.' Fortunately Jim was exempt from the service and the course was condensed from six to four years. 'We'll need lots of good doctors in the years ahead,' the Dean announced. 'Keep up your grades, boys, and you're a step ahead of the draft.' Still, they were required to take officer's training and assigned a position immediately after graduation. With 'cum Laude' printed on his diploma Jim Lindsay could've entered any famous medical centre. However his 'Mecca' was an army camp in Manitoba.

    'Who knows where this painful sojourn into the management of sore feet, piles and venereal disease will lead if the war continues for a few more years,' he wrote to his father, 'but it has sufficed for surgical training in a veterans' hospital.'

A few years later an American Superfortress dropped the first atom bomb over Japan. Before the second fell on Nagasaki Jim became engaged to Merri. They were married on V.J. day and moved to Toronto where at Christie Street Hospital, introduced to a ward of hideous disabilities and fanciful reconstructive procedures, Jim made his life-long decision. 'At least one can observe the results of an operation,' he chided a fellow novice interested in internal medicine. 'Once a pill is past the lips and over the gums it's by guess or by God. No, I'd rather deal with tangible problems.' A few years at Oxford studying 'cold' musculoskeletal deformities - long enough to pick up a British Fellowship - qualified Jim to write the Canadian certificate examination. Sub-specialization was in vogue. 'Orthopaedic Surgery' was fairly new and he loved it. Consequently passing the certificate examination had not been difficult. A steeper hurdle was obtaining acceptance by Shipton's physicians and surgeons. They were not keen to have him. Probably because of a lack of confidence in their own knowledge. 'I've been setting bones since 1910,' Doc Skinner maintained when Jim first met him. 'Nothing you know I don't, young man.' Shortly afterward the old G.P. died of pneumonia, complicating a hip fracture he refused to have pinned.

During this setting-up period the Lindsays' had three extra pairs of shoes to buy and money did not come easy, not until Jim had won the locals' respect. Nothing dramatic happened to shower him with accolades. Just a steady start which he credited to mixing knowledge with common sense. 'Don't knock yourself, Jimmie,' Merri said, when he felt shameful for borrowing a little extra from the bank. 'You have the uncanny ability to apply everything you know, and you know an awful lot. Someday you'll be a terrific provider.'

Her forecast proved correct as had his father's reminder which antedated Merri's by a dozen years. 'How do you think I'm able to pay for your keep?' His old man asked while the two of them stood on the platform waiting for a train to London. It was a question put forth on several occasions, like the day Jim kicked a football through the living room window; this time the elder Lindsay was smiling. 'I just happen to know more about my business than my clients. Knowledge is power son. Get off to university and eat it up.' Too bad his dad hadn't lived to see the fruit of his advice; he would've been impressed, but to Jim money was a fringe benefit.

Curing an affliction, relieving pain, suffering and fear were more satisfying.

So he thought, until lately. Now he wasn't sure. One unredeemable fact precluded all else - the absence of permanency.

A patient, cured, comes back tomorrow with a recurrence or another problem and the day after dies. He was merely temporizing, fighting an organized retreat, made more aware of his own mortality by the impermanence of his accomplishments and the inability to predict. From a life of hard work what would be left? A stack of files, documenting the existence of a series of problems that because of their confidential nature could never be divulged? He was resentful and the feeling was growing. Why? Was it kindled by incompetence to offset his own transiency? Possibly. Were these perceptions behind his consideration of a trip to Afghanistan? Training other doctors to carry on one's work had some degree of perpetuity. He might establish orthopaedics as a specialty in that country - if politics or Father Time and Mother Nature did not intervene. Perhaps Jason was right, a pyramid, a cathedral or a submarine could last for centuries.

Disrupting the curious silence befallen his father Jason queried, "How did it go in Toronto last week? The scoliosis case."

Jim slowly shook his head. "The surgery or the postmortem?"

"Postmortem! You mean she died?" Jason hadn't associated such a finality with the patient until that moment. The mechanical treatment of lateral curvature of the spine had been explained to him more than once. He was intrigued by the placement of metal rods along the backbone to bend it to one side or the other and hold it firmly until a graft welded the bones into the correct position. Much like suspending a bridge or the planking operation they were about to undertake. It never occurred to him the scoliosis involved a human being.

Observing his son's anxious expression Jim explained, "No, the patient did very well. I'm sorry my facetiousness confused you. The postmortem was Geoffrey Robb's dissection of my examination result."

Unimpressed by his father's failure to pass an exam at the age of forty-three Jason nodded dully, "What did he say?"

"He gave me the diplomatic run-around. Said my paper had been excellent but the oral borderline. I'm to repeat it in the spring. He apologized, saying they could only pass forty-five percent. Told me what I already knew. Whether or not I passed wouldn't interfere with my income. 'We know you've a British Fellowship and have already passed the certificate,' he said. 'but it won't hurt you to wait till March.' "Who the bloody hell does he think he is?"

Jim's glistening red face would have frightened anyone other than a member of his family. Jason started to snigger but sobered as his father continued.

"Funny thing. He mentioned how Dr. Best made out. An indiscretion, I reckon. Neither his business to say, nor mine to hear. Told me what a fine Christian gentleman Beecher is and how lucky we are to have him in Shipton."

"Who's Dr. Best?"

"Oh! I'm sorry, Jase. I thought you were listening when your mother and I were talking at supper the other night."

Jim's first impression of Dr. Best had not been favourable. Embarrassed by revealing his feelings over a personal matter and loathe to gossip, he chose not to digress any further. "If we're going to stand here palavering all morning we'll never finish this job."

Jason pointed at the skeleton. "I made the frames, chine and battens yesterday but can use your help."

"Your mother told me. Where were you?"

"Out with Hotshot."

"Rich Mosley?"

"Yeah. We went to the show."

"How's Rich doing?"

Jason's friend was two years older and nowhere near as bright. The only thing they had in common was a shine for basketball. While Jason had skipped a grade in public school Rich had to repeat his 'senior matric'.

"Not bad. He's working harder this year- has to. Things don't come easy for him."

"Has he any plans?"

"Yep. Wants to go into medicine."

"Why?"

"Says it's the highest paid profession."

Jim's eyes narrowed as Jason went on. "He'd like to talk to you sometime when you're not busy. Says his parents can't advise him. Neither has been to university. I think he wants you to give him a recommendation."

"What's his dad do?"

"He's a factory foreman. Makes good money. Rich has no brothers nor sisters. His dad has promised to pay his tuition; he'll need it. There's no chance of his winning a scholarship."

"To make money is as good a reason as any. As long as he's worth it. But it's putting the cart before the horse. If he proves he's any good the money will follow. Sure I'll speak to him Jase, some weekend or over Christmas."

Rich Mosley was a pleasant lad with a lot of street sense. But to get into medicine and stay there he needed more than parental encouragement, financial backing and a character reference from Dr. Lindsay. In Jim's opinion the boy didn't have the intelligence. But he wouldn't be asked to comment on that aspect. Anyway, Jim thought, who am I to judge. With a genuine interest and a ton of application Rich might make it.

"What movie did you see?"

Jason was on his knees fidgeting with a pair of gudgeons. He put them in a small paper bag and laid it aside before answering.

"'How The West Was Won.' 'The Longest Day' was at the Odeon. But the line was too long. So we went to the Capital."

"Any good?"

"Yeah but it was sad."

"How's that?"

"Almost everyone in the picture died. There were some exciting scenes, especially the buffalo stampede and the final shoot-out. It spun out a century of American history. I learned something but it left me cold. Families grow up and move out. Grandchildren are born. Parents die. I guess we should've waited to get into 'The Longest Day'. It's all about the invasion of Europe."

"I think you made the right choice."

"Why?"

"It gave you a better perspective of life. From what I've heard, 'The Longest Day' is nothing more than a theatrical account of D-Day. Very exciting if you like a lot of noise. Apparently it doesn't depict the real horror confronting the individual. Again one might look upon modern warfare as impersonal. Bombs are dropped from great heights. Artillery shells land many miles away so the man who pulls the trigger never faces his enemy."

Jason, level in hand, was going over the framework apparently not listening. His answer caught his father by surprise.

"Yes and getting killed in a war is expected, there's a purpose in dying. Death in peacetime is not. It's unthought-of and rather selfish."

For a young person never subjected to the anguish of losing someone close, the remark was profound. Both of Jim's parents died before Jason was born. Jim remembered the bitter resentment when his mother passed away. His small wet fists had pounded the headboard nights on end until sorrow gave way to anger and the tears dried. She had always been around to comfort. Suddenly she was gone and he felt betrayed. Parents should never die. They should fade away slowly. Better Jason be exposed to this empty feeling on the silver screen. In real life such stress can be agonizing.

"It's the time element Jase," he proposed. "When a film director jams three generations into a four-hour show he plays up the captivating scenes. Other events in the lives of the characters are either omitted or sped up disproportionately."

"All of life's experiences are relative," He went on. "As are the interactions of one person with another. A day in the life of a newborn is ever so much longer than his parents. It's a whole lifetime. Talk to any old person and they'll tell you the older you get the faster time flies. Let me prove it to you mathematically. At one year of age a week is roughly one fiftieth of the total length of time you know. A week in your life at fifty is fifty times fifty, or one twenty-five hundredths of your total experience. Or two thousand five hundred times shorter. Which ever way you look at it. A person lives within a time frame. Not outside where it can be viewed objectively like in the movie you saw. There is definitely an awareness of acceleration but the point of infinity seems a long way off."

Sensing his son might be a trifle bored with his dissertation he added whimsically, "but not all heavenly bodies are inanimate, cold and remote. What about Debbie Reynolds?"

Intent on his father's homespun theory of relativity Jason missed the connection. "What about her?"

Jim's grin broadened. "Wasn't she in the picture?"

"So?"

"Doesn't she have a heavenly body?"

Jason smiled tolerantly.

"Okay I quit. Where are the planks you wish to steam?"

"Out behind the garage. I knocked half the ends out of two used water heaters from the junk yard. Then placed them on their sides high enough to get a fire underneath. We can run the planks through the open upper section and fill the lower halves with water. We've lots of wood and Mum bought a chunk of kennel coal."

While he was speaking Jason backed through the trap-door and down the ladder.

Two feet behind, sneakers to fingers, Jim followed.

"I've been reading a bit." Jason remarked. "The instructions recommend white cedar for planking but the boards have to be steamed in order to bend them. The question is, for how long. Using the old hot water heaters is my own invention. I hope it works."

Emerging from the garage Jason pointed upward, "We can pass the planks through the left-hand dormer. I loosened it yesterday."

CHAPTER FIVE

Behind the garage a wooded slope descended to the edge of a pond. Thin wisps of morning mist and sunlight danced on its leafy surface. Jim gazed south, beyond the bench of land and the escarpment to the cloudless sky.

"What a beautiful day! It was just like this nine years ago. The first time your mum and I came out here. Old Percy was on his last legs, diabetic and crippled with arthritis. His seventeen acres hadn't been cultivated in years. All he managed was a small vegetable patch; the buildings were in terrible shape."

Jason was not listening; he was thinking of building a dock. A large oak uprooted by erosion had settled into the pond. Beside it where the bank was less steep his father had placed a pump to draw water for the lawns. He pointed at a concrete pile supporting the intake line. "I'll moor her there. Next to that fallen tree."

"It's as good a place as any Jase." Where the boat would be anchored was immaterial. On Jim's mind was the problem of getting it out of the garage. He glanced back at the house trying to visualize what the property had looked like previously. "Many people had been around to buy this place but old Percy wouldn't sell. Your mother thinks we were the first who didn't try to steal it from him. Although she disagrees I think he took a fancy to her. Showed her all around. Took our offer of two thousand an acre; when we left he gave her a bushel of butternut squash."

"Why did you tear down the barn?"

"We had to. It was dangerous and full of rats. Besides we didn't need it." Jim was thinking of Julie's fall through a rotten board resulting in a broken forearm. He had set it without an anaesthetic and never did let on, as the sweat rolled into his eyes that this simple greenstick fracture had filled him with more dread than a bloody disc removal. They burnt the barn the following day.

"Why did we move out here anyway?"

"Don't you like it?"

"Oh yeah, I love it! But Mum's not keen at times. She does a lot of driving. More than when we lived in town."

"Yes but she enjoys nature, and the privacy." Jim had never taken his wife's complaints about taxiing kids too seriously. He felt beneath her grumbling she loved the land and would live no place else.

Jason regarded the barn's remains, a stone foundation and a stack of boards. In a clump of dried nettles nearby stood a rusty ploughshare. "Why don't we farm the place?" he asked.

"Sure. We could plant crops and an orchard or two. But who's going to look after them?"

"Hire someone."

Jim shook his head. "No one will work for the kind of money I can pay. It's better to carry on with what we're doing, subletting to J.C. Chatsworth to grow hay and pasture his sheep."

"I still think we need a barn," Jason looked concerned.

"Why?"

"A place to store my boat and we could keep horses. Jennie and Julie would be happy."

Sitting on a plodding nag is a far cry from dressage. After a stilted ride over the Rockies Jim was doubtful if Jenny enjoyed riding horses, either. Although Jason was interested he preferred to play golf; having explored the magnificent course at the Jasper Park Lodge Jim couldn't blame him.

Jenny was on cloud nine. Two hours on the trail she crashed to earth spiritually wounded when her mount stumbled in a marmot hole. For three days the two of them swung on the backs of a couple of nags until their thighs rubbed raw. With no space to ride abreast over inclines unsuited to anything faster than a walk they would have been bored out of their skulls had it not been for the spectacular scenery. 'The view must have been breathtaking,' Merri had commented, 'up in all that unpolluted air.' Jenny was unable to contain herself. 'Sure was Mum. Ask Dad. He rode behind my mare and she farted each step of the way.'

"Maybe Jase," Jim partially agreed. "Some day when each of you want a house of your own we can subdivide the land and you can do as you please. If your future lies elsewhere you can sell your share, likely at a profit. Good land is a precious commodity and property like this will become much harder to find in the future. Actually its main asset is investment although I consider elbow room a greater one. Still, we're not entirely sequestered. We have quick access to the city. It takes less than ten minutes to get to either hospital and your mother's able to drive you kids to school and your various activities without inconvenience except when she has to be in two places at once. Which reminds me, when do you take your driver's test?"

"Friday afternoon."

"Well you better pass. We need an extra chauffeur and you'll do fine." Jim had no doubts about his son's driving. Jason was careful, trustworthy and had been making his own decisions since kindergarten. How subtly time changes, Jim thought, studying the respectable young face; the black dash of brows knotting with curiosity; hard muscle replacing pubescent fat; and thickening through the shoulders. Jason was no longer a boy but responded with boyish exuberance to Jim's question. "How about a swimming pool? Then the whole family will have something to enjoy."

Jason had been loading his arms with maple logs. In his delight he let them roll at his feet. "You mean it? When?"

"Next summer. There's a contractor in Toronto. Spraying gunite, he takes only a week - Meakin; Meakin's Monolithic Pools. His name reminds me of that honey-dipper we had around to clean out the septic tank. What's his face?"

"Whitty." Jason smiled.

The name meant nothing to Jim as he vaguely recalled a man of short stature bent over a divining rod. "Oh yes, the Super Septic Suction guy. What a character!"

The man's likeness to a chimpanzee with a runny nose came quickly into focus and Jason snorted. "You should've seen the look on mum's face when he walked in the back door in plastic coveralls and a gas mask."

"Before or after the job?" Jim chuckled.

"Before. He stuck out his hand and said, The name's Whitty, mam, rhymes with Shitty. I'm here to suck out your tank."

Jim laughed. "He has to have a sense of humour. The funniest doctors I know are obstetricians. They get showered with all kinds of crap. Anyhow while we're wasting time fetch a hose from the back yard, long enough to reach your boilers. I'll go prime the pump."

It started as soon as Jim turned on the switch. By the time he scrambled back up the slope water was gushing from a ground faucet.

"We're lucky the pipes weren't frozen Jase. There's a thin layer of ice on the pond. Remind me to drain the system when we're through."

Jason grunted in agreement and turned off the tap. Between them they connected the hose and directed the nozzle into one of the boiler troughs. While the water level rose Jason shoved kindling underneath and Jim slipped into the garage to reappear in a moment with a gas can. He sprinkled some of its contents on the split logs, waved Jason out of the way and tossed a lighted match.

Whoosssh... black clouds billowed skyward. The troughs were quickly smudged and began to waver in the heat of combustion. Father and son stood mesmerized by the leaping flames until the blackness cleared and tongues of crackling yellowish smoke licked the bottom of the boilers. Slowly the fire-wood began to glow.

"We've got a fire," Jim drawled, "but it'll be awhile before we have steam. Why don't we go shoot some baskets?"

"Good idea!" Jason replied and dashed toward the house for a ball.

While he was gone Jim removed a tarpaulin from the cedar planks stacked against the garage. There were ten altogether, one-by-tens, eighteen feet long and not a knot in the soft clear grain. He leaned a plank against the wall and bowed it. When the force was reduced it readily straightened. He repeated the manoeuvre a few times until he became aware of Jason watching.

"Matchless wood but my it's tight! Are you sure steaming's going to work?"

"Sure, I'm sure, Dad. Furniture companies bend heavier stuff than this."

"When did you get it?"

"Wednesday while you were in Toronto. Mum and I picked it up in the station-wagon. It was ordered months ago. The lumber yard would've had it earlier if it weren't for a train wreck in British Columbia." Jason paused. "That was the excuse the salesman gave."

Jim put down the plank and walked over to the boiler. He placed his hand in the water and looked up at Jason impatiently. "Huh! It's not even warm. Load some coal on the logs and we'll leave it for a half hour." Holding up his hands, he added, "Toss me the ball."

Jason fired a backhand shot from his waist trying to catch his father off guard. But the old pro caught the ball easily and tucked it under his arm.

"See you out front," Jim called over his shoulder and sauntered onto the pavement. His first try hit the backboard and bounced off the rim into the middle of the driveway. It was smartly recovered and he was gauging the distance for another shot when Merri hailed him from the screened-in porch.

"Isn't this the day you wanted to go to church?"

"What for?"

"To hear about Afghanistan."

"Damn it! I forgot." He pulled up the sleeve on his jersey and consulted his watch. It was ten o'clock. Reflexively, he shouted, "What time is church?"

Merri's mocking laughter neither surprised nor offended him. "Eleven, you mean it's been so long since you were there you can't remember when it starts?"

In her nightgown, housecoat and slippers she felt chilly and started to shiver. Hugging herself, she added, "the smoke you're creating is blowing through the house. What are you trying to do, burn it down?"

"There's no danger. Everything's under control. It's dying down. Come take a look."

"It's too cold. I'll see it later."

"Ah come on," Jim urged. "Get your coat. You can warm yourself by the fire."

"I'll see it after church. I have to get the girls ready."

"It'll be too late."

"What are you doing?"

"Come and have a look. Come, come," he teased. "I'm not going to tell you. You'll have to see for yourself."

Woman's curiosity finally got the best of her. She took Jim's suggestion and returned in a leather coat. Her shapely legs were bare down to a pair of doeskin moccasins which stained when her feet touched the wet grass. She stooped, removed them and skipped sprightly across the driveway. As high as the tip of her husband's nose, slim and quick, she was soon dependent on his shoulder to re-apply her slippers. Her voice was soft and low.

"They're brand new. The dampness will ruin them," she said, brushing off the dew. The skin of her legs had tiny goose bumps and needed a vibrant massage. When warmed to her satisfaction she tilted her chin for a kiss and smiled."Good morning my darling."

Merri's face was not what the average person would call cute or exotic. It exuded the quiet beauty of intelligence, with deep set sensitive eyes, a noble forehead and a firm wide mouth.

Jim looked down at her chestnut hair and the healthy glow on her high cheeks enhanced by a late fall sun. He reciprocated with a casual peck on her pursed lips. Completely taken by surprise she was suddenly swept off her feet.

"Put me down, you dodo!" she protested. "Jim! What do you think you're doing?"

"Just trying to keep your feet dry." He grinned. "This is not the time, nor the place for a ravishing. Stop squirming or you'll put my back out. Persist and I'll have to throw you over my shoulder."

Back of the garage, his mouth open, Jason watched them approach and blinked. "I don't believe it. Where did you pick up that trick? I hand you a basketball and you come back with a babe in your arms."

Merri balanced nimbly when Jim let her down. Peering inquisitively at the smouldering water heaters she asked, "What's that?"

Jason looked his mother straight in the eye and made up a word. "A Plankensplatz!"

"A what!"

"A thingamabob."

"Oh I see."

Merri could take teasing but it annoyed her to think men considered women incapable of comprehending mechanical things, particularly when she was an expert at managing household affairs, mechanical or otherwise. This time it came from her one and only son and his humour amused her.

"You're pulling my leg," she winked.

"It's a steamer," Jason smiled. "I'm going into business and in the tradition of Meakin and Whitty have alliterated the name of my company, 'Lindsay's Lumber Limpery for bending boat bottoms.'"

"How about 'Let Us Torque Your Totem.' Jim interjected, giving his son's neck a gentle twist.

When the gadget had been fully explained, he added, "We've a slight problem."

"What?"

"We're going to church this morning."

Jason regarded his father in disbelief. "You're cracking up."

"No I want to learn something about Afghanistan."

"In church?"

"Dr. Best's recounting his experiences; I'd like to hear him."

"But I'll need help in getting these planks up to the loft."

"I know," Jim agreed. "I'm sure we can manage both."

In disgust Jason kicked a large chunk of coal under one of the boilers. He should have asked Rich to help him but it was too late. His friend had gone to a football game in Buffalo. "Ah nuts! Is it really important?"

A rise in the shifting wind swirled smoke against the barn. Merri backed off to avoid it. Jim was enveloped momentarily. His eyes began to smart and he coughed. "Look Jase, I think I've got it. We can all go to church. By the time we change our clothes the water should be boiling. We can place the planks in the steamer. If the water is left running slowly the troughs shouldn't boil dry. When we get back from church the planks will have had plenty of steam. What do you say?"

Jason wasn't happy. His father was determined to go to church and he might as well go along with him. He grabbed one end of a plank and waited for Jim to pick up the other.'

Merri turned toward the house. "Hurry up, you guys," she directed, "Let's not be late for the service."

CHAPTER SIX

Dr. Lindsay rushed through the gothic arch of St. Matthew's and opened the double glass doors. Before parking the station-wagon he'd left his family on the side walk, expecting to catch up in the vestibule but it was impossible to locate them through the maze of crimson-gowned choir members assembling at the back of the church. Rather than thread his way conspicuously into the nave where they might spot him Jim chose to wait unobtrusively near the guest registry.

For some inexplicable reason he never felt comfortable in church. Self-consciousness inhibited him from the moment he entered. Consequently on Sundays before Merri dragged the children off to the eleven o'clock service at St. Andrew's Presbyterian he was rounding on hospital wards with a promise to join them if he could, a rare happening except on festive occasions. Even then an emergency might come to his rescue. Now where are they? He wondered, hopefully in a rear pew. When the processional hymn began and the choir proceeded down the main aisle he might sneak in behind it.

Luck was with him. The sexton, Waddington, was an old patient. The hypochondriac had haunted Jim's office since the day it opened when the consulting room was a partitioned section of the residence and Merri dubbed as a receptionist-secretary. Waddington had recognized Merri and the children immediately and observed an usher had conducted them to a row of seats near the back.

"Take the left aisle next to the wall", the sexton pointed. "There'll be less disturbance."

"Thanks," Jim nodded.

Waddington smiled. "Welcome to St. Matthew's, Dr. Lindsay."

The greeting was accepted with polite indifference. Carelessly Jim asked, "How are you Wally?" As the words passed his lips he wished he'd kept them shut. Too late, the question was taken literally, an opportunity Mr. Waddington couldn't resist.

"I'll have to get in to see you soon. My calluses again," Wally whined. "They're killing me."

There was no question Waddington had bad feet. The man's problem dated from the long route marches he underwent during boot camp. It was probably nothing more than ligamentous strain easily corrected by proper fitting shoes or a period of rest. Knowing the man better, Jim suspected Wally had talked himself into an unnecessary

Do Unto Others 69

operation and likely the surgery legitimized his complaints. He was permanently crippled and discharged 4-F. Forever after he claimed poor health to get out of uncomfortable situations and the Department of Veterans Affairs faithfully paid his bills.

Jim sighed in frustration. "Call the office next week and get an appointment. Tell Betsy you were talking to me in case I forget."

The instructions didn't matter. Whether he called or not Waddington would be the first patient to show up Monday afternoon and there was nothing Dr. Lindsay could do about it, short of cancelling the whole lot. The man irritated him. 'You shouldn't let him get to you,' Merri chided. 'Sure he's wasting your time but he is rather pathetic.' Waddington was not the only odd-ball Jim was forced to see. There were others. Betsy knew them all and spaced them, the most notorious at the beginning of the day's list to let her boss dispel his misery early.

The Lindsay clan occupied almost a half a pew and to the casual onlooker was a picture of salubrious solidarity. They reshuffled when Jim took up the aisle seat so Merri could sit next to him. Their five offspring were strung in order of age, the youngest beside her.

Farthest away sat Jason. His eyes, deep set like his mother's, were fixed on a sharp curve in the balcony railing. The wood must have been steamed for the carpenters to have managed such a bend, he reckoned, restless to be back at the barn. Rolling the church bulletin between his palms he fashioned a paper spy glass thinking, if there were no unchartered waters left, he'd sail to the moon.

In the middle on tip-toes Heather was hanging by her elbows from the pew in front, rubbing her sensuous lips against a mink stole and breathing into the lacquered coiffure of its late middle-aged owner. Jennie reached out to unhook her. However to do so she had to lean in front of Julie. Julie had the same idea. There was a minor commotion when their heads bumped. Something metallic hit the floor and the two of them giggled.

"Shush and be still," Merri hissed without taking her eyes off the chancel. Busy admiring the colourful scene in the stained glass window, she did not notice Kathyrn vanish under the pew.

Jennie sobered first. Minus a hair clip, a long blond lock had fallen across her face. "Get my barrette Julie," she whispered. "It fell under your seat."

Before Julia could move a small clenched hand unfolded and a voice piped up from the floor, "I got it Jen."

Without a word Merri took the offering, clasping the small limb gently, she guided Kathryn back onto the bench. "Now what was that all about?" she asked.

Jennie and Julia, wide-eyed and fish-mouthed like a pair of synchronized swimmers, turned toward their younger sister, still chinning herself on the back of the pew.

Merri sighed and slowly shook her head. An abrupt tug on the back of Heather's coat ended the gymnastics. "Now pay attention, all of you," she directed.

It was the only cue required. Alert they poised on the edge of an oaken pew, straight and expectant, save for Heather who sat in rapture, brushing her cheek with an angora mitten, quietly sucking her tongue.

Jim noted their discipline with amusement. He'd been watching other late arrivals bow their heads in silent prayer and wondered if he should follow suit. Though he didn't feel the need a short one for the health of his patients and security of loved ones could do no harm. If there was an omnipotence taping his thoughts mere respect should suffice. He closed his eyes but the music interfered with any attempt to communicate. Perhaps it was an adaptation of Barber's Adagio for Strings, he wasn't sure. No matter, it was so spellbinding and appropriate God might have composed it himself. Suddenly the long chords ceased.

In flapping scarlet the little organist pounced on 'Rise Up Oh Men Of God', beating his holy instrument with all four extremities at once, so fervently the pipes lining the chancel bristled like a stockade vibrant in the throes of battle. A cannonade or the smell of smoke wouldn't have been out of place as the column of crimson choristers spearheaded the main aisle.

Jim felt Merri's hand on his arm. "There's your friend," she whispered.

Doctor Best was easily spotted. While the curate and minister were draped in clerical robes he wore the Ivy-look: a dark blue worsted suit, skimpy white collar and narrow orange tie. Boyishly handsome he was certainly not boyishly shy as he winked at someone in the front row before submitting to the opening prayer.

Following a round of scripture readings, the litany, choir and solo anthems, announcements and two more hymns, the last of which

Do Unto Others

was, 'In Christ There Is No East Or West', the reverend Garwood Trussell D.D. addressed the gathering. He was bespectacled, elderly and balding, his stern resonant voice in tune with the amplification system.

"Friends," he said, punctuating his introduction with pauses, "there will be no sermon today. Rather we'll hear directly from one of our missionaries, Dr. Beecher Best."

The minister looked down at the seated young man, smiled and turned back to the audience. "T'is indeed an honour to have him among us. Having known his family for years, gladness fills my heart as I welcome him back."

"Dr. Beecher Franklin Norman Best"- Reverend Trussell pronounced the names slowly and interspersed another of his dramatic pauses - "is a man of sacrifice, a man of God; one whom this congregation may look up to for inspiration and leadership. Several years ago, as a neophyte physician he ventured off in the fashion of Livingstone and Schweitzer to a secluded valley in a far-flung corner of the world to practise his profession in a place where God alone was his mentor. Joining forces with the Christian Mission School our church has been supporting in Bamiyan, Afghanistan, he has devoted himself to the work of the Lord. Now he has returned to his place of birth and baptism, to his rightful church, bringing his recently acquired skill in the field of orthopaedics."

"That's the best 'ad' I've heard in years," Jim mumbled at Merri's raised brow.

A prolonged hush fell. Even the coughing, nose-blowing and prattle of children stopped as Reverend Trussell concluded, "Dr. Best, it is most kind of you to come and address us."

Beecher thanked him perforce. With constraint he crossed the podium to lurch up the semicircular staircase leading to the pulpit. Grinning broadly, confidently, he placed a few sheets of paper beside a glass of water on the lectern.

The vertical stained glass window high above the altar on the back wall of the chancel refracted a colourful channel of light directly at the speaker. Truly the highlight of an auspicious occasion for cloud extinguished the glorious path from Heaven and the ceiling spotlight had not the same effect.

Beecher gestured, palms upward, chin tilted and began to speak, his words floating down on the sallow faces lining the concentric pews. "Thank you, Father," he prayed, "for your eternal blessings. Thank you for the wondrous gift you have bestowed upon me - the art of healing - and the opportunity I have this day to share my experiences. 'Neither do men light a candle and put it under a bushel,' Jesus said, 'but on a candlestick and giveth light unto all in the house. Let your light so shine before men that they may see your good deeds and glorify our Father in Heaven.'"

Dramatically Best hesitated while he fondled the lectern Bible. Then he looked out at the congregation saying, "and Jesus also said, 'Therefore all things whatsoever ye would that men should do to you do ye even so to them.' For this is the law of the prophets."

There was a lull while his hands sank into his back pockets and he swept the nave with a gradual rotation of his head.

"God's Golden Rule. Love thy neighbour as thyself. How well the church of St. Matthew's has adhered to this holy law. Your generous contributions -"

"I don't believe it," Jim muttered. "This guy's right up there on the mount. He's too good to be true."

"Ssssh," Merri cautioned. "Not so loud. Give him a chance. He's just getting started."

"That's what I'm afraid of!"

"Oh you!" She could not find a word to fit and let the exclamation die.

"Your generous contributions," Beecher repeated, "have made it possible for my wife and me to cure all manner of sickness and all manner of disease among the people of an underdeveloped nation." He cleared his throat and repeatedly waved an arm in a great circle above the congregation.

"Almost halfway round the world lies Afghanistan, a territorial crossroads rather than a country because its boundaries are unnatural and cut through ethnic and linguistic ties. Its backbone is the Karacorum and Himalayan mountains, and it covers an area the size of Alberta - about a quarter of a million square miles - a reasonable comparison because like Alberta it has plains or steppes as they are called in Asia, plateaus, and tortuous mountains."

"We worked in the Hazarajat, the central region, named after its inhabitants, the Hazara. These people are fortunate in respect to their unity. Amir Abdur Rahman Khan's arbitrary boundaries, established in the late nineteenth century, has not divided them like some of the northern tribes, for instance the Uzbaks who inhabit both Afghanistan and Russia or the Pathans, the mountain men living in

Do Unto Others 73

the eastern region who have been split by the Durand line into Afghanis and Pakistanis. Indeed the Pathans are still fighting to form an independent nation."

Dr. Best intuitively glanced at his wife seated in the front row and read her lips as she was frantically telling him to slow down. Eventually he got the message and continued at a leisurely pace, stressing what he considered the more important points and pausing between them.

"There are two major languages in Afghanistan, Pashto and Farsi - or Persian. It is interesting they are spoken mainly by tribes at opposite ends of the peck order. Pashto was bestowed upon the nation by the Pathans who are at the head of the line while the poor Hazara who ironically speak Farsi, the language of the elite, come last as simple peasant farmers, shepherds, goat-herders and coolies. The Hazara often tend the flocks of their sedentary Farsi-speaking neighbours, the Qizilbash, who are truly of Persian descent. The Qizilbash are more a class of people than a tribe, and the business of running the country falls on their shoulders. Both of these Farsi speaking groups are Shi'ites, the lesser of the two main divisions of Islam."

Beecher smiled like the cat who ate the cream. "In comparing Mohammedanism to Christianity, I like to think of the Shi'ites as being similar to Protestants. Both sects have broken with tradition, the traditional lines being the Sunni Muslims and the Catholics. Compare Ali, the son-in-law of Mohammed, to Martin Luther. Mohammed, the Prophet, was of the Quraish tribe but Ali wasn't. Nor was Luther an Italian; he was German, and certainly not the son-in-law of a Pope."

His grin broadened expectantly. When there was no laughter to his intended witticism he burst into an explanation. "Just think of a celibate priest having a daughter to give to a renegade of the Faith."

An applause meter might have detected a few scattered titters. Beecher's smugness faded but only for seconds. He squinted at the congregation and paused thoughtfully. "But I will not confuse you with any more details." Then smiling he raised both arms. "We'll forget the trees and stick to the forests, the three great religions, Judaism, Christianity and Islam. A blackboard would make it easy to point out their main similarities and differences but I have none."

Wheeling he turned his back to the audience and pointed high on the chancel wall, above the large cross in the stained glass where the ceiling peaked. "There," he said, his arm remaining on target as he swung around to face the congregation. "Up in the peak is God! Directly below in the middle of the cross is Jesus, his son, who gave us Christians the 'word'. On the left trace the ceiling down to where it meets the side wall - where the valance lighting is. See! It's in line with the left arm of the cross. Imagine Moses seated there with his stone tablet containing God's word to the Jews, 'The Ten Commandments'. Over on the opposite wall beyond the right arm of the cross is Mohammed with the 'Five Pillars of Wisdom' or God's word to the Muslims. Down at floor level directly beneath each of these divine works man has organized religions. To reiterate, firstly on the left we have Judaism, Christianity in the centre and Mohammedanism on the right. For people trying to interpret the word of God we have the Torah, the Bible and the Koran respectively, all written by disciples of each faith in an effort to apply God's Holy Law, for instance the parables so familiar to Christians."

"From the Koran or Hadith the Shari'at was created which really is no more than a fundamental code for social behaviour. In the eyes of the three major religions God is one and the same. All Muslims believe in the Koran and accept the Five Pillars of Wisdom. Mohammed like Moses was deemed to be a Prophet nothing more. Only we Christians recognize our prophet to be the Son of God."

Beecher had been tossing his words like a fire-and-brimstone preacher, diverging from his text. His forehead knotted as he paused to study Lil's notes. Scribbled along the margin in indelible ink he read 'ad lib'. For a moment he discarded the script to add a personal note. "The only time we came across a drug problem was in the capital. Lil and I were sitting in the jeep, parked outside the post office in Kabul when a young western couple approached. They were barely out of their teens and almost out of clothes. The woman held a child the same age as our Michael, swathed in rags, flies crawling over its thin face. Her mate unveiled a bronze statue of the Hindu God Kali. He would have taken anything for it. They were starving and probably spending all their money on drugs. It would have been better to give them food. A very sad scene and there was nothing we could do but pray for their souls."

He took a sip of water from the glass on the lectern and resumed, vigorously plunging into a detailed description of Kabul and its climate. Then he smiled and started again.

"We arrived in the capital, the fall of '56. Waiting for us at the British Embassy was Tom Bereskin. We liked him right away. His peaceful blue eyes set in a ruddy face radiated happiness and trust, and we came to know him as a man who asks little and gives a lot."

"We went on to the valley and arrived as the sun set. Such colourful rock I'd never seen: turquoise, beige and deep brick red. Within a half hour it was gone and in the darkness we pulled into the mission, an abandoned caravanserai." He hesitated and closed his eyes as if in a trance before interjecting, "Thank you once again dear Father for all the beauty of this earth."

Beecher paused to take a sip of water, slyly glimpsing another of his written notes. "The Mullahs had asked Tom on more than one occasion to pack up and be off. But he stayed to help the peasant farmers harvest their crops, tend their livestock, offer practical advice and cause no harm. Eventually he earned their trust. Still the priests or Mullahs hounded him, particularly after he had coaxed a few kids into his school. There was no retaliation, partly because Tom did not place a cross anywhere and partly because there is no hierarchy in the Islamic faith, such as we have in our synod."

Beecher gulped down another sip and smiled. "In Bamiyan there are farms operated with the most primitive tools. Wooden ploughs are pulled by oxen or women. Farm labourers are tenants or rather feudal serfs, and could be compared to share-croppers in the United States. Crops have not changed for centuries. A diet of rice, lamb and a flat unleavened bread called nan is invariable. Many of them can't afford the lamb. Consequently roughage is a problem and creates a high incidence of bowel problems." Beecher grinned broadly, "I once operated on an old Afghan with a volvulus and he did quite well."

Then he looked up from the lectern and diverged from the script. "In the rural areas there are no paved roads. Donkeys and camels replace the car."

"Incidentally!" he snickered. "I discovered the Farsi word for donkey is car, spelled K-h-a-r!" He paused expectantly but when their was no reaction added, "they don't rust like Fords."

While speaking he had leaned forward till his forearms were flat on the lectern, unaware that his slim orange tie had become un-clipped and fell into his water glass. The soaked end drawn across his indelible notes left an undecipherable blur. Furtively he searched, but the words Lil had so carefully chosen were illegible. Horrified he stiffened as the cooling wetness penetrated his shirt.

"Ah ah," he stammered, spontaneously realizing the cause. "There are many things I could tell you about Afghanistan but I'm afraid due to limited time I'll have to skip a few. Many interesting and fascinating experiences." Quickly regaining his composure, Beecher nonchalantly drew a handkerchief from a pant-pocket, wiped the end of his tie, blotted the dampened composition and turned to the next page. As he buttoned his jacket only a few astute souls were conscious of what had happened.

His "ahem!" was aimed at the balcony. "Once we were invited to a wedding, by the father of the bride. He was an influential Pathan, a Maldar, or chief of the nomadic Ghilzai tribe and the ceremony took place in a secluded vale not far from our caravanserai. We were billeted in a black goat hair tent where bed rolls were spread on thick maroon rugs. His daughter was being given to the son of another Ghilzai chieftain who had summered in the same mountain pastures for years. It was a lively one, and as the music makers stepped up their pace," - Beecher beamed at Lil seated apprehensively on the edge of the front pew - "we got into the act with a demonstration of North American square dancing."

Lil frowned back. It was another of his grand-standing ad libs; he never did tell the whole story. In his effort to impress the Ghilzai he clumsily stomped her foot. The lump his boot raised never did recede. While he returned to the script she rubbed it subconsciously against the opposite heel.

"On the third day the party moved back to the groom's tent. This time both participants rode the horse, the bride veiled and dressed in a long carmine gown, riding in front of the groom. He dismounted first and was taken to a low platform where he sat on a pile of cushions. She joined him, led by a maid carrying a tray of henna. Someone lifted her veil and a mirror was placed in front of the them. We were told it was to allow the young couple to see themselves for the first time. Islam considers studying one's image, under other circumstances, a sin. I did not understand what was said but apparently both replied to the Mullah's question with 'I do', just as in our marriage ceremony. The word 'obey' still remains, and likely will for a long time. The man answered without hesitation. That the girl had pledged her freedom probably never entered her mind."

"The vows were spoken, their little fingers painted with henna and guests began tossing candied almonds." Beecher put his hands in his side pockets and began to chuckle. "A far more

Do Unto Others

nourishing method of supplying the gonads than tossing paper confetti and not nearly as unsightly as the bits blowing about the grounds of the church this morning."

His chuckle was echoed by a wave of mirth from the pews followed by a stronger one when he added. "Must've been a big one yesterday."

"They play all kinds of games," he continued in a sportive mood. "Tag, Blind Man's Bluff and war games - similar to Cowboys and Indians. Girls have dolls and boys, marbles, called bujul, made from sheep knuckles. A favourite game of the men is Karoms, much like our pool, but without cues. They also like to bet - though it's against the Shari'at."

"Chess has an avid following, but the game generating the most enthusiasm is Buzkashi. It is played by two competing teams and involves carrying a headless calf by horseback. The aim is to drop the carcass into a circle about ten metres in diameter after dragging it from one end of the field to the other."

"I could go on for days," Beecher smiled. "There are many things I haven't mentioned. So much to tell, but I must close and leave the rest for some other time, which hopefully the Lord will provide." His tone saddened markedly. "Seated on the plane, waving good-bye to a crowd of friends, patients and families who had come to wish us well gave me a feeling of fulfilment I have never known before."

After a moment, he bid the congregation to rise and recite the Lords Prayer.

Before announcing the recessional hymn Rev. Trussell invited the members to join him for refreshments in the basement auditorium where Dr. and Mrs. Best could answer their questions.

CHAPTER SEVEN

When the Lindsays emerged from St. Matthew's the Sunday traffic on York Street was quiet but not the weather. Tumultuous clouds obliterated the sun, biting gale force winds whipped leafy flakes and sent them hissing in the gutters while power lines, like dropped base viols hummed tempestuously, clashing with the creak and groan of shop signs.

In the midst of this polar ferocity Jim, Merri and the four girls quaked and chattered by the curb, waiting for Jason to pull up in the station-wagon.

"Let's huggle!" Heather pleaded, drawing her two older sisters around her.

No one needed persuasion. Instinctively the whole family including Jim and Merri circled, hugging and huddling in a spiralling cocoon of closeness.

"Nothing pings like propinquity!" Merri stuttered her favourite phrase, an amusing sweet nothing invented in dalliance on her wedding night.

Kathryn, a head shorter than Heather, squeezed into the centre. Addressing the waist of her mother's muskrat coat she asked, "What's pro - pink - tea?"

"It's a hot drink with alcohol in it like Irish coffee," Julia advised with the reassuring air of a first year high-school student.

"Jul-ee-ah!" Jennie scolded. It means nearness. Look it up."

"You're all wrong," Jim's eyes, in tears, twinkled from the cold. "Propane Kitty was a night club entertainer in the Gay Nineties. Her sister Fanny danced the 'Can-Can'. Fanny by gaslight they called her."

"You're impossible," Merri chided.

At that instant Kathy squirted loose. "Here comes Jasie!" She cried and darted out into the road.

Her mother cupped her mouth with her hands and hollered against the wind. "Careful! Wait till he stops."

It took but seconds to load the wagon. There were no arguments about who should sit by the windows. Everyone was satisfied to be out of the cold.

"Jason, drive by the office. I'd like to check tomorrow's schedule."

"Can't you do it later Dad?"
"I'd like to save a trip if I can."
"But the planks are steaming."
"It'll only take a minute."

Dr. Lindsay's office was located on James, two blocks south and parallel to York. In contrast to York, plotted by a meandering heifer years ago, James street was shorter and straight. Methodically designed by early settlers when Shipton was a port on the old canal it flashed a broad grassy median planted in evergreens, birch and Japanese maple. For six blocks it was flanked by spaciousness and a handful of large red and yellow two story brick dwellings with wide semi-surrounding verandas. Halfway down the middle of the street Jason parked beneath the limbs of a dead elm, ghosting the Lindsays' previous home.

Jim opened the car door, striking it on a cast-iron horse trough entrenched in a strip of mown weeds between the side-walk and the road. "Whoa," he warned. "Either that useless thing goes or we trade it for a gas pump."

The Lindsays had been offered good money for the 'receptacle of ditched junk' by an antique dealer. If he had approached disguised as a junk pedlar they would have gladly given it to him but his showing up in a natty pin-striped suit and putting a value on it created resentment. They subsequently kept it, speculating it might be worth something.

Jim side-stepped the trough, crossed the cement walk and unlatched a low gate in the surrounding wrought-iron fence. A slate path dividing an expanse of lawn led to the porch. He was on it in a bound and disappeared inside the house.

Merri turned to her son. "How did you like the service?"

"It was nice but Dr. Best sure is a clumsy jerk. He almost fell up the stairs into the pulpit. I could hardly keep from laughing when his tie flipped into the water glass."

Merri being more intent on the context of the sermon missed the incident but the girls hadn't. Julia and Heather bubbled over when Jason mentioned it.

"Did you see him wring it out," Julia spluttered. "He buttoned up his jacket right away so nobody would notice."

"Don't be so critical," Her older sister scolded. "I bet if you people were to get up there you'd be so nervous you couldn't say a word."

"Maybe so!", Jason exclaimed. "You'll never have a chance to prove it. Nobody will get me to stand up in church and give a sermon."

"It wasn't really a sermon," Jennie continued. "It was his own story and interesting if a trip to Afghanistan turns you on." Directing her remarks to her mother she appended. "I liked the service and the music, especially Mrs. Simmons, the soloist. She's so nice and the church is so elegant."

Merri nodded in concurrence with Jennie's opinion. She and Jim were traditionalists and St. Matthew's exemplified the modest orthodoxy of Protestantism but on a grander scale than the church she was brought up in. "I love the architecture too," she said, "the gothic arched doorways and turret-steeple with the minarets adorning it."

"It's a Minnie Mouse House." For an enchanted moment the listeners awaited Kathryn's clarification.

"A what?" Jason asked.

A round of amusement accompanied Kathryn's delightful harping. "It's a Minnie Mouse House, a Minnie Mouse House, like on television."

Heather was more serious. "She's right. It looks just like it."

Sensing the gaiety surrounding him when he climbed into the car, Jim asked curiously, "what's going on?"

"Kathy thinks St. Matthew's looks like a Minnie Mouse House," Merri informed him.

He chuckled at the child's delightful imagery and suggested, "They should change the name to St. Disney's."

"Did you get what you wanted?" Merri asked.

"All set! Let's get the show on the road."

His son reacted by pressing the accelerator to the floor and the rear wheels spun on the leafy pavement.

"Jason! Hold it down!" Jim reprimanded. "You trying to break Breedlove's record."

Like a straight man in a minstrel show, fully expecting another of Jim's one-liners Merri inquired, "Who's Breedlove?"

But her husband wasn't kidding. "Craig Breedlove, the current Barney Oldfield, set a land/speed record on the Bonneville salt flats a short while ago. They clocked him at four hundred and seven miles an hour."

"Wow!" Jennie exclaimed. "That's almost as fast as Mum drives."

"You sure you don't want to stop at one of the hospitals Dad? We'll be passing St. Mary's any minute."

"Don't be smart," Merri warned, detecting a note of sarcasm in her son's voice.

"I'm sorry but I'd like to get home and finish what we started this morning. For all you care my planks might be burnt to ashes."

Jason chose the middle bridge across the old canal. To reach it he turned right at the end of James and proceeded along Brock. Before he made a left across the waterway, the traffic light changed to red.

"What's going up there?" Merri asked. A lattice of structural steel was being erected opposite St. Mary's hospital.

"An apartment," Jim replied.

"Funny I didn't notice it before. It's quite high."

"Eight floors, I've heard. Three more than the General and one more than the Shipton Hotel. It'll be the tallest building in town. Extendible crane puts 'em up almost overnight. Look!" Jim exclaimed. "Up there. I don't believe it. There's a guy riveting a girder. In this wind, he's a damn fool."

Jason laughed. "Mohawk! There's a gang of them working overtime. We watched them yesterday. They're fearless of heights, a steel beam is as wide as a football field."

"Nonsense! In this weather, I don't care how agile he is the man is courting disaster." While Jim expressed his disapproval a violent gust lifted the billboard in front of the construction site and hammered it against a tool shed. Merri twisted to read it as the light turned green and Jason revved the engine.

"Brock Towers. Suites available April '64," she noted.

"Yes and that crazy Indian, poised on his pedestal, thinks he's General Brock himself."

Under other circumstances Jim's remark might have been funny but his opinion was strongly voiced. No one spoke.

The bank on the far side of the bridge was steep and curved. Beyond it the road lay flat and straight. Farms made idle by the season swept by; here an orchard, there a field, withered and gradually whitening with snow.

Jennie, quiet throughout the drive, leaned forward as if she had something confidential to say. She placed her elbows on the back of the front seat. Resting her chin on her thumbs she spoke quietly. "Why don't we join St. Matthew's?"

"You mean transfer our membership?" Jim queried.

"Yes."

"We'd have to change our denomination."

"So what! One Protestant church is the same as another."

"That's an argument for staying where we are. What's wrong with St. Andrew's?"

"Nothing. But St. Matthew's is more sophisticated."

"You mean the ceremony has more frills, not that it has more to offer."

"Well sort of. It's the music. The choir has more talented experienced people and I like the sound."

"That's not all you like." Jason winked at his mother. "I think she has a crush on a tall red-headed guy."

"Who?" Jennie blushed.

"Bradley Coleman. I saw you and Julia chatting him up in the auditorium after the service."

"He's cute." Julie interjected smiling.

Jenny scowled. "We weren't chatting him up or whatever you think. He's a friend who happens to play trombone in the school band."

"It appears someone has an ulterior motive," Jim grinned.

"Da-aad!"

"It's as good a reason as anything you've put forward so far. Perhaps even better."

Merri remembered seeing Jennie and Julia talking to a handsome young man but she had been too busy trying to meet Dr. Best to pay much attention to them. "Invite him home sometime Jen," she suggested, "so we can get a closer look."

Jennie sighed and sat back in her seat. Her, "Oh you people" was ignored.

"By the way, who was the cute little old lady you were flirting with Jim?"

"The one in the wheelchair?"

"Was there more than one?"

"Winifred Trussell, the minister's wife. She has rheumatoid arthritis and I'm planning an operation for her hands. The younger woman with her was Lillian Best."

"I met Mrs. Best," Merri acknowledged. "She was with Beecher when I finally got to talk to him. Even accounting for her dowdiness I'd guess she's five years older."

"I got that impression myself and their personalities are poles apart."

"Seems so, my dear, but appearances can be deceiving. What did you think of his talk?"

"It was interesting. Very well composed and full of meat. Not the sort of address one expects to hear from the pulpit." Jim nudged Merri's shoulder. "Stayed awake for the whole thing."

"I noticed." Merri nudged back. "An unusual treat! But then the subject material was more to your liking. He might have submitted it to the National Geographic. Then you could have fallen asleep in your easy-chair, reading it."

"His theatrics bothered me" - there was a momentary silence when the wagon's rear wheels began to skid. "Better hold it down Jase," his father warned. "The road's beginning to ice."

"I got it Papa." Jason's tone was full of self assurance. He kept his foot off the brake and let the vehicle roll forward at it's own rate of deceleration.

Merri gently grasped Jim's thigh and patted affectionately. "Tell me my darling. How did his theatrics bother you?"

"They may be appropriate for church but I hope he doesn't carry them over to the practice of medicine. Frankly, if I'd had his experience I'd rather keep it to myself. No doubt this would be impossible, for sooner or later a colleague would con me into speaking. But if I did I'd rather do it with slides. The spotlight would be on the screen and not me. Even then it could be misconstrued by envious people as being show-offish."

Merri patted his thigh again. "Sweetie, you're too modest," she bantered lovingly. "You'd rather hide your light under a bushel."

"No, just shy." The proximity of her hand warmed him. "Particularly when it comes to you, my lovely wife." He gave her a one armed hug and pecked her cheek. "I think I'll hide you under a bushel."

"Shy! My eye! After five kids you've got the nerve to say that. You've got to be kidding."

Merri returned to the topic under discussion. "What Reverend - whoops! I mean, Dr. Best said at the beginning of his speech was certainly fitting and what one expects to hear from a pulpit. After all," she reminded, "he was sent as a Christian missionary."

"I suppose your right," Jim agreed. "It's not my style."

"You should be thankful - I am. Why criticize him?"

"One of his remarks bothered me. I hope he doesn't believe it himself and it was said to impress the audience."

"What's that?"

"God's Gift. The art of healing. Healing must be treated as a science, not an art. It's an innate force physicians can only nurture. The ultimate power to heal resides within life itself. If there is a God in Heaven who supposedly created life then God alone has the power. The word "Art" implies the ability to produce something beautiful which could include the art of dressing a wound and should not take precedence over logic. If a doctor ignores these principles in favour of pleasing himself or his patient anything can happen. He must keep these principles in mind at all times or be guilty of negligence."

Merri chaffed, "You mean a good bedside manner is not important?"

"I didn't say that. What I meant is: if there is no indication for any kind of treatment based on scientific facts the need of a patient to have something done or the need of the physician to do something has to be ignored."

"Furthermore," Jim added, "the Golden Rule is only as good as the judgment of the people practising it; judgment is the sum total of man's intellectual and emotional reactions. Call it common sense for lack of better words. Some have it and others don't."

"You're starting to sound like a preacher yourself."

"Thank you Father Meriel," he smiled.

His wife forced her voice deeper than her normal low. "You're welcome," she laughed.

"Anyhow, Best has asked me to show him around and I've arranged to meet him tomorrow morning."

A moment's silence followed, to be broken by Jason. "We're home," he declared, pointing the station wagon up the Lindsay driveway. It slithered to the top of the hill and skidded around the traffic circle.

Do Unto Others

Merri took her time. She checked out the kitchen and followed the girls upstairs. From the master bedroom Jim could hear her organizing their activities while they changed from their 'church-going' clothes. "Lunch is in a half hour. I'll make some shrimp chowder and grilled cheese sandwiches."

"Good!" Jennie exclaimed. "I get the 'grand' Julie."

"You had it yesterday. It's my turn."

"Julia," her mother interfered. "Jennie has a conservatory examination in two weeks. Use the old upright in the rec. room or practise your flute. This afternoon you can switch around."

"Mum you're forgetting 'patch'," Julia reminded.

"No I'm not. You're not due at the arena until three thirty. There's lots of time - where's Heather?"

"In the bathroom," Kathy volunteered.

A tap turned, water splashed, and the toilet flushed before an opening door discharged the sibling in question.

"Heather! You have an oboe lesson Tuesday and you haven't played a note all week."

"Ah mum. Do I have to? I hate it."

"Don't give me a hard time, Heather. Do as I say or go to your room. No skating either."

The older girls needed no prompting. Jennie was a self-starter and capable of managing herself. Julia though less dynamic followed suit and accomplished a lot with deceiving imperturbability.

Heather was a problem; she possessed a classic artistic temperament. With a perfect ear she had tremendous potential and it was mainly for the child's benefit her mother stooped to concentration camp tactics.

"You speak to her," Merri ordered, as Jim brushed by in the upper hall.

He was pulling on a heavy knit sweater, blindly groping for the stair well and complied. "Okay Heather, do as you're told." His words were muffled in wool.

"A lot of help you are," Merri called after him.

"I'll talk to her later," he shot over his shoulder. "We've got work to do." Hurriedly he slipped through the kitchen, grabbed a wind-breaker and went out the back door.

Jason was waiting for him behind the garage. The coal had reduced to smouldering ashes, and steam rampant in the cold air swirled madly about, partly obscuring the horizontal water heaters.

A blast of wind cleared the view and Jim could see the protruding planks. "Appears no harm done," he said. "Come on, let's pull one out and have a look."

"Careful," Jason advised. "It's hot. I've already tried. Here, put these on."

Jim accepted the worn leather mittens and recognized them as part of his skiing equipment. He shook his head and pulled them on fingering a hole in the sweat-stiffened palm.

"I'll get you a new pair for Christmas, Dad."

"Forget it Jase. I guess they've had it anyhow." Changing the subject, he asked, "What about the dormer window?"

"I opened it just now."

"Let's go. Grab the other end as it comes free."

The board sagged like a rubber sword. "How about that!" Jim exclaimed.

"Hot spit! It really worked."

The flat board was so floppy they had difficulty balancing it. Once turned on edge it was easily paraded around to the front of the garage. Placed against the wall it leaned drunkenly.

Jason climbed into the attic workshop and when he reached the opening began to haul it in while Jim steadied it from below. At the halfway point the board bent ninety degrees and had to be lifted over the sill.

Jim watched while it was drawn in and the window shut, then rejoined his son upstairs. "It's uncanny! I've never seen a thick piece of wood bend so much without breaking."

Jason was ecstatic. "Terrific eh! We better clamp it before it cools off."

Eagerly the two of them secured the plank to the frame, Jim holding while Jason positioned and tightened the C-clamps. When they were satisfied it was accurately placed Jason sawed off the excess extending beyond the stem and transom. The manoeuvre was repeated three times till both sides of the hull had been formed.

"After lunch," Jason announced, "I'll take 'em off, trim them so they fit better then screw and caulk them."

"I'll give you a hand." Jim offered. "If I don't get a call."

"I can manage."

"No trouble," Jim was insistent. "I'd like to. Haven't had so much fun since gramma died."

Jason was wondering how silly the old man could get when Kathy surprised them. She was hidden by the transom, her inquisitive eyes deep in the shadow of her parka.

"Watcha doin' Jasie?"

"Making a boat."

"It doesn't look like a boat."

"It's not finished."

"Mum says if you want something to eat come right away."

"Okay," said Jim. "We're coming. Mind you don't fall down the ladder."

Indignant she moved toward the hole.

"Better let me go first," Jason volunteered. "I'll help you."

"I got up myself, Jasie. I can go down." Before she could place her tiny feet in the opening her brother was through the trapdoor and waiting. He steadied her while she backed down the rungs. Safe at the bottom, he helped with her mittens and they started for the house.

CHAPTER EIGHT

In the family room Heather stood by the bookcase pouting. Merri, Jennie and Julia were seated at the table.

"What's the trouble?" Jim asked.

Merri was disgusted. "All she wants to do is watch television. Instead of practising her oboe she turns on 'Sunday Afternoon at the Movies'. Now she won't eat. Just stands there sulking because I told her she can't go skating."

"Heather. Go to your room," Jim demanded.

"No!"

He was much less tolerant than his wife and used to having his orders obeyed. He strode over to Heather.

She glared, openly defiant. "I won't play it!"

"You will." Jim bid and his eyes went frosty. "Then get up to your room this minute."

Unintentionally he had forced the situation beyond the point of return. Again she refused and the colour drained from his cheeks. Angrily he enunciated the words. "Get going!"

She did not budge, not even to blink an eye.

Incensed, he spun her off her feet, backside up and whacked her bottom. Labouring toward the front staircase he carried her kicking and squirming until she nearly got away. At the landing she bit his arm but he held on tenaciously and made it to the upper hall and her room where she was flung on her bed. Jim retreated, slamming the door.

"You're staying there until you learn to behave," he roared.

Alone Heather for the first time began to cry.

Inwardly trembling and rubbing his arm he traced his steps back to the dining table.

Julia broke the silence. "You shouldn't have hit her."

His violence had been the result of an involuntary emotional response and it fostered remorse. Jim had been sorry from the moment he made his move but he was committed to see the action through. Julia's comment did anything but console him. In fact it sucked him back to the brink of an ebullient inner cauldron and he had to fight the strongest urge to send her packing as well. He ignored her interference. No one else spoke.

The shrimp chowder was delicious but burned his gut. He did not attempt the grilled cheese sandwiches. When he saw Jason had finished and was getting up to leave, he nodded. "I'll be along in a while."

The other children hastily departed and Merri began to clear the table.

"May I have some more coffee?" he asked.

She poured him a fresh cup and he lingered, stirring and sipping and stirring until his equilibrium returned and compassion for Heather infused him.

The child had curled into the fetal position when Jim re-entered her room. She looked unwanted and unloved.

"I'm sorry Heather," he said, almost choking on his words.

She pushed herself up when he sat down on the bed beside her. The explosive application of his hand had been shockingly therapeutic and produced at least one desirable effect. Her defiance had disappeared. She needed the comfort of another human being and moved closer to him. Though her hair was streaked with sweat and tears she was no longer sobbing.

"Did I hurt you?" he asked.

"No," she maintained.

Jim drew her close and caressed her damp tresses. "We love you Heather," he murmured. "All we want is for you to do what's best for yourself."

"But I hate the oboe, Daddy. I won't play it."

"Why Heather? Why do you hate it so much?"

"I can't play it. That's why. I can't stop the squeaks."

Realizing frustration and lack of confidence were the root of the child's stubborn behaviour, Jim humoured her. "You should have heard Jennie squeak on her clarinet when she first started playing. Once she did it on stage during her festival piece with a whole bunch of people listening. If you really want to hear squeaks," Jim smiled, "let me try it. I bet I can't play a single note without squeaking. Just a sec. I'll show you."

He stood and with a cursory glance failed to see anything vaguely resembling an instrument case. "Where's your oboe?"

The instruments were kept in a cadenza next to the old upright piano in the recreation room.

Beethoven's "Fur Elise" was giving Julia a battle. Jim excused the intrusion, picked out the oboe case and a music book for beginners. Before he located a stand, Heather was searching beside him.

"We best go into the den, Julie needs to concentrate. Here, you put it together," he said, handing over the case, at the same time attentively prodding her towards his study. "I don't know how."

The oboe was assembled with diligence. "You have to wet the mouthpiece," she spoke with difficulty, the thin flattened wooden tube soaking up her saliva. When the double reed was adjusted to her liking she blew into it and produced a clear mellow concert A.

"Not bad," said Jim. "Let me try it."

He puffed frantically but not a sound was heard, not even a squeak.

Heather's diffidence lessened. "Tighten your lips and pull the mouthpiece out a bit." she advised.

Jim blew again and a loud harsh blast abruptly transformed into a high pitched irritating noise. He looked surprised. "There, I told you I could make it squeak."

Heather laughed. Jim smiled back more pleased with his daughter's returning poise than his ability to produce a note. He decided to give back the instrument and placed a music book on the stand.

"Can you play a scale?" he asked.

"Yes," she replied timidly and began at 'A' in the bass clef, covering chromatically not just an octave but the instrument's entire range. Though her oboe had a tendency to quack like a duck each note was distinct and effortless. Only when she reached the higher ones did strain grimace her face. At high 'D' Heather took a final breath and nothing but wind issued from the bell.

"See I can't get it," she blurted and her countenance fell again.

Jim offered more cheer. "Sure you can. It just takes lots and lots of practise. You'll get it eventually. Even a vibrato. Why don't you try something easier and more fun? How about this?" He had opened the book at 'I know where I'm going' an American folk-song in F major. "Come on, try it," he coaxed.

Reluctantly Heather gave in and performed the piece with a gifted interpretation. Though there were a few mechanical errors marring the smoothness it was obvious even to Jim's untrained ear his daughter had a natural talent, a shame to be wasted.

"Play it through one more time," he suggested. "Then we'll try something else."

They went on together, Jim turning the pages and upholding her confidence until Heather had covered everything she had been taught. Still she was not completely prepared for the approaching lesson. Discreetly he decided to call a halt.

"We'll do it again tomorrow night. Okay?"

Shyly she nodded in agreement.

"You'd better try some of mum's soup now. It's almost time for the arena." He left her while she was dismantling the instrument and ambled back to the kitchen.

Merri had finished placing the dishes in the automatic washer and was making a pie. "Special request," she disclosed.

"Who's?"

"Kathy's. Who else?"

"Me!" Jim grinned and for the second time removed his quilted wind-breaker from a hook near the back entrance. Gesturing toward the den he added. "She's all right now. Guess I'll go help Jason."

Before his fingers could grip the door knob it turned unexpectedly in his palm. Equally surprising was to be pressed like a bushel of grapes against an inside wall by an agitated son.

"Where's Dad?" Jason fumed.

"Right behind you," Merri countered, rather astonished with her wild-eyed offspring. "You may have broken his nose."

"Maybe I should, it's all his fault."

"What's my fault?" Jim asked, un-wedging himself to force the door closed.

"The wood! Its dead! Dried out! Every time I put a screw in those damn planks they split. There are cracks two feet long and still spreading. We've killed the grain thanks to you." Jason was so disappointed and angry, he was on the verge of tears. Totally vexed he continued. "The boards were steamed too long. I should have stayed home and done it properly. But no I had to let you drag me off to church. Damn it all Dad."

There was an audible silence while Jim regarded his son's disenchantment. Merri opted not to get involved in spite of the provocation to correct Jason's language.

"We'll just have to do it again and do it right," Jim sighed. "It is my fault Jase and I'm sorry. Tomorrow you can order four more planks. In the meantime we'll have to use what's left and try again. That's the way things are son. You win some, you lose some. Experience is a painful teacher."

Although he accepted his father's apology with receding hostility, Jason dismally turned away muttering to himself, "It'll take months to get them."

CHAPTER NINE

From its inception the General Hospital had branched and re-branched like anagrams played by successive governors. The board was a piece of subdivided real estate between York Street and the old canal. Properties acquired were replaced by hospital expansion. A memorial plaque, adorning a wall of the foyer, was all that remained of the homestead where Jonas Clark first set up a ward to treat indigent and friendless patients. In the aerial photograph hanging beside it the hospital looked like a skeleton key, two of its three wings aimed at houses to the south.

Fronting York a single storey accommodated administrative offices, including a rapidly expanding Medical Records Department, much to the chagrin of the Medical Advisory Committee. 'At one time this place actually housed patients,' Committee Chairman Dr. Edgar Atwater complained to the governing Board. 'It's easier to get a room by hiring-on than getting sick. Before the war one person filed records. She also looked after Admissions. Now you have at least a dozen and each has to have an office. Where in hell are we going to treat our patients? The irony of it is we rarely use the hospital's records. We keep our own.'

Although in agreement with the allocation of space Jim Lindsay argued against Ed's last point. Hospital typists were useful. They made copies of all his dictations: the histories, physicals, and particularly the operative findings and progress notes. Like the Chairman he kept his own records but a large number of them originated in the hospital. If anything irritated Jim it was the high-handed way the Hospital Administrator, Bert Smith, dealt with the few 'Docs' who were lax in completing their charts. 'Regardless Bert,' Jim hotly contested, 'submitting names to the Governing Board to have admitting privileges lifted for the sake of one missing signature just isn't fair.'

'Every time the Administrator takes on another assistant' - Chairman Atwater wasn't through bitching - 'each has to have a separate room for a personal secretary, another of Murphy's Laws no doubt.'

The front section did have a few amenities: a doctors' cloakroom and lounge, and a spacious oak panelled Board Room graced by the portraits of previous chairmen.

The basement beneath held the X-ray and Pathology Departments, Medical Laboratories and an Outpatient Clinic. As land contours diminished in height from York Street to the bank of the old canal the basement was exposed at the back of the hospital and opened onto a parking lot.

The most recent extension, situated at the extreme east end of the front section, had five floors; all wings were represented alphabetically from east to west. From a sun-deck on the top of 'A' wing one could look over the whole complex from the separate Taylor Nursing Residence, bordering the old canal, to 'C' wing where the Stevenson Psychiatric Unit was located. The Unit had its own entrance onto York and was linked to the rest of the hospital by a concourse over the ambulance port.

The game recommenced when the present governing Board decided to erect a double corridor addition as high as the 'A' wing but in line with York Street. An architect was chosen, tenders called and a contractor hired. Ceremoniously his Worship the Mayor kicked off a public fund raising campaign while his wife in orange dungarees, self-chosen for the occasion, stomped a chrome-plated spade.

Before the foundation could be excavated a neighbouring filling station had to be demolished. 'Creeping substitution' Jim called it, borrowing an orthopaedic phrase referring to the absorption of dead bone and replacement with fresh osteoid. Though the comparison was abstracted by his erudite mind he was forced to observe the proceedings with the ignominious awe of a medieval serf. The scene had that effect, for armed with a Brobdingnagian flail a wrecking crane caterpillared and clanked its way into position. Pointing accusingly it swung at the marked and forsaken garage.

Jim felt the blows through the pavement, cataleptically held by the huge oscillating ball. A white wall, ashen in the grey light of dawn, quaked and fragments of bricks and mortar clattered in all directions. In spite of his fascination he was alerted by the clamorous antics of the machine's operator. Jim ducked in response, thinking himself in danger but his wariness passed an instant later. The man's whistling was not meant as a warning but to attract a bevy of student nurses emerging from the Taylor residence. His watch read 7.29 am. They were almost late for class; time for a round before meeting Dr. Best.

The wind began to bite. Jim shrugged, adjusting his turned-up collar, and plunged his bare hands into the pockets of his trench-coat.

Turning to enter the hospital, he remembered an x-ray jacket left in the Pontiac and dashed back to the doctors' reserved space behind Emergency. He reached his car as the last student was struggling with an armful of books, the wind and her blue and white striped skirt caught in the exit of 'B' wing.

The Pontiac was not locked, unlike the pretentious four-wheel throne parked next to it and the sleek red Corvette preventing him from opening the driver's side of his car. Jim wondered why Gerhardt Fast had parked so close. The three of them owned the only vehicles on the lot. Either the man was in an awful hurry or he had visual problems.

Frugal when it came to automobiles Jim considered them merely a means of transportation. Keep them in running order and insured but don't fuss over them. If someone was desperate enough to steal his crate why worry? He kept no medical bag full of syringes and drugs to entice the kooks. Nothing of value. His dusty light grey sedan did not even bear the customary M.D. license plates. Perhaps it was best. At least he wasn't embarrassing the profession.

He squeezed through the passenger door, careful not to scratch the regal finish on the Coupe de Ville; the Cadillac had cost Paolone a bundle.

Jim smiled, thinking the current Chief of Surgery, Joseph E. Paolone, had probably arrived at seven fifteen, punctual as usual, and vexed because the usurper of 'his spot' had not been molecularized.

Joe was a swarthy late middle-aged squab with the physiognomy of a parakeet and rhetoric just as repetitive, though his paraphrases were grandiloquent. He could talk forever. When a single word would suffice Paolone used a paragraph.

Physically short he liked long words, gaudy ties and expensive cars. There was an cushion behind the wheel, enabling him to see the road beyond the hood. How he reached the foot pedals was a question no one had the nerve to ask, barring Andy Cruikshank, his tormentor and arch rival. If Crooky enquired, it would've been for the want of information and not because of facetiousness for the Chief of Surgery at St. Mary's was a bantam himself.

To Jim, from the height of his athletic frame, Paolone had to be a comical curiosity but the man's aggressiveness and buoyancy demanded careful appraisal. Colleagues often embarrassed by his exuberant verbosity regarded Joe 'a pain in the ass' except when his recalcitrant remarks were directed at government interference with the practice of medicine.

To his many patients who clung to each superfluous syllable the 'Doc' was Caesar. Notwithstanding his parentally induced egocentricity and inherent weakness for words, Joe did have redeeming qualities. His industriousness, indefatigable pursuit of perfection and timely compassion were beyond reproach. His tailoring father and dressmaking mother had raised Joey, their only child, in three small rooms above a clapboard shop on a downtown side street. The day he graduation from medical school was a proud and gala event, but his parents penultimate joy came the day Joseph E. Paolone, Physician and Surgeon, nailed his shingle to a stately James Street residence.

Jim reached for the large yellow jacket and backed out awkwardly. His coat rubbed up against a dirty fender. As he bent to brush it off the wind, returning to gale proportions, almost tore the bundle of x-rays from him.

Weatherwise the morning had begun like the day before, clear and crisp but much colder with patches of snow. The ill-fated boat planking had commenced under similar conditions and ended in a storm of protest. That was yesterday. Think of the present and plan ahead, common sense advice but hard for a pricking conscience to heed.

Consoling Jason was no easy task. How many times in his life had Jim been forced to rely on unpredictable human behaviour? Hardly a day went by he wasn't disgruntled by the indifferent attitude of a patient, nurse and colleague. But they were pardonable. Failing himself was harder to take, failing his son inexcusable.

He gained the sheltered threshold of the basement entrance when a piercing blast slammed the door behind him. Inside a handful of names radiated from the call board in the dim companionway. Absently he switched on his light and before striking off for the X-ray Department contemplated the others. There were two obstetricians, an anaesthetist, Paolone and Gerhardt Fast.

The label 'Physician and Surgeon' was no longer in vogue. In the post-war era doctors were bred as General Practitioners and Specialists and expected to limit their practices accordingly.

A lamentable trend to Joe Paolone and he didn't wish to conform. He was not alone. Of the ninety doctors on the Active

Medical Staff of the Shipton General one-third considered themselves capable of treating everyone from the cradle to the grave.

A few by informal training with a preceptor in the field of general surgery added to their know-how more sophisticated and dangerous procedures. This elite group included Dr. Paolone.

Attesting to Joe's knowledge was a certificate from The Royal College of Physicians and Surgeons of Canada. He had received the paper the day after 'UNCONDITIONAL SURRENDER' headlined the Shipton Shield, merely by applying. No examination had been required. Joe framed and hung it - for all to see - in the vestibule of his office. As Crooky commented derisively, 'If it wasn't for the College's Code of Ethics prohibiting advertising Joe would've displayed it on a billboard along with a life-sized photograph of himself, smack in the centre of his lawn.'

Vexed by fellow practitioners of lesser ability who asked for second opinions from other locals, including himself, Dr. Paolone knew his own limitations and sought help elsewhere on occasion. But his problems were sent out of town in fear of losing prestige.

Dr. Lindsay slapped the oversized envelope on the counter beneath a bank of illuminating view boxes in the deserted X-ray Department thinking, there you go Ben. They're all yours. Send them to Toronto and collect your money.

He drew a handkerchief and cleared his nose still smarting from the cold wind. Misplaced films were a constant source of irritation to the radiologist, Ben Nickerson, and the administration office, particularly films taken of injured workmen. The envelope lying on the counter containing a myelogram was a case in point. Ben had been bugging for its return since the day after Jim had signed it out. Until x-rays films were safely in the hands of the 'W.C.B.' no one would get paid. 'Another bureaucratic inroad harassing doctor-patient relationship,' Ben would say, shaking his full head of black hair, 'and it leads to errors and misconduct.' Too often surgeons frustrated by delay and confused by forgetfulness were forced to take another x-ray of their patient, prepped, draped and deeply anaesthetized on an operating table. All because a menial clerk, adhering to rules, had mailed the initial films to the Board. Routine x-rays were of no serious consequence; films of a broken bone could be repeated. The increased amount of anaesthesia and radiation to the patient were undesirable but not excessive. But for special procedures such as a myelogram - so special its performance required authorization from the Board beforehand - being out of reach jeopardized the patient.

In addition not every practitioner was given the green light to treat the Board's cases. 'When you're dealing with the great Loa of Industrial Disease,' Ben declared, 'you're invoking a voodoo priest par excellence. He puts a juju on all of us; honest docs don't have a chance. His free reign decimates the field and the fallen bellyache like they had a gut full of pins.'

Every time he thought of this interference Jim exploded. Due to an unavailable myelogram he had to decide whether to proceed with his surgery or discontinue the anaesthetic and send his patient back to the ward. He chose to forge ahead, relying on memory and the accuracy of the radiologist's typed report. Fortunately at operation a large piece of ruptured disc was found exactly where it was seen on the myelogram, but he had perspired more than usual. Following this alarming experience, he confiscated all x-rays of his patients under active treatment. If his actions bothered anyone he could care less.

Warmer now Jim removed his trench-coat, slung it over a shoulder and left the viewing room. The basement corridor echoed the beat of his brogues back to the stairwell.

Gerhardt Fast was on his way out. He flipped a switch and his name disappeared from the call board.

"That was a quick trip Gary," Jim commented, recalling how Dr. Fast's red Corvette had effectively sealed access to the driver's side of his Pontiac minutes after he arrived.

"Nah! been here all night," replied the young practitioner, his handsome angular features and brown hair enhanced by the red glow of the exit light.

Jim mounted the first step pensively and stopped. "Really!" he exclaimed and stared, waiting for an explanation. He hadn't been in the hospital more than ten minutes himself. The man was either lying or had gone out temporarily.

"Yeah! Tough life C.J." Fast grinned. With no further explanation he drove his hip into the bar latch and shouldered the door saying, "gotta go, see you," his words mingling with the sibilant wind.

A probing current filled the stairwell and high above in the drafty recesses the air shrieked synchronously. From the landing Jim watched the younger doctor hustle across the parking lot, thinking of the noncommittal reply and trying to remember if he had ever had a straight answer from Gerhardt Fast. Finally, accepting it was none of his business, he continued his climb to the first floor.

Three registered nurses conferring in front of an elevator blocked his way to the main hall. He recognized the head of the Emergency Department, Jean Milligan, and Mrs. Anslow, the Night Supervisor. They nodded congenially, smiled at his apology for intruding and parted to let him through. At a casual glance the two women were much alike: matronly, broom-height with blue tinted hair. Both wore steel-rimmed spectacles and starched, white, black-banded caps, placed well back on their heads. While the Night Supervisor was dressed in a belted white uniform, Mrs. Milligan wore a loose-fitting operating gown. Where Jean was robust Mrs Anslow bulged pliantly.

Before he passed them, Jean's scalloped grin broadened and she asked, "Have you met our new O.R. Supervisor Dr. Lindsay?"

Jim stopped to acknowledge the third woman. She was small, unfathomably attractive, different from the conventional Anglo-Saxon beauty with high cheek bones and slanted amber eyes. Her nose was straight and a tantalizing ringlet dangled in front of each round ear. As sweet as a lollipop, he thought, though her heart-shaped face would have looked better balanced by a Peter Pan hairdo than the fashionable lion's mane she had adopted. He fully expected to hear a high pitched immature voice, however her greeting was Garbonian and unctuously seductive.

"Hi! I'm Tanya Harrington."

Like Anslow, the O.R. Supervisor wore a white uniform but it was beltless, short sleeved, modishly feminine and contoured a youthful curvaceous body. A flared skirt ended at the knees.

Jim looked directly at the face beneath the stylish cap, nestled in her hair-do and answered dispassionately. "Pleased to meet you, Miss Harrington."

She corrected him in the same buttery tone. "It's Mrs. Harrington!" Her eyes, shone with amusement, as she squeezed his hand.

Dr. Lindsay stopped, deliberating his words. How should he know she was married? Then he noticed the safety pin clasping a pair of rings to the front of her dress. "Oh I see."

"I believe you know my father-in-law," she added, "Robert Scofield Harrington." The name was clearly pronounced and drawn out.

'Bosco' Harrington was a household name. Of Shipton's upper-crust he was the most powerful. President and General Manager of Harrington Steel Works, Bosco had been Chairman of the Hospital Board since before the war. Moreover he owned the pulp and paper mill supplying the Shipton Shield and a host of other identifiable enterprises. In addition many benevolent Societies had come under his ardent leadership including the Heart Fund and the Cancer Foundation. As Dr. Lindsay had never had any personal contact with the man he replied, "I don't believe I do."

Tanya's eyes widened, losing a pinch of their oriental flavour, as she questioned, "You don't?"

"Well I know who he is," Jim commented, "but I've never had the opportunity of meeting him."

"Huh!" Her jaw clenched and a look followed, aimed at registering him on a lower social level.

Jim cordially nodded at the new O.R. Supervisor and smiled. "My pleasure, Mrs. Harrington. I hope you'll find your job satisfying."

"I'm sure," she replied, in a voice so low it was almost inaudible.

Turning to Mrs. Anslow, centring the trio, Jim derided. "Please don't disturb me for an insomnia problem. You're lucky Merri took the call. I'd have burned your ear off."

"But Dr. Lindsay!" Her whine followed him down the hall. "You left no order for a repeat sedation."

He paused as if he'd forgotten something and when he looked back his sternness had faded. "Sing them to sleep next time Anslow."

Jim strode down the hall, thinking Mrs. Harrington was doubtlessly qualified or she would never have been considered, but the idea of having the daughter-in-law of the Chairman of the Board in charge of the Operating Room outweighed any positive points. It was strange he had not heard of this appointment before. Apparently none of the doctors knew or the word would have been passed around. Bert Smith asserted he was running a public institution governed by democratic principles. Again opinion from the Medical Staff had not been solicited. Another farce. His suspicions were aroused.

Bosco Harrington might not have had a direct hand in it but he probably telegraphed his message loud and clear. Perhaps on a chance remark, 'Of course if she is selected I will be proud indeed.'

Jim frowned, although Mrs. Harrington's addition to the staff would be welcome her shouldering such a responsible job wasn't necessary. He and his colleagues had believed if anyone were to take over it would be Chalmers and there was no urgency. It had only been since September the previous Supervisor had retired and under the affable Chalmers everything was running fairly well. She had been second-in-command for years and nursing was her whole life. He shrugged. Why on earth Tanya Harrington wanted the job was a puzzle. Financially she didn't need it.

CHAPTER TEN

Paolone was seated at the far end of the huge mahogany conference table partly obscured by an untidy stack of hospital charts. Jim saw him upon entering the room. The little Chief was busy thumbing through typewritten pages, scrawling his signature oblivious to anyone else.

Jim crossed over to the opposite honey-combed wall, found his own slot and removed a handful of neatly folded reports. "Morning," he said, tossing them on the table. There was no reply.

Jim scraped a chair into position and sat solidly upon it. Paolone failed to look up. Jim's knees jarred the table. "What'sa nice'a wop doin in'a dump'a like'a deez?"

That did it. Joe cocked his head and fluttered his flat black eyes. "Hey pisano!" he sang, stroking his parrot-like beak. "Your Italian's improving." His smile smacked of mockery as he added. "Ah, this is a memorable occasion. To what do we owe the honour and pleasure? The Sisters throw you out?"

Paolone's exchange shot found its mark. Though Dr. Lindsay openly preferred to work at St. Mary's there was an insinuation anyone who did cared less for the General which was not true. He divided his energies equally between the two; most of the specialists did. Any resentment was personal, deep-seated and prevalent among the G.P.s who had limited privileges from the day St.Mary's opened.

The religious Hospitalers had met some opposition. The General had been established first and demanded certain loyalties. But Paolone's accusation that St. Mary's was an autocrasy, not in the best interests of the public at large, was unfounded. An opinion, Jim found hard to understand because the little Chief was a staunch Roman Catholic. The nuns in charge were dedicated. At the General this philosophy was often overruled by individual pursuits.

Jim did not reply immediately. Before pocketing his reports he perused them until he came to the annual application for reappointment to the Medical Staff.

"What do you think Joe? Shall I sign up for another year or let the place go to pot?"

Paolone squared himself, combed his stubby fingers through his thin grey hair and without a trace of humour replied. "With my expertise, inimitable charm and envious looks it never will."

Jim laughed. It was hard to tell if Joe really meant what he said. He had baited Paolone and got a typical Paolonean response. Laying the application on the table he signed the bottom. "Mind witnessing this?"

The little Chief pursed his thin lips and twitched. "Not at all," he said patronizingly, "even the added clause where you vow not to split fees."

Sensing he was in for another dissertation on medical ethics, Jim decided it was time to leave. He had heard it all before. The little man was dead set against kick-backs or fee-splitting. His denunciation of such a deplorable act was so stinging a perpetrator would never have the courage to proposition him. Consequently from personal experience it was Paolone's belief this unethical practice was not going on. 'Albeit,' he would say. 'The temptation is there abetted by a loose system of fee collection through third party insurance companies. When doctors bill their patients directly they can be asked to justify their fees but when a patient authorizes an insurance company to pay one Doc, money changes hands like ships passing in the night. Besides it's a two edged sword that cuts both ways! On the one hand a frustrated aggressive operator hungry for cases can be coerced into offering kick-backs for a steady source of referrals while on the other an unscrupulous practitioner fattens his purse at the expense of an inferior surgeon.'

'Then there's the foxy folk,' Paolone would go on, 'who won't authorize direct payment to their physician and abscond with the cheque, a misdemeanour played on every Doc at least once and by seemingly innocent people.'

'Let the government take over medical insurance as they have hospitalization,' Joe warned, 'then we're in deep trouble. Everyone: doctors, patients, administrators and the government will become greedy, dishonest and totally unconcerned. The cost will become insurmountable and guess who'll take the blame? Us! For what politician is going to finger himself for advocating bankruptcy? He would malign his constituents, the same people he'd duped into thinking medical care is a right, regardless of cost and available for all, not a privilege of the undeserving rich. What person doesn't take all he can get for nothing? The handwriting is on the wall,' Joe prophesied, 'and we're responsible. We should never have accepted third party payment in the beginning.'

Jim stood up, tucked the application in an envelope and stashed it in an inner pocket of his sport coat.

"How come all you orthopods wear brogues and Harris tweeds? Last spring I went to an orthopaedic convention in Chicago - not for the tax deduction mind you - and every doc who walked into the auditorium wore brogues and a heavy wool jacket. Haven't you guys got any individuality or imagination?"

"They're rugged, like mineralized bone," Jim replied and added, "You know, we're the oldest branch of surgery. The first operation was performed in the Garden of Eden by God Himself."

"How's that?"

"The extraction of Adam's rib."

"Yeah! yeah! yeah! smart ass," Joe chuckled. "Where did you hear that?"

"From an orthopod with an imagination," Jim drawled and saluted as he angled toward the door, "See you, Chief."

Shunning the elevator Jim took the stairs two at a time to the fifth floor and entered A5. The Paediatric Ward did not believe in lying-in. There were little people all over. He located the nurse in charge, checked the charts for temperature elevations and began rounds. Three of his four patients were comfortably arrayed in the rumpus room. The seven-year-old with the broken leg was managing his crutches satisfactorily and could be discharged. The other two were infants and could have passed for sisters a year apart with fair hair, blue eyes and congenital hip dislocations. Incisions were checked through a window cut in their casts. There was no redness or swelling but it was too early to remove their stitches. He stroked the older one on the head and handed her a compressible toy elephant from the floor.

His fourth patient, a ten-year-old boy, was confined to bed with a fractured femur. From the hall Jim heard him crying in pain and realized what was happening before he'd reached the bedside.

"Who in Hell removed the weights?" He growled.

The student nurse following him was speechless, pale and petrified, so he repeated himself with less candour, still glowering, "Who took the weights off this boy's leg?"

"I, I, don't know," she stammered. "Nothing was said at report."

"Well find out," Jim growled, "and fetch the weights."

The young woman was frightened, seemingly glued to the spot, and moved only when he turned his attention to the boy.

How many times had he lectured to the nursing staff and orderlies on the principles of balanced suspension and traction? He had lost count. The Thomas splint used to support the limb was at right angles to the floor so the child's leg pointed to the ceiling. He adjusted it to the intended position almost parallel to the bed. A pin had been placed through the bone below the knee and the ends of it were clamped in a metal bow. Rope usually tied to the bow trailed uselessly, partly covered with sheet. It was untangled and he threaded it through a pulley, hanging from a cross-bar at the foot of the bed.

The boy's thigh was swollen, tender and shortened, indicating the broken ends had overlapped considerably. Very gently he pushed the padded ring at the upper end of the Thomas splint against the child's groin and maintained a manual pull on the traction bow until the nurse returned.

"It was the night supervisor Mrs. Anslow," she said, handing him the weights. "The boy's heel was resting on the bed - he was uncomfortable and she was afraid he'd get a pressure sore."

Jim gave her a blank look and tied the weights to the free end of the rope. The child had stopped fretting. "There you go," he reassured. "Everything's going to be all right."

It had to be Anslow, he thought, upon leaving the room. She was a kindly soul and in her mind she had done what she thought was right. He could hear her excuse, she was full of excuses. 'But it was hurting him Dr. Lindsay!' There was no use making an issue of the incident. No serious harm had resulted. It was incredible! Anslow awakened him at two a.m. for a sedative because there was no written order, but without an order she had the audacity to play around with a gadget she knew nothing about. Jim would speak to her later; meanwhile he'd go back to the counter, write in the chart and inform the nurse in charge no one was to adjust traction without his permission. Before he had a chance to do so a speaker in the corridor ceiling blared his name.

Jim picked up a phone at the nursing station and dialled 'operator'. The line was busy. Impatiently he began to pace back and forth between the elevator and the counter, alternatively pushing the 'down' button and dialling zero. He got the girl at the switchboard first.

"Operator," she oozed.

"Lindsay here. You were paging me?"
"Oh yes, Emergency's looking for you. They say it's urgent."
"What time have you got?"
"Five after eight."
"Do me a favour and call the lounge," Jim demanded. "Leave a message for Dr. Best. I'll be a few minutes late."
"Dr. Who?"
"Best. Dr. Beecher Best."
"He's not on our list. Is he new?"
Jim hesitated. "No," he replied, "just a visitor."
"Sure thing Dr. Lindsay."
The elevator arrived and he darted for the opening.

In the Emergency Department Jean Milligan was tearing the metal cap off an intravenous bottle. The creases parenthesizing her wide friendly mouth faded, as she announced, "We've got two patients for you Dr. Lindsay and they're both badly hurt."
"Car accident?"
"Not exactly. One is a motorcyclist who collided with a car."
"Tibia?"
"No. His foot was torn off. The ambulance driver brought in his shoe. The foot's still in it. He's in number four." While Jim frowned, thinking how futile reattaching it would be, she added, "The other man is in the large room. The x-ray technician is developing his films. Seems his back's broken. He can't move his legs. We've a call in for Finny but his answering service can't locate him."

Jean paused and regarded Dr. Lindsay quizzically, before she said. "Your friend's with him."
"My friend?"
"He introduced himself as such - Dr. Best - says he's an orthopaedic surgeon."
"How come he's there?" Jim sounded as if he were talking to himself. "I was supposed to meet him in the doctor's lounge."
"Came in the back way," Jean explained. "Helped the ambulance men unload the stretcher," then she asked quietly. "Does he have privileges?"
"Why do you ask?"
"Well, he's in the midst of starting an IV and wanted a paracentesis set-up. He's ordered a type and cross match for three units and called for a catheterization tray."

"I see," said Jim absently.

"I checked the Active Staff list and he's not on it. What'll I do?" As a department head Mrs. Milligan knew the rules. She had every right to have Best expelled from Emergency but the patients' problems were more pressing.

"Better go ahead with the lab work anyhow," Jim advised. "It's got to be done. I'll speak to him later."

The large room was brightly illuminated by recessed fluorescent ceiling fixtures. Five wheeled stretcher-beds with tightly sheeted mattresses were visible from the door. They were equally spaced, unoccupied and placed perpendicular to the long back wall. Drawdrapes forming a cubicle around the sixth were not long enough to hide several pairs of trouser and nylon sheathed legs.

Dr. Lindsay drew aside the heavy cotton to catch Dr. Best in the act of removing a long needle from the upper abdomen. Failing to aspirate blood, Best tried a second tap a few inches below the left rib cage. Again the procedure produced negative results. Two more jabs into contralateral sides of the lower belly were also unrevealing. Throughout the procedure Best was bent over; when he replaced the syringe on the paracentesis tray he noticed Jim.

"Dr. Lindsay! How are you?" Beecher grinned broadly.

"What's going on?" Jim demanded, ignoring the inappropriate social formality. If there was anyone to be asked the state of his health it had to be the poor man lying on the stretcher. From the speed at which Dr. Best was working it was doubtful if he'd taken the time.

"This unfortunate fellow has severed his cord," Best declared, scratching the patient's foot with a splintered tongue depressor. When nothing happened as the sharp piece of wood stroked the skin of the sole he added, "See! A pathological reflex already! A Babinski! His cord must be completely divided."

Jim glanced quickly at the patient's face. The eyes remained shut. If Beecher's observations had been heard they caused no detectable alarm. It was the face of an old man, weather-beaten, wrinkled, and reduced to an ashen colour. Beads of sweat glistened on the smudgy forehead. Jim glared at Best. "We can discuss the problem outside," he suggested, forcefully. Then scanning the other faces in the cubicle asked, "What happened?"

"Wind!" One of the ambulance men revealed. "At the 'Landmark site' on the other side of town. A tool shed fell on him. The edge of the roof caught him across the middle of the back. He was pinned down when we got there. It took a gang of Indians to lift the shed before we could get him out."

Jim solemnly shook his head at the group around the stretcher and inquired. "Who's his family doctor?"

There was no reply and while Jim searched their blank expressions the old man opened his sunken eyes and sniffled, "I don't have one."

"Then we'll have Dr. Atwater take a look at you," Jim suggested, "if you have no objections - he's an internist."

The patient nodded slowly, his frantic eyes shut and he appeared to drift off again.

Trying not to cause any further discomfort, Dr. Lindsay went about re-checking Beecher's neurological findings and supplemented a few tests of his own. While he was engaged in his work the x-ray technician returned from the Dark Room and waited for him to inspect the exposed films.

Beecher had strolled into the hall; seeing her enter the cubicle he followed.

"Let me have a look," he insisted, tugging at the frames of wet x-rays.

She delayed, hoping Dr. Lindsay would intervene. By the time Jim realized what was going on Beecher was holding a film up to the fluorescent light. "T12-L1," he announced. "Fracture dislocation."

Once again Jim contained himself but the look he gave the impudent Dr. Best would have cowed a bull. His orders cracked like a sheet of ice. "Take the x-rays to the cast room. Put them on the view box. I'll be there shortly." Addressing the two nurses quietly standing by, he ordered, "Make the patient comfortable. Hang 1000 ccs. of normal saline. Get an orderly to put in a Foley catheter and transfer him to the ward. I'd like one of you to stay and check his vital signs every fifteen minutes."

Jim cursed under his breath. It was precisely this type of situation that merited an Intensive Care Unit but Administration saw fit to use any available space for itself. He barked at the two women. "If neither of you is free hire a 'special' and ask the Supervisor to have a Stryker frame made up. We'll need it right away."

To Jean Milligan who had reappeared he asked. "Have you heard from Finny?"

"Not directly. He's doing a craniotomy at St. Mary's."

"What for?"

"Brain tumour. He doesn't know when he'll be finished. Possibly eleven."

"Okay." Jim exhaled. "Would you please get hold of Ed Atwater. Ask him to call me after he has seen this patient; call the O.R. and tell them to set up for an emergency laminectomy and fusion. We should be ready by noon."

"Fine," said Jean. "Shall I book the motorcyclist too?"

Dr. Lindsay had almost forgotten the second case. He thought a moment, his features sagging with pessimism. "I suppose you should alert them," he answered dully. "It can wait awhile. Sounds like a straight-forward amputation. Where is he?"

"Treatment room four," Jean reminded. "His parents are with him."

Jim stepped across the hall to the cast room where Best had taken the x-rays.

The films were on the view box but Best was unaccountably absent. Jim studied them intently. The backbone had been broken in half and markedly displaced, producing a step-like deformity. The cord had to be anatomically, as well as physiologically, transected. "Son-of-a-bitch," he muttered. "What's the use?"

There was no point involving Finny. The patient was beyond neurosurgical help. Severed cords did not heal even if the halves were accurately approximated and sutured microscopically. A laminectomy wasn't indicated but stabilization was, if the man would ever sit in a wheel chair.

The door to the adjacent room partly opened and Best showed his smiling face. "You coming to see this guy?" he asked.

E. R. 4 was the same size as the cast room, fifteen by twenty feet. Instrument cabinets, treatment stands, anaesthetic equipment and a scrub sink lined its pale green tiled walls. Upon a centrally placed operating table lay a youth, gasping with pain. Terror filled his eyes and he was bundled in a woollen blanket. A hulking woman sat on a stool beside him. She had dressed hastily, her shabby maroon coat was unfastened revealing a chunky kimono-clad thigh.

"My poor Bobby, my baby," she wailed over and over, her dishevelled tresses swabbing his wet dirty cheek.

Behind her stood a slight man in patched denim pants, tenderly patting her arm. He held a yellow hard hat in front of his tattered blue wind-breaker and was staring at a curious towel wrapped package. It was about the length of a size ten shoe and rested on the Mayo stand.

Grimacing, the youth tried to raise his head when the doctors entered the room. Agony contorted him further and he groaned and fell back. Whereupon the woman hugged him fiercely, smothering his plangent cries with tears.

Jim was frankly surprised to hear Beecher introduce him and the woman ceased to wail.

"Mr. and Mrs. Hardy, and Bobby. This is Dr. Lindsay."

The formality was artfully executed in a hushed amiable tone.

"Friends of yours?" Jim asked.

"No. Yes, er well, what I mean is I just met them."

The confidential manner flashed off momentarily and Beecher's closely-set, pebbly orbs, pin-balled as indiscriminately as his speech, landing anywhere but on the people in the room.

"Oh I see," Jim drawled, wondering what had transpired while the good doctor had been conversing with these miserable people. "Then you know Dr. Best," he added, addressing the three of them.

"We know him," Mr. Hardy spoke up. The slight man moved out from behind his massive wife. "He's already told us. Says he's your colleague. Glad ya could come, Doc."

Jim nodded, smiling tacitly. He was beginning to get the picture. While he had been across the hall examining the old man Best had boldly presented himself to the Hardys. What was wrong was Best's presence.

Mr. Hardy whined. "Ya gotta help us Doc. Our son." He choked and gestured with his headgear at the youth. "He's all we got. Doc Best says you can sew his foot on. Is that right Doc? Can ya do that?"

Jim did not reply but he wondered. Had Best actually advised these poor unenlightened people, a completely severed foot could be rejoined? If so, there was nothing he could or wanted to say under the circumstances. Any comment would have to await his appraisal. He had invited Beecher out of courtesy to meet him in the doctor's

Do Unto Others *111*

lounge prepared to acquaint him with the hospital lay-out. Now he wished he'd never offered. Without hospital privileges Dr. Best had ordered treatment, performed a minor surgical operation and implied to the parents of a patient he was a trusted associate. Best had become a pesky intruder; Jim wanted to be rid of him. In a pressing tone he asked, "Would you take Mr. and Mrs. Hardy out to the waiting room and send Mrs. Milligan back? I'll need her. By the way, Beecher" he added, searching his jacket pockets, "Please take this to Administration. It's my annual application to the Hospital Staff. While there you might as well fill in your own. Wait for me in the doctor's lounge."

Beecher regarded Jim through half closed lids, "As you wish," he mumbled, "But what about the boy? His foot has to be prepared right away if we're to restore it."

Every muscle in Jim's face contracted simultaneously and he had trouble emphasizing, "Please do as I ask. We'll discuss the boy later."

CHAPTER ELEVEN

It had been a morning of deprecation. Prysniuk had asked for a priest. Half of his body was in a quagmire and he was afraid. Predictably his condition remained the same.

Mrs. Hardy had wept plaintively, beseeching the Almighty to save her son's foot but the practical fulfilment of her prayers was up to the doctors. When Jim gravely rendered advice she became hysterical and required sedation. Her husband had been bitter and argumentative. He could not understand why Dr. Lindsay refused to re-attach the foot. Nor did he understand the doctor's suggestion of removing more by cutting through healthy tissue higher up the leg. Recently the misguided Mr. Hardy had seen a picture in the Shipton Shield. A young girl had sustained a similar injury to her arm when she was run over by her father's tractor. The tragedy received widespread publicity when a team of specialists at a University Hospital made a sensational effort to connect the severed parts. After eight hours of surgery the fragmented humerus had been restored, the damaged arteries and nerves repaired, and pinkishness and warmth returned to her hand. Not reported was the inability of the child to flex her unfeeling fingers after the operation, and the likelihood she never would to a useful degree. It was also improbable the news media would inform the public months later when the stiff, ulcerated limb was replaced by a plastic and metal prosthesis.

A numb indurated foot subjected to the pounding pressure of body weight had a poorer prognosis and was sure to break down.

Jim had wasted his words. Crooky was hailed for a curbstone consultation and agreed with the proposed treatment.

Still the elder Hardy, deafened by hope, kept insisting, 'Dr. Best says ya can put it on so what ya waitin fur?'

'Who the hell is Dr. Best?' Crooky had blurted, 'God Almighty?' Lowering his voice, he reminded himself it was not the sort of thing a man of his professional stature was expected to say, particularly in front of the worshipping laity.

He suddenly hung his head and a florid blush accentuated his snow white hair. Away from the eavesdropping clerk, he listened to Jim's explanation.

Further reasoning with the Hardys was useless and their son was packed off to a University Hospital in Toronto where the greybeards surrounded by a brilliance of progressive young minds and the

Do Unto Others

most up-to-date technical equipment might assuage Beecher's influence.

At noon the orderlies wheeled Prysniuk into the operating suite and left him premedicated in the holding area, resting comfortably on a Stryker frame. As the anaesthetist was tied up with another case the nurses covered the instrument table and went to lunch.

By one o'clock the surgeon's locker room was empty save for Drs. Lindsay, Finny and Best, dressed in scrub suits and waiting. Beecher had tagged along upon Finny's invitation irrespective of Jim's negative feelings. Exclusive of the Paolone team all of the doctors involved in the morning's operations had finished and left.

Hooking a rangy leg over the arm of a soft leather chair Jim recessed with a pipe while Beecher sat at a table reading the newspaper. The coveted sofa in the alcove settled under the bulk of Dr. Elton Finny, thumbs stuck in the arm holes of his greens, his fat fingers interlaced across his heavy chest.

Finny was no Ben Casey, the stern, aloof, restrained, melancholy, secretly passionate, unrelenting, fervently dedicated brain surgeon depicted on T.V. In fact he was quite the opposite: loud, profane, rustic, jovial, disgracefully uninhibited, emotionally labile, and downright repulsive at times. Fortunately for him his chosen field was limited and highly specialized. When the population grew enough to support a second and third neurosurgeon Finny might have to take a back seat. In the meantime his supporters were tolerant. He belched; his recumbent corpulence quivered and a noisy fart permeated the conditioned air. There was no I beg your pardon, excuse me or other tasteful apology offered. He simply lay at the seat of his subconscious, his ruddy face bowing before a dun tufted crown.

Jim slid further into his chair wondering if the neurosurgeon ever considered anyone other than himself. 'At least Finny is honest,' Crooky would argue. 'He doesn't stick his head in the sand when there's trouble brewing and try to cover up his mistakes.' Dr. Cruikshank's opinion was based on Finny's daring intervention, undoubtedly saving a life. The episode occurred shortly after Finny's indifferent welcome and consolidated Crooky's stand on the necessity of having a neurosurgeon on call. The patient, one of Dr. Cruikshank's closest friends, had sustained a splitting headache, lapsed into coma and was hauled off the golf course to St. Mary's where a spinal tap performed by Crooky himself - later Finny criticized him for doing it - indicated a cerebral haemorrhage. The man was placed under close observation. Bleeding continued and as increasing intracranial pressure plunged the base of his brain into its exit from the skull, one by one vital reflex centres became depressed. His blood pressure rose and his breathing waxed and waned rhythmically. Death was imminent, minutes crucial. Transferring him to a distant neurosurgical unit certified his inhumation. In desperation Finny was asked to see him and in less time than it would've taken an ambulance to reach Toronto he clipped the leaking aneurism and the patient began to recover. There had been instant jubilation. Never before had such courageous surgery been performed in Shipton. Finny was proclaimed a hero, showered with congratulations and ostentatiously basked in glory. That evening excitement was offset when the patient lapsed into coma. Finny had to leave a cocktail party at the Cruikshanks where he was being feted. He astutely assessed the problem and re-opened the patient's skull. A clip had worked loose and had to be replaced. Some of the staff had reservations, possibly tinged with jealousy. There were a few innuendos. As Paolone suggested, 'the first clip was improperly applied.' But Crooky spoke up in Finny's defence, 'It takes guts to admit something might have gone wrong but a lot more to do something about it.' His friend survived and from then on the Chief of Surgery at St. Mary's supported Dr. Elton Finny 'carte blanche'.

While Jim sucked his pipe he remembered the Sisters' attitude. They were not so easily convinced, although in the beginning they were elated the first brain surgery ever performed in Shipton distinguished their hospital. In due course Finny's alpha nature proved to be incompatible with their best interests and they were not unhappy when he began to do less at St. Mary's and more at the General. No one would ever convert Finny. At the General his flamboyant eccentricity became a pleasurable diversion.

Finny's name was on Sister Bernadette's tongue earlier when Drs. Lindsay and Best were ushered into her private office. In recalling the conversation Jim ran the last three hours through his mind.

She ended a telephone conversation with, 'the man's impossible', hung up and swung around to greet them.

'Sister, Dr. Best would like to meet you.' Jim's presentation had been terse and to the point. 'He's planning on practising orthopaedics and wants an application.'

The Administrator flashed Beecher a deceptively sweet smile and rose from her desk. 'How do you do Dr. Best?' she said, rustling a voluminous habit as she skirted her desk to welcome him with a soft hand. Framed by a long white veil and starched coif her greying eyebrows arched pleasantly.

'Your associate, Dr. Lindsay?' she inferred blinking behind a pair of rimless glasses.

'No!' Jim replied, 'I'm just showing him around.' He had been asked the same question by Bert Smith at the General and suspected, through discursiveness, Best had left Bert with the same impression, also the Hardys. Jim was becoming more annoyed; his hospitable gesture was being misinterpreted. Jason would be his associate someday. 'Sorry Sister', he said, evading the issue, 'but I have a few patients to see,' and while leaving, added, 'when you're through, Beecher, meet me in the doctor's lounge.'

Jim damned himself for procrastinating. The opportunity to end Beecher's allusion had come in the car on the way from the General but he had put it off preferring to extract more information on Afghanistan. After the Administrator's assumption he was more determined.

They had re-convened to tour St. Mary's Hospital and were returning to the General in Lindsay's Pontiac.

Beecher was commenting on the efficiency of St. Mary's impressed by the segregation of surgical sub-specialities onto separate wards when Jim interrupted. 'There are a couple of things I must tell you,' he said. 'You will have to obey the rules. Until you have been accepted as a member of the Medical Staff you have no more privileges than a visiting layman. What you did this morning was illegal.'

Beecher put his arm on the back of the front seat and turned to ask innocently, 'What are you talking about?'

For a moment a traffic light delayed them and Jim locked directly into Beecher's inquiring eyes. 'You truly don't know.' he said and striking a pointed index finger on the steering wheel slowly ground out the facts. 'Though you might get away with examining the patient in the Emergency room, provided you had his permission -

which you did not - you certainly had no legal right to treat him. Your starting an I.V. on Mr. Prysniuk and tapping his abdomen was against the law.'

'You're kidding!'

'No, I'm quite serious.'

'You mean to say if a person is critically ill or injured such as the man I saw this morning, and being trained to render life-saving therapy and carry it out, I could be charged for it?'

'Precisely! Assault! Furthermore the hospital would be deemed negligent for permitting you.'

'Huh! What if I were the only doctor in town?'

Jim frowned and started the car in motion again. 'In that case it would be a very small town with a more flexible set of by-laws. If they had a hospital, you might be granted temporary privileges. Anyhow,' Jim added, 'there are no guarantees against law suits. Many a patient has tried to make a buck off the very people who try to help them. Thank God suing hasn't reached the proportions it has in the States. Down there a doctor stopping for an accident risks his financial security just to be a good Samaritan. I'm sure you've read of incidents.'

On York St. they encountered a brief traffic jam and Jim remained silent while they passed through the downtown business section. When the street was clear he began again, his voice a trifle higher in pitch. 'Another thing, watch what you say in front of patients. A glib comment can be demoralizing.'

Beecher jerked his head defensively.

'If you're going to associate with me,' Jim continued, 'which is what you want everyone to think, you'll have to learn restraint. You made a pretty devastating remark in front of the old man. He wasn't out in left field as you appeared to think. Or maybe you weren't thinking at all when you said, 'This unfortunate fellow has severed his cord.' He heard every word of it and he understood. Your inflection helped. In my opinion it was neither the time, place, nor way to tell him.'

'Something else,' Jim's voice was becoming more tense. 'You obviously don't know what a positive Babinski reflex is. It doesn't occur until long after the spinal cord has been severed and is elicited by an up-going big toe when the sole of the foot is stroked. As you noted the big toe didn't react at all.'

Whether or not Beecher was absorbing Jim's fault finding remained a mystery for an inexplicable grin crinkled his eyes and he did not answer.

'Finally,' Dr. Lindsay added as he turned off York and drew into the parking lot at the back of the General. 'You should never promise patients something you can't deliver, even if the odds look good. Have reservations. Anything can go wrong. Whoever told you an avulsed foot can be rejoined successfully?'

'Ah, ah, nobody,' Beecher hesitated. 'It was my own idea. I think it's worth a try.'

'Well that's encouraging!' Jim smiled wryly. 'I was beginning to question your professors.'

'I still do,' Beecher argued, stubbornly clinging to his original point of view. 'What more has he got to lose?'

'Time!' Jim exclaimed.

The Pontiac ground to a halt and before exiting, he expanded. 'Months, years, forever. Eventually he'd resent you like an animal in a steel trap. In case your professors didn't tell you, there have been other attempts by very capable surgeons. It just isn't worth the effort.'

Jim opened the car door and hoping to put an end to the conversation said, 'I must get on with my business. You'll have to excuse me, I have a few calls to make. It looks like I'll be tied up all afternoon and I'll have to cancel my office.'

'Mind if I scrub.?'

Most of an unenjoyable morning had been spent with Dr. Best and Jim had enough. Further time with him would be an imposition; other things of importance took precedence. As it was he was not looking forward to the operation. It would not be easy. Having to put up with the shenanigans of Finny was a strain he was forced to endure. 'Sorry Beecher,' he replied quite openly. 'There won't be enough room around the table. Besides I'd have to clear it with the Administrator and I haven't time to chase him down.'

'Then may I lunch with you?'

The answer, an impartial shrug, did not completely disguise Dr. Lindsay's displeasure. The cocky bugger was just too much.

While they were eating sandwiches in the hospital's snack bar Jim listened sceptically.

Beecher, in an effort to exonerate himself, prattled on about the latest orthopaedic innovations. He was extolling the virtue of a 'hanging hip' operation he'd read about in a recent issue of the Journal of Bone and Joint when Jim bluntly cut in.

'I do McMurray's osteotomy for osteoarthritis of the hip. It succeeds if it's done properly and the head of the femur is allowed to roll into a more congruent position when the shaft is displaced.'

'But you have to break the bone and it takes months to heal,' Beecher pointed out. 'In a hanging hip all you do is cut the attachments of the muscles crossing the joint. It's easy. The patient is up and about in a few days.'

'Easy eh', Jim argued. 'What about the femoral artery, and sciatic and femoral nerves?'

'No problem,' Beecher reassured.

'Have you ever done one?'

'No.'

'Have you seen it done?'

'No.'

'Then what makes you think it's so easy or it works?'

'It has to! It's a mere anatomical dissection to relieve tension on inflamed tissues.'

Dr. Lindsay had to concede it was a rational treatment but was not fully convinced. It didn't sound as reasonable as the osteotomy he'd been performing over the years. Many articles had been published in the journals by men of repute with supposedly sound judgment. However not all of the suggestions they put forward were reliable, a sobering fact which he'd discovered early in his career. Later he gathered a few writers produced papers for the sole purpose of seeing their name in print. Beecher was going to find this out for himself; judging from the supercilious expression which the young surgeon wore, Jim wondered if he ever would.

'You should keep abreast of the literature,' Best imputed. 'It's a good way to relax.'

The counsel, if it were made in good faith, was insolent in light of the difference in age, position and experience of the two men. Yet, Jim accepted it without malice as a stroke of one-up-man-ship. After all, duty-bound or not, he had been the first to draw the line. Besides he felt guilty, regarding his lack of current information, emphasized by the Fellowship examinations. 'Perhaps I should read more,' he said. Still he brooded, feeling overburdened. The younger surgeon needed someone to watch over him and keep him out of trouble. Jim would rather mind his own affairs. What precious energy he had at the end of a day was devoted to his family.

Beecher's aggressive behaviour was not an oddity. Most successful surgeons were aggressive individuals; they had to be. The chances were Beecher would get through his early years as others before him without any serious misadventures. Of course he'd get his fingers burnt, but hopefully he'd learn not to repeat his mistakes. In the meantime the wary Dr. Lindsay conscientiously resolved to keep the unseasoned surgeon in line whenever the occasion arose. Still it was galling he would have to start today; and with Finny to contend with as well.

Why in hell the neurosurgeon agreed to Best's request to scrub was beyond him; perhaps he needed a theatrical audience. Jim smirked as he thought how they were a team - like Abbott and Costello.

CHAPTER TWELVE

While Drs. Lindsay, Best and Finny were waiting to start their case the hall door opened and Charlie Simpson, struggling with a pushcart, limped into the dressing room. He had the shy air of one who is well-known yet desired not to be. 'Simp the gimp' as he was affectionately called by nurses and doctors alike, had been hustling things about the operating room for almost thirty years. He was short and slim with sparse grey hair, most of which was hidden beneath an ever present O.R. cap. His narrow wrinkled face was traversed by a scar, gracing him with an undying smile. Pushing the cart over to a corner table he loaded it with the empty coffee urn and proceeded about the room, gathering dirty cups and soiled scrub suits. Now and again he had to bend down and the movement was awkwardly executed.

Beecher, abandoning the newspaper, watched him with curiosity. "What happened to your leg?"

"Dieppe. German grenade burst my knee," Charlie explained. "They fused it at Christie St. My leg's two inches short. Have to wear this built-up shoe," He demonstrated his custom-made boot with a tug on his white trousers and added, "It doesn't bother me none. Been like this for twenty years."

"Then why do you look so distressed?" Beecher asked.

"It's my other hip. It's getting stiff. Hurts when I walk."

Jim had been eyeing the two of them through a screen of aromatic smoke and interjected. "Saw you marching Armistice Day and you were stepping right along Charlie."

"It comes and goes, Doc. I've been meaning to make an appointment with your office."

The intercom cut in. "Dr. Lindsay?"

"Yes."

"They're ready for you in O. R. 3. Is Dr. Finny there?"

"Yes! God-dammit! It's about time!" Finny catapulted off the couch and stood akimbo, yelling his words at the ceiling speaker. "Where the hell is Larson?"

"Starting your anaesthetic," the woman's voice replied.

Her answer was echoed by Paolone who entered during the commotion.

Finny snarled, "For Christ sake Joe. What took you so long? It's taken you four fucking hours to ream out one lousy ass-hole."

Paolone looked haggard, his eyes flatter than usual. "Rectal carcinoma," he rasped. Glands involved. Had to go into the belly as well. She bled like the deuce. Larson won't move her until the anaesthetic has worn off. He's down in your room now."

Finny didn't wait for Paolone to finish. He stormed out with Beecher at his heels and Paolone found himself directing his brief apology to Jim. "I'm sorry, it was a tough case."

"Abdominal perineals usually are," Jim agreed. "Who was assisting?"

"Pearson and Morrisey. They're in the nurses' lounge."

"You should've have had another surgeon," Dr. Lindsay commented, knowing Pearson and Morrisey were G.P.s. "Would have been easier with two teams."

Paolone shook his head drearily. "I couldn't get anyone else."

While Jim pulled himself out of the leather chair Joe asked. "What are you up to?"

"Back. Nasty fracture with cord damage."

"I should have known. You and Finny working together." Lowering his voice and large upper lids, Paolone confronted Jim privately. "You must have the patience of Job to put up with him."

Jim laughed and turned to go.

"Hey Lindsayello," Joe called after him. "Don't forget the meeting tomorrow night."

Jim held the door ajar. "What meeting?"

"Department of Surgery. It's important. We're going over the final plans for the new addition."

"A lotta good that'll do. You can't change anything now. They've broken ground."

"It's about bed allocation. Better be there."

Jim sounded indifferent. "I'll see," he said. Tuesday night was saved for pick-up basketball with Jason and his friends. He hated to give it up. Slowly his stare shifted from the floor to Paolone and he mumbled, "I suppose, if it's important."

"Say, who's the pup following Finny around?"

"Best. Beecher Best, a local boy. He's an orthopod."

"Another one!"

"Yes," Jim sighed. "Another one freshly certified and raring to go. You'll hear all about it. See you later." Before Paolone could ask any more questions Jim left for the sterile area.

At the reception desk a harping clerk reminded him everyone was waiting and handed him a pair of boot-covers. No apology was offered for holding him up for the past two hours. The thought had never crossed her mind.

Jim stepped into the glare of O.R.3. It was a big pure white room except for the shiny stainless steel fixtures. The large American operating table had been moved to the corridor and the spotlight was on a Stryker bed. Asleep from an injection of intravenous pentothal Prysniuk lay supine, strapped to one of its padded frames subtended by a chrome-plated cradle.

Larson's long bony fingers were busy with a strip of adhesive, taping an endotracheal tube to the patient's forehead while four nurses hovered about, one assisting him.

Running water and the muffled sounds of Finny and Beecher came from the far side of the swinging door.

The anesthesiologist looked up, his blond Nordic appearance evincing everything was under control. "Almost ready to turn him," he remarked as Jim approached.

Miss Chalmers had offered to circulate and was standing next to Reif, holding a pair of eye pads. He squirted a dab of lubricating jelly on them before taping them to the patient's face.

"Where's the other frame and the wheel blocks?" Jim asked.

Chalmers pointed to a side wall. "All ready."

"I sent Finny and your friend to scrub," Reif disclosed, "figuring it takes only one person to flip this contraption."

"Two," Dr. Lindsay corrected. "Turning it is simple but we need one at each end to pull the pins and set the blocks in place."

"You take one end. I'll get the other and the girls can look after the wooden blocks." Larson suggested.

Chalmers placed the other frame over the front of the patient. It was similar to the one on which he was lying, complete with side-to-side canvas straps and a thin sectional mattress. She bolted it at each end to a pivotal circular plate. An axle in the centre of the plates allowed them to rotate on the stationary cradle. They were prevented from doing so by metal pin-locks. When Prysniuk was sandwiched between the frames three nylon belts were wrapped around to keep him from falling out. Larson then disconnected the tube from his anaesthetic machine and the pin at the head of the bed While a nurse steadied the moveable frame, Jim pulled the pin from the foot end and on the count of three the patient was quickly rotated one hundred and eighty degrees. After reinserting the pins, the frame which had previously supported Prysniuk's back was unbolted, and the endotracheal tube connected to the gas machine. Finally each end of the cradle was fitted into wooden wheel blocks, converting the frame into an operating table of comfortable height.

"Shave and prep from his shoulders to below the buttocks," Jim ordered, "and strap a cautery plate to his thigh."

The sheet was pulled down and Jim saw the back for the first time. In fear of causing more damage he had purposely neglected to turn Prysniuk when he examined the old man in Emergency. "Come here," he said, beckoning to scrub nurse Keefer and two graduates idly chatting in a corner. "You should all see this for it can result in a serious nursing problem; not the 'gibbous' or hump in the middle of his back and the bruising around it where the break has occurred. But look!"

Jim palpated a raised whitish patch of skin the size of a small pancake above the buttock cleavage and professed. "That welt is the beginning of a pressure sore."

Larson leaned on the cranial end of the frame and stretched to see. "Huh! It doesn't take long," he commented, "another couple of hours and he'd have a slough for sure."

"Right!" Jim exclaimed. "A complication to be avoided. This method of turning him is much easier and effective than propping him with pillows. What do you think Miss?" He asked the older of the two chatty nurses. Busy pouring hexachlorophene soap, she was not thinking and did not reply. When Dr. Lindsay gave the order to shave and prep she had reacted automatically, her concentration neither on his short discourse on pressure sores nor on a routine procedure.

"What do you think you're doing?" he demanded.

Rousing from wherever her mind had wandered she was slow to answer. "Getting your prep basin ready."

"Well start again," Jim ordered. "Next time cover the stand with a sterile drape before you put the basin in it."

"Yes Dr. Lindsay," she said in a bored acrimonious tone.

Jim bristled. Concentrating on another concern he kept his ire under control. "Where are the films?" he asked.

"I've called for them but they haven't come from X-ray," the younger graduate replied and dared to suggest, "May I uncover the instrument table now?"

"Not until the patient has been draped and we're all gowned and gloved," Jim asserted and wondered when they would ever get his routine straight without having to inquire each time. Turning to the scrub nurse he asked, "Everything on?"

Keefer had backed off to a less congested corner than where she had been standing when Jim first entered the room. Her gloved hands were clasped in front of her waist and Chalmers was tying the back of her gown. As far as I know," she replied. "Mrs. Harrington picked out the instruments herself. The girl who set them up was sent to relieve in the case room."

Jim held his breath, peevishly determined not to break his own rule. Finally he proposed, "I guess we'll have to wait and see," and headed for the scrub room.

He found a spot and crammed in while Finny and Beecher were finishing the suds and rinse routine. Talk around him concerned the 'Cloward Procedure'. Finny, having learned Beecher was familiar with the neurosurgeon's technique of anterior interbody fusion of the cervical spine, was in a histrionic mood. He chortled above Jim's spraying faucet, expounding raucously until he decided his hands were clean enough then bunted his chest against the swinging door to the O.R.

Keefer handed him a towel. Bowing in the manner of a venerable oriental, Finny clasped it, squinted and chinked his words comically. "Ah so, and how are you Miss Lotus Bottom?"

Chalmers giggled as she helped him into a gown. It barely covered his back and she had difficulty fastening the ties.

Before he had finished forcing his fat fingers into the recesses of his rubber gloves, Keefer offered him one end of a folded table sheet and together they spread it over the lower half of the patient. A second sheet was similarly opened and laid over Prysniuk's shoulders before the large fenestrated cover was superimposed. Its square opening allowed access to the operative site and after its upper edge had been clipped to a pair of I.V. poles the seated anaesthetist was completely screened.

Throughout the draping Beecher had been left to 'drip dry'. When he was eventually invested as a sterile member of the team Finny bade him stand opposite himself on Prysniuk's left. Then with the knife poised like the baton of an orchestra conductor about to dive into Beethoven's Fifth he bellied up to the Stryker frame, received a reassuring nod from Reif and swept into the opening. The skin was incised for a distance of eight inches down the mid-line. With a few deft strokes the fatty layer was parted to expose the fibrous tissue, enveloping the spinous processes, muscles, and a large clot.

Bleeding was profuse. Keefer opened the sterile suction tube and handed the tip to Beecher along with a gauze pack. She also provided a diminishing supply of arterial forceps. When she was about to run out of them Finny demanded the 'Bovie'.

"The switch is next to your right foot Dr. Finny," she answered, unravelling the connecting wire and passing the electrocautery needle to Dr. Best.

Finny straightened, belched loudly and felt the floor with his grounded boot. Satisfied with the hum emanating from the lighted console whenever he stepped on the switch he summoned Beecher's assistance. "Touch my forceps when I give the word." Then pinching an oozing vessel between the tips of his instrument he cried, "on", simultaneously closing the circuit with his foot.

Beecher made contact and held it but nothing happened.

"Up the power," Finny shouted and Chalmers responded by turning a dial on the console. When sparks leapt from the end of his forceps, blackening a minute area of surrounding tissue and producing a faint curl of smoke, he shouted again. "That's high enough! Damn the torpedoes, full speed ahead!"

Dr. Lindsay had reappeared and outfitted for operating was inspecting the glittering assortment of orthopaedic instruments. To his dismay the graduated set of straight and curved Lambotte osteotomes were missing, as were the Hibbs' gouges and Wilson plates.

Keefer who was standing at his elbow detected their absence as soon as the cover had been withdrawn. Too ashamed to mention it, she watched his forehead gather into fissures of consternation and retreated to her Mayo stand at the foot of the table on the pretence Dr. Finny needed a fresh scalpel blade. But Finny, busy cauterizing, paid her no heed.

To Keefer's relief chastisement was not in the offing. The fissures evened and if Dr. Lindsay had any feelings whatsoever they were concealed in the depth of his steady brown eyes. "I would like to have a word with Mrs. Harrington," he said quietly. "Would you please have her come in?"

"And," he added, sharply interrupting while Keefer was relaying his request to the younger graduate, "don't come back without the x-rays."

In the time it took for the girl to scurry away, nervously crumpling the instrument cover to drop it in a hamper on the way out, Jim had edged alongside Beecher.

"There's your fracture Jimmy baby", Finny exclaimed, scooping a cupful of clot from the bottom of the wound. "And there's his cord, completely pulped!"

No sooner had he spoken than the end of his nose collided with Beecher's brow, thrust forward attempting to see.

"For Christ's sake!" Finny swore.

"Perhaps you'll be able to get a better look from the other side," Jim suggested, forcefully bodying Beecher out of the way.

The cord was indeed pulped. Moreover it was torn apart. Shredded strands of collapsed dura were identifiable within the neural arch of lumbar one. The adjacent twelfth thoracic vertebra was jammed forward the width of the spinal column and lay buried in bone debris hidden under the overlapping distal half.

Finny fiddled and cursed the traumatized nervous tissue, then tossed his neurological forceps on Keefer's Mayo stand.

"Pretty God damned hopeless," he bellowed.

Beecher had done as Jim suggested and was standing on Finny's right, closer to the head of the table. "Why do you say that?" he asked. "You haven't seen the proximal segment yet. Maybe you can dissect the frayed ends and suture the two halves together."

"You're either pulling my leg or full of shit!" Finny declared. How do you suppose that's going to help?"

"According to a Toronto surgeon," Beecher expounded, "it is possible to repair the damage and regain function."

"I've never heard of such crap," Finny interrupted. "Peripheral nerves? Yes. But the spinal cord never."

Incredulously Jim listened as Beecher continued the argument and was intrigued to hear his own questions being posed for a different purpose.

"Have you ever tried it?" Beecher asked.

Finny was silent.

"Have you ever seen it done?"

"Never!"

"Then why not try it?"

"Negative results. That's why. Don't be so God damned ridiculous!"

Finny's generosity was fading. Spittle wet his face mask which stuck to his lips. He spluttered. "It has failed in the dog lab. So what makes you think it will work with humans?"

"Man is a different animal," Beecher protested.

"There's no doubt about that," Jim chuckled. "Some are even lower on the scale of intelligence." Then in a serious mood, he commented. "If I recall it is the lower forms of life that are more adaptable to injury. Divide a planaria and both halves will generate the missing part. A salamander pup if amputated through the tail will develop a new one. But only if the nerve roots are left intact. Destroy the central nerve supply and the phenomenon does not occur."

"Forget the academic bull!" Finny cut in. Eager to get on with the job, he had run out of patience. "Hand me the Jesus Lion Jaws Keefer," he demanded.

A pair of huge locking clamps were provided and Finny attached one of them to the posterior arch of 'L1'.

"Here," he instructed, "Steady this Lindsay. I'll bring the twelfth to meet it."

Beecher's uninvited counsel had drawn a tight little crowd and Jim found himself trying to avoid contamination from a graduate flanking either side. Meanwhile Chalmers had parked a stool next to Larson's gas machine and mounted it, steadying herself with a hand on the anaesthetist's shoulder.

Fishing into the cavernous hole the neurosurgeon blindly put the bite on a piece of backbone. Without warning he heaved upward. Nothing happened. When he slackened his pull everyone around the table honed in curiously.

"Angle more cephalad," Jim advised.

On the second try Finny yanked violently.

The clamp sprang loose in his hand and the abrupt release of tension forced his elbow into Beecher's midriff. Beecher tottered. Tripping over the cautery wire, he made a grab for the mobile I.V. pole supporting the drape. Its rolling base slammed into Chalmer's stool. She lost her balance and crashed into the anaesthesia machine, launching it across the room. Larson caught her before she hit the floor but in doing so he left the patient unattended. The cost was an uprooted endotracheal tube.

Larson recovered it quickly, disconnected it from his machine and held it above the screen. "Such revolting developments," he proclaimed facetiously. "Look what we have here!"

"Jesus Christ!" deplored Finny with visions of having to flip the patient back into the face up position in order to reinsert the tube. Without a closed system it was impossible to accurately assess gaseous exchange and assist ventilation, especially with the patient lying prone. Freed from the respirator, lack of oxygen and the build up of carbon dioxide could be lethal. Prysniuk could drift through the twilight zone irretrievably. It was urgent the tube be replaced.

"Any suggestions?" Jim asked.

Larson delayed his answer until he checked out the tanks, gauges and connections. Then he said with mild relief, "Nothing broken. I'll see what I can do" and dropped out of sight below the drapes.

Lindsay and Finny faced each other fearing the worst but in a twinkling Larson was back on his stool. "All fixed," he declared, so off-handedly his colleagues would never suspect how ecstatic he felt in replacing the tube with such little fuss. He would never tell them it had involved a lot more luck than skill.

"Way to go," Jim beamed, greatly relieved.

"Give me a few limbo lessons," twitted Finny, "I'll become an anaesthetist and intubate all my patients upside-down."

Larson could contain himself no longer. The picture of fatback Finny 'ooching' his mountainous belly under a knee-high bamboo pole was more than he could take and he laughed until he had to blow his nose, and again and again throughout the rest of the case whenever the mental picture reappeared.

During the confusion Mrs. Harrington had slipped into the room. Appropriately she demurred by the view boxes until contingency permitted her an opening. As Jim picked up the misdirected Lion Jaw and groped for a purchase on the bone she approached the table and caught his eye. He didn't recognize her at first. The last time they'd spoken it was only for a moment and she was wearing a white uniform, her assiduously dressed mane not bound by a green O.R. bonnet. He did remember the sexy voice.

"I have the patient's x-rays Dr. Lindsay," she said. "The Wilson plates are in the autoclave. They should be ready any minute."

Jim put down the clamp and folded his arms while Chalmers accepted the x-ray envelope from Mrs. Harrington and moved toward the view box. He started to follow but stopped and turning to Mrs. Harrington asked, "What about the Lambotte's and Hibbs'?"

"I sent them back to Zimmer," she replied. "According to our records they haven't been sharpened in six months."

Jim was furious and shouted, "Who said they were dull? They've hardly been used. Besides I re-sharpened them last week."

"What difference does it make?" Mrs. Harrington went on, coyly lowering her heavy lashes. "You've osteotomes and gouges on your table. I picked them out myself."

"What difference?" Jim lashed out, "I'm taking a graft from the iliac crest and the instruments you've chosen are useless."

"The other surgeons don't think so," she contended. Her speech had lost its seductiveness and was taking on the steely ring of authority. "If they can use them why can't you?"

Jim rose to the challenge. Towering over her he asked, "How do you know? Today is your first day on the job." Glancing at the large stop-clock above the scrub room door he calculated, "You've been here six hours! How can you possibly know that?"

For an immeasurable interval Tanya Harrington gaped, mute and immobile, like a jade Buddha with gleaming yellow eyes.

Chalmers broke the spell. "If you wish Dr. Lindsay, I'll call St. Mary's and have them send their set by cab."

CHAPTER THIRTEEN

Paolone looked around the Board Room, casually counting heads and asked the two doctors seated to his right, "Where the hell is Lindsay?"

"Presumably playing basketball," said Pearson, a frail scholarly-looking man who had been in private practice since the depression of '29 and dressed the same way, apparently unable to find anything better.

Dissatisfied with Pearson's guess Paolone rephrased his question."Does anyone know where Lindsay is?" When no one else answered he ranted, "Christ, this is an important meeting and he's the only one not here."

Morrisey, flanking the bushy-eyed Pearson, had a broad waxed moustache that looked like a layer of cloud bisecting his pink face whenever he smirked. He spoke up in order the rest in the room could hear, "if he's not playing B-Ball he's out jogging."

"He's nuts!" Fat, unimpressed Finny, jeered whenever he heard of Jim's self-sparked fitness regime. "What's he trying to prove? He's some kind of super-jock who'll outlast us all! Who's he kidding? Longevity is in the genes. Take 'em off and I'll show you who can go the longest."

Among the snorts and guffaws following Finny's remarks Paolone grew pensive. Secretly his faltering libido caused him concern. He was past his prime. So was his voracious free-speaking wife Angie who openly commented it would not bother her in the least if her husband dispersed his excess seminal fluid in a brothel, releasing her from the arduous duty of a sexual gymnast. Ten short years ago Joe had as liberal an appetite for intercourse as Finny but unlike the neurosurgeon preserved his physique exercising out of bed with equal vigour. Now, where well-toned recti muscles once drew in his waist an elastic girdle allowed him to wear a forty inch belt. Vanity boiled in Paolone, and Lindsay's fastidious self-discipline made him jealous.

When Jim finally showed up at the Department of Surgery meeting the loss of intern accreditation was being rehashed. There appeared to be no way around it unless a connection with a teaching program could be arranged.

Paolone was discouraged. "Those jerks in Toronto are as secretive as postpartum cats. I've offered to set up a service on my own time at my own expense and they haven't the decency to reply.

Furthermore," he added, "it means the end of the Outpatient Department. From now on all non-paying patients will have to be seen in your offices."

"What's wrong with that?" The little chief was interrupted by the soft voice of his Vice-Chairman Alligood, conspicuous among the surgeons for his apologetic height, mild manner and indecisiveness. Because of seniority Alligood was slated to head the department when Paolone's five year term expired. A By-Law, constituted against Paolone's will, ruled a chief could not succeed himself and Dr. Lloyd Alligood dreaded the day. He had trouble trying to decide whether a red hot belly needed to be opened. Smiling shyly, he withdrew a lengthy neck between a pair of bony shoulders, his dark eyes focusing on a tithe of musician's fingers thrumming soundlessly on the massive mahogany table. "I've been seeing non-paying patients in my office for years," he stated. "In my opinion having no interns to look after welfare cases is not the problem. What is more important, the hospital is without a resident doctor to cover emergencies."

"Do you have a suggestion?" Paolone asked sharply, suspicious the Vice-Chairman was about to steal his thunder.

"No!" Alligood replied, keeping his head down, concentrating on his graceful hands. Though he might express an opinion, to initiate a discussion or get involved in an argument was against his nature. "Maybe someone else has something to say." he added.

Paolone asked for more dialogue and three quarters of an hour later not one member of the Department had come up with an idea appealing to the majority. They were in agreement on one point only, the injustice perpetrated by the Accreditation Board.

Gord Shorter was the most vociferous dissenter. "Pee on them from great heights! Yesterday I was kicked off Staff because I'd failed to sign a discharge note. Why? Because of a ridiculous By-Law, that's why! A By-Law the god-damned Accreditation Board recommended to Administration. They do it every three bloody years. When they come back, if their recommendations haven't been instituted, the hospital loses its accreditation. I don't get it. Where do they get so much power? Who asked them around in the first place?"

Gord the biggest man in the room with a big booming voice was merely warming up. "After putting in five years of 'Wallah service' for the Urologists at the Mayo Clinic and twenty-five on my own I'm expected to spend the rest of my life doing a part-time internship in the Shipton hospitals. Piss on it! Let the G.P.'s do it. Damn it all! They didn't slave around as long as we did. That kind of crap is more in their line anyhow."

The matter went unresolved and Paolone, before he turned to other business, assured them he would take it to the next meeting of St. Mary's Medical Advisory Board and express their adamant disapproval to the heads of other departments.

In a lighter vein Mrs. Harrington's name came up and Joe officially informed the 'dirty dozen' encircling the huge table at long last the hospital's governors had appointed a permanent O.R. supervisor. Most of the surgeons had already met her and were meretriciously affected. With fawning femininity Monday morning she had catered to the little chief's ego during the troublesome abdominal perineal resection and won him handily. To Joe, in spite of his advancing decline, her attitude, like her new look, was a spark from a radiant orb. He worshipped youth. Her postgraduate nursing degrees, as he read them off, "are like a halo around the moon."

"Which could mean we're in for a storm," Jim inserted, adding his dissatisfaction with her performance during the Prysniuk case and her marital relationship to the chairman of the Board. But his comments fell on deaf ears.

Even Finny who witnessed his ordeal the day before thought he was a bit of a 'prick'. "She's just making it hard for you in the hope you'll stick it to her. Give the lady a little time Jimmie baby. She's slightly green. Like your friend Beecher."

Dr. Best, being brought into the conversation, Jim was obliged to outline the young orthopaedist's career from the time he left medical school up until the present.

"He didn't tell me he was a preacher!" Finny snorted before Jim had finished.

"Credit one for Beecher," said Jim, "You'd have eaten him alive." Inwardly he granted Dr. Best some discretion, sparse as it was.

When they arrived at the main item on the agenda, bed allocation, there was as Jim suspected little to do about it. The new five-floor extension was to be a double corridor wing with private, semi-private and ward rooms. It boosted the total number of beds, including the Psychiatric unit, to six hundred. The surgeons were allowed to use one hundred and eighteen, roughly ten beds apiece, half of which were to be housed in the new wing. There was no agreement on segregating surgical sub-specialities and assigning them to separate wards so, as far as Dr. Lindsay was concerned nothing worthwhile had transpired.

The past week had been much more taxing than usual. Looking back on it while snacking alone in the cafeteria at St. Mary's, Jim realized he could not have worked in another case if his life depended on it. In addition to Prysniuk's mortifying spinal injury and his elective surgery, exclusive of Monday, averaging three procedures a day, five other emergencies had extended his list of operations. These included two broken hips which required pinning. The second on Tuesday evening had kept him late for the Department of Surgery meeting - no great disappointment. He smiled to himself. Nonetheless it had been good for a laugh or two - the usual stuff - with Eldridge's snoring and falling out of his chair and Finny's jokes, particularly the one about the guy who was run over by a truck - his wife had been feeding him dog food and after every meal he sat on the centre stripe, licking his balls. Jim had thought it worth repeating and told it to Merri at two minutes after twelve when he crawled into bed. Though she laughed, her remark, 'is that all you guys have to talk about', precluded a scolding for not calling her earlier. 'Anyhow, Jim Lindsay', she teased. 'If I ever hear of you fussing around with one of those nurses I'll run off with Algernon after serving you a tin of Dr. Ballards.'

If I had my 'druthers', Jim thought, the evening would have been spent playing basketball.

Wednesday his voluntary work at the Crippled Children's Centre was postponed in order to fit in office appointments cancelled Monday because of Prysniuk's emergency.

Munching on a western sandwich, Jim wondered why he bothered with the Crippled Children's Centre. In its current stage of development it was not really a centre but two small rooms in the basement of the General managed by a women's service club, offering parental relief and allowing anxious mothers a couple of 'free' afternoons a week. Jim recalled Crooky's remarks: 'The centre's nothing more than a glorified baby-sitting service. Most of the patients are cerebral palsy cases and there's bugger all you can do for them.' 'True,' Jim agreed, 'but only from a surgical point of view. A bit of physiotherapy doesn't do them any harm and now and then the physios need direction.' 'You're right,' Crooky said adding, 'please don't quote me. If it gets back to those service club women they'll claim I'm against motherhood.'

The third emergency occurred Wednesday evening, an open fracture of the arm, and was promptly treated at St. Mary's. But close to midnight was spent pacifying the apparent cause of the mishap, the driver of the vehicle. The injured man, a vagrant reeking of alcohol, had stepped off the curb in front of the Shipton House as a car was passing. The extremely upset driver followed the ambulance to the hospital. 'Didn't see him until the last minute,' he kept repeating to the night clerk in Emergency. When the driver learned Jim had examined the victim he had clutched the orthopaedist's arm. 'It wasn't my fault Doc, honestly; don't let him die. I don't want him on my conscience.' Jim had calmly broken the driver's grip, looked him square in his frantic face and asked, 'If it wasn't your fault why should he be on your conscience?' What Dr. Lindsay didn't ask was, 'How fast were you going and were you paying attention to the road?' Jim had gone off to notify the O.R., thankful liability determination wasn't his job.

He drained his first cup of coffee and sat thinking. Human beings, how disgusting we can be. Look after us Lord and let us quit bashing each other about!

Thursday an axe-head glanced off a frozen trunk striking the tender lad who had swung it, producing a nasty compound fracture. The incident had happened shortly after school was out and was booked for 6 pm. After the case Jim had arrived home tired and late for supper but happy and pleased there was nothing to prevent him from staying there - a pleasant state short lived! He hadn't arisen from the table when there was a subsequent call.

It was Crooky. A twelve-year-old had fractured both bones of her forearm. He tried to reduce the deformity himself by a gentle manipulation to no avail. In his opinion it needed an open. 'I agree,' Dr. Lindsay replied. 'Do it.'

'I can't. What I mean,' Crooky sounded very apologetic, 'she's my granddaughter and I'd rather not.'

So that's the way it goes Jim acknowledged, pushing himself up from the small round table. You never know when they're going to do it to you. I haven't had a night at home all week.

In spite of this demanding role and the bitter cold he had doggedly gone for an early morning run, firmly believing this strenuous 'relaxation' essential for his well-being, but few if any surpassed the workload and responsibility he chose to carry. Andy Cruikshank attempted to put the whole business in perspective. 'The more you put in, the more you get out. Regardless Jim,' he warned, 'life's a game of poker and you never know what the dealer's going to turn up.' It had been a sensible reminder and passed undisputed. Instinctively he knew his limit. The problem was to confine himself.

CHAPTER FOURTEEN

Dr. Lindsay paid for his lunch and within minutes was seated behind the wheel of his Pontiac headed for the office.

Having learned not everyone attached to his cases felt as responsible as he did, Jim refused to book surgery on Mondays unless it was absolutely necessary.

The problems were usually minor: delays in getting patients from the wards, too much time between operations, a piece of essential equipment temporarily missing and assistants generally not paying attention. All of which rarely resulted in a calamity but was sufficiently stressful to irritate and possibly delay a patient's recovery.

The Prysniuk fiasco was a good example. If it had not been for Reif Larson's deftness and the calm deliverance of Miss Chalmers, the patient could have died on the table or the surgery cancelled and the fusion never achieved. As it turned out the instruments arrived from St. Mary's and the surgery ended successfully. But prolonging the procedure potentiated infection and diminished the old man's chance of survival.

If I had a free hand, Jim thought, I'd fill the operating room from eight till five Tuesday, Wednesday and Thursday and spend the other week days examining patients.

The car heater was turned on full blast. Following Sunday's devastating winds more polar air crystallized the heavens and without an insulating layer of cloud near record breaking temperatures ensued. Where last week serene water bordering the Lindsay property had mirrored the flight of migratory fowl and Orion skulking in the northern hemisphere, there was now an abeyant sheet. Earth was dipped in frost, bark shrank and the battered shoreline echoed the rumble of expanding ice. Happily little snow had fallen and the pond was ideal for skating.

Jim's spirit gradually rose with the barometric pressure. His colour improved and he smiled easily, expecting a relaxing weekend at home, perchance a game of bridge or shiny with the kids. Although he was physically beaten this euphoric feeling ignited his power of concentration, added spring to his gait and made him more sociable. If Jason passed his test they might take in a movie. As it crossed his mind the boy was probably already out with the examiner.

Veering his shabby sedan to miss a police cruiser, Jim slowed, noting there was no one in it and crept up the driveway, leaving a narrow space behind Betsy's coupe, enough room to let him in the side entrance. In the building he climbed a short flight of stairs behind the reception desk where Betsy was preparing a chart on a new patient. He stopped short of the hall leading from the waiting room back to his private office. A glimpse beyond Betsy on any day other than Friday might have depressed him. The waiting room was full. Casts, kids and crutches littered the floor. A group of men stood near the front door talking, laughing or periodically leaning against the wall and the coat rack. At the opposite end of the room before a tall mirror, stretching from the mantle to an ornate ceiling, a woman was refreshing her make-up. Everyone else had found a seat somewhere.

Betsy was hunched over her work and awkwardly handed him a list of phone messages, without turning, bobbing or shaking a curl of her jet black hair. "The Bailiff's here," she said, addressing her pen. "Came in with a police detective. They're waiting back in your office."

"That accounts for the cruiser," Jim grinned. "For a moment I thought someone was disturbing the peace."

Betsy smiled. "There was but I took care of it." Her black presbyopic eyes, enlarged by heavy horn-rimmed glasses, contracted. "Another subpoena I suppose; as if you didn't have enough to do without being dragged into court. Who is it this time?"

"Beats me," Jim replied.

"The mail's on your desk. You got a letter from Afghanistan. If you don't mind I'd like to have the stamps."

Thinking of Merri's philatelic fancies, Jim replied, "We'll see," and motioned for his secretary to follow. Behind a divider, screening the cloak closet from the waiting patients and out of sound, he hung up his trench-coat and in a half whisper asked. "How many have we got?"

"I booked twenty-nine. A few more don't have appointments."

"Who?" Jim murmured, mildly annoyed.

"A fractured collar bone, a broken ankle and a sprained knee. You saw them in the E.R. last week and suggested they report in today." Betsy shook her head in disgust. "What if we had to cancel again, like Monday. How can I get in touch with patients if I don't have names and telephone numbers?"

Jim apologized. He repeatedly forgot to jot down names. When he did remember, the slips of paper were often in a jacket hanging in a closet back home.

"How can I bill them when I don't know who they are?" Betsy reprimanded. "If they don't show up in the office I never hear from them."

"That doesn't happen often," Jim commented.

"No! What about the woman Dr. Atwater had you see in St. Mary's yesterday?"

Jim rubbed his forehead saying, "She's going to die; she has advanced carcinoma of the breast. Her spine is riddled and she has a pathological fracture of her femur. There's nothing anyone can do for her. I put her in traction."

"Well, she has insurance," Betsy declared. "Dr. Atwater suggests you bill her. He phoned this morning. Says he wants a call back. His number's on the slip I gave you. Thanks to him you'll get paid."

"Very considerate." It was only Tuesday he asked Atwater for a cardiac evaluation on one of the old ladies with a fractured hip, knowing full well she couldn't afford the operation let alone the internist's appraisal. "Guess I owe Ed a favour Betsy," Jim added. "A lot of people owe him favours; he rarely complains."

Betsy picked the top three folders from a pile and followed. "The Ireson baby's in the plaster room," she said, handing the charts to her boss. "Mrs. Trussell's in the first examining room. There's a younger woman with her. The disturbance you were kidding about when you came in is in the second, a woman and her noisy brats. They were making such a racket the other patients were getting restless. Only one of the kids needs to be seen. The sooner the better. I'd like to get rid of them."

"Betsy! What kind of talk is that?" Jim teased. "I thought you were dedicated?"

"Dedicated! To what? The doormat club! Every time you're late I'm the one who has to listen. The complaints they have are not the same you hear. They're worse. Non-medical. Usually about the unpunctual doctor I work for. When you show up they turn on their best behaviour, sweet as pie. One of these days I'm going to" - her remark was drowned by a ringing phone. "Oh dear!" She sighed and scurried back to her desk.

Jim watched her go. She was dedicated in spite of all the abuse she had to take, a loyal shield in an endless fray. She absorbed it well and because he recognized her value did not exact secretarial perfection. Though her grammar and spelling were jarring, typing was rattled off at good speed and she was rarely behind in her work. There was no doubt about it Betsy earned her keep and she was kept generously. If she quit he knew it would be difficult to replace her. Probably need two girls, he surmised, pushing open the door to his private office.

The Bailiff and the detective were imposing men and deflated the limits of his inner sanctum. After returning his greeting they introduced themselves.

"Have a seat," Jim motioned, after he managed to get around them and settle behind a fortification of medical books and strewn letters on top of his desk.

"We won't take up much of your time Doc," said the Bailiff, "we know you're very busy. The sergeant has a few questions to ask. I grabbed a ride over with him to serve this subpoena. Here's eight dollars for your trouble."

Jim chuckled. "A windfall! Thanks a lot." He broke into laughter reading 'Kowalski versus Scott'.

"What's so funny?" the Bailiff asked.

"Oh nothing," said Jim. "Besides it would be unethical of me to tell you."

Unfolding the official document, he reviewed the case. So Kowalski's going to sue; I'm to go to court and testify on his behalf. Tell the court how much pain and suffering he went through or how a few years down the line he will become permanently crippled. Already he has had advice from a lawyer who told him he didn't have a leg to stand on. "Huh," Jim grunted, perusing the subpoena - Delivered this 22nd day of November, 1963. The funny thing is, Jim mused, Kowalski has a leg and claims he can't stand on it which is a lot of hogwash. What's even funnier, Kowalski was headed the wrong way on a one way street, riding his unlit bicycle in the middle of the night in a blinding snowstorm. Now he's suing the driver of the car he struck.

"Thank you Sir," said Jim, still smiling. "Now what can I do for you Sergeant?"

"It's about the accident victim you looked after Wednesday night." Detective Robinson replied.

"The man in St. Mary's?" Jim queried. "Donohue, the man who was hit outside the Shipton House?"

"Yes. I understand he was badly hurt. You mind telling me the extent of his injuries?"

"As long as I'm not quoted in the newspaper," Jim nodded and smiled, leaning back in his chair while he rattled off: a compound fracture of the left humerus, fractured left ribs, a contused lung and a broken pelvis, then expounded on his treatment.

The sergeant made notes and asked, "is he able to answer questions?"

"I believe so."

When the two men had left Dr. Lindsay looked over his list of telephone messages. An asterisk opposite the names indicated the urgent calls. Mrs. Blum's finger's were numb and swollen; her broken wrist was in a cast which likely needed splitting. The operative wound over Mrs. Pennington's bunion had spread slightly and she was alarmed. He buzzed Betsy and asked her to call both patients and have them come in later. The rest of the messages were less important and could wait. He chose an open line and dialled Dr. Atwater.

"Eddie old bean, what's up?" He asked when the receptionist had put him through.

Atwater was sucking his pipe and a gurgling sound was audibly transmitted. "Not much, comparatively."

"What do you mean comparatively?"

"Haven't you heard the news?"

"What news?"

"Kennedy's dead! Someone shot him."

"Kennedy?" There was silence while Jim determined to whom Atwater was referring. "You mean President Kennedy?"

"Yeah. Down in Dallas. It's on all the radio and T.V. stations."

"Who on earth would do that?"

"They haven't found out yet."

"Sorry to hear it." Jim was moved though he was not keen on the Kennedy administration. In his opinion the president had been

Do Unto Others *141*

born with a silver spoon in his mouth. It was okay for him to give away his wealth; forcing other Americans through legislation was against Jim's principles. But Kennedy had some good ideas. "Just last night I was reading a condensation of the Shriver report on Kennedy's Peace Corps. I think it's excellent sending young people to help out around the world."

"Have you sent in your credentials yet?" Ed asked.

"For what?"

"Your trip to Afghanistan with S.E.R.V.E. You asked me for a reference. Remember? You're still going?"

"Oh yeah! Well...No." Jim was still mulling over Atwater's shocking revelation. "I haven't made up my mind. There are a lot of factors to consider. Actually I doubt if I will."

"That's too bad."

"Why?"

Ed's pipe gurgled on languidly. "I was looking forward to giving your shots."

"Thanks very much!" Jim laughed, "What did you really want? Sounds like you called to borrow my pipe cleaners."

"That bad eh?"

"It's either your pipe or a runny nose."

"My apologies! I'll put it away." Atwater got down to business. "Two things. Your friend Prysniuk is in bad shape. Gram negative septicemia. The blood cultures came back this morning. The bug is sensitive to chloromycetin so I'm socking it to him along with a massive dose of hydrocortisone. We'll know in the next few days whether he's going to survive. I'm heading for the General and will look in on him. Oh yes, I almost forgot. I'm sending you another rheumatoid hand, like Mrs. Trussell's. Typical ulnar deviation and subluxed metacarpo-phalangeal joints. The sed rate's down and the patient is fit for surgery. Put your secretary on."

"Sure," said Jim, buzzing for Betsy to lift the extension. "As a matter of fact Mrs. Trussell is waiting to see me. Plan to put her in hospital next week."

"Yes," Betsy cut in.

"Dr. Atwater wants an appointment for a patient. Will you look after him?" When Jim heard his secretary ask, "How about next Tuesday at 4:00 pm.?" he hung up.

The Ireson baby was due for a cast change and a two o'clock feeding. His mother was leaning over the high work table supporting a bottle when Jim walked in. "How's Johnny?" he asked.

"Fine! He's growing like a weed." The young woman replied, and plucked a squirting nipple from the infant's gums. She lifted the baby from a plastic basinet, blotted a bubble of milk on his chin and laid him on the arborite surface.

"No doubt about it," Jim agreed. The tiny toes, beyond the plaster were slightly edematous.

"Isn't there another way?" She pleaded. The sight of the electric saw alarmed her. Through the whirr when it was switched on, she shouted, "The noise is frightening!"

"Sure," he shouted back, "but time consuming. You can soak it off."

Jim watched her expression of relief turn to puzzlement. "Next time," he explained, turning off the saw."Before you come in soak the cast in water for an hour or so. It will soften and you'll be able to unravel the bandage yourself."

It took a minute to run the vibrating blade down both sides of the plaster and the cast opened like a pod. The baby was startled but did not cry.

"There now. He's getting used to it." Jim grinned.

"Maybe he is but I'm not," groaned Mrs. Ireson. "I'm always afraid you'll cut him."

"Not likely, though it is possible - the blade oscillates rather than spins. Let me show you," he suggested, flicking on the switch.

The surfaces of his thumb and index finger closed lightly on the cutting mechanism. When the power was shut off they were seen to shift back and forth as the vibrations slowed to a stop. His skin was unscathed and his eyes twinkled as he offered the saw to the young mother. "You wish to try it?"

"I'd rather not!" She was still apprehensive though her curiosity had been aroused. "How come it cuts plaster and not skin?"

"Plaster like bone and nail is stiff. It does not have the resilience of skin. The saw-teeth scratch their way through. If I'd held the blade tighter my fingers would have been marked."

The cast was discarded, the padding beneath torn free and the club foot bared. Jim massaged it gently, manipulating the heel and ankle and twisting the forefoot outward. "Coming along nicely," he remarked. "Today we'll go to work on the heel. A few more weeks and we'll be able to stretch the Achilles tendon."

"How long will it take altogether, Doctor?"

Jim paused, before Mrs. Ireson had been discharged from the obstetrical ward he had answered the same question, outlined the proposed management and advised the Iresons of possible difficulties to be encountered along the way. Either he had failed to make himself clear or she was losing her patience. He decided she needed encouragement. "Don't worry. In the end he'll have no trouble." Taking a fresh roll of pressed cotton and wrapping it around the left foot he continued. "Though there's need for correction casts now, possibly night splints later and special shoes until he has finished growing he'll do alright. Rarely does a club foot deformity require surgery. As long as we persist in what we're doing he should have a near normal foot."

Mrs. Ireson frowned. "What do you mean 'near normal'? You're saying it won't be perfect."

Jim ignored her temporarily. He was wetting a two inch roll of plaster. As it was a fast setting type he delayed clarification until the tiny cast had been moulded and he no longer needed to concentrate on holding the limb in its corrected position. "Functionally it should be perfect. There may be some discrepancy in size, giving rise to shoe fitting problems. But nothing to get excited about."

Mrs. Ireson was becoming apprehension. "I should think there is,"

"What?"

"Something worth getting excited about. Wouldn't you want your child to have a normal looking foot?"

"True," Jim agreed. "But we can only do so much."

"What about surgery? You said, 'near normal' and 'without operative treatment'. Maybe he should have an operation."

Jim tightened his sensuous lower lip and shook his head, realizing he had clarified nothing and had confused her. He decided they both needed help. "I think you should have another opinion Mrs. Ireson," he suggested softly. "If it's okay with you we'll arrange to have him seen by one of the orthopaedic men at the Paediatric Hospital in Toronto."

"I must speak to my husband first if you don't mind."

"Right. Have him give me a call. In the meantime let's carry on as we have."

"Sorry to be so much trouble Dr. Lindsay," she ventured. "I do appreciate you're trying to help us. But I want him to have the best treatment possible."

Halfway out the door Jim spoke without looking back. "Betsy'll give you an appointment for this same time next week. She'll be here in a moment. If you should make up your mind before next Friday let me know."

The second examining room was a few steps away. Dr. Lindsay was barely inside when a four year old clambered up his leg. He raised the child and plunked him down on the table. The youngster quickly wriggled off. With a resounding slap he landed on all fours and scampered behind the door to join a toddler actively engaged in creating obscene sounds with the door-stop.

"He's not the one you're s'posed to see Doc."

The informant was a bored insouciant woman seated beside the washbasin. With an elbow resting on the rim she flicked a lighted cigarette into it and pointed at the stripling standing by the window. "It's Billie! Com'ere son. Take your pants off and show the Doc your knee."

Billie climbed onto the examining table.

"Where does it hurt?" Jim asked.

"On the lump," the boy answered and indicated a swelling three grimy finger breadths below the kneecap.

"Doc Morrisey says he's got 'Goat Slaughterer's Disease', his mother added, "But I don't believe him. Billie's never been near a farm."

Jim snickered, trying not to laugh."You mean 'Osgood-Schlatter's disease. Have any films been taken?"

"Huh! Any what?"

"X-rays."

"Oh yeah! Down the street at the Clinic. Didn't they send them to you."

"No," Jim replied. He strongly suspected this lazy dishevelled woman had been requested by her doctor to pick up the x-rays and consciously forgot.

The tibial tubercle was enlarged more than usual and as Jim pressed the swelling the boy winced. "How long has it been sore?" he asked. Did you bump it?"

"I dunno."

No light was shed by his shrugging mother.

"When did you bang it?" Jim altered his wording.

"I didn't. It just started hurting."

After a thorough clinical assessment which included checking the boy's temperature Dr. Lindsay turned to Mrs. Crump.

"Would you mind picking up his x-rays and dropping them off when you have a chance?"

"I would!" she said indignantly. "I haven't time to traipse all over town. Why do you want to see them? Doc Morrisey read me the report on the phone. Says Billie should be admitted to hospital for a cast. You're the one who's supposed to do it."

Unbelievable! It hadn't taken long for this woman to learn all the tricks. Admit her son to hospital for a cylinder cast! Take up a hospital bed for a minor procedure he could do in the Outpatient Department. Why? So she wouldn't have to pay a cent. But the taxpayers would at a basic rate of fifty dollars a day in addition to the cost of treatment.

For an eternal second Dr. Lindsay held his breath. Though he had plaster in his office he kept only small rolls suitable for infants with club feet. He did not have material to undertake a cylinder cast for an active adolescent. If a cast really was necessary it would have to be applied in the E.R. and it was unlikely the poor woman could pay for it. Eventually the Sisters would have to write it off as they had done for others with charitable satisfaction. He sighed deeply, thinking the matter not worth stewing about and reached into a drawer for a piece of felt and a tensor bandage. After holding the felt over the bump with the elastic bandage he patted the boy on the head. "That ought to protect you Billie. Try not to bump it and it will heal on its own."

Facing the troubled mother, indolently seated beside the wash basin, he advised. "If that doesn't work we'll put him in plaster but give it a chance. The condition usually burns itself out. I'll send Dr. Morrisey a note."

Before she could answer Jim was gone.

Betsy met him in the hall with a Physician's Services Insurance card in her hand.

"Mrs. Trussell has P.S.I. She gave me her number."

"Isn't that nice," Jim drawled. "But she doesn't need it. Who ever bills a minister's wife?"

"Maybe her husband felt guilty or proud," Betsy proposed. "I had to transfer her to your office. Mrs. Feldman developed another of her convenient spasms. She's lying down in the first examining room."

"Is she alright?

"Nothing a swift kick in her fat backside won't fix. She's gone this route before. It's the quickest way to be seen. There were twelve patients ahead of her. Now she's fourth; let her lie there till you've seen everyone else. It'll do her good."

"What's her problem?"

"The usual. Lower back. Shortly after she came in the pain became excruciating and according to her it will go away if she can stretch out."

Jim grinned. Betsy had a knack of hitting the nail on the head. "Okay, when I need the room I'll see her."

"Oh" Betsy almost whispered as he moved away."You'll enjoy this. Mrs. Richardson paid the last instalment on her account. Walked in without any support. She's happier than a lark and says if she ever breaks her other hip she hopes you'll be around to fix it. She's started to save in case."

Jim's face lit up. "Thanks a heap Betsy. You've restored my suffering faith." He laughed and the glow of gratification remained as he hailed the two women patiently waiting in his consulting room.

"Well Doctor you seem in a good mood," Winifred Trussell observed.

Jim's smile widened. "I suppose I am. How about you?" he asked while inspecting the gnarled shiftless fingers held in his palm.

At one time the minister's wife had been a vibrant woman, the centre of many a parish social. At sixty-five any physical attraction resided in her charming face for her fingers were grotesquely twisted and she was confined to a wheel-chair. Cocking her head stiffly, she said. "Mentally and spiritually I'm fine, but what can you do for them? I'm unable to grip my wheel-chair. Will I ever be able to manage the contraption?"

"I can straighten your fingers and relieve the pain," Jim advised. "You'll have to pray for strength; there's nothing I can do about it. How about your arms?"

"Oh they ache at night. I can't get them over my head. My elbows swell and won't straighten but I can still feed myself." She sighed and lowered her voice slightly. "Doing my hair is a problem. Lil did it this morning. You have met Lil, I believe?"

Lillian Best had been standing by the window, secretly admiring the large backyard through an opening in the Venetian blind. She dropped her hand nervously and the shade began to bang against the pane. "Dr. Lindsay," she coughed self-consciously. "It's good to see you. I was having a peek at your back yard. There's enough space for a pool."

"We thought so once while we were living upstairs," said Jim silently studying her. She had to be approaching forty, short, a little wide in the hips, not a bad figure - if one found roundness appealing - with a shy faultlessly plain face and grass coloured eyes. Recently she had a permanent. At St. Matthew's he had paid little attention to her; he did recognize the same olive tweed suit. "But we decided against it," he went on, "until we found a spot more to our liking."

"Though I shouldn't be prying," said Lil, appearing less bewildered than she had a moment before. "Would you mind telling me how much this place costs?"

"Why not? Any real estate broker knows. Twenty-five to thirty thousand at today's prices. You'd never guess after the war I got it for ten. You want to buy it?"

Lil blushed and stammered. "Th', there's a house very much like this across the street. Beecher wants it. They're asking thirty-seven five."

Jim's friendly expression didn't changed. "They'll probably come down, though not much. Business has never been so -"

Winifred Trussell interrupted, "Getting back to my problem Doctor. I know you're busy and we mustn't keep everyone waiting. But what about this operation? How long will I be in the hospital and what about after?"

"About five days," Jim placated. "You'll have pins in your fingers for three weeks-"

"Whoa!" Mrs. Trussell suddenly blanched. "Sounds awful Doctor! Don't tell me any more."

"The rest is easy." He told her about the post operative occupational therapy, posed questions pertinent to the drugs she was taking, and after suggesting, "we'll do one at a time, otherwise you'll be completely indisposed," asked, "Any questions?"

"You have my head spinning. I'm sure I've forgotten to ask something I need to know and won't remember till I'm back home."

"Then give me a call," said Jim politely and watched as Lil began to back the wheelchair toward the door, "Say!" he exclaimed, detaining them. "I did enjoy the service, particularly Beecher's talk. I think he's missed his calling."

"I'll tell you a secret," Mrs. Trussell winked, her neck too stiff to turn and look back at her aid. "Lillian wrote it. That's why it was so good. Beecher just delivered it. She studied anthropology before going into nursing."

"Now, now, Winifred," Lillian spoke up protectively. "Beecher's been so occupied lately he hasn't had the time."

"It makes no difference. Congratulations to both of you," said Jim. "The experience you've had is invaluable. I'm quite envious."

While he was speaking he got a signal from Betsy, prancing impatiently in the corridor. "Dr. Lindsay," she called over the head of Mrs. Trussell. "Take the private line. It's Dr. Atwater again. Says it's extremely important."

Jim bid the women goodbye and grabbed the phone. "Eddie," he said in a teasing mood always happy to talk to his friend. "You in some kind of trouble?"

There followed a brief silence before Dr. Atwater responded and when he did he was not in his characteristic mood. His words were hoarse and ominously far away. "I've some bad news Jim. Your son has been in an accident. He's in the E.R. at the General."

Dr. Lindsay was out of his office post-haste. He reversed down the driveway, spun the wheels of his Pontiac and proceeded east on James Street, wondering if he was over-reacting. After all they had been confronted with family emergencies before. When Jenny was four she cut her chin on an aluminium tray. It was a small laceration and he had no qualms, suturing it himself. Heather broke her arm, falling off the elevated hearth in the family room. Having treated severe supracondylar fractures of the humerus, the slight greenstick break presented no challenge. It seemed nonsensical to ask a colleague to look after such a trivial thing.

If Jim was cool under pressure Merri was polished marble. The day Kathy lost the tip of her index finger in the meat grinder, her mother stemmed the bleeding with a towel and methodically sifted the contents of the bowl until she found the tiny vestige. Plunking it in a bottle of water with a pinch of salt, she packed the child along with her parted Peter Pointer into the car and introduced herself to a nurse at the E.R. Jim was tied up in the O.R. but Crooky was available to repair the damage. The terminal tuft of bone had to be shelled out and the remaining skin used as a graft. The finger healed and although it was a little shorter the defect was barely noticeable. Ever after Kathy looked before she poked.

Jim shrugged. It was a rough way to learn a lesson. When he compared the worry he had then with this current one his fear returned.

"Don't think about it," he whispered. "You're fearing the unknown. You'll find out soon enough."

Diverting his attention, he turned on the radio and caught an excited newscaster transmitting the shocking death of President Kennedy. "Lee Harvey Oswald, apprehended minutes ago in a Dallas movie theatre for killing a police officer, is being interrogated as the chief suspect in the Kennedy assassination." Despite his own consuming suspense Jim harkened to the course of history as if he were attending a pagan sacrifice along with the rest of the confounded world.

Jason and the driver-examiner Mr. Rossetti didn't have a chance. A west-bound car carrier blew a tire and the driver, trying to control the cumbersome vehicle, hit the brake. As it jack-knifed on the Queen Street overpass one of its spanking new automobiles came loose, hurdled the guard-rail and crashed down on the roof of the Lindsay's stationwagon. Jason's death was instantaneous. The tremendous weight crushed his skull and impaled him on the steering column. Mr. Rossetti never regained consciousness and died in the ambulance.

Part Two

*Sunday, March 1, 1964
to
Saturday, Aptril 25, 1964*

Dr. Lindsay & Mahmud

CHAPTER FIFTEEN

The D.C.6 left Tehran the eve of February 29th and was due to touch down in Kabul at 10.30 am; ten hours before church bells proclaimed Sunday morning services in Shipton.

Within the big plane Jim pressed his brow against the window. Twinkling Iranian towns could have been galaxies millions of miles away. Even time seemed suspended, lulled by the incessant drone of the engines. He withdrew to see a ghostly face with hoary sideburns staring back. How much whiter were his temples than three months ago when Jason died! The suffocating feeling returned; it was always stalking, ready to pounce.

The second day of the funeral brought a thaw followed by a north-east gale and freezing rain. The combined families distended each room with activity and the house became a bedlam rather than one of mourning.

Jim's nephew Billy was most distraught. The previous Labor Day Jim and his brother-in-law had taken their sons fishing in northern Quebec. It had been fun and they were all looking forward to another trip. Jim found the boy sulking by the pond; after the lad flushed out his sorrow he took him into the house for a game of pool.

Merri's parents, halfway round the world had no choice but to complete their tour. Determined to book a flight home they could find nothing enabling them to arrive in time for the funeral.

Freezing rain kept falling. For a third sleepless night a cracking wind flung glazed and broken twigs against the roof. By morning it had gone but the rain continued. All Jim could recall was the crowd of young people who attended the memorial service in the Smallwood Chapel.

As their son was lowered beneath wet plastered leaves Jim, Merri and the four girls huddled under umbrellas, mindless of the Minister's sympathetic intonation while overhead in a shivering tamarack a cluster of sparrows harmoniously ruffled against the cold and dark clouds pitched like blue whales spouting pewter sea

In the afternoon at the Lindsay home condoling friends and relatives watching American Television saw a replay of the morning's pathos when Air Force I dipped its wings at a wooded knoll in Arlington.

Something moved behind the haunted image in the pane. Reflexively Dr. Lindsay turned to discover the smiling Afgan stewardess with a tray of steaming cups. He took one, returned her cordial greeting and sipped the highly sweetened drink. Although he would have preferred black coffee there was an enticing aroma to the hot liquid warming his hands. Tea, the beverage of the East, prized by the British and consumed in quantities from Persia to the Sea of Japan was in his household a generation removed. After a few sips he began to relax and the fingers of sorrow slowly released their hold.

The aircraft was fairly new and comparatively empty. There were sixteen passengers including himself, a third as many as there had been on the flight from Beirut to Tehran when the plane was full.

The Lebanese capital had been a treat due to the hearty welcome he received from Crooky's niece. Her husband, Dr. Donald Shaw headed the Cardiovascular Unit at the American University Medical Centre. They had been living in the capital for the past six months. Hearing Jim would be passing through Beirut on his way to Afghanistan, Crooky asked him to ring up the Shaws and deliver a packet of wedding photos. Shortly after landing Jim was taken to dinner; Crooky's pictures were presented over a sumptuous meal at a gourmet restaurant.

They were delighted, and with the anecdotal Dr. Cruikshank in common, enjoyed a most pleasant evening. Unfortunately Jim couldn't stay the night and by the time he boarded the Ariana Airline flight felt he'd known the Shaws all his life.

The passengers were counted again - the second tally with more interest as Dr. Lindsay tried to deduce who they were. The semi-darkness of the cabin made his pastime more challenging. Everyone but the young blond man two rows in front had been on the plane from Beirut. Boarding in Tehran seconds before the hatch was secured, the newcomer doffed a beige Persian lamb cap and threw it along with a carry-on bag, brief case and great coat on the overhead rack. He strapped himself into the seat, turned on the ceiling lamp and adjusted an air-jet.

Other than the elderly couple across from Jim, a family of Sikhs sprawled unconsciously over the first few rows and two men, jabbering an unfathomable language at the back of the plane, all were apparently travelling alone and most were trying to sleep.

In the seats directly across the aisle the elderly couple, undisturbed by the invisible bumps, dozed like a pair of large mouth bass. In rumpled grey tweed the old man could have passed as an

English country gentleman; the woman supplemented his scrawniness with oodles of chin and an upsweep of grey-blue hair.

The newcomer was one of two persons besides himself whose ceiling beam was lit. Jim had not quite decided the other, further forward on the opposite side of the plane, was a farmer when the man turned off his light to relax through the remainder of an abnormally short night.

At the same time the latest arrival ran a pair of strong hands through his blond hair and straightened to a height of six feet. A slim charcoal business suit accentuated the breadth of his back and shoulders. He removed his suit jacket, folded it carefully and stretched, unaware anyone was watching. A swimmer, Jim surmised, from the thick-rooted neck and prominent jaw, or a football player.

The young man laid his case on an arm-rest, unlocked the combination and took out a sheaf of papers. Possibly a lawyer as well, Jim guessed, German or Swedish from his appearance except for his hooked nose. Then he could be American or Russian - or a spy on Her Majesty's Secret Service. Nah! A diplomatic courier perhaps, but the fellow would have been handcuffed to his case and never leave those valuable papers in the overhead compartment or unguarded on the seat as he was doing. While Jim continued his sly observation the young man, groping for the tops of the seats guided himself aft toward the lavatories, limping almost imperceptibly. A student, Jim thought, giving his guess one last shot. No definitely not. He was too deliberate to be a student. "I give up," he muttered, and returned to the window. The stars were beginning to fade.

In fact the newcomer was a student and introduced himself upon his return. He hesitated between Jim and the elderly couple, surveying the forward end of the cabin until he noticed Jim's friendly nod and dropped into the aisle seat.

"Sir," he said, "I hope I have not trespassed on your privacy." His accent was mellow, though he strangely enunciated the 'ed' in 'trespassed'. "I heard you speak to the stewardess. You are American?"

"No," Jim replied, welcoming the opportunity to while away the flight. Getting to know people was his livelihood. Most could be trusted and he regarded the handsome stranger with the intense blue eyes without suspicion. "No," he repeated, "I'm Canadian."

A frown drew the young man's eyes but quickly disappeared. "Ah," he smiled, exposing a set of even teeth. "Vous parlez francais? Oui? Je suis content de vous rencontre. Je m'appelle Darius Abdullah Mahmud."

Jim chuckled at the man's inference and explained, "No, I'm an English speaking Canadian from Ontario." He offered his hand. "My name's Lindsay, James Lindsay. Happy to meet you Mr. Mahmud."

"Mine's Dari," Mahmud said, before letting go of Jim's hand. "From where I come people are known by one name."

"Iran?"

"No. Afghanistan."

"You're an Afghan!" Jim was openly surprised. He had an impression from the National Geographic, describing Kipling's romantic adventures, and Beecher's account of a tall turbaned hillsman in baggy clothes with dark flashing eyes, black hair and a fierce red beard, quite removed from the well groomed sunny headed young man to whom he was speaking. Actually he knew better from reading S.E.R.V.E.'s reports. The capital, Kabul, was a modern city of three hundred thousand. Although civilization in isolated mountain villages had not advanced beyond the thirteenth century it was reaching the larger towns. From his appearance and manner Darius Abdullah Mahmud could live anonymously in any western society.

"It's too bad." Mahmud looked troubled.

"What's too bad?" Jim asked, wondering why being Afghan should be a problem or he had thoughtlessly offended his new acquaintance.

"You cannot speak French."

"Sorry!" Jim half smiled. "I can read and understand what I hear provided it's spoken slowly but I can't converse beyond an elementary level."

Dari looked disappointed. "It's required where I'm going; for a moment I thought I'd have a chance to practise."

"Where?"

"Kabul University."

"Really!"

"Yes. It does appear strange. At home we speak Farsi, Pashto, a little Russian, German and English. Now to study medicine I must be fluent in French."

It was another fact Jim had learned from speaking to Washington. He had been advised the University might ask for his opinion or call upon him to lecture. The Medical School had been established with French AID and classes were being taught in French by French professors. He had not paid much attention to the information for his purpose was to teach post graduate students at the Avicenna Hospital. There the Americans had influence; interns and residents were required to know English. Apparently there was little communication between the Medical School, run by the Ministry of Education, and the hospitals under the Ministry of Health. The long range plan was to train Afghan counterparts to run their own show. He felt sorry for the young man, empathizing as he thought of possible problems in store for himself. Then it was best to look at the positive side, Afghans were being taught regardless. "So you want to become a doctor!"

"Yes." Dari sounded resigned in spite of the barriers.

"Where did you study premedicine?"

"At the American University of Beirut. I was accepted into their Medical School and have almost completed my first year."

Jim was confused. "If you don't mind my asking why are you not finishing your course in Beirut?"

"My father is ill and I must study closer to home. I was investigating the possibility of transferring to Shiraz University in Iran but it is still too far away. If I am to continue it will be either at the University of Kabul or Nangrahar in Jalalabad. Nangrahar is quite new. I would prefer to study there as the courses are in English.

"Is your father a doctor?" Jim asked.

"No. You westerners would call him a 'jack of all trades'. My father is a Provincial Governor and a Senator. So was my grandfather before he died. Our family has held land at Kapisa and Bamiyan for years. And you?"

"I'm going to Kabul for a month."

About to ask why, Dari paused. Like all ferangi this man's whereabouts would be general knowledge shortly after arrival.

"I'm an orthopaedic surgeon," Jim explained, "with S.E.R.V.E. Medicare. I'll be working at the Avicenna Hospital."

The Afghan's impartiality vanished; although he tried not to show it, his eyes widened with astonishment. Of all the people he should chance to meet here was a man who was not only practising a branch of medicine which especially interested him but might have influence as well. "That is very good," he declared excitedly and paused briefly before adding. "But you won't like it."

"Why?"

"It is a dirty place and there is no decent equipment."

"You talk like you've seen it."

"I have." Dari scowled and shook his head. "Almost five years ago. Perhaps it has changed. Why do you want to go?"

The question was one to which Jim had no answer. He was not sure himself. Before Jason died he felt like trying something different. His practice had become a treadmill and his patients increasingly fitted into a series of irritating problems, incurable with the means he had at hand.

After talking it over with Merri they had decided to postpone long trips until the children were sufficiently mature and could fend for themselves but Jason's death altered that decision. Bitterness and depression came in sleepless nights and Christmas passed before the shock dissipated to a point where either of them regained any enthusiasm for life. Even then they'd find each other awake and they would weep, tangled together, until mental exhaustion gave way to sleep.

In the interim Jim saw to his patients mechanically. While he began to recoup a degree of zeal acceptance of other attitudes deteriorated to an all time low. He was argumentative and morose. Passing the orals did nothing to raise his spirits if anything it depressed him further. The examination had been a farce. Before he faced the other examiners Geoffrey Robb had approached him in the hall, 'You'll do just fine,' he said. - as if Robb had some inside information - 'nothing to worry about.'

The questions had been straight forward and Jim answered them with the same aplomb he'd shown in November. Later in the evening, a week before he left for Afghanistan, he was called into a closed session with all of the other candidates and presented with a slip of approval admitting him to an exclusive fraternity. This accomplishment did not make him as proud as it should have. Somehow Paolone found out from Beecher, Beecher through his close association with Dr. Robb, Jim suspected. 'It's only a piece of paper Lindseyello. Someday they're going to do away with that damned examination. There's talk now of combining the Certificate and Fellowship examinations into one. They'll have to in order to keep the tail from wagging the dog. Mark my words, my friend!'

In the end Merri had pushed Ed Atwater's suggestion. 'Jim should get away. A change of environment will do him good' - advice doctors had been prescribing to patients suffering emotional fatigue for years. Not entirely convinced, Jim had agreed.

Merri stayed home with the girls. With a lump in his throat he saw them wave good-bye, bunched together in the departure lounge at the Toronto Airport. This last minute scene had been so moving he left his carry-on luggage behind, barely remembering it before the plane took off. Jennie had met him inside the gate where she was trying to persuade an attendant to take it on board. Jim had given her a final hug but couldn't speak for the lump was still there.

"Why I'm going so far away is difficult to say. I need a change, S.E.R.V.E. wants volunteers and the deal sounds like a great adventure."

Fair enough Mahmud thought, studying the soft brown eyes of the 'ferangi'. They were gentle and cognitive with a capacity for humour. It was doubtful if one could fool them about anything; they didn't have the look of a subversive, an entrepreneur, or a religious fanatic. He smiled. "Let me welcome you, Sir."

"Thank you," Jim grinned. "I'm looking forward to this."

"Do you have a family?" Dari asked.

"Yes. A wife and four daughters." Dr. Lindsay's face abruptly drained of expression as he confided, "our son was killed in a car crash last November."

"I'm very sorry. It is indeed a tragedy when a man loses his only son."

How little does he know, Jim thought and turned away to look at the brightening earth. "Ah its getting lighter!" he exclaimed. "There's a pink glow on the horizon."

Both were silent until the first rays of dawn penetrated the unshaded port windows. Then Dari asked, "What about your patients? I assume you have someone to look after them?"

"A new doctor in town has offered." Jim felt suddenly uneasy. "As a matter of fact he has been to Afghanistan himself. In the late fifties he was a medical missionary." Recalling Beecher's narrative, he went on. "In Bamiyan, yes, I believe that's where he was."

"Christian?" Mahmud hissed and sucked in his breath, tense with hatred. His knuckles blanched as he pressed hard against the chair-back in front. The man could only be the missionary doctor responsible for butchering his foot.

Puzzled by the young man's behaviour, Jim asked, "anything wrong?"

"No. No, I have a cramp," Dari lied. "Parasites, amoebae, we all have them." Anger darkened his brown face and he queried in a tone short of impertinence. "Do you trust him?"

"Who?"

"The man who has taken over your practice."

It was a leading question and answering it truthfully would have been avoided under normal circumstances. Conversing with a total stranger half way around the world provided confidentiality. In fact the same thought had been plaguing Jim from the day he met Dr. Best. His choice of leaving Beecher in charge of his patients was not made easily because it was also a test of his own judgment. If Best was not reliable there would be those less forgiving who would blame Dr. Lindsay if anything went wrong. But there was no one else available. Fortier, now working to full capacity, had refused. Either Jim referred his cases to Best or walked out on them, a highly unethical thing to do. Well, it was too late now. Any goof-ups would be waiting for him when he got home.

Jim shrugged. "Odd you should ask, Dari. I'm not sure of the answer myself. If he isn't trustworthy I'm afraid I'll have a few problems when I get back."

"Problems! What sort of problems?"

"He's very stubborn, insensitive and unwilling to take advice. Too keen to operate I'm afraid. 'Do unto others as you would have them do unto you,' he preaches but seems unmindful of the golden rule of surgery, 'Do no harm.' Twice he's proceeded contrary to conservative advice. Unless he curbs his attitude he's bound to get into trouble." Jim frowned and continued, " Before I left there were a couple of incidents where I thought his judgment was not good but giving him the benefit of doubt the contentious issues more likely were due to inexperience. The man has a lot to learn."

Mahmud boiled with contention. "You Christians are too generous. We Muslims prefer the Old Testament version of your Golden Rule, 'Do unto others as they do unto you.' Treat someone decently and you'll receive the same treatment in return. Kindness begets kindness et cetera. Perpetrate evil and you deserve likewise.

We do not believe in turning the other cheek." Dari laughed. "It would be making the same mistake twice."

While Jim mulled over Old Testament teaching, likening it to the attitude of the western legal profession, the young Afghan curiously asked. "I would like to learn more about these incidents."

"Sure," Jim replied. "How much anatomy have you had?"

"Too much," Dari chuckled. "I want to get into the clinical aspect of medicine."

"Well," Jim drawled. "I'll tell you. There were two occasions. In the first instance he came to me with an x-ray of an ankle, showing considerable calcification in the Achilles tendon. He said a middle aged tennis player was having localized pain and swelling. Beecher wanted to excise the calcium. I told him if he did a fair amount of the tendon would be sacrificed, making it prone to rupture. I suggested he leave it alone, treat the patient symptomatically by adding a heel-lift to his shoe and prescribe anti-inflammatory pills. If raising the heel of his shoe wasn't enough I told him to go for broke and lengthen the tendon surgically. Far less difficult than dealing with a natural tear. No matter, he went ahead and removed it. Three weeks later the heel cord ruptured the first time the patient stressed the tendon. He thought it was quite a joke. A major reconstruction to right the situation became necessary. From a surgeon's point of view, it wasn't a serious error but it put the patient out of action for a longer period of time. How he explained the complication would be interesting. I found out later he took the man to the hospital chapel and prayed with him before the second operation."

In Dari's mind, the man had to be the one who'd operated on his foot. "You said there were two incidents?"

"Yes. The second case involved a broken leg. The shin bone was fractured about two inches above the ankle, a site which is slow to heal."

"He wanted to operate, "'I'll just put in a compression plate and screws and pack it with bone chips.'"

"'I'd never heard of such nonsense. Just put the leg in a cast from the thigh to the toes, I told him, and chances are it will unite without a scar or any serious complications."

"'What complications can you possible get from such a simple operation?'" he'd argued. "Non-union and Infection, I'd said, but he didn't listen. He did the case the day before I left. The more I think of him, the less I think of him. The man's a fool."

Jim became quiet, thinking both of these situations had been irritating but weren't abrasive enough to incite a punitive frame of mind. There was still hope Beecher's well documented intelligence would temper him. The plate he intended to use had been developed by the Swiss to compress the bone ends and produce rigid immobilization, a state necessary for bony union. *Maybe Beecher'll end up a hero and I'll be a stick in the mud.*

A clatter in the forward galley alerted them to the preparation of breakfast trays and Dr. Lindsay smiled. "If you'll excuse me Dari, I'll go freshen up."

Mahmud looked up as Jim passed, "Before we land, may I have your address? At your convenience I would like to show you Kabul. Friday is the Muslim Sabbath. Prayers are held in the Mosques. Some places close but the bazaars are open."

Jim gave the young Afghan an approving look. "I'd like that very much, Dari. Thank you!"

In the direction of the lavatories a dark-skinned Muslim in flowing white robes and matching turban was about to kneel on the floor. Sensing Jim's approach he snatched up his prayer rug and stepped out of the aisle.

When Jim emerged from the washroom the fellow was facing west, away from the nose of the plane and the rising sun."Huh!" he marvelled. *The man has an uncanny sense of direction; after we took-off he bowed to the east. Somewhere in between we must have overflown Mecca.*

He saluted a good morning to the old Englishman and to Lindsay's surprise he was greeted by a deep southern accent, "A good day to you too, Suh." - good was broken into three syllables.

Stumped again Jim conceded, unable to repress a smile. *So they weren't English but Americans.*

He had barely buckled up when the same girl who had served him tea reached to unlatch his table. Gesturing at the window she smiled, "We are passing over the Iranian Plateau. Below us is the Dasht-i-Kavir, a great desert surrounding our country."

Jim searched for dunes but couldn't distinguish any.

The precooked omelette was not very tasty. After a few mouthfuls he gave up, preferring to take in the ever changing scene beyond the window. The backbone of middle Asia paraded in staggered columns, pushing higher until its frosty peaks punctured the clouds.

"The Hindu Kush!"

Jim recognized the voice as Mahmud's but did not turn around. He was completely transfixed by the scene in front of him. From west to east as far as he could see were tremendous mountains. Their purple bases splitting into tortuous ravines, buff and brown in the morning sun. Here and there a flash of light signalled the presence of water.

"Where are the trees?" Jim asked, mindful of the evergreens at the foot of the Canadian Rockies.

"In the valleys. Fir, on the mountains. Poplar and larch, by the river banks. What's left of them."

After awhile the big Douglas shuddered and banked over the jagged rim of a huge valley, allowing a topographers slant of the ground.

"There's the air strip and Kabul!" Dari pointed. The city lay like an oversized horse-shoe tossed into a prodigious pit. As if the shoe had barely landed a haze of dust hung over mounds of earth. The mounds, dwarfed by a majestic backdrop, were technically mountains themselves comparable to the Laurentians, actually higher for their base was a mile above sea-level. From Kabul, the river flowed eastward across an open plain toward a gap in the rim.

The aircraft levelled and drifted lower, circling shale encrusted slopes, then down over an irregular bottomland chequered with farms.

"Juis!" Dari remarked, pointing at a crisscross system of irrigation ditches.

"Are those Caravanserai?" Jim asked.

"Where?"

"Those mud-brick fortresses."

"No, qalas. Caravanserai are much larger, about the size of an entire village; they're farther apart, the distance it takes a caravan to travel in a single day. Qalas are comparable to castles. In the past when feudal wars were common, harassed villagers sought refuge under their landowner or Khan. Each tower signifies a complete unit with adjoining living quarters, granaries and stables. The surrounding wall is much higher than a man can reach and keeps out thieves and marauding wolves." Dari singled out a large flat roofed complex with five square turrets. "Ours is much like that."

While the D.C.6 rounded for the final approach Mahmud buckled himself in the seat next to Jim. In the recent past he had been home once - ten months ago before his father became ill. He might have made the trip more often, but it was only within the last year U.S.AID had loaned the Afghan government funds to purchase aircraft for international flight. Getting back to Kabul by land was tiring and time consuming. He had left the bulk of his belongings with a friend in Beirut, hoping his father's illness was temporary. His deep blue eyes melted with the thought of seeing Roxane.

The day he left for Beirut she had shed her chadri, encouraged by a proclamation from the Queen and as other Afghan women were doing dressed in western clothes. Since then she had almost completed a course in modern languages and was working part time for a newspaper. He remembered the crowded airport. She was on tip-toes and disregarding Muslim propriety kissed and clung to him in desperation. The silk kerchief he'd given her fell back on her coat and he had looked down on her blue black hair and wished she'd hang on forever. Now he was back and blazed with anticipation.

Dr. Lindsay noted the young man's preoccupation. "I guess you're happy to be home!" he said and added. "If you can come to our teaching rounds at Avicenna get in touch. The address is on this card."

"Can we drop you there? We've lots of room."

"No, but thanks just the same," Jim smiled. "I expect to be met by the Medicare people."

Dari pocketed Jim's card and there was a gap in their conversation during the landing.

When the aircraft stopped near the terminal they wished each other well and Mahmud went ahead.

Jim did not see him disembark but caught a glimpse through a window. The Afghan was striding across the tarmac in a steady uneven gait. A remarkable young man, he thought, waving off a twinge of pain as he was reminded of Jason. But why the limp? He kept on watching, fascinated. Either Mahmud was wearing a prosthesis or had a fused right ankle and foot.

CHAPTER SIXTEEN

Dr. Lindsay stood inside the open hatch, allowing the elderly couple to pass. While he waited, marvelling at the towering splendour, a pungent mixture of burnt wood, body odour and sewage assailed him. This 'brown scented air', as he recalled later, fit the environment for everything from the snow-line down was a shade of brown: the shale, the boulders, the earth, the trees, the grass, the faces and the uniforms of soldiers guarding the airport.

At the immigration queue he overtook the jowly man whose bald head was covered with a smudgy sun helmet. Without baggage, Dari had cleared out and the officer was conducting a prolonged interrogation of the elderly couple. The delay was apparently frustrating the tanned-faced man because he kept stepping out of line to look at the travellers in front of him. A canvas bag was strapped to an epaulette of his safari jacket and he was impatiently snapping an American passport between his teeth. Turning around he pointed his pug nose at Dr. Lindsay muttering, "They've probably got the wrong visa."

"Is there more than one?" Jim asked. His tourist visa was obtained by S.E.R.V.E. and he had given the matter no thought.

"Entry and Tourist," the man replied.

"You've been through here before," Jim grinned.

"Uh huh!"

"What's the difference? How can one be a tourist without entering the country first or vice-versa?"

"It's not like the States," the man replied, "where every Tom Dick and Harry can move in and take out papers. They don't like foreigners settling here. The only way you can become a citizen is to marry one. So you know who gets to stay. The women! Believe it or not I met a guy who's got seven wives."

The man's earnestness was too much for Jim and he couldn't resist, "and each wife has seven cats."

There was no change of expression in the tanned face. "Well," the man corrected himself, "maybe three of them are concubines. He's a big Uzbak. Owns a spread the size of Long Island and raises Karachuls."

"So he has the women and his help have the sheep," Jim chuckled facetiously.

The man couldn't repress a smile though he continued to press his point. "It's not as funny as you think mister. Here some guys take all the women. Others get none. Those who have none take each other."

Out of smart remarks and disinclined to carry on this line of conversation Jim returned to the previous issue. "What about the visas?"

"If it concerns you, an Entry visa is for business purposes and does not entitle the holder to leave Kabul without reporting to the police. With a Tourist visa you can but it expires in thirty days. Under special circumstances they'd likely renew it." The informant regarded Jim quizzically. "Where're you staying?"

Dr. Lindsay's reply, "the U.S.AID Staff House" altered the man's attitude. His lids opened a trifle and a faint glow rounded his cheeky face. "Deemstra", he said. "Hank Deemstra. I'm going there myself if we ever get out of here. I'm supposed to be in Pul-i-Kumri tonight but I doubt if I'll get any further than Charikar. Hope there's a jeep packed and ready to go. If the plane'd been on time I'd be there by now. Want to share a cab?"

"Maybe. Lindsay's the name." The closing sentence of a letter he'd received from the mission chief, Al Keele, read, 'You'll be met at the Kabul Airport by a member of S.E.R.V.E.' "Perhaps we can give you a lift Mr. Deemstra," he suggested. "What's your business?"

"Agriculture," the man replied and went on to describe a wheat project north of the 'Kush'. "Plenty of Ruskies there too," Deemstra continued. "The Afghans hate them and I can give you a few reasons, the most important being they're afraid of a take over, particularly with all the Russian military strength sitting on the north bank of the Amu Darya. Another is Russians don't mix with Afghans; their advisors remain aloof and live in separate compounds. Also - a fact which is not as much anti-Russian as pro-American - our equipment is superior. Look around and you'll see Russian trucks breaking down all over the place." Deemstra smiled. "Regardless, I've seen plenty in this post war era and nowhere have I witnessed the two ideologies cooperating and competing under such friendly terms. Take this airport, half Russian and half American. The landing strip was paved by the Americans with seven thousand feet of runway to accommodate larger craft. The Russians built the terminal and the control tower but they forgot radar. That's why there are no night flights. Even daylight flights are dangerous; there are mountains in them fleecy clouds."

"Thanks a lot!" Jim shuddered, "Think I'll walk home."

Deemstra shrugged. "I shouldn't be so hard on the Ruskies." "There's another airport built entirely by Americans - a beautiful job in Kandahar - just finished it. There's no radar there, either. Also while our Helmand river project is trying to irrigate the desert to the south the Russians have been busy elsewhere building a grain elevator, a cement factory and a bakery, all functioning properly. The bakery's not too popular; most Afghans prefer home-baked nan. It's a flat unleavened bread full of roughage. Don't eat too much. It'll blow you to smithereens."

Slowly the passengers trickled through immigration and customs until it was Jim's turn. He was not delayed long in spite of a painstaking search of his belongings and rejoined Deemstra at the taxi stand.

The crowd jamming in and out of the terminal was far in excess of what one would expect for the number of passengers arriving. Most were men: tall, dark, slim and supple with quick black eyes. Their long heads and noses varied as much as their facial hair. There were flagrant moustaches, long scraggly beards and manicured goatees. Those dressed in occidental clothes were generally clean shaven and sported tightly-curled lambskin hats. Nor were all the noses prominent and coarse, typical of the semitic and arab races. A few were straight and finely chiselled. Others, broad and flat apportioned a pair of slanted eyes. Besides the khaki clad milita dallying with their rifles and policemen wearing blue greatcoats, the majority were dressed in the national costume: Filthy turbans sloppily wrapped with a free end trailing down the back or over a shoulder, western suit jackets and loose-tailed shirts, flapping and fluttering in the wind like their voluminous trousers. Traditional coats were of tanned sheep skin or colourful striped heavy cotton whose designer forgot to include lapels and made the sleeves too long. With no means of fastening them some wore weskits of rich velour.

At one end of a rectangular reflecting pool decorated with flags several baggy suited types, seated cross legged or squatting on their heels, were tossing small white balls into a circle.

"Karoms", said Deemstra. "Or marbles. One of their favourite pastimes. Play it in their teahouses instead of pinball and darts.

"I'm told the balls are made from sheep knuckles," Jim said.

"Yeah." Deemstra's two-tone forehead wrinkled in surprise. It was the sort of information not generally available in the books about Afghanistan. "Where did you hear that?"

"From a medical missionary who worked in Bamiyan."

"Those jerks! Why the hell they want to come here and jam Christ down Muslim throats is beyond me. Most of the Afghans I know would just as soon slice a missionary's throat to keep from listening." The agronomist paused and redirected Jim's attention to the circle of Karom players. "Someone over there is picking up a bit of change," he snickered. "You'd think because they copy the westerner in dress they're learning his vices. Not so. They've been sinning since time immemorial. The Koran forbids them to gamble, charge interest, drink alcohol and eat pork. The entire grape harvest used to be dried into raisins and shipped out, most of it to Russia. With French know-how vineyards are being cultivated for winemaking. From what I've heard it's not bad and the few bottles they don't export must be consumed locally. I dare say, the only rule the modern Afghan is not breaking is eating pork though I've seen dead ones on the road, here and there."

To one side of the boulevard leading to the city, sheep and goats were rapaciously attacking the early blades of spring. Bunting, bleating and munching they swarmed onto the thoroughfare where they merged with an assortment of roaring trucks, buses, foreign cars and bell ringing bicycles with festooned wheels, all adding impetus to the swirl of life.

Suddenly Deemstra exclaimed, "Oh Oh! There he goes."

"Who?" Jim asked.

"The Mullah," Deemstra pointed. "He's cracking down on that gambling ring."

"Isn't he the one from the plane? He was praying in the aisle this morning. I almost tripped over him."

"Could be. They all look alike to me."

A tall, grey-bearded chap in a white turban and long white robes was striding in the direction of the circle of men when his advance was cut off by a black Mercedes. As the Mullah dodged it the driver got out and opened the doors for a family of East Indians standing well back on the side-walk. The black bearded head of the household was topped by a tightly rolled pink turban, cresting high in front like the prow of a ship. He stepped to the curb and motioned for his wife to hurry. She waddled behind in a pale blue sari, herding three youngsters clothed as if they were on a Sunday outing in Shipton.

"They were on the plane," Jim asserted. "Sikhs, I believe."

"Yes," Deemstra agreed. "Wealthy ones too. Sikhs are a lot like the Jews, very industrious sensitive intellectuals with the knack of making a buck. Most are successful merchants in Kabul. They worship their tools, work for themselves and remain aloof. This is not such a strange place when you compare the population and social pattern of Afghanistan to the United States. The people are much the same, mixtures of different nationalities and races. Here the process has been going on much longer and the product is fairly constant but prototypes surface from time to time like a kettle brimming with inadmissible ingredients. Even the British tried to leave a trace but more of their blood was shed than mixed."

Jim engrossed in Hank Deemstra's dissertation had forgotten the Mullah and the game going on across the road. When he looked back at the median neither the Mullah nor the players were in sight. "Now where did they go?" he mumbled, squinting suspiciously at the back of an overcrowded bus. Possibly one of the three figures, clinging tenaciously to an open door was wearing white robes but he was not sure. The players seemed to have melted into the background of long faces and spacious cloth.

"Never underestimate the wrath of Allah my friend," said Deemstra. He grinned and gave a consenting nod to the operator of a Volkswagen taxi. "Come on Lindsay let's go. Looks like your friends aren't going to show."

Before Jim could decide his bag was loaded under the hood and he was crammed into the back seat next to the anxious agronomist. Deemstra instructed the driver in Farsi and the small car swung west along the broad airport road.

As they careened toward the city Jim attempted to identify the leafless trees lining the recently paved road and remarked, "I didn't realize soft maple grew outside North America."

"They're plane trees," his companion corrected. "Back home we call them sycamore or buttonwood.

Hearing his fares speak English, the driver motioned to a height of land off to the right. "Bemaru," he said. "In 1504, Babur the tiger fired warning flares and sent his mail-clad horses galloping down on Kabul. That is also where the British were defeated. Three times we defeated them. Now the Americans and Russians are trying to win us with aid."

"Huh!" Deemstra grunted disgusted with what he thought was an ungrateful remark.

"Do not misunderstand me, Sahib," the driver demanded. "There is no doubt we need help but it is only because your company is enjoyable you are welcome. We do not want American or Russian Imperialism any more than British. We value our independence but to all countries we are equally friendly and while we go on happy to have aid, put the hateball in the side pocket."

Jim smiled at the driver's distorted axiom and asked. "Where did you learn your English?"

"I work part time at U.S.Embassy," the driver explained.

The traffic thickened and the Volkswagen slowed behind two man-drawn vehicles apparently racing each other. Beeping the horn frantically had little effect in clearing the way. Not until one of the contestants tired and dropped back allowing the second to precede did they have clearance.

"What the deuce are they?" Jim asked.

"Karachies," Deemstra replied. "They make them out of used axles, stolen wheels, anything that rolls."

From a projecting pole the length and breadth of a light standard each man must have been pulling half a ton, Jim estimated, judging from the size of the boulders teetering on a platform mounted above the wheels. "It must take a lot of strength to move them." he commented.

"Or stopped!" Deemstra added. "They're a traffic hazard."

Past the residence of His Majesty Mohammed Zahir Shah the airport road abruptly ended at Pashtunistan Square, a wide intersection centred by a fountain. They had come to the closed end of the city, the point where the prongs of the horse-shoe met. Traversing it was like a trip through the trenches of Arras. Ahead of them Jim saw a jumble of mud-brick buildings the colour of dead bracken, slender minarets and graceful domes. Terraces and adobe houses had been built on the steep slope of the central mountain.

Zigzagging through the heart of the city, back and forth over an assortment of bridges, the small car eventually turned onto a wide street, skirting the south side of the central mountain.

At a stoplight an old man shuffled by in up-toed shoes bent under an enormous back-pack stuffed with carrots similar to a sack slung across the rump of his trailing donkey.

The light changed but before they could proceed the intersection was blocked by a file of camels led by a grimy man and a dark handsome woman in a full length, patterned red skirt. A black shawl hung below her buttocks and from her neck and waist strings of gold and silver medallions glittered attractively.

"Wears the family fortune wherever she goes." Deemstra whistled softly. "Bet those coins are worth a few bucks."

She was the first afghan woman Jim had noticed since they left the airport. Fascinated, he watched till her graceful carriage and swinging hips came abreast of a coven of veiled creatures waiting on the opposite corner. The last camel loped by and the spooky figures, like children masquerading at Halloween, darted toward them. "Chadris!" he exclaimed, wondering what lithe spirits were trapped within the pleated cloth.

Deemstra leered, his flexed arms resting along the top of the back seat. "How's that grab you? Follow them home and you'll catch a slug of lead in your ass. It isn't worth it. Most of them look better with those things on than off. I know a lot of women back home who should wear them."

As if Allah chose to avenge their lusting, the rear of the Volkswagen split open and three heads whipped back and forth. Jim felt his neck snap, saw headgear fly and heard his fellow traveller groan. The little car pitched wildly, snorted like a stuck pig and died. Deemstra, minus his sun helmet and contorted with pain, was miserably clutching his right shoulder. A tongue of wood was snug against the seat where his arm had been.

Through a rent in the shattered engine compartment Jim sighted along the offending pole to a grey bearded face looking as bewildered as his own. Recalling Deemstra's livid denunciation of Karachis, he scanned the pole again to find the face had disappeared and at the far end on a caisson of sorts was a battery of bricks.

Tumbling out of his cab, the driver stomped to the rear to survey the damage. Though he spoke in Farsi his angry inflection was common to all languages. In staccato bursts he berated the bearded drayman until the chap's penitent manner turned to rage.

By the time Jim could plan what to do for Deemstra, the two Afghans were stuck into each other and their struggle was hard to ignore.

Deemstra swore his arm must be broken. It was painful, useless and stuck out from his chest.

"Mind if I have a look?" Jim suggested, unbuttoning his companion's shirt wide enough to admit his hand.

"Do I have a choice?" the agronomist moaned.

There was no room to remove Deemstra's jacket and lay him down. Getting him out of a two door cab the size of a Volkswagen without giving him something for pain or slinging the arm was impossible.

He felt the outer collar bone until his fingers found a hollow below the tip of the shoulder. The head of the humerus was lying at a lower than normal position. "I think it's dislocated," said Jim, then taking hold of his companion's flexed elbow, rotated the arm. The upper end moved in continuity and no grating was felt. "It shouldn't be broken; relax and I'll put it back."

Sweat puddled on the man's scalp and his nostrils dilated with each breath. "Go ahead," he laboured. "But take it easy."

Without releasing his grip Dr. Lindsay began a steady downward pull, gradually levering the flexed forearm outward while Deemstra ground his teeth and tensed his good arm.

Jim murmured. "Put your arm down and stop fighting."

"I can't. It hurts too God damned much."

"You'll have to try."

"That's easy for you to say, mister. It's not your bloody problem."

Seconds dragged by as the arm wrestling intensified. When it appeared to have reached a draw, a crescendo in the quarrel outside unsettled the agronomist and he lost his hold. There was a clunk, the joint relocated and the agronomist sighed with relief.

"Stick your hand in the front of your shirt for now. I'll sling it when we're out of here."

Without a word Deemstra bowled over the front seat to escape through the driver's door.

CHAPTER SEVENTEEN

Neither of them got very far. A mob had gathered to see the fight and like an amoeba was flowing around its stimulating nucleus, engulfing gawky bystanders.

The combatants had backed off and were spitefully eyeing each other. The Karachi man had the advantage in weight and though he was shorter his turban alluded to height.

"Looks like the cabby is taking a licking," Deemstra observed. "I don't think the cut on his cheek is from the accident."

Inclined to agree, seeing the Karachi man wipe the blade of a knife on his baggy pants Jim asked, "Why doesn't someone stop them?"

"Don't get any heroic ideas my friend. This is no place for a meddlesome 'ferangi'. That mob would just as soon stone us." Deemstra's warning was followed by a hasty order as he gestured toward the car. "Grab my pack and load me up."

Jim draped the khaki bag over the uninjured shoulder. He also had his doubts about the crowd's reaction but felt his companion's statement seemed a bit far fetched. He shrugged, hauled out his own luggage and hustled after the agronomist.

"Less haste and more speed," Jim advised when he had overtaken Deemstra. "What do you think will happen?"

Deemstra twisted around to check, more concerned with the possibility of pursuit. The crowd was dispersing and he spied a blue coated policeman. "Nothing much," he chuckled, "the marines have landed," and kept barrelling along doubling his pace, unaware Jim had returned to the scene of the accident, until he paused and looked back. "What the hell are you trying to do? Get yourself put in the jug!" he cried when Jim finally caught up.

"We forgot to pay him."

Deemstra stared, contemptuously. "Christ! he shouted. "The son-of-a-bitch should pay us for the inconvenience. How much did you give him?"

There was no use telling Deemstra he had donated an extra American ten toward the cost of repairing the Volkswagen nor ask him to share his charitable act. The tanned faced man was in no mood to understand. So he lied. "Two hundred afs."

"Jesus! Four times as much as the fare and we have a mile to go."

Jim changed the subject. "How's the shoulder?" he asked and glanced about for another cab. Deemstra, still shaking his head in disgust, was loath to answer till Dr. Lindsay re-phrased the question.

"You feel well enough to walk?"

"How else are we going to get there?"

"What about that?" Jim grinned, pointing at a curious horse drawn cart clopping slowly toward them.

"A Godi! Are you kidding? We can crawl faster."

The agronomist's meagre patience drained. Pivoting on his heel, he mounted a bridge.

On the south side the bank of the Kabul river was retained by a cement wall. Between the river and the shale base of the southern mountain a main thoroughfare ran east and west. Once they were on it Jim thought he recognized a building to their left from the pamphlet S.E.R.V.E. had sent. "What street is this?" he asked.

" Maiwand," Deemstra growled.

"Isn't that the Avicenna Hospital?"

Deemstra paid no attention. Turning right he kept on walking and Jim had to catch up again.

"We can drop in and find a sling for your arm," Dr. Lindsay suggested. "You really should have it x-rayed."

"Look Buddy! It's my arm. Let me worry about it. Nobody's going to get me into that hole."

Jim granted Deemstra the right to treat his body as he wished. Arguing was a waste of time and he lapsed into silence to conserve his strength.

They trudged onward, the base of the southern mountain to their left. Dominating the city, a rocky ledge on its shadowy slope held two antique cannon and from this prominence a decadent wall rose and fell to the east, stepping upward and over a barren peak, piebald with snow. Jim had read about it - the ancient Kabul wall- once wide enough to accommodate chariots. Fascinated he looked up until pain in his stiffening neck deterred him.

There was a park on the north side of the river where the bank was less steep and the water shallow. Men women and children in varying degrees of nakedness were wading in the languid current washing their cars, donkeys, laundry and vegetables, or for sheer enjoyment were gaily splashing about, their capacious clothing reefed into diaper-like shorts. Up-river a lad was watering camels while nearby, apparently spying on them, a man squatted behind a boulder.

Do Unto Others 175

Another of their strange customs Jim supposed, wondering what the man was really doing.

Deviating away from the mountain Deemstra led on across another bridge and five minutes later, dusty and weary, they approached the chain-linked fence of the U.S.Aid compound.

At the main gate a sentry popped out of a black and white striped guard house. He recognized the snub-nosed agronomist at once, admitted them with a perfunctory salute and waved at a long yellow building when Dr. Lindsay asked about the Infirmary.

"Christ I've no time to go there," Deemstra objected. Without a word of thanks he took off toward a block of corrugated steel sheds to hunt for his jeep.

The ground was covered with patches of sublimating snow but Jim was sweating from exertion. He set his luggage down on the shady side of the Infirmary and contemplated the receding little man whom he would add to his list of insufferable suffering. He did not like Hank Deemstra. During their close association the churlish fellow was so bent on his own purpose not a question did he ask. Jim smiled, wondering how Deemstra would refer to him in the future. Probably as the interfering bone setter who bought a well-used cab.

The Infirmary was empty, the Dispensary locked and the Commissary closed for the day. The only activity within the compound came from the direction where Deemstra had gone. Not keen on crossing paths with the man again Jim walked back to the main gate and explained his situation to the sentry.

"You've come to the wrong place Sir," said the young marine. "The U.S.AID Staff House is on the other side of Darulaman Boulevard in Karti Char. If you'll wait till I'm off duty I'll give you a lift."

"You're on," Jim replied and a half an hour later he was beside a similar sentry post, boxing a wary Afghan and controlling access to a stately white house with a grey shallow pitched roof. The house was set well back from the street and a paved walk led up to its wide terrazzo porch.

"Dr. Lindsay I'm terribly sorry." The apology was offered by Al Keele in the pleasant surroundings of a spacious lounge. "I was going to meet you myself but there wasn't a car available. Welcome to Hardship Post."

Keele was a raw-boned six-footer in his mid-forties with black eyebrows and bristly white hair. Like a cowpoke blown in from the range he was typical pioneer America and as out of place in the luxury of the staff house as the staff house was out of place in its impoverished environs. The setting provided comforts unaffordable to its civilian residents in their own homes, back home. There was a modestly furnished dining room in addition to the snack and liquor bars, a pool table and a dance floor.

At the registration desk Jim was allotted a key to a room in the annex, a stone and white-washed plaster building next door.

The houseboy ran ahead with the luggage and mounted a porch to enter the front hall. On the second floor he put down the suitcases and waited for Jim and the mission chief to catch up.

Keele indicated a row of wall hooks in the vestibule. "When you leave the building hang your key by the front door. The baccha will need it to clean your room. Lock your door and take the key to bed with you."

From the bedroom a door opened onto a balcony. Keele walked out into the sunlight and leaned on the ornamental concrete balustrade. "You can trust the bacchas. They'll look after you, your laundry and shine your shoes. But don't tip them too much. You'll spoil it for the next guy. If you think they deserve more, pay them at the end of your tour."

While Keele was talking the lad who had carried the suitcases appeared in the courtyard below. He picked a stone from the gravel path, fitted it into a sling and let fly at the jagged green bottle glass partly embedded in the top of the wall. A crystalline report assured his aim had been true and he skipped merrily past the security guard into the street. "Kids are no different here than in the States," said Keele lazily. "They're just not as well off. In Arizona he'd have an air rifle."

The strain of two days' travel was beginning to tell. Jim's eyes glistened and when he yawned tears wet his cheeks.

"Why don't you get a couple of hours sleep," the mission chief suggested. "I'll be back at seven to pick you up. By then I should have a car. We'd like to have you over for a drink. There'll be other people; some you'll be working with; others you should get to know."

Keele called back from the stairs. "If you need anything the Commissary is well stocked. You can buy liquor there tomorrow."

Suddenly remembering, he frowned. "I forgot you're Canadian. You're not allowed to use it. Never mind. Give me a list of what you need and I'll have it put on our tab. We'll settle up later."

After Keele left Jim unpacked his belongings and lay down on the bed exhausted but too fired up to sleep. The expensive Conterax bought to take slides was sitting in its case on top of the dresser. He wondered why he'd packed it in his luggage. There were so many interesting things to shoot. Closing his eyes he acquainted them to memory. Within minutes he was dozing.

A faint tapping sound awakened him and when he heard it again he opened his eyes. The strange surroundings confused him and he consulted his watch. Having forgotten to advance the hands baffled him further. He lifted his head from the pillow and soreness in his neck immediately reminded him of the karachi and Deemstra. There it was again, a gentle knock on the door. I'm not dreaming, he thought, but was uncertain as the tapper looked like the southern gentleman who was on the plane. "Yes, he asked, curiously?"

"I'm Ames, Leroy Ames," the visitor replied. "I hear you're an orthopaedic surgeon and hope you won't mind having a peek at my wife, Blossom. We're staying downstairs. It's her back."

Jim closed his eyes and opened them slowly. He had come half way round the world to escape low back pain, whip-lash and pernickety old women. How far did he have to go? The muscles tightened at the base of his neck. "Sure thing, Mr. Ames," he reluctantly agreed. "I'll be down in a few minutes."

Ames turned out to be Dr. Ames, a retired ophthalmologist voluntarily attached to the Eye Clinic. He was old and feeble and should have kept his lumpish wife at home in South Carolina. The rutted sideroads of Kabul were no place for an elderly couple. Their taxi had hit a pothole and the jolt produced a persistent pain in the centre of her spine. All her decrepit husband could do was help her to their room.

Upon seeing the doctor, Blossom tried to sit up but couldn't tolerate the position and fell back in bed. She smelled of perspiration, perfume and Johnson's baby powder. Her upswept hairdo had collapsed and silver wisps fell on her huge breasts. Jim with Ames help rolled her semi-prone and gently percussed her spine. When his fist thumped the middle of her back she complained. "Probably a simple wedge compression of T 12, Doctor. Keep her in bed and make her comfortable. Give her an analgesic if you have any. If not they should honour your prescription at the Aid Infirmary. Find her a good stiff corset and she'll settle down."

Excluding the smiling Afghan waiters, the staff house dining room was deserted. Jim had a bit to eat and was fondling a second cup of coffee when a feeling of longing came over him. He sauntered back to his room and began a letter to Merri and the girls. By the time Keele returned it was finished and he was advised to give it to the Medicare driver for posting in the morning. Yar Zamir also knew where to change black market money. He would be around at 8.00 am. each day to transport Jim to the hospital and nearby places of interest, acting as an interpreter.

The home of the mission chief was in Charti-Seh five blocks away and much like the house for volunteers but smaller. In addition to the glass crested walls the court was defended by a pack of yapping dogs. Jim gingerly waded through them and backed onto the porch. Keele kicked the largest and the rest slunk away.

Smoke and an assortment of people shared the living room. The affair was no different from cocktail parties thrown in Shipton. Jim shook his head, thinking a fruitful conversation with anybody, interesting or otherwise, was out of the question. He suspected the place was teeming with small talk, political manoeuvring and flirtatious overtures. Superficially it was an all-American do for the invited Afghans were indistinguishable in western clothes. Only the servants wore national garb, masking any resentment with incurious glances.

Al's gregarious wife Judy introduced Jim to the other guests. Her puffy eyes crinkled while she laughed and her laugh was loud and throaty, at times so effervescent tears wet her florid cheeks.

Before she excused herself to gossip with the Vice Consul Jim learned the Keele's had three children attending the American school. There were no summer holidays for the academic year ran from March to December. They loved Afghanistan, loved bus trips down the freshly paved Khyber to Peshawar and skiing at the Salang pass where the Russians were completing a tunnel two kilometres long through the Hindu Kush. Geraldine Billings, wife of the Peace

Corp doctor, hinted Judy was an alcoholic, dying to return to Tucson but wouldn't spend a nickel to get there.

John and Betty Disher were quiet and friendly. The droll Dr. John reminded Jim of his friend Atwater, also an internist. As the senior full-time medical officer Disher captained the team.

Mrs. Disher presented Jim to Ambassador Jake Newton, a tall slim man who fitted nicely into the Afghan scene with his long thin face. In college Newton injured a knee playing basketball. Lately it had been swelling. When he discovered Jim was a 'B-Ball' enthusiast he shouted at the only solitary figure in the room, a man leaning against a wall partially hidden by a clump of medical trainees. "I want Dr. Lindsay to examine my knee tomorrow, 2 pm. Arrange it." Jim subsequently found out the man was the infirmary physician, Ezra Tomarin.

While Tomarin searched his pockets for a note book Newton moved on and Jim was introduced to an attractive young woman judged to be in her late twenties on the arm of a swarthy man.

"This is Amir Kash," she announced. "You'll be working with him. He is the most experienced house surgeon at the Avicenna Hospital. I'm Peggy Dolan, Peace Corp, nurse in charge of the operating theatre."

Amir clicked his heels, bowed low and retained the orthopaedist's hand so tenderly and for so long Jim became embarrassed. It was not the firm shake and break he used himself. While his eyes were roving about the invited guests, contemplating how to diplomatically let go, he realized the act was a local custom, for other Afghans were doing it. To his relief a waiter intervened with a tray of drinks. Jim accepted scotch and raised his glass to wish Amir good health.

The chief resident repeated the salute and remarked, "scotch is vedi good drink."

"I thought it is against Allah's will to consume alcohol," Jim asked.

Amir smiled slyly and cast a disdainful look at another house officer talking to Miss Dolan. "Muslims are like Christians," he said. "While Baptists abstain it is the custom for Romans to drink. Is it not? We too have sects within our religion. I am Sunni. Noor there is Shi'ite."

"You amaze me with your knowledge of our faith Amir. Have you ever been to a Western country?"

"No, but I would like to go vedi much to United States. It is beautiful place, like Afghanistan, wide open spaces but not old and used up. I saw a movie at the AID compound, 'How The West Was Won.' It was vedi good. Have you seen it?"

The room the smoke and the din diverged as distantly as the stars and Jim felt the cold nudge of emptiness. Jason saw the film and had been upset. They had discussed the characters in it and he remembered trying to explain the relative acceleration of life, an eventuality his son would never know.

Amir was saying something about a cousin's vineyard near Istalif, of how the man was making wine and selling it to a Catholic priest at the Italian Embassy but the disclosure didn't register. Gradually the universe reverted; he regained a normal perspective and sensed Keele's tow-headed ten year old tugging at his elbow.

"Supper's ready Sir. You're s'posed to help yourself."

An adjoining room had been opened revealing a huge table topped with great platters of roast lamb, canned meat from the commissary, rice, raw carrots and cooked vegetables of many varieties. There were slices of pineapple, nuts and nan, tantalizing to an empty stomach. But Jim had already eaten. It never occurred to him the invitation included dinner. Keele's request was vague. There was no hint of anything special aside from the number of important people present. Not until the guests had served themselves and corks began popping.

"Welcome to our twenty-fifth my friends," Al proclaimed, holding out a glass of bubbly. "To my twenty-five year old bride."

Judy couldn't stand up to appreciate the applause. Her words were slurred. "Tha's right. I've been twenny-fife for tha pash thirdy years."

"Just as well she sat!" Jim overheard Geraldine Billings whisper to her husband. "She'd have fallen flat on her face."

"If I don't get to bed soon," Jim chimed into Art's other ear. "That's exactly what'll happen to me."

After congratulating Al and Judy Jim begged their leave and decided to walk back to his room while he was still able.

Night had fallen. Curfew was in effect and few electric lamps bathed the deserted streets. In the cold air packing the big valley isolated sounds echoed far off identifying themselves as man, animal and machine. Constellations were brilliant and reassuring. In the east high above the Kabul wall a sinister moon crossed the mighty Orion. The heavenly hunter had traced a path from Southern Ontario to the Kohi-Baba where he was soon to set and the darkening mountains, like humble monks, paid homage.

    The jingling of metal startled Jim and he spun around in time to see a mounted patrol enter a gap between two houses, their progress down a narrow lane, marked by barking dogs. As they rode on toward the southern mountain he gazed up at the crenellated walls, mysterious in the moonlight, and had a notion to climb it before he left.

CHAPTER EIGHTEEN

Standing apart from the crowd on the terminal roof, Ghubar the Tadjik scanned the grey sky for a sign of the Ariana Afghan plane. He was jubilant, the feeling hidden behind a stoical face. But it was there, broadcast by his angled eyes, and had been from the moment he learned Dari would arrive from Beirut.

It was only this morning Malikar had summoned him to the library. He remembered how peculiar his master behaved. 'Dari my beloved youngest son is coming home. Fetch him from the airport and bring him to me. It is imperative I know why.' As Malikar spoke he rose from a long table where he was labelling artifacts. Suddenly his face drained of colour and he coughed, 'Bring him here immediately or you'll.' The elder Mahmud slumped forward as Ghubar tried to support him, barely succeeding in breaking his fall. As if nothing happened Malikar looked up and concluded. 'or you'll go back to the stables.' There was neither malice nor humour in his tone just a moist expression which Ghubar could not decipher. The harshness of the words stung. The Tadjik was bewildered and stared in disbelief. Not since he was a baccha three generations ago had anyone in the household of Mahmud threatened to punish him. His loyalty was beyond question. The man was either out of his mind or there was something drastically wrong. Confused he watched Malikar return to his labelling.

Action bustled on the tarmac below. The hull of a D.C.3 was being stuffed with bales of cotton. The cowling had been removed from one of its twin engines, displaying a circle of cylinders, each the size of a litre can. Closer to the terminal a biplane started up. Ghubar watched as the pilot tested its rudder and flaps while taxiing toward the runway. Aeroplanes and their management fascinated him.

Not so long ago, about the time Malikar started flying, Ghubar had tried to get into the Ariana Airlines Maintenance Training Course. His application was turned down. Too old, they said. He had been around almost as long as the piston engine; why shouldn't he be more familiar with it than the young men whom they preferred. He had Dari's grandfather, Zulfikar Mahmud, to thank for it. Now there was a man! Ghubar sighed remembering: horseman, soldier of fortune, Governor and visionary. If he were anything less, the Tadjik reflected, I would not have exceeded childhood and lived so long.

Zulfikar, realizing the potential of motorization, invested in a fleet of trucks. Ghubar, barely fully grown, was Zulfikar's batman, having been elevated from personal baccha. As he had tended the master's horse so well, he was chosen to mind trucks and became a skilled driver-mechanic. Later over other motorwans he was entrusted with consignments of goods. Bright green lorries with Mahmud & Sons emblazoned with gold leaf, singly or in serpentine columns, back-firing up and down the dusty passes from Turkestan to Peshawar were Ghubar's duty, and he had delighted in it for almost forty years.

Not until the Afghan-Pakistan border closing of '61 had there been any sign of a slow down. Even that was inconsequential because Malikar, the present owner of the company, was every bit as crafty and enterprising as his father. A baksheesh in the right pocket opened less travelled routes through Pathan territories.

Craftily Malikar had himself included in a trade delegation to Russia. While there he bought a Daimler and secretly arranged an airlift of the Afghan fruit crop through Indian and Lebanese airlines. 'Why go around a fence,' he told his sons, 'when you can hurdle it.' Grapes and nuts were flown to Amritsar and Beirut in return for other commodities. Before the border re-opened all whom Malikar had personally involved: the growers, exporters and airlines, made a profit.

It was during the time Ghubar was making frequent trips to the Begram and Kabul airfields, his love-affair with flight flourished. He would climb the stairs to the roof of the new terminal as he had done this day and watch the mechanics work on their Dakotas or occasionally larger craft.

The present task was a twofold pleasure; the four engine plane, gracefully cutting through the clouds, was bearing his master's son whom Ghubar had nurtured and dearly loved as his own. Dari might just as well have been because Malikar seldom had time to teach him. Ghubar with his reservoir of practical knowledge had taken over. To Dari he was a walking encyclopedia and he returned the Tadjik's affection with admiration and respect.

The D.C.6 descended through the brightness, banking slowly. While watching Ghubar's face gathered like lines in an electromagnetic field, fixing his mouth in a static grin. Twice the plane circled before gliding into the final approach; its thunderbolt blue fuselage and white body stripe rising and charging like a bayonet. Through the smoke and screech of rubber the nose wheel finally touched and the plane headed for the apron.

When he was sure the passenger in the dark grey suit limping across the tarmac was the one he sought, Ghubar pulled the loose sleeves of his chapan around him, descended the stairs and headed for the car park. A few minutes later he moved the landrover closer to Arrivals where Dari had no trouble finding him.

They embraced warmly, planting kisses on each other's cheeks and when they were alone the younger man gripped the Tadjik's thin arms and searched his face. Although Ghubar's beard was more white than grey and his skin had become patched with pigmentation, his eyes still held a sparkle of intelligence. They veiled when Dari asked. "How is my father, kaka-jan?"

"I saw Malikar this morning. He is not himself but swoons and says strange things. I think his mind is affected. He no longer hunts and has given up flying. Only his antiques interest him. Most of his time is spent in the library admiring them. He has given up the living world for the dead. Maybe he wants to die."

Dari let go of the old motorwan and turned away. The last time he was home his father had looked ten years older than his real age, suspected as being sixty-five. Although Malikar did not complain it had been obvious normal exertion was difficult and he was urged to see a doctor.

Dari threw his attache case in the back of the rover and climbed into the passenger seat. "Who's looking after him kaka-jan?" he asked.

Ghubar laughed and shifted into a higher gear. "Who? Who other than Malikar's wives, concubines, daughters, servants and I take care of him?"

The question was answer enough. Ghubar would've known if a physician had been treating Malikar. Switching to other concerns Dari asked after his brothers.

"They're well," Ghubar replied seriously. "Kamal is at the qala. Ahmad and Khushal will be home for Nawruz; so will the rest of the family, including Zulfikar's half brother, Zor."

Wrapped in his personal problems Dari had forgotten the Spring celebrations. If he wasn't worrying about his father and his own future, Roxane was stealing his thoughts. He had written he'd be home for the holiday but failed to tell her when because at the time of writing he was unsure. Thinking of past Nawruz festivities he became silent.

At Pustunistan square Ghubar turned north-west passed Zarnegar Park and the onion-shaped dome of Amir Abdur Rahman Khan's mausoleum. He continued along a northern prong through the quiet residential area of Shar-i-Nau. When the road forked at the foot of a hill, crowned by the brilliant Bagh-i-Bala Palace, the old Tadjik skirted it and drove on between two lesser hills to enter the Koh Daman plain. Regarding his passenger, he commented. "Your father hasn't seen a doctor if that's what's troubling you."

"Maybe he can be persuaded."

"Perhaps, but he is as stubborn as your grandfather; Zulfikar did not believe in doctors either. He put his faith in Allah and the amulet you're wearing. Did I ever tell you how he came by it?"

"No," Dari lied partly to humour the old man but he did enjoy the telling. Often he had heard the tale and each time it was different. Though Ghubar's fictitious embellishments were creating a legend somewhere in between lay the truth. Besides a 'yes' would not have discouraged the Tadjik. Resigned to listening he lay back in his seat.

Ghubar was in rare form. A broad grin brightened the driver's scrappy yellow teeth. "It was once a medal awarded for bravery by a British General to Ali Mahmud, your great grandfather, or Zulfikar's father."

Dari smiled. This was a new version. "I have been led to believe the taw'iz was made from a Safi slug."

"True, Zulfikar was wearing the honour over his heart when he was hit. The medal saved his life. Take a look at it. There are flakes of lead embedded in the silver.

Curiously Dari fished the talisman from inside his shirt while Ghubar spoke, "If you look closely you will see a citation."

There was no distinct engraving. The object was roughly circular, dull grey, the size of a silver dollar with a bleb on the inside. Where one might expect a corresponding dent on the outside there was a globular smear of darker grey. Cracks and fissures radiated to its irregular circumference. Possibly there were the numbers 4 and 2 inscribed near the edge but Dari couldn't be sure. "Go on kaka-jan,"

"According to Zulfikar, Ali Mahmud led a brigade of Qizilbash cavalry. They rescued a number of British prisoners being held for ransom in Bamiyan.

Dari looked at the Tadjik doubtfully. "Why should Afghans help the British?"

"You forget. The Qizilbash are not tribesmen. They were mercenaries imported by the Safavids over two hundred years ago. It has been only since Rahman Khan they have gained power and influence in Afghanistan."

Dari's scepticism bested him. "How did you learn about the medal?" he asked.

"Zulfikar told me."

"Are you sure he didn't pinch it? Or Ali Mahmud steal it from a British corpse."

Ghubar was astonished. "I never knew Zulfikar's father; he died before my time. But Zulfikar was honest and just. I believed him. Why shouldn't I? He was kind to me."

"Tell me more about the medal," Dari asked.

"Zulfikar wore it for as long as I knew him. From the day I entered his harem."

"The incident of the bullet. When did it occur?"

"Not long before his death. It was in the early days of a Pushtun Safi revolt. Though the taw'iz saved his life it lost its power and didn't help in the end. Perhaps in changing shape it lost its charm."

Dari pondered Ghubar's supposition and smiled. "Then why give it to me?"

The Tadjik nodded and answered. "In being transferred to another soul it becomes reincarnated."

Dari snickered. "You mean recharged like a battery?"

"Why not?"

Ghubar's zeal was more than Dari could take and he burst into a fit of laughter. When it had subsided he said. "Kaka-jan, I too will wear it as long as I live but only for sentimental reasons. If it brings me luck I will be happy. Tell me again how it happened?"

"The Safis struck as we were approaching the Laghman. Zulfikar was at the head of the column. The force of the bullet took his wind and knocked him off his horse. I had been riding beside him; while he was gasping for air I managed to drag him behind some rocks. The bullet had fragmented and a piece of metal lay beneath his skin. The wound was ragged. I extracted the fragment and sealed it.

"How?" Dari interrupted.

"With my knife and the gun powder I sprinkled into the hole. When the powder had burned I packed the hole with one end of my lungi and wrapped the rest around his chest. It was a flesh wound and not too painful. Later we slipped away in the darkness. He could not get over his good fortune and from then on wore the taw'iz regularly."

"But in the end it didn't help?"

"Correct. He was wearing it two years later when he died in an explosion. The Safis had fled north almost into Nuristan and we were right behind. I was driving the Rolls. A shell blasted us into the air. Praise Allah I was thrown free but Zulfikar died instantly."

"I don't agree kaka-jan. I'd consider my grandfather extremely lucky. His death was instantaneous and heroic; He's probably in paradise. I'd prefer to have mine the same way. Wouldn't you?"

Ghubar took a hand off the wheel and scratched his beard. After a lengthy interval he gave in to Dari's logic. "You may be right. I buried him where he fell and made my way home, leaving Zulfikar where his spirit had left him. The rest of the story you know. I returned to Kapisa to your grieving family and gave you the amulet. You were six at the time."

"Almost six," Dari corrected, "and I've rarely been without it in fifteen years."

CHAPTER NINETEEN

Ghubar drove in silence, giving his young master a chance to question him further, however Dari abstained. After a while the Tadjik asked, "What was it like on the big bird?"

"Out of this world kaka-jan! The plane flew so high I could almost make out the curvature of the earth. Many things below were too small to see. It really is like a big bird; I got the impression the trailing edge of the wings fan out like feathers and reduce air speed, making it possible to land in a shorter distance. Like the hawk you killed so many years ago. Remember, you were teaching me to shoot."

"Yes," the Tadjik grinned, "it would take more than a long rifle to bring down a D.C.6."

Cresting a hill the landrover surprised a large herd of goats prancing down the road. To avoid them Ghubar braked with force and the 'rover' fish-tailed. His full concentration was required to keep the vehicle on the road. Dari, rebounding between the gear box and the door, bumped his head against the frame. Seeing his passenger rub his scalp, Ghubar asked. "Are you alright?"

"Sure kaka-jan. Nothing a neurosurgeon can't fix."

Unable to comprehend, the Tadjik shrugged and returned to his driving. Now and again he glanced at his dozing passenger, thinking of the immense advantages open to the young man. As he regarded Dari's handsome features the truth of having revolved full cycle in the household of Mahmud became more apparent; Zulfikar was close to Dari's age when they first met.

Their relationship began following a squabble between two Tadjik tribes. The winter had been unusually severe and spring did not come soon enough for the Andarabi living north of the Khawak pass. Their sheep and goats, starved of pasture, were allowed to descend upon Panjsheri land. Arguments developed and the angry Panjsheri countered by slaughtering a few sheep. To avenge the loss of their animals the Andarabi returned a few days later. Shooting followed. Remarkably no one was hurt.

The dispute occurred shortly after Zulfikar became tax collector of Parwan province. Tadjik territory came under his jurisdiction and because the hillsmen were remiss in their payments he decided to teach them a lesson on the pretence of ending their argument. It took two days to muster a lashgar of Qizilbash and ride to the seat of the trouble. Unfortunately word preceded them and when the lashgar entered the valley it was ambushed by the combined Tadjik tribes. Resentful of his intentions the Panjsheri and Andarabi set aside their grievances to tackle a common enemy - no central government was going to subjugate them. But their defense was no match for Zulfikar's highly trained cavalry. Though they stuck like leeches the Tadjik were forced to withdraw when their leaders were picked off, and young Ghubar and his mother became prisoners.

He'd never been able to drive those dark days from his memory. During his youth as Zulfikar's personal baccha and stable boy he managed to subdue them. As batman and motorwan they were forgotten. Now in his dotage the old servant looked back upon the beginning with bittersweet memories. His father and uncles had been taken from him before he was old enough to have a lasting image of their faces. Their properties were confiscated. For a few pounds of silver the same land was resold to his mother's relatives who had survived the attack. This fact came to light months later and the discovery rankled. He found himself hating the greedy Panjsheri-Tadjik more than Zulfikar. There was no doubt his captor was ruthless in amassing wealth, but surrounded by the peace and security of the compound, Zulfikar's sensitivity and love were unlimited.

As a prisoner Ghubar was hostile and would have murdered Zulfikar Mahmud and his mother's puzzling attitude was no consolation. Her openness to their abductor was annoying. Ghubar felt neglected, adding jealousy to indignation. 'I'm only doing it for your survival,' she said, when the cause of his whinging became apparent. 'We are his slaves. Act like one or run away. Go ahead. Beg in the streets. Catch birds and sell them in the Charikar bazaar.'

A stunning woman older than her philandering abductor, she had no trouble attracting him nor competing for his lavish attention. Not enough! She wanted more than sex and the trinkets he doled out to mistresses. She wanted a commitment, preferably marriage with all its prerogatives. Still she would settle for a concubine's assignation as a compromise. Cohabitation with power in any role bestowed more influence and protection than she had as a peasant's wife. To achieve, she chose to stay out of her abductor's bed as long as she dared but not out of touch. It worked. Her air of not to be had was plain aphrodisiac. Her slanted eyes scorned his dominance with the haughtiness of a queen. He could have taken her easily at any time and with self-righteous justification but Zulfikar was an honourable man.

All the while she extracted favours for her son - a useless exercise for Ghubar performed well on his own. Indeed he became his captor's personal baccha. From the childless women of the harem he learned of Zulfikar's fancies, particularly politeness and expediency can go a long way. Charm can open new doors and become an exit for misunderstanding.

Ghubar made up to his captor and the discomfort gradually subsided. Mistrust gave way to pleasure when Zulfikar allowed him to ride. 'You'll make a fine horseman my boy,' his master had said and in sincerity added. 'An officer, perchance a job in the business.'

'A futile hope!' his mother had declared, 'like leading a donkey, because Ghubar you are Tadjik. You do not have a drop of Qizilbash or Mohammedzai blood in you. Never will you be accepted into the Amir's cavalry or given an administrative post in Zulfikar's new trading company. To achieve you must marry into the family.' But his mother's plan had no guarantee.

Among Zulfikar's increasing offspring Ghubar found the competition difficult. Still there was always the unforeseen. Allah might have a treat in store for him. In fact he was forced to rely entirely on Allah because fate intervened to thwart his mother's plans.

It happened during the Kafiristan campaign. Zulfikar was recalled to lead a brigade and her chance to become his fourth wife was lost forever. Tahmina, the flaxen haired Nuristani, won out. Zulfikar brought her back from the war, toting Malikar, their new born son, on his shoulders.

The Nuristan conquest was despicable, Ghubar had gathered, eavesdropping while sitting cross-legged in the anteroom waiting to serve veteran campaigners.

In his story-telling Zulfikar would pause, smiling whether or not his squat sibling was among the listeners. 'It was Zor who saved most of the Nuristani, my brave little half brother.' To the trusted he would bare his soul. 'I'm tired of fighting the Amir's battles. In nine years I've ridden from Herat to Badakshan, Zabul to Fariab, herding thousands of conquered tribesmen from one end of Afghanistan to the other, first as a stable boy - an exciting time,' he'd waffle. 'Zor and I were always together. We went around the bazaars stealing melons and eggs for the Colonel's horse, and we'd pick up a few things besides ticks and lice.' 'Women,' Zor would interrupt, adding, 'But you were better at it than I.'

The details of how Zulfikar acquired Tahmina were never mentioned. Whether she was abducted like Ghuber's mother or given to Zulfikar by a grateful father, the Tadjik servant never found out.

After the Khan's death Zulfikar Mahmud accumulated parcels of land in Gulbahar and Kapisa, presumably in the name of the new Amir, Habibullah. From a practical point of view the properties were his as long as he continued to collect taxes and had the strength to hold them.

Upon a prominence overlooking the Ghorband and Panjsher rivers he built his qala and tucked in his harem. Other than routine policing of feuding tribesmen he could apply himself to trade and rear his youngest son.

Bonny and adventuresome Malikar was a child of five when Ghubar was placed in charge of him. Ghubar liked him from the start and cultivated a relationship with patience and generosity, the same response Zulfikar's kindness had induced in him. Consequently the Tadjik slave was no longer treated as a lowly baccha but a friend and companion. When Zulfikar took his son hunting and fishing, Ghubar was there. When they went to visit Zor at the Bamiyan compound Ghubar, with little Malikar on his shoulders, was allowed to explore the ruins, scale the Buddhist cliffs, dive into the cold blue water of Band-i-Amir and sun themselves on the calcium deposits.

Till then the Tadjik felt he was leading a charmed life. Allah had been most beneficent. His life could not have been better. Even his scheme to marry into the family was shaping up. He had matured into an amiable handsome young man, turning the heads of most of the women in the harem.

Guriz, the daughter of Zulfikar's first wife, was one of them but her guile was Ghubar's undoing. She enticed him into a sexually compromising position and they were caught in the act, unfortunately by her half brother Zabuli, resentful of the Tadjik's popularity. Zabuli had his truckling servants overpower Ghubar and before anyone could intercede the Tadjik slave was castrated.

Zulfikar was trading hides in India. When he returned and heard of the calamity he was enraged, not because of the dishonourable conduct of his daughter; Guriz was suspected of disgracing the family for some time with transgressions worthy of stoning. The evil deed of his son tore him apart. If Zabuli had not fled to Iran, Zulfikar would have given him the same treatment.

The old Tadjik turned right at the traffic box in the centre of Charikar. Only twenty miles to go, he judged. Beyond the Panjsher river lay Gulbahar. How many times had he passed it's wall - he couldn't say. 'We're almost there,' he whispered, realizing his charge was sleeping.

Half an hour later they had crossed the river and were approaching the qala. Built on a rocky summit it was an imposing structure with a tower at each corner and a keep rising from their midst. The landrover advanced along the powdery road up to a massive wooden entrance. A turbaned lookout, recognizing it, descended from the crenellated parapet to open the gate.

In the spacious courtyard Dari, awakened by a raspy handbrake, made for the entrance to the qala. Before reaching the twin doors they parted and a baccha appeared. Ghubar lingered outside until Dari's belongings had been taken in and the dusty vehicle washed. A nap was on his mind and he headed for his quarters.

Restraint chilled the vestibule. Dari's stepmothers with maids and household staff welcomed him in subdued tones.

Malikar's first wife, Halima, answered questions regarding her husband's health. Gesturing toward the great hall, she said, "He had another of his spells this morning and is resting on the couch. Ghubar was with him at the time."

A lofty room opened off the central hall. Entering it, Dari smelled smoke and heard the crackle of dried wood. Malikar was lying under a heavy blanket on a couch in front of the fire; he sat up suddenly and frowned. "The student has returned! What for?"

Dari wanted to say, you sahib. I have come to be of help, but remained silent knowing his father's pride. Before he could think of an answer Malikar asked, "How do you like Beirut?"

Dealing with this question was simpler. "Fine, sahib. I'm enjoying medicine and am certain I've made the right choice. It is not particularly difficult but the amount of memorization is wicked."

Malikar had lost weight and strength. The dapper flamboyance had faded and his scant hair was as white as the Koh-i-Baba. Allah had been kind bestowing him with four sons and nine

Do Unto Others 193

daughters all healthy and successful. Dari was the last and still unsettled. Attempting to growl, his voice became little more than a hoarse whisper. "You're not planning on giving it up!"

"No, sahib, never."

Malikar nodded and a faint smile graced his thin face. "I'm very happy," he smiled, grateful of how benevolent Allah had been. An intelligent man he valued higher education. His affluence had sired influence, enabling him to obtain admission of his first three sons to English schools and from there, university. Kamal had studied commerce and finance at Oxford and was capably running the trading business. His second son Ahmad graduated in law from Cambridge. Ahmad, a member of the Ministry of Justice, had been appointed to the Constitutional Committee and was busy completing a draft of the new constitution. Khushal went to Farnsborough where he learned to fly and was piloting for Ariana. Dari the youngest was studying medicine.

Yes, he thought, Allah has been bountiful. Profits afforded shares in the Bank-i-Melli and dividends were invested in his family. His own future hopefully would be paradise. In his entire life he had not purposely harmed a soul.

Malikar had become a connoisseur, a collector and patron of the Arts. Slowly he rose and turning toward a glass encasement, covering an entire end wall of the room, fumbled for a light switch. Illumination flooded the shelves, full of artifacts. "There is a fortune here Darius," he said. "But we don't need it. When you finish all of my sons will have become educated and should be able to provide for themselves. Marriage arrangements for your sisters have turned out better than satisfactory."

He picked up a carved elephant tusk and rubbed it against his cheek. "Knowledge is far more valuable than these material treasures," he continued. "No one can steal it. Artifacts can disappear over night, reducing their owner to ignominy no further ahead than the earth where he and his treasures began."

Malikar Mahmud paused momentarily contemplative, then added. "But everyone should enjoy these beauties. They should go to the Museum."

While speaking he was standing, facing his son. Suddenly his eyelids fluttered and he folded unconsciously. Dari caught him and carried him to the couch. Once recumbent the elder Mahmud came around quickly and quite surprisingly carried on talking, as if there were no interruption."Yes. Don't you think it is a good idea?"

Perturbed by the whole sequence Dari had lost the thread of conversation. "What?" he asked.

"Giving these relics to the museum."

"Oh yes, if you wish," Dari agreed, rearranging his father's blanket. Suddenly, he decided to bring his feelings into the open and brook the consequences. "But there is something more important I'd like to discuss with you," he proposed, while choosing his words. "I want to find the cause of these spells you're having. They may be curable."

Without waiting for a reply Dari went to his room and returned with a stethoscope and sphygmomanometer.

"What have you there?" Malikar asked.

"An instrument for measuring blood pressure."

When Malikar did not object Dari wrapped the cuff around his father's arm and moved the pressure gauge so he could easily read it. "Nothing wrong there," he commented when the test was finished. "Now let me listen to your chest."

Malikar reluctantly undid a few buttons and opened his shirt. "If my pressure is normal," he remarked, "how can there be anything wrong with my heart?"

"Quiet," Dari cautioned, positioning his stethoscope. "I can't hear when you're talking." There was a swishing sound over the precordium radiating to the base of the neck. Dari's eyes narrowed in concentration. After a moment he spoke encouragingly. "Sahib, you can be helped. There is reliable treatment for your problem. You must see a cardiologist."

"No my son. My fate is in the hands of Allah. I'm prepared to die. My time is coming soon."

"You are being selfish, sahib. You are not considering anyone else, especially what you have to give of yourself. Choose death and you take an irretrievable step. Stick around awhile," Dari smiled. "We enjoy your company."

There was silence throughout the rest of the examination. "I think you have stenosis or narrowing of your aortic valve, where the blood leaves your heart to circulate through the body. You should have a chest x-ray and an electrocardiogram. There are good doctors at the Avicenna who could tell you more. One arrived on the plane with me. Part of the Medicare team, he is an orthopaedic surgeon and

Do Unto Others

invited me to attend rounds. In exchange I have offered to show him Kabul. Heart disease is not his specialty but probably he can refer you to the right person."

Malikar was staring above the fireplace at the mounted head of a Urial. Two saber-like horns cradled a Winchester carbine, only ten pounds fully loaded. One more shot, he thought, one more trophy would be marvellous. His son's advice attracted him. If he could hang on a bit longer, watch his grandchildren mature, take in the natural wonders of heaven and earth, hunt again or fly his plane. He smiled, it would be interesting to learn just how astute Dari was as a diagnostician. If his youngest son was correct and something could be done to prolong his life Allah should not mind. There was nothing in the Shariat to condemn this choice.

Dari discerned a gathering interest in his father's eyes. "I have seen an operation performed at the American University Hospital in Beirut by a cardiac surgeon. If the aortic valve is giving you trouble it can be replaced. The operation is serious but with all the modern equipment and in this man's hands the success rate is quite high. You really shouldn't pass up the opportunity, sahib."

Malikar looked up at his son. He had heeded advice from Ahmad, Kamal and Khusal. Why not from Dari. "You're right," he nodded. "It can't do any harm." Then he smiled, "but tell me what really brings you home?"

"I'm transferring to the University of Kabul."

"Why do you want to do that?" Malikar frowned.

Dari blushed and the ridges on his father's forehead flattened. A shrewd smile drew one corner of Malikar's mouth and he added, "I see, you want to be closer to Roxane?"

"Well - er - maybe." If Malikar were dying he did not want to spend his time elsewhere. Before he could explain Malikar started to speak again.

"You knew her father, Mir, my best friend."

"Ah yes, Mir Ghulum. That was long ago but I remember her mother's second wedding to Rishtya better. It was the beginning of many good times we've had."

No sooner had Dari commented than his last trip to Bamiyan came to mind. The one ending in a nightmare of disillusion. He cursed under his breath. The stump had started to ache again as it did whenever he thought of it. 'Phantom pain,' a surgeon called it. Repressed anger bottled within him began to simmer. He needed action, a work out or an assignment deadline. If not it would get worse.

While he was recovering from surgery hatred kept him going. But after the leg healed he felt the same hatred sapped his strength. In the past when the dark mood appeared he would withdraw to be alone in a cloistered place, alone to plan his revenge, his catharsis. How to accomplish this became a problem. The chances of running into Best were as remote as having his foot restored. Busy studying, trying to find solutions to more solvable problems had left little time to brood. Now that the mood was upon him again he'd give big Herk some exercise."If you don't mind, sahib, I have a few things to do."

As Dari stomped toward the stables the pain began to lessen. In the morning he would take his father to Dr. Lindsay for an opinion. Unless their conversation on the plane had been fantasy the man must know Dr. Best. "Perhaps now he had a chance to get even." Dari smiled, he felt better with each step and began to whistle.

CHAPTER TWENTY

Janet Schocker felt a cold spurt wet the crotch of her panties and run down her thigh. She crossed her legs and swung around to find Beecher on one knee hiking her skirt with a 20cc syringe.

"You bastard!" She giggled, pulling the mask from her pretty face. "What do you think you're doing?"

"Cooling you off baby." He laughed coarsely. "Must be on your toes when you're working with peachy Beechie."

She deigned a "ha, ha," whipping her soapy fingers at his eyes, and made a grab for the syringe.

He was quick to react and hung on so tightly neither of her prying hands could wrest it from him. She got inside his grip and encircling arms.

Teasingly, he switched the syringe to the other hand and loomed over her like a tunnel of surf as she spun, pressing her butt backwards and forcing his hips against the scrub-room wall to restrain him with the grinding action of her rump. "Give up yet?" she asked.

Beecher was nowhere near giving up. He was enjoying every second.

Schocker, a size larger than petite, was short waisted, wide in the shoulders, broad in the beam and fairly well endowed up front. She fitted into him nicely. For reasons unexplained and not without snide comments from the other operating room nurses, she chose to wear petite back-fastening gowns which popped open with the slightest hunch of her shoulders to expose a delicate spine spanned by colourful lingerie. This evening she wore a bold fuchsia brassiere with a metallic sheen.

Beecher spied it and let go of the syringe. "Okay I give up. You win," he conceded.

"Thank you Sir," she said, accepting the syringe, and proceeded to shove her dark brown bangs under her O.R. cap. Provocatively she twisted her head and smiled.

Beecher wore an imbecilic grin. Something else was about to happen, she suspected while re-preparing her hands and knew as quickly as it did. There was a light tug, a snap, and her breasts sagged.

"Pretty neat!" Schocker exclaimed; "and with only three fingers. My! You're skillful doctor."

"Thank you," he replied, grinning lecherously.

Janet moved to a neutral corner and brought her hands up behind her, the syringe held in one of them, and tried to re-hook her bra.

In a stride Beecher was half way across the room. "I'll help you," he offered.

"No way, big boy."

"Ah come on," he coaxed, continuing to advance.

"No," she insisted and produced the syringe. What was left of its contents discharged in his face.

"Hey! What's up you two?" Duggan called from the theatre. "We're ready and waiting."

"Coming," Beecher hollered back and fumbled through a chrome-plated jar above the sink for a cap and mask. As he put them on he winked at Schocker. "I'll fix you later doll."

"Delighted doctor. Just tell me where and when."

"Behind the cathedral at dawn."

Janet giggled. "Pistol or sword?"

"I'll put it to you anyway you wish and in any position."

"My, you are a dirty old man."

"Half right."

Janet roared, "So you're old but not dirty?" She had refastened her bra. When she leaned close to the tap to rinse her forearms it showed again. The look in his eyes told her he had seen it. "Sorry," she smiled. "I meant to put adhesive tape across the back of my gown but I forgot." Raising her hands to let the water drip from her forearms permitted the gap to close. She moved toward the doorway.

"How about we go for a ride later?" Beecher spoke in a near whisper.

Schocker was peering through the glass into the operating room. Her head lifted thoughtfully, as one elbow pushed against the door. "Maybe," she said, without glancing back."

Dick Duggan thought Agnes Bennett resembled a figurine, the high stepping ballerina he'd given his wife for Christmas. She was lying flat on her back on a fracture table, her arms outstretched and her left thigh and knee flexed as if she were about to pirouette on her right toes. The stance was to accommodate an x-ray tube, directed at the inside of her right hip.

The old lady looked up at him and pulled at the lower end of her hospital gown, unable to lengthen it as far as her naked hips. She disliked Duggan. He'd withheld things from her. 'You'll only feel a little prick,' he warned but said nothing about the possibility of a sudden shock-like sensation in her legs when he withdrew the long needle from her lower back. She was lying on her right side then, and held for a few moments before being rolled onto her back. When Duggan felt the spinal anaesthetic had taken he asked she be transferred to the fracture table. An orderly helped the doctors move her; they'd proceeded with surprising care. But the ache in her left hip remained. It had bothered her while her outstretched arms were being confined to boards and Dr. Best was flexing her left knee over the x-ray tube. Agnes mentioned it to him and understood his reply, 'Don't fret my dear, the pain will go away once the anaesthesia has taken.' But it was still there.

She lifted her head from the small pillow nurse Adams had provided and saw she was trapped between two vertical posts. Both were padded, one parting her labia, the other, pressed against her right side, kept her on the table. Her left elbow had an IV attached to it and was secured to an arm board. After wriggling out of the confining strap, her right upper extremity was free to explore and she reached for the second post feeling the top of it below the flare of her right hip. Lifting her head a little higher she could see her extended right knee and the adjustable stirrup gripping her foot. There was no sensation in it but the right lower extremity looked as if it were being stretched.

"Feeling any pain now Agnes?" Dr. Best had reappeared and was standing beside her, wiping his hands on a green towel.

"Yes," she told him. "In my left hip," adding, "Please take the tube from under my knee." He was not listening and turned to the nurse, "If you don't mind Adams, re-strap her right hand." He winked at Agnes, "Nothing to worry about my dear. When you're back in your room you'll feel fine."

Beecher almost grasped her hand before remembering he'd already scrubbed. His eyes crinkled warmly about two feet from hers. "How did you come to break your hip Agnes?"

Mrs. Bennett retained a fair portion of her faculties in spite of having received a dose of premedication. She answered dully, having difficulty articulating. "I tripped over Patsy, or maybe the doormat. We'd just come in from a walk."

"Who's Patsy?"

"My Pomeranian," she replied, as if he should have known. Everyone else of importance knew her darling Patsy, then she rationalized it was the first time she'd ever met him. How should he know of her dog? She smiled adding, "My neighbour has her now. She'll keep her until I get out of the hospital. How long will that be doctor?"

"Two weeks maybe. As soon as your stitches come out."

"Will I be able to fend for myself. I live alone."

"Certainly. The physios will have you walking in a few days."

Dr. Duggan cut off any further questions by placing an oxygen mask over Mrs. Bennett's nose.

"Dick, when you have a minute," Beecher directed. "Give her an analgesic,"

"I already have. She's had 50 mgm of demerol plus phenergan." Duggan's reply was sharp. He was fed up. There had been too many delays. In his opinion the operating room was not the place for a social visit nor to be discussing a patient's prognosis. The woman should've had her surgery hours ago. She'd been seen in Emergency by an associate late in the afternoon. After receiving the x-ray report he was notified at the clinic. That was about 5.15 pm. when he was seeing his last patient and would've been free to do it before supper. Best had been consulted, and confirmed the x-ray technicians findings, indicating he'd tee up the case. Duggan went home to eat; later he phoned to learn the hip pinning had been scheduled for 8 pm. Thinking the surgery wouldn't take more than an hour and he could be home by nine to watch the end of TV hockey, Duggan had arrived twenty minutes early. To his disappointment Paolone had booked a bowel obstruction and the hip pinning had been bumped. Paolone preferred to work with his own anaesthesiologist, so Duggan and the hip pinning had to wait. Then Joe had run into a belly full of pus which required a cleansing of the whole room when he'd finished. Adams had called Mrs. Starling the night supervisor about setting up one of the other major rooms but the night supervisor had declined. Thus it was 10 pm. by the time Duggan was able to inject the spinal anaesthetic, another ten minutes to set up the x-ray machines, ten more to take and develop the check films and fifteen waiting for Beecher to quit clowning around in the scrub room. Yes Duggan was bothered and about to tell the surgeon to mind his own 'effen business' but the patient was wide awake. Instead he grumbled. "She'll be all right. Just get on with the job!"

While Schocker was helping him into his gown and gloves Beecher asked, "Where's Clayton? He was supposed to assist."

"He phoned while you were scrubbing," Adams ventured. "Told me to tell you the clinic was full and it will take him till midnight to finish house calls."

"What's Byers doing?" Beecher asked.

"It's his night off."

Typical, Beecher thought. It was no different in the evening than during the day. G.P.s just weren't interested in assisting unless there was an ulterior motive like getting out of the house for some reason or other. Lindsay had warned him. 'No matter how anxious you are to get going never start a case until all the help you need is present. Like x-rays. They're important to have around even if you might not use them.' Lindsay never seemed to have any problems. The men who referred him cases were mostly in solo practice, old-timers whose patients were almost family.

"Then we'll have to manage on our own," Beecher smiled. He'd learned during his residency doing without an assistant was no handicap, particularly when pinning hips. It was the one operation attending consultants turned over to the house staff except if the patient happened to be one of their friends or a V.I.P. Best had done a fair number of them on his own. As long as there was a scrub nurse available to hold retractors the operation was a piece of cake.

He walked over to the view box and took another look at the films. In neither of the two views could he see the faintest suggestion of a crack. The upper end of the thigh bone was canted downward at its normal angle in the A.P. film and tilted very slightly forward in the side view. The ball fit into the socket perfectly.

Duggan had followed and peering over Beecher's shoulder commented. "Looks too good to be true."

Best feigned modesty when he saw Schocker and Adams had come for a closer look. "Yes. Not bad," he agreed. "Now we'll slam in a nail."

Adams had seen a lot of hip operations during the war. Before Dr. Lindsay introduced the Jewitt device with its angled and fused plate the general surgeons had used a two piece gadget held together by a bolt and lock washer, the nail and plate sections being named after their inventors. "What kind of a nail do you need?" She asked.

"A Jewitt."

Adams had been pinning hips on the three till eleven shift for years. "I've put everything in, including the prostheses in case you change your mind," she sounded as if she dared him to do just that.

Beecher did not appreciate her wit nor her practicality and ignored her as he stood baffled by the post reduction films.

"How can you tell which apparatus to use if you can't see a break in the bone?" Duggan asked.

"I saw it on her original x-rays, the ones taken in Emergency when she was admitted. The break is through the trochanters."

The technician Stan Pecak had been listening and before Dr. Duggan had a chance to ask him pulled the original films out of a folder and put them on the view box. The break was clearly visible on both views at the tip of a lead arrow stuck-on the film by the technician. In one corner below the date was the letter 'R' indicating the views were of the right hip.

Beecher decided to sit for the operation so Adams placed a couple of swivel stools beside the table and adjusted their height. With Schocker seated to his left, Dr. Best's right hand was unimpeded.

Adams watched while the skin was incised for a distance of five inches, commencing at a point about two inches below the joint and extending through a layer of fatty tissue along the outside of the thigh.

When the muscles were exposed Beecher separated their fibres in line with the skin incision by bluntly tearing them lengthwise. A relatively less bloodletting procedure, until the surgeon decided to take up the knife and cut an artery next to the bone. Schocker was close against him, pulling the wound apart with a pair of deep right-angle retractors and the front of her gown and Beecher's shoulder were splattered.

"A branch of the circumflex femoral," he declared when it had been clamped and tied off, adding, "Now for the cobras and a guide block." Once the S-shaped retractors had been inserted and stretched the muscles aside, the block was held against the upper femoral shaft. Into one of its three rows of holes, angled to correspond with the average downward tilt of the femoral neck, a wire was inserted and tapped home with a mallet. Beecher, listening intently to the sound of each rap, stopped when a solid thud indicated the wire had invaded the harder hip socket. "Okay, time for x-rays," he announced.

Schocker shoved the instrument table out of the way and covered the wound with a sterile towel. Doing the lateral view first, Beecher received a cassette from Pecak, placed it in a sterile cloth cover and clamped it against the post next to the flare of the hip. Then he stepped behind a protective screen with Duggan and the two nurses.

The technician donned a lead apron and moved as far away from his machine as the cord would allow before pressing the switch. There was a buzz, and another minutes later when the A.P. view was shot.

Duggan watched Pecak scoot for the dark room, hoping the result would be satisfactory. There had been too many delays as it was. He checked Mrs. Bennett's blood pressure and pulse again, reconfirmed she was comfortable and opened a copy of 'Time magazine'.

Adams and Schocker rechecked the instruments to make sure nothing was missing while Beecher paced slowly back and forth.

Pecak was back from the dark room in six minutes with two views of the upper end of the femur at right angles to each other. The only difference from the previous set was the presence of the quide wire about one foot long extending from eight inches outside the bone, up the middle of the head and neck of the femur. "Perfect!" he said, holding them in front of the view box by their drying frames. "You couldn't have placed it any better with radar."

Best snickered. "Interesting comment Stan. Someday we'll be using something similar, a T.V. monitor."

"Really!" Adams exclaimed. She had seen scarred and cancerous fingers from fluoroscopy. "Won't that be dangerous?"

"No, the amount of radiation will be much less; a lead screen won't be necessary." Beecher laughed, adding, "no more slap and tickle with the anaesthetist."

"Ah, that'll take the sport out of it Beech." Duggan, thinking his long evening was drawing to a close was in brighter spirits. "Did you hear that Agnes," he said. "You should've waited five years to break your hip. You would have been a T.V. star."

Mrs. Bennett knew Dr. Duggan was speaking to her but the last dose of medication was annoying. "Please give me a glass of water," she rasped. "My mouth is so dry I can't talk."

"Not a glass but you can suck on this," the anaesthetist replied, placing a wet cloth on her lips. Turning to Best who was still admiring the x-rays, he remarked, wryly. "Okay Beech, finish the gah gah and get it over. I've missed the Eleven O'clock News, maybe there's time for the Late Show."

Schocker had rearranged the instrument table and was waiting to hand Best a ruler when he slipped into his seat beside her. Their knees met deliberately and she pressed a satiny thigh against his.

"How would you like to pin this one?" he asked once the appropriate length of nail had been determined and a threaded driver screwed to it. "See," he said holding the device up to the overhead lamp. "There's a hole clear through from the butt end of the driver to the sharp end of the nail. That's to accommodate the guide wire." Beecher fitted the nail over the wire and twirled it like an old fashioned car crank. "This is the blade section," he went on, "the angle it maintains with the nail corresponds to the angle between the shaft and the neck of the thigh bone. Notice the holes in the blade. They're for the screws." His eyes gleamed. "If you've never screwed hard bone before, Schocker, you're in for a treat."

Duggan rolled his eyes at Adams. "For Christ's sake, Beech, stop frigging around and let's get on with it."

"Hmm," Best coughed and finished explaining. "The screws fasten the blade-plate to the femoral shaft." Then he introduced the point of the nail to the outer layer of bone supporting it with his left hand while his right kept the plate parallel to the thigh.

"Grab the mallet and give the butt end of the driver a sharp crack. Once it's on course, hammer it all the way in."

"I'd prefer you do it Dr. Best," Janet's voice was low and even.

Beecher reached impatiently behind her for the mallet lying on the instrument table. He was not sitting in the centre of his stool and the seat tilted slightly on the swivel, tipping him enough to misjudge his reach. The mallet was knocked to the floor.

"Holy Christ!" Duggan hissed. No one else said a word.

Adams made a brief assessment of the instrument table. Nothing else, other than a couple of haemostats had fallen.

Beecher scowled at her angrily. "Get me another."

"There isn't another one sterile. I'll have to flash this."

"Don't you have one packaged?"

"No."

"Why not?" Beecher demanded. Several times he had investigated the storeroom to see what was available and discovered certain instruments were packaged and shelved for expediency. "I don't understand."

Adams picked up the remaining fallen articles wiped them on her skirt and paused at the door. "Dr. Lindsay borrowed the extra set of osteotomes to take to Afghanistan. The mallet was with them."

"Who gave him permission?" Beecher asked.

Adams shrugged.

Duggan took a long thoughtful look at his colleague. The dolt was shifting the blame for his clumsiness."It was probably the sister's Governing Board," he suggested. "Lindsay's one of their chosen few."

"If so they had no right without consulting the other surgeons." Beecher sounded like a peevish schoolboy.

Schocker decided to throw her hat in the ring.

"Why not? It's their hospital. I guess they have the right to lend instruments. Besides she appended, "It's for a worthy cause."

"What?" Beecher asked.

"Going off to help in the third world. I wish he'd taken me."

Duggan lowered his magazine and sniggered. "You're not his type."

"Why is it you guys think women are good for only one thing? There must be plenty a nurse can do and it would be fun to travel to another part of the world."

"That last bit sums it up." Duggan smiled. "The travel appeals to you."

There was no point in arguing with these two, Schocker thought. Basically they had her tagged. She was a fun-loving type who wouldn't mind a little sight-seeing. What was wrong with gaining a bit of enjoyment in exchange for doing something worthwhile? Besides the work had to be more exciting than her present job and she wouldn't have to put up with their shenanigans. No matter, their behaviour was partly her own fault; she did like to provoke them. "I think it's admirable that's all."

Beecher scoffed. "You mean Lindsay's trip to Afghanistan?"

"Yes. I admire him for it. Everyone should."

"Not me."

"Why not?"

"I got it out of my system years ago." Beecher's tone was degrading. "Third world conditions aren't for me. I'll take civilization and everything it has to offer anytime. Lindsay should know better. When I went there in the mid fifties conditions were so primitive there was little one could do."

Her question was an exclamation. "You went to Afghanistan!"

"Yes. Right after my internship."

"On a trip or to work?"

"As a medical missionary."

Janet was doubtful and laughed. Dr. Best did not fit the role. She was about to tell him in a respectful way, knowing how far to go with teasing, when Adams arrived with the steaming hot mallet and began to cool it in a kidney basin.

Andy Cruikshank was on the phone in Emergency, trying to raise the switch board. He had dialled several times with no result. Standing beside him, nervously tapping a ball point pen, Dr. David Bagley looked concerned as he contemplated an emergency aneurysm.

"Damn and to hell!" Crooky growled, slamming the receiver into it's cradle. "Come on let's go."

They met the operator at the elevator, a tea cup in her hand.

"Why the hell don't you plug in your phone?"

"Sorry Dr. Cruikshank. I've just this minute come on. Didn't Violet answer?" She asked without thinking. "She should be there."

Why the three till eleven operator had not waited for her replacement to show was not Crooky's problem. He had an old patient shocked by an abdomen painfully distended with blood. The man was still in x-ray where they'd left him following an aortogram.

"Who's the night supervisor?"

"I heard it was Starling."

"Where is she?"

"I don't know. I told you Dr. Cruikshank, I just came on."

"Find her. We have to operate immediately."

Both elevator cars arrived at the same time. Bagley stepped inside the nearest and held it.

"Tell her," Crooky called, "We'll need six units of blood and a lab technician. Also to meet us in the O.R."

The doors closed and the car began to rise. Crooky's eyes were on the floor. "How many aortectomies have you done?" he asked.

Dave looked down at the wisp of white hair on Crooky's pink scalp and grunted. "To be honest, on my own not many, maybe half a dozen. Not having a senior cardiovascular surgeon around to help, I still need a second pair of skilled hands. You will assist?"

Crooky felt the elevator stop as they reached the fifth floor. "Do you think I'd run out on you?"

"No. I'm sure you won't but it did happen to me once and I had an awful time. The patient bled out, right on the table."

"Where 'bouts?"

"A small town in West Virginia. My assistant had to see his lawyer and the lawyer would only see him if he came right away. Seems he delivered a baby with cerebral palsy superimposed on Down's syndrome and he was being blamed for it. He and I helped each other in the O.R. frequently. The kid died. Actually a blessing as the boy was a very ugly sight. He was not only a musculo-skeletal cripple but had two reasons for being mentally retarded as well."

"Barely into my case - in fact we were scrubbing - my assistant excused himself. Apparently, the plaintiff's lawyer claimed the infant was not properly resuscitated and had an expert witness to substantiate their argument. Contrary to Steven Leacock's definition of an expert, this 'son-of-a-bitch' was a jealous competitor from downtown. It would have been best if the child had never been conceived. Theoretically it was the parents' fault - they provided the genes. That's when I decided to come home. Seems like all the docs down there are too busy covering their asses to help each other."

"Having him run out on me probably didn't matter. My patient likely would have died anyway. If you have to operate on aortic aneurysms the mortality rate is a lot higher when one has to insert a prosthesis as an emergency procedure."

Bagley had been talking all the while they were changing into scrub suits. There was no one to be seen; voices floated from a room down the hall.

Crooky opened the intercom. Whatever was happening in O.R.3 was creating plenty of hilarity. "Could we have a nurse right away?" he shouted.

"Who's that?"

"Cruikshank. What's going on in there?"

"A little ole' hip pinning Crooky. Whatcha got?"

Andy recognized Best's voice. He had invigilated all of the six cases Beecher had to do under supervision. Overlooking the question he fired one of his own.

"How long you gonna be?"

"Five minutes." Duggan broke in. "Come have a look. A perfect reduction. We can't even see the fracture line."

Adams materialized. Before Andy could turn off the intercom she asked, "You have something urgent Dr. Cruikshank?"

"Aneurysm. I'm afraid it can't wait until you've cleaned up in there. We'll have to start in another room."

"Have you spoken to Mrs. Starling?"

"No, where is she?"

"With a patient in severe acidosis on the third floor."

"You'll have to call in a second team."

"But I don't have the authority Dr. Cruikshank. You'll have to talk to either Starling or Sister Bernadette."

"Well do me a big favour and find Starling." Andy was becoming agitated. Starling would get an earful if he contacted her himself. She had been present when his case was admitted and knew it would likely go to surgery. Leaving Bagley behind to take care of the details he strolled to O.R. 3.

"Now lets see this perfect nail you're bragging about," he called from the door.

Best nodded and left his stool. Sidestepping the fracture table he lumbered over to the view box. The films were resting on the floor, leaning against the wall. "Pick them up," he said grinning at Crooky. "They're all there. Have a look."

Crooky didn't have to sort them out. The technician had numbered them from first to last. There were four sets. He put up the fourth and final A.P. and Lateral views. Sure enough there wasn't a fracture line to be seen. Hard to believe, Andy thought, and started working backwards until he came to the original set taken in Emergency. The A.P. of this pair of films was larger and clearly revealed the whole pelvis to include both hips. He checked the marker and found the broken hip was indeed the one with the 'R' on it. The break was below the articulation, a long spiralling line extended down

Do Unto Others 209

the shaft a distance of three to four inches. He went back to the final A.P. film and held it alongside the original. Something was missing. A small round calcification next to the bone of the broken hip seen in the original A.P. but missing throughout the subsequent films.

"What do you make of this?" he asked pointing at the upper outside of the bone. Here you see it. Here you don't."

Beecher did not immediately connect the significance of Crooky's observation with the splendid reduction he had obtained. "Calcification in the bursa," he replied smartly.

"Probably in the tendon," Andy corrected. The point Best failed to grasp; the calcification was a natural marker and didn't jive with the lead marker placed by the technician. To Crooky it was evident the 'R' had been mistakenly placed on the left side. If Best had pinned the wrong hip it was better Best find out himself. The consequences were too serious to ignore. Eventually Crooky would have to give his opinion and it was better here than in court.

While Beecher returned to the table and finished closing the wound Crooky went to look for the patient's chart. He found it at the head of the table, stuffed under a pillow. Clayton's notes were skimpy. He had recorded her chief complaint as a painful hip but didn't specify which side; all he had covered in his physical examination was the heart and lungs. Routine blood and urine checks were ordered along with a type and cross-match for two units of blood. There was nothing written by Dr. Best. Andy then turned to the patient's chart and found under 'medications administered' '50 mgm of demerol given for severe pain in left hip.'

"Dr. Best," Crooky asked, feeling surly but keeping himself in tow. "Did you examine this patient?"

"Certainly." Beecher's reply was prompt and sounded indignant.

"Then where are your notes?"

"I haven't had time to write them."

"Was she complaining of pain on the left side? The reason I ask is the nurses recorded they gave her demerol for pain in the left hip."

Beecher was about to ask what he meant when he remembered Mrs. Bennett had also complained to him of pain in her left hip and he had not seen her before Duggan had given the spinal. He had not examined her nor correlated her complaints with any physical or x-ray findings. As he thought of the operation itself there had been no haematoma. In all the intertrochanteric fractures he had pinned there was a collection of blood at the fracture site. In most of them he had encountered the break directly. He put down the needle holder and went back to the view box. He stared at the films growing more dumbstruck. It couldn't be but there it was, a tattling speck of calcium and the stupid technician had put the 'R' marker on the wrong side. Why had he not examined the woman himself? Being too busy was no excuse. If he had the evidence would've been there - shortening of the leg with a rolled out foot.

"Shit!" he shouted, "shit, shit, shit!"

CHAPTER TWENTY-ONE

Moira Finan kept important news till last. Her superior Patty Goleski listened patiently as the Glaswegian rambled on about who had required oxygen, pain medication, repeat sedation, the bed pan or just plain tender loving care. Five patients apparently had a good night or rather they did not bother her.

"Did you look in on them?" Mrs. Goleski asked.

"Not since I came on shift at eleven," Moira answered pushing a black lock away from her freckled face.

"Then how do you know? They could be dead in their beds."

The superior's two assistants smiled and tried to hold back the snickers. Moira caught them and fumed with vexation. "They were all sleeping soundly," she replied. "Not once did a light go on. I'm sure they wouldn't have appreciated my waking them."

The answer was insufficient. Night nurse duty was mainly vigilance and Patty was about to chew her out. Miss Finan's voice rose with spite.

"What I was about to tell you Mrs. Goleski," she explained, harshly pronouncing her superior's name, "is we had two bloody admissions during the night and I was busy running my tail off."

"Well why didn't you say so?"

Finan chose to ignore Goleski's question. She had a mind to demand an immediate apology but it could wait. Once the day staff heard the juicy scandal surrounding the new orthopaedic surgeon they would never have listened or paid attention to the mundane part of her report. "Dr. Bagley ordered a special for Mr. Sewicki, the ruptured aorta in 26," she continued. "He came back from surgery at 04.00 hours. During the operation he received six units of blood. The seventh is still running and the lab is holding another two. However, according to Bagley, they likely won't be needed." Moira paused waiting for questions. She smiled adding, "the second admission is in 31, an old lady with bilateral fractured hips. She was in the O.R. four hours and returned around midnight. Dr. Best was the surgeon."

Patty Goleski's eyebrows raised. It was the first time she had ever heard of a patient having two hips pinned during the same operation. "How is the poor dear?"

"Okay. The spinal wore off by the time her surgery ended. She bled a lot. Dr. Duggan says spinals usually do, something to do with paralyzing the peripheral circulation. She had two units upstairs.

The Lab called in a special donor for an extra pint. Her vital signs are stable and she's on saline. Her daughter and son-in-law are with her."

Moira had called Dr. Best fifteen minutes ago and told him the Hughes were anxious to speak to him. Now she saw the surgeon stepping out of the elevator. He turned in the opposite direction toward room 31. Before she could alert the others the phone rang. Sister Bernadette was on the line.

"Tell Dr. Best I want to see him before he leaves." The Administrator said, not quite masking her anxiety.

The door to his patient's private room was open when Beecher walked in. He gathered the middle-aged couple standing on either side of her bed were the relatives of whom Miss Finan had spoken and grinned confidently. "How's grannie this morning?" he asked.

"That's what we'd like to know doctor," the woman replied.

Oxygen was hissing from a nasal tube, dangling from the metal headboard. Dr. Best heard it and reached for the valve connecting the tube to the piped-in supply. He bumped the bed in the process of closing it and his patient opened her eyes. "I see you're awake," he remarked.

Mrs. Bennett, heavy-lidded and half asleep, looked up at him and asked with effort. "How are you this morning Doctor? You must be worn out."

"Not really," Beecher smiled and turned to the man beside him. "Mr. Bennett, I'm Dr. Best. I was looking for you when we finished operating but was told you had left."

"We've been waiting here since nine o'clock last night," said the man lethargically. His jaw hardened. "Agnes is my mother-in-law. I'm Dick Hughes."

"And I'm Shirley, Mrs. Bennett's daughter. "I'd like to know, Doctor, why it took so long?"

Beecher looked straight at the concerned crease dividing Mrs. Hughes' baggy eyes. "We pinned both of her hips."

"She broke both?" Shirley was confused. She distinctly remembered Dr. Clayton said her mother had broken the left hip.

"No." Beecher answered directly.

"Then why operate on both?"

Dr. Best glanced at his patient. "If you'll pardon me, Mrs. Bennett," he said and turned to the daughter. "Your mother is old."

"You don't have to apologize Doctor," Mrs. Bennett interrupted. "No one knows it better than I."

Beecher disregarded Agnes' comment and went on. "She has osteoporosis. Her bone is brittle. Rather than wait for her to break the other we decided to reinforce it. She's a tough old bird in every other way, prolonging the operation hasn't done her any harm."

While he was talking Mrs. Goleski touched his arm from behind. "Pardon me, Dr. Best" she said. "The Administrator would like to see you."

Behind an expanse of desk Sister Bernadette looked drawn, troubled and preoccupied. The healthy blush was missing from her cherubic cheeks and she prayed over her rosary, twiddling a gold crucifix hanging from it. At midnight Mrs. Starling had awakened her to advise a second team was needed in the O.R. Before it was light she had put in a call for Dr. Best. That was an hour ago and he had not answered. In the meantime she had Mrs. Bennett's chart brought from the third floor, open in front of her. She began turning the pages, perusing for any impropriety. There was a hand written History and Physical by Dr. Best; the anaesthesia chart indicated the patient's general condition had remained satisfactory throughout the four hour ordeal. There was a brief operative note, also by Best, outlining what he had done. Discovering Crooky had registered an opinion as well she dialled the switch board.

"Would you please locate Dr. Cruikshank. He was up most of the night and is probably at home. Perhaps you should try there."

No sooner had she hung up than the door opened and Beecher swaggered in.

"Your welcome, Dr. Best," she invited, as he was already seating himself in the plain hard backed chair in front of her.

"You wanted to talk to me?" he asked.

"Yes," she replied her eyes narrowing slightly. "You must have got the message some time ago."

"I did," Beecher confirmed. "But I wanted to finish my rounds first." He did not mention fifteen minutes had been spent coaxing the Hughes down to the chapel to pray for their mother's recovery. Sister Bernadette would find out from one of the nuns who had seen them.

The administrator stared at him cooly. Doctors were always too busy to come when she wanted them. Usually she did not insist but in serious matters she could be impatient.

"If it's about last night," he proceeded. "I've seen Mrs. Bennett and she's doing fine."

Sister Bernadette took a deep breath and commented icily. "Let's hope for the benefit of everyone she continues to do so."

The remark was cynical and Beecher kept quiet.

"Pinning the wrong hip is negligence; putting an elderly patient through such a lengthy operation, particularly when it was unnecessary, is misconduct."

"There are those among the orthopaedic surgeons who would disagree." Beecher smiled, "An ounce of prevention is worth a pound of cure. There are many examples, for instance straightening bow legs in a child will prevent arthritis of the knee."

"Maybe so, but a child is more resilient than an eighty year old and Dr. Best you fail to see the point. You made a mistake."

Averse to admit he was in any way to blame Beecher spoke out accusingly. "The X-ray Technician put the marker on the wrong side."

"Apparently. But surely in your examination you would have noticed the left hip was broken."

"Not necessarily," Beecher contested. "She had no deformity."

"Then why was the x-ray taken in the first place?"

"I didn't request it. The referring doctor did."

"Well," Sister Bernadette let out a deep sigh. "She must have complained of some pain."

"She didn't," Beecher lied. "When I arrived Duggan had already given the 'spinal'. Her legs were numb and paralyzed. I didn't expect her to have any pain. Even if she had it could have been due to some other cause such as osteoarthritis."

The Administrator rubbed her sleepless eyes. The man had an answer for everything. Although she sensed he was not telling her the whole truth there was no way of proving it. Any further discussion would be useless. But she carried on, "I see you've recorded your findings," she said glancing over the history and physical sheet, "and your operative notes. When did you write them?"

"When I'd finished the surgery."

Do Unto Others

For the first time the sister believed him. It was a routine with which she disagreed. A detailed story of the patient's complaints and physical findings, if not accompanying the patient upon admission, should be in the chart after the patient reached the ward. The surgeons were particularly slack, contending most of their cases were urgent, frequently going directly from the E.R. to the O.R. For the sake of expediency and to simulate cooperation the sister's governing board, upon legal advice, had drawn a twenty four hour limit. "I see," she said, silently granting he was within his rights, then swivelled her chair to face the window. Outside a heavy snow was falling. Brock Street, wet and slushy, splattered with morning traffic. The sky was grey and street lamps were still burning. A depressing sight in keeping with her mood.

"Will that be all?" Beecher asked and stood to leave.

Sister Bernadette nodded, turning around. "Yes, for the time being." Then forcing a smile she said wearily, "Thank you very much for coming."

Beecher had the door open when abruptly she changed her mind. "Not quite doctor," she called after him. "I have one more question to ask." It was more like a challenge. "If you'd operated on the hip she'd broken first would you have pinned the other?"

Beecher pretended not to have heard and closed the door behind him.

The day shift was going off duty when Andy Cruikshank strolled into the foyer of St. Mary's. He shook large snow-flakes from his overcoat and smiled at a few familiar faces. He had cancelled his Thursday afternoon curling at the golf club, believing the business at hand was more important than informing a team-mate he was unavailable. Sister Bernadette had seen him come up the walk relieved he had kept his word and was ready to greet him with a sunny 'hello' when he walked into her office.

The Administrator was always happy to see Andy Cruikshank. Since the nuns had appointed him Chief of Surgery they never had a reason for regret.

"I hear you had a terrible night," Sister Bernadette remarked. "Did you ever get to bed?"

"About five," Andy replied. "But I did get more sleep after you found me at home."

Sister Bernadette looked concerned. "I'm sorry about waking you but I've been quite upset. There has been negligence, incompetence, call it what you wish. I'm afraid we're in for a law suit. Dr. Best came in this morning and blamed the whole fiasco on the X-ray Technician. I've also had a chat with Stainsbury, the new Radiologist. He told me the original films were taken in the late afternoon by Susan Herzog a girl on his staff. She is the one responsible for the 'marker' goof up. Stainsbury had a look at the films himself to confirm the facts. The girl came to see me. She really feels badly and begged we let her stay. Also, it's true the orderly pushed the table into the room the wrong way round. In fact he was following the nurses' orders to set up for a right hip pinning. The orderly can't be blamed nor can the O.R. staff. They were all following the doctor's orders. The big question is did Dr. Best examined the patient."

"How is she?" Crooky asked, temporarily avoiding the issue.

"Quite stable. Although she lost blood it has been adequately replaced. Her temperature is up a bit but I guess we can expect it for a few days. We'll pray she doesn't get an infection. She's a lovely old soul. It could finish her, keeping her down longer than need be. I've seen so many elderly people just fall apart when they're confined to bed."

Andy was thinking if a suit developed a smart lawyer could tack on extra bucks for the complications, pushing the damage clause up considerably. He nodded in agreement and yawned, politely covering his mouth. Then lit another cigarette. "The only one who could possibly make anything out of Clayton's note would be a plaintiff's lawyer if Mrs. Bennett chooses to go that route. More than likely she won't, but don't put anything past her family, especially if inheritance is involved."

"Dr. Best is already working on them," the Administrator interjected. "Sister Magdalene saw him taking the relatives into the chapel around eight this morning. Only God knows what he told them."

"Sister," Andy smiled teasingly, "Perhaps he really is sincere. You Catholics don't have a monopoly on prayer."

"Touche! Dr. Cruikshank," the sister laughed. "I should give him credit." Then she sobered, "Any one covering up as he appears to be doing is suspected of hypocrisy as far as I'm concerned."

"How do you mean?" Andy asked.

"Did you see his preoperative write up.?"

"Nope," Crooky replied and scratched his head, thinking. About 11:45 pm. when he looked at the patient's chart there was only Clayton's skimpy note, nothing by Dr. Best. "Please may I have the chart?" he asked.

The write-up was dated Tuesday March 3rd, 1964, the exact time deleted. After several minutes reviewing it Andy read aloud, "'When I saw Mrs. Bennett she was complaining of pain in both hips.' Best goes on to describe an undisplaced fracture of her right hip and some early signs of osteoarthritis in both. But he writes 'no shortening nor deformity noted'".

The operative description was dated March 4th, 1964, Andy noticed, and the preoperative diagnoses concurred with Dr. Best's physical findings. What held Andy's attention were Best's comments on the x-rays. 'Post reduction films showed no sign of a break and I assumed the fracture had been set perfectly. A routine pinning of the right hip was then carried out.'

"'Just before closing,'"Andy read aloud, "'I discovered the x-ray marker had been placed incorrectly. The fracture was on the left side. The patient's general condition remaining stable allowed me to proceed.'"

"Is he a good surgeon?" Sister Bernadette asked.

"Technically I'd say so. I watched him perform his first six operations under mandatory supervision."

"What were they?"

Andy grunted, "not much," then clarified his statement. "Three of them were bunionectomies. Two involved the lower leg : an ankle fracture and a calcification of the gastocnemius tendon. The sixth one I questioned."

"How's that?"

"I'd never heard of it. An excision of the os trigonum in a young basketball player. It's a small accessory bone behind the ankle. Some people are born with it. Dr. Best contends it's not a separate bone but a piece broken off the back of the talus, one of the ankle bones. Apparently his patient was having pain in his heel cord. Best quoted an article he'd read. I meant to ask Jim Lindsay about it."

"Did Dr. Lindsay ever supervise him?"

"I think so, but I'm not sure. Best zeroed in on me. I guess he figures I'm a safe bet, not having studied orthopaedics to the extent he has."

"You've got to admit his write up had a lot to be desired," Sister Bernadette commented, returning to her first concern.

"What did you think of my consultation?"

The administrator had to admit she had not read Dr. Cruikshank's note and apologized adding, "I should."

"Well, there's something in it which may advance your suspicions. When I examined Mrs. Bennett between her operations I found her left side was deformed. The foot was turned out abnormally and the whole left lower extremity was adducted - drawn towards the mid-line. In my mind there was no doubt. It was a direct contradiction to what Dr. Best states he found on March 3rd, 'no shortening or deformity noted.'"

While looking for Crooky's comments the Sister came across Best's written report. "Very interesting," she remarked. "He's dated his preoperative note the 3rd of March but I distinctly remember him telling me he had written it after the surgery which would make it the 4th, the same date as the post op. note. Why would he do that? He also told me this morning Mrs. Bennett was not complaining of any pain when he first examined her after Dr. Duggan had given the spinal. Though in his preoperative work up he states Mrs. Bennett complained of pain in both hips." Sister Bernadette's frown remained as she concluded. "The man has told so many lies, he doesn't know the truth himself."

CHAPTER TWENTY-TWO

Jim lay in bed listening to the yelping dogs, the only sound the early hours had to offer. It resounded like a festival of discordant arias, yapping, snarling and growling. There were solos, duets, trios, double trios and double triple trios. The compound next door entertained a gnawing sextet, and including the courtyards facing the street behind there were enough ensembles to muffle the Mendelssohn Choir. He looked at his watch which read three thirty and was amazed he had actually slept through six hours of incessant noise.

Stuffing his ears with toilet tissue he rolled over, covered his head with a pillow and tried to sleep. His breathing was still irregular. Tossing the pillow aside he flipped over and concentrated on remaining completely quiet. It was impossible. His heart pounded and he could not control his breathing.

His breathing! Something peculiar had happened. As he lay, conscious of each inspiration, a suffocating sensation bewildered him, like the tightness induced by his recent anxiety. He got up and turned on the light, stretched, touched his toes a dozen times, lay down and began to read. The urge to breathe gradually recurred. With effort he could regain his wind but when he stopped actively expanding his chest there followed shorter and shallower involuntary breaths until breathing ceased. This cycle of under and over-breathing kept repeating alarmingly. Whether it had occurred while he was sleeping he had no way of knowing, though he suspected it probably had. 'Air Hunger' he decided, diagnosing his own disorder, most likely due to the altitude. People raised in the mountains had evolved a compensatory number of red blood cells and weren't affected. Outsiders adapted in time. Not to worry! He settled against the headboard and started to thumb through an Afghan tour guide. The necessity to increase his breathing was too compelling. To hell with it! Better to keep moving he decided. If it's lack of oxygen a run should do the trick.

He slipped into a pair of sweat pants and tennis shoes. While scrambling into his cotton pullover the sleeve snagged on his watch showing a half hour later than when last checked. It was too early for a run, too dark. Someone might mistake him for a fugitive. Postponing the exercise he sat at the small writing desk, found a pen and paper and began a letter.

'Thursday, Mar.5th/64
Kabul, Afghanistan

My Dear Merri,

This is my second letter in a week, although the first was rather short, mainly to let you know I arrived in one piece.

Many times you've listened to me describe strangers and events till you were bored out of your mind. You called me your window to the outside world. From this distance an astronomic telescope would be more fitting as I zoom in on these novel characters. So here I go stretching your patience again, discussing people whom you'll likely never meet because if you accompany me on a return trip most of the present company, on two year contracts, will be gone.

The flight was long and tiring but interesting and subsequently useful, notably meeting Crooky's kissing cousins in Beirut. Since then I've called his nephew Dr. Donald Shaw to refer a case. The patient is the father of Darius Abdullah Mahmud - of whom I've written - and has a cardiac problem.

Dari brought Malikar to the Avicenna the day after I arrived, a working day for both Moslems and Christians. The Muslims take off Friday, their Sabbath, but work the rest of the week while Christians, mainly voluntary people, take off Sunday as well giving them an extra day.

Lucky for Malikar there is an excellent internist with the S.E.R.V.E. Medicare team. I was introduced to Dr. John Disher and his wife Betty the evening I arrived. At the last minute the Keeles - you'll recall Al Keele, the mission chief, from my last letter - invited me to their 25th wedding anniversary. Everybody was there. From what I gathered the only one not present was Disher's surgical counterpart. Missing one party is nothing. There are at least two a week.

Last night I went to my second, this time a diplomatic affair given by the U.S. Ambassador. Included was a Russian. Rather than a last minute invitation it was more a 'summons' personally conveyed by the Ambassador himself - probably payment for having examined him. He has marked bowing of a leg with arthritis of his knee, the result of an old medial meniscus tear. Unfortunately I could offer him nothing more than advice and a shot of cortisone.

The 'Conestoga Complex' Keele has coined their nightly gatherings, comparing them to western settlers drawing prairie schooners into tight circles. The custom is more for comfort than protection - if their tabs at the U.S. commissary are any indication. With an endless supply of provisions they can hold out as long as it takes to convince the natives the American way is best. Relying on their commissary the way they do is ridiculous to other foreigners who know the Kabul bazaar has a larger selection and sells everything - at reduced prices - from Dutch chocolate to Norwegian sardines. Yar Zamir, whom S.E.R.V.E. Medicare assigned as a driver, took me there; I'll go back bargain hunting with him and Dari tomorrow.

Dari's father, Malikar, lives like an upper class North American. He looked apropos in a grey pin-striped three piece worsted suit, white collar, maroon tie and shiny patent leather shoes. After his electrocardiogram he sat on the edge of the examining table, his deep set eyes searching our faces for an answer to his question, "What do you think?"

When Disher told him he had a chronic heart condition, probably the result of rheumatic fever, the reply wasn't sufficient and Malikar surprised us with 'aortic stenosis I believe you call it' and turned to his son. 'Darius you were right! You make me very proud.' He has every right to be. Dari is a bright young man, mature beyond his years. How sadly he reminds me of Jason.

Regarding us critically, Malikar asked. 'What more do you have to offer?' After John went on to describe how surgery could correct the condition, Dari said he had seen an aortic valvular replacement while studying medicine at the American University of Beirut. More coincidental, the operation was done by Dr. Donald Shaw. I sent a night telegram immediately and the reply came back yesterday. Malikar has an appointment with Shaw sometime toward the end of March. Malikar was pleased and has requested we visit his qala during the Nawruz (Mar.21st) celebrations. He is impressive, candid and sincere, a true patriot and a poet. As he was leaving he turned and said, 'Doctor, the Afghans are a wonderful people with an over abundance of three wares they cannot sell or give away: magnificent mountains, customs and poverty. I hope you enjoy your stay.'

At first glance the Avicenna looks modern compared to its archaic backdrop. I've heard it was built by the Russians between the first and second world wars. A two story building, ironically shaped like a Christian cross, it contains eighty beds, forty allocated to surgery, half of which are occupied by orthopaedic cases.

When I first entered the dingy front hall I wondered why I left Shipton's relatively immaculate facilities. Single light bulbs fed by an inconsistent supply of electricity are strung sparingly. Floors are swabbed daily in an antiseptic routine, but the murky water only transfers filth from one corner to another. The linen is dirty as are the mattresses, sagging in line with their rope springs. Flies constantly pester dressings, frequently reeking of pus.

But these obstacles can be overcome and the gratitude of the patients is rewarding.

John Disher tells me the lack of basic sciences makes it difficult for the residents to understand the reasons behind treatment. I have found this true on the surgical side as well. Patients are not undressed for physical evaluation and while haphazard questions are asked concerning their ailments a single x-ray is held up to a window. The doctors haven't learned it is essential to take two views at right angles to each other to gain a perspective.

I have been lecturing in the morning and demonstrating applied anatomy in the afternoons. My pupils write down every word, partly because they're diligent but chiefly to improve their English. The better ones act as interpreters. Generally, Afghan doctors are courteous, cooperative and anxious to learn but they can be put off by criticism - who isn't - more so by western female nurses. The trainees in anaesthesia are especially affected; their impatient mentor should be sent home.

The full time S.E.R.V.E. doctors have been encouraging the Afghans to take the ECFMG examinations held once a year in Kabul. Passing them could be a ticket into an American centre for further studies where they may remain. Perhaps a residency exchange program might be better; it would allow Canadian trainees to see diseases they only encounter on the flat pages of textbooks. There's nothing like studying pathology in three dimensional living colour.

Besides heart disease - there is lots of it here - John Disher finds typhoid and dysentery are problems and will continue to be until more preventative measures are taken. Although Keele's task to improve water supply and sewage is making headway it has a long way to go.

John tells me it is almost impossible to do an autopsy because patients are whisked out of hospital before they die. There are several reasons but it boils down to two: religious practice and costs. A Muslim must be buried intact. Leaving part of him behind in a glass jar is unacceptable. Likely financial reasons are more important. Burying relatives in the hills avoids the expense of a formal funeral in a public cemetery plot. Taxi drivers charge ten times more to transport a dead person from the hospital so why not hit the road while they're still breathing. When it comes to saving funeral expenses things are the same the world over.

It reminds me of the time I happened to be available to pronounce an old man in the General's Emergency. You must remember the story! There was difficulty stretching him out due to rigor mortis, meaning he'd been dead for some time. The nurses asked me to speak to his tearful wife. After telling her he was dead I asked when she had last spoken to him. 'On the way to the airport in Miami,' she answered, adding, 'he passed out and it was hard to get him from the cab to a wheelchair.'

'The stewardess was so kind. She propped him in a seat and covered his head with a blanket. Better let him sleep.' she said.

'We brought him straight here curled up in the back of my son-in-law's stationwagon.'

He had terminal cancer and she'd taken him to Florida for one last fling. I nearly cracked up when she said, 'He was just dying to get home.'

It irks Disher, there are certain patients who appear near death but have a reversible condition such as diabetic coma. Relatives taking them home negate any chance of recovery. When the Afghan-Pakistan border was closed medical supplies like insulin were held in a Peshawar warehouse. With it's re-opening the crisis has passed.

John doles out no more pills than necessary for three days of therapy. Otherwise they'd be sold in the bazaars. If patients need more they have to come back.

His most notable case, Habibulla Ansari, left hospital Monday. He is an important member of the constitution committee which by appointment of His Majesty is drafting a more liberal government. Ansari's large bowel perforated through an abscessed diverticulum and required a life saving operation. As expected the man developed medical complications. Besides spending hours restoring the fluid and electrolyte balance John had to discuss every move with a couple of Moscow physicians. Luckily Ansari survived.

At the Ambassador's party, a celebration of Ansari's recovery, I met one of the Russian doctors. He spoke fluent English and was quite entertaining, ordering two rounds of expensive brandy each time the waiter appeared, the second for his friend who never did show up.

Busy in the O.R. I was late getting to the Red Crescent building across the river. Art Billings, the Peace Corps doctor, spends most of his time there and manages to find a few orthopaedic cases. Having one hundred and fifty healthy Peace Corps volunteers to look after he has little to do. Tuesday I showed a film on disc surgery. Art saw it and gathered together a dozen patients with back pain. In each case, symptoms were due to T.B. There was not a ruptured disc among them.

When I first saw the small O.R. and scanty equipment I thought it wise to avoid highly involved procedures. Consequently I discharged a three year old girl admitted for surgical correction of dislocated hips. The chance she'll develop a post op. infection is so high it isn't worth the risk. She waddles but still gets around.

Yesterday I was surprised to see the Afghan senior resident, Amir Kash, perform a very difficult procedure to eradicate a tuberculous pocket in the thoracic spine. He cut out the abscessed bone and replaced it with rib. Though the patient is an old man, partially paralyzed and will likely die of his disease, the operation offers him a chance to walk again.

While watching the back surgery I wondered if I'd done the right thing in discharging the child. In denying the Afghans the opportunity of learning a new procedure I was not fulfilling my teaching obligations. But I'd hate to make her worse and leave her to suffer alone.

A serious problem is the lack of a portable x-ray machine. As this involves patients who need re-checking following the setting of fractures, they must go to the X-ray Department. Not only that, the number of plaster rolls must be accurately calculated beforehand. I was lucky to set a broken shoulder and hold it overhead like the 'Statue of Liberty', amusing the students for it was the chap's right, and he became a social outcast. No sharing of the communal bowl; his left was needed for toilet paper.

So much has happened and I haven't been here a week! I'm totally consumed. When I've the time to compare all of this with what I have, I count my blessings. Hug the girls. I miss them.

Jim signed the letter with love and added a postscript: 'I've still to meet that gal, 'Ellen' what's her name, the nymphomaniac in Mitchener's 'Caravans'. But I'm not looking.'

He folded the twelve pages and sealed them in an envelope. Clapping it between the leaves of his passport he strolled onto the sun-deck to absorb the freshness and first streaks of dawn. In the west, beneath a fading moon, the Koh-i-baba loomed like a colossal crate of eggs. Closer at hand the city, brindled in shadow, was beginning to stir and life, smoke and dust flickered in the morning light.

Across the street a brown figure steadied a bundle of fire wood precariously balanced on the chine of a plodding donkey. On the first leg of his run Jim passed them in front of a tiny shop where stacks of flat bread cooled on a window ledge, its delicious aroma mixing with fumes arising from a slimy juis beside the road.

The baker's boy who had come to expect him each morning hurdled the ditch and marked time on its muddy bank until the target of his mimicry turned out of sight.

Other dark faces followed him southward on Darulaman Boulevard in the shadow of Sher Darwaza where the spectacle of his swinging by in a green track suit extracted more humour.

At the intersection of Aliabad he doubled back and found himself behind a horse drawn wagon. Its shallow box was ringed with challenging Afghans and to humour them he lengthened his stride. Shouting gleefully they cheered him on, prompting the man at the reins to step up the pace, though try as he could, the driver thwacked no more than a spastic trot from the straining nag. Down the stretch they ploughed, buck-board and hooves versus running shoes, for a quarter of a mile, spurred by the happy gang bouncing in back.

Near the staff house their routes parted and Jim dug in his toes to sprint ahead. A hawking pedlar watched him slant off to cut a corner and snorted when a tell-tale splash declared the winner had failed to clear the murky juis.

The muck stunk like an outhouse. After scraping it off Jim showered and dressed for breakfast in the dining room.

As per usual he ate his first meal alone but received companionship from the kitchen staff because no other boarders were present at the time he chose to eat. There were others. The night before he'd met a bunch of engineers from Qandahar and left them revelling until the wee small hours.

The waiters would bait him to speak Farsi, repeating his simple English courtesies. Whenever he attempted an afghan word they would correct his pronunciation, laughing unaffectedly at the zany sounds he made. At eight o'clock one of them announced the driver of a Fiat parked out front was asking for him.

"Tashuckur, Bahmonay Khooda," said Jim, rising to go.

"Thank you, goodbye," they translated in unison like a kindergarten class about to recess for the day.

CHAPTER TWENTY-THREE

Yar Zamir was another study in brown from karakul cap to squeaking sandals, except for the phosphorescent smile. He was short, slightly built and fitted comfortably behind the wheel of a Fiat. Dropping Jim at the hospital, he promised to post the doctor's letter and be back by noon.

Dari awaited Jim's arrival. The student was grinning from ear to ear and had been from the moment he spotted the Medicare car. When the two had exchanged greetings and Jim had received news of Malikar's health, the younger Mahmud dismally exclaimed. "I can't get into Avicenna without a pass!"

Jim made light of his friend's predicament. "You should have told them you were a visiting professor."

"I did. I also said you are my friend but the man at the door didn't know you."

"He recognizes me by the camera," Jim smiled. "Since I took his picture he's never had his eyes off it. Follow me," he winked and was soon excusing himself to a harem of purple chadris arrayed on the steps.

The resident staff were gathered in a small room. "Where do we start?" Jim asked, after Dari was introduced and the customary hand-holding had ceased.

Amir Kash's fawn coloured face was as void of expression as his English was minced. "Men's ward," he replied. "Two new admissions. One is neurosurgical patient. Other is general. You will see?"

"If you'd like, but I bet you know more about those specialties than I."

"One is gunshot wound. Spine is broken."

"Paraplegic?"

"Yes. Afterward, we have two cases for O.R. - triple arthrodesis and bone tumour." Amir ended with, "I would like vedi much you operate."

"We'll see," Jim nodded, and while the group moved down the hall learned from Amir the two patients for surgery were seen at the Red Crescent Clinic, Jim himself recommending their treatment.

The men's ward was on the second floor, facing the street. It was a long room and contained a dozen beds arrayed along its shabby walls. They were full, several containing more than one patient.

Peggy Dolan was showing the nurses how 'not to change a dressing' when the doctors appeared. Terminating her instruction she received approval from Amir Kash to have her students join his rounds, then wriggled her way next to Dr. Lindsay at the front of a semicircle of men ,listening to a second year resident present his management of a third degree burn. During a pause in the discussion she nudged Jim who was focusing his camera on the patient's blackened hand, and announced, "I found a Stryker frame!"

"Where?" he asked.

"Down in the dungeon - the basement. Someone donated it a couple of years ago. It's never been used, covered with dust. No straps nor mattresses, otherwise it's all there."

"What do you know!"

"I thought I saw one. Monday when you mentioned the need for it I went looking."

A game old Pathan had suffered a pelvic fracture in a road traffic accident three weeks earlier. He had lost control of his bowel and bladder as well as the power and sensation in his legs. Following admission the poor fellow had been placed on his back in a girdle with a rope connecting it to a forty pound sandbag slung over the foot of his bed. For twenty-one days the position was maintained. Not once had the skin over the buttocks been examined until Dr. Lindsay rolled the patient on his side. A complete breakdown of flesh over his sacrum had occurred and the odour was pathognomonic of gas gangrene.

The man was delirious; a friend of equal years knelt beside him, holding his hand and fanning the sweat from his brow.

"His friend never leaves his side. Sleeps on the floor." Peggy whispered to Jim while the house staff gathered round.

The sight was pathetic. The patriarch was not long for this world. It was his friend who needed consolation. Dr. Lindsay took a deep breath and let it out slowly. After a moment he launched into a short dissertation on the difference between wet and dry gangrene. How the wet type could be cured by timely surgical intervention and a sensitive antibiotic. There was no cure for the dry type; it was caused by the blockage of a major artery. When he finished he asked

Miss Dolan, "When can you have the Stryker ready?" thinking the problem should have been discovered sooner.

"Tonight or tomorrow morning. If no one can sew the straps I'll do it," she answered. "But I'm not sure of how many or where to place them. Are you?"

"No, though I'm willing to help," Jim replied cheerfully. "I'll go down and have a look this afternoon."

The girl's attitude pleased him. Physically she reminded him of Merri, slender and supple, not as tall. In her late twenties he imagined. She had the same fine chestnut hair with a flip curl at the nape of her neck, but not rolled inward like his wife's.

They moved on to the next bed where Dr. Kash, pointing an index finger at his own temple and twirling it, exclaimed, "the man is crazy."

"How's that?" asked Jim. The rest of the doctors were gawking at a young man sitting cross-legged on a blood-stained sheet.

"He cut off his penis!"

"He what?"

"Yes. He is one the cases admitted during the night."

"How did it happen?"

"It was no accident. He did it himself. He wants to be woman." Kash discharged one of his rare smiles and went on, "to please his friend who is motorwan."

"What is a motorwan?"

"Truck driver. His friend is truck driver."

"I see," said Jim. "What do you intend to do?"

"Nothing. Suturing it would be useless. He would cut it off again. Also it would not function. Maybe as a surgeon you have some ideas."

Jim snickered, recalling an indecent joke. "I'm afraid not Amir," he said. "He needs a psychiatrist."

"Vedi interesting. We have no such specialty."

"Then let him be a woman." Jim shrugged, adding facetiously, "Or maybe Allah has some spare bones lying around."

Kash did not appreciate his visitor's humour and said so. "Including Allah in a joke is a sacrilege. The Beneficent and Merciful is not to be ridiculed. You are right and you are wrong," he flashed. "Let him be woman yes! It is too late for him to be man; even if Allah himself changed his mind he would not give him back his penis."

Jim's face flushed. His remark had been out of place. In poking fun he had unintentionally slighted Kash's religion. The more he thought about it the more insulting it appeared. After awhile he realized his faux pas worried him more than it did Amir and he would remember not to do it again.

The practical session progressed in a disorganized fashion, each young doctor taking his turn at presenting and practising his English, with Jim listening carefully and interrupting to clarify a point or take a picture of an interesting case. He was in the midst of changing lenses when the second recent admission was introduced.

The patient, a beardless man in his mid thirties, had been shot but not in the back. The bullet had arrived by a circuitous route. He could neither feel nor move his legs. An A.P. x-ray indicated a bullet overlapped the eighth rib; the entry wound was at the front of his chest.

"They say he crossed his father-in-law," Amir volunteered. "What do you think, Dr. Lindsay?"

"Having heard only part of the foregoing presentation, Jim answered absently. "Firearms are very dangerous - " He had wanted to mention how many men he had seen with cartridge belts and long rifles, but everyone in the room was laughing. Embarrassed, he blushed again, this time believing he had inattentively missed something. Amir Kash was laughing convulsively. "Vedi funny! Firearms are dangerous." Unwittingly Jim had hit upon a form of Afghan humour; emphasizing the obvious. This too was put away for future use.

Not a drop of blood exuded from the chest wound. Quietly Dr. Lindsay percussed the lung fields and listened to the man's breathing, then palpated the belly. After returning his stethoscope to a suit coat pocket he commented. "There doesn't appear to be any serious internal bleeding. The missile was probably deflected by a rib and followed it around to the spine. I think you should get another x-ray Amir. This time have the technician take a lateral view. From the two films we can get a better idea of the bullet's location. Do you have any myelographic dye?"

"No" Miss Dolan intervened. "But we have a spinal tap tray and a manometer."

"Great! Go get it and we'll do him in bed."

The exercise was carried out with only one hitch - it took extraordinary strength to flex the patient's lower back. Eventually this was accomplished with the man's head tucked between his thighs. There was such an extreme range of motion in the hip joints, flexing the thighs produced very little leverage. "Most likely because the patient has hunkered all his life," Jim proposed, thinking, constantly moving a hip through its full range of motion was beneficial and may be a reason why Afghans have a low incidence of osteoarthritis.

A long hollow needle was eventually inserted between two lumbar vertebrae and punctured the sac of fluid enveloping the nerve roots. After obtaining a few drops, Jim was pleased to find no blood.

"Why is the test significant Sir?" asked Dari.

"It means the bullet has not entered the spinal canal and caused bleeding around the cord."

The rate of flow from the needle gradually tapered and Dr. Lindsay connected the glass manometer tube to the needle and held it vertically. "Someone put their hands around his neck and squeeze," he asked, simultaneously observing the fluid level in the tube.

Miss Dolan complied. When the level did not rise she was asked to squeeze harder and her second effort almost choked the patient. Still the level did not change.

"He's blocked," Jim declared. "Prepare him for surgery, Amir. The bullet should come out."

Kash looked puzzled. "Why?" he asked.

"When Dolan squeezed his neck she increased the venous blood flow to the choroid plexus in the brain and hence the formation of cerebral-spinal fluid in his lateral ventricles. The pressure of the fluid can be measured by a manometer. Squeezing the neck should have increased the CSF pressure and it should have risen to a higher level in the manometer. As it did not I assume there is a block in the system. If there is a chance of recovery he should have the bullet removed."

The procedure used up most of the time allotted for rounds and the group disbanded, Drs. Lindsay and Amir with Dari going to the O.R., the remainder to their various duties.

The operating rooms were equipped with Russian tables, obsolete gas machines and portable lamps. Their combined floor space was less than the room used for orthopaedics at St. Mary's. But by North American standards they were functional and would tolerate a reasonable list of cases if instruments were available. As it was there were barely enough to run two rooms.

Having selected the bone tumour to do first, suspecting it was probably a malignant growth, Jim cut off the crumbly upper four inches of humerus. His provisional diagnosis was based on the patient's age, what he had seen on the x-rays and the development of increased swelling and pain in the upper arm. There was no means of speedily identifying the mushy material he sampled; the lab was not equipped to do a frozen section. It was not equipped to do any sections, not even the routine ones, as there was no microtome, nor stains nor slides. He simply excised what he thought was enough, including part of the shoulder joint, and left the patient with a flail arm. If the wound healed he would still have the use of his hand. If the tumour was aggressive the man would die. Thus ablating his arm would make no difference.

Leaving Amir with a junior to close the incision, Jim chose from among the used instruments those needed for the next case, gave them to the circulating nurse for re-sterilization and proceeded into the corridor where the second patient was being held.

A scruffy porter brooding beside the stretcher backed against the wall, making room for Dr. Lindsay to carry out an examination. Dari followed and watched Jim unsuccessfully attempt to force a stiff, atrophic foot into a relatively better position.

"Why does he need a triple arthrodesis?" The student asked.

"Polio. He has a 'drop foot' resulting from paralysis of the shin muscles. See how his foot turns under and downward", Jim elaborated. "We call it an equinovarus contracture. His foot needs to be realigned with the leg and brought back to its normal weight bearing position. It can only be done by surgical correction and fusing three of the joints in his foot."

"Is it a dangerous procedure?"

"Not particularly if it's done properly. Accuracy of approximation and a minimum of bone removal are most important - just enough to correct the deformity. See these joints." Dr. Lindsay pointed them out on an x-ray film held up to a bare bulb suspended from the ceiling. "Their cartilaginous surfaces have to be removed and the raw bone brought together and held tightly till the gap is bridged by new bone. I brought some staples with me," he smiled. "I thought they might come in handy. The same principles apply to the healing of fractures, mainly setting the fragments in position and holding them long enough. 'Long enough' means until there is no movement and a gap is no longer seen on an x-ray. Correction of a foot drop deformity entails more carpentry because reshaping the foot as well as stability is involved. In other words the joint surfaces must be wedged rather than cut straight."

"Is it done for 'club foot'?" Dari asked.

"If you mean the kind present from birth, occasionally in untreated or resistant cases but only when the foot has matured. Nine out of ten can be improved with casts or splints in the early months of life."

Peggy Dolan had come up behind them and was waiting to give Dr. Lindsay his camera. That she was there would have gone unnoticed had the porter not sucked in his breath and perceptibly stiffened. Jim detected the man's carnal gleam aimed over his shoulder and turned around to be greeted by the smiling Miss Dolan. "You left this in the ward," she said. "You're lucky it wasn't stolen."

"Many thanks," He replied, placing the strap around his neck. "Just in time for a shot of this foot."

While Jim set about taking pictures the porter again withdrew, and stared lustfully from Peggy to the camera, reeking and scratching his black wiry beard with long dirty fingernails. An electronic flash uncovered him and he muttered something in Farsi and took off down the hall.

"What's the matter with him?" Jim asked.

"He thought you were taking his picture," Dari answered, "and cursed you for doing it. Most Muslims consider photographs sinful."

"Odd," Jim replied, "I thought everyone enjoyed having his picture taken. Either the chap's a bit shy or has a police record."

Miss Dolan beamed. "Right the first time Dr. Lindsay. Since he started to work here he follows me around like a stray pup, staying far enough away to see what I'm doing. He has to be strange. I'm not the type to entice a man to swim the Hellespont."

Jim was not so sure and didn't share Peggy's self-appraisal. The nursing instructor was well favoured by any standard of beauty and attracted many admiring glances. He smiled, looking down at her plain white dress. She had adopted the Afghans' long white silken pantaloons, worn beneath her dress. The material floated seductively on the surface of her legs. She was lovely and there was no doubt in his mind the porter's steely stare was salacious. "Aren't you afraid?" he asked.

"Afghans are grateful for what we do for them. He's no different. I've been spat upon in the bazaars but only by the traditionalists; though they don't respect their women as much as their horses they do them no harm. No one has ever tried to molest me. Darn it," she laughed, adding. "How's it going?"

"Not bad. We'll be another two hours."

"Then you'll be down to look at the Stryker?"

"Yes. In fact we could use two of them."

"Maybe not," Peggy sighed. "The old Pathan hasn't responded in twenty-four hours and his breathing is very shallow."

"Too bad. The proper type of treatment might have saved him."

"Look at it positively Dr. Lindsay. If it hadn't been for his crisis the Stryker frame would have rusted in the dungeon. At least we'll have it ready for the next time."

The next time! There's not always a next time, if so it's never the same, Jim thought, while staring after the fluttering form.

The special order of white cedar for the boat Jason was building arrived a few days before he had left on this trip. He had picked it up at the lumber yard and transferred it to the work shop over the garage where the skeletal frame was still laid out on the wooden floor, the relic of an un-launched dream. "You win some and you lose some, Jason. We'll have to do it again and do it right "-

"Pardon?"

"Huh! Oh I'm sorry, Dari. I was talking to myself."

"Sir, they are calling for the patient. If you have finished your photography I will wheel him into the theatre."

"Would you like to scrub on this one?" Jim asked.

"You honour me Sir, but I must go soon."

CHAPTER TWENTY-FOUR

Amir Kash had prepared the skin with mercurochrome and was forcing air into the tourniquet when Dr. Lindsay marched in, hands dripping wet.

"How should I position him?" The chief resident asked.

"On his back with a sandbag under his hip. Use stockinet and don't drape below the knee. The leg should be free to manipulate."

"We have no stockinet," Amir replied. "The last case finished it."

"Then we'll use towels and sew them to the skin edges."

"We have only paper ones. They do not conform well."

"They will have to do. The skin is a potential source of infection and must be covered."

The drapes were made in Japan, greyish blue with a faint gloss to minimize absorption. To Jim it seemed like an expensive method, particularly in a country where cloth was as available as paper was scarce. He had discussed the matter with Al Keele and the response was discouraging. 'We can't even keep the place supplied with sheets for the wards. They're stolen right off the truck before they reach a bed. It's a poor country Jim. Not enough locks to go around.'

"What are the complications?" Dari asked while watching his mentor expose the outer surface of the bones below the ankle.

Dr. Lindsay ceased dissecting and glanced over his shoulder. It was a shrewd question, an important consideration before planning any undertaking. From what he had observed, complications were all too frequently relegated to minor significance by inexperienced surgeons more interested in doing the job than in the harm they might cause. Now here was a second year medical student already seeking the pitfalls. His opinion of Darius Abdullah Mahmud rose another notch.

"There are early and late," Jim answered and turned back to his scalpel and forceps, dividing his attention between them and an impromptu lecture.

"What about gangrene?"

"Gangrene!" Dr. Lindsay had listed every thing but.

"It would be highly unusual. There are two kinds, as I mentioned on rounds. You all witnessed a case of wet gangrene. It's caused by a gas producing bacteria found in manure. Dry gangrene, the other type, is death of tissue in the absence of putrefying bacteria, for example the severance or occlusion of an artery. It would be very unusual to have it occur as a complication of a triple arthrodesis because there are two arteries supplying the foot. Even if one were damaged the other might be sufficient. It would take a very ambitious surgeon to cut them both."

The remark produced as much laughter as 'Firearms are dangerous' from Amir and the second assistant but Dari persisted. "Where are they?" he asked.

When the locations of the anterior and posterior tibial vessels had been pointed out, Mahmud became thoughtful.

"Of course a tight plaster can cause gangrene too," Jim commented for the benefit of Amir, seated at a table writing post op. orders. Make sure it's well elevated and have the nurses check the circulation in the toes. If there is any impairment split the cast it's full length down through the dressing to the skin."

"What kind of an amputation would you do if gangrene occurred?"

Jim regarded Dari sharply. The vision of the student limping across the tarmac returned and it dawned on him Dari's line of questioning might be personal.

"A Lisfranc or a Symes," he drawled, "depending on the level of demarcation." While speaking he watched Mahmud closely. If Dari had a problem, simply asking would permit him an opportunity to share it and if the problem was solvable possibly Jim could be of assistance. But Dari's handsome features remained stubbornly noncommittal, not at all like the jubilant person who had shown him such friendliness on the plane. Jim was puzzled. Whatever secret the Afghan harboured was stashed away. He decided not to pry. If Mahmud needed help he would ask.

"I do appreciate your hospitality and have learned much this morning. Now, if you will allow me the pleasure, tomorrow I will take you on a tour of Kabul."

Jim graciously accepted. He had no plans for the Muslim Sabbath. To see the city with someone who knew it, would be a treat.

Once arrangements had been made to meet in the hospital at 9.00 a.m., Dari thanked him again and left while the surgical team moved on to the gunshot wound.

An hour and a half of meticulous exploration resulted in removal of the bullet and decompression of the spinal cord. The incision was closed and after a padded dressing was applied the man was transported to a small recovery room.

In an awed and complimentary mood Dr. Kash remarked, "that was vedi nice surgery. You think he will regain function?"

Jim was sitting on a bench in the doctors' dressing room massaging his aching legs.

"It's difficult to say Amir," he replied. "There was no apparent damage to the spinal cord when we opened the dural sac. After the bullet had been removed and the sac was closed, pulsation occurred on both sides where the bullet had entered the canal. But we can't be sure. The cord has definitely been transected physiologically. It may wear off and recovery take place. If it does, function will return. Let us hope for the best."

"I think we should keep him in the recovery room for special care," Amir suggested. "More hands to turn him and empty catheter bag."

"Fine," Jim agreed and commented, "It's been a long morning my friend."

"Yes. Is after one. More than long morning," Kash laughed.

The corridor was empty and the quietness uncanny.

"Where is everybody Amir?" The place is like a morgue."

"Is Thursday afternoon. Like Saturday afternoon in America begins week-end. Everyone is gone home."

On the ground floor the two men separated, agreeing if any danger signs arose with regard to the patients Dr. Lindsay was to be contacted immediately. Amir went to relay this instruction to the resident on duty and Jim started toward the administration offices at the rear of the building.

In the small room assigned to S.E.R.V.E. Medicare Yar Zamir was reading an Arabic newspaper. The back of his chair was tilted against the wall and his swinging feet were crossed. When Dr. Lindsay barged in, whistling in a carefree manner, the little man hit the floor, slapped his sandals on the tile and respectfully removed his cap. "Doktar, you are ready?"

"Shave all your hair off and you'll look like Yul Bryner," Jim teased, and when the driver responded with a blank stare was obliged to explain. "He's a movie actor."

"Ah, a star like Hopalong Cassidy!"

"Sometimes," Jim smiled.

"The car is outside Doktar. Where do you wish to go?"

"Home - er. I mean the staff house. I've had it Yar. Time to tie my feet to the ceiling."

Baffled, the Afghan continued to frown while he fished in his baggy suit for the car keys. Repeating the phrase "tie feet to ceiling" Yar shook his head.

A sand lot separated the hospital from a row of smaller buildings. The Fiat was parked in the middle of it.

Neither of them noticed Peggy Dolan's hunkering 'stray pup', the evil-eyed porter, licking the edge of a cigarette paper. At the sight of the tall man with the camera he tensed, dropped his hands to the ground and glared viciously. A clenched fist crushed the flimsy roll and his whole body extended, slithering slowly upward against the wall. He spat when he thought Jim was in range.

The spittle fell short of its mark. Its sound dampened by Dr. Lindsay saying, "I'd like to get a picture of that." He was referring to the cook-house across the lot. Under the shed roof shading its doorway the kitchen help recessed around a large copper samovar. The building had no chimney and the only means smoke had of escaping was through a window facing the hospital. Soot blackened the mud wall above it and to the casual onlooker the place could have been gutted by fire. The scene was worth a thousand words.

Yar Zamir misread Jim's purpose.

"Yes!" he beamed. "They would like that. Take them now when they are not working."

Jim declined. A shot of the chefs in the midst of preparing a meal when their cook-house was full of smoke, suited him better. Besides he was anxious to get back to the conveniences of the compound. The thought of using the hospital toilet was as effective as a dose of paregoric. A white enamelled metal plate set flush with the floor, its foot grips centring a hole leading to God knows where, was unappealing.

"Tell me Yar," he said, turning away from the cookhouse and nodding up at Sher Darwaza,"What's at the end of the Kabul wall?"

"The Citadel - Bala Hissar!"

"Before I leave Afghanistan I want to climb the mountain and follow the wall, starting from this end at the noon gun. Is it far?"

Yar shrugged and hollered at the kitchen help. After an exchange of words and gesticulations which included a pantomime on the loading and firing of a cannon complete with the plugging of ears he answered, "Two hours. I have never gone to Bala Hissar that way."

"Why don't you come with me?"

"No. It is no good. Some people go up there and are never seen again. Take the road around the mountain."

"In broad daylight! How could anyone come to harm?"

"Maybe you would rather see the dog fights." Yar smiled as he suggested an alternative. "They are held Friday morning on the flats by the noon gun."

The idea did not appeal to Jim. He had a sympathetic detachment for dumb animals and would sooner watch a boxing match or some form of human sport. Ducking into the Fiat he asked, "Why are you Afghans so bloodthirsty?"

"What is bloodthirsty Doktar? The spilling of blood means nothing. Blood does not frighten us and we don't drink it!"

The mini car was backed around to face the rear of the hospital. In the dazzling brightness the black bearded porter with the nasty eyes had not altered his stance.

"Now there's a bloodthirsty chap if I ever saw one. He's glaring at us like the Devil himself."

"A strange one," Yar admitted, as they waited for a break in the traffic on Jaedi Maiwand. "Never speaks. Always alone. They say he lives up in the ruins and is possessed of a Jinn. Where I do not know."

"What is a Jinn?" asked Jim.

"An evil spirit. In America you call him crazy."

The Fiat moved forward slowly. Trying to ford a stream of bicycles required more attention than the driver could devote to his passenger's peculiar pronunciation. Nor was Jim bent on talking, his abdomen was rancorous.

When they swerved off Darulaman Boulevard and the staff house was a stone's throw away he remembered a promise to Peggy Dolan.

"Damn it, Yar," he snapped. "I have to go back and inspect the Stryker frame. Wait for me."

Five minutes later Dr. Lindsay reappeared, walking less rapidly than before.

"This won't take too long," he said. "Sorry to hold you up."

The driver nodded patiently and asked, "did you wish to leave your camera in the car?"

"Not at all."He had been in such a peristaltic rush he had forgotten it. "But it's just as well," he added. "I can use it."

A picture of the Stryker frame with its sheep skin straps and whatever Miss Dolan had contrived for mattresses would make a terrific slide. Tomorrow with a patient on it he would take some more.

En route Yar returned to their previous discussion. "We are not blood thirsty, Doktar. Spilling blood in a fair fight is not wrong. It takes more than one to fight. Strength is right. To lose is to be weak. You believe it too, so do the Russians. If you did not there would be no arms race."

"By 'you', you are referring to the Russian and American Governments," Jim smiled. "I'm less than a pawn and you're forgetting Kennedy's nuclear test ban treaty."

"It means nothing. It is cover up. Because they do not test it does not mean they are not making weapons."

"Yes," Jim sighed, gazing out the window. "No doubt what you say is true." They were passing Deh Mazang and the park by the river. The same park he had observed from the opposite bank during his trek with Deemstra. People were enjoying themselves in its pleasant setting, possibly the same ones he had seen before.

"Hmm," he exhaled slowly. "What about the meek? The humble, gentle people who really delight in the simple life and shun bloodshed and fighting. Will they inherit the Kingdom of Heaven?"

"Bah! It is New Testament Christian teaching, like turn the other cheek. It means nothing. Allah takes only warriors to paradise. We will all inherit a plot of ground, the losers sooner." He grinned at Jim. "No man can follow your Christian belief and take from life all that is his without fighting."

"Then you believe in the survival of the fittest?"

"Yes. I believe in power and strength. So do you but do not admit it."

Yar's argument was basic logic - the outlook of an aggressive individual struggling to stay alive in a country with little to offer. Dr. Lindsay in accepting the driver as an uneducated lackey had underestimated the man's practicality. "You win," he drawled as he collected his camera equipment and added "Yar, you are a wrangler of formidable strength."

Perplexed by what his passenger said, Yar shook his head and submitted. "You wish me to wait again, Doktar?"

"Yes please. I'll not be long."

Jim attached the electronic flash to his camera, switched it on and held it to his ear listening for the high pitched hum which indicated a potential charge. Satisfied he slung the camera over a shoulder and strode into the hospital.

The building was more deserted than it had been forty minutes ago. The back entrance was unlocked and the offices were empty. Why a guard was posted at the bolted front entrance and none at the back was a security inconsistency. Adapting his vision to the dim interior he made his way to the junction of the halls. Where the open stairwell led either up or down a muffled sob broke the stillness. Peculiar, Jim thought, delaying his descent into the basement and giving ear to the Paediatric Ward above.

In the five days he had been at the Avicenna not once had he heard a cry of anguish from the suffering. The stoicism exhibited was unbelievable. Rarely did a patient require heavy amounts of narcotizing drugs. 'The Afghan doctors have no mercy.' Miss Dolan complained. 'They never prescribe narcotics and it is the right of every patient to be relieved of pain.'

'Our way of life provokes you, not your compassion,' Dr. Kash had answered. 'Patients need no analgesics. Pain does not kill.'

There it was again. A muffled whimper coming from somewhere below. Suddenly a terrified shriek, a woman's scream, shrill and piercing, resounding like a high speed drill. Jim crouched on the staircase peering into the semidarkness until he dared to move.

Cautiously he stepped down the darkened stairs until he could see a beam of light from a window cutting a square on the concrete floor. "What's wrong?" he cried, wary of his own sound and the response it might bring.

The shrieking ceased. Metal scraped the cement floor and a voice shouted his name. "Dr. Lindsay, he's got a knife!"

A shadow darted across the sunlit patch and rushed up the stairs. It was almost upon him. In panic he gripped his camera and a blinding flash lit the stairwell.

In the blackness afterward a figure stumbled up the stairs, more intent on escape than inflicting wounds.

CHAPTER TWENTY-FIVE

Peggy screamed bloody murder and was unharmed but she felt partly responsible. The Stryker was too heavy for her to lift and she'd asked him to accompany her to the basement. His name was Hashim or 'Hash the masher' as Art Billings called him. 'No matter what strange customs have lead to this, I find it difficult to blame the guy entirely.' The Peace Corps doctor commented. 'A red-blooded male with fewer hang-ups than Dolan's thwarted rapist might have made a pass at her. But a pass is not the same,' he'd added jokingly. 'Sex at knife point is a bit one sided. As for Jim Lindsay firing his camera.' Art shook his head in wonder. 'Real cool, like in a movie I saw, a Hitchcock thriller'. Having recalled the cliff hanger Art would never be convinced Jim's flash was an accident. 'It makes no difference,' he added. 'According to statistics, the ruckus saved her eventually.'

Some admired her courage and ability to react. Unscathed she was living proof of their comments. What she did not reveal was how she dealt with her attacker, of how resolute he was to avenge his pride. She had come close to a violent end but chose to keep it to herself.

When Dr. Jim did not come to help with the Stryker frame Peggy went looking for him. In the hall she met Amir Kash. He told her the visiting orthopaedist was last seen heading for the administration offices and she hastened to find him. Neither Jim nor Yar were there. Disappointed she tried the parking lot to learn from the kitchen staff the 'tall ferangi' had left for the day. "Damn!" she sighed and turned to see Hashim, hunkering in his grimy clothes.

'Come with me, I need your help,' she ordered in Pashto and like a pointer sniffing the wind, he followed.

In the gloom at the foot of the stairs he hesitated. She had indicated he was to carry the revolving bed from the basement up to the administration office where she could finish it in better light; to make his task easier she began to disconnect the frames.

Hashim's eyes widened as she glided from one end of the apparatus to the other, bending and twisting, her gyrations tantalizing him. Stealthily he slipped behind her, creeping closer until he was within touching distance.

She was attempting to lift the second frame; its sudden release caused her to back into him. Surprised when her silken buttocks brushed his loin he reacted by wrapping an arm around her.

'What are you doing Hashim? Let me go!' she ordered. The smell of his breath and body were offensive. 'Let me go or I'll scream,' she repeated. He clasped a hand over her mouth and tore at the front of her dress, his smelly beard rasping her cheek as he hunched forward. She struggled to pull away and tried to scream through his greasy palm muffling her sound. She thrust backward bunting with her rear; but the more she bucked, the more excited he became.

He let go of her mouth to tug at her pantaloons; she cried out but her screams were smothered in a turban wrapped around her face. Without relaxing the turban he pulled her closer.

Desperately she pushed backwards, grabbed his distended penis and wrung it through the soft folds of his baggy pants, her fingernails sinking into the sensitive flesh. Screaming she spun, still clinging to his shrinking phallus and while he tried to break her grip she kneed him in the groin.

He buckled and stumbled to the bottom step, blocking her path of escape. She screamed louder, shrieking at him, augmenting her shrill echoes with endless screeching. To her horror he revived and from the depths of his sash drew a curved knife, vaguely gleaming in the darkened room. Pointing it at her he crouched, forcing her to retreat behind the Stryker frame where she continued to vent her ringing indignation until Dr. Lindsay appeared on the stairs.

Jim had not asked any questions. Her ruffled state spoke for itself. There were no tears nor sobs, just an overly relieved smile. 'Pardon me if I don't rush into your arms. I'm a little shy.' Her dress was tattered and she had covered her chest with her hands. 'Would you mind lending me your jacket till I find something else?' she'd asked.

That evening Hashim's transgressions had been reported to the local authorities by the hospital administrator, contrary to a request from Al Keele. The S.E.R.V.E. mission chief feared an international scandal and firmly insisted that because Miss Dolan had come to no harm, the incident should be forgotten.

The nursing instructor was back in her role the following morning as though nothing had happened.

Friday morning Peggy arrived early and had two Afghan nurses bring the Stryker frame from the basement to the corridor outside Recovery. While Drs. Lindsay and Kash were rounding on their post op. patients she finished attaching the buckles.

Those of the house staff who did not have the day off were curiously inspecting the revolving bed when Amir and Jim happened by. One of the interns was lying face down on the ventral frame and Miss Dolan was adjusting the straps under his forehead and chin.

"Stay right where you are," said Jim. "We'll give you a spin."

The dorsal frame was placed over the young doctor's back like the top half of a hot dog bun, and three large belts were wrapped around the frames to secure him. With Dolan at the head and Jim at the foot, the spring-locked pegs were pulled out and the intern was rotated face-up.

Dr. Kash laughed and tried it himself. Everyone got into the act, cutting into line like patrons at an amusement park.

Mahmud showed up in the midst of this clowning and Jim singled him out, chattering like a side-show hustler. "Come here my good man. See for yourself. Don't be bashful. Step right up. Here we have the 'Shipton Spinner'. The keenest ride in Kabul. More kicks than a Kuchi camel. Stand aside there my friend; let the gentleman pass. Okay, climb aboard. Now hold tight." Jim maintained the patter as Dari was buckled. "Guaranteed to give you the thrill of your life or your money back. Hold tight! Here we go!"

Dari was spun until he was dizzy and the fun ended there as the stitching of a strap gave way and had to be repaired. Dolan was not dismayed. It was a minor calamity, a compromise worthy of the demonstration. There was not a soul in the narrow hall who did not know how to operate her frame.

"Now that it's christened," Jim drawled, "we should have a celebration. Miss Dolan! Would you like to join Dr. Mahmud and me for supper at the staff house tonight?"

"I'd love to," Peggy smiled, "but I can't. My room mate and I are off to Jalalabad for the weekend," she paused for a moment thinking and added, "we'll be back Sunday afternoon. Why don't you bring your friend to our place for a fancy Afghan dinner."

"Okay, Dari? I just got us invited for a home cooked meal."

The student was hesitant. He thanked Dolan for her kind offer, expressing he could not say until he made a few calls.

Dr. Lindsay interrupted his thoughts. "Ready to roll?"

Mahmud looked apprehensive. "I hope you don't mind taking a bus or walking Sir. I do not have a car."

"Don't worry. We've a limousine and a chauffeur parked out back." Jim's playful exaggeration brought a sigh of relief from the student who took him literally. Dari was used to luxury at Gulbahar. There was always a spare vehicle and Ghubar available to drive. In Kabul any form of transportation was welcome. A car was a car no matter what the make. He was using a bicycle.

Another agreeable day forecast a pleasant trip. It was warm, dry and the sky was magnificent. At the sand lot Yar Zamir, perched like a leprechaun, bounced off the hood of the Fiat and opened a passenger door.

When the three of them were tightly packed into the little car Dari asked, "where would you like to go?"

"Well, where did you have in mind? How about you, Yar?"

The driver shrugged and turned to face Dari in the back seat.

"The Doktar would like to see the noon gun fired and follow the wall to Bala Hissar." He checked his watch. "We have three hours until midday."

"Make a circle," Dari suggested. "Out to Paghman and Kargha Lake then back to the central mountain. If the doctor would like to visit the bazaars he might do so this afternoon."

"How far is Paghman?" Asked Jim as they were tossed about by the roughness of the street.

"About twelve miles," Dari answered.

"I take it 'Jaedi' means street."

"Yes. You are right Sir. The one we are now on was named in honour of Maiwand after the first tribal chief raised the banner of independence in Kandahar."

"Who was Maiwand?"

"I beg your pardon Sir."

"Maiwand. The chap, the street is named after."

"Maiwand was not a man," Mahmud smiled. "It is a place. A village northwest of Kandahar in southern Afghanistan. It is where the Ayub Khan almost annihilated a large British force in the second Anglo-Afghan war. I am surprised you did not know. You are a British subject?"

"Yes, but we like to think of the Empire as a Commonwealth. If your ancestors had not been so independent your country would also enjoy the advantage of membership."

"That would be nice Sir but there are too many factions preventing unity among my people. We love freedom, like the Americans; and like them we would have broken away, if we had been subjugated."

They gassed up and headed west toward Paghman, north of a main prong of the Kabul river. Potholes were numerous and Yar was forced to slow down to avoid breaking a spring.

"There is much history around Kabul," Dari commented as they drove through a village of mud-brick walls. "There on the right is a shrine. See the pennants flying above - the Shrine of the Bride and Groom. A legend surrounds it."

"Do you know it?" asked Jim, anxious to learn all he could about afghan lore.

"Yes," Dari smiled.

"Tell me about it."

"This time of year there is not much to see. A grave is all that remains. Years ago a young man of the village married a girl and they had their reception in the garden of Khaja-Mosafer - There! We passed it."

"The wedding party was broken up by messengers, arriving to warn of the approaching enemy. Rather than being slain, the bride prayed to Allah, asking that her loved one and she be turned to stone. They were, and in the presence of their family and friends. Since then, an innocent bride, embracing the statue will have her wish fulfilled. If she is evil, the statue will fall and crush her."

In the ensuing silence, Dari added, "I know many others. Afghanistan abounds in legends. Some of the oldest involve giants and castles, dragons, handsome princes, beautiful maidens, good kings and bad kings. It is a world of make-believe, sprinkled with history and geography. Much of our background is legend by word of mouth. Only recently has our history been recorded; Sohrab and Rustum is the most famous story."

Ah yes!" said Jim approvingly. "I'm familiar with the poem by Matthew Arnold."

They were driving past dormant gardens. "A month from now this place will be fragrant with pink and white blossoms," said Dari, continuing to smile. "You should visit us in the growing season. You have come when the land is cold and barren."

"Yes, but it's still eye-catching," Jim appended.

Back on an open stretch, the highway dipped into a broad valley where bare foothills formed an immense sheltered bowl. A multitude of sheep and camels dotted the low area and off to the left, half a mile away, low black tents surfaced like a fleet of submarines.

"Hold it," Jim shouted, "there's a picture I want."

Yar had barely stopped the car on the soft arid shoulder when a small boy in a beaded green beanie crept from the ditch. Growing inquisitively taller, the lad advanced to the opposing traffic lane and propped himself on a lengthy staff.

"I'll take one of him too Yar, if he'll agree."

The boy surmised what was about to happen and after smoothing a thatch of ratty hair replaced his sparkling cap and ventured closer.

"I am sure he will, Doktar but someone else is about to interfere."

Jim was bent under the lid of the trunk rummaging through his utility bag and had not seen the dark-eyed woman who had also materialized. On hearing Yar's comment he twisted to see a swirl of nomad red. Bespangled from head to toe, she was a gaudy spool of silver. Rings pierced her earlobes and bands ringed her arms. One nostril pricked by a golden charm flared brightly in tune with her angry jangling. Behind, lukewarm to her steamy mood trailed a donkey on a rope. She made for the boy, swaying with each swishing step. Not wishing to be dragged off, he yelled when she yanked his coat. His outburst caused the animal to balk and for a twinkling she was stretched between them like a paper doll.

It was a tempting shot which Jim missed waiting for her permission. By the time he talked Yar into asking her the domestic crisis had ended. With a kick and a cuff from the woman the trio scampered back into the ditch.

A short time later mother and son, or sister and brother - whatever their relationship might have been - were seen skipping off to the encampment on the plain.

It was beginning to break up. Black goat skin tents were being struck, rolled and lashed to the spines of couchant camels. From a knoll, mounted for a better view, Jim watched the graceful desert ships awkwardly slip their moorings, stern legs first. Then their forelegs, flexed beneath a curved prow straightened, and up they bobbed, pitching and yawing, to sail away in a broken line. Through his telescopic lens Jim saw a man on a white horse dash madly ahead of the column. Women and children straggled behind, struggling with their donkey-laden possessions. Grazing flocks of fat-tailed sheep, tended by boys and bearded old men, flanked the procession and spilled over the land, as unsettled as droplets on a bowl of stew.

"Those bustle-tailed woollies are the most peculiar sheep I've ever seen," Jim commented, back in the car. "Looks like they're suffering from severe prolapse."

Mahmud smiled. "The 'bustle' is where they store moisture and energy. Like the hump of the camel it allows them to go long distances."

CHAPTER TWENTY-SIX

At Paghman they saw a multitude of landmarks, man made and commensurate with Afghan life, bleak in early March. Ascending higher, the road passed other monuments and buildings, another square, terraced gardens planted in bleak cherry orchards, arghawan and tulip bulbs. There was a bandstand where a band played for King Amanullah during the summer months.

"It was much different in those days," Dari ventured. "Our present ruler, Zahir Shah, is a constitutional Monarch; he chooses to influence rather than command. Under the guidance of his cousin Daoud we are into our second five year plan. He enlists aid from East and West to improve roads, airports, transportation, power plants and communication and has been successful, but he has overspent his first five year plan and there is much to be done."

"Just this year," Dari continued, "His Majesty decided to separate the crown from the government and we will have a new constitution embodying the division of power among three branches of state: Legislative, Executive and Judiciary. Like the United States we now have political parties and election by universal and secret ballot. The new constitution will grant equal rights to all Afghans, men and women. None of the Royal family may become a minister or member of parliament or hold a position on the supreme court."

"If that is the case all Afghans do not have equal rights," Jim interjected. "You discriminate against your king. You have put him on a shelf; the first stage in getting rid of him. When he's served his purpose he'll be asked to leave."

"Not exactly, Doktar," Yar disagreed. "He put himself on the shelf. Maybe he prefers not to be assassinated as his father was."

The comment brought laughter and when it had subsided," Jim asked. "Is there any communist activity in your country?"

"Communism is not outside the law," Yar answered hesitantly, "But it is not favoured by our people. Our government is composed of a two party system but it is still run by those with money."

"When the wealth of the upper class is depleted by high taxes and too much governmental spending," Dari inserted, "there will be anarchy and despotism. Either we'll go back to our old feudal system, or swing to the extreme left."

Yar drove into the parking lot above a cafe and stopped beside a thick cylinder of stone.

"Are there any elephants around?" asked Jim, unaware of seeing any.

"Only for entertainment," Dari replied, "but we've had them in the past. There is a story one fell wounded at an entrance to Kabul long ago when the Arabs were attacking. The city was held by a Hindu, Shahuja. Of course the city was taken."

Jim affected an English accent. "What do you say we drop into that cafe for a spot of tea, old boy?"

"If you wish Sir, but may I suggest we go on to Kargha Lake. It is more pleasant and there is a restaurant with a better reputation."

Doubling back through Paghman, Yar wheeled the tiny vehicle onto a road lined with spacious villas, dormant gardens interspersed with artificial ponds and rising landscapes set against the rugged snow crested Sulaiman mountains. Finally, where the road curved around the southern end of a lake they came to a new dam wide enough for crossing vehicles. On the far side Yar brought the Fiat to rest.

In the courtyard of a Chaykhanah Dari summoned a round of sweet tea and nan. Jim was beginning to suspect the impure flour used in its baking was the cause of his current malady and he was uncertain how much food he could take. "Order a meal if you want," he suggested. "We haven't time to visit the bazaars before noon."

The Afghans welcomed the opportunity and on short order the waiter brought a steaming platter of rice and stewed lamb. While Mahmud and Yar scooped up the food on chunks of unleavened bread Jim ate sparingly.

Dari brought up the Kabul wall. "Truly no one knows who built it or when," he commented. "It likely dates back to the White Huns. They poured in from Russia across the Hindu Kush and overran the Kushan Buddhists. Later the Persians and western Turks took Kabul and must have had a go at restoring the fortification. No matter, the wall, though incomplete was in place when the Arabs gained control."

"According to legend," Dari continued. "The wall was built by the last king of a dynasty of Turks called the Ratbils. He was a tyrant and conscripted workers from his oppressed subjects. No one dared oppose him in fear of death. To carry out his orders, especially being conscripted to build his wall, was a death sentence in itself for the work was excruciating. Those who did not pull their weight, through laziness or weakness were either killed or buried alive in the depths of the construction. Imagine being compelled to listen to the pitiful cries of your entombed friends until death silenced them."

"Among the populace, so the legend goes, was a young bachelor. His obsession for his sweetheart made him weak and cowardly and he hid in fear of the king's men, believing he would die on the wall or be immured forever, never to enjoy his love. The girl had more courage than her fiance. While he hid in terror she took his place, passing as a man alongside the workers. One day when the king arrived on inspection she purposely drew a veil across her face. When he asked why a woman was there working with the men her reply was to throw a rock, knocking him off his horse; he died on the spot. This act of bravery became the signal for an uprising. The king's men were beaten. There was great rejoicing and the people descended from the hill never to return to the wall again.

"What happened to the girl? Dr. Lindsay asked.

"She went back to her fearful lover."

"Interesting yarn," said Jim, draining his teacup, "I know a few liberated women who will relish that one."

Returning to the roaring rhetoric of the city, the little car entered the stream of life, corpuscling its way toward the southern mountain. High above, and sparingly covered with snow, the top of Sher Darwaza sparkled in the noon sun. By a winding lane Yar urged the Fiat up the base, toward a jutting ledge where two decrepit cannons poked their muzzles over Kabul. His eyes fixed on the narrow road he motioned for his passengers to take a peek at Babur's tomb, lying at the foot of the slope. Then, skirting the ledge he parked on the fringe of a cramped plateau.

They were right on time. The wizened gunner was ramming home a wad of cloth. Silently he acknowledged the visitors, laid down the eight foot ramrod and stood beside a cannon wheel, probing his vest for a pocket watch. Steel-rimmed, the wheels were taller than the patriarch and splayed on their axles, were packed in rubble to prevent the carriage from recoiling. After plugging his ears he cupped the timepiece in his hands.

"Go stand beside him," said Jim, stepping backward to fit the entire length of the cannon in his viewfinder.

"Let me take the picture and you stand beside him," Dari proposed. "If you'll show me how it works."

"Okay," Jim agreed, and after adjusting for light and distance so Mahmud had only to press a button, ambled toward the gun.

Head bowed, eyeing his watch, the patriarch was unmindful of the ferangi's putting an arm around his shoulders, or of Yar Zamir crowding his other side.

There was a click and Dari hurriedly handed the camera to Jim, urging him to be ready for it was almost noon. Jim was in no rush. Being familiar with the operation of his Conterax he followed close on the heels of the fastidious old man, shooting each stage of the loading.

Several small boys had sprouted from nowhere. A clump of mushrooms in their oversized turbans, they were more captivated by the photographer than the daily event. Wide eyed they watched him lean against the business end of the barrel his camera aimed at the priming charge as it poured from a ten pound bag.

When the gunner was satisfied a sufficient amount of black powder had entered the vent he rolled the residual in an oilskin, placed it aside and lit the punk.

Jim was focusing on the touch-hole from behind when Yar cautioned. "Best stand back Doktar. The bang will break your ears."

Baroooooom! The explosion almost blew Jim off his feet and swallowed him in a cloud of white smoke. Coughing and grinning he faded in a moment later. "That one ought to win a prize," he crowed, his ear drums still humming.

As the echo resounded over the city the mushrooms uprooted themselves and spread out on the flat. When they saw the ferangi slip the old man a tip they regrouped, transforming into a circle of beggars. "Piquetur Sahib, Piquetur for baksheesh," they cried. "Baksheesh Mistah. Baksheesh."

"You'll have to do something for it," Jim demanded and moved to the spiked second gun. "Climb up here," he said, stroking the barrel.

Eventually they understood. Straddling the huge cannon, they strung out along its length, save the smallest who was left to tend a mean looking mongrel. Holding tightly to the leash, he too had his picture taken.

Jim gave them each ten afs and ten more to the boy with the dog and returned to his friends, trusting the little beggars would leave but they hung around like pilot fish.

"Now for the wall, Dari," he grinned. "How about it?"

Mahmud tilted his head at the crumbling rampart, "I'm sorry Sir, but I 'd only hold you up." He frowned, "I have a problem with my leg."

The opening Dr. Lindsay awaited had finally surfaced. Curiously he asked, "What sort of problem?"

"It's a long sad story and I do not wish to discuss it."

Jim felt let down. He preferred to have someone accompany him. The thought of Dari being unable had never occurred. However, he'd planned on the hike and wanted to take it. "Too bad," he said. "Is there anything I can do?"

"No Sir. I have no pain. I can walk fine on level ground. Only irregular surfaces give me a problem."

"Sorry you must pass it up and please don't think I'm unsociable; from the top of Sher Darwaza the view must be terrific."

"Not at all, Sir. I have many things to keep me occupied. Later, if it is still your wish to visit the bazaar I will meet you at the Bala Hissar. If not I will see you at the staff house tonight."

"Okay," said Jim. Turning to Yar, he advised, "It should take me about three hours," and set off along the path.

The boys followed, in spite of the old gunner's order to stop pestering the 'Ferangi'.

Rhapsodizing the execrable 'Baksheesh', this entourage soon outwore its welcome. Patience and endurance paid off and several hundred yards on, after he'd shown them his empty pockets, they began to trickle down the mountain.

One lad persisted farther. With a pathetic expression he took off his shoes and held them up to his gullible victim. There were holes in the soles large enough to admit three fingers. It was a performance executed with Machiavellian finesse and Jim dipped into his wallet for an American five.

The boy's feet were as agile as his mind and he skipped down the sharp shale slope, shoes in hand, like a sure-footed goat, needing footwear like a hole in the head.

As Jim watched, feeling a mixture of reproach and admiration, the boy stopped. Gesturing upward he shouted, "Koob nez! Koob nez!" and spun on the jagged stones to disappear behind a boulder.

Literally translated, no good, no good, was either a criticism or a warning. Perhaps the bill was not enough and he had been told off. Remembering Yar's words of the day before, 'some people go up and never come back' Jim began to wonder if the boy had been pointing at the peak.

Half a mile further the land began to level and Jim paused at a cleft in the wall to look at the sprawling city. The venous blue Kabul river wound through the heart of an urban metabolism, pulsating with anachronisms.

Directly below, outside a mosque, a waving field of men were bowing in the street, reminding him it was the Muslim Sabbath and also of his aversion to organized religion. Jim felt sorry for them. Such regimentation had to be stifling. How could anyone get closer to his Maker than standing in reverence alone on a mountain surrounded by a miraculous gift of natural beauty. Possibly the men on the ground gained as much gratification from prostrating themselves but he couldn't believe it. He paused and took a few pictures.

In Jim's mind there were only two forces which affected him 'pull and push' each having its own synonyms, but in the final analysis boiled down to love and hate. Either in excess was harmful. There were positive and negative thoughts, attractions and repulsions. Individual tastes impossible to argue lay somewhere in between. To him the bent bodies, cringing in the dirt, resembled a group therapy class and from his present elevation their concerted calisthenics seemed utterly mad. He had accepted long ago there was a divine omnipotence controlling the universe, an energy to be respected, an impersonal one, undeserving of the selfish petitions of man. When plagued with guilt, a feeling commonly experienced by surgeons, he'd asked the Creator for guidance to overcome a ticklish problem which he himself had created, feeling even more guilty he lacked the perspicacity and endurance to solve it. Even then he did not need a church. There were no spoken prayers, just a communicative thought.

Pain, physical or emotional, and fear had never driven him to seek the Almighty either - until Jason was killed. Fear had overwhelmed him the instant he suspected something disastrous had happened. Once he knew the irreversible truth it dissipated and he was full of despondency and the pain of pity and sorrow for Merri and the girls. Comforting them caused more misery. A tragedy had passed through their lives. There was nothing they could've done to prevent it, nor could it be cancelled or rectified. If there was a Heaven above, he rationalized, Jason surely hadn't been denied entrance for the boy was innocent. If so there was the possibility of a reunion, so the Bible would have him believe. But he couldn't conceive of a life in the hereafter. If he didn't believe in Heaven or Hell why taint his sanity with false hope? Jason was gone in every sense, only the memory of him lived. Neither God nor Beelzebub was about to return his son, not for anything he might offer in exchange, the least of which were his eyes now beset by a magnificent view. For a moment the scene was tainted with bitterness and he would've sold his sight to have Jason back.

At the summit Jim crossed through a gap to the north side of the wall and continued his trek southeastward, coming upon a low rectangular enclosure farther along, possibly an outpost in by-gone days. Ramparts thick and disintegrating contained a drift of irregular earth highlighted by moguls of packed snow, sand and crumbling stone. Attracted by the strange unevenness he entered the grounds and began poking around. The inner surface of the walls were pitted and pocked and partially excavated in places, with holes large enough to admit a man. Interestingly, where the mud-brick veneer had been eroded there was not the expected gravitation of earth beneath. Some thing or person must have pushed it away from the base into the central area. Someone looking for something? Maybe an archaeologist trying to unravel the Ratbil legend? Mechanically he began to kick and scrape at a friable clod beside him. Espying a white object the shape and size of a wrist bone, possibly from a workman buried in the rubble, Jim picked it up but it was merely polished stone.

He left the fort the way he entered through a rent in the northern rampart and regained the path, now shaded from the afternoon sun. The climb in the light air and the glare and heat of midday affected him. Sweat was running into his collar and his sport coat weighed a ton. He removed it along with the camera and loosened his tie, thinking it was time for a breather and a cool drink, then chided himself for leaving the water-bottle back in the car. A smudgy patch of snow beckoned like an oasis. He knelt beside it, scuffed off the icy scum and scooped up a handful of the cleaner snow underneath. After licking a pint he sat down at the base of a buttress, cushioned by his corduroy jacket and set his camera aside.

Several feet beyond the shadowed outline of the wall the ground dropped off steeply. From where he was seated, leaning back against the rampart the whole plain east of the city came into view, from Bemaru heights, commanding the left, to a moat south of the Bala Hissar. Fascinated he took it all in, unleashing his imagination: British emissaries, riding on brightly caparisoned chargers, carrying Generals Pollock and Roberts through lines of pompous red uniforms; splendour on the Citadel's walls. For several minutes he sat, fantasizing the past, enthraled with the panorama of 'snowy summits old in story', mentally reciting Queen Victoria's poet laureate, 'blow bugle blow, set the wild echoes flying: blow bugle; answer echoes, dying, dying, dying.'

After a while his shirt dried and he removed his slackened tie. Since he had been resting the shadow of the Kabul wall had moved to within a yard of the brow. Pondering it, he noticed where it was marginally straight before there was now a bulge directly in line with his head. Although he felt ridiculous because no part of him was exposed to the sun he wagged his head from side to side, expecting the shadow to move. It didn't. If anything it had grown smaller. He twisted around to scan the top of the wall but there was nothing accountable. Whatever caused the bulge had gone. Odd, he thought, trying to shrug off a feeling he was being watched. Twice more it appeared. Reinvestigation revealed nothing. Next time he calculated, I'll wait.

There it was again and getting larger. Someone or something was climbing the rampart behind him. Whoever, or whatever was making no effort to communicate, certainly not by phonetic means. In the hush he began to pivot, slowly keeping an eye on the shadow until suddenly it leapt to the edge of the drop-off. "Gotcha" he guessed, swiftly springing to his feet and completing the turn. The sight was terrifying. Standing on top of the wall was the black bearded Hashim, wild-eyed with madness, raising a huge rock.

Everything happened so fast Jim could never be sure. Later he remembered, pressing hard against the rampart, reducing the target to the size of his head and protecting it with his encircling arms. Reaching higher to fend off the inevitable missile, to sweep it away or pull it from Hashim's grasp, madly beating the space above until he came up with a pair of ankles. It took all his strength to dislodge them but failed to prevent the rock from smashing his left arm. The pain was excruciating, worse while countering with his right to catch his assailant in the stomach. The blow landed as Hashim skidded down the face of the wall, paralyzing his diaphragm and doubling him with breathlessness.

Limp and bleeding, Jim watched the man roll off the edge and land on a less penchant incline farther down. He struggled to the rim wondering if he could detect any sign of consciousness but all he could see was a contorted body and staggered back to the wall.

CHAPTER TWENTY-SEVEN

"Maybe he went back to the noon gun."

It was the first time Yar Zamir had spoken English since he left Dr. Lindsay on the far side of the mountain several hours ago and an indication of his impatience. The delay meant nothing; it was the worry. A large part of his job with S.E.R.V.E. was spent in limbo, waiting upon the whims of a visiting specialist or his wife while he, she or they bargained in the bazaars or debated where to go or what to do. Today he had allowed one of them to explore a place where criminals and estranged members of Kabul society were suspected of hiding. Reverting to English was a subconscious effort to share his feelings.

After depositing Mahmud at the dormitory Yar went home for a couple of hours. Later he returned to pick up the student and drive through the city, skirting Sher Darwaza, to end up in the public cemetery at the opposite end of the wall. From here, in the company of Kabul's dead and departed below the desolate towers of Bala Hissar, the two Afghans were able to keep the south side of the eastern rampart in view.

Dari did not respond to the driver's suggestion immediately. He was busy watching a rabble of goats; the giddy miscreants were irreverently foraging the burial ground, frolicking over the rocky mounds. One of them, cavorting on its hind legs was trying to pinch a scarlet streamer, flying in remembrance of a beloved soul, the only distinguishing mark the grave-site had. When he finally spoke, his tone did not suit the desecrating indifference surrounding him.

"No. I do not think so. He would not deliberately change his plan. Something extraordinary has happened I fear."

While Dari was speaking he swung his feet out of the car and began to roll up his right pant leg. "If you think he went back to the noon gun then go and see," he said. "I will start the climb from here."

The statement came as a surprise to Yar who had heard the student turn down the Doktar's invitation on the grounds he had a problem with his foot. Speechless he turned to scrutinize his passenger whose leather-cuffed thigh was fully exposed. A steel hinge on either side of the knee connected to a flesh coloured foot.

"I can manage the slope better without this," Dari continued. "With it on I have to walk sideways uphill because it has no ankle joint. Some things I can do more easily without it." He smiled, "it is ideal for traversing a hill provided I go counterclockwise."

About to withdraw his stump from the socket he added cynically. "I leave this infernal device with you. It is the work of a Jinn. So do not worry if someone steals it. The thief will get what he deserves."

"No," Yar objected so emphatically Dari twisted around to face him, thinking the driver had taken him seriously.

"I see him. There," Yar pointed, "by the bend in the wall."

Recognizing the familiar bronze corduroy jacket casually draped on the advancing form their uneasiness lessened. The driver's tense declaration drew it back like a loaded bow.

"There is something wrong!" To Yar an indefinable flaw warned him something was not right and he feared the worst. "The man is hurt!" he cried.

Before Dari could re-apply his prosthesis his companion had cut the distance to Dr. Lindsay in half.

Jim saw them coming and would have waited for help but the gradient dropped him faster than he could go. He was forced to run and while he clutched his left arm his jacket and the Conterax slipped from his right shoulder and dragged him off balance. Down the incline he bolted out of control until an abrupt encounter with level ground brought him to his knees.

When Yar got to him he was rocking in a sitting position hugging his useless arm. Pain glazed his eyes and a handkerchief wrapped around his left elbow was soaked with blood.

When the limb was splinted and tied with cotton pennants, borrowed from the cemetery, the two Afghans helped Jim into the car. Not wishing to cause embarrassment both refrained from asking questions.

Yar started the engine. Fearful of jostling his injured passenger, he cautiously reversed onto the gravel road bordering the moat where there was room to swing the Fiat around. Automatically he steered for the Infirmary at the U.S. AID compound. It was not until they were almost there, Jim offered an explanation.

"It was Hashim." In spite of the splint his arm throbbed and he winced. "The man tried to kill me. He's probably where I left him."

The driver's normally serene features hardened at the mention of Hashim. He let Dr. Lindsay continue uninterrupted while Dari leaned closer from the back seat listening intently.

"I was sitting at the base of the rampart with my back against the wall when he crept up behind me." Jim paused to suck in a breath. "Luckily his shadow gave him away and I was able to turn at the last minute or he'd have bashed my skull. Instead the rock hit my arm. There's no doubt the bone is broken; a fragment is protruding through the skin and my elbow feels out of place. It will need an open reduction."

"What is 'open reduction'?" Yar asked.

"An operation," Dari said. "To put the bones back in place."

Jim closed his eyes, grimacing as he futilely strained to bend his arm. A wave of nausea passed before he reopened them and went on stammering, "Hashim lost his footing and slipped off the wall. I hit him in the pit of the stomach, knocking the wind out of him. He fell over the edge and is lying on the slope unconscious. Possibly he was breathing but I couldn't tell." Jim sighed. "He might need help."

"Let the vultures pick his bones," Yar hissed. "He was the aggressor. You had the right to fight back." Harshly the Afghan continued. "It is written in the 'Sura of the yellow cow'. Fight in the way of Allah against those who fight against you but begin no hostilities for Allah does not love aggression. The one who attacks you, attack him in the manner he does unto you and know Allah is on the side of those who ward off evil."

"Someone should treat his injuries, we can't leave him there."

"Let him be, Doktar. It is not up to you to help him. If Hashim ceases to be aggressive, Allah may be forgiving and merciful."

Dr. Lindsay did not have the strength to pursue the issue. He wanted to lie down. His mouth was dry and he needed water. The Fiat's constant bobbing made him dizzy; he felt like retching.

What remained of Jim's strength and the breadth of Mahmud's shoulders got him onto his feet and upstairs to the Infirmary. The only patient on the ward, fully clothed and folded like an accordion, he was angled into a standard sized hospital cot.

His colour returned with recumbency, sips of water and a warm blanket thrown over him by the portly nurse who had met them at the front door. Subsequently she excused herself to notify Dr. Tomarin.

Ten minutes later the AID physician rushed in, flushed from a game of tennis, and Jim was obliged to narrate the preceding events all over.

Dari and Yar listened, unwilling to leave until a definite plan had been outlined. They idled at the foot of the bed while Ezra Tomarin lent an unwilling ear, as if the story were interfering with a message he was receiving from the strumming wind. Vacillating from the urgent matter of the man lying in front of him to the incriminating circumstances putting him there, he hemmed and hawed, eventually blurting, "Maybe Hashim will lay countercharges. The Canadian Consulate should be alerted. In an impartial law court it would be his word against yours. Though from the man's behaviour, I do not think anyone will believe him."

"To hell with legalities." Jim's voice rose in pitch. "We don't even know the full story. The man is either dead or lying up there in dire straits. Why can't someone go have a look, if for no other reason than to relieve my conscience."

"Your conscience or your curiosity?"

As Ezra intended, his cynical remark irritated. In a placating tone he added. "Certainly you do not feel responsible for the fate of the madman? He attacked you."

Jim eyed the AID physician sharply. The strain of arguing had stiffened his muscles and he groaned as a spasm seized his damaged arm. When it passed he replied. "Yes my conscience. Not for what happened up there. I know it wasn't my fault. I didn't push him off the crest but I left him with possible fatal injuries expecting to get first aid. Sure my conscience bothers me and will until someone can be persuaded to look after him. No man is perfect, neither is one worthless."

Ezra scowled. He was slightly built, in his early forties. Whether or not he believed Dr. Lindsay's sincerity was impossible to read in the expression on his bony face. His authority was limited to the Infirmary but he could ask the sergeant in charge of securing the compound for a detail of off-duty guards to scout Sher Darwaza. As soon as the idea formed the AID physician dismissed it. He hated to meddle and the move might back-fire. The sight of an Afghan being escorted by a party of uniformed Americans would raise a lot of questions, be difficult to explain and might draw allegations upon himself. He was not listening and Mahmud was forced to repeat his offer to take on the task twice, before it finally sunk in.

Raking his fingers through his hair, Ezra studied the young man before nodding, "Go ahead. You can borrow a First Aid pack but be sure you return it." He slanted his head toward the portly nurse standing in the doorway. "Mrs. Collins will lend you one."

"A stretcher might be useful," Jim added, "he'll need someone to help." Puzzled, he shifted from Ezra to Mahmud. "What about your foot?"

Dari ignored the question and took Dr. Lindsay's hand. "If I need help I will ask my friend Sayyid. We live together at the dormitory. First I will go and see, starting from Avicenna."

The student's easy smile imparted trust as he backed toward the door saying, "I will do all in my power to allay your conscience Sir. There is nothing I can do for you here. May Allah guide you!"

It took an hour to run the routine laboratory tests and develop a set of x-rays. Dr. Tomarin performed the screening himself. When he returned from the darkroom the verdict was as suspected: both bones were involved. The force of the blow had fractured the ulna, proximal to its mid-shaft. That much was already evident; a jagged end had come through the skin. However the x-ray did more than confirm the bone was broken. The break was straight across and the two fragments were overriding. Jim looked at the films himself and concurred with Ezra's finding, adding another. "The head of the radius is displaced. It's not where it should be."

"There it is," Jim muttered. "Dislocated. You can see the radial head lying in front and above the capitellum. A Monteggia fracture dislocation - extension type"

Dr. Tomarin wasn't as sure. Holding the dripping films up to the window a second time, he tried to place the capitellum. Somewhere at the lower end of the arm bone, there was a rounded knob he vaguely remembered from his anatomy. Tracing the humerus to its junction with the two forearm bones Ezra came across it, or what he thought it to be. Something looked out of place and he was still trying to figure it out when he heard a dejected Dr. Lindsay ask, "where do I go from here?"

Ezra closed his eyes and cupped his nose pinching the bridge, seemingly in seance with the supernatural. "It's up to you," he

Do Unto Others

said finally. "I have not much to offer besides advice and if you want my opinion go see the nearest orthopaedic surgeon." Ezra flashed a weak smile and added soberly, "there isn't one between here and Teheran other than yourself. Perhaps in New Delhi but the trip would be too strenuous."

"What about a plane?"

"There are no flights to India till next Wednesday. You'd best leave tomorrow. Take the Ariana D.C.6 to Beirut or London. Either place is on your return ticket and won't cost you an extra fare."

Jim frowned, took a deep breath and let it out airily. A specialist flown in would have the same flight problems. Unless there was a private aircraft available and if so it was quicker for him to fly out. "It'll be too late," he fussed. "This wound needs attention now or I'll end up with a bum result. If it's open another day it'll get infected."

Ezra regarded his patient encouragingly. "That can be taken care of. I will cleanse, debride and close the skin with a local anaesthetic."

"No. No, please don't misunderstand. The head of the radius needs accurate replacement. The longer it remains dislocated the more difficult it will be to put back and the greater the likelihood of arthritis developing later. No. It must be fixed now."

Ezra's thin skinned features wrinkled further and the high points of his cheeks glowed. "I'm sorry," he said, sounding determined, "but I'd be doing you a disservice. I'm not prepared to take on that kind of responsibility nor do I have the equipment. A simple debridement is what you need and the wound closed. The fancy operation can be done later by an expert elsewhere."

It was sensible advice. Dr. Lindsay, in light of his experience and looking at the situation as objectively as he could was compelled to disagree. Although it was chancy the initial treatment would have to be definitive, the management of which he couldn't carry out himself. He recalled how Merri had kidded him on pinning so many hips he could do the operation blindfolded with one arm tied behind his back. Now cursed with a similar handicap and being blinded by pain and personal involvement he was in a position to prove her point. Hip pinnings were far more common than open reductions of the elbow. Impossible. Somehow the odds had to be improved. What he needed was an extra pair of hands to do his bidding; to this end a general anaesthetic was out of the question. "Have you had any experience with brachial blocks," he asked.

Dr. Tomarin frowned and turned away. "Yes," he answered, "during the Korean war I did a number of them. That was over ten years ago."

"How would you like to brush up your technique on me?" Sensing an aversion to his proposal, as Ezra failed to reply within a reasonable time, Jim continued, sounding as if for most operations all one needed was a do-it-yourself kit. "If the rules can be bent to grant Amir Kash temporary operating privileges, I'll put myself in his hands if I'm able to direct them. A brachial block should be ideal. It will anaesthetize my whole arm, relax the muscles and permit the use of a tourniquet. What do you say?"

Ezra was on the verge of tossing in the adage 'Any man who tries his own case has a fool for a lawyer' but settled on a more practical argument. "There's the instrumentation! We've nothing but soft tissue stuff. No plates, screws nor intra-medullary rods."

"They may not be necessary," Jim was quick to point out. "If someone can bring a set of bone holding forceps and retractors over from the Avicenna they'll be all we'll need. Just in case, there is a graduated nest of Rush pins in the O.R. cupboard. Amir can bring them as well. I'd prefer not to have any metal put in at this stage as it increases the danger of infection." He smiled again before adding, "Hope you've got lots of antibiotic."

Dr. Tomarin was no gambler and had a chimeric fear of errors of commission. Unmarried, to the disappointment of his Jewish parents, he withdrew from as much personal responsibility as he could and enlisted in the marines, spending the Korean conflict as second-in-command of the sick bay on an aircraft carrier anchored off Seoul. Following the war Dr. Tomarin transferred to the Department of External Affairs and was assigned to his present position. Subordinate to higher authority and to his own inferiority complex, the AID physician enjoyed a measure of emotional relief. The forceful manner of Jim Lindsay was rocking the foundation of his security. To save himself Ezra had to make a move before the orthopaedic surgeon went over his head. "All right," he mumbled, "I'll have to get in touch with the Embassy."

Twenty minutes later in a sombre mood, Ezra returned to relate the Ambassador had been contacted and gave his permission. He'd phoned Art Billings also. Although the Peace Corps doctor was initially appalled he'd replied exuberantly and would be more than happy to assist Dr. Kash. A third call failed to reach the nurse-in-charge of the operating room. The AID physician groaned, "I'll have to set up the O.R. myself." Handing Yar Zamir the list of instruments which Dr. Lindsay considered absolutely essential, he ordered the driver to fetch them as soon as possible, along with Amir Kash and Rabia, the most competent scrub nurse at Avicenna.

CHAPTER TWENTY-EIGHT

Delighted by Dr. Lindsay's choice, Amir Kash was briefed on the operation.

At nineteen hundred hours the autoclave timer buzzed as Jim was being positioned on the table: face up, his chin tilted to the right, his splinted left arm beside him.

The coldness of a swab on his neck caused second thoughts. Perhaps he should call the whole thing off, take Tomarin's advice and head for home. He regarded his intact right arm, tempted to pull it from the gauze strapping holding it down. What if the block didn't take? Could he stand the pain? If it worked would it allow sufficient muscle relaxation? What if the tourniquet gave out? He'd lost a fair amount of blood and there was not a bottle of his type in the refrigerator. If the tourniquet worked he wouldn't need any.

"I'm going to raise a wheal," he heard Ezra say. "You'll feel a pinprick and a shock-like sensation will shoot down your arm."

Jim twitched when the needle struck bone. In a few minutes his tingling fingers turned numb. It was strange not to feel the constricting pressure of the tourniquet or the Afghan surgeon's hands removing the splint from his limb. With returning courage, alert and almost comfortable, he saw his floppy arm no longer a functioning part of him, being held aloft and doused with methylated spirits.

The first stage began with an irrigation of the wound. The ragged skin edges were trimmed and debris discarded. Using a direct pull, with Dr. Billings providing counter traction, Amir was able to place the ulnar fragments end on; but when the traction was released they wouldn't stay. After several attempts had failed, Jim suggested, "you'll have to reduce the radial head first. Once in position it will act as a natural distractor and keep the ulnar fragments from overriding."

Amir tried to manipulate the head of the radius with his thumb but it wouldn't budge. "There is soft tissue in the way Doktar," he proposed. "I will have to open the elbow."

Jim bit his lip. "Then approach it anterolaterally and be careful not to injure any vessels or nerves. "Make a lazy S incision. Start it above the lateral end of the distal humerus then curve it across the front of the elbow and extend it distally along the inside of the forearm. Do not start it too far distally and keep it close to the radial joint line. I don't want you damaging my supinator nerve. The head has probably poked through a rent in the joint capsule and won't go back because the edges of the tear have closed around the neck. It's the same as the slit in a shirt for a button and like a button hole you'll have to pry the tear open to reduce the head. Use the elevator as a lever and make the rent bigger by extending it. You'll have to pull down the length of my arm as well."

Each step was reiterated as the operation proceeded until Amir, sweating profusely, straightened and regarded Jim quizzically. "I have done everything you say but it will not slip back into joint."

"Can you feel the head of the radius?" Jim asked, lifting his shoulders off the table and straining to see over the obstructing drapes. If his right hand had not been securely fastened he would have reached into the operative field. He glared at the intravenous tubing leading away from it.

"Yes. I can also see it." Amir's masked face was almost in the wound.

"Can you see the neck?"

"No.

"Then you'll have to enlarge the hole in the capsule."

"I do not know this word 'capsule'."

When describing the operation to Dr. Kash Jim had assumed the chief resident knew common anatomical terms. He closed his eyes and asked, "Do you know what fibrous tissue is?"

"Like sinews?"

"Yes. Just like sinews. It's the tough whitish substance connecting muscles to bone and bone to bone. A capsule consists of a thin layer of the stuff. It surrounds the ends of the bones forming the joint.

"Ah yes. I understand and can feel it now," Amir nodded.

Jim lifted his head to see what Kash was doing and discovered the surgeon had a scalpel in his hand directed perpendicular to the joint. "Don't cut it like that," he exclaimed. "Not crosswise and don't use a knife. Take a pair of scissors. Push the closed points into the tear and spread them open."

One look at Amir's eyes revealed the chief resident was confused. "Please do as I say," Jim pleaded. "It's very simple. All you have to do is spread the tear open in line with the capsular fibres. If you feel more comfortable using a knife then do so but make the cut longitudinal." Jim shook his head and dropped back on the slender pillow. A second later he heaved himself up again and continued in a raised voice "I mean up and down, not across. Once you get the radial head in its proper place a longitudinal incision will be easier to close and may prevent the head from popping out again."

Moments later Amir announced. "I have widened the hole but it will not reduce."

"Try pulling harder. It's got to go back." Jim began to sweat. It had to reduce. The only thing he could imagine preventing replacement of the radial head was muscle spasm. "Art," he demanded, "get a grip around my upper arm so Amir has something to pull against and you Amir while you're pulling with your left put your right thumb on the head and push it back through the rent in the capsule."

Unable to feel Jim sensed the developing tug of war through Billings clenched teeth. A dull clunk broke the tension.

"Ah, we have it!" Amir cried puffing from exertion. Unfortunately he relaxed his hold and the elbow promptly re-dislocated. "But it will not stay!"

Jim partly raised his head but it was impossible to see around Billings broad back and he slumped on the cushion. Don't let it get to you, he told himself. There's something you're forgetting and instantly he knew. "It's the biceps!" he declared. "You'll have to relax it. Reduce the head but this time before you let up on the traction bend my elbow as far as it will go and supinate my forearm. That will put the biceps in a shortened position; it won't be able to contract."

The chief resident, obsessed with reproducing his previous feat had not been listening but Art had. When the radial head clunked into its normal position he clasped the wrist, flexed the forearm and twisted the palm so it was facing the patient's shoulder. "Match point and game over!" he exclaimed. "Now what?"

Jim barked "Hang on for God's sake! Don't extend my elbow an inch. Not even to set the ulnar fragments and close the incisions. Keep it there till the plaster hardens." He grinned with relief adding, "let go and I'll break your arm."

Art's face rounded with amusement, crinkling his blood speckled mask. "Is that any way to talk to a lowly assistant? Such bravado! I should put it back the way it was and let you try." Art chuckled at the absurdity of his remark and carried on. "Here I've been for the past hour, clenching my fingers to the bone, pouring out buckets of sweat and tears and - "

"My blood," Jim interrupted. "It's all over your face. What happened to the tourniquet?"

Before answering Art had to round off his remark. "That's all the thanks I get," then he laughed. "Nuthin! It splattered out of the wound the first time Amir reduced the head. You had enough haemoglobin in your joint to support an elephant on cardiac surgery."

Suppressing his cynicism, Ezra Tomarin had remained out of the conversation. He had become party to an outlandish escapade he had openly tried to avoid and would likely never be convinced. Squeamish by nature he had not left his post at the head of the table to check on the brutish aspect of the operation, best carried out in a butcher shop as far as he was concerned. Keeping tabs on the patient's general condition had been his job and it had not been easy. Lindsay had been springing up and down like a 'Yo-Yo'. While the cast was being applied he looked down at the large brown eyes, shining with self reparation and confidence, qualities he had never possessed. But he felt no envy, rationalizing Jim Lindsay was an aggressive, reckless fool who could have done more harm to himself. It was pure luck the operation had succeeded. Sarcasm took over. "What other miracles can you perform, J.C.?"

"It's C.J.," Jim corrected, "and neither initial stands for 'Jesus' or 'Christ' if that's what you're intimating."

Dr. Billings buoyed above the current of innuendos and burst out comically, "Wait till he sees the scar, Ezra, and has only himself to sue." The Peace Corp physician was a born optimist and because of his surgical inexperience hadn't shared Dr. Tomarin's misgivings. Fat, short, jovial, apt to be cast as a court jester, water boy or cheer leader, Art Billings had signed on with the Peace Corps, dragging his wife and three kids to Afghanistan where he hoped to play a role overshadowing the aura surrounding him. Unlike Tomarin he wasn't envious but quite open. In future fantasizing he'd identify with Jim Lindsay, embellishing the story of the arm-chair orthopod to legendary proportions. His boyish face was still shining with admiration as he helped his idol assume a semi-reclining attitude on a pillow banked cot in the room.

After leaving the US Infirmary Mahmud walked north until he came to a bridge over the south branch of the Kabul river. There he sat for several minutes considering alternatives. Beyond the far end of the bridge a curved road ran between the central and southern mountains which would bring him to the Avicenna. Closer to the bridge was the lane past Babur Shah Park leading up to the noon gun. Some distance to the west was the University and his room-mate Sayyid, if he happened to be there. Thinking his friend was probably attending a party at Kargha Lake, he hadn't bothered.

Mahmud swung his legs loosely, striking his heels on the concrete balusters. The task he had wilfully undertaken would have to be done alone. Listening to the thud of his fibreglass foot he began to wonder why he'd got himself into this predicament. Climbing was not as easy as he had told Yar Zamir. It was true he could climb better without his artificial limb but without a foot he lacked propulsion. His gaze wandered to the jutting plateau and the muzzle of one of the cannons. The slope above it was steep but manageable.

Pride and resentment had caused him to decline Dr. Lindsay's genial invitation. He had prepared to meet the occasion by loading his sports peg in a bag on his bicycle but to satisfy his conscience when reneging he rationalized the orthopaedic surgeon saw an excessive number of cripples in his daily routine; why expose him to another on his free time? Still if he had gone along with Dr. Lindsay the vicious assault likely wouldn't have happened and there would be no need for this reconnaissance.

Dari arrived at the courtyard behind the Avicenna, relieved to see his bicycle was still chained to the rack. He dropped the kit Mrs. Collins had given him beside it, unlocked the leather bags on either side of the rear wheel and took out several items: traditional garb, a scabbard, sheathing a knife, a running shoe and a rubber tipped hollow wooden peg. In the shadow of the cook house his suit and prosthesis were exchanged for baggy pants, a tunic and mismatched footwear. Before putting on the tunic he slung the scabbard's strap from his right shoulder and adjusted it against his right side, bringing the hilt of the knife level with his waist. Turning his attention to the kit he removed a few gauze dressings and pocketed them, thinking they could be useful. "I might need them for myself," he smirked.

Above him the Kabul wall had grown a mane of golden dust, swept by a late afternoon wind on the crest. Looking at the bare boulder strewn slope, he picked out a path of ascent, locked his valuables in the leather bags and slipped through the back entrance to the hospital.

At the emergency desk Mahmud left the canvas kit with the nurse in charge, telling her it belonged to the U.S. Government and must be returned to Miss Dolan in the morning.

Scrambling up the steep northern slope Mahmud fumbled under his tunic to ensure the knife was in place; It was still there when he reached the path, paralleling the wall. Burnished by the setting sun the whole complex could have been a heavenly shrine but Mahmud knew better. Aware of the dangers within the decadent ramparts he proceeded slowly, pausing at regular intervals to study the terrain.

Not far from the top something off to his left looked out of place. Lighter than the greyish brown rock, it lay on a flatter piece of ground; above it the grade steepened. He crouched against the wall and stared. The unknown seemed to move.

More cautious now he resumed his climb, his perspective broadening until the heap became an oblong shape and the movement, cloth quavering in a gust of wind.

Pulverized debris spilled from a rampart; Dari used this spill to mount the wall for a better look. Once on top he could see within the enclosure. Satisfied there was no one there he moved a few yards further along until he came upon a gouge as though a rock had been moved out of place. A flash of colour caught his eye and he looked down to see Dr. Lindsay's green and yellow tie. Dari lowered himself and picked it up. Nervously he shoved the tie inside his tunic and crawled to the brink.

Squinting through the increasing gloom, Mahmud peered at the fluttering form. It had to be Hashim. Who or what else could it be?

The man was either deep in coma or dead. Trying for a reaction he selected a handful of pebbles and tossed them in the man's direction. Nothing happened, not even when a careless shot careened into the victim's groin. He shouted 'Salam'. There was no answer. After another session of tossing and calling Mahmud gave up. The only way to be absolutely sure was to get within arms length.

It took minutes to reach the traverse and soon he was pegging his way over shale. A circuit around a clump of rocks allowed him to approach from a concealed angle. A dozen more steps and his wooden peg came to rest beside the unyielding body. Although the forehead was abraded the features were unmistakably those of the porter whom he had seen for a short time the previous day, except the hostile expression had vanished. The mouth, like the eyes, was open and secretions had dried on his beard.

Mahmud felt for a pulse but couldn't find one. He poked at the ribs with his peg, like a hunter testing a kill, and repeated it. Still nothing. Kneeling he put an ear to the chest and heard his own breath.

There was nothing more to do. Without an autopsy the cause would never be known. Possibly a fractured skull or a broken neck! He closed the stiff unblinking eyes.

Leaning against a boulder Mahmud looked out at the eastern plain almost invisible in the dusk and contemplated what to do. Should he report to Dr. Lindsay, S.E.R.V.E., U.S.AID, the Kabul police, next of kin? He sighed deeply and turned back to the corpse. Who was he? Had he any identification? Roughly he went through the ragged clothing and found nothing of value: two ten af coins, soiled cigarette papers, a book of matches, an empty tobacco tin and a curved knife wedged in a rope waist band.

He put everything back and decided to bury the body. Hastily Mahmud removed the dirty outer garments and placed the hands in a position of prayer. The tattered grey turban was shaken out and spread to cover the corpse. It took until dark to collect bits of rock and shale but a bier was eventually formed. When it was finished he bowed his head and murmured. "Who is thy God? Allah. What is thy religion? Islam. Who is thy Prophet? Mohammed. May Allah forgive thy soul."

He stood idle for a moment, surveying the starlit mound of rubble before pivoting to head for the path.

Much later in the chill of the night as he pedalled for the dormitory Mahmud made a lasting pledge. Hashim's fate would be kept to himself. He would dissemble his report. There would be no further investigation.

CHAPTER TWENTY-NINE

Maude Collins was a practical nurse of limited scope, having absorbed the basic sciences in an accelerated program immediately following Pearl Harbor. An outgoing muscular woman, self-endowed with a liberal layer of fat, she was neither clever nor well-informed. In accordance with her naval experience she prided herself on strength and devotion, especially when it came to carrying out orders. Her husband was a Midway veteran and died in Bethesda Hospital where he had been convalescing for fifteen years. Maude specialed cases and upon his death, liberated, childless and menopausal, invested his pension and sought a means of extricating herself from a dull existence. With Washington connections she succeeded in landing a contract with U.S.AID.

Afghanistan suited her fine; the environment was captivating; her duties were easy; she had only to do as she was told.

Dr. Tomarin had been content with her performance and late in the evening conveyed his faith in her judgement to Jim Lindsay after the orthopaedic surgeon had recovered from his brachial block.

"You're in good hands Sir; Maude has been nursing for years."

Having bandied words with specials recommended by the Shipton Nurses' Registry Jim didn't share Ezra's confidence. Enemas and sedatives were the extent of his reliance. Even these innocuous procedures could be mismanaged if left to the discretion of someone determined to get as much sleep as his or her patient before dawn relieved them of a disagreeable duty. Mrs. Collin's bovine recognition of Dr. Tomarin's esteem did nothing to reassure him. There being no other choice he covered his doubts with an innocuous blink.

Jim leaned back on the pillows. His arm was beginning to throb and he felt cold and despondent. The shaded lamp beside him burned conspicuously. It illuminated the top of the night table and scribed a paler circle on the ceiling.

The faces of Ezra and Mrs. Collins blended with the enveloping darkness. Amir Kash's swarthy countenance was less easily distinguished. That he was there at all was disclosed by a set of teeth articulating with Dr. Tomarin.

Orders were listed on the chart and observed by Maude after the doctors left. The circulation, sensation and movement of the fingers were to be checked at hourly intervals, demerol was to be injected intramuscularly every three to four hours, depending on the degree of pain - its requirement left up to her - and a barbiturate was prescribed for sleep.

She gave Jim a sedative capsule and a shot of narcotic at 9.00 pm., elevated his cast, adjusted the ice pack and retired to an adjacent room, believing her charge was settled for the night.

Contrary to her hopes this didn't occur. On her midnight round she found his drawl more pronounced and he was pacing the floor.

"The itch in my fingers is driving me nuts!" he protested.

This unexpected symptom and the patient's aggravation muddled Maude. She stalled in the door-frame, fidgeting with a thermometer, her corpulent outline screening light from the passage. The emotional tranquillity, well-being and euphoria the drug was supposed to bring about weren't evident. She had never heard of it having an excitatory effect or causing peculiar behaviour. The demerol was simply not holding him and he needed more.

"Climb back into bed, Sir," she urged, steering him toward the cot. "We'll get your cast back in the sling and elevate your arm. Walking with it hanging down is making the pain worse."

Jim agreed finally and accepted another injection after leading her several turns within the limited space of the room.

When she departed he curled on his side and clasped his head in an effort to shut out the distressing impulses congesting his brain. In a while his mind rewound to half a world away, to a frozen pond beneath a bluff, a stand of bare maples and the warmth of a sandstone house. It was late afternoon. No one was about. Merri must've gone to fetch the kids from school. Sunbeams played on the ice and a fan-shaped window over the door erupted into brightness. These impressions were confused with the yellow swath of the ceiling light.

No! She was home. There she was, head bowed, amber in the night lamp's gleam, gazing down at him, her eyes shimmering with longing. Or were they his mirrored in hers. They closed and her delicate lips parted beseechingly. "God I wish I was home!" he uttered, desperately dragging out the words.

"Here. This will take care of it." Mrs. Collins had reappeared. She was holding a hypodermic. "It's time for another needle," she said and raised the short sleeve of his night shirt.

Disoriented, Jim argued feebly. "I don't need it. The pain has gone."

Ignoring his objection she jabbed his arm. "There now, you'll feel better. I'll drop in, off and on. I have to check your fingers. If you're asleep I won't disturb you."

The empty syringe was quickly withdrawn and replaced on a tray. With a parting, "sleep tight" Maude turned off the lamp and a halo of gloom descended.

For a moment Jim blinked at the crack of light beneath the door. It was not bright enough to trigger another hallucination and the melancholy vision of Merri failed to show.

Stuporous with sedation he eventually fell into a fitful sleep, exacerbated by shivering and a vivid illusion-

He had to see for himself if Hashim were dead and started up the mountain. It was very dark and the darkness was felt not as the absence of light but as a cryptic force, condensing on a cold slope thick with mist and stygian shapes. Full of doubt he probed the soil, searching for a sign, some emblem of life. Up he crawled on his bare hands and feet, gripping the slippery shale while the sodden chips like snails gliding on their secretions, slid noiselessly down the incline. Attracted by their motion he clawed at them but no creature emerged, nor root, nor stem, nor leaves, nothing to offset his seclusion. The earth was empty of everything but silence. Even his breath, drawn in fear he was the last being alive, made no sound.

Higher he climbed amid the rocks, some possessing human form, a welcome sight, and he ascended faster to stagger over their dark greasy surface. No reciprocating warmth assured him, no communicating link, nothing! Except there, lying at the foot of an outcrop was a grey petrified shape sculpt like a man lying on his back, pointing with a jagged arm, pointing like a sign post to an eerie incandescence farther up.

He inched more steeply now, clinging to a granite surface, pulling his body up and over a ledge. Vapour swirled about him like steam from a huge cauldron, coming from the entrance to a lighted cave. The opening, a few yards ahead, was wide enough to admit a man. He peered inside at a brilliance, bathing pictures painted on the opposing wall, etchings of animals and men. Whether they were human scribbles or mere fluorescent veins impregnating the rock he never discovered for in the space of half a step he plummeted downward. Dizzily downward, then up, then down again, at a strange uneven rate as if he were re-passing the centre of the earth.

Downward he fell through an endless duct, dry-lined with murals of decadent civilizations, innumerable faces floating life-lengths beyond, grey faces, the faces of patients whose broken bodies had been temporarily patched, unfamiliar in death, passed by in quiet succession. Among them were his friends: childhood playmates, a cousin, two uncles killed in the war, and an aunt. He gasped upon recognizing his parents. When he came to Jason he screamed, but made no sound.

Mrs. Collins found him on the floor, his plastered arm thrashing the empty air. She bent down and shook him, wondering how much sedation it would take to keep him in bed. Putting her arms around his chest she pulled him to his feet and during the lift up onto the cot a crack was noticed in the cast. It was only a line incompletely circling the plaster and no damage to the underlying limb had occurred but Mrs. Collins' uncertainty on how to deal with it forced her to contact Dr. Tomarin for specific orders. Otherwise she'd have gone on needling narcotic until her patient was blue in the face.

Ezra came immediately, distressed by what had happened. He reinforced the defect with a fresh roll of plaster and checked the nurse's record. Observing there was nothing wrong with the amount and interval at which demerol had been given he advised, "You'd better not give him any more. The drug has an adverse effect. The U.S.Aid physician left at 3.00 am. after Jim's hallucinations had cleared and he'd fallen into a deep even sleep.

On the drive back to his quarters Ezra wondered about the night nurse's competence. Collins should have known better than to go on giving medication, obviously not working. Even worse was her continuance in light of its effects. Apparently she had made no effort to look up the drug's harmful reactions, listed in the pamphlet accompanying it. Ezra shrugged. Maude was another average human unable to cope with something apart from the ordinary. Why should she care? There was always a higher authority to take responsibility. The lack of absolutes in dealing with health problems was too much for Maude. She would never comprehend the words 'never' and 'always' could not be used in their absolute sense because when dealing with life, as diverse and unpredictable as it is, there are 'almost' but never 'always' exceptions to the rule. His faith in Maude dropped. She was going to need closer supervision. Better she be transferred.

The nightmare recurred several times, particularly when Jim was waking from a deep sleep. Though it was as vivid and iniquitous as the first time it didn't last as long. Unlike most dreams, immediately forgotten in the conscious state, he could remember every agonizing detail. Dozing would bring it back and he was in its throes Saturday when the Infirmary's day nurse entered. A firm slap on the cheek snapped him out of it.

Jim grunted awake. Bewildered, he looked up into a mouthy face. The features belonged to a tall slim woman and improved slowly as she withdrew her head. "I'm Jane Andrews," she smiled. "Time for lunch!"

Jim frowned. "You're not waking me for a sleeping pill?"

Jane cleared her throat and when she swallowed her Adam's apple rose and fell noticeably. "Why would I do a silly thing like that Dr.Lindsay?" She said and bunched the pillows to support his back.

"Because", he was about to transfix her with his opinion on the nonsense of certain nurses when she placed the bed-table across his thighs and offered him some food. The poached eggs were steaming, the smell of bacon and freshly baked American bread irresistible. "Hmm," he substituted, "The quickest way to a man's heart. Thanks! I haven't eaten since yesterday morning. No wonder you got to me." Between mouthfuls, he asked, "What's new?"

"Not much. How's your arm?"

"Aches a bit when I move my fingers." His reply was accompanied by a casual smile but with concern he inquired. "Any news from my young friend, Dari?"

"Peggy sent a message from Avicenna this morning." Jane's voice had a mannish pitch and she continued speaking in a breezy cheerful fashion which took one's breath away listening. "She has one of our First Aid packs. Says the nurse-in-charge of the E.R. got it from a crippled medical student with instructions to return it to us. She thinks it was used as there were a number of disposable dressings missing; also a pair of scissors which she wants back."

Chattering on merrily as if she had nothing else to do and enjoyed talking, she continued, "When I told her of your bad luck she had already heard it from Amir. She's worried stiff. If her own experience with Hashim upset her yours has been unnerving. Says she'll never go anywhere alone again. We room together. Now she won't go home without me so she's coming here as soon as she gets off duty. It's not like her. We went through high school and nursing together. Athletic, aggressive, attractive and charming. She could have any man she wants. It was her idea to come here. I'm just Plain Jane, the follower."

The day nurse finally paused, allowing Jim to comment. "A follower can also be a pillar of strength P.J. Likely she's counted on your support. Don't belittle yourself."

She blushed, acknowledging his compliment, and he followed by quizzing her regarding her background. Her answers were dispensed in the same light-hearted fashion and he soon found Miss Andrews to be a remarkable, well rounded individual with knowledge on many subjects far greater than his. Inadequacy in these fields came as no surprise for Jim had been reminded more than once in speaking with intelligent people, schooled in disciplines other than medicine, there was more to life than the mending of bodies.

In addition Jane was loaded with talent, being a skilled artist - proving her forte by sketching him during their conversation who sculpted and played the piano, things he'd never attempted. The morning passed rapidly and before Miss Andrews left to assist Dr. Tomarin in the Dispensary Jim decided her brains and aptitude more than made up for her plainness.

His surliness later in the day contained Mrs. Collins.

Miss Andrews returned in the evening with a potted geranium and Peggy Dolan. "I would have brought you some tobacco," she said, "but there's none in the Commissary and no bouquets either. You can give this plant back when you leave. I'm sure you won't have any room in your luggage and you'll look ridiculous carrying it on a plane."

Tickled with P.J.'s practicality, Jim turned to Peggy Dolan. It was clear she had changed. The gaiety and spunk he had admired were gone. She offered him a fleeting smile and mechanically asked how he was.

To demonstrate he could still function Jim raised his cast from the supporting pillow and attempted to sit on the edge of the cot but a paralyzing pain charged up his arm and he rolled back. Steeling himself, the sharpness subsided and he regarded his visitors.

Peggy had taken a seat by the window and Jane moved in behind her, placing a comforting hand on the more attractive woman. Dr. Lindsay stared blindly at the ceiling, listening to Miss Dolan's version of what had become of his assailant. No accident victim fitting Hashim's description had been admitted through the E.R. nor had the surgical residents been called upon to treat him. She'd inspected the wards in case the man had gone there directly. Venting her rage, she exclaimed, "I hope he's dead. He deserves to die!"

"Now now," Jim scolded, tongue in cheek. "He just got a bit carried away. You shouldn't have teased him so. Don't you know the effect you have on men? Besides we're supposed to be saving lives not taking them." His half-hearted grin vanished. The sequence of the last two days had left him with mixed feelings. He'd faced a treacherous foe and come away the winner, a thrilling sensation difficult to turn off. Subconsciously he rubbed the knuckles of his good hand like a boxer entering the ring. Thank God his fist had found its mark or he wouldn't be reliving this momentary elation. It was an extraordinary pleasure, outweighing the guilt of possibly having killed the man.

What if this combat had taken place in a battle with the same result? How much mercy would he have shown? He had often thought about it during his brief stint in the army and had never decided. He sighed deeply. It didn't concern him in the least if Hashim were dead. Vengeance or wishing the man dead was another matter. His feelings didn't run that high.

Reflecting his assailant might still be alive and left to his own resources, Jim concluded his original thinking hadn't changed. If the man was injured someone should see to his immediate needs, otherwise he was better off dead.

"Believe me Peggy," he added, "Hashim has come along to try us. Though I do understand and sympathize with your sentiments, if the man is still alive we must try to help him."

Whether Jim's noble approach gained a following was hard to tell because neither of the women voiced an opinion.

Jane took Peggy by the arm, coaxing her out of the chair. "Come on," she implored, smiling broadly, "let's go home and bake the doc an apple pie. Maybe there's some ice cream in the commissary." At the door she called back. "Pleasant dreams, Chief."

Good idea, Jim thought, hoping he could. Any kind of dream would be better than his recurring nightmare.

A messenger brought a parcel from Dr. Billings during the lunch hour with a note saying he had to make an emergency trip to Mazar-i-Sharif to treat one of his Peace Corps workers who had come down with dysentery. It had contained a pictorial book of Afghanistan. Art had added a postscript. "As you are unable to see the sights I'm sending them to you." Jim lifted it off the night table but with one hand to hold it he soon tired and closed his eyes.

Moments later Dari found him sleeping. Showing more consideration than Western well-wishers, bellowing their presence from the hall, the student knocked quietly on the open door. He held a shopping bag in the crook of his elbow.

There was no response. Dr. Lindsay remained doubled on the disquiparant cot. Not wishing to disturb him, Mahmud was about to leave when he barely heard an audible groan. It was a fearful sound and grew into a succession of disconsolate gasps. He could not turn away and looked on helplessly until the noise suddenly ceased and the patient straightened and covered his face with the sling.

"I did not mean to awaken you Sir," said Mahmud gazing on curiously.

Jim shook off his apathy, swung his legs over the side and sitting up slowly regarded his young friend. "Dari! Nice to see you!" He saw a bundle under the Afghan's arm, not much bigger than a man's head and didn't know what to make of it. His first reaction was it had something to do with his assailant and all sorts of macabre thoughts crossed his mind. No, Dari wouldn't have cut off Hashim's head to prove the man was dead. Why not? He had witnessed some strange Afghan customs and he was barely a week in the country. His horrified expression was fortunately misinterpreted.

"Sir you look surprised and not so happy to see me. I am sorry to break in on you in such a manner. I will return later."

"No. Please don't go. I am very glad to see you. Stay! I insist."

Now fully awake and very anxious to hear what Mahmud had to say, Jim wasn't about to let him walk off without disclosing it. Perhaps Dari had a change of heart and decided not to go. It was a hazardous undertaking. Smiling casually he offered his hand.

In deference to clasping it Mahmud pulled a package from the suspicious looking parcel. It was exquisitely wrapped in silver paper. "A gift from my father," he said, solemnly half bowing and gave it to Jim.

"Very kind. But he needn't have," said Jim, curling his good arm around the box and placing it on his lap.

"Maybe I should help you open it Sir?"

"That won't be necessary," Jim affirmed, locking the package between his thighs. "My it's heavy! What do you suppose is in it?" The temptation to shake the present and turn it upside down or sideways was offset by having one useful arm. A card had been inserted under the artfully tied blue ribbon. Jim read.

Gulbahar
Mar.7/64

To Dr. James Lindsay FRCS(C)
My Honourable Friend.

With deep regret I learned of the tragedy on Sher Darwaza. Such depravity is a blemish on my country. To make amends my compatriots will have to sacrifice.

Please accept this gift with my greatest respect. It was to be donated to the Kabul Museum. The certificate within the box is authentic and the export papers have been authorized by customs.

I would be most honoured and grateful to have the pleasure of your company at my qala during the Nawruz festivities two weeks hence.

May Allah the Beneficent and Merciful bless you with a prompt return to vigorous health.

Your humble servant,
Khan Wali Malikar Mahmud

Jim passed the note to Dari saying, "what do you make of this?"

Mahmud looked at the message briefly and explained, "The box contains an antique my father intended to donate to the Kabul Museum. By giving it to you he is depriving them of an invaluable gift. He thinks it fair compensation for the service you have rendered to the Afghan people. In fact it is a double deprivation. Hashim by taking you out of action has deprived his countrymen of your favours."

While Jim struggled with the imaginative bow Mahmud offered, "Here, let me help you," and carefully removed the ribbon without tearing the wrapping. "Paper as fine as this is a rare commodity and can be used again," he added folding it neatly.

The lid was opened and the packing removed. With one smooth tug Mahmud extracted a bronze bust of an ancient Greek soldier about eight inches across the base. "Graeco-bactrian, circa 2nd-3rd century B.C., helmeted warrior," he read from a label stuck to the undersurface adding, "This antique was recovered in Kapisa on my ancestor's land."

Jim could barely contain himself. "It's magnificent, simply astounding. I hope your father knows what he's giving away."

Mahmud laughed. "He's been collecting artifacts for years. One living-room wall is covered with them. That's not all," he continued, extracting a leather pouch from the bottom of the box. Loosening a draw string he dumped its contents onto the cot.

"My God!" Jim exclaimed. "Are these real?"

There were half a dozen roughly circular silver coins. On the obverse and reverse sides were various scenes and figures. One shakel revealed a king running with a bow and javelin in his hands. A tetradrachma had the wreathed head of Athena stamped on one side and her symbol, the owl, on the other. There was Zeus with his thunderbolt, Heracles, Hercules and Demetrius I - wearing a helmet shaped like an elephant's head - and Hermaius the last Greek ruler of the Kabul valley. Jim was flabbergasted.

"I just can't believe it," he said. "What a rare treat!"

"We come across these quite often while working the land. Most of them are not so well preserved. Some are difficult to identify and classifying them is even harder."

"That may well be." Jim was thinking any scrap of metal remotely resembling an ancient coin would be treasure enough for him, but these pieces were worth a fortune. "How can I ever thank him?"

"My father will be satisfied when he hears how much pleasure you have derived from his gift. That is all! Now I have something for you from myself." He smiled as he fished a green and yellow paisley tie from a suit coat pocket.

Jim recognized it immediately.

"I believe this is yours Sir."

"You found it at the base of the wall near the ruins?" Dari nodded.

The opportunity had finally arisen and Jim had to know. "Was he dead?"

Mahmud's cool blue eyes met the orthopaedic surgeon's directness. "He has gone. No sign of him."

Jim exhaled slowly and turned to the window. It was getting dark and he could just make out the tennis court. It may relieve my conscience, he thought, but it doesn't remove a danger. Until he was airborne he'd be looking for a filthy unkempt madman.

"Thanks. It was a brave thing you did going up there after him. He could've attacked you too. Also not very easy for you. That's an artificial leg you're wearing."

Mahmud flushed with humiliation as he related, "The story goes back a long way. To the time of my birth. A congenital club foot necessitating a Symes amputation. It was removed five years ago after becoming gangrenous from a triple arthrodesis."

Jim frowned asking, "Iatrogenic?"

"Yes." Dari was going to tell the whole story but decided against it. Dr. Lindsay would have to find out for himself. He switched to his father's invitation. "Will you be able to come to Gulbahar?"

"Though I'd like to very much I think it's best I cut short my stay. Actually there is little I can do other than tour around. To stay here solely for that purpose would be frivolous without sharing it with my wife. No, I'm going to book the next flight out. Please convey my appreciation to your father. He is awfully kind. Tell him I'll come back some day and if he ever visits Canada he must stay with us." After pausing, with glistening eyes he added, "so should you my friend."

CHAPTER THIRTY

It was dusk when the landrover entered the qala's gate; five floodlit towers streaked the courtyard with light.

Ghubar stopped by the heavy front doors, released his passengers and wheeled for the carriage house at the rear of the keep.

"The qala is packed. There is light in every window," Dari observed, reaching for the bell cord.

Roxane had not seen her family for several months. If Dari hadn't taken 'call' for a friend they would've arrived Thursday afternoon. Now the festival was half over. Better late than never, she thought, and her frustration gave way to radiance. "Looks like a launching pad", she cried. "Everyone must be here."

Broad and squat, Sayyid was also excited but for another reason. Traditionally Sunday was set aside for the Buzkashi and the Hazara had his heart set on picking up a prize. He grinned, thinking of the event and loosened his chin straps, allowing his thick fox-brimmed helmut to rest on the back of his neck. "But we're still in time for the game!"

Dari gave his friend a knowing look. "Tomorrow will not be as easy as you think; the contest is to be held in the river."

"Buzkashi-yi-darya?" Sayyid's mouth fell open, emitting a low whistle. A soaking wet calf carcass must be awfully slippery. He had always played on the mayden. Hoisting one hundred pounds and dragging it leg-locked round the pommel was tough under dry conditions. "You can't be serious?" he asked.

Mahmud nodded in reply. "I wasn't supposed to tell you. Nobody was to know until the teams saddle up in the morning." Dari chuckled. "I wanted a preview of your reaction. You're to keep it under your fuzzy fez or I'm in trouble. Not that forewarning you will make any difference other than allow you a moment to bite your nails."

"Ha! Ha!" crowed the Hazara.

"But the price is right," Dari went on. "Malikar is donating five hundred afs per goal and scarlet turbans to the winning team."

The great doors opened. A youthful baccha refulgent in a gold and maroon vest received their coats in the dark panelled hall.

"Food is being served Sahib," he said and skipped through to a germanic room sparkling with French crystal and English silverware. Scores of people clamoured boisterously around a long table spread with Irish linen and porcelain tureens simmering with international cuisine. A host of bacchas hovered over them, replenishing goblets and plates. Elizabethan England, Roxane thought, having recently written a precise on the subject. A number of smaller tables were set for the children.

Soroya saw her daughter immediately and jumped up for a hug. "They're here," she shrieked, vibrating with pleasure.

"Come, my boy. I've been saving a seat beside me," Malikar beckoned through the turmoil.

Sayyid shyly backed off. Except for Roxane's family from Bamiyan he didn't know the other guests. Her cousin spotted him and waved from the far end of the table.

"How's the educated farmer?" Nur asked, crowding along the bench to let Sayyid settle between himself and his sister Fabia.

The Hazara's flat round face lit up. "Have you taken to drinking wine too?" he asked seeing Nur's glass half full of red liquid.

"It's only grape juice, bobec," Nur smiled. "Which is what we're all drinking except those English schooled gentlemen yonder." He looked toward Dari's brothers at the opposite end of the room.

Dari dutifully kissed his stepmothers, Halima and Farah, and moved on to his grandmother Tahmina. He hadn't seen her since his trip to Nuristan. Sunrise shining on a marble lake was caught in her long white hair. She raised a set of gnarled fingers from her black woollen skirt to stroke his face. He held them for a moment, catching a measure of her love.

"My, you've turned into a handsome young man," she creaked. "The image of your grandfather. Don't you think so, Lysander?"

Dari's great uncle laughed. Every time his sister saw Dari she said the same thing. "A man's strength and courage are his beauty, not his girlish eyelashes." Lysander winked,"You must come again soon; we don't see you enough. The river is full of fish and the mountains abound with snow-cock. My tazi points them at a quarter of a mile."

"Sure Pak, but I don't know when. Medicine is taking most of my time. Maybe when - " Dari hesitated, "- or if I graduate."

Roxane's stepfather Rishtya was listening and having no doubt about Dari's ability interrupted. "When you're finished you must come to Bamiyan. We haven't had a medical man since Ferangi Best, five years ago."

Mahmud frowned at the reference to his malefactor. The arrogant fake wasn't a doctor.

"Why not?" Soroya demanded, misinterpreting the strange look replacing Dari's pleasant one. To have Roxane return to the fold was no secret. A sure way of recovering her would be to entice him.

"We also need a respectable hospital," Rishtya continued, wondering if Malikar would support the cause. Dari's father had given a bucket of afs to the Cotton Company's hospital at Kunduz and it was quite likely the elder Mahmud would contribute more if his son was involved. Becoming more enthusiastic with the idea, Rishtya yelled above the din at the head of the table. "How would you like to build a hospital in Bamiyan for him?"

Malikar smiled and shouted, "If that's what Dari wants."

Old Zor on Malikar's left, rheumy eyed and unaccustomed to alcoholic beverages, sounded upset. "What does the young pup want now?" he rasped, adjusting his hearing trumpet.

"The hand of your granddaughter," Malikar teased. "Isn't that your wish too? You primaeval camel!"

Zor brightened. If only he could live to see the wedding and tell Zulfikar in the beautiful garden beyond. "When?" he cackled.

"Good question. We can't let him leave the country without a wife. He might not come back."

Roxane was about to ask what's to prevent me from going alone. She had been out of chadri for sometime and was soon to receive a degree in languages. She could look after herself married or not but kept her thoughts to herself.

Dari removed his taw'iz and swung it under Zor's nose. "Pardon me Baba, can you tell me where this came from?"

The old man took the amulet in his shaky hands, bit it and squinted until his memory connected with his bloodshot eyes. "It belonged to your grandfather, my stepbrother Zulfikar."

"Where did he get it?" Dari asked.

"From our father Ali Mahmud."

"And how did my great grandfather get it?

Eventually Zor replied, "It was presented to Ali for bravery by the British. There is a citation on one side."

Dari took back the ta'wiz and re-examined it. "I don't see an engraving. Only a distortion where it was struck by the Safi slug."

Zor plugged in his ear horn. Leaning forward until the funnel was inches from his great nephew, he shouted, "You doubt my word?"

"No Baba," Dari answered and smiled with reassurance.

"He tells you the truth my son. I have read it," Malikar intervened. Then resuming his conversation with Zor he motioned along the table. "My other sons married before they went abroad."

After the meal, comfortably entrenched in the drawing room's leather chairs the men resumed their discourse.

"You were saying business has never been better, Kamal," Dari commented. "I've heard it was best in grandfather's day."

"True, but relatively." Kamal ran his stubby fingers through a thinning crop of dark hair. He had developed a slight paunch; it twitched when he spoke. "Zulfikar was better off than the average Khan - I'm referring to overall wealth - and Daoud's second five year plan has been as successful as the first. The Salang pass will open any day, cutting the time of transportation north to the Amu Darya and Russia in half. Last year the war with India ended and the border has reopened. It was never really closed as we managed to sneak a few loaded trucks across; now trade with India is more brisk than ever."

The half-brothers, Kamal and Khushal, physically were at opposite ends of the pole. While Kamal was short and heavy, Khushal had a lanky appearance.

Gaunt, lined cheeks perpetuated Khushal's grin and a receding crown dipped approvingly as he took over. "The tonnage of dried fruit and nuts we fly to India is greater than ever. Last year the Kabuli merchants made a profit and topped two million." The creases in his face deepened when he smiled. "Father is away ahead of the Ariana Airlines and leases his own planes. He has even sold grapes to Eastern Europe via Russia. Who says the Soviets aren't capitalists!" "Let's face it. We are at a geographical disadvantage. Air cargo is the most expedient way out. Twice a week I fly a D.C.6 loaded with karakuls destined for New York. They're unloaded in Frankfurt and transferred to Pan American jets. It won't be long before we have jets too." Khushal, also a Colonel in the Air Force, was keen to expand his aerobatic skills. Flying transports was a bore. "With all that air space why confine oneself to a single corridor?"

Roxane had slipped into the circle and sat on the arm of Dari's chair. The other women had retired elsewhere. She knew it was a brazen act but she was as knowledgeable as any of them and preferred men's conversation. "If Khushal thinks flying transports is dull he should try cooking." She interjected, "or raising babies." Everyone but Khushal laughed.

Brothers-in-Law had also joined the group. Raqia's husband Ayub manufactured knives and scissors and sold them to the shops. He posed a question for Kamal. "Where would you advise us to invest our afs?"

"Right here - the north end of the Koh Daman plain. It will soon become an industrial centre. Russian money and expertise is building a dam at Naghlu on the Panjsher, an extra sixty thousand kilowatts of hydroelectric power to supplement the station at Jabal-us-Seraj."

Ahmad the lawyer, Kamal's full brother tittered. "If you are right Kamal, the value of land is going to rocket. I can make a fortune just drawing up deeds."

"But the government will probably take it over," Roxane commented, sarcastically. "Unless you can guarantee the right to free enterprise in the new constitution. By the way, how's it going?"

Except for a lighter bone structure Ahmad was the spitting imagine of Malikar, darkly pigmented, slightly built but with a goatee in addition to a mustache like his father's. He stroked it thoughtfully. "Our internal struggle is closely linked to the outside world, to the Cold War, in spite of what the Mullahs will have us believe. From their religious point of view the answer is cut and dried. We are Muslim. The Christian Americans and Russian atheists are infidel nations. Resistance to their interference is simply adhering to the truth of our own faith."

Once he started pontificating it was hard to turn Ahmad off. "As far as communism versus capitalism is concerned either system depends on a strong central government which we do not have. In this case to our advantage. Even though Amir Abdur Rahman Khan organized us into a nation technically, tribal feelings run high. 'Might' is still right and outweighs the vote. Communism and capitalism will eventually neutralize each other anyway. In either system the leaders seem incorrigible with imaginative productive minds. But they lean more to power than what's best for the people. Their outlook is no different than our tribal chiefs. They just play the game on a bigger field. So the mass of mediocrity without the will nor independence to act for itself will continue to switch from one ideology to the other, levelling the opposing philosophies and losing their freedom in the process, which is our major problem."

Ahmad continued. "We also have the haves and have-nots, an expanding middle class and a great rift between the uneducated people and the literate few. The new dormitory at Kabul University - to be opened next semester - will allow for an increased enrolment. But will this body of a thousand extra students be able to afford their tuition?" He stammered, adding, "Plus they are a perfect media for subversives."

Roxane frowned. "Are you implying students don't think for themselves?"

"No. It's just at times they can be easily led. A perfect medium for training subversives. You asked me how the constitution is progressing; we've completed a new draft. For the past year I've been working with the Law and Political Science Faculties at the University. Often we've interviewed individuals and groups from all ethnic, social and occupational levels. We've even consulted with a French expert though I don't know why as the French have produced more unacceptable constitutions than any other nation on earth.

There were no more questions and Ahmad would have gone on forever if Malikar hadn't chosen this moment to appear.

"I'm very pleased you have all come. You have turned this Nawruz into something special, a complete family reunion." He was thinking it might be his last. The forthcoming trip to Beirut could lead to a termination of his leadership. Looking over the intelligent attentive faces of his sons he was unable to chose a successor. Life in Afghanistan was becoming complicated. In the rapid expansion of knowledge not one of them would be able to master as much as he had in his day. They would have to trust each other. Smiling he announced. "Now for some music," and clapped his hands. "Abdul! Bring us the instruments."

The baccha went to a large cabinet standing against the opposite wall and carefully removed a woodwind, a few stringed resonating boxes and a drum which he placed before his master.

Malikar kept the Dhol. Crossing an ankle over his thigh he placed the two-headed drum across his lap, put the suspension strap around his neck and cinched the cord to stretch the goat skinned membranes. He beat the drumheads with his hands and tested the percussive effect on the wheat seeds trapped within.

Kamal chose the Surnai and blew through its double reed while Khushal and Ahmad tuned their stringed instruments. When satisfied with tone and pitch the 'entrepreneur' turned to the audience. "What'll it be? Western, Country Western or traditional Persian."

Before anyone answered Kamal began warming up with a plaintive rendition of 'Yesterday'. Soon his brothers joined in, Ahmad picking out the melody on his lute while Khushal chorded on the Dhamboura.

For an encore they played another Beetle tune, 'Strawberry Fields', Malikar gently adding a beat with his drum. When the piece was finished Khushal switched to a plectrum and plucked out the range of the instrument before settling on half a dozen choice chords. As he repeated them rhythmically he asked. "A poem! How about it Kamal?"

"No. he objected. "Ahmad is the intellectual, the literary one."

The lawyer blushed. "There are a lot of illiterate Afghans who can compose poetry better than I."

"Ahmad is much too modest," Malikar declared. "Come. Let us hear some of your Sufi mystique. Surely the alcohol has lifted your inhibition. How about ad-libbing on this:

'My love, have a few more rounds of wine.
It will quench your last night's thirst and mine.'

Ahmad was not to be persuaded. He knew his lyrics would be too solemn for this festive group. It was better they dance. He broke into a pleasant melody, bowing his Sarinda with such a compelling rhythm a number of the men were soon on their feet, shuffling, twirling and clapping their hands overhead.

CHAPTER THIRTY-ONE

Supported by the back of a drawing room chair, Roxane leaned to whisper in Dari's ear. While her shifting tresses coyly screened an eye, her tone was serious. "Let's go somewhere for a private talk?"

"Talk?" Dari smiled flirtatiously. "My room, or yours?

The one eye he could see glinted flatly back as Roxane's expression faded. "It doesn't matter where we go in this rambling excuse for a prison, someone will be watching. Why not the chesterfield in that far corner?" She flipped the errant bob behind an ear and stood up. "At least we can get away from this noise."

They had barely sunken into the plush cushions, Dari at one end and Roxane in the middle, when Sayyid took up the remaining space. He had exchanged his dark suit for a quilted chapan, woollen breeches and a pair of scuffed and muddy knee-high boots.

"You're wet!" Roxane noticed, feeling the arm of his chapan. She was about to tell him they were having a private conversation and wanted to be left alone but hid her frustration by politely asking, "What have you been doing?"

"Riding."

"You're joshing!" Dari feigned disbelief. Sensing his friend was not his usual easy-going self he apologized quickly. "Seriously I know you're keen to win a prize tomorrow but on a moonless night, you weren't really scouting that treacherous course?"

"The stars are out!" Sayyid smiled.

"You must be crazy!"

"Possibly. But it wasn't difficult. The horses are so well trained they know each rock, pebble and grain of sand, even the deceptive pools to avoid. They're uncanny. The one I've chosen may not be as fast as my Mercury, but he has endurance and is sure-footed."

"You didn't wear him out?"

Sayyid smirked. "No, I just gave him a little exercise. I left Ghubar and the chapandaz refuelling him with a bag of barley, butter and raw eggs. They call him 'Zeus'."

"Zeus! I didn't think he could be tamed."

"Just a trifle high-spirited. It took them seven years to work him into the game. Now he has all the moves." The Hazara was elated. Buzkashi was his passion and he had just discovered a responsive, powerful mount. Pretentiously, he added, "Provided he has a good rider."

Dari was intrigued. During his childhood he watched while Ghubar and the chapandaz tried to break Zeus, the colt, and begged to ride him. But the Panjsheri Tadjik in his wisdom disapproved and forbade it. "I'll trade you," he insisted.

"For what?"

"Hercules."

Sayyid did not respond so Dari spiced up the offer. "Hercules, my Remington and a case of cartridges."

Very generous, Sayyid thought. Hercules was seventeen hands from hoof to withers with twenty years experience, fifteen of them under Qabir Khan, a former champion. Hercules and the Khan were one being, a joy to behold. Malikar had paid plenty to present the horse to Dari on his son's sixteenth birthday to counter his brooding over the loss of a foot. Dari had ridden Hercules only a few times before going off to the University of Beirut. Since then the splendid beast, still in its prime and under the tutelage of Ghuber and the chief chapandaz, spent more time in pasture than on the maydan. Zeus was younger, not as tall but had the hind quarters of a jumper and endurance as well. The choice was experience versus age. The Remington almost tipped the scales. Sayyid had borrowed it to clean out a pack of wolves attacking Rishtya's sheep. It was more accurate than the cut down Mosser the Hazara had been using. The offer was a magnanimous gesture on Dari's part. What had he to lose? Pride? The pride of winning a prize or two? Or was it propriety? It didn't matter. Both animals belonged to Malikar. Had he been a bit hasty in presuming he could pick his own mount?

Sayyid flushed. "All right. You take Zeus and I'll ride big Herk. But I'd rather you keep the gun."

Now it was Dari's turn to feel guilty - Sayyid clearly had his mind set on riding the younger horse. In addition to disappointing his friend he embarrassed him. "No. Let's just forget I said anything. You take Zeus."

Sayyid's tongue rolled in his round face. There was only one solution. "How about tossing a floren? Heads I stick with Zeus and you keep big Herk and your gun. Tails I'll take your offer." He sifted through his pockets for a coin and handed it to Roxane. "You flip."

She eyed them both, uncrossed her slim thighs and pulled the hem of her blue silk dress below her knees. The coin was tossed in the air to land on the carpet at her feet. She watched as it circled on its edge to land reverse side up. "You, my dear," she scowled at Dari, "are going to break your bullish neck. Sayyid has just won a gun and a chance to live."

She bent down and picked up the floren, adding. "If he doesn't get pneumonia from sitting in his cold wet clothes."

The Hazara's brow knotted and he stood up. "So! You want to be rid of me." The outcome of the toss had unsettled Sayyid. He had really wanted Zeus. What possessed him to gamble? The opportunity to give his best friend an even chance? He silently shrugged off fate. It was still age versus experience and he had a fifty-fifty chance of winning the Buzkashi. "See you in the morning," he smiled. "I'm going to bed."

"Well", Roxane sighed when Sayyid was safely out of ear-shot.

"Well", Dari echoed as he caressed her forehead with his own. "You are a patient little donkey."

Patient! Roxane thought. Now I must be presumptuous. She pulled her head away and faced him squarely.

"You had something you wanted to talk about?" He asked.

"Us."

The fire had died to a flickering blue. Though a number of the performers had retired, the dancing was still in progress.

Dari yawned sleepily. He was unaware of a problem. They were a perfect match. There was complete understanding between them with or without dialogue. They were inseparable companions when time and distance permitted, honest and open. There was also honour in defiance of a mutual lust held in stony abeyance like a pair of Greek statues awaiting the blessing of Eros. Though lately after prolonged separations it was becoming increasingly difficult to resist. Kisses, caresses and embraces heightened lasciviously. Aroused by his thoughts Dari became fully alert, conscious of a provocative hip snug against his. He answered his own question. "Us? All we need is a Mullah, a Koran, a king-sized bed and I'll be the envy of all my friends."

Roxane giggled. "You're not proposing?"

"Why not?"

Her coyness faded. "It's late. You're tired and not in the mood to appreciate what I have to say, however I must get a few things straight."

"You've got something to confess," Dari teased.

"No. Be serious. If you truly respect my opinion then you will understand my answer. No. I don't want to get married."

"Never?"

"I didn't say that."

"Then you must tell me why."

"Exactly what I want to talk about." Roxane looked down and opened her palm, exposing Sayyid's coin. Her fingers were steady, warm and dry. Tightening them around the coin she continued. "In our hearts we married long ago as children, carefree and innocent, no selfish consuming interferences. Just each other. But now our lives have changed. You are going off to Beirut for at least two years. Longer if you specialize. I love you and I always will but I won't tie you down. Nor do I want you to feel obligated to me. Malikar and Rishtya would use me to that end. Force us into a final consummation. I would become your burden, an anchoring weight, progressively heavier with each pregnancy. For wherever you go I would follow. Nor am I ready. I don't wish to be tied down either."

"Then why not come with me?" Dari interrupted. "Married or not, free to go whenever you wish."

"I do not wish to leave Afghanistan. I'm not fully prepared."

Dari looked confused as Roxane went on to explain. "Up till now I've never had to sacrifice because there have been no choices. You have sacrificed our companionship by choosing Beirut over Kabul for medical training. I too have been provided with an alternative. I've been accepted into broadcasting. The job is with Radio Kabul and appeals to me. It will be an exciting challenge.

She looked at Dari's face closely and her eyes began to glisten, reading his disappointment. "The chances are you will come back, which reinforces my decision. Forcing you back through marriage may risk the opportunity of your finding a more rewarding career somewhere else. I trust you Dari and will pray to Allah you will return to me. Also I am prepared you might meet someone else, a ferangi perhaps. You might even marry her and bring her back to Afghanistan. Though I do not wish to share you with anyone else, That, I could live with. But losing you altogether, I'm not so sure."

"I love you too Roxane." Dari's voice broke and he reached for the coin in her hand. He smiled. "Tell you what. Let's make it an even chance. Heads we get married. Tails we - "

Roxane placed her hand over the floren and pressed her palm against his, interlocking their fingers. "No. I won't change my mind." As he stared at her in disbelief she encircled his neck and drew him close to whisper softly. "Let's go find a king-sized bed."

His only uncertainty was where. Dari's room was next to his father's on the second floor of the central living quarters. An armed baccha guarded the corridor and there was no way to get by him unseen.

"Come on," Roxane beckoned, "I know a cosy place." After supper her sister Raqia had shown her guest bedrooms above the banquet hall which the Rishtya family was to share. There were a number of rooms on that level. Alone on her way back Roxane had explored them. Several doors led into separate apartments. Her mother and Rishtya were occupying one, two other married sisters and their families another. The third was hers, and the fourth was empty save for a number of stored articles, including bedding and a heap of rugs on the floor of an alcove. Intuitively, she locked the door and took the key.

Outside the great hall Roxane removed it from her purse and showed it to Dari. "The key to our love nest," she purred. "It's for the third floor, last door on the left, passed the central tower. I'll go ahead. If I meet anyone I'll pretend I forgot something and come back."

Dari clasped her arm. "No, wait. There's an easier way. You don't have to go alone. We'll take the tower recess on the main floor."

"But it means passing the entrance to the great hall and the party's not over."

"Don't worry. We'll be taking a casual stroll. If we meet anyone we're just on our way to the top to gaze at the stars. There's nothing surreptitious in that."

Roxane squeezed his hand. "Sneaky."

"Sneaky? It seems to me you're the sneaky one."

Nothing disturbing happened and they reached the recess leading into the tower.

An echoing ring from the bottom metal step cautioned them to remove their shoes. There was nobody in the third floor passage; in no time at all Roxane had the door to the vacant apartment open and they were inside, breathlessly holding each other like a couple of slaves who had not quite stolen their freedom.

The tiny vestibule was dry but cold. Roxane shivered. "Hug me for a minute."

"Here. Take my jacket." Dari suggested and cloaked his suit coat around her trembling shoulders. "Too bad we can't chance a fire. No matter, I haven't any matches."

He began to grope for an identifiable object.

"There are some blankets about four paces left of the door we entered," Roxane advised, "and some rugs piled nearby."

Dari found the outside wall and almost tripped over them. They lay beneath a bay window. He drew apart the drapes and soon his vision accustomed to the starlit room. "I found them" he breathed, recognizing a familiar pattern.

"I've got the sheets," Roxane added.

He was kneeling on a rug, checking its depth when her silky thigh brushed his cheek. Instinctively he put his arm around her legs and buried his face.

"First I must cover these dusty rugs with fresh bedding. Then we can be cosy! It'll only take a minute."

"Make it half a minute."

When the last blanket had been spread she stood up and reached for him. His jacket slipped from her shoulders as her arms linked their chests. "Now you can unzip - " Before she could finish their mouths met; automatically her arms were around his neck. They kissed, their passion building gradually until Roxane began to moan, her body swaying against him.

Dari withdrew his lips first, his probing fingers settling on the downy back of her neck. The swish of a zipper was barely audible above the surge of their breathing. In a cascade of sparks her dress crackled to the floor.

Roxane's eyes shone in the dim light. "Now it's my turn," she hummed, unfastening his tie and the buttons of his shirt. She loosened his belt, heaved a shirt tail from his trousers and pulled the collar down across his back.

"The undershirt too," she spoke softly, breathlessly and tugged it over his head.

There was another sparkle of electricity and Roxane giggled, "My, we are charged tonight!"

During the tugging and heaving, Dari's pants had fallen uncovering his prosthesis. "This too," she murmured, unbuckling the strap above his knee.

The stump shaken loose of its stocking was pressed against her lips. He could barely see her eyes looking up at him reassuringly as she sat heels drawn under her on the floor.

"Why did you do that?" he asked.

"Maternal instinct."

Pulling at his underpants she declared, "and I have others." Dari was highly excited and his penis throbbed in tumescence. She fondled the phallus; rubbing it against her cheek, she kissed it.

Her caressing tickled him and he backed off, surprised that she was not completely naked. "I'd like another turn," he sighed, but she twisted away from him onto the makeshift bed.

"You can have another turn in here." She whispered pulling the covers over her head.

There was a lot to discover and each exploration led to something wonderful - the blend of his muscles from the broad base of his neck through the upper chest down over his shoulder blades and across the flank leaving a spicy hollow beneath his arm where she could snuggle her face on the soft ribbed surface and count the spines in the furrow of his back.

She was not as frail as her delicate gowns deceived; the smoothness of her skin, felt in a handful of breast, poured over the breadth of her shoulders, surprisingly as wide as her hips with a waist he could encompass in the crook of an elbow and wrist. Her buttocks were two melons rolling slowly beneath him and she smelled like honey in heated milk.

Wriggling into an agreeable position Roxane twisted the kinky coils of dark hair covering his chest, growing thick in his underarm. "I want you Dari," she murmured. "Now."

She thrust her pelvis upward and clasped his body with her legs, digging her heels in the back of his thighs, while he entered hard and tight until she was stretched beyond her limit. The tear was sudden and searing. She closed her eyes tightly against it and felt a trickle of stickiness run backward, pasting her to the sheet. In a moment the pain subsided.

Dari was through and winding down. Her eyes flew wide open. There had to be more to it. She struggled out from under and nestled an ear on his chest, clinging to him. Hearing the beat of his heart slow and even, within the gentle rise and fall of his ribs, she drew a leg across his lower body and ran it up and down over his flaccid organ, listening until his heart began to quicken. His waist tightened and there was a resurgence of the roll of flesh beneath her thigh.

      The second time there was no pain nor disappointment. But a sad empty feeling followed the height of her ecstasy. She was not so sure of her decision to remain in Kabul. From now on she would need Dari more than ever, more than any career.

CHAPTER THIRTY-TWO

Sanding a boat deck proved to be good therapy. The range of motion in Jim's left elbow had increased steadily, though he still lacked hyperextension and arm girth. Smiling to himself, he thought it's already mid April. To be scientific I should have measured myself before as well as after the assault. "Ah, who cares! - I feel better."

He switched off the belt sander, placed it on the work bench and started down the ladder. Merri met him outside the garage.

"I was coming to fetch you for lunch," she said. "You have some interesting mail."

Rubbing the slight ache in his stiffening arm, Jim smiled. "Coincidentally my stomach is giving me the same message."

"How's it going?"

"A good dusting and it's ready for an undercoat."

"I mean your arm, Dodo."

"Great! No problem."

"Then why are you favouring it?"

Jim had been tightening the muscles and pumping the joint since the day after Sir Edgar had operated. "I'm not really. The more I work it the better it gets."

When he had slowly bent the joint to its maximum, Merri hooked her arm in his and towed him toward the house.

"Rick Mosley still wants to be a doctor. He called an hour ago and would like to come out and talk to you. I told him perhaps later this afternoon but call first."

Jim wondered if he could spare the time. Andy Cruikshank had indicated he needed to speak confidentially on a matter not to be discussed over the phone and was coming along for a drink before supper.

Rick had dropped by New Year's Day asking for references to go with his applications. The lad could talk the leg off a mule and had stayed all afternoon, watching the Bowl games. He would have sat through the Orange Bowl as well but Merri turned off the T.V. at ten thirty, decreeing everyone in the Lindsay household was going to bed. That was three months ago and Rick had not been around since.

Jim shrugged and his comment, "I doubt if I'll be able to fit in Rick," was followed by a sigh of relief from his wife.

"Frankly my darling, I'm glad. To throw your own words back at you, 'he's a pain in the ass.'"

"Did I say that?"

"Yes. Also he's too nosy. More interested in our affluence than the work you're doing."

"How uncharitable of me."

"A bit out of character but probably an accurate observation."

"Who wrote the letters?"

"There's one from England and two from Afghanistan." Merri winked. "I thought I detected perfume."

"Oh!" Jim smiled. "On which one?"

"Which ones do you think?"

"The ones from Afghanistan naturally."

"You old reprobate. You told me you didn't run into Ellen Jasper."

"She may have been hot off the press but not as hot as some of the other chicks I came across."

Merri giggled. "Tell me how you really came to break your arm, Dr. Lindsay. Was it falling out of bed or twisted by a jealous husband?"

"You'd never believe it."

Inside the kitchen Jennie was bouncing on the balls of her feet. "Guess what! Bradley Coleman invited me to the school dance."

"When?"

"Now!" cried Julia. "He just hung up."

"I mean when is the big event?"

"Tonight." Jennie's ponytail bobbed and her eyes were beaming.

Jim regarded her doubtfully. "How do you expect to get there?"

"I thought you'd drive us, Dad."

"But how are you going to get home?"

"You can pick us up on the way back from the movies."

"What if we decide not to go out tonight?"

Jennie stopped bouncing and her face fell. Julia resurrected her hope. "There's a mystery thriller at the Odeon, Dad. You'd like it."

"Yeah. It's real scary." Heather put in.

"Who says so?" Jim asked.

Kathy was standing in the middle of the group 'Kitty' in her arms, stroking the soft black fur with her chin. "Emily Masters," she answered. "Her parents took her to see it last night."

Jim's eyes widened. He covered his face with an arm and began to tremble. "I don't think I could take it. It'll give me the creeps."

Everyone laughed.

"OK, that's settled," Merri announced. Heading into the family room she added,"Soup's on!"

After lunch when the kids had cleared the table and vanished, Jim caught up with his mail and read aloud parts of it to Merri. The Afghanistan letters were from Dari's father and Art Billings.

Malikar's surgery had been successful. The text of his letter covered the events from his arrival in Beirut to his joyous return to Gulbahar. He was very appreciative, no longer having fainting spells and the pain in his chest had disappeared. He had nothing but praise for the surgical genius of Dr. Shaw. Dari was with him throughout his ordeal and had remained enrolled in third year medicine at the University, further delighting the elder Mahmud.

The envelope from Art Billings included an aerogram addressed to Jim from Donald Shaw. The cardiologist greeted him pleasantly and went on to describe in detail how he had opened Malikar's heart and repaired the constricted aortic valve. His prognosis, following an uncomplicated post operative period, was for an eventual return to normal activity. He sent Alice's regards and love to Crooky.

Art provided a follow up of the patients upon whom Jim had operated. Though the triple arthrodesis was still in plaster the wound had shown no signs of sepsis. The patient with the bone cancer died a month after the amputation. Sorry about that, Billings wrote, but there's better news to come. The young Afghan who was drilled in the chest by an angry father-in-law started to wiggle his toes shortly after you left, and is expected to be walking soon. Lucky you were here to treat him. The next paragraph was devoted to news of the friends Jim had made among the 'Ferangi'. Peggy and P.J. left for the States. They didn't feel safe with a madman on the loose even though Hashim apparently has disappeared. Art ended the letter restating his admiration of Jim's courage and hoped his arm was on the mend. You all come back now, you hear? You still owe us three weeks of volunteer service.

"What are you smiling about?" Merri asked.

"One of the characters I ran into over there."

"Who's that?"

"An American named Billings, a real comedian. Helped put my arm back together. Speaking of which it's time for more therapy. I better get up to the loft."

"You should rest after a meal. Take it easy. Read a book or lie down. I might even join you."

"If that's a proposition I'm for any kind of therapy."

"That's not what I had in mind, Jim Lindsay. You don't need that kind of treatment. At least not in the middle of the day."

Jim grinned. "I'm glad you qualified your statement. Thought for a second you were about to deprive me of my nuptial rights." He stood to go, noticed the third letter and sat down again.

"What's that?" Merri asked, adding. "Don't tell me. A letter from Sir Edgar begging I should leave you and live with him on his hundred acre estate."

"Sorry my dear. It's only a bill."

Merri pouted in jest. Sir Edgar Ramsey was forever a gentleman. He had kissed her on many occasions. The first time in a hospital cot a few hours after Jason was born. Jim was standing beside the bed cradling his son in his arms. 'So there Squire Lindsay. A buss from a knight of the realm. Get thee hence and tend his horse.' Jim had been reminded of the remark six weeks ago in the Departure Lounge at Heathrow. Sir Edgar had driven them to the airport and seen them through the Check-in queue. Before leaving he put his arms around their shoulders and kissed Merri's cheek.

"Why is it the people to whom we owe the most we can never repay?" Jim's question was not to be answered. It was a statement of fact. While he had been studying at Oxford, the English orthopaedic surgeon had literally taken him under his wing or 'into my wing' Sir Edgar would say, a twinkle in his puckish eyes. 'The west wing of our house.' Jim and Merri had lived with the Ramseys for close to three years and found the man to be more than an eminent teacher; he was a modest most obliging confidant imbued with decency and the unconquerable British spirit.

"No doubt you're referring to the Ramseys."

"Who else? I'll never be able to repay the man."

"He doesn't expect it. Your passing on his good will to those less fortunate is his reward. He was pleased to hear of the work you were doing in Afghanistan. I watched him closely while you were talking. He lit up like a Bonzai tree on Japanese New Year."

"I suppose you're right. But I feel so indebted."

"What else could you have done my darling?"

"True. There isn't a surgeon I trust more than him. Accepting his professional help gives me no qualms. It's his hospitality."

Turning to the Englishman in his hour of need was as natural as a ship seeking haven from a storm. Edgar had answered his distress signal with a reciprocating wire and was on hand when the Ariana flight landed at Gatwick. During the drive north to Oxford they caught up on the past fifteen years and discussed the pros and cons of fixing his fracture with a pin. In the end Edgar agreed to do it the following morning. When they arrived at the Ramsey estate Merri was there waiting for him, having caught the first plane out of Toronto after she received his telegram and a phone call from the Ramseys telling her everything had been arranged. Margaret would be along to fetch her. All she had to do was go to the Meeting Place and wait. A week later, with a promise someday the Ramseys would come to Canada for a visit, they left for a short holiday, touring the Midlands in a rented car.

"So who's sending us a bill?" Merri asked.

"It's from the Inn where we stayed in the Cotswolds."

"You're kidding. What for?"

"They're invoicing us for the meals we took in the restaurant."

"How stupid." Merri looked puzzled. "I thought you paid the restaurant separately?"

"I did. But they're claiming I signed our room number to them. Number 302."

"That's the number all right," Merri asserted.

It had been an antique room in a 'circa 16th century house' with warped plastered walls and a slanted floor, so inclined, when Jim crawled out of the high downy bed in the middle of the night he lost his balance and almost brained himself on a timber in the ancient ceiling.

"There must be some error," she proposed. "What'll we do about it?"

"Ignore it. Someone else has obviously signed his name to our room by mistake."

"Or on purpose."

Jim laughed, "you reckon?"

At two minutes to five Andy Cruikshank parked his Volvo on the shady side of the towering blue spruce centring the circle out front. Merri admitted him and sent Julia to get her father. In the living room when the two were seated she asked, "How's Celeste?"

"Better than nothing."

Merri smiled at Crooky's humour. The poor man had trouble with an invalid wife. "And your daughter and sons?"

"Fine. So are the grandkids. They're over at our place at the moment, baby sitting Celeste. During the week it's not so bad. A woman takes care of her. She does the housework and gets my meals as well. And the boys are okay."

"Jim just received a letter from your niece's husband."

Crooky brightened. "He's a great lad. Anything interesting?"

"He asked to give you their love. Most of it dealt with the operation he performed on an Afghan friend of Jim's."

"Yeah, I heard awhile ago. How did it turn out?"

"Very well. There was also a letter from the man himself. He's back home and very pleased with the outcome."

The sound of the back-door being shut caused Merri to cock her head. "He'll be here in a sec," she declared and asked Crooky if he wanted something to drink, "Tea or coffee, perhaps?"

Jim loped in wearing jeans and a worn plaid shirt. "I think Andy prefers Rye and Ginger," he advised. "I'll get it."

"Make it a Rye and water," Crooky corrected and combed his nails through a thin layer of silver, screening his scalp. He waited until Jim returned with his drink, plus a scotch and ice for himself then asked, "What have you been up to?"

Jim looked down at his worn pants. "Forgive the appearance. I've been out in the garage working on a boat."

"What kind?"

"Sail. Jason began it. I'd like to launch it this summer as he had planned." Jim did not mention how depressed he had become each time he viewed the Snipe propped on its uprights like an emaciated body in suspended animation, and the urge he had to burn it. Time was healing his wounds. It would be better planked, coated with paint, dressed in rigging and afloat on the pond where the southwest winds would blow life in its sails. He regarded his older colleague and raised his glass. "Cheers!"

Andy answered the salute with his customary, "The better for seeing you," took a sip and placed his glass on a coaster provided by Merri. "How's the arm?" he asked.

"Better."

"When are you coming back to work?"

"Monday. Full time." Jim sighed. "I spent all of last week at the office cleaning out paper. There was a ton of correspondence to answer, mostly medicolegal and W.C.B. - a heap of misery. I hated to dump all that typing on Betsy but there's no alternative."

"You need another girl?"

"I don't think so. She can handle it. Likely finish it over the week-end. She's had close to a two month break; the extra work won't kill her. Looking over my appointment book, next week looks pretty light. Other times when I've taken off I come back to an office load of patients. It could be seasonal. April's usually a slack month." Jim smiled. "Blame it on the miserable climate. A lot of people are down south basking in the sun. They forget their ailments. Who wants to waste time in a doctor's office when the golf courses are open."

"That's one of the things I wanted to talk to you about."

"How's that?"

"There's more to it."

"For instance?"

"Your patients are going elsewhere."

When Dr. Cruikshank noted his statement had drawn no more than a blank expression from Jim he went on to explain. "So are some of mine. Not many mind you. I only have a few orthopaedic cases. It's Best. He's stealing them."

A smile slowly spread into a broad grin and Jim began to chuckle. "I was accused of stealing patients when I first came to town, remember."

"That's right, I remember." Crooky nodded. "But your behaviour was more ethical. You only took referred patients. Once I was miffed when Mrs. Calderwood went to see you with her arthritic hip. I'd been treating the old biddy for years. You operated on her and I was mad as hell. I didn't learn she'd gone to see you until I saw her on your O.R. list. Her family doctor, a friend of mine for years, had sent her to you. I asked him why. In clear devil-be-damned English he told me it was her idea. Bloody well made a fool of myself. I must say I was a bit jealous when she got a good result. But I learned something. You taught me how to do the procedure, a 'McMurray osteotomy', when I asked you to assist me on a similar case."

Andy paused and his bushy white eyebrows lowered. "But this guy Best is something else. He's right behind every ambulance entering the E.R., grabbing every case walking in the door. Even sees his follow up patients there so he doesn't miss some business. Administration should charge him rent." The colour of Crooky's face was vermilion.

From a vest pocket Andy drew a packet of 'Players', lit a cigarette and stuck it to his lower lip. His eyes began to water and he dabbed at them with a pocket handkerchief. "Something happened while you were away" he went on. "Beecher made a serious mistake and dishonestly tried to cover it."

"Omission or commission?" Jim asked.

"A combination of both."

"How's that?"

"He failed to examine a patient, then proceeded to do the wrong thing."

"That's misconduct."

"I suppose the College might call it that."

"What's being done about it?"

"Nothing!"

Crooky drew in a large breath of smoke and exhaled slowly. "There's nothing we can do without exposing some well meaning souls and the Hospital to a law suit."

"Sounds complicated. Tell me more."

"It is, but understandable. Actually there were a series of mistakes made by a number of people but the fault lies with Best. He pinned the wrong hip."

"Really!"

"Yes, Beecher isn't very thorough, or wasn't in this case. He didn't examine the patient before she was taken to the O.R."

"Unforgivable!"

"Sure," Andy agreed. "We all know it, even Best himself. That's why he lied. Wrote up the history after he'd done the surgery and predated it."

"How do you know?"

"I happened along during the operation. The post pinning x-ray films had been taken. Proud as a peacock, Best invited me to look at them. I couldn't see the break. In my experience pinning hips I've never seen post reduction films without some evidence of a fracture. I became suspicious when I detected a small calcific deposit near the greater trochanter was present on the preoperative set of x-rays but absent on the subsequent films. I mentioned this to Beecher and he had a fit."

"Weren't the films marked?"

"Oh yeah. Another part of the story. The X-ray Technician goofed. She placed an 'R' marker on the left side and very prominently, just above the hip socket."

"Wheew, what a mess! And the patient?"

"She's fine. Didn't turn a hair. Lost a bit of blood as expected having two major operations at one go. But no complications."

"You mean he just went ahead and did her other side."

"I don't think he had any choice."

"How did her family take it?"

Crooky threw up his hands. "I really don't know. There must have been a lot of interesting questions asked. Rumour has it Best told them she had a deteriorating bone condition and to prevent the same thing happening to her right hip he had braced it with a pin."

Jim found it difficult not to smile. "Prophylactic treatment!"

"Yeah." Crooky smirked. "But hardly in the same ball park as forcing a guy to wear a condom to prevent him from getting the clap eh! It's really not very funny."

"That's not what tickles me. It's the man's gall."

"No doubt about it. He's full of it. Full of something smelly too. Sister Bernadette is nobody's fool. It was she who caught him lying. He told her he'd written his preoperative work-up at the same time as the post operative note, which was obviously after the surgery. Yet he dated it the evening before. She thinks it was to cover his mistake."

"Perhaps. But how many times have you dictated your history and physical at the same time as the op. note?" Jim argued. "We're all guilty of it. Sometimes even after the patient has been discharged."

"Okay. Play the Devil's advocate if you want. But we've not fiddled with dates." Crooky paused. "I don't know about you but I haven't."

When Jim failed to commit himself Andy carried on. "My point is he purposely predated his work-up because he'd never done a preoperative examination. If he had there's no doubt in my mind he would have discovered the fracture was on her left side."

"You said Sister Bernadette spoke to him. Anyone else?"

"No. At least I doubt it, unless it was Sister Magdalene. Not being medically trained it's highly unlikely she would tackle our friend, particularly after hearing of his intractability from Bernadette."

"For a week or two the incident was number one on the hit parade. If Bernadette told Magdalene what she told me then there is nothing the Board can do for the moment. If they take Best to task it means admitting the X-ray Department also made a mistake. Two wrongs still don't make it right. But is it right for the hospital to bear the financial brunt if there's a law suit which is likely. The X-ray Technician was one of the hospital's employees and it was the Sisters, through their own Governing Board, who gave Best the privilege to use their facilities. Any old 'which way', the Sisters stand to lose. My bet is they have had legal counsel from the Lay Advisory to do nothing until they're forced. Let the patient make the first move. If she does it will most likely be against Best. He's the hospital's first line of defence." Crooky chuckled. "Who said life is simple."

"Or easy," Jim interjected. "Frankly Crooky, and this is between the two of us, I don't like Beecher any more than you do. Nor do I trust him. I wish he'd gone elsewhere. But we're stuck with him. If it turns out he's a blemish we must eliminate then somehow we'll have to cut him off. But that's risky. I'm going to mind my own business. I've got six mouths to feed, four people to educate and a practice to run. Best can get himself into all the trouble he wants."

Andy exhaled a large cloud and sucked in another litre of smoke, thinking whether Lindsay liked it or not, as a responsible member of the medical community, he would have to get involved if it came to censuring Best. "Though I have to agree with your attitude," he coughed, then coughed again and went into a paroxysm of coughing. "Yeah," he sputtered. "He'll probably get away with it this time but sooner or later he'll - "

"You might like to try my English muffin pizzas, Dr Cruikshank." Merri interrupted. A tray of English muffins with melted cheese, pimentoed olives and pepperoni slices was set down on a coffee table next to their guest.

The little chief leaned forward, stubbed his cigarette in an ashtray and looked up at her appreciatively. "Sure, I'd be delighted," he sniffed. "Smells great."

How Crooky could smell anything but the smoke around him, for the sake of politeness Merri didn't ask.

In a few minutes she was back with a coffee pot. "I caught part of the six o'clock TV news just now," she disclosed. "Saw something that would interest you, Jim. The German ex-S.S. officer you treated. The man who slashed his wrists."

"Eckheusen? Hans Eckheusen," Jim surmised

"Yes. That's the name I heard. He went over the Falls. Some tourist was standing by the railing and took a movie of the whole affair. The man jumped into the current and was over the brink before any one could stop him. Quite horrible!"

"That's all?"

"Not exactly. Eckheusen's wife was with him.

"She committed suicide too?"

"No, she was in the car at the time. Apparently he asked her to drive by the Falls. She'd been to the Sanatorium and was taking him home. He left his wallet on the front seat and told her he wanted a closer look."

Jim turned to Andy who was chewing a mouthful. "I sorted out the guy's tendons and median nerve. A psychiatric case, he was admitted to the Stevenson wing after slashing his wrists. Really mixed up. His wife found him in the bathroom, a bloody mess. Her boy friend brought him into Emergency."

"Her boy friend?" Crooky had to gulp down a morsel of muffin before commenting. "Sounds intriguing."

"Yeah. She was fed up with his depression and found attention elsewhere. Can't blame her. The guy was a wreck, loaded with guilt. The Psychiatrists pieced it together. Apparently Eckheusen wasn't his real name. He chose it to escape going to prison after the war. Aaron eventually transferred the man to Woodholme Sanatorium. There was nothing more he could do for him and from what's happened neither could the 'shrinks' at Woodholme." Jim smiled, "I guess I'll never know how my repair turned out."

Andy laughed. "I'll bet you never got paid for it either?"

Part Three

Saturday, March 18, 1967
to
Friday, November 17, 1967

Dr. Lindsay & Dr. Best

CHAPTER THIRTY-THREE

The prize-winning post and beam sat on the clay bench at the foot of the escarpment. Set in a clearing the house overlooked a conventional middle class neighbourhood. Its flat-top was not beautiful and questionably practical but it had won an award for a Shipton architect and prestige for its owners. Like a king-sized container waiting to be off-loaded at a warehouse, Jim thought, spinning the wheels of his ageing Pontiac up the heated driveway. Hard to tell the front from the back. The adjacent garage held a Cadillac Seville for Paolone's every day use, Angela's Buick and a used compact. He stopped beside a walkway possibly leading to an entrance, stepped over a bank of late March snow and followed the concrete to steps on the north side. They climbed to a wooden deck, splitting the big box into a sandstone lower level and an upper wall of thermopane. Just which panel opened confused Jim for they were all backed with heavy brown drapes.

A deck encircled the house. Dr. Lindsay was on his second time around, looking for a bell-button when he met Paolone coming the other way.

"Hey Pisano! Whatsamatta? Yousa lost?"

"Your place has to be the most burglar proof I've ever seen."

"Not really," Joe squinted and the tip of his beak straightened a notch. "You're not used to these modern conveniences. Each glass section has sliding doors; in summer it becomes a gazebo."

"What about winter?" Jim frowned. "Must cost a mint to heat!"

"The drapes help." Paolone did not sound convinced and reached for a nylon cord, hanging from a fir beam. "For attention one must pull this," he instructed.

A gong resounded somewhere within.

"Westminster chimes!" Jim smiled and shook his head in disbelief. "What else you got new and exciting, Joe?"

Paolone turned toward the front lawn with its dun crested tufts and pointed to the top of a thirty foot pole. "The flag!" he exclaimed.

In the stillness it looked like a blood soaked rag. "Pearson's pennant! What's new about that?"

"I know, the queen unfurled it some time ago but it's new to me and hard to get used to - that ridiculous maple leaf! Christ the

Americans have more maple trees than we do - disappointing is the exclusion of green for us Italians."

Jim laughed. "The French wanted to include blue and no doubt had more justification. Why are you flying it?" he asked, unable to understand why Joe had gone to the trouble. It did nothing for his commercial looking house other than transform it into a Federal building, like the Tourist Information Centre.

"Patriotism," Joe spat. He didn't want to admit his politically active wife had needled him into hoisting the damn thing. Suddenly the morning sun burst through the overcast and his eyes began to water. "It's Centennial year," he explained, wiping his lids on a shirt cuff.

"My God, you 'Ities' are emotional," Jim teased. "Imagine crying over a flag."

"Oh crap!" There was no use telling Lindsay the brightness had caught him off guard. "Come on," he grumbled. "Her Highness is waiting."

The floor off the deck was obviously for living, recreation and entertainment, divided by sectional furniture and moveable bookcases. A large television screen sat in the centre next to an acorn fireplace, partially hiding a dining area. Parquet floors were polished to a cinnamon sheen and sunbeams played on a stovepipe cut through the ceiling. Even the large fully equipped kitchen was exposed. One permanent wall cordoned a powder room and a study; parallel to it a broad open stairway led down to the sleeping quarters.

In the master bedroom Angela lay on top of the covers in a full length white lace gown, her upswept black hair, head and shoulders on lacy pillow cases; a casted right leg was propped on yesterday's copy of the Shipton Shield.

Jim ambled across the green shag rug to her far side and noticed she rested on a posturepedic cedar box. To one side was a matching chest. Indeed the room was without clutter. Recessed ceiling lights flooded a magnificent renaissance tapestry, hung on a grass papered wall and next to a spacious closet was an adjoining bath finished in black Italian marble. He took it all in as she smiled misanthropically and swore, "Not a God damned window on the floor! How's a body supposed to get any sunshine and fresh air? Fingal must have been standing on his head when he came up with this design. Triumph of the architectural year they call it."

"The conditioner's fan's on full blast," said Joe.

"So what, I can't see out."

"Plenty of view upstairs," he argued. "This room's for sleeping. Get off your fat ass and use the crutches the physio gave you."

"My ass isn't any bigger than yours Joe Paolone. In fact there was a time when you treated it with more respect. Our passion pit, or 'fornicatorium' which you call this place, is nothing more than a sterile 'Fingal's cave' or 'black hole of Calcutta'.

As for fornication - Jim cut in before the argument got too personal. "Angela, what's the problem?" he asked looking down at her, wondering why he had agreed to see her at home. He detested housecalls. The last one had been three years ago in Afghanistan when Dr. Ames prevailed upon him to see his blubbery wife. With the exception of her grey hair the woman bore a resemblance to Angela. That was it, he thought, a special favour to a fellow doctor.

"I want you to take this thing off," Angela ordered.

"I can't."

"Why the hell not?"

"It keeps your broken ankle in place."

"But it's quit paining. I want it off."

"Angela if I take your cast off now the ankle mortise will spread and you'll end up with arthritis."

"Which in your excessively heavy state," Joe added, "is inevitable anyway."

"Oh shut up, you twit. I've a speech to make next week and I'm not crawling up on the platform with this abominable weight.

"Why not?" Joe smiled. "Think of the extra attention it'll bring and the by-line in the Shield: 'Undaunted Angela Throws Cast In Ring.'

"Sorry," Jim apologized. "Take it off at your own risk. I recommend at least two more weeks, followed by an x-ray. I'll take it off when we get back from California."

"You're going to the Surgical meeting too?" Angie huffed. "Joe's leaving for San Francisco tomorrow. Taking two of the O.R. nurses with him." One side of her mouth elevated sardonically. "A menage de trois."

Paolone looked sheepish.

"No", Jim replied seriously. "I'm off to Disneyland with Merri and the girls. Should be lots of fun." He regarded the churlish face framed by a lacy pillow and changed the conversation. "I read in the paper your high school chum is going to be the new Justice Minister."

"That Bastard! After the next election he'll be Prime Minister. Mark my words. Him and his 'Quiet Revolution'. A so-called Catholic! Encouraging divorce and homosexuality. Back in those days he also supported communism. Abortion is the only thing he advocates I agree with."

"Maybe you should run against him Angie," Jim smiled. "A staunch conservative like yourself."

"First things first, my good man, I've an aldermanic seat to contest."

"Doesn't matter who's in power," Joe scoffed. "Look what the conservatives have done, commissioning a biased white paper on medicare. The Feds have us by the short and curlies, socialized medicine right across Canada. Wait till it hits Ontario."

The moment had come to leave. Joe was revving up for a bash at his favourite grievance, government interference in health care. Jim excused himself from Angela and slipped through one of the invisible panels back to his car.

Joe was right on his heels. "By the way, Crooky wants to call a special meeting of the surgeons. A peer review of Best. Has he spoken to you?"

Jim had to roll down the car window to answer, "Not to any extent. He called me yesterday but preferred not to detail the problem over the phone. I'm on my way to his office now. Apparently some of Best's cases are giving him cause for concern."

In semi-retirement, Dr. Andrew Cruikshank had sold his large office rooms on James St. and rented one of the basement apartments in the Landmark building across from St. Mary's. He had given up operating, opting to assist the more active surgeons and was devoting his time to medical legal work.

He greeted Jim with, "Glad you could come," and conducted the taller man into his private office.

"I don't have much time," Jim apologized. "We're due to fly in a few hours - school break. Besides I've still rounds to make."

"Sorry but what I've been collecting on our friend Beecher is lengthy. Perhaps you can take this and look it over," he said, sailing a few stapled sheets of copy-paper across his desk.

Jim accepted. There were a dozen typed pages, containing summaries of patient's hospital records.

Crooky lighted a cigarette and coughed. When he had finished, Jim advised, "You should give them up before they kill you."

"I'm too old to stop," Crooky sputtered, "Why give up a pleasure when I haven't much time to enjoy it?"

"How's Celeste?" asked Jim, hoping to get on to a less morbid subject. "I saw her walking your hound the other day. Out our way, by the old church."

"Yeah that would be her," Crooky smiled. "She's taken to hiking. Doing her a world of good."

They were an incongruous couple, Celeste being taller, more slender and frail, a few years younger than Andy. Rarely were they seen together, the extent of their socializing being a private party with intellectual types at their tastefully appointed Georgian home when her health permitted. Merri had invited them many times but her overtures were turned down. How they got together in the first place was a mystery to her, let alone how Dr. Cruikshank stuck it out. But Crooky was devoted to his Celeste.

He sat in silence as Jim started down the list. The first patient was Trish Lucas, a three month old girl with a diagnosis of congenital dislocation of the hip. Best had admitted her to perform an adductor tenotomy, a minor procedure to lengthen the muscles of the groin. Afterwards, to keep her thighs spread she was placed in a double plaster spica, a cumbersome cast encircling the waist and both lower extremities down to the toes. No x-rays were taken either before or after the procedure. Jim turned the page.

"Hold it there," Crooky demanded, "let me tell you something he hasn't written. When I saw this girl on the O.R. schedule I wondered why such radical treatment. So it was a minor operation but how many two month old kids with CDH have you operated?"

"None."

"Me neither, and I've seen a few cases over the years. This kid was done under local anaesthetic!"

"You must be joking!"

"No I'm not! I've never heard of such nonsense. How he prevented her from wriggling all over the table beats me. Any anaesthetic in a two month old is risky, but a general is safest, particularly in the hands of an experienced person, and it would have made the operation easier."

"Actually a frank dislocation can be determined by clinical examination alone. But one should get x-rays to prove it or differentiate it from other anomalies such as congenital absence of the upper femur. In a kid this age," Jim was thinking aloud, "if the hip was completely dislocated, corroborated by x-rays, I'd examine her under a general anaesthetic, gently reduce the dislocation and hold the corrected position in a plaster similar to what he did. In fact I would not be averse to doing an adductor tenotomy at the same time."

Mentally Jim reviewed the problems faced in hip dysplasia Finally he said, "But there are various degrees of pathology in congenital hip dislocation, Crooky, ranging from no dislocation per se to a frank dislocation. The milder conditions become manifest later, usually at one year of age when the infant begins to walk. They can be detected early by clinical examination. The thighs are difficult to spread. Usually I treat these kids in a pillow splint. After six months or certainly by the time the child starts to walk, the head of the femur is well seated and the socket has begun to form. Before these commercial jobs, I used casts, similar to the one Best applied." Jim stopped and summarized his remarks. "Of course a lot depends on the degree of pathology, whether the hip joint was completely dislocated at birth or partially, with a shallow socket. If the only pathology found in this case was tight thigh adductors, she has been over-treated."

"There is no way of determining the degree of pathology," Crooky interjected, "without taking x-rays of both hips, the normal side for comparison, which he failed to do."

"Right."

"Well, there may have been no films taken at the General," Dr. Cruikshank smiled, "but films were obtained at Ben Nickerson's X-Ray Clinic by the paediatrician who referred the kid. I got Nickerson's permission to borrow them." Crooky pulled a small X-ray jacket from his desk drawer. "Have a gander."

Jim held the two films up to the light. There were two views taken from the front, differing only in that the baby had her lower extremities in line with her trunk in one and spread in the other. In neither view was a dislocation evident. Both the femoral heads were just beginning to appear as tiny opaque spots equal in size and consistent with the patient's age. The cant of the socket was normal.

Do Unto Others 319

If there was anything out of line, the left thigh was not spread quite as far as the right.

"The kid might have some tight adductors on the left," Jim admitted, frowning his indecision "But this could also be due to the way the patient was positioned at the time of x-ray."

"Exactly!"

"To give Beecher the benefit of doubt, let's say the kid had slight tightness of the left hip adductors. Then all he had to do was keep her thighs abducted in a pillow splint for a few months and take another x-ray. Certainly he didn't need to lengthen the tendons."

"My sentiments too!" Crooky was emphatic. "There's a definite pattern through the other cases. I've collected about a dozen. The man's too aggressive. Fortunately none of his patients have died." The desk jumped as Dr. Cruikshank brought his fist down. "I think the time has come to confront him officially."

"Andy, why document this stuff?"

"After the Bennett fiasco when he pinned the wrong hip I tried to give him some fatherly advice but might as well have talked to the moon. He's oblivious to any constructive criticism, leastwise from me. Probably thinks I'm an outdated old toot and I find his attitude disturbing. If the man is salvageable I can put my personal feelings aside and trust he pays some heed to the collective advice of his peers. Drastic perhaps, distasteful and time consuming but it might work."

"So if we hold a Peer Review and discover he is unsalvageable or uncover a more serious defect, say poor judgment or find he's negligent, incompetent, or guilty of misconduct, then what?" Jim asked. "What recourse do we have?"

"Lift his privileges."

"That means going to the Board."

"Right and it wouldn't end there. The Board would have to uphold the recommendations of the Medical staff and report him to the Ontario College. In turn the College will likely send investigators to find if there is a legitimate case against him. A trial at the College would follow and could be unpleasant with all kinds of nasty repercussions. It could totally exonerate him and make us look like idiots. If he's found guilty the sentence could range from an unregistered reprimand to permanent suspension of his licence. Or the College may modify the penalty to allow for re-instatement, forcing him to seek further training, even choosing a mentor."

Dr. Cruikshank shrugged and the cigarette stuck to his lower lip bobbed like a Willie Wagtail. "The toughest fight would be right here, trying to get unanimity among the doctors. Have you ever heard of their agreeing one hundred percent on anything? The variety of opinion is proportionate to the number of docs on the staff. In this case the whole bunch would be asked to vote. Ludicrous, when the opinions of unqualified persons have to be counted but that's our democratic system. What the hell does a G.P. know about the finer points in the management of congenital hip dislocation? Nothing! They'd have to be educated. They might very well let their emotions guide them. Who wants to be party to taking a man's livelihood away?"

"Besides, getting the surgeons' agreement is one thing but Alligood would have to convince the chiefs of all the other MAC departments as well. Can you see him doing that? He's about as convincing as a fly. The damn fence sitter."

Jim chuckled and stood to go. "Crooky, you shouldn't have resigned," he said, folding his copy.

"I had to. The Board introduced a five year limit - a chief cannot succeed himself - ten years late in my case. Alligood is next in line."

"Well you sure paint a distasteful picture." Jim placed the list of cases in his coat pocket adding, "Poor unsuspecting Alligood. Does he know?"

"I've talked to him privately, like yourself."

At the door Jim dallied. "Tell me Crooky, is it worth it?"

"When you've finished looking over the list, get in touch. Chances are you'll withdraw your question." Crooky patted Jim's shoulder. "Have a pleasant trip and love to the family."

Sister Magdalene was conferring with head nurse Penner in the nursery section of the Paediatric Ward. Seeing Dr. Lindsay was about to leave, she broke up their discussion and hailed him. "We have a serious problem," she said in a strident voice, so foreign to her normal dulcet tone.

"Oh?"

The sister was a tall woman with a wide friendly face. This morning tautness overruled. "The baby in bed 2 has been wailing all night. We've given him as much morphine as we dare and it doesn't hold him. He hasn't been seen by a doctor since he went to the O.R. yesterday. Please have a look."

Jim checked the wall clock, reading an hour till noon. He should have been dictating letters for Betsy to type while he was away. "Who ordered the morphine?" he asked.

"Byers," she answered, sounding distraught. "We tried to reach Dr. Best, but he's signed out to their Clinic for the week end."

"Did you try his home?"

"Yes but there was no answer."

"Who routinely covers for him?"

"The Clinic I suppose."

"I mean which orthopod?"

"I couldn't say. He rarely comes here. Most of his cases are done at the General. Come" she begged, reaching for Dr. Lindsay's arm. "The boy's beside the window. Please see him."

Sister Magdalene's grip was more compelling than her words and there was no choice but to follow.

The child's crying increased when Jim lifted the blanket. His little hands began to tear at the cast. It incorporated his whole left lower extremity down to the toes and he was trying to push it away.

A cursory glance was all Jim needed and he sent the sister to get the cast cutter. The nail beds were as white as the underlying sheet; most odd the foot of the cast was rolled outward compared to the knee. "What in hell have we here?" he growled and after Magdalene returned, promptly sent her back for the chart.

The oscillating blade cut through the cast from above downward in the mid-line. Three finger breadths above the ankle it hit a metallic object hidden in the plaster. The baby screamed.

"Read me the operative report," Jim ordered.

"There isn't any nor is there a preop note," the sister declared. "All we have is the anaesthetist's record and the nurses' notes."

Jim swore and grabbed the chart. At the top of the anaesthetic sheet he read the admitting diagnosis, 'Congenital club foot'. There was no indication of what procedure had been done, but he did get an inkling from the admitting clerk's handwritten note. It was dated Mar. 16/67, the day of admission and distinctly read, admit for a rotational osteotomy of the left tibia.

"Damn! If I hadn't run into the pin I'd never believe it."

"Believe what?" Sister asked.

"Anyone would break a four year old's leg to correct a club foot deformity."

He switched on the saw a second time and worked his way around the pin distally, along the inside of the foot, then put his fingers into the split and pried the plaster open. Magdalene handed him a pair of heavy scissors and he cut the entire length of the padding beneath. The colour of the toes did not improve. A silent watch for five minutes added nothing. Letting out a deep breath, he turned away mumbling, "He'll have to go back to the O.R."

More easily said than done, the sister reflected. Today's Saturday. The supervisor would have to be notified, the O.R. team called in and most repulsive to her was informing the baby's parents.

"You'll have to speak to them Dr. Lindsay."

"Who?"

"The Iresons."

"Good God!" Some three years ago he had to contend with the Iresons. Not them, it was the wife, the baby's mother. He had never met the father and recalled his last encounter when she agreed to make an appointment with someone in Toronto, but couldn't remember to whom he had sent them. They had never come back. He tried to focus on the last visit and it was suddenly obliterated by a more crushing memory. It had been on the day Jason died.

Then, he thought, perhaps I'm jumping to conclusions. They're probably not the same Iresons. Looking at the child's face more closely gained nothing.

"Get them on the phone Sister and I'll speak to them before surgery." On second thought, he added. "Better ask the Iresons to come in an hour from now."

"It's Mrs. Starling." Janet Schocker, sitting naked on the edge of her Queen sized bed whispered with a hand over the phone. She removed it and pressed a finger to her lips, warning Beecher to be quiet.

He was lying equally stripped, face up, a pink sheet partially covering the lower half of his body.

"Shit!" he exclaimed, after she had put the phone back on its hook and told him there was an emergency. "For Christ sake, we're just getting started."

"Like hell. We've been at it all night."

He wasn't about to divulge he had a bet with Husselman he could lay her twenty times on a week end. So far, since midnight when their sexual marathon got off with a mutual climax, he had come seven times in eleven hours. With about thirty hours to go he could make it.

"OK, let's try for eight," she giggled, jubilantly straddling him. "This one's on you." It took a minute for her to reach a climax, grunting with ecstasy. A final thrust and she bounced off, leaving him to finish his emission alone.

"Hurray! Another winner, Beechie boy. You stay right where you are until I get back. Chow!"

While Janet showered Beecher was quiet until his curiosity got the better of him. He wrapped the sheet around him and went into the bathroom.

Janet turned down the shower in order to hear him. "You asked what's up? Lindsay has a redo. Some four year old, who was operated yesterday. Seems there's a problem with the circulation. Starling says he might have to open the leg and explore the artery."

She stepped out and began to blot with a bath towel dragging it up through her crotch and between and over the roundness of her breasts. The action set Beecher's juices flowing. "Now hold on Peachie, little Jany baby will be back to take care of you real soon." Pretending to rinse her mouth she took a glass from the back of the sink and filled it with cold water. Before he realized what she was doing, the water was poured down the front of him and his manhood began to shrink. "That ought to put you on hold." She laughed and began to dress.

Twenty minutes later Beecher was listening to an Elvis Presley record when Janet rang.

"Hey Beech. You better get in here fast. The redo is the Ireson kid you operated on yesterday. Lindsay's split the cast. There's no toe movement and he can't feel a pulse. The parents are climbing the wall. They told Sister Magdalene they won't have anything to do with Lindsay. He hasn't talked to them yet and is due back in fifteen minutes. You've still time to get here before he does."

"Christ, he can't just walk in on my patient. How did he get to see him?"

"How should I know. Just get your balls in here! There's a serious problem and the kid's your responsibility." Janet hung up, wondering why she had anything to do with him. She smiled to herself. One thing for sure, Beecher was the best sex she'd ever had.

But there was more to it, she thought, while setting up for the operation. He gave her the impression life was not to be taken too seriously and made her laugh, which her dour husband never did. If Peter smiled his face would fall off.

Mr. and Mrs. Ireson were bent over the crib, trying to fathom Dr. Best's medical jargon. His eyes were swollen and blotches of redness highlighted his puffy cheeks. He spoke lethargically. "I did what I told you, a minor operation. Put two pins in his leg, parallel to each other, about three inches apart and cut the bone between them through a very short incision. The lower pin was then rotated outward so it formed a ninety degree angle with the upper one. Both pins were left sticking through the skin and I incorporated them in the cast. Everything was fine when I checked him last night and this morning."

Although he was speaking in a low reassuring tone Mrs. Penner caught his lie. Her mouth fell open and she blinked. If he had slipped in to see the child no one had seen him, at least it hadn't been reported. Some doctors did occasionally but most often they checked with the nurses. He might have come unnoticed if the baby were sleeping but then he was not asleep - at report she was told the patient had been screaming all night.

"I don't know why Dr. Lindsay has all but removed the cast," Beecher paused frowning. Glancing at the blanched and bloodless skin the reason was obvious. Not about to admit it he continued. "He had no business splitting it."

"He wants to operate." Mrs. Ireson wept into a hankie. "Please stop him."

"Certainly."

The ensuing moment was broken by his name being bellowed from the passage. "Dr. Best come out here immediately; I want to talk to you."

Jim had difficulty keeping himself from barging into the nursery and dragging the good doctor out by the scruff of the neck.

Beecher obeyed and started toward the door, hollering for no other reason than to impress the Iresons. "Dr. Lindsay. You're not taking this boy upstairs."

Jim closed his eyes and held his breath; there was a violent desire to plant four knuckles on Best's haughty nose. "That's right," he glared as Best faced him, "But you are!"

"If you gentlemen wish to discuss this problem, it's better you do it in private." Sister Magdalene intervened, leading the two of them into an empty storage room adding, "I'll bring a couple of chairs."

"Never mind Sister, what I have to say to Dr. Best is not going to take very long." Jim's jaw was set so tight his teeth ached. "You stupid son-of-a-bitch. The kid's got impending gangrene and you stand around like a bloody imbecile. First thing you do is give him a spinal, it might help dilate his arteries, then de-rotate your pins back to a normal alignment. If the circulation doesn't improve you'll have to split the fascia over his anterior compartment, allowing the arteries to expand. Chances are that's where the boy's problem lies if you didn't bugger the blood vessels when you cut the bone. No matter, the odds are it's too late now. After six hours muscle tissue deprived of it's blood supply starts to die. According to my calculation it has been over eighteen. The child will be lucky to get away with a few contractures. But his leg will never be normal. What beats me is your having been duly admitted to the Royal College of Physicians and Surgeons as a Fellow by examination, you bloody well should know."

Beecher was aghast. Usually he had a comeback, but Dr. Lindsay's blast smothered him.

Jim had not waited for an answer. Beecher was on his own. Braced against the store room wall, he was thinking of his next move. For the moment he had none.

CHAPTER THIRTY-FOUR

"Darling please turn off the light. It's awfully late."

Jim twisted on the pillow, struggling to peer over his newly acquired reading glasses and nodded. "In a minute sweetheart. I've half a page to go."

"You've been poring over those cases since we left home." Merri sighed.

"Not really."

When he walked out of Dr. Cruikshank's office Jim had not intended to give the former chief's data a second thought until the Peer Review. But his private confrontation with the younger orthopaedic surgeon alarmed him. Crooky undoubtedly had been stuffing a can of worms and was about to blow the lid. He had perused the list on the plane. Once into the material he was unable to let it go.

Merri couldn't get to sleep for the lack of it. She needed the warmth of Jim's body, her security blanket, ever comforting, for they had been together since they were very young. 'We're so lucky,' she had said dreamily, 'to have such a strong attraction for each other.' More than once they had joyfully proclaimed their mutual good fortune. In the course of their lives they'd seldom been apart for any length of time. 'You're my favourite person,' he'd drawl, as he was hers and they intended to maintain this status till death parted them. Whatever Jim wanted to do was fine because she truly enjoyed the same activities whether they were sporting, musical, social, philosophical, or doing nothing. She didn't go along with him for his sake alone. 'You shouldn't dote on him so much,' Martha had reprimanded, repeatedly misjudging her daughter's behaviour. 'Why not?' she'd replied, amused her mother was reluctant to grant her one weakness. 'I'm happy looking after him, just to be near him makes me happy. He's not demanding, never was and I doubt if he ever will be. Happiness comes from within, our mutual attraction brings it out. We're damn lucky.'

It had been an exhausting day. The take-off had been delayed by three hours due to ice in Detroit, the one stop on their route to Los Angeles. It was past midnight before everyone was settled in their hotel rooms, the three kids occupying the adjoining suite and her parents in a double across the hall. Merri's father was a worry. He'd been discharged from the Hospital the day before having had four pints of blood to jack up his haemoglobin. Cirrhosis, Dr. MacLaren had told them several months ago, giving Dr. Cunningham another six months, possibly a year to live, provided he gave up drinking altogether which puzzled Merri as her father never had been a heavy drinker. 'Then,' the internist had proposed, 'he must've had viral hepatitis or damaged his liver with some toxic chemical, possibly a disinfectant. He told me he was a veterinary.' The thought of her father being an alcoholic was repulsive. He was thin and frail and had sat with his swollen ankles and pinkish yellow cheeks, waiting to be pre-boarded on the sleek new Boeing jet, waiving his right to a wheel chair or any assistance from the stewardess. The trip in store was not strenuous: three days of fun in Anaheim - breaking the long drive from L.A. to Carmel with an overnight stop half way up the coast - exploring the Monterey Peninsula and San Francisco in the time remaining.

Checking on the three girls, Merri wound out of bed into her tartan dressing gown and tip-toed into the adjoining room. They were asleep, Heather alone in one bed, Julie and Kathyrn in the other. Jennifer had passed up the trip; she was in the second year of an Honour Science course at University and up to her neck studying for final exams. So she said! But Merri suspected differently. Her oldest daughter was in love with Brad Coleman - she had taken her final two years of high school in one to catch up to him. In addition they had promised the trip to Merri's parents as a forty-fifth anniversary present. She had just left the older couple in the room across the hall.

When Jim turned out the light she threw her dressing gown over a chair and slid in beside him. In a few minutes she was curled on her left side with her back against his chest, his right arm around her. Their touch was so natural there was actually no feeling except for a sensation of belonging, as if each owned the other's skin. Her breathing deepened and Jim knew she was asleep.

He was wide awake and restless. After a few minutes he rolled on his back and stared at the bare shadowy ceiling occasionally lit by street lights as a faint breeze disturbed the curtains.

Tomorrow was a new day and a promising one. He was as excited as the kids about Disneyland. But the anticipation had little room to develop in his troubled mind. Try as he could to concentrate on something pleasant the events of the past day, his ruckus with Best and Dr. Cruikshank's implications kept passing in review. The pages of names and circumstances he had just put down reappeared. The first case had been gone over three times in addition to the short discussion he had with Crooky concerning the indications. There was no doubt in his opinion the two month old Lucas baby had been improperly treated. Best shouldn't have cut her thigh muscles but he had.

The second patient's problems were more acute. She needed treatment and urgently.

Mrs. Anna Gillies, age sixty-five, was admitted to the Shipton General Hospital on April 15/65 with multiple injuries caused by an automobile accident. The record showed she was in shock upon admission, her pelvis was broken in two places, four ribs were fractured with bleeding into the chest cavity and spiral breaks had occurred through the mid shafts of both thigh bones. Less than twelve hours following the accident, with her blood pressure hovering at 80/60, Best took her to the operating room. Either he chose to ignore her shocked condition or failed to recognize and treat it before commencing a seven and a half hour procedure under general anaesthesia. Her shock could have become irreversible and she might have died; if it hadn't been for Duggan's pumping blood and monitoring, she surely would've. What startled Jim was Best's aggressive manner in treating her fractures. He cut both of her thighs, put the fragments back in place manually and held them with not only one long plate and screws but two! Incomprehensible, when both fractures could have been treated adequately by traction, certainly until her shock had cleared. Then, one after the other, they could've been opened a week or so apart. The most aggressive treatment Jim could accept was doing both femurs at once and putting a single plate across each break, but only after she was out of shock. Miraculously the patient survived.

The third case had many features in common with the second. Mrs. Georgette Hayton also had a fractured femur similar to one of Mrs. Gillies'. The line of the break spiralled down the shaft for a distance of seven inches. Due to Mrs. Hayton's senescence - she was eighty-nine - her bone was considerably osteoporotic and lacked calcium, phosphorus and protein. Her routine x-rays showed faded bone and foretold delayed healing. Jim shook his head in disbelief as he read how Beecher had also performed the same type of open reduction on Mrs. Hayton as he did on Mrs. Gillies, placing two plates along the shaft at right angles to each other. Any bone surgeon could have told him there was a good chance the screws would pull out before the break had healed.

There were three patients with back problems upon whom Dr. Best had operated with adverse results. While studying them Jim fell asleep.

In the Tonga room of the Fairmount Hotel Joe Paolone and Tanya Harrington were dancing up a storm. How convenient it was for Chalmers to come down with the flu the day before they left Shipton, permitting them this interlude, Angie would have said had she known. But Joe had no intention of telling her.

The guitarist humped into 'You ain't nothing but a hound dog' and Joe decided to call a halt. During the evening as the orchestra floated up and down the lengthy pool he had fox-trotted, waltzed and nearly split his lumbosacral support on a tango.

"Time to turn in Dr. Paolone?" Tanya asked in her soft seductive voice. She smiled and raised her eyebrows. "We've a busy day tomorrow and it's well into the wee small hours." Her Jackie Kennedy mane had been traded for a stylish short cut, highlighted with blond streaks. But she hadn't given up her mini skirts and the gent at the next table had a glorious view of her bottom whenever she crossed her legs.

Joe would've given his last buck to get into her pants. On the plane he'd suggested sharing expenses, mainly rooms. She turned him down. To be expected he rationalized. With all the money she has, he was small potatoes. He rented a Jaguar at the airport and told her he was prepared to make her visit to San Francisco memorable, if she cared to join him. She did and his wave of hope began to crest. It swelled further while they were checking into the hotel and she agreed to have dinner with him. Twenty minutes later the doorman saw them off to Bavarian cuisine at a restaurant near the base of Coit Tower, ending in the Fairmount lounge. It had been a superb evening. "Enchanting," she purred, pulling her mink collar over her ears. She did not mention she had been through it all before.

He escorted her across California street and up to the fourth floor of their hotel where she edged discreetly through the door to her room turning down his offer of a night cap. Before she closed it, he took another shot announcing, "After the meeting we'll drive down to L.A. along the coast. There's an interesting Inn at San Luis Obispo - like a scene from Snow White! You'll enjoy it."

When she murmured, "Wouldn't it be wonderful. Good-night Dr. Paolone," his expectations rose to greater heights.

Tanya, lying alone on the bed in her glittering room, reminisced. The Inn at San Luis had been where she spent the first night of her first honeymoon - no one in Shipton knew she had been married twice before she encountered Noel Harrington, not even Noel. Beau, or Buster as her friends called him, had left the world long ago. All of his relatives were farmers in Montana. Fat chance of meeting them here and it would be fun to revisit the scene. She might even stay in the same room, maybe the same bed.

Her marriage to Shipman B. Lee had been a matter of necessity. The night at the Inn had occurred two months too late. She was sixteen and a virgin when Buster, a navy gunner, banged her in broad daylight in the cypress woods behind the Palace of the Legion of Honour. His impetuous salvo impregnated her and two weeks after they were legally wed Tanya had an abortion. Outraged by what she'd done, his leave over, Shipman First Class Lee left her with no intention of returning. He was drowned in the Mariana Trench. When that short chapter in her life ended she returned to San Francisco and her mother Halena at the Bocci Bowl where the two of them sang operatic arias while waiting on customers. Financially they were still fairly well off.

The Count and Countess Chernofsky had been white Russians and escaped via Vladivostok during the revolution, having a taste of unbearable hardship. Their story had been told by Halena many times, instilling a mere idle curiosity in Tanya. If printed it would have been a best seller. 'The terrible conditions on the railway trains were all true,' Halena would say. 'We had to share our excrement with other refugees in a crowded cattle car. We didn't feel safe, even on board an American trawler destined for the U.S., not until we landed in San Francisco and were lost in the crowd. Then we knew and began to feel comfortable.' All of which might have happened on another planet as far as Tanya was concerned.

Before the Czar's death, the Count transferred his securities to a European bank. He recovered them and moved his family into a rambling villa overlooking the Golden Gate. Tanya was born in the mid twenties. Four years later the great depression followed and her father lost everything but the house. He blew out his brains rather than face the dishonour of doing manual labour. The reason given to

Tanya when she was ten was he just got tired of living. Later Tanya entered Hubbord's finishing school for young ladies where Halena honestly believed her daughter might learn self discipline as well as refinement. Tanya smiled. It had been there, through a delinquent friend, she'd met Buster.

After the Count's death Halena sustained them, singing and by selling her jewellery. Though her voice was relegated to minor roles at the Opera House the high mark of her career was performing as Annina, Violetta's maid. Taking her bows gave her a taste of fame but she never had a starring role. Disappointed but not discouraged she continued to take lessons and practise. The work at the Bocci Bowl gave her a chance to sing, still hoping to be discovered as a great soprano. Each night she would pour out her soul in a climactic performance of 'One Fine Day' from Madame Butterfly or Mimi's swan song, from La Boheme - she loved Puccini. Tanya as a little girl would listen from a curtained room at the back of the bar.

Instinctively Halena knew her profession was not for Tanya. 'You make up for everything in looks,' she would remark, 'You've been attracting men from the day you were born.' Tanya recalled the tight look on her mother's face as Halena advised, 'but it's skin-deep security! I know!' How vainly her mother had tried to hang onto her own beauty - twice she had a facelift. Plastic surgery had pulled the corners of her mouth outward smoothing the turkey wrinkles in her neck and broadening her smile but when she relaxed the operation had added only a permanent strained expression to her wide handsome face. Halena's 'You need something substantial and as you're not smart enough to go to University it will have to be Nursing.' Tanya had never forgotten the comment; regurgitating it angrily in her mother's presence upon receiving a Bachelor of Science in Nursing fifteen years later when she was on her third marriage.

Her second husband didn't last long. Brent, was a light weight, a budding tenor hanging out at the Bocci Bowl. Halena was quite taken with him; he was right for her daughter. Tanya married him when she was twenty four and employed by a hospital in the Mission District. They took a flat nearby so she could walk to work. Three weeks after the wedding he came home early to find her in bed with an intern and attacked the man with a nine iron. The young doctor, a black belt in judo, easily disarmed him and delivered a swift and punishing beating.

A short time later Bosco and his son arrived. Noel Molyneaux Harrington, named after his French Canadian grandparent, drank too much, even then. The pair had come to San Francisco for no apparent reason other than to sell pulp to the newspapers and soon fell into Halena's clutches.

The old man, an opera buff, needed a housekeeper for his dying wife. He offered Halena the job, sweetening the pot with assurance as a board member of the Canadian Opera he could find her more interesting work. Halena did not take long to decide and when he had completed a deal with the Herald they flew to his mansion on the Niagara River.

Tanya continued to serve customers, playing hard to get with Noel. In black tights and a white satin blouse split to the waist she presented a spectacular figure. Noel prized what he saw and offered her a thousand dollars to join him in Reno for a week-end. Much to his surprise she refused the offer. He doubled the price. 'No thanks I'm not that kind of girl'., she answered with a tincture of resentment.

As she receded beyond his alcoholic mist he burned with desire. How much would it take to get her into bed? Night after night he frequented the bar, increasing his offer. Again and again she refused. She drove him crazy with lust. Back in Canada he chased her by wiring flowers, telephoning and mailing presents. She accepted everything but wouldn't come across. He found business excuses for returning to California and would spend an entire week-end getting drunk on cappuccinos. In a hundred different ways he told her he loved her. Oddly she said she loved him too. Finally in sheer desperation he asked her to become his wife. 'I will,' she replied.

Back in Niagara events moved rapidly. When Bosco's wife died it was plain Halena could not go on living in the house; Harrington did not want to lose her too. She was more amusing than a brood of baboons, great at entertaining his friends and business acquaintances, sitting at the magnificent grand piano in the drawing room, belting out everything from ribald ballads to Lucia. There was only one way in his conventional mind of holding her, marry her. Sure and why not, she thought, any woman would leap at the opportunity. 'Certainly darling,' she said and placed a wet kiss on his moustache. A few hours after the proposal, long enough for him to hire a clergyman and secure the necessary documents, they were wed in the chapel by the river.

Noel arrived home with his bride the next day, having tied the knot, surprisingly to a relative. There was nothing in the good book against marrying a step sister, provided your father was not her real father.

Bosco loosened his collar as if the living-room were becoming a vacuum and berated his son, 'You lost Alice through meanness and drink. She had plenty of right to leave you. Bugger it this time and I'll throw you out.'

In May the two couples boarded the old man's twelve meter sloop on a delayed honeymoon and sailed to Toronto for a weekend of celebration. The air was fragrant with blossoms and from the lake the Niagara fruit belt was a lovely sheet of pink and white, dividing the deeper blue of the water from the colour of the sky. The latest Harringtons were off to a new and favourable start.

But Noel could never give up his old ways; to counteract his selfish nature Tanya had given him plenty of leeway. She told him how wonderful he was whenever he came home, regardless of the hour. She accompanied him to the Bahamas, delighted with the glitter and gambling. When he lost over twenty-five thousand in one night she gave consolation rather than censure. In bed, pleasing him was most difficult. She had to take it slow and easy lest her experience betray her. She had led him to believe she was uncommonly pure and simple but in his haste for satisfaction he didn't know the difference. From the first night his performance was shameful and far below her standard, ejaculating with a squeak, prematurely at times before she could bury his organ. 'I'm sorry,' he'd slobber. 'You're so damn sexy.'

That Noel was a poor lover was an understatement. His excuses were gambling losses, business failures, tiredness, never he might have had too much to drink. Her lack of sexual gratification became irksome and difficult to hide. She needed a lot more than him; and with this frustration grew a gnawing fear her true feelings would be revealed. Either she found fulfilment elsewhere or sublimated her desires. She asked if she could go back to nursing, take a postgraduate course. The first step was to get back into circulation; she was now in her forties. To her surprise he agreed.

For three years Tanya had been employed by the Shipton General Hospital as the Operating Room Supervisor. During this period she had only one affair. Gerhardt Fast had been the answer to all her prayers, sexy and undemanding. She ran her fingers over her smooth face, rejoicing in the absence of wrinkles, then down, caressing her slender body. Why screw up my life with Paolone? Why not? She smiled, pulling the sheet over her. The chief of surgery was kind of cute and attentive, a mesmerizing conversationalist, anything but a bore which Gary could be at times.

CHAPTER THIRTY-FIVE

The day after the Lindsays left for California, Beecher called Dr. Robb and arranged a transfer of the Ireson child to the Paediatric Hospital in Toronto. The boy's leg was in a precarious state As Jim suggested, Dr. Best had removed the cast and splinted the limb in a normal position but nothing changed. Still, Beecher declined to operate, believing there had been a slight improvement in the colour of the toes. But no movement nor sensation returned which worried the parents.

It was Sunday morning and Dr. Robb wasn't eager to take on the problem. He'd heard of osteotomizing the shaft of the tibia to correct club foot deformity but he could find no reason for doing it himself. Whatever indications Dr. Best conjured the boy was in danger of losing his leg. 'All right', he condescended, 'get him over here as fast as you can and don't forget to include his x-rays and a copy of the hospital record.'

The distress call had been made at 7 am. Immediately afterwards Beecher took the patient's chart to Administration to have it photocopied. The office was closed and Mrs. Starling had to unlock the door. She turned on the lights of the Xerox and un-clipped the chart from its metal backing. Beecher's eyes narrowed, watching the machine spit out the pages, thinking the nurses' notes should disappear or be destroyed.

He spied a number of yellow manila envelopes on a supply shelf; helping himself to one, he asked, "Mind if I take this?"

Starling shrugged. Permission was not hers to grant; as long as he was using it for hospital business who'd object? She turned away from him and began to run more pages through the machine.

The Night Supervisor was content with her job. St. Mary's had become her passion the day it opened. Her husband had died of cancer, leaving her childless and detached. The nuns had been very perceptive; she readily accepted their offer. Working nights was better than lying awake alone at home without Sam. Spending days on her own was a routine to which she had become accustomed when Sam was working. To Bess Starling, unlike many of her married associates, the night shift was her salvation. Off duty she would retire at 8.00 am. and be awake by 2.00 pm. She'd time to putter in the garden or have tea with old friends or go out for a meal if she chose. Nor did she mind the 'one in three' week-end duty, her current responsibility. If anything bothered her it was the crankiness of doctors and she was continually on guard. Dr. Best was pleasant. "Not at all." she said, thinking the hospital could afford it.

"Thanks." Beecher grinned. "If you'll excuse me I have something to do on the fifth floor. Please put the copy in this," he said, snatching a second envelope from the shelf and flying it at her. "Send it to Paeds," he added, "I'll carry it from there."

Mrs. Starling nodded, feeling a bit resentful. Exactly what she intended to do! Did he think such routine was beyond her? She closed her puffy eyes and a huff of indignation swept a page onto the floor. Wearily she bent to pick it up.

The hospital was more hushed on weekends; the Doctor's Lounge was empty. Seated behind the open door Best was virtually hidden but he could hear every sound in the hall. He listened for the clatter of the administration door being shut and locked, followed by footsteps growing louder as Starling came toward him. When she turned into an adjoining corridor to stop before the main elevators he quickly tossed the extra yellow envelope on a rack in the closet and took the stairs, arriving a dozen yards behind her as she entered the second floor Paediatric Ward.

Johnny Ireson was lying on a stretcher in front of the nursing station; his parents standing by, worried by their pending trip to Toronto but stoically resigned to it. Sister Magdalene and Mrs. Penner were trying to cheer them up. The head nurse was saying, "I'm sure, Dr. Robb" -

"Dr. Best asked me to give you this," Starling interrupted, delivering the yellow envelope to Penner. "It's a copy of the boy's record; they'll want it in Toronto."

By then Beecher had caught up to her. "I'll take it", he said, grabbing the envelope from the Supervisor. Ostentatiously he licked the flap and sealed it.

Mrs. Starling appeared affronted, but said nothing and stepped behind the counter to drop the clip board, containing the original record, into its slot in the portable filing cabinet. No one else needed it for the moment, she thought. Dr. Best had written the discharge order earlier. Later in the day the chart would be removed, placed in a folder and sent to Medical Records.

"Let's go", Beecher ordered, pushing the stretcher away from the nurses. The Iresons jerked after him like a tow rope.

Do Unto Others 337

"If you'll wait a minute Dr. Best," Sister Magdalene hollered, "we'll get an orderly to help."

"Not enough time," he called back. "I'll handle it."

Beecher paused with a sudden afterthought, x-rays would have to be gathered, meaning another trip to the fifth floor. "OK", he shouted at Magdalene, and manually held the vibrating elevator doors. Turning to the Iresons, he ordered, "wait for the orderly; he'll be here soon. I almost forgot Johnny's x-rays. It's important you take them to Dr. Robb in Toronto. Meet me outside, by the main entrance in five minutes." He let the elevator doors close, clenching the yellow envelope to his chest.

The filing system in the X-ray Department was familiar to Beecher who had worked it frequently on his own. He readily found Johnny Ireson's index card, jotted a number on Starling's yellow envelope and entered the storage room. Before starting his search he closed the door, ripped open the envelope and removed the copies, including the nurse's notes which he creased and switched to a pocket inside his jacket. While he was restoring the rest of the chart Alex Pecak opened the door and nearly caught him in the act.

"Can I help you?" the technician asked.

Beecher stuttered apprehensively, then quickly recovered his composure. "Yes. I'm trying to find Johnny Ireson's films. I've written his number here."

Alex reached for Beecher's yellow envelop but he wouldn't give it up. "It's 10-03-6740," he said, adding with a pompous smile, "my memory serves me well!"

Alex went to a row of shelves for the pertinent jacket. Checking to make sure the films were within, he inquired. "Where are you taking them?"

"To a patient who's going to Toronto." Dr. Best's brow knotted briefly; the technician would ask him to sign for them, meaning his signature would be recorded. His first thought was to avoid it. If it came out later, the nursing record was missing he might be suspect. When he realized signing for x-rays had nothing to do with the chart he asked. "Where's the book?"

Back in the office, Alec put a boney finger on a line. "Write here," he instructed, "I'll fill in the blanks" and watched unconcerned as the young surgeon wrote an illegible word.

Pecak, tall, slim and balding with slit-like eyes and a long thin face was a Yugoslavian refugee. During the war he had fought as a Chetnik against the Germans and later against the Partisan Communists, his own people. When General Mihajlovic was shot for treason in 1945 Pecak escaped to Canada, unharmed but forced to abandon his homeland. He was cautious and suspicious. What Dr. Best had been doing cloistered in Film Storage was none of his business but he highly suspected the surgeon was up to something.

Before catching up to the Iresons Beecher went back to the lounge on the main floor where he'd cached the spare yellow envelope and exchanged it for the one presently holding copies of everything but the nurses' notes. He placed the fresh envelope on the conference table, sealed it and scribbled Robb's name in large letters on the front. The used one was torn into small pieces and discarded in a waste basket.

Outside Admitting Mr. Ireson was fidgeting beside his car when Dr. Best found him. The orderly had placed little Johnny on the back seat with a pillow under the cast. Mrs. Ireson supported the upper half of him on her lap.
    Beecher gave up the packets of notes and x-rays and saw the worried father into the driver's seat. "Everything's going to be all right," he reassured, "You'll see," and patting Mr. Ireson's shoulder through the open window added. "The movement will return in a few days."
    Neither Beecher nor the Iresons saw Sister Magdalene framed in a main floor window.

In his Toyota on the way to the General, Beecher wrestled with his growing entanglement with Schocker. The affair had started a few years ago and shouldn't have lasted so long. He might as well have been married to her. Thank God she was separated. If she weren't he could have a problem. Just like getting involved with a patient; it took only one irate husband to charge him with 'Alienation of Affection' and his licence could be revoked.
    Schocker was still a safe bet, bright, sexy and available. She fed his ego and he ate like an ant in a sugar bowl. How sweet she was, buying him presents at Christmas and for his birthday, sending him funny suggestive cards. She had a million ways of getting his

attention, most quite novel and open like the colourful brassiere straps she displayed, now concealed under more fitting attire in keeping with her associates in the Operating Room.

There was not a nurse at the hospital who didn't know what was up, the way Beecher was carrying on. He would bring pizzas or doughnuts in the evening on the pretence of treating the staff and hang around until she was off duty at 11 pm. Sometimes after the other girls had left they'd have a lively session on the couch in the Doctors' Lounge or the vacant Recovery Room. If they made it to their cars there'd been the university parking lot or a back road in the country where once their knickers were down she would cross over to the passenger's side and bridge his naked thighs. She was light and solid sitting on his lap, arms outstretched and palms against the top of his shoulders. He'd nothing to do but watch her eyes. Surprisingly they had never been caught.

In return he'd given her an occasional dinner in Buffalo or Toronto, followed by a romp on an inexpensive motel bed. He listened to her broadcast the latest gossip, mainly about the miscues and quirks of other surgeons. She talked quite a bit about her own life as well. A great deal concerned her sexual experiences and her eroticism though not extraordinary, other than in the telling. She had been laid by her boyfriend's older brother at fourteen. The first time was extremely painful but a second penetration a week later had felt like a drive through paradise. Afterward the younger brother didn't have a chance, definitely not when she tried to relay what she'd learned and he was too shy to take advantage.

Janet couldn't get along without sex. It was the answer to everything. At nursing school she'd given freely to a classmate's fiancee though the girl had been her best friend. She'd kept giving, trying to win him till her last effort which left him breathless on the washroom floor during his marriage reception. Apparently her classmate never found out for they were still the best of friends.

Janet's own marriage wasn't worth much. Admittedly she gained a boy and a girl but Peter had been useless as a lover. Unfortunately he'd come to the hospital one night to catch her with Dr. Fast. She hadn't cared much for Fast either; his performance was too one sided and brutal. Peter couldn't deal with the situation and left. A period of reconciliation arranged for the sake of the children also failed and he left again. Separated, his only responsibility was to pay half toward the costs of rearing the kids. Actually he owed her nothing as she'd no regrets for what she'd done. 'Why should I?' she said. 'It's just the way I express myself.'

Now Beecher wondered if he should reciprocate, tantalize her a bit, something less traceable, cash perhaps.

At the General quick rounds disclosed no complications. Dr. Best's patients had been accommodated in the new 'E' wing. Every bed and piece of equipment from the night tables to the stainless steel portable food carts and dressing trays were new. He enjoyed being part of the whole scene and alone in the elevator he mumbled, "Praise the Lord for all things bright and beautiful!" At the parking level he got off. It was time to go home.

Everyone agreed the Bests required larger quarters. Though the house was big the entire downstairs was taken up with office space. At first it was adequate. The den served very nicely as a Consultation Room and required no renovations, and the spacious living room provided a place for patients to wait. Till then they had the use of the kitchen and dining room. A year ago Beecher hired a contractor to transform these remaining areas into examining rooms. Subsequently they were forced to do what they could with the upstairs and that hadn't amounted to much. There had been five bedrooms and a bath. Two continued to be used as bedrooms, one for Lillian and Beecher, the other for the two boys. The third was for recreation and had a small dining table. The next bedroom was converted into a kitchen and a small filing office was allocated to the fifth. After they'd acquired the house and Beecher set up shop, Lil became a receptionist-secretary-bookkeeper, an immense task which grew more tiresome day by day. She made all the appointments, typed letters, booked operations, collected and paid bills. In between she cared for the kids. This arrangement was still in effect and she was fed up, more accurately depressed. Fed up, she thought, implied having the guts to do something about it, which she didn't.

Over lunch Beecher announced it was time they found a separate place to live. He'd heard of a country lot for sale near the escarpment and wanted her approval. Surprise! He'd actually thought of her before making a decision. Lil was elated!

After lunch they went to look at it. Michael climbed all over the old house, actually finding his way to the roof. Beecher felt compelled to haul a ladder from the barn and climbed after him.

Robby had stuck to his mother from room to room. Awed by the size of the place, he found a spot for an electric race car track. "This isn't for sale," Beecher had to tell him. "It's the acre next door."

From the second floor of the derelict dwelling they could look out on adjacent land. The lot had a brook traversing it and was a lovely piece of property. But very expensive, according to the sign.

From home Lillian learned more. She called the sign-posted number and talked to the vendor who was also a daughter of the deceased owner. Before dying the man had severed the piece for a retirement home. "This type of real estate is hard to come by," the lady said. "That's why we're asking so much. If you pay the full amount you'll likely get it." Lil smiled. If Beecher did she could stay home. A replacement could do her job, except for the bookkeeping which she'd no intention of giving up. Oddly, Beecher didn't care. He seemed preoccupied.

CHAPTER THIRTY-SIX

Monday morning Beecher left the house before Lil and the boys were up. His first stop was St. Mary's. He obtained the key to Medical Records from the switch board operator, pretending to do some dictation.

As anticipated the Ireson chart had been sent down sometime the day before. Beecher had no trouble finding it. He took it into a booth, closed the glass door and fitted a fresh belt in the dictaphone. Johnny's History and Physical were lengthy as were the Progress Notes, manufactured with precise detail, far more than Beecher'd done before they were photocopied. Then he ripped out the Nursing Record and purposely failed to sign the Discharge Summary, which could've proved he'd at least touched the boys chart after it had left the ward. If a legal witch-hunt ensued he would be the prime suspect. Now there was no evidence; who could prove anything?

Finished dictating and out of the booth Beecher locked the door to the hall and tore up the Nursing Record. Smugly satisfied he dumped the remnants in a waste basket, unlocked the door and walked across the hall to a phone booth. He dialled Schocker's number.

One of her kids sleepily answered.

"Is your mother there?" he asked.

"Just a sec'," the small voice replied. "She's in the bathroom."

"I thought you'd still be in bed panting for me," he chuckled when Janet finally picked up the phone.

"Sure," she snarled, stretching the word. "What the hell do you want?"

"We have some unfinished business." He chuckled again.

Janet was in no mood for horse-play. The night before she'd argued with her estranged husband who returned their kids from his shared weekend, covered from head to toe in dirt. 'We had a great time mum,' her boy exclaimed. 'Dad took us hiking and we camped out over night.' Typically he hadn't hung around and refused to give her extra money for the kids who were badly in need of clothes.

"For Christ sake Beecher," she snivelled, "Bugger off. You guys are all the same. Take all you can get and give nothing."

"What do you want?" he asked. He'd never caught the effervescent Schocker on a down swing before.

She began to cry. "Money! What else makes the world go round?" She felt like a whore for mentioning the word.

"How much do you need?"

"Don't tell me you'll lend me some?" Her voice sounded hollow.

"Sure. I'll give it to you. No strings attached. How much?"

A silence followed so he asked again. "How much do you need?"

Liar, she thought. Of course there'd be strings attached. Every time he felt like a good piece he'd be around to collect. Accept his offer and she was a kept women. As she mulled it over she realized she couldn't manage otherwise unless she took Peter to court. Beecher probably wouldn't stick around much longer anyway. She was surprised he'd lasted as long as he had, being a womanizer from the word go. Well a bird in hand is better than two larks in the bush.

"How about two hundred for starters."

"When do you need it?"

"Immediately, you dope!" Schocker almost yelled when she realized he wasn't pulling her leg.

"Okay honey." About to add he would bring it around later Beecher felt a tap on his shoulder and immediately clicked off to be confronted by an impatient Dr. Bagley.

"You mind?" said the vascular surgeon, crushing into the booth before Best had a chance to free himself. "I must make an important call."

"Go right ahead." Beecher looked befuddled.

Bagley dialled, nonchalantly asking Best, "What brings you in so early?"

"Nothing."

His call connected before Dave had a chance to consider his colleague's senseless reply.

Every Monday morning Lillian did the laundry. Once the automatic washer was stuffed she would start emptying pockets, setting aside clothes for the Cleaners. In the process of tossing Beecher's jacket around the nurses' notes fell out and she put them on the dresser.

For a life-time it seemed, they'd been living above Beecher's office. He'd bought the old Wilkerson property on James Street across from Dr. Lindsay's. Beecher had suggested his mother move in but Lil would have no part of it. Fortunately the old girl preferred to go on living in the family home in the Spruceridge area. Thank God, Lillian mused. As things turned out there wasn't enough room.

Lil straightened from the pile of sorted clothes and caught a glimpse of herself in the mirror. Grey strands were streaking her hair. Perhaps she should start colouring it before they became too noticeable. Lines had formed beneath her grass-green eyes and she pouted reflexively, "When the good Lord came to giving out looks he skimped on me. Maybe I should see a beautician."

A draft of wind moaned through the window and the papers she'd put on the dresser went sailing. She snatched one in mid air. A line stood out, 'still screaming, medication not holding, unable to contact Dr. Best.' Curiously she read on, '3.00 am. March 18th' - two days ago. Beecher should've been available. He said he was home all week-end. It was all he'd said and transferred the spotlight to her. She had plenty to tell about the nursing convention in Toronto.

Friday afternoon they had dropped the boys at their grandmother's. Jessie agreed to keep them until Lil got back. Afterward Beecher drove her to the Bus Depot.

Where was he? Sitting on the edge of the bed, she read all three pages. Finished she threw herself backwards and stared into space. Where had he been from supper time Friday till noon the next day? The nurses tried three times to get him. His answering service reported he had signed out. Byers had eventually covered for him and Dr. Lindsay felt it necessary to split the Ireson boy's cast. Why had he bothered to make these damning photocopies. Should she ask him? If she did he'd think she'd nosed through his pockets purposely, even read them, which wasn't entirely true. Did Beecher have a girl friend?

Lil felt edgy and depressed. Her husband had an extramarital affair before. He didn't deny it. He even apologized profusely vowing he would never do it again. That was before he became a successful surgeon. A chilly blast of wind entered and she got up to close the window. She'd return the papers to his closeted jacket and pretend the incident had never happened.

But it had. Her feeling of insecurity remained. What if he asked for a divorce? It was the last thing she wanted. She felt like throwing up! For self-preservation and the sake of her children proof would be needed. Before she put the papers back she would sneak out and re-copy them. Sneak out! The repugnance was unnerving but not strong enough to break her resolve.

The E-wing elevator stopped on the fifth floor. Beecher emerged and walked over to the holding area. His patient, Charlie Simpson, was dry from premedication. The O.R. orderly, awaiting hip surgery was surrounded by a group of familiar faces: Jean Milligan, Keefer, another scrub nurse, and Betty Chalmers, all offering encouragement.

Chalmers was the only one wearing a mask. She pulled it below her chin to blow her nose. Her eyes were red and swollen. She gave Dr. Best a sullen look, thinking it would be better if she were home forcing fluids. But with the O.R. Supervisor off to California and one of the other girls on the gynecology ward with a threatened abortion, the O.R. was short staffed and she'd been asked to oversee.

The group parted to let the surgeon through. Beecher promptly held Charlie's hand. "Mornin' Simp, how yah doing?" When his dried out patient had difficulty replying. Beecher added. "Who's going for coffee to-day?" Still Charlie said nothing.

Charlie'd been serving the doctors for over forty years, except during the war. His hazel eyes were unrevealing. He wished they'd get it over. He'd had surgery before. A field unit at Dieppe had cleaned out the shrapnel and saved his leg. The fusion three years later at a Rehab hospital had stiffened his knee permanently but it eased his discomfort. What he dreaded most was the bloody pain after the operation.

Beecher tried again to humour him and when his remark, "You look right at home in that cap," likewise brought no response he spun on his heel and made for the dressing room.

Jean Milligan flashed her parenthetic grin. She'd known Simp for most of the time he'd worked at the General and wondered why the orderly had decided on a newcomer rather than choose a experienced surgeon but hadn't asked. "It's not too late to change your mind, Charlie. You don't have to go through with it."

Simp reflected her smile and closed his eyes. "My mind's made up," he whispered.

Four years ago he'd sought Dr. Lindsay's advice and had been told he'd eventually need a hip replacement. The operation was in its infancy and Jim felt in time the innovators would perfect it. 'However' he added, 'If your hip bothers you I suggest an osteotomy.' Charlie understood Dr. Jim's explanation; his femur would be cut below the hip and would take a few months to heal. To languish in bed was not Charlie's idea of relief. So he continued to make monthly trips to his G.P. for muscle relaxants, anti-inflammatory and pain pills. Once when Dr. Morrisey was on vacation he went to the new clinic near the General and was passed on to Dr. Best. Beecher had looked after him since. When his condition became worse he was advised to have a different operation. It entailed only soft tissues: lengthening all the tendons, muscles and ligaments surrounding the joint. A 'hanging hip' Dr. Best had called it, designed to eliminate stiffness and pain. Charlie was reluctant but after a visit to one of the new orthopaedist's patients he submitted. Now he thought otherwise but due to his pre-medication was unable to speak his mind.

Both Byers and Clayton had been recruited as assistants, one to hold retractors and help stem the bleeding, the other to manipulate the leg. The operation was to be performed with the patient on his side, the affected hip uppermost. Keefer had scrubbed and a new girl called Tallmadge circulated. Duggan was administering fluothane.

Beecher had made several incisions around the joint, cutting deeper into the sinews controlling hip movement: the adductors on the medial side, followed by the hamstrings in back and the glutei along the outside. Bleeding was generous, cutting ceased while Drs. Best and Byers stuffed the wounds with hot wet packs and began a meticulous arterial suppression, ligating and cauterizing vessels.

The delay didn't relieve Clayton's strenuous task of lifting and manipulating the weight of the entire leg. "How much longer you gonna be?" he asked.

Best regarded the bigger man sharply. "Have patience my little jackass said the Camel."

Clayton didn't enjoy the surgeon's sense of humour. If an arm had been free he would have driven a fist into Beecher's mouth. Beads of perspiration dripped from his bushy black brows. "Come on Beech," he exhaled loudly. "Move your ass."

"We're almost finished. Just the tendons in front to go," Byers assured. "Hang in there old buddy."

As each sinew was severed Clayton felt the mobility of the hip increase. Still the limb was heavy and it was hard to keep the knee from buckling. Tallmadge wiped his face.

He rolled his head back and closed his eyes trying to blot out the ache in his arms by visualizing something more pleasant. He was in the tropics on a windsurfer, a cool breeze blew from the sea.

Do Unto Others 347

Clayton could feel the strain on the boom. A wave broke over the bow and splashed his face. It felt quite warm.

"Christ! What have you cut?" The voice was Byer's and it was raised in panic.

Clayton's eye's opened, the spell over. A red stream had hit his mask and his partner was trying to plug the source.

"Must be the femoral artery," Beecher deduced, not particularly agitated.

"What do we do now?" asked Byers.

"Locate it and clamp it off."

"Christ he'll end up with gangrene. Why not suture it back together."

"That's the next step," Beecher said calmly. "We have to find and control the proximal end."

"Did you sever it completely?" Byers hadn't recovered from his initial fright. "Maybe we should call in help," he added. "Frankly, I don't like this Beech."

"Cool it, Ron. I know what I'm doing, and I'm in charge here."

Bob Clayton had reached physical depletion. "I don't give a damn how you resolve this problem, Beecher. I can't hold this leg another second."

"Okay, put it down and we'll have a ten minute break." Beecher had finally found the cut artery and was nipping the flow with a clamp.

"You could use a rubber shod bulldog," Keefer suggested. "It'll cause less damage to the artery." Before Beecher could answer Tallmadge dashed off to a supply cupboard. Unable to find a resemblance she went to the nursing station.

Chalmers listened to Tallmadge's tale and put in a call in for Dr. Bagley who was in the cafeteria having coffee with some of the staff. He quickly answered and the operator put him through.

"I wish you'd come and help unscramble this mess," Chalmers pleaded. "Dr. Best wants to repair the femoral artery. He'll have to use your equipment and I don't think he's ever used anything like it before."

The O.R. was a shambles. Blood was everywhere. The drapes were soaked. Clayton's face was a mask of red. Instruments lay on the floor and Keefer's table was a mess. Beecher was attempting to sew the cut ends of the artery together. Each time he removed his clamps the vessel burst like a worn garden hose. He was on the verge of giving up and tying it off when Dr. Bagley appeared.

Dave rapidly sized up the situation. A bypass was mandatory. Charlie's artery was riddled with plaques and the same diameter as a pipe stem. When and wherever Beecher passed a suture it crumbled like cheese.

The patient was lying on his back, a deep hole in his groin. Duggan was busy pumping a plastic blood packet and the respirator bag. The patient's pressure dropped so low he couldn't get a recording and the pulse felt rapid and thready.

"If you don't mind I'd like to give it a try", Bagley suggested.

Best wasn't happy with the change in command but agreed and moved to the opposite side of the table. Clayton declared he'd had enough and excused himself. Byers decided to remain.

"First," Dave ordered, "I want the patient re-draped. Clean up your table, Keefer and get my set of prosthesis and special instruments. This calls for a five eights Teflon graft."

Fifteen minutes later all was set for a restart and within an hour the prosthesis was anastomosed to the femoral artery above and below where it had been cut.

Bagley closed the large anterior incision and gave the needle holder to Best. "Here", he said. "As you made the others you have the privilege of closing them."

Beecher turned to Byers, "If you'd rather I'll hold the leg."

"Tell me where you want it positioned and I'll look after it; anyway you're quicker at suturing than I." Byers paused, adding, "likely more weary."

Bagley remained to make sure old Charlie was adequately resuscitated. While cutting the excess suture he watched Beecher fumble through his one handed ties.

When the operation had finished the three men accompanied their patient upstairs to a private room in the new Intensive Care Unit.

Bagley ordered a special nurse. His concerns were the accurate monitoring of urinary output, fluid replacement and a check of the circulation in the leg every ten minutes. Of the slightest drop in blood pressure he was to be notified immediately. He asked Beecher for a private talk and together they went into one of the empty rooms.

Dave managed to control his exasperation. "I don't know what you were doing," he said. "I've never heard of a 'Hanging Hip' operation but I'm not an orthopod. I do know there was no reason to cut the femoral artery." He was seething to say Christ man! Don't you know your anatomy? Then thought better of it. It would betray how strongly he felt and do nothing but distance the orthopaedic surgeon. Convincing other surgeons he'd something special to offer, hadn't been easy. Referrals were few and far between. Orthopods were more apt to pick up arterial trauma. Treating Beecher with a little tact and understanding might prove useful. He smiled diplomatically. "I guess we're all subject to accidents. In future, Please feel free to call me."

Beecher didn't bat an eye. "Sure," he replied. If he'd appreciated Dave Bagley's rescuing him from a tight spot there should've been some conveyance, either by expressed word or conduct but there was nothing. In fact he'd expected a dressing down. Bagley's attitude left him with no argument. The surgery he witnessed wasn't difficult. With the right instruments and Teflon grafts he could've done it himself. His mistake made not the slightest dent on his conscience. He walked into the hall whistling.

Byers was leaning against the nurses' counter. Beecher smiled. "Sorry Ron," he said. "It was a misadventure and could've happened to anybody."

Ron Byers was also a diplomat but for other reasons. He and Beecher had been to school together and shared the mistakes of growing up. Having heard Beecher's rationalization, he was reluctant to criticize. "A stroke of bad luck Beech. Forget it."

CHAPTER THIRTY-SEVEN

Beecher rarely got home before noon. Lillian was surprised to see the tail-end of his Toyota pull into the garage. Michael was throwing stones at the neighbour's cat and quit to greet his father. Lil couldn't hear their conversation; but whatever her husband had said caused the lad to frown with disapproval and skip around to the front of the house.

The Simpson case had taken a lot out of Beecher. He was slow to get out of the car, and plodded through the office. Lil heard his heavy feet on the backstairs. She was busy when he entered the kitchen.

"Hi", he called from the doorway, sounding winded.

She didn't turn to greet him; doubts of his fidelity earlier in the day lingered.

He was heaving and asked, "What have I done wrong now?"

"Nothing." Though her voice was under control there was an unusual strider as she tried to maintain herself. She had a strong urge to denounce him with her suspicions but hadn't worked out how to go about it and couldn't face him.

"What's for lunch?", he asked.

With the back of her hand Lillian brushed a wisp of hair and turned away. "Fish and chips".

"Call me when it's ready. I think I'll lie down."

Beecher dragged himself into the small recreation room. She heard the chesterfield creak as he settled on it, and muffled talk with Robby whom she knew was there reading.

Regarding his older son Beecher grimaced in disgust. Robby was approaching ten and had the motor age of a two year old; he was wearing plastic shoe horn splints to keep him from tripping and they were in constant need of repair. Without them he could barely navigate. The heel cord elongations of Dr. Robb had helped for a while but a growth spurt had negated the result. He was sitting with his feet drawn under him, balancing a large illustrated book on his juxtaposed thighs. From the waist upward he'd developed normally and his I.Q. tested average. He'd rather handsome features, a broad face and forehead, presently crowned with a crash helmet, and widely spaced deep blue-green eyes. His engaging mouth had spread into a welcoming smile when his father entered.

"What did you learn at the Centre this morning?" Beecher asked, surmising his son had been for physiotherapy at St. Mary's. Likely the boy had just returned. Three mornings a week Lil took Robby for treatments. Beecher had not liked the idea; a stigma was attached to the word 'cripple'. He preferred his son be in the main stream and attend a public school. The lad did in the afternoons and mornings of the days he didn't go to the clinic. 'Attention won't do him any harm,' Jessie had pointed out and as usual had her way.

Robby did not answer his father's question. "I like it better."

"Like what better?"

"St Mary's. Sister Magdalene is nice."

At the mention of her name Beecher's mind reverted to the day before and Sister Magdalene's involvement in the Ireson case. Vividly he recalled the entire incident and where he'd stashed a copy of the nurses' notes. Reflexively a hand jerked to the inside breast pocket of his jacket. An uneasy feeling overcame him. Where in hell were they? He went into the bedroom. They weren't on the dresser. Maybe Lil had already found them. If she'd read them she would wonder why he hadn't answered his calls. Cold sweat trickled down his neck. He stood for a full minute looking anxiously about the room. Then he remembered changing outfits. The suit he wore yesterday must be in the closet. There it was and the papers were still in it. He quickly removed them and thrust them into a trouser pocket. Later he would destroy them.

Was the stress of lying getting to him? Beecher felt like he'd just given himself away. Now he was obliged to take another chance. If he went to the bank to get the money for Schocker he'd need an excuse. So, he gathered checks from a drawer, more than enough than the two hundred dollars he'd promised and told Lil he was going to the General to check Charlie Simpson. "I might be late getting back," he said. Nothing was disclosed regarding the difficulty he had with the 'hanging hip' procedure and how a major artery had been severed. He'd tell her about it later.

Apprehension lured him to the General, his main concern being the patient's circulation. Charlie was resting face up, totally conscious and having surprisingly little pain. After Beecher had checked both pulses in the foot and found them to his liking he grinned at his patient and said. "We'll have you up walking in no time."

"Why is it you guys always say 'we' when you talk to us patients," Charlie had asked seriously. "Haven't you got the guts to take responsibility? Always hiding behind each other!" His mouth had twisted wryly. "I know you didn't do the job by yourself anyhow, Doc. Dave Bagley was in and told me he did part of it."

"Oh that!" Beecher said and disguised his error with confabulation. "Bagley has some special prostheses - artificial arteries - and I needed one so he brought them along. You see Charlie, your problem wasn't as cut and dried as I told you. It wasn't only your hip giving you pain. The circulation was also a problem. You have a lot of degenerative arterial disease. The muscles around your hip weren't getting enough blood. We call it intermittent claudication. Comes on when you're exercising - like walking. The muscle requires more oxygen and in your case it couldn't get enough due to the narrowing of your blood vessels." Beecher paused theatrically, "and it sure was bad! The lack of blood to your muscles was causing you as much pain as the arthritis in your hip." Then he chuckled. "You might call this a two in one operation Charlie."

When his patient sat up as though someone had just handed him a raffle prize Beecher left, wondering how he was going to explain Bagley's bill.

After leaving the General he dropped in to see Schocker. She was getting ready for work and the baby sitter was due to arrive any minute. Beecher didn't stay long and felt awkward in the presence of her two kids. They sat, side by side, like a pair of vervet monkeys trying to decide if he had peanuts to pass out. Janet was genuinely pleased and tucked the dollars down the front of her uniform. "What will I have to do for the next payment?" she said, and when he did not answer, laughed as she was closing the door. He could still hear her.

The waiting room was full when Beecher showed up and Lil was in better spirits. She had cut off any conversation with the patients beforehand, an idiosyncrasy of hers that bugged him. Often she would get tied up with informalities and delay giving him messages. Talking to people made her feel good. It was the most enjoyable part of her job, of her dull demanding life, but he considered it unnecessary. 'Business first,' he would assert, how can I run through this mess if you spend all your time gabbing?' This afternoon for a pleasant change he was smiling.

"Mr. Simpson's okay! No complications! How many have you lined up?"

"Quite a few Beech. We'll be here till well past six. What took you so long?" The question had become a habit. For a fleeting moment he looked guilty and she was reminded of her earlier suspicions. Why should he have to account for every minute in his life. She forced a smile. "Did you run into any other problems?"

"Nothing serious", he replied and turned to study his list of appointments.

Interrupting him, Lil said, "Please give Dr. Robb a call. He phoned while you were out."

Within a few minutes Beecher had the Toronto orthopod on the line. It was as expected about the Ireson case.

"The lad you sent over definitely had ischemia. We operated on him yesterday and split his tibial fascia."

"How do you know that's what he had?"

"He had no pulse. One of our radiologists stuck radiopaque dye into his femoral artery and took a few pictures. None of the dye reached the muscles in his leg."

"How do you think it happened?"

It was a question Beecher wished he'd never asked for his operation had been the cause. Cutting the mid-shaft of the tibia had produced bleeding into the soft tissues, particularly muscle tissue held against the bones. Unable to expand because of the tightness of the cast they developed an inner pressure, and further anoxia. The result was a vicious cycle, only relieved by a decompressing operation.

Geoffrey Robb sounded annoyed when replying to Beecher's moronic question. "If you don't know, my explaining isn't going to help. I'm terribly sorry Beecher. I think we've saved the boy's leg but it will never be normal. As he grows he'll develop clawing of his toes and a foot deformity. The leg won't grow as fast as the other and it'll end up a few centimetres short. Further surgery will be necessary in the years to come to correct these problems." Dr. Robb paused momentarily before summarizing. "The parents are anxious to get him home. We'll discharge him in a few days. You can take the stitches out in a week or so. By the way," he asked. "Don't your nurses keep any records?"

Beecher paused before replying, "Ah, ah, why do you ask?"

"There weren't any with the material I got."

"That's odd. I know they do. I've read them myself. I'll ask Records to send you another copy."

"Won't be necessary." Robb's brusque remark ended with a click and the line went dead.

CHAPTER THIRTY-EIGHT

Disneyland was great, eh Dad?" Kathy chirped from the back seat. She was right behind him and beside her grandparents, her elbows resting on her father's shoulders.

"Yeah, really great!" Jim tossed her a loving smile.

She put her arms around his neck. "My Daddy!"

"What did you like best?" he asked.

"It's a Small World."

"My favourite too."

"Same here", Julia agreed. She was planted between her parents in the front seat. "How about you Mum?" she asked.

Merri gave Julie a squeeze. "I agree." She said, thinking how beautiful the ride had been. They were in a life-boat, floating through large gilded rooms tinted with soft pastels, full of puppets who sang a sweet uncomplicated heart warming tune. At each bend in the canal there was a new adventure. Every culture of every country in the world was on display with an abundance of cute and comical accents.

"Not me," Heather contended. "I liked the Pirates of the Caribbean." She was boxed by the luggage in the back of a rented suburban. Dr. Burl Cunningham turned to regard his granddaughter. "It was fun, absolutely marvellous." For Jim's benefit he added. "Actually I've enjoyed myself immensely. You're lucky to have such a generous Pa. Not many kids have a chance to come here."

The comment made no impression on Heather. She had no concept how much anything cost and never bothered to ask. When she was in grade two her mother had tried to teach her a lesson. Someone or something had upset her and she refused to go to school. It had worried Jim enough to visit the principal who also had no idea what was wrong. Heather had been as stubborn as a mule. Merri had taken over asking the child what she wanted more than anything in the world. 'Incredible Edibles', Heather had replied, confusing her father and forcing his wife to explain. 'It's a machine to make Jube-jubes in the shape of monsters.' 'How much does it cost?' he asked. 'Not much. About sixteen dollars.' Jim had dug into his wallet while Merri demanded, 'Just give me a one. She's not getting it all at once. A buck a day is all, for every day she goes to school.' The scheme had worked. In just over three weeks Heather had enough to buy the machine. But the incident did nothing to change her attitude toward spending. Suddenly she declared. "Next year we're going to the Calgary Stampede."

"Who's 'we' Heather?"

"All of us."

Dr. MacLaren had given her father six months to live, at best a year. Vacantly she answered, "Wouldn't that be nice."

Looking sympathetically at her daughter, Martha Cunningham had the same thought. She twisted to face her granddaughter. "Let's play a game, Heather. How about licence plate poker. Most of the cars we've passed have California plates, usually with six numbers, so we'll play six car stud. You get the first draw."

Jim was travelling at the speed limit when a big purple Lincoln cut in front. The windows were tinted and he couldn't see in. He did notice the licence and started to howl. So did his father-in-law. The numbers on the plate had been replaced by the letters FATCAT.

"There goes a misdeal!" Jim smiled.

Continuing to chuckle, Burl Cunningham added, "I'd say it beats all."

It would have taken five hours to make the trip from Anaheim to San Luis Obispo had they not dropped into a movie lot. "We used to go to the flicks every Saturday when I was a kid. For only a dime," The Doc. stated. "They kept us coming back by showing serials, stopping them at an exciting moment. There was no sound either. No scary music, just a piano player knocking out a few thunderous chords."

The kids had looked at him as if he were loony. They had never seen silent pictures. Most films were of marathon length, sometimes with an intermission included, and all had an ending. They were more interested in Julie Christie's dressing room and the props used in Dr. Zivago.

It was late afternoon when Jim signed the Inn's registry. Julia accompanied him. Merri and her parents remained in the 'Wagon' while Heather grabbed Kathy and went to explore the main building. The place was steeped in atmosphere; each room was created from large full logs and rounded boulders with crude furniture.

"Oh I see you're from Canada too," the desk clerk noted, upon reading the back of Jim's credit card. She smiled adding warmly,

"I'm giving you the last three rooms I have. They're in Section C. Welcome to our Inn."

The clerk's 'too' interested Julie and she asked. "What part of Canada are you from?"

The bubbly lady erupted with laughter. "Me? Heavens no! I was referring to the couple who signed in before you. They were in the dining room a few minutes ago. You'll probably meet up with them."

"What time do you stop serving meals?" Jim asked.

"Oh Suh, we're open most nights till midnight."

He took the three keys. Though the hour was late it was imperative they stow their bags and get freshened up before supper. He needed a shower. Shaving could wait till morning. "Go find the kids Julie," he ordered, "We're in thirty-one, two and three."

By eight-thirty they were on a semicircular leather upholstered seat in the huge dining room. Including the high beamed ceiling everything was a shade of red: the pink table cloths, the leather upholstery and the carpets with matching drapes. Even the upper halves of the heavy glass tumblers and the chandelier shades were tinted pink. Antiques and American memorabilia had been nailed to the walls and hung from the rafters. Exclusive of the attendants the Lindsays were the only people in the room.

"Must be off season", Jim commented.

"Or the food's no good." The waiter had set a shrimp-cocktail in front of Dr. Cunningham. His sarcastic tone drew Merri's attention. Noting the familiar twinkle in his eye she knew he was teasing. The old man was back to his usual self, and appetite as well.

"It's such a pretty place," she said. "Surely the food must be good."

"Probably the only thing not pink in this room is the middle of my steak."

Merri accepted another sample of her father's wit with a grin and watched Jim cut into a juicy piece of sirloin.

"Ugh!" Julie made a face. "How can you eat it? The blood's still running out." Her Dover sole almondine arrived and she didn't wait for an answer.

Mrs. Cunningham had the fish as well, and a fourth order was divided between Heather and Kathy.

"I didn't want this stuff," Heather complained. "I want a hamburg and chips."

Earlier her mother had explained they were having dinner and a hamburger was not on the menu. As the child had not chosen anything else Merri had decided for her.

"Mum, you never listen to me." Heather was beginning to sulk in one of her obdurate moods.

"I'll give you another choice. Eat your fish or go to bed." Merri could also be resolute.

The child glared then impetuously demanded, "Give me the key, Dad. I'm going to our room."

Jim regarded her thoughtfully. "Try some of my steak," he suggested. "It tastes like hamburg."

Heather pouted and stood up. Her "No" was emphatic.

"Ok", said Jim handing her a key. "But don't lock the door. It's the only one we have."

Before Unit 30 in section C, Dr. Paolone and Tanya Harrington were lounging on the lengthy verandah in padded wicker chairs, sipping aperitifs, engulfed in musical talk and the fragrance of the California countryside when a young girl climbed the steps in front of them and proceeded to the adjacent Unit. They took little notice of her until it became apparent she was having difficulty unlocking the door. Joe went to her aid but his luck wasn't any better. The key just didn't fit. He checked the figures with the number on the door.

"It's the wrong key young lady. You'll have to go back to the desk and get the right one."

"No I don't", Heather maintained, "we have three rooms."

She moved on to the proper door and let herself in while Joe returned to Tanya with a puzzled expression.

"The kid looks familiar. I'm sure I've seen her before."

He had during the previous summer when the Lindsays had invited Angie and him to a barbecue but Joe couldn't remember.

Tanya smiled, wondering if the suave Dr. Paolone had lost his marbles. It was the fourth time in four days, ever since their second night at the Mark Hopkins, he'd recognized someone from home.

There was the woman at the Opera House whom he swore was Dr. Cruikshank's tall wife, slender and frail. An absurd comparison he had to agree later when Tanya said she had positively identified the woman as a friend of her mother's from the good old days. They had sung together at the Bocci Bowl. She had taken Dr. Paolone to the bar for lunch the following day to prove her point. The manager was the only person she knew and he had hailed her with joy. Following a few entertaining arias, including a provocative version of Carmen, supplied by Tanya herself, Joe was pleasantly surprised. Afterward they had driven around town with Tanya pointing out places of interest, the house where she and Halena had lived, Twin Peaks, the Palace of the Legion of Honour and Mary's Help Hospital. She was careful not to mention anything about her previous husbands.

Then there was the man at Fisherman's Wharf who looked like Joe's old room mate from University. He had walked past them as Tanya was reading the dinner menu in the window of Torantino's. Joe was so nervous at the possibility of a reunion with such a close friend, they had gone across the street to Dimaggio's.

The third incident happened while they were strolling down Market Street. 'Christ, he looks like Alligood!' Joe had exclaimed. It was a natural assumption. Alligood, as a member of the American College of Surgeons, could've been at the meeting though Joe hadn't seen him there. He herded Tanya into a shop, costing him a bottle of expensive perfume and several pairs of panty hose. The episode had made Joe fearful they were being followed. Maybe Angie or Noel Harrington had hired a private eye.

'What difference does it make as long as we're not caught 'in flagrante delicto'?' Tanya'd laughed at his concern after he'd made love to her three times, 'I've got a lot more at stake than you have.'

Joe was unsure. Tanya might lose a fortune if she was caught, but Angie would kill him.

The kid had him worried. Intuitively he went inside on the pretense of getting more ice. Tanya joined him a few minutes later. "You were right this time. It's one of Lindsay's kids. I just caught a glimpse of him and his wife. I'm sure they didn't see me."

Joe began pacing about. "What'll we do?"

"Nothing," she sighed. "Stay right here until they've gone."

Jim stopped at the Wagon to collect a road map and make sure the vehicle was secured for the night. He had a good look at the Jaguar beside it and noticed a rental sticker. Who in hell would want to drive that gas guzzler? he thought. The Wagon he'd leased was a gas guzzler too but at least it held more people.

When he joined the others inside, Heather was talking excitedly.

Julie interrupted her story. "Dad, you'll never guess who the other Canadians are."

Jim shrugged.

"The Paolone's and they're staying next door."

"It figures", her father grunted, "Nobody else I know would rent a car like the one he has."

"Not the Paolones, Julie," Heather corrected. "Just Dr. Paolone. There's a lady with him and it's not his wife. I know Mrs. Paolone. Once she came to the school to judge our public speaking contest. Member mum? You were there."

"You've been watching too many soaps." Merri glowered. "Now get to bed!"

CHAPTER THIRTY-NINE

The glasses kept sliding down Burl Cunningham's nose and he'd stop to push them up. Jim was admiring his father-in-law from across the garden, thinking how closely Merri favoured him. Even their gestures were alike. Merri would replace her tortoise shell rims in exactly the same way, running the bridge of her glasses with the tip of her left middle finger up the crest of her nose until it fell in line with her eyes. Another inheritable trait, Jim hypothesized.

Cunningham pulled a handkerchief from a shirt pocket and began to mop his brow. He looked well, not so pasty and he'd put on a bit of weight. Whether the increase was healthy fat or edema was hard to tell. Spiritually, the California trip had done him some good.

Jim turned off the roto-tiller and called, "Brahms, have you had enough?" A peculiar nickname, short for 'Brahman'- after the herd. Burl had earned it during his football days after a display of strength caused one of his team-mates to remark,'Burl Cunningham is so strong he could pin a bull with his bare hands.'

"Yeah," the Aggie Vet replied. "Let's go in. I'll buy you a drink." Delighted with the irony of his suggestion, he chuckled, "Non-alcoholic! If I can't have a beer neither can you."

"But my liver's in better shape Pop!"

"So's your whole body Jimmie. Not that I'd like to have all your muscle. I haven't the energy to run it."

The Doc lifted his straw hat and went on mopping. The top of his head was covered with large freckles and sweat glistened from his brow, permanently wrinkled as if it were straining to keep the flesh from falling down his face. After dabbing a while he glanced up at the sun almost to its zenith and exclaimed, "My what a glorious day. If this weather holds through the week-end we'll have the whole works planted."

"I hope you're right Pop. I'd like to finish it, weather or not. It should have been seeded by the 24th. Anyway it doesn't matter. This time last year we had snow."

They turned toward the porch where Merri was kneeling, sorting boxes of spring flowers grown from seed in her room over the garage. Behind her daughter, Martha was seated in a cushioned chair and felt like giving up her knitting at the sight of her husband's wasted frame. The bulky sweater she had started weeks ago seemed to outgrow him day by day. Why had she knit such a heavy one? He would have no earthly use for it in the middle of the summer. Was it a token of hope he would outlast the year and need it in the colder months? Now she sadly wondered if he would be alive to receive it. As the men entered she frowned singling him out.

"My goodness, what have you been doing? You've boiled over!"

Brahms removed his battered hat. "I was composing!"

Martha had ceased to laugh at her husband's favourite pun years ago but couldn't help smirking.

"It's true," Jim intervened. "He was composting a garden."

"You're not so funny," his mother-in-law commented and sobered, "taking a sick man out in the sun and working him into a state of idiocy. You should be ashamed of yourself."

Jim regarded Martha fondly. At seventy she was still attractive. He liked the way she tilted her chin when she pretended to be angry and her face was as straight as a preacher's.

"How about a drink?" Merri asked. "What'll it be Pop?"

"Sasparilla," the old man drawled and selected a lawn-chair next to his wife.

"Gary Cooper eh?" she asked whimsically, having heard her father mimic the actor many times.

"Nope. It's Super-duper Cooper the Pooper-scooper!" Jim exclaimed. "Which reminds me Whitty is due back any day to clean out the septic tank. He was here with a divining rod, trying to locate it while we were away. Just before we left for California I drove a stake in the ground where we found the tank last time. Anyhow he chose to ignore my marker in favour of his magic wand. When we got back I checked it out." Jim stopped as if he'd forgotten something important and it was too late to make amends. "My God! That was two months ago. Since then he's dug at least four holes, looking for it. Not one was within ten feet of my stake. I found it myself the other day and cleared the hatch. All he has to do is remove the lid and suck out the tank. My-o-my the joys of country living!"

"Sorry Dad! We haven't any sasparilla." Merri interrupted.

Suggesting, "make it two cokes," Jim stretched his legs, brushing Julia who was sitting on the floor opposite him. Instantly she popped her big brown eyes over a book and offered, "Take my chair Dad? I'll move into the family room."

"I wouldn't think of it, sweetie."

"Then have this pillow," she suggested pulling it from behind her.

"Thank you," he smiled, sliding further down the wall until his entire length stretched out and her offering could be bunched under his head.

When comfortable Jim regarded his father-in-law. "Tell me Pop," he asked, "have you ever done any back operations on animals?"

"A few times, mainly Dachshunds," after a slight pause he elucidated. "They get trouble with their discs and as they get older arthritis sets in. The vertebral canal narrows and the pressure on their nerve roots paralyzes them."

"That must be the trouble with Emily Master's dog," Julia suggested.

"No," her father corrected, "Kelly's an Irish Setter. They're prone to hip dysplasia."

Dr. Cunningham stroked his dewlap. "Does he have a wetting problem?"

"I don't know Grandpa," Julia giggled. "What dog doesn't wet the floor when he's not let out in time?"

"You're right," Brahms smiled, "but when a house-trained dog reverts to wetting it could mean there's a back problem; particularly if he drags his hind legs too."

Jim was about to explain why he had introduced the subject when Merri arrived with the drinks and set them on coasters, announcing she was going back to the kitchen to prepare lunch. In the doorway she stopped pensively and turned around, "Jim do you remember the German S.S. Trooper you treated a few years ago?"

"I'll never forget him."

"Was his name Eckheusen?"

"Yes, Hans Eckheusen. He's the one who committed suicide going over the Falls."

"He left a wife didn't he?"

"Yes. Why do you ask?"

"I just heard on the radio she was in a car-train accident. It happened at a level crossing near Dunnville. Her boyfriend died on the spot. Apparently she escaped without a scratch."

Brahms couldn't contain his curiosity. "What was that all about?"

"Once upon a time I had a patient," said Jim whimsically, as if it were a Fairy Tale, "a German ex S.S. officer. He tried to kill himself by slashing his wrists. I patched him up. He was on the Stevenson ward for several months until the local psychiatrists transferred him to Woodholme Sanatorium. His wound had healed but he still had no movement nor sensation in his hands and needed physio. Six months after being admitted to Woodholme they released him for a week-end in the custody of his wife. On the way home he asked to drive by the Falls. He got out of the car, claimed he wanted a closer look and jumped the rail a few yards from the brink. Of course he was swept over. A tourist taking a movie of the Falls recorded the whole affair. The film was peddled to a local TV station and shown on the eleven o'clock news. Merri saw it. I never did find out how much function he regained in his hands but he must have had some to haul himself over the rail."

Dr. Cunningham smiled. "Did you ever get paid?"

"That's a cold-blooded question," Jim remarked - the lack of remuneration for a job well done had crossed his mind. "Not so far. I did send a bill but I consider the story itself worth the fee."

"Well," Merri appended optimistically, "His wife escaped injury in this latest episode. She must still be living in the area. You may get something yet. Send another bill." Anxious to get lunch underway, she didn't wait for Jim's reply.

As she headed for the kitchen, he called after her. "No way, she's got enough problems and too much time has elapsed."

"Her boyfriend might have been loaded," the Doc suggested. "Maybe she's been left a pile of dough."

"Not likely." Jim spoke with resignation. The matter no longer involved him. "Say Brahms," he said, determined to put the conversation back on track, "let me feel you out on something confidential."

"As long as you don't pick my brain. There's little left."

"Promise it won't hurt," Jim smiled, "and I doubt if it'll bore you. It concerns a young orthopaedic surgeon who has to be toned down. There's a Peer Review Meeting set for next Thursday evening. We aim to confront him with a number of his cases. Cruikshank has collected most of them. I have a couple from '64 plus a more recent one. They certainly deserve airing. He's done some strange things; it's amazing he's got away with them."

"Sounds nasty already, not the sort of business I'd like to be in. Lucky for me animals can't talk or I'd have been in trouble myself. He waited patiently while Jim loaded his pipe. "How many bowls will it take?" he asked.

"That depends," Jim grinned. "How much you want to hear, and how many questions you ask." After tamping the tobacco with his thumb until the force required to draw air was to his liking he regarded the older man. "From your droll statement I assume you've never been sued by an owner."

"Once. Didn't I tell you?"

"Nope."

"You wanna hear about it?"

"Is this going to cost me one pipe or two?" Jim rolled his tongue in his cheek."

"If it takes more than five minutes I'll buy you a tin of tobacco."

"Shoot."

"Nothing to it really. One evening I put down a Pekinese at the owner's request, or I thought he was the owner. He didn't tell me his wife had just divorced him. She was furious. Poor little Perky was part of her settlement. She claimed I had no right to do such a horrible thing as she would never have given her permission. We found out the date of the decree. It happened to have been the same day."

"Who's we?"

"My legal consultants. Apparently she had taken the guy for all he was worth and went out to celebrate. Stanley, her ex-husband, snuck back to the house and grabbed the pooch. The dog looked pretty sick when Stanley brought him in. Possibly it had been poisoned a touch, not enough to kill it. There wasn't anything I could do to help and went along with him. I put the little fellow to sleep and at the guy's insistence gave him a bill. He presented it to his ex-wife the next day. I never heard a word from her but I did from her lawyer."

"So how did it end?"

"It cost me another pooch. I offered to give her the next healthy stray I could find, vaccinated, castrated or spayed, whatever her heart desired, but it wasn't enough. She claimed her dog was a grand champion, siring other champions, a champ of all champs, and her lawyer produced a picture of Perky wearing a heap of ribbons and medals."

"Did you have to appear?"

"No, it was settled out of court. My insurance covered most of the costs."

Before her husband's third start on the Best topic, Merri reappeared and advised, "Better let it wait till later. Lunch is on. Also Whitty's holding the line. He wants to speak to you."

"For God's sake. Tell him the tank has been bared and all he has to do is clean it out."

"I did," Merri insisted.

"So when's he coming?"

"He didn't say. Just asked if you were sure you'd found the septic tank."

"My God," Jim sighed. "Go back and tell him, it certainly wasn't King Tut's Tomb. If he doesn't want the job we'll get somebody else to do it."

"Suppose he calls your bluff. Who will you get? There aren't many people in his line of business."

"Sorry sweetheart," Jim nodded. "You're right. But I can't speak to him; I've lost patience. Tell him I've had an emergency call. If he comes at two, I'll be in the garden and will talk to him then."

"Fine! Just don't invite him into the house."

CHAPTER FORTY

Later was a long time coming. Jim didn't get another chance to introduce the Best affair until after supper.

Before dark Martha, Merri and the girls went to watch a Victoria Day fireworks display, leaving the two men free to talk uninterrupted for as long as they wanted - if Jim could keep the old boy on course.

They were seated in easy chairs opposite each other in the den. Jim reloaded his glass with more ice and a tot of scotch. He opened the discussion while the Doc was still on his first Molson's.

"It'll be interesting to see how he reacts to our criticism."

Brahms had been berating the government for spending money on centennial celebrations and believed his son-in-law was referring to the Prime Minister. Orienting himself he asked, "Who? You mean that fellow Best?"

"Right."

"What's he done that's so wrong?"

"You name it."

"Okay. You mentioned he fouled up a couple of backs. Go on!"

"In fact there were three, the only three he's done which indicates his lack of experience. Before the first case he let it be known it was his first back operation. Both Ramamurti and Fortier offered to assist but he ignored them and chose a general practitioner. The surgery lasted over three hours."

"What's the average time?" asked the Doc.

"Depends on the problem Pop. A laminectomy and discectomy takes me less than an hour. I've removed a disc in under twenty minutes but it was a big extrusion - an easy one - wedged between the nerve root and the dura like a gall in the crotch of a tree."

"Pardon my inexperience, but what is an extrusion?"

"My apology. I thought you might have run into a similar situation in animals."

"I've seen prolapsed or herniated discs. The term extrusion never."

"What exactly do you know about discs?"

"They're the flat round pads between the vertebral bodies; the vertebral bodies are a long line of spools making up the front of the back bone."

"That's right .There are thirty-three of them in the human, called vertebra and make up the neck, chest, lower back, pelvis and tail bone. These divisions account for the four curves seen on a lateral x-ray. The ones in the neck and lower back curve foreword and are called lordotic while the other two are kyphotic or bend backward."

"Animals are different," Doc Cunningham interjected. "From the base of the neck downward their backs are more of a C curve."

"Like new born kids," Jim smiled, adding. "At the back of each spool and attached to it is an arch of bone. These arches are fused in the sacrococcygeal region but free to join each other throughout the rest of the spine. The arch of each vertebra is jointed to the one above and below forming a long canal which protects nervous tissue.

"The Vertebral Canal - Now that I've heard of!" Doc Cunningham exclaimed. "I once thought I'd write a book about a trip through the Alimentary Canal but maybe the Vertebral would be more interesting - all those messages going back and forth, up and down between the body and brain. It would be more exciting than working as a switch board operator at the Playboy Club."

"Really Pop!"

"Sorry about that. You asked me what I know about discs. Well, here's some more. Within the arch, the nerve fibres are called roots, because they anchor the spinal cord. Their free ends pass out of the canal through a hole formed by two adjacent vertebrae. The cord ends in the upper lumbar region and the roots form a tail below, called the cauda equina."

"Correct."

"Discs are spongy and act like shock absorbers. But they're really joints and hold the vertebral bodies together. This is the case in four legged animals. They don't usually put weight on them by sitting or standing. The centre of a disc is soft and pulpy. Sometimes their fibrous outer rim develops a weakness and the soft centre pushes the rim out to form a bulge - called a herniation or prolapse." Brahms beamed like the brightest student in the class. "How's that?" he asked. "Do I pass?"

"Right," said Jim, smiling at the merriment in Brahm's jaundiced eyes. "But an extrusion goes one step further. The fibrous outer rim ruptures and the pulpy centre is squeezed through the rent to lie in the vertebral canal. I like to compare it to the inside of a grape being popped through its skin. It starts with pain in the back often radiating down the back of the leg due to it's irritation of nerve roots. The roots get caught between the bulge and the side wall of the arch, or pedicle as we call it. The back wall is the lamina; that's the part we have to partially remove to get into the vertebral canal. Between the pedicle and lamina is the apophyseal joint - rarely the cause of pain. If the rupture or herniation occurs in the mid line of the body - I mean smack in the middle of the back - the pain can be down both legs. This doesn't happen often for the back of the rim is reinforced by a tough ligament which runs the full length of the spine. Fortunately we have this anterior longitudinal ligament or there would be more people paralyzed by disc extrusions. More commonly the bulge happens to be either right or left of this ligament to compress one or two nerve roots."

"Dr. Lindsay. I think you're showing off. Just because your patients are higher on the evolutionary scale you think you're smarter. So what's Dr. Best done that's so bad?" he asked.

"I don't profess to be smarter than you. If anything I'm an undeserving protege."

"Tish! Tish! Jimmie boy, such humility."

Jim blushed, realizing the old man had been pulling his leg. He coughed nervously. "I believe he's incompetent."

"Prove it to me in plain language like you're going to have to prove it to God knows how many others before anyone is going to do anything about it."

"Firstly, he operated on a thirty eight year old labourer. Possibly the man's name was Wolenski but as I can't remember let's call him John Doe 1. Compensation patients are notorious cry babies and should be handled with kid gloves."

"Another funny?" Brahms interjected and chuckled. "Cry babies and kid gloves!"

"I wasn't thinking in the same vein. What I meant -"

"I know what you mean son. I like puns." The Doc's smile vanished. "Please go on."

"Three weeks after the injury Best operated on the man's back. Apparently the patient was having only back pain. There was no leg pain whatsoever, no compression or irritation of his nerve roots."

Brahms shook his head, "You called it an injury. I'd say a so-called injury."

"What do you mean, so-called?" Jim asked.

"Didn't you say all he did was bend over at work and pick up some weight?"

"I didn't say that. You assumed it." Jim had difficulty suppressing a smile. "But you're probably right. Having your back give out at work is an accident, at home it's simply bad luck. The Workmens' Compensation Board has become sticky about the definition of a back injury lately and a worker has to prove he was subjected to some unnatural physical stress at the time - which stimulates all kinds of innovative stories."

"Unnatural, Bah! A person can throw his back out with a good sneeze."

"Doesn't matter. The most important point in the case of John Doe 1, is Dr. Best showed extremely poor judgment in his management of the man's problem. He should've given the guy more conservative treatment before jumping into an operation. Also, when Best decided to operate, he should've requested help from a more experienced surgeon. As I've already said both Ramamurti and Fortier offered to assist him. He admitted it was his first back operation. Instead he asked Olga Laskowitz, fresh from an internship. If that isn't bad judgment I'll eat my shirt."

"How many lady docs have you got?"

"Four, including Sylvia Packard who's semi-retired. They're taking more women into medicine now than they did in my day. Makes no difference."

Jim shrugged and continued, "Getting back to John Doe 1, there was no need for Best to do extra investigative procedures - a myelogram and discograms. The patient didn't complain of leg pain nor did routine x-rays show any signs of disc degeneration. In other words there were no indications for doing the operation. But Best proceeded. He tore a hole in the dura and permanently damaged nerve roots."

"Of course the man was much worse," Jim continued "and suffers intractable pain in his leg. The case was referred to Ramamurti for a second opinion. Poor Mehendra! Best wanted to re-explore the guy and Mehendra had no choice but go along. Nothing much to see other than a lot of scar tissue. Ramamurti ended up fusing him. Why, is unclear, although in both Best's and Ramamurti's preoperative notes mention is made of instability of the lumbosacral spine as a complication of the first operation. One year later John Doe 1 is worse than ever. The WCB are taking full responsibility for him and will go on paying as long as his disability lasts, which could be indefinitely."

"Frantic to get him off the disabled list and settle his case - anything to get him out of their hair - the Board sent him to a neurosurgeon who diagnosed 'intraneural fibrosis', a fancy way of saying permanent scarring of the nerves. So a third operation was performed, cutting the nerves higher in the spinal cord to stop painful impulses from reaching his brain. During this third operation motor nerve fibres, in addition to the sensory ones conveying pain were cut, resulting in partial paralysis of the uninvolved leg."

"How can you blame Best in this case? The man was bent on self destruction. If Beecher hadn't buggered him someone else would've. He'd have shopped around until he got his operation come hell or high water. John Doe 1 had plain given up. He wanted an excuse for an immutable remittance."

Jim was forced to agree with the old man's wisdom but in his opinion the patient couldn't be blamed entirely; he didn't have training that Dr. Best had and Best triggered the man's circumstances. "Okay," he said. "On to John Doe 2."

"Mr. Fred Overton was born in 1940. That would make him about twenty-seven or eight. He was also complaining of low back pain. Once again there was no pain in his legs. He was employed as a sanitary engineer. Some time before he went to Dr. Best a diagnosis of Charcot-Marie-Tooth's Disease was made at the neurological clinic in Hamilton. A medical doctor there had prescribed a back brace. Dr. Best admitted him to hospital and did a myelogram which according to Ben Nickerson showed nothing abnormal."

"What's Charcot-Marie-Tooth Disease? You're losing me. I've never heard of it."

"It's a disease that runs in families and affects muscles of the leg and foot, sometimes the hand. It's a muscular dystrophy and can be confused with Poliomyelitis in that muscles are affected but differs as the paralysis is symmetrical and not caused by a virus like Polio. Also patient's suffering from it don't have peripheral pain."

"By 'peripheral' you mean the part of the nerve after it leaves the Vertebral Canal?"

"Yes, and almost all peripheral nerves are mixed." Jim added. "They convey sensations like pain, touch, temperature and position of the body to the brain and relay muscle impulses, the motor impulses for contraction. Mr. Overton had paralysis of the muscles in his legs which prevented him from lifting his foot and caused him to walk in a peculiar way."

"You mean, he had a foot-drop."

"Right. A herniated disc in the lower back can cause the same thing. Dr. Best mistakenly thought the man's paralysis was due to a disc problem and decided to operate. He removed a disc and botched the surgery, not only in making the wrong diagnosis but again tearing the dura. He recognized his error this time and patched the hole with a piece of fat. Of course this heroic gesture came after he had already removed a normal disc."

"What harm can come from a hole in the dura?"

"Usually none. But it can result in a chronic leakage of cerebral spinal fluid and headache similar to that following a spinal anaesthesia. I suppose one could end up with a more serious problem, like meningitis."

"So his blunder might cause no harm but it's not doing the patient any good," Brahms frowned and added, "It sounds like Best is a bit heavy handed."

"Apparently the patient is still having low back pain, has to wear his brace and blames the discotomy for making him worse."

"Jim I'm going to have another beer. I know I'm not allowed another but listening to you talk makes me thirsty."

"Have you had enough?"

"No, tell me about the third case."

"As soon as I get back."

Jim mixed another scotch and handed a beer to his father-in-law. Toggling the cubes in his short glass he resumed his discourse. "The third case, Jane Doe 1, was in her mid forties when he attacked her."

"My, sounds like an ungentlemanly thing to do."

"The more I think about what he's done the angrier I get. In this woman's case he could've been a hero. She was referred by her family doctor and did have a ruptured disc. A portion of it had broken away - sequestrated and extruded - and was lying up against the nerve root between the 4th and 5th lumbar vertebrae - the second joint from the bottom of the movable spine. She had all the classic symptoms and signs with pain down the back of her leg, plus a foot drop similar to the Charcot-Marie-Tooth case. But Best missed it. He went in at the right level, opened the posterior rim and scraped out the nucleus but failed to locate the extruded piece that was causing the trouble. It

Do Unto Others 373

had been lying outside the rim, more laterally than he could see. I figure he couldn't visualize it because he hadn't removed enough of the lamina. Fortier came to her aid a week later. After reassessing the situation, Marcel decided Best had missed something and re-operated. It took a bit of courage. He might've been wrong. The extruded piece of disc was discovered and removed. The patient was most grateful. Back from vacation Best made a housecall but she'd have nothing to do with him."

"How do you know?"

"She told Marcel."

"Can't say I blame her." The Doc took a sip of his beer, then asked. "So what's this leading up to?"

"A Hearing but a Peer Review Meeting first. Actually it has more positive features than negative. I don't think anyone is trying to get rid of Best. From everything I've read and from my own dealings with him there is no doubt in my mind he's extremely aggressive and needs to be curbed. He's a sanguineous type. People with this temperament are usually quite remorseful once they are faced with their shortcomings."

"What makes you think he'll admit them?"

"That's the unknown factor and the negative aspect of the meeting. He may clam up, thinking we're out to get him, negating any constructive criticism."

"Well aren't you?"

Jim paused, wondering if his father-in-law might be right. "I can't honestly say. I don't like him though a lot of people do. He's outgoing and talkative at times, warm and personable. But I think he's egocentric and a compulsive liar."

"Them's fightin' words son." Doc Cunningham laughed. "Putting your feelings aside, he shouldn't be allowed to carry on the way he is."

"Actually Pop I'll be glad to get the damn hearing over. I'd just like to mind my own business."

"Doing anything new and exciting these days?"

"As a matter of fact yes. We've purchased an Image Intensifier at St. Mary's. It is an X-ray machine with a TV screen. Do you remember the fluoroscope?"

Brahms chuckled. "I literally burnt my fingers on that gadget."

"It has the same uses, but there's less radiation. Hip pinnings are a snap now. And I plan on doing a different hip replacement. Acrylic cement holds the components in place. The immediate results have been gratifying. How it will stand up five years down the line is the sixty-four thousand dollar question. Though I'm not overly keen I've booked one for next week."

"What don't you like about it?"

" Mind you, so far the results are good but it's anchored with cement which might lead to adverse tissue reactions and sloppy carpentry."

"When we were talking last you were doing the 'Ring.'"

"Yeah and before that the 'MacKee Ferrar'. This cement type allows for discrepancies in the fitting."

The old man stood up and stretched. "Well Jimmy boy I think I'll hit the hay. It's past ten."

"I didn't realize."

Brahms shuffled toward the door leading to the front hall and the stairs. He and Martha stayed in Jason's room when they came to visit. The only thing different was the addition of a second single bed. His grandson's pennants, posters and trophies were still around, cruel reminders of a lost hope. Brahms lived from day to day and dwelt on how life was, not on how it might've been. "I reckon the others will be home soon," he said. "See you in the morning."

"Goodnight Pop," Jim called after him, satisfied it had been a productive day. Thanks to the efforts of Jenny and Brad the garden had been planted. The pair were home from University for a couple of weeks but Jim hadn't seen much of them. Jenny hoped to pick up a job life-guarding at the 'YWCA'; while waiting she was giving swimming lessons in the back-yard pool and Brad was working at the Agriculture Experimental Station.

The septic tank had been cleaned. Whitty had blown in shortly after three and Jim led him to 'the discovery'. The man was unconvinced until the lid was removed and he plunged his head inside. Jim smiled, recalling the episode. He didn't need an Ear, Nose and Throat Specialist to tell him 'Scoop' Whitty had anosmia.

He'd also had a chance to vent his feelings on a confidential matter, troubling him. Brahms was more than Merri's Dad. He was a trusted friend to whom Jim could speak openly and receive sensible advice, a terrific sounding board. He loved the old man and glowed as he thought how attuned the Doc had been. How succinctly the old guy had summarized the situation. 'Disregarding your feelings, Beecher shouldn't be allowed to carry on, certainly not in the way he does.'

CHAPTER FORTY-ONE

The week of the Peer Review Meeting started warm and wet, an ideal clime for germination and growth, benefitting those lucky enough to have finished their spring planting. Blossoms had dropped, revealing a promising glut of young fruit and the growers were happy. But when the temperature climbed into the nineties and high humidity followed even the most enthusiastic began to wilt. By Thursday the weather reached an unbearable peak and as fate would have it the meeting was called off indefinitely.

On the morn of that fateful day the sun hung behind an oppressive shroud. The atmosphere was so dense it was doubtful if light would ever break through. Nothing changed till noon and ever so gradually when the air began to move. It came from the southwest, sluggish at first and fitful, lulling now and again to catch its hot breath as if the heaviness were too much for it. Then gaining confidence it began to push harder, softly whimpering and moaning, its spasms lasting longer and coming closer together, bearing down more powerfully, screaming like a she-devil in the throes of birth. It clutched at the fresh green orchard leaves, shredding them like a herd of hungry elephants, trumpeting and shrieking, lasting halfway through the afternoon. Then all at once, fully dilated it blew itself out. From the stillness came the cry of the newborn, roaring overhead.

Desperately in search of sustenance the beast came to earth near the west end of town and for a quarter of a mile it twisted, on and off the elusive railway line, sucking the breath out of everything in its path. Small frame houses, paralleling the tracks, imploded with such force there was nothing left but fragments of board, plaster lathe and tangled plumbing. Further along the street, the walls of another constructed of hollow clay tiles virtually exploded. The lumber yard on the opposite corner looked as if a giant had lost a game of pick-up-sticks and for spite had tossed the warehouse roof frisbee-like into an adjacent lot.

The semblance of a Vauxhall landed, wheels up on a neighbour's concrete porch, squashing the neighbour's cat. Whitty's pick-up truck, recognized by 'Super Duper Pooper Scooper' painted on its sides, was crushed beneath a toppled billboard and four other private vehicles would never be used again.

Shattered glass lay everywhere. Telephone and hydro poles had fallen like tooth picks, their tangled wires flicking tongues of lethal sparks. The sparrows perched on them moments before mysteriously disappeared.

Tending his own business, the west end drunk had been walking down the street, counting the cracks in the pavement when he was blown off his feet. Herbie came to rest twenty feet off the ground lodged in a maple tree. He merely crossed his legs and relaxed in a dead weight.

The monster escaped at the bridge over the old canal as if the stench of the mill's sluice had been more than it could bear and spiralled into the covering cloud. There was disruption with the loss of electrical power. Offices were in darkness; gasoline pumps were useless; both hospitals had been forced to switch to auxiliary generators; and phones were out of order. Human damage varied. Most had abrasions, cuts and bruises but there were a dozen more seriously injured, and two had died.

A Station Street survivor recovered the bodies of an elderly couple from the rubble of their stucco cottage within an hour after the tornado had passed. Other people were still missing and it was feared three children, heading home from school, had been dashed from the high level bridge. Everyone else was accountable. "If it had struck during rush hour traffic many more might have perished. We're really fortunate," Dr. Alligood told a reporter from the Shield after appraising the casualties brought into St. Mary's.

What the Chief of Surgery omitted was if Reif Larson and Dave Bagley had not been around to resuscitate the death toll could have been doubled.

The O.R. Supervisor broke the alarming news as Reif was about to start his seventh anesthetic of the day. Consequently they were in the E.R. to do initial assessments when the ambulances arrived and for a life-saving few minutes were the only doctors available. While Reif intubated two unconscious patients with stove-in chests, Dave cut down on their shocked vessels and pumped in blood.

The rest of the staff had been in their private offices. Those who could be contacted reacted promptly and an hour later the E.R. looked as if the twister had returned. Both minor theatres and the cast room were going full tilt. The five gurneys in the small E.R. Recovery were occupied and extra stretchers, bearing less acute cases lined the hall.

At the General the picture was less congested, although an equal number of victims had been taken in. The spacious new Emergency was more accommodating, actually twice the size of St. Mary's. It contained a holding area and an additional chamber, carpeted and comfortably appointed, almost chapel-like in atmosphere, where consultations could be handled privately with relatives. Most important, giving the new E.R. a decided edge, was the proximity of the X-ray Department.

The ominous wail of sirens subtly tapered off and by 6 pm. when the last of the stretcher cases had been admitted the city was strangely quiet. At the General's E.R. nursing counter a small group, including two ambulance attendants, Jean Milligan, a younger nurse, the ward clerk Mrs. Wheeler, and Dr. Cruikshank were discussing the disaster.

"The neighbourhood looks like it's been hit by a cyclone," an ambulance driver commented quite solemnly. He had used the word 'cyclone' figuratively, not having been informed of the fact, and went on to defend himself. "How should I know? I've never seen one," rather put out as the younger nurse had laughed, pointing out that was exactly what had happened. 'Ninny' was on the tip of her tongue but the ward clerk beat her to it.

Mrs. Wheeler had always been an obnoxious nag in Dr. Cruikshank's estimation. She was fat and lazy, reluctant to get off her butt and look for a nurse when he needed one. On rare occasions when she did her nylon clad thighs rubbed together like grating cheese. He went to the ambulance driver's rescue. "We don't have them here either as a rule, certainly not the same as where I grew up. Maybe because it's flatter there. If we do get one it doesn't travel as far because of the buffeting effect of the escarpment."

When the call had gone out Crooky was looking at x-ray films in the Radiology Department. By the time he had reached the trouble zone there were a number of other doctors and nurses in attendance, all younger than himself and full of zip. A Triage had been established, grouping the acute, semi acute and ambulatory cases. Best and Fortier were already looking after the musculoskeletal injuries. There was no need for him to hang around.

Crooky was leaning on the counter, his back opposed to the noisy waiting room and had to cup his ears to catch a question from the nurse who had ridiculed the ambulance driver.

"What are you doing here Dr. Cruikshank? I thought your loyalties were with St. Mary's."

"They are young lady." Probably he'd heard her name once but couldn't remember.

She glanced at him unable to fathom how anyone would want to work in a Catholic hospital. She had enough of nuns and their strictness during her training at St. Michael's in Toronto. "Are you a Catholic?" she asked.

"No," Andy smiled, "Scots Presbyterian."

The girl raised her brows.

What use was there in explaining the reasons for his loyalty. They went back a long way - over ten years - before the hospital was opened and he was selected to head up the surgical department. The nuns had wanted only qualified men on their staff. It had been a bitter struggle. But in the long run the standard was upheld and patients benefitted. Most gratifying, the General adopted the same policy eventually. Now excellence was out of his jurisdiction - so he thought - until Dr. Beecher F.N. Best came along.

At the main entrance Crooky halted. So much had transpired in the last few hours he had forgotten the special meeting scheduled for 8 pm. Damn, he cursed under his breath. The whole business was a weight on his conscience and he wanted it done and over.

With the Best affair preoccupying his mind he turned, curious to find out what the younger orthopaedic surgeon was doing and experienced a sudden sharp pain between his shoulder blades. It cut his breath and he straightened and rotated his back in the opposite direction, thinking if something had temporarily gone out of place it would be righted. But the pain was still there. "Damn, now what have I got," he murmured. Over the past few months he'd an ache in the centre of his spine. It bothered him at night and he blamed it on arthritis, the result of abuse he'd imposed upon himself during his younger days, bucking the line or the hundreds of miles of back-packing he'd done. Instinctively he braced himself against the wall and the sharpness gradually subsided.

Gritting his teeth Andy retraced his steps to the nursing station, aiming for the back corridor where all the action was. However, turmoil in the front hall blocked his path. A shoddily dressed man lay upon a stretcher, cursing everyone and everything within hearing.

"Do you recognize him?" Jean Milligan asked, her grey eyes sparkling with amusement, as Crooky attempted to circumvent the obstacle lying between the rubber boots of two members of the fire brigade. He had no idea who the man was until he heard the voice. "Fer Chrish shake Doc, I wan the hell out of here."

"Herbie! Herbie Smith." Crooky grinned. He hadn't seen his former patient in years. Operating on the old sot's bunion was an incident he would never forget for Herbie had the worst case of scabies he'd ever seen and none of the nurses would go near him. Crooky had to prep the foot himself. "What brings you in here?"

"He was blown up a tree, Doc." the fireman nearest Jean replied. "Someone spotted him. We got the call some two hours ago. Getting him into the rescue bucket was like netting a sixty pounder with no room in the boat. I thought he was dead, snagged on a branch but old Herb was deep in the land of nod. When he did come around he was swinging. For a while I thought it might be easier to remove the tree."

Jean giggled. "Why didn't you shake him loose?"

"We thought of that but we'd left the trampoline back at the station and the fall might have killed him. I got his legs into the bucket in the nick of time - his coat buttons let go and he slipped out of it like Gypsy Rose Lee. It's still up there, no more the worse for wear than old Herbie. We don't think he's hurt but we don't know. So we brought him in."

"Better take him back to the West End Lounge and buy him a drink," Crooky suggested. "Here," he added, advancing a ten, "if I were stuck up a tree for two hours a pint would be the first thing I'd ask for. If we keep him here without a drop he'll go into the DT's."

Marcel Fortier was in the first cast room in the midst of setting a broken wrist. He saw Dr. Cruikshank passing and hailed him.

"Hey Andy. Come here a sec."

"You called?" Crooky asked, reversing his steps.

"Yes, I have here a bilateral fracture of the wrist." Though Marcel was aware Dr. Cruikshank was a general surgeon who didn't possess the same qualifications he appreciated the older man's experience. "The eighth this evening. The others were not so bad. This guy has a trans-scapholunar fracture dislocation on both sides."

Crooky said nothing but went to the view box. It was an unusual type of break and he could not recall treating more than two or three in a lifetime of practice. With both wrists and elbows stiffened in flexion the patient resembled a praying mantis. Andy asked, "How's he going to wipe his bum?"

Marcel laughed. "Ask him."

The anaesthetist had done a brachial block and told the man in fifteen minutes he would have no pain. That was not entirely true and Dr. Fortier had supplemented a shot of local.

Crooky wanted to say relaxation under a general anaesthetic would have made the procedure easier but refrained. Instead he said, "I'd like to see your post reduction films if you don't mind."

"Sure." Marcel beamed. "When they're done." He had a strong jaw and cunning brown eyes with hair to match, parted to the left of centre and combed back in a series of waves. "I wouldn't normally do it under a brachial block but with a belly full of pea soup a general is risky. There's not enough time to do things properly but I think an attempt to reduce his wrists is warranted. With urgent work piling up this man's injury could be put off but the swelling he'll get will make it more difficult."

Nodding in agreement and backing toward the door, Crooky tossed a parting, "Good luck! Hope you get some sleep," before proceeding to the second cast room.

In fear of running into an encounter with Best, Andy halted in the doorway. Beecher had his back to him as he bent over the foot of the table applying a long cast to an elderly women's lower extremity. The orderly spied him.

"Dr. Cruikshank! I haven't seen you in ages. How are you?"

"Fine Sid. Looks like you got your hands full tonight."

The orderly was providing counter-traction to the upper thigh while Best rolled plaster. Crooky silently waited until Best faced him. "What's she got?" he asked.

"A fractured tibia," came the curt reply. "This is a temporary measure. I'll open it Monday."

"Mind if I have a look?" the senior surgeon suggested, stepping into the room. An x-ray film lay across the patient's chest. He took it and held it up to the ceiling light. The break spiralled two thirds of the length of the shin bone. The fragments were undisplaced, allowing plenty of opposing surface for union to occur and the bone was of good quality. The ideal treatment in Crooky's estimation was simply immobilization for a reasonable length of time and the fracture would likely heal in a good position. It did not need setting, just a full length cast. "What in heaven for?" he hooted.

Beecher grinned. "She wants to get back in the saddle again. The wind unhorsed her." He chuckled and added. "If I plate it she'll be up walking in a couple of weeks. Otherwise it will take months to heal."

"About two and a half," Crooky growled. "What if she gets infected from your operation?"

"None of my cases get infected." Beecher conveyed no emotion. If anything his eyes narrowed slightly as he thought Andy Cruikshank had an awful lot of nerve to criticize. The former Chief was undoubtedly the one behind the trouble they were lining up for him. He continued with self assurance, "I've used the compression plate a hundred times and not one has got infected. If I do, I'll just remove the plate and put the patient on continuous antibiotic irrigation and drainage. It works like a charm."

Dr. Cruikshank's tone was derisive. "One hundred cases! I don't believe you. Tell me Sir," he hissed. "I'm sure you're aware people have lost their legs as a result of bone infections. Is that the sort of treatment you'd chose for yourself?"

"Darn right. I've given her a little sedation, 50 mgms of demerol IV, enough to take the edge off her pain and as soon as I can get her into the O.R. I'll fix it with a plate."

Andy couldn't believe his ears. "It's going to take a God-awful long one." He remarked, adding. "At least a dozen screws to hold it."

Beecher shrugged. The device he'd use would create a compressive force across the break, stimulating new bone formation. The method had been invented by the Swiss and was in general use.

Dr. Cruikshank had tried the technique a few times and liked it but he believed its over-use could lead to abuse. Conservative treatment was best in the long run. He regarded Beecher icily. "Well, he grunted. "It's your choice." Andy could feel a pulse throbbing in his head. It was time to go before he said something more damaging in front of the patient. He had wanted to tell Dr. Best this was another example of what he and a few of the other surgeons were worried about. Beecher was jeopardizing his patients. He might have been spared the business of an accounting tonight but the committee wasn't finished. However before leaving Crooky broke that ethical rule and snapped in front of the patient. "I wish you luck, Sir. What you've planned for this woman I wouldn't do to my dog."

As he turned into the hall the pain in his back recurred and he had to stop again for relief.

In an operating room on the fifth floor Joe Paolone snarled at the circulating nurse. "For Jesus sake, Tallmadge get me some God damn abdominal packs."

"I'm sorry Dr. Paolone, there aren't any more. You'll have to wring them out and use them again."

Joe was deep in an abdomen, trying to swab a ruptured liver. "Christ," he exploded. "We're not operating in the Third World. Get me a ton of oxycel gauze. If you haven't got it then a packet of gelfoam. Try the E.R. or bloody St. Mary's. Get it anywhere you can and make it snappy."

He kept his gloved hands over the huge rent in the capsule brooding over the absence of Tanya Harrington. Where in hell had she gone? With no night duty she was usually around till five. Of all the times to take off early! Why was no one able to contact her?

After returning from California Joe had become acutely aware of Tanya's intrigue with Gerhardt Fast. At first he had shrugged it off, thinking once she had him she would have no one else. Inviting her to the surgical meeting in San Francisco was a ruse; he had got what he wanted. The sex had been great. Her body would make a mummy sit up and take notice. The greatest thrill had been getting away with it. It was exciting to take a risk, maybe the loss of everything he owned, for Angie would be spiteful as hell. Maybe he had done it for no other reason. Angie was so God damn virtuous, he'd found a little slap and tickle elsewhere.

Tanya had been an outlet and an extremely enticing one. She was no longer the forbidden fruit, the unapproachable, enchanting him with her classical beauty. She was flesh and blood and oh what flesh! A generation ago her company might have been tolerable but the bottom line was he did not like her as a person. She carried on with the air of a diva, mentioning important people for whom she had sung before coming to Canada. It had been his choice. He believed a good screwing was what she needed and to pull her down a peg or two gave her his best shot. He even thought he'd have another go at her when nobody was looking, she still had that much appeal. But he had let the affair drop, carrying on in Shipton was too dangerous. It had been stressful enough in California, worse almost running into Lindsay. Joe resolved to maintain this new perspective until he saw her embrace Gerhardt Fast before she got out of the G.P.'s flashy Porsche.

It infuriated him; he'd been nothing more than intermission entertainment. Why was he so blind? But then, what if Gary was screwing her on a regular basis, he had his moment of triumph and beaten the younger man at his own game. It left him feeling rather smug.

A few days later, Scott Morrisey and Paolone were donning scrub suits, closeted in the O.R.'s locker room, their conversation centring the inefficiency of O.R. nurses. Scott had been complaining of a delay caused by an inaccurate tally in the number of sponges demanding a recount. He had his back to the door and didn't see Gerhardt go into the toilet but Joe had. In an inflated voice the Chief of Surgery interrupted his colleague loud enough for Gary to hear. 'Now that I've had my way with the supervisor things might improve!'

'Who? Tanya', Morrisey had shouted. Realizing the dialogue was meant for his ears alone, he spoke more softly. 'You didn't. Not in San Francisco!'

'Yeah.' Joe smirked, 'her ass is in the palm of my hand.'

Following the episode he thought he'd win her back. His pride was at stake and he began to court her, not quite as gaudily as he did in San Francisco, nevertheless with some sincerity, much to the amusement of the rest of the O.R. staff.

Tanya ignored his overtures; she needed nothing from Dr. Paolone, not the chocolates, nor the opera tickets and especially not his fawning over her in front of the other nurses. Once he had grabbed her around the waist and planted a garlic scented kiss on the back of her neck. Afterwards she dogged him like the miasma, always being somewhere else. Her side-stepping caused him to look for excuses. The fact Gary was in the prime of life, handsome, athletic and available made no difference. It had to be something else. Perhaps Joe wasn't spending enough and for lack of funds was losing by default. Inconceivable! He'd show her.

His chance came last evening when Angela and he were at a cocktail party at the Harringtons. The estate with its mansion and boat-slip on the Niagara River were definitely out of Joe's range. Halena had planted a gushy kiss on his cheek. Disregarding Angela she led him into the pink and silver living room where the Paolones mingled with an assortment of Shipton's elite.

    Joe had bowled his way to the very hub of the party, chatting it up with the old boy himself. Harrington was Chairman of the Hospital Board and could be very useful. There were also plenty of other influential souls to exploit. He was soon on his third martini and expounding his favourite anti-socialized medicine kick, not caring who was listening nor where his wife had gone.

It took Tanya the whole evening to plan, time, and execute the scene. After cutting Mrs. Paolone from the flock she had guided her through the solarium onto the rambling lawn. Under the rose arbour by the dock they had lingered to admire the flowers. Dr. Fast with Joe in tow were walking toward them. Before the two had reached the limit of her voice Tanya went into her act, rounding each word effectively. 'Your husband is a bit too bourgeois in his tastes, particularly music. Take my friend Gary there. He's an expert on everything. German composers for example, not the old tacky ones like Bach and Beethoven, but Mahler and Anton Bruchner. When it comes to judging artists his insight is exquisite.' Her speech changed at a startling rate as the two men came in range. 'Your husband has no class at all.' Tanya gave Angela the full glint of her amber eyes and hissed, 'Get him off my back.'

    Gary and Joe eventually caught up. It was the first time Angela had crossed paths with the elegant doctor and she was still paralyzed and speechless from Tanya's cat-like pounce.

'A highly unusual state for the aldermanic candidate, Mrs. Paolone,' Joe commented gleefully, later in the sanctum of their bedroom.

    Following his remark she'd let him have both barrels. A night lamp narrowly missed his head and slammed into the expensive wall hanging. He ducked behind the cedar box, expecting the other lamp to find its mark but there was nothing more fearsome than her derisive laughter. She had jumped on the bed bouncing like an overweight puppet on her bad ankle. He'd never seen her so physical.

Then she came down with a crash, landing on her very adequate bottom.

'You really are a stupid ass Joseph Edgardo Paolone,' she had shouted, 'Playing up to the little tramp. She's taking her husband for everything she can and she's hunting around for more, Fast for instance, with the only asset she has and you know where she keeps it. You've lost your chance and you'll lose more than your balls if I ever hear of you taking her anywhere else. Jesus Mary Joseph! Use your head.' Angela had laughed loud and long after her outburst; she was quite pleased with herself. 'You won't ever hold that little tart,' she added as a final twist. 'Take a good look at yourself. Go ahead. Use the bathroom mirror.'

And so it had ended. Mrs. Noel Harrington was just another cog in the surgical wheel as far as Paolone cared. Now, why was she not around when everyone needed her?

The ripping of a paper packet brought him back to earth and Joe turned to see Tallmadge unload its sterile contents. "Gimme it," he demanded, snatching the coagulant from the instrument table. "All of it."

Joe stuffed the gelfoam sheets into the wound, regarded Scott Morrisey, his assistant, and ordered. "Keep your hand on this for a while. I'm scrubbing out to see what's going on."

Dr. Morrisey wasn't happy with the chief's departure but there was nothing he could do about it. He had done a few gall bladders and appendectomies in his day and knew how to close an abdomen. The worry in this instance was when could he be sure the bleeding had stopped? His partner was pumping a fourth unit of blood into the patient. "How's she doing Fred?" he asked.

Dr. Pearson was elevating the foot of the table to keep the patient from drifting into deeper shock. "She's mainly on oxygen," he replied. "I don't want to give her any more anaesthetic if I can avoid it." He stuck his head over the drape, separating him from the surgery. "Looks like it's stopped. Why don't you close?"

"I'd just as soon let Paolone make the decision."

Fred Pearson said nothing. The longer his partner put off suturing the belly the more shocked the patient would become. He also knew if the wound was closed and further bleeding detected the patient might have to be brought back for a re-exploration. It was a damned if you do or don't situation. "Tallmadge," he said. "Ask Dr. Paolone to come back. I want to talk to him."

Every room was in use. Even the ophthalmologists were hard at it. Twiddle claimed he had never seen so many dust inflamed conjunctivae which were nothing compared to the corneal puncture in a young lad who was blown against a thorn bush by the high winds preceding the tornado.

Dr. Paolone left the eye specialist and ran to O.R.4., to see what Phil Barnofski was doing. Plastic surgeons irritated Joe. They took too long to sew up skin and made their living per stitch, closing excisions of worts and precancerous moles. Joe had never realized how many potentially malignant skin lesions there were, until Barnofski came to town. He took a peek at the face beneath the plastic surgeon's nimble fingers. There were three large lacerations crossing the cheeks and forehead; the deepest had severed the upper lip down to the gums. "How long you gonna be?" Joe asked.

Barnofski was slow to reply. He was concentrating on a stitch, wondering where to sink it without contorting the flaps. He looked up deliberately and with imperturbable calm asked, "Why?"

"We need the room."

"He's got a broken jaw and I've got to wire the teeth when I finish these cuts."

The local anaesthesia was beginning to wear off and the patient twitched as the plastic surgeon nipped the skin edge with his forceps. "Look Paolone," said Phil, "you won't spare an anaesthetist so it's going to take time. This man should have had an endotracheal tube. I'm doing my fucking best." There was nothing sanctimonious in Phil's choice of words, only their delivery.

Joe was frankly embarrassed and left for O.R. 2. Vulgar words referring to sex deflated him.

Eldridge, Olesiuk and Smith were battling with a splenectomy. After changing his gloves Joe burrowed next to the surgeon to have a look and hollered at Chalmers to get him a footstool. The patient's guts were swimming in blood. To secure elbow room he bunted Eldridge aside. His runty left hand dove into the belly and grasped the splenic artery between thumb and forefinger. "Gimme a curved Kocher," he demanded, "and get the God damn suction tip out of here Igor. We can use this blood. Save it! Nothing better than transfusing patients with their own haemoglobin."

Chalmers slapped a clamp in Joe's hand. On a second attempt he closed it on the artery, and the bleeding stopped. Composed he said, "Now Igor, get a small basin and dip it into the pool."

Olesiuk nearly dropped the first draught. After dipping a few times he managed to salvage a fair amount.

"Enough Igor. Go back to your sucker. Put the tip next to my finger so I can see what's going on."

Eldridge had begun to dissect the spleen before Paolone arrived. He should've controlled the blood supply to the organ first. Joe could see the surgeon's cut and a tear into the splenic pulp. "Looks like we've got the major bleeder under control," he declared. "Now stand back. I don't want anyone jarring me while I tie this off."

Once the ligature was secure Joe asked, "Eldridge, you sure there's nothing else ruptured?"

"I had a good feel around," came the soft reply - Bob Eldridge was ten years Paolone's senior but a couple of decades behind in experience.

"That accounts for all the blood," Joe scowled. "You should have gone after the trouble first. Stopped the bleeding, then have a look around." Simple common sense, Joe thought, but kept the condemnation to himself. Tallmadge butted in to tell him he was wanted back in O.R.1. Morrisey wondered if it was safe to close.

Joe stepped down from the stool, sighed audibly and peeled off his gloves. "Get this guy closed pronto," he ordered. "We've got two more injured bellies to go plus a probable appendicitis."

"What'll I do with this blood?" Smith asked. The anaesthetist was holding the basin in his lap on a sterile towel."

"For God's sake man. Put it in an IV bottle and pump it back into the patient."

"What'll I do about the clots?"

"Didn't you put heparin in it?"

"Nobody told me."

"For Christ sake!" Joe was exasperated. Morrisey couldn't make up his mind whether he could safely close an abdomen and now this imbecile hadn't preserved the patient's blood. "Throw it away." he muttered.

CHAPTER FORTY-TWO

Gerhardt Fast lived in a huge white frame house, owned by his family for almost one hundred and fifty years. It had been built following the war of 1812 by Colonel MacDougal, a predecessor on his mother's side. The two storey structure faced the lake, the mouth of the Niagara river and the American flag waving from the opposite shore. From a widow's walk Gary could point his telescope at Toronto and read the red sign of the Royal York Hotel.

    He was the last of his lineage. His father, a Captain in the Princess Pats, had been killed in Korea. Cancer took his mother during his final year at Queens, leaving him heir to a fortune and there was no practical purpose in working. He loved music and it had been a toss up whether to become a doctor or a concert pianist. Being intrinsically lazy he chose neither, full time.

    After receiving a call from his answering service he lay on top of his bed, thinking he needed to shower before rushing to the General. The temperature and humidity had to be in the high nineties. Ten minutes rest he thought. Hell, there would be plenty of bodies around to take care of the victims. They would never miss him. "God it's hot!" he muttered. "Hotter than the loft we used to play in as kids."

    Gary and Noel had been friends since infancy, born in a town not much bigger than a village between the Falls and Lake Ontario. Though the Fasts owned two large farms with colossal concrete barns Noel's Dad was even richer. The Harrington line stemmed from an immigrant paternal grandfather, a hard drinking blacksmith turned garage mechanic, and would have continued in ignominy had the youngest son Bosco not left to make his fortune elsewhere. He had the luck of the angels and discovered a gold mine in the Yukon, literally making buckets. 'Prospecting wasn't for me,' Gary heard him say. 'While my friends were lighting cigars with ten dollar bills I bought up forest and sold to the Pulp and Paper Industry,' adding, 'Money is to be respected - it makes more money!'

    Gary rolled off the bed, stripped and headed for the bathroom. The floors creaked and the hot water tap was leaking. The old place was certainly not as elegant as Noel's. It was during the depression of 29 that Bosco had purchased his estate and years later the second of the huge Fast farms, the first having been expropriated by the government. Gary recalled how his family had done very well by Bosco, accepting shares in Harrington Enterprises as payment. The provincial money they received for the first farm remained invested. After the deaths of his parents he had nothing to do but move his capital from pile to pile and watch it grow. Old Bosco sure knew what he was talking about!

The water was refreshing. He preferred it cold like the river where he and Noel had spent their youth, swimming, sailing and fishing. It was as if they were blood brothers and fitting as Bosco claimed, since neither had a brother nor sister. As inseparable as David and Jonathon they were as dissimilar as night and day. Gary was the accepted leader, smarter, more courageous, daring and talented - a Coward, Borge or Liszt at the piano, while Noel was simply happy to tag along, proudly slapping his idol's broader shoulders.

Everything was fine until the fairer sex entered their lives. After graduation Noel had gone to work for his father. Gary with a few years of medical school left had to find other amiable playmates. Women melted as he turned the full force of his personality their way. They liked to touch him, stroke his curly brown hair and plant kisses on his cheeks. Noel would become envious whenever the two were in mixed company. He did not have the same angularity - the lean coiled spring look. He was soft, podgy-faced, barrel-chested and full across the shoulders, giving him a heavy bloated appearance, and he walked with his knees slightly knocked and pigeon-toed. To him, Gary was God, even after Noel married Alice.

The wedding had been arranged by Bosco and Alice's parents to incorporate the Franklin's foundry. Noel admired her at first. Her intelligence and artistry reminded him of his only friend. But she loathed flying, fishing and hunting, any of the outdoor sports Noel loved. Plainly they were mismatched. She was an introverted perfectionist and her passive aggressive tactics caused him to balk like a steer in a branding chute. By the time Gary had finished his internship and set up practice Noel had taken to the bottle. Gary's friendship saved him from becoming an outright lush. When Noel was down, Gary picked him up, often dead drunk from the floor of the Yacht Club. Alice became the symbol of all the evil in the world and when he had too much to drink he'd go after her with his bare hands. Twice he tried to strangle her but failed, falling at her feet, asking forgiveness, a perverted sense of love and hate. Finally she sued for divorce and Bosco gave her all she wished and more.

After Alice, Noel moved back with his parents. It was like old times. He and Gary were buddies again. They sailed regularly, the windier the better, scudding across to Toronto in a stiff southwester, tacking back in the middle of the night and feeling their way upriver to Bosco's private slip. They shot pheasants at a game farm and put on a spectacular display of aerobatics at the annual Air Show. Between these escapades Noel clung to the booze.

Essentially this relationship did not change. They were still close, so close acquaintances often suspected they were queer which was only partly true.

Slipping into his grey slacks, Gary chuckled at the allusion they had created. Eccentric yes, but not homosexual, the slander-mongers could forget it. If anything they were asexual except for an occasional binge, like Noel cracking up in California. Getting married again had not been his intention. It quelled the gossip regarding their sexual preference but created an emptiness in Noel. Tanya had concocted the whole thing. Why? Was it for a chunk of Bosco's money, or some malicious satisfaction? She must have known her eroticism was too much for him. 'She can drive a studhorse up the wall,' Noel would confide, almost pleading. 'She's spading my grave with a back-hoe.'

So Gary had taken her on and his friend continued to drink. Tanya had wanted Gary from the day she met him at the Harrington's pool, clean, lean and gleaming, with a fascinating butt.

She swerved her Sunbeam around the fountain in front as a sudden gust of spray topped the convertible's wind-shield and wet her face. In a moment Tanya had parked, fought the phenomenal wind to the lee of the porch and entered the house.

Gary was sitting at the full sized Steinway in the sunroom playing the 'Appassionato.' He seemed totally immersed and she watched, entranced by his fingers gliding over the keys. At the end of a dynamic run he stopped abruptly and turned around, his pale eyes piercing the air between them. "What do you want?" he asked.

"The usual," she answered, "You." He reeked of sexuality, the most gorgeous man she had ever seen with his sculpted face and the conditioned body of an Olympian. At night in bed, thinking of Gary she would attack Noel's sogginess with passion, leaving them weak and sweaty.

Ancient history. She had not participated with the same relish since Gary had brought Noel home from the club, slobbering drunk.

It had been after midnight and she was wearing next to nothing. They had put Noel to bed and before the doctor left she had asked him to play for her. It was much the same as now. He was wearing a white cotton shirt open to the middle of his chest with a knotted red scarf. She stood behind him, slowly getting up the courage to touch him. Her hands slid inside his shirt front and she pressed her body against his back. He had turned around just as he had now and playfully asked her what she wanted. "You," she'd ventured.

"Only a part of me pleases you." The words came out in a low steady voice lacking expression. "Get lost Tanya. You don't need me; you've never needed me. You're a sexy bitch who wants a virulent soul once in a while and I've been obliging because I felt sorry for you. Now it's over. You're a selfish slut. You took Paolone out to your old stomping grounds and over-heated him. He's lucky he didn't have a heart attack."

"Who told you?" Tanya began to tremble. One look at her and Gary knew the truth. Her pupils were dilated and the pulse in her temporal artery was racing. "I have to go now," he said. "There's been a tornado. The whole staff has been called in. You should be there. It's your duty."

"Please Gary. Don't leave me. Not now. Not like this. I want you. Do you know how much I love you?" she was on her knees imploring.

He ignored her overtures and stood. Apparently she had not listened to him. He repeated the devastating news . "A tornado! A mob of people have been admitted to the General." He smiled as though he were about to say something funny, "The General expects every soldier to do his duty. Come on Tanya, put a little effort into it."

"I could make you happy," she said mournfully.

He walked over to a chair where he'd thrown his blazer. She followed whimpering, "It's because of Noel," her voice was high, "Isn't it? He's your pal and you don't want to hurt him. Is it right to give up our lives for a good for nothing? I shouldn't have married him. I don't love him. I'll tell him about us tonight. I'm leaving him."

"No you won't Tanya. You'd be losing all those charge cards, the shopping trips to Toronto, that convertible parked outside. No my dear, you won't go so far."

She watched him leave and as his black Porsche skidded around the fountain, suppressed anger welled from her throat. "You bastard," she screamed and filled the empty house with curses.

By mid-afternoon Jim had examined a dozen patients and needed a break. Betsy brought him coffee and he relaxed at his desk with his feet upon a pull-out typewriter slab, looking over his mail. Most of it was junk, advertising from pharmaceuticals and instrument manufacturers. Two letters interested him, one from his lawyer, the other - probably from Dari - was covered with Afghan stamps. He opened the 'Harrison, Bartlett and Samuels' envelope first. It was a writ and very brief. The reference grasped him unexpectedly. 'Ireson ats Lindsay'. His feet hit the floor. "What the hell is this!" When he finished he could not believe a word of it and read it over again, not once but twice. He was being sued for assault. 'At noon Saturday the 18th of March, 1967,' it informed him, 'you took it upon yourself without the expressed permission of the parents to remove a cast from the leg of the infant son of Mr. and Mrs. Thomas Ireson. As a result the boy has been crippled for life. Your action was abhorrent in view of your professional status.'

Jim slammed the writ on his desk and buzzed for his secretary.

"Get me George Bartlett right away," he demanded.

"Sure," Betsy replied. "Anything else?"

"No!"

"Jennifer's here. She's brought you a patient."

"Send her back."

Jim was not prepared to meet anyone until he found out why his lawyer was suing him, not even his daughter. He glanced at the signature. The typing beneath it read, 'J. Cohen.' So it was not Bartlett himself but someone in his office. It seemed unethical.

Jenny entered with a five year old clasped to her bosom. She was taller than her mother, blue-eyed, blonde, with hair down to her shoulders. She was grinning. "Hi," she said, soothing the child on her lap. "He fell."

"Oh! So what's the matter?" Jim sounded as if he cared less.

Jenny frowned. "I'm sorry to barge in on you like this Dad. I guess I should have taken him to the Emergency."

Jim blinked and apologized. "So am I, Jen. No trouble. It's just something irritating me."

"What's that?" she asked.

"It's a long story. I'll tell you about it later - as soon as I find out what it's all about."

He rose, skirted the desk and knelt in front of her. The child looked frightened. Jim smiled.

"His wrist," said Jenny, extending the boy's arm. "I think he's broken it."

"Maybe. What happened?"

"The wind's terrible at the house. It flattened him!"

"One of your pupils?"

"Yeah, this is Jimmy Banwell. His mother dropped him off. She wasn't home when I called her so I brought him straight in. He hadn't even got into the water."

Jim raised his brows. "You got insurance?"

Jenny didn't get the implication until after she'd thought for a few seconds.

"Of course," she said grinning. "You!" then added. "You're better than insurance. That's why I brought him here."

"Ah Jen." Jim couldn't decided whether or not his daughter was serious. He shook his head and added, "Give me a break."

Jennifer laughed. "I am."

"Oh ho, then I'm going to put you to work." Jim's lips turned in. "Hang on to his arm," he directed. "Until I tell you to let go."

The forearm, wrist and hand resembled a classical dinner fork. The deformity had been caused by a displacement of the lower growth plate and experience told him it would go back where it belonged without too much fuss. Jim looked straight into the little fellow's eyes; tears streaked his face. "How brave are you?" he asked.

The child turned away, snuggling against Jenny, one apprehensive eye on the doctor. Jim gently grasped the fingers. "This will only hurt for a second," he said his voice as firm and gentle as his grip. With one motion he pulled hard on the fingers and pushed the distal radius forward. The deformity disappeared and he flexed the hand. The boy was more surprised than pained. He let out a sharp cry and tried to pull away, but Jim held on firmly. "Take it easy son," he went on comfortingly, "it'll quit hurting soon."

Jenny regarded her father admiringly. "That was neat. Now what?" she asked.

"A cast. Don't let him move his arm," Jim cautioned, "Come on let's get some plaster."

Betsy joined them while Jim was applying stockinet. "The phone's dead," she said. "I can't get through to Mr. Bartlett."

Jim had momentarily forgotten the Ireson business. When Betsy reminded him the thought occurred he was presently setting himself up for another suit. He had no permission to treat Jimmy's arm.

"Damn," he muttered.

"Did I do something wrong?" Jenny asked, wondering if she had not held on tight enough and the reduction had slipped.

"No. I'm sorry." Jim paused. "I was thinking of something else." It had been a demoralizing day. Yesterday he'd operated upon a teenager with a deformed elbow. He had cut the bone close above the joint and taken out a wedge to correct a cubitus varus deformity, the result of a badly set fracture. The case had been referred to him by Cecily Williamson who assisted during surgery. Today it had been noted the patient could not extend his fingers, indicating damage to the radial nerve. The paralysis was probably transient and caused by a retractor, but he was not entirely sure and it worried him. He had not told the boy's parents and how to go about it was bothering him. Now he had this ridiculous writ.

When the plaster had set Jim sent Jenny and the boy off to St. Mary's to get a check film and was on his fifth patient when they returned.

Jenny left the boy in the car and burst into the examining room. "Dad," she blurted. "The X-ray Department was jam packed. There's been a tornado. The place is in an uproar. I ran into Sister Magdalene. She asked me to tell you you're needed." By now Jenny was puffing, "Pecak, the X-ray man, told me to bring Jimmy back tomorrow."

"A tornado?" In his fifteen years living in the Peninsula he had never encountered or heard of one. "You sure?" he asked.

"Yeah. It hit the west end an hour ago. They say it did a lot of damage."

"Accounts for the phone not working," he assumed. How often had he heard trouble comes in threes? In addition to his two worries it sounded like he had a hard night ahead.

"Okay Jen," he said, "Tell Jimmy's mum I'll call her when I get a chance. Make sure he gets an x-ray tomorrow."

"If there's any trouble at home," he shouted, "Let me know."

CHAPTER FORTY-THREE

Halfway through the night the disaster was compounded by a breakdown in the central boiler at St. Mary's depriving the autoclaves of steam. Though the resultant delay was rectified within a couple of hours the sterile linen supply ran out and most elective procedures scheduled for the following morning had to be cancelled.

By 10.00 am. Dr. Lindsay was on his fifth emergency, a fracture dislocation of the hip. The head of the thigh bone was displaced into the pelvis and punctured the bladder. Working with Gord Shorter he managed to extract the head and push it back into its damaged socket.

While repairing the rip in the bladder the Urologist asked, "How do you expect to keep it from displacing?"

"With a pin."

Shorter, alias Shortie, was six foot six, had a large frame, a St. Bernard face and a proclivity for clowning. "A safety pin?" he asked.

Jim was not in a jocular mood and over his reading glasses glared at the big man, ten years his senior, thinking the urologist had it easy during the operation and could afford to be funny. Gord had gone home to bed at midnight, requesting to be called when the present case was under way. Jim had been up all night except for forty winks under a blanket in the doctor's dressing room. By mid-morning he was so tired he could barely stand. Sensing the difficulty, Gord asked a more reasonable question. "Why not plate it?"

Dr. Lindsay had considered the possibilities beforehand. The anterior pillar of the pelvis had been pushed inward, carrying the smashed socket with it. When the head of the femur had been extracted from the bladder he was able to pry the inverted piece of pelvis back in place. He thought it could be held with a traction pin driven from front to back through the upper end of the thigh bone. A weighted rope, pulling it sideways, ought to hold the fragments in place. Later he might reconsider an open reduction. He had ten days to think it over. If the traction pin and weights did the trick the second operation would not be necessary. Plating it now would add more time. The longer the wound was open the greater the chance of infection and Gord had yet to finish his part. Jim frowned at the taller man and grumbled, "Just get on with your sewing."

"Yes Sir, Sonny," said Gord, like a parent scolding a spoilt child.

Jim spent another half hour in Recovery, setting up traction. Shock blocks were placed under the wheels, elevating the bed on the patient's involved side, and the nurses were warned not to level it under any circumstances. With thirty pounds of lateral pull the patient might end up on the floor. Everything seemingly under control, he went off to the wards.

On Paediatrics he joined Cecily Williamson who was urging their young patient Ivan Sinkilovich to move his thumb. Dejected she turned to Jim saying, "He can't straighten it. What do we do?"

"Wait."

"For how long?"

Jim did not answer and drew a pocket-knife from his jacket. After removing an inch of plaster from the base of the boy's thumb, he said. "Now shut you're eyes Ivy," purposely misnaming him.

The gangly youth objected "My name's Ivan. Ivy's a girl's name. Don't call me that."

"Sorry," Dr. Lindsay smiled. "Okay Ivan, I want you to tell me if you can feel this point but you must keep your eyes closed."

"You're going to stick it in me."

"Have no fear," said Jim adding, "I'm just going to touch your skin. But if you feel you can't trust me Dr. Williamson will cover your eyes with her hand." Then nodding at Cecily, he went on. "Say 'yes' whenever you feel it."

The tip of the blade was applied to an area at the base of the thumb and with each contact the youth attempted to grasp Jim's arm with his un-casted extremity.

"That wasn't so bad," said Jim, emitting a breath of relief. "You'll be able to hitch a ride in a few days."

From the Paediatric Ward Dr. Lindsay took the elevator and entered the X-ray Department. Alec Pecak was scrutinizing films of the Banwell boy.

"Sprained wrist?" he asked, unable to discern anything wrong with the bones.

"No, a slipped epiphysis," Jim replied. "I reduced it in my office about the time all hell broke loose."

"I remember. Your daughter was with him." Alec's slit-like eyes were barely open. He shook his head, apologizing, "it was

Do Unto Others

impossible to fit him in," commenting, "You did a nice piece of work on that broken knee too. "How is she?"

"So far so good," Jim replied, thinking he still might have to split the woman's cast. One thought leading to another the Ireson boy sprang to mind and incited him to go to Medical Records to examine the child's chart.

The Doctors' Lounge was crowded with staff members, listlessly discussing the events of the past night. Jim nodded at a few, checked his mail slot and crossed the hall to Medical Records. After a few minutes a clerk located the Ireson chart and he settled to read it. His own note was easily identified, so were five hand written entries on the Progress Sheet by Dr. Best, two of which antedated Jim's seeing the child, one the evening following surgery, the second at 6.30 am. on the first post operative day. Curious, he scanned them. Beecher's writing was hard to decipher but in essence recorded there had been no problem with the circulation and nerve function on both occasions. Remembering Mrs.Penner's statement, indicating the nurses had tried to contact Dr. Best from the time the patient had arrived on the ward until Jim was asked to interfere, he searched for their notes. Unable to find them he pointed out their absence to the clerk.

"Sorry Dr. Lindsay," she replied. "That's all I have."

Where were they, he wondered. Surely the nurses had recorded everything they'd done.

Jim signed for the chart and took it back to Paediatrics. Mrs. Penner had the day off; he called her at home. "Can you remember who was on duty the night of March the 17th?" he asked. Realizing it had been over two months ago, he reminded her. "The day the Ireson boy had his operation."

"I think it was Sutherland. She wanted to be home with her kids during the 'spring break' and was doing extra time."

"How is she at record keeping?"

"Very thorough. Why do you ask?"

"Well," Jim paused. He had not counted on being interrogated in return and commented offhandedly. "Apparently the nurses' notes are missing from the boy's chart and Medical Records has no idea where they are."

Isabel Penner's memory suddenly cleared. "Why don't you call Mrs. Starling. She took the chart for photocopying. The Ireson's needed a duplicate to take to Toronto. Dr. Best took the copy from

Starling and gave it to the Iresons himself. If our records have been misplaced, Toronto should have a copy."

"Where did the Iresons take their boy?" Jim asked.

"To a Dr. Geoffrey Robb at the Paediatric Hospital."

Jim thanked her and with a sinking feeling hung up. Geoffrey Robb was a self-righteous stuffed shirt, but he was honest and expertly sound. He would have to be to get accepted into that institution. He dialled zero and asked for another outside line.

"The Doctor's still in surgery and is not expected until later this afternoon. Shall I have him return your call?" Robb's secretary asked.

"No, I'll call back." Jim knew most doctors returned a call at their convenience, sometimes long after working hours, after a game of golf, or whatever!

Discouraged as well as exhausted he dragged himself to the office on time for the afternoon session.

"Betsy," Jim ordered. "Get that son-of-a-bitch Bartlett on the line. I want to talk to him."

Betsy's saucer-shaped eyes expanded. In her twelve years with Dr. Lindsay she had never heard a profane word; nor had he been as officious and rude.

She adopted the same attitude with Bartlett's secretary. "Dr. Lindsay says," she stated politely, "if Mr. Bartlett doesn't return his phone call within five minutes he'll never get another medico-legal report." After clicking off Betsy thought over what she'd said and smiled. It was an ultimatum Bartlett's office would have to seriously consider. She hated pounding out those six page reports.

"George, who is this jerk Cohen you've got working with you? Jim asked two minutes later.

From Lindsay's tone George Bartlett was unsure of the implications and hedged. "Cohen! I don't understand."

"You damn well do George. If not, then what kind of a shop are you running?"

"Jim. Would you please cool it. I haven't got a clue what you're talking about."

"You do have a Cohen working for you?"

"Yes. He's a junior member. Not a partner."

"Well," Jim sighed. At last he was getting somewhere but he still didn't know how Cohen came to be involved. "I don't understand," he continued, "how a law firm with whom I've been dealing for fifteen years can be suing me. Don't you have any ethics?"

"Okay, Okay" - George sounded as if he were a Bank Guard trying to control an unruly queue of patrons who wanted their money back - "What's this about?"

"I have a writ under your letterhead, accusing me of assault and conduct unbecoming of my professional status by the parents of a patient I saw for five minutes in the hospital. I tried to improve the circulation in the kid's leg and I'm being sued for it."

George Bartlett paused, "I'll have to consult with Cohen and call you back."

"Well make it damn snappy," Jim barked and slammed the receiver.

Sunday began with a promise from the weatherman. The rains, soaking the peninsula in the wake of Thursday's tornado, had passed and sunny weather was expected.

Before church Beecher drove through the west end of the city with Lil and the boys to view the wreckage. A work force had cleared Station street and the debris dozed into piles where houses once stood looked like a block in the Spruceridge neighbourhood after being prepared for a shopping mall.

As the service would not start for an hour he decided to take a quick trip into the country for another look at 'their' house - after he'd signed the 'offer to purchase' Beecher felt the property belonged to him.

Between cloud patches blue sky was visible to the north. As the Toyota climbed the escarpment the sun burst through, shimmering on the wet branches and bringing spring colours to their virescent brilliance.

In the back seat Robbie had a headlock on Michael. The younger brother was bent on grabbing the dinky toy Robbie'd been running along the top of the front seat. Michael was the same size coordinated and agile but a loser once within Robbie's stronger arms.

Lillian turned to break them up and noticed a small car trailing close behind. A woman drove, possibly two children sat beside her. It was difficult to be sure; they were constantly bobbing up and down and she could make out only one small head at a time. A family like themselves out for a Sunday jaunt, she thought, confiscated the mini-truck and relaxed in her seat.

The car overtook them before Beecher pulled off the road into the farm. The driver honked and a boy and girl threw themselves at a back-seat window and waved.

"Who are they?" Lil asked.

"Who do you mean?" Beecher's voice faltered and he looked pale. "The people in the car? I dunno. Never seen them before."

Lil felt he was lying. He stopped the engine and the boys crashed out of the back onto the wet grass.

"Now don't get all muddy," she called, "We're still going to church."

Dr. Lindsay did not ordinarily operate on Monday morning. Andy Cruikshank had gone to St. Mary's hoping to catch the surgeon on rounds. When he found Jim was scrubbed in the O.R., Crooky poured himself a coffee and proceeded to fill an ash tray with butts.

Jim had been called to treat the unconscious survivor of a motor vehicle accident. If she'd remembered to buckle her seat-belt she likely wouldn't have been admitted, let alone sustain a depressed fracture of her skull and an open shattered knee cap. Finny had already seen her and booked an elevation. Jim had asked Dr. Mehendra Ramamurti to assist. The Asian had been most willing. It was a chance to collect two fees for one operation, almost as much as either of the surgeons.

Mrs. Burwin appointed Janet Schocker to scrub while she herself circulated.

Finny had made a semicircular cut at the front of the skull, and with Mehendra retracting the skin flap, attempted to lever the bone fragment into position. For no apparent reason he asked. "Why does your brother wear a turban?"

"Because of his faith," Mehendra replied.

"Why don't you wear one?"

Ramamurti restrained himself, any answer would give Finny an opening. The man was asking personal questions to cause embarrassment. Mehendra was not going to tell him his choice had been a great sacrifice. He had come to Canada from Africa, stopping long enough in the United Kingdom to obtain a medical degree and an English wife. He and Elspeth had been passionately in love. No cultural, religious, or social barriers could dissuade them. They had settled in Toronto and during his residency she had borne two sons named Clive and Kim. Now his sons were grown, a living part of him but in a new world he did not completely understand, nor did it understand him, forgivable, for he was unsure of where he belonged himself.

His wife was taking more frequent trips to Devon. Each time she stayed away longer to visit her aging parents, her brother and sisters and friends she had left.

He longed more for Tanzania, the wide open spaces of his youth: uncluttered horizons, vast migrating herds of Wildebeest, the astonishing beauty of the skies, purple, gold and crimson as the sun set. Now he was a man without a religion, without total social acceptance and the vast land of his birth.

His brother had sacrificed nothing. The snowy bearded Surji kept his emblems: the dagger hidden beneath his tunic, a turban and a sari clad wife, idiosyncrasies that invited derision.

"The bandage you will wrap on this woman's head will resemble a turban," Mehendra said, "and she'll look more peculiar because women don't wear them."

If he meant to be funny, Finny couldn't tell, for the Asian's deep-set eyes were dark and unrevealing. Finny made no further attempts to bait the Sikh and pried the bony fragment into position, holding it with a few well-spaced wire sutures.

"Okay my friend," he said, bunting the instrument stand with his belly and shoving it in Ramamurti's direction. "Do a nice plastic closure. I'm going out for a crap."

Rounding the table Finny goosed Schocker and she blushed. "Say, didn't I pass you out in the country Sunday morning?" he asked.

"What time?"

"Ten," Finny snickered. "Before or after the rendezvous?"

"Must have been with my kids," she explained.

Finny ripped off his gloves and gave them to Burwin. "Now Marigold my dear," he said, looking down his nose, "You can strip me and draw my bath." Turning to the anaesthetist, deep in 'War and Peace', he commented, "no doubt you'll keep her in ICU. Tell Molly baby I'll be in to see her later."

Reif Larson nodded indifferently, used the interruption to recheck the patient's vital signs and went back to his book.

CHAPTER FORTY-FOUR

Finny had left St. Mary's long before Jim and Mehendra moved into the O.R.'s lounge. But Crooky was there, half asleep in an easy chair. "Tough case?" he asked.

Jim took up one end of the chesterfield and raised his feet onto a naturally distressed coffee table. "Not really", he replied. "A compound comminuted knee cap. The extensor expansion was torn."

"What did you do with the patella?"

"I was thinking of circumferentially wiring it but it was badly smashed. We threw it away. The soft tissue came together nicely." Jim looked about the room. Seeing it was empty, he asked, "What's on your mind Andy?"

"The cancelled meeting." Dr. Cruikshank frowned. "Both Alligood and Paolone think it's better they talk to Beecher first. The Peer Review has been put off."

"I take it you're not in favour?"

"That clown Paolone is very impressed how Beecher conducted himself during the disaster and Alligood thinks all Best needs is more supervision."

"Who's going to provide it?" Although his question had been directed at Crooky Jim regarded Dr. Ramamurti. "What do you think Mehendra?"

"We do not have a separate Orthopaedic Department. Let the general surgeons monitor him."

"You can't do that," Crooky growled.

"Why not?" asked Jim, "you guys won't let us have our own department. You look after him."

In the ensuing silence Dr. Lindsay thought of how the Shipton surgeons had treated him initially. There were a few distasteful memories. Paolone had stolen a case from him shortly after the General Hospital had granted him privileges. The patient had a broken wrist, a simple Colles fracture, and Jim was unaware Scott Morrisey was the family doctor. The nurses had tried to reach Morrisey but were unable. For the sake of expediency they had asked Jim to take care of it and he agreed. Somehow Paolone found out and barged into the cast room, erupting like Vesuvius. "I look after all of Scott Morrisey's surgical problems," he claimed. "What the hell do you think you're doing?" Rather than create a scene Jim backed off.

Do Unto Others 405

Afterward the only referral from Paolone had been his wife, Angela, and much to Jim's surprise Joe hadn't told him how to treat her.

Dr. Ramamurti had taken over the other end of the chesterfield and spoke up quietly, "I don't think Dr. Best has had enough experience doing back surgery, neither have the general surgeons."

"Am I to infer you would be willing to oversee him on that score?" Andy asked.

"Not necessarily," Jim intervened. "We've already offered to give him a hand but he's refused. He could bring his back cases to one of us and learn privately or refer them out of town where he might not receive the same interest. Quite frankly Andy, I doubt if either situation is suitable as nobody has the time."

"That is true," Mehendra declared. "Before his first case he told me he had never operated on a back. I offered help. He preferred to get Olga Laskowitz. I doubt if she has ever observed spinal surgery, let alone assist on a case. The patient ended with nerve root damage, likely permanent, and from what I recall the indications for the operation were not there. I have heard he went out of town to a neurosurgeon with his last case."

"Would you have helped if he'd asked?"

Mehendra paused, momentarily deliberating how to answer Andy's question. "Yes and no. If I thought I might learn something, a new procedure, something I'd never seen before, I would." Mehendra stopped abruptly and bit his lip as if he remembered something causing him regrets, then continued, "I did help on the second operation - the second time he operated on the first patient. In my opinion the second procedure was necessary. The patient had been worse following the first; possibly something had gone wrong. Actually I didn't know of the torn dura and excessive bone removal from the facet joints until the re-exploration. I thought a fusion would do the patient no harm. At least it would produce stability. But he didn't improve with the second operation and went to Toronto to have the nerves cut at a higher level."

"You haven't got down to the real problem Andy." Jim said while he got up and closed the dressing room door. "The big question, is the man's judgement. I think it's defective or he hasn't got it and he's dishonest. You detected it yourself when he pinned the wrong hip and wormed his way out of it." Jim hesitated and wondered if he should go on. An accusation without facts could be misconstrued as gossip. "A while ago," he continued, "Beecher did a rotational osteotomy of the tibia on a four year old boy with club foot. The day after the operation I found the kid in a terrible state. There was no movement nor circulation in his foot and probably no sensation either. I took it upon myself to split the cast and had planned to do more when out of the blue Beecher appears. The nurses informed me they had been trying to contact him all night to no avail. I told him to take the kid back to the O.R. and return the foot to its normal alignment - he'd twisted it outward almost ninety degrees. I thought the boy had spasm of the arteries. Certainly the cause was more complex than a tight cast; splitting it made no difference. Beecher did absolutely nothing. Just let the kid sit and transferred him twenty- four hours later to Toronto." Jim paused adding, "I got hold of Robb yesterday. I wanted his copy of the nurses' notes. He told me he hadn't receive them."

Crooky looked pleasantly surprised. He had given Jim a pile of evidence. This case could be added as another example of Best's misconduct. Perhaps the sceptical Dr. Lindsay would be willing to do something now, but there was obviously more to the story, and he asked, "Why did you need the nurses' notes?"

"I'm being sued."

"What!" Andy snapped.

"Yeah, you heard me! By the parents of the kid. I didn't have their permission to touch the boy and that constitutes assault."

"What the hell!" Andy had trouble understanding. He'd been solicited for medical opinion by the law profession plenty but he had never come across anything quite like Ireson ats Lindsay.

"That's not all," Jim added. "I'm liable for everything including the kid's contracture and all the late complications when they become manifest. Robb never received a copy of the nurses' notes and told me he took the boy to surgery, removed Best's pins and released the anterior compartment. He said the muscle was so pale it looked as if it were under a tourniquet. The superficial circulation has improved but there is definitely loss of muscle tissue. In other words Crooky, the kids got Volkmann's ischemic contracture and will have trouble the rest of his life."

"And you're responsible for it?"

"So the parents think." Jim continued, "I saw the boy as an infant. The deformity was mild, no more than an intrauterine positional problem. When I tried to explain to the mother she got confused. I sensed she didn't trust me and sent her out of town. I never saw her son again till now. Evidently she and her husband are going to get me come hell or high water." Jim shrugged adding, "The catastrophe wouldn't have happened if they'd listened to me in the first place."

"You're no doubt right but you can't blame yourself for people disliking you. We can't all be politicians or diplomats. Some folks will toss a law suit because they don't like the colour of your tie," Andy looked at Ramamurti briefly and added, "or your skin. But tell me, why is the nursing record so important?"

Jim was holding a lighted match to his pipe. He blew it out and explained, "It would prove the boy had the problem when he returned from surgery, long before I split his cast. The record has vanished ; Robb should have received it. I think, and damn me if I'm wrong, Best had something to do with their disappearance. I suspect he stole or destroyed the nurses' notes and the copies. The last time Starling saw a copy, it was in the envelope intended for Toronto and Beecher had taken it from her."

Crooky was beaming. "So in summary," he said. "If I may paraphrase. Dr. Beecher F. N. Best" - Crooky chuckled interjecting, "I think the sound of his middle two initials befitting - is an incompetent rogue. What are you going to do about it?"

"I haven't finished," Jim declared. "There's more to the story. The Iresons went to a junior member in the firm of Harrison, Bartlett and Samuels. - I've been employing them since I came to town. Not often but as needed, like when we bought the farm - I told Bartlett about Cohen sending me a writ, and Bartlett has ordered Cohen to drop it. Now the little bastard has referred the Iresons to Husselman and the fight goes on."

"I'll put the question to you again." Crooky laughed. "What are you prepared to do about Best?"

"Kill him!" Jim made the suggestion in jest. "Crooky, I'll tell you something," he continued. "If I've read the data you've collected once I've read it four times. I've discussed it with old Brahms. Some of it seemed far fetched. But now, but now," Jim repeated, thinking of the survival of his family, "I'm ready to believe every word of it. Perhaps Mehendra will go along? We'll help get rid of Best but we want something in return. Something vital to the welfare of everyone. We don't want to get into another nasty situation and the only way to avoid it is to have our own orthopaedic department, completely autonomous with a vote on the Medical Advisory equal to any other department and the power to recommend who'll be allowed on staff. Assure me of this Andy and I'll go overboard to help you."

Crooky's mouth dropped open. He had not banked on Jim's pragmatism. The request was neither irrational nor untenable. Why not, but where to start. He would go on badgering Best; the man was a menace to medicine perhaps to society. He shouldn't be allowed to operate. He was willing to give Paolone and Alligood a chance to change the man's attitude but Crooky firmly believed the problem went much deeper. The man was his own worst enemy. He'd get him sooner or later; if he lived long enough.

"Swing it Andy," Jim smiled, "and you'll hit the local archives as the first Chairman of Orthopaedics."

Paolone and Alligood had decided to meet with Best Saturday morning after the clinical conference. Jim Lindsay had excused himself because of a promise to take his family to the Ontario Museum. All the other surgeons were there including Drs. Cruikshank, Fortier and Ramamurti plus, a few of the general practitioners associated with the Department of Surgery. In the aftermath of the tornado there was an abundance of personal achievement and everyone wanted to be heard.

Alligood had organized the meeting and led with a scholarly dissertation on the management of the multiple injured patient. He brought charts and x-rays of a handful of cases requiring critical care and stressed treating the airway first then haemorrhage and brain damage followed by trauma to the abdominal contents. Bladder and musculoskeletal injuries came last. He emphasized not to neglect a fracture if it could be approached under the same anaesthesia as tracheotomies, body cavity explorations and burr-holes. To emphasize his point he presented two patients Larson and Bagley had treated. Both had crushed chests from walls collapsing on them. In addition to requiring immediate correction of breathing difficulties both had other injuries, one a concussion and the other an open fracture of the femur. He also stressed thoroughly appraising a patient before operating.

One by one the doctors were asked to comment and the meeting was conducted on a reasonable level of professionalism until Paolone took over when it became a 'show and tell'. He had every patient admitted moved to the main hall. Joe pontificated for twenty minutes, castigating everyone for inefficiency from the Emergency Room to the O.R. staff. The administration had not been prepared to handle the crisis. There were not enough packs; the lab had been too slow to type and cross match blood for transfusion; the circulating nurses had taken too long to find what Joe needed; an ambulance driver had broken a patient's ribs giving CPR when the patient had merely fainted; the O.R. supervisor was unavailable when she was needed. Observing Joe's attitude toward Tanya Harrington in the recent past, a few brows raised over his last comment.

Paolone had nothing but praise for the doctors. "Morrisey and Eldridge were superb," he said, very seriously. "We would have lost a couple if it had not been for them."

Listening, Andy rolled his eyes. An ash dropped on his lapel and he leaned forward to brush it off. The sharp pain between his shoulder blades recurred and he pulled himself straight, forcing his back into the chair. It was time to get an x-ray.

Behind a curly black beard Ben Nickerson was sitting in front of a bank of view boxes studying an upper GI series.

"Mind doing my back?" Crooky asked.

"Not at all," said Ben. "Have a seat. I'll be with you in a minute."

Crooky watched and listened while Ben looked over the films, simultaneously jabbering into a dictaphone.

Finished, the radiologist smiled. "Okay," he said, stroking his bushy face. "Let's go find a technician."

"You should shave it off."

"Now why should I do a stupid thing like that?"

"Because of those white streaks on each side of your chin - You look like a skunk."

The Lindsays had a very pleasant outing and were home by supper time. The phone was ringing when Jim opened the door. Heather ran through to the kitchen to answer it. "Dr. Cruikshank!" She yelled.

Merri looked at Jim with a mixture of annoyance and disappointment and sighed, "Not another emergency!"

"I don't think so," said Jim. "He probably wants to tell me how the meeting went."

"Couldn't it wait till Monday?"

"He's worked up over Best; so am I. Paolone and Alligood were to speak to Beecher this morning. That's probably what it's all about."

"I know you are darling," Merri smiled, "almost obsessively so. Ever since you received the writ."

Jim motioned for quiet and picked the phone from the kitchen table. "What's up Andy?"

"Could I impose upon you?"

"Certainly."

"It's a personal matter I'd rather discuss with you privately."

"Sure Andy. How about Monday? I'll come to your office."

"Jim, as I said it's personal. It's got nothing to do with our friend Beecher and it has me worried." There was silence on Jim's end of the line so Andy went on. "I had an x-ray of my back today and I'd like you to have a look. Can I come out?"

"Okay but give us an hour. We're about to eat." Jim felt Merri tugging at his elbow. "Just a sec," he added and placed his hand over the transmitter.

"Why so urgent?" she asked.

"He says it's personal."

Merri shrugged and did not looked pleased. Jim turned back to the phone. "Yeah, it's fine Crooky. Get here when you can."

"Thanks Jim, thanks so much! I'll be there at eight."

Andy came right on time and Jim led him into the den.

"I'm really sorry to bother you like this but if you'd give me your opinion on these films I'd be most grateful."

"What's the history?" Jim asked.

Crooky hesitated, "I've been having a lot of pain lately, in the middle, between my shoulder blades."

Dr. Lindsay took the x-rays out of the envelope and held them one at a time over the top of a lamp shade. "You sure have a lot of degenerative arthritis," he commented.

"What about T7." Crooky was going to put the end of his finger on a vertebra in the thoracic region but held back as if the spot were contagious. The bone instead of being rectangular was slightly wedged and there were holes in it, likely caused by a malignancy.

Knowing how heavily Andy smoked, cancer was highly suspect. Jim pretended to study the x-rays further, wondering what to say. Andy had been a father figure, helpful and encouraging, supplying hints on where to send patients for orthopaedic appliances, how to get referrals, of whom to trust. He had taken Jim around the hospital, introduced him to the Administrators and permanent staff, supplied a reference for his applications and had been generally kind and courteous. The realization his good friend had an incurable condition was hard to take. Andy's days were numbered. How could Jim give his opinion and give him hope when he had none himself. "Have you seen anyone else about this?" he asked.

"Nope."

"What about Ed Atwater? Why don't you go and have a complete check up?"

"I don't need to."

They were standing in the middle of Jim's den. Andy looked up at the younger man and without a trace of doubt stated, "I've got cancer," then smiled. "Now we've settled the diagnosis let's get on with the treatment. What do you suggest?"

Jim was more outwardly shaken than the little chief. If Andy did have cancer of the lung it was too late for a resection because the tumour had spread to his back bone. Radiation therapy was the best way of slowing down the growth but it was not a cure. "I still think you should see Ed," he nodded. "If he agrees," Jim had difficulty finishing, "it's the Cancer Clinic."

"Okay, now that my problem's solved," Crooky grinned, "how about pouring me a stiff one?"

"Rye?"

"With ice and a splash of water."

Dr. Cruikshank stayed till nine, never mentioning his prospective treatment. Celeste and what his children were doing were his main topics. He finally got around to reporting on Alligood and Paolones' proposed tete a tete with Best. It had taken place in the snack bar and lasted as long as it took to down a cup of coffee. Crooky had sat with Ramamurti and Finny at a table purposely chosen for eavesdropping. Lloyd Alligood, saying little sat at another table jotting notes while Joe and Beecher did most of the talking. They had left as if exiting a stage, the star performer going ahead with maestro Joe slightly behind, hanging on to Best's shoulder, eyes on his shoes, exhibiting a contrived indifference to the audience. As Crooky described the scene he had fully expected Beecher and Joe to return for a curtain call.

Other than that the only things missing were applause and Alligood, who had faded into the background like a stagehand.

After Jim had seen Crooky off he returned to his den, alone with his ghastly thoughts. Of the people he had met in Shipton he would miss Andy Cruikshank the most, next to Ed Atwater but only because Ed was closer to his own age and they had been to school together. Losing Crooky would be to a lesser extent like reliving the passing of his mother and father, sorrows worn thin with time. Even the shock of Jason's death had lessened and there was a time when Jim thought it unlimited. Each grievous parting had seized a portion of his spirit. He wondered how much he would have left if Merri were to go first, and thinking of Merri his mind roamed to her Dad. Old Brahms was more than a father to him; he was Jim's ultimate mentor. Brahms' days were running out. He closed his eyes and tried to drown his melancholy in the painless, weightless, nothingness of sleep.

Jim became aware of Julia waving a familiar envelope under his nose. Blinking awake, he asked. "Where did you get that?"

"On the floor of the Pontiac."

It was the letter from Afghanistan. He must have tossed it absently on the seat when he had rushed off to St. Mary's the day of the tornado.

"Can I have the stamps?" she asked.

"You'll have to ask your mother. She's the collector," Smiling he added, "but I don't think she'll mind."

Jim moved to his desk, turned on the lamp and found a letter opener, a souvenir of his Afghanistan trip. He slit the stamped end and removed the postage. "Here," he said. "Someday they might be worth a pretty penny."

Extracting the letter, Jim found it was from Dari. The last time he had written to the Afghan was six months ago on the back of a Christmas card. He had received a short note in reply but the letter in front of him was lengthy and accompanied a formal wedding invitation.

He read, Roxane and I are to be wed the end of June. We would like very much for you to be present. But we will understand if you can not come.

There will be opportunities for us to visit in the future. You remember I told you I wanted to become an orthopaedic surgeon. You advised me to write to Sir Edgar Ramsey when I was ready. You told me you had written to the great man on my behalf, asking if he could help me receive further training.

Jim had written to Sir Edgar. He put Dari's letter down trying to remember what Ramsay's answer had been. Not being able to, he returned to the letter and read on. Sir Edgar recommended me to one of his proteges, Mr. Wilfred Durnford, presently the Chief of Orthopaedics at a University Hospital in upper New York State.

I am excited to be accepted. One of my professors in Beirut, an internal medical specialist, took his training at this same university and is very competent. He also acted on my behalf.

I have passed the Afghanistan and the ECFMG examinations and finish my internship in one month. I am eager to get on with my training. We will fly to New York immediately after the wedding.

The next few pages were newsy, much to do with people who were at the Avicenna hospital when Jim was there. The Medicare arm of S.E.R.V.E. remained in operation; though most had moved on, but Amir Kash was still around.

'Afghanistan, continues to play the West against the East and reap a reward of aid from each side, but for how long?'

'Malikar is pleased with his new heart valve, my brothers get richer and I ride in the Buzskashi, but not as well as Sayyid.' Dari signed off 'Inshallah.'

He took the letter to Merri in the family room, a piece of crochet on her lap, her eyes on the TV. "Interesting," he said. "Do you want to read it?"

CHAPTER FORTY-FIVE

Malikar, with Dari and Sayyid trailing, strode into the morning light. The day was warm, the sky clear and a pleasant breeze descended from the rugged peaks. Behind them, the keep shimmered like an Olympic torch in the sun's reflected rays. Preoccupied with the approaching contest the elder Mahmud headed toward a path and several large paddocks bordering the eastern rampart.

The track led to a narrow opening in the six foot wall of the first enclosure. Twisting sideways to enter it, Malikar looked back at his qala, awash in the Panjsher's beams. The sight was comparable to an aurora he had seen on a trip to the arctic circle. Incredible, he thought, and pointing a gloved hand at the central tower exclaimed, "A good omen! Allah blesses us this day!"

The gap admitted them singly into the first paddock and they crossed it's sun-baked surface to other slit-like openings and adjoining paddocks strung in a northerly direction for a quarter of a mile. The last gap opened onto the shady front of a stable where they paused before an open field to admire a score of horses. Fully harnessed and tethered by short ropes, each was attended by a syce.

"The Baghlan mounts," Malikar declared.

"Is that all they've brought?" Dari asked.

Misinterpreting his son's remark, his father frowned, "These beasts don't appeal to you?"

"No. I mean, yes they do; I thought there would be more of them."

Malikar smiled, "I'm sure they have reserves." The elder Mahmud was dressed in doeskin riding breeches and dark brown leather greaves, fitting his role as the official host. A narrow brimmed fedora darkened his deep black eyes and he wore a green tweed jacket to match.

Before entering the stable to check their own mounts the trio strolled into the field for a closer look at the oppositions'.

"Aren't they beauties?" Malikar claimed. "They belong to an Andarabi Tadjik, a friend I've had for years. Look at them, brushed to perfection, manes and coats as glossy as silk." While he was admiring their broad round chests and deep shoulders a tall grey stallion raised its head. "By Allah there is strength and endurance in that beast," he commented.

"All I see are horses and grooms. Where are the chapandazi?" Dari replied. The Gulbahar horseflesh was as good as what he saw staked out before him. Malikar's chief chapandaz, Ikander, was extremely fussy when it came to selecting breeding stock, but of greater importance were the men who controlled them. "Where are they?" he repeated.

"Having tea." Sayyid's slanted-eyes crinkled but sobered as he added, "planning their strategy. When I was growing cotton in Kunduz I rode with them, forceful brutes with strong wrists and thick fingers. They go mad on the open plains." He grinned in a wolfish way. "But the river! That takes more skill and a whale of a horse."

Dari was listening to Sayyid's comparison. "So brader-jan, you are an expert on Buzkashi-yi-darya. I remember the first time we played the Panjsher, three years ago. How come all of a sudden you're an expert?"

"Ah, but I've learned my lessons since."

"Swimming lessons?" Dari smiled.

Clopping hooves drew their attention to the stable. Syces were moving the Gulbahar string into the paddocks.

Ghubar, the skin of his face now parchment thin and criss-crossed by the scourge of time, was leading big Herk. A younger groom had Zeus in tow and handed the black's reins to Sayyid. "Your horse Sir."

Sayyid frowned, wondering if there was some mistake. "I've been riding big Herk for over three years."

Dari smiled. "I know, but Zeus is rightfully yours and I've decided to return him."

"Really!"

"Yes really. He's too much for me." He was about to say his future plans did not include Buzkashi but decided against it. "Please take him in exchange for Herk," he added, "and keep the rifle."

Sayyid couldn't believe his ears. To have Zeus back! He was delighted but hid his feelings behind a mask of indifference. "If you prefer," he concluded, curious to know why.

Ghuber smiled and his eyes shifted admiringly from the big chestnut to Dari. Now he clung to life to exercise his memory and render help with a body increasingly letting him down. Money was no problem. Malikar had given him a stipend, one hundred thousand afs, in recognition of his loyalty, fully expecting him to quit. But it was better to be occupied until he dropped. Being forced to do nothing would magnify his loneliness and be more degrading than the life of a stable hand or a baccha should he voluntarily reduce himself further. He had no family of his own nor place to go. His smile widened as he handed the reins to Dari. "You would like to exercise him yourself, Sahib?"

The younger Mahmud nodded. His eyes no longer full of scorn for the Baghlan horses softened to reveal a mixture of admiration and pity for the old Tadjik. "Thank you Kaka Jan," he replied and the old man backed away.

Dari was soon walking his horse, dressed like the other members of his team in a blue cotton shirt gathered inside black woollen breeches. The fox-fur rim of his tartar helmet was also black, the colour of his rough leather jerkin and boots. The right riding boot differed by having a calliper which fitted the stirrup and was hinged to allow knee flexion. At its upper end a leather cuff encircled his thigh, and the prosthesis could be removed like a scabbard by undoing the laces.

In contrast, the Baghlan players wore quilted chapans and silver turbans.

The area for the Buzkashi, an hour's walk from the qala, included a big open valley and three lazy bends in the Panjsher river. It was roughly rectangular in shape, four furlongs in length from north to south by three furlongs across, and boxed at its northern and southern ends by a narrow gorge with steep granite walls. Ikander had picked the site. 'The game is meant to be played on horseback and horses should be allowed to run,' he protested. 'Let the Panjsher be merely a barrier like the rocky outcrops, not the whole field.' He voiced his objection after the first river match ended in a waterpolo contest, neither side being able to win.

A whitewashed circle, ten metres across, represented the goal. It was situated on a hectare of flat land to the west of the middle bend in the river. Here, the current was weak, its irregular bottom deep, but a low bank made fording less treacherous.

Close to the Circle of Justice there was a shallow pit to hold the body of a decapitated calf. Two flagged staves, the length of the playing field apart, were driven into the muddy east bank to ensure the carcass would have to be carried across the river twice before being dropped triumphantly in the circle.

The site curved three hundred metres to its farthest point east of the river where a precipitous ridge, continuous with the gorges at the extreme ends of the valley, made a superb backdrop. West of the river the surface slanted gently, readily accessible by a winding dirt road.

An English friend of Kamal's once remarked, 'I should think this 'mise en scene' more conducive to staging rock concerts, an opera or ballet, lolling on the grass with a bottle of wine and a basket of bread and cheese without a care in the world.'

Khushal had smirked knowingly and remained silent. Other Englishmen had impressed him as being peace-loving poofters but four years at Sandhurst had taught him differently; plenty of them beneath their supercilious veneer were as full-blooded as himself.

A conglomeration of gaudily painted lorries packed with spectators blocked the western access. Clambering turban-clad males were everywhere, roaring at the unfolding scene and today's commotion was not confined to the lorries. A few Baghlan supporters had scaled the rocky brow to the east and from this enviable perch were determined to make their presence known, yelling at their favourite team.

A hush descended and heads turned to the south. The first horseman, Baghlan's chief chapandaz, magically appeared. In a silver turban he sat tall on a tall grey steed. Recognizing their hero, the smattering of fans on the eastern ridge greeted him. "Kanji, Kanji," they cried, streaming their head gear like ticker-tape.

Following him filed the rest of the troop in grey quilted chapans of various shades and design, their identical turbans bonding them as a team.

Ali Mohammed did not mind. The Baghlans' rag-tag appearance made it easier to distinguish individual riders and today his older brother was among them. From the height of the eastern ridge he yelled Rafiq's name. Unable to hear above the deafening crowd the horseman rode on solemnly, whip in hand, his tough leathery face the colour of brick.

Then came the Gulbahari led by Ikander on Caucasius, a white stallion. The horsemen wheeled to face the opposition across the Circle of Justice and three riders cantered down the slope toward them. Malikar in his western garb was easily identified; the other two were from the militia. Fit, and wearing an Air Force Colonel's uniform, Khushal brought his Arabian thoroughbred to a standstill between the circular goal and the shallow pit. He relaxed while his khaki-clad batman rolled a calf carcass into the depression.

Malikar was jubilant. It was his birthday, the eighteenth of June. Within a week his youngest son would be wed and he had arranged this game to honour the happy event. Noting the calf had been placed level with the edge of the hole, he tapped his third son on the shoulder. "It is your duty to direct and referee this game fairly. I am sure you will! Above all, you must remember the Baghlan chapandazi are my guests. If there is any uncertainty they should have the benefit of doubt - understood?"

The vertical lines on Khushal's gaunt cheeks gave the impression he was incessantly smiling and made it difficult to judge whether the Colonel had taken his father seriously. He nodded in agreement, allaying any misgiving. Turning to the horsemen he stated the rules:

"No chains, no knives and no drowning. Any infractions, or purposefully unseating an opponent, will cause a halt in play while I sort out the offenders. Perpetrators are deserving of punishment and I will be the judge and executioner. There will be no time outs and a two hour limit to the length of play. Neither horses nor men can be substituted but a player can exchange his mount for any riderless horse found wandering about the course. Should the injured or otherwise dislodged horseman return to find his mount has been seized, he has no choice but to scour the field and look for another or remove the rider who has taken his own, provided he doesn't use a chain or a knife. It is to be a best of three series. Each round will begin at the crack of a pistol. Two shots indicate a foul, three the conclusion of a round. Members of the winning team will receive green turbans and two thousand afs."

Few of the horsemen paid any attention. Ringing the pit, they oozed around the carcass like a snake bent on swallowing itself, packed so tightly it would burst. It did when a shot rang out, and erupted into a colourful mass, rising and falling like a slick on an ocean wave.

Only Malikar's red-bearded chief chapandaz held back. He heard the lead-tipped lashes, whipping frantically, ripping into faces, muzzles, withers and flanks. Mounts reared. Now and again he caught sight of the carcass amid the confusion as it was snatched from one hand to another. It slid over horses' rumps, dangled and fell to be trampled and grasped again. He saw Dari, hanging by a single stirrup, throw himself across the mane of a Baghlan horse in a effort to retrieve it and Sayyid, under the belly of Zeus take it from the same opponent. But neither were able to hang on to the slippery hide.

Ikander waited and when the fray moved toward him he backed off, reining his great white stallion. The wild ones were expending their energy getting nowhere; soon a horse and rider would break away and then he would make his move. His eyes narrowed, peering into the dusty air, and he bit the handle of his whip. Caucasius sensed it was time and made a bolt for the melee but the chief chapandaz jerked the reins and his mighty horse shook its magnificent head and balked in disapproval, neighing, rearing and thrashing. "Not yet Caucasius, my beauty, my white wonder," he cried, his voice lost in the pandemonium.

The atmosphere was thick with dust, the smell of horses and sweat so stifling Ikander retreated again to catch his breath. For a moment he lost sight of the carcass. When he spotted it the whirlpool was spinning off and the Baghlan leader was galloping furiously toward the north end of the field; the others following like a pack of wolves.

Kanji wedged the carcass between his thigh and the saddle, and spurred his animal to a frenzy of speed. Rather than stay close to the river and hope for a safe crossing he made a bee-line for the bank opposite the north pole where the water was shallow but lined with semi-submerged boulders. Together they could make it; his stallion had the agility of a goat and he the assurance to drive him across. A quick look over his shoulder revealed the main body had fallen back but he was unable to increase the distance between himself and two hard driving Mahmud riders. Further back he spied a white horse fording the river.

Dari and Sayyid caught up to Kanji when Pamir shied from the bank. Wary of a headlong plunge into an irregular bottom, the grey recoiled. Fearful his mount might break a leg Kanji turned, hoping to escape up the slope but the move came too late. Within seconds he felt a handful of lashes shear his chapan, was brought to bay and slowed to a walk, a horseman on either side, tugging at the reins. Before being completely overcome Kanji rose to his full height and heaved the carcass to Rafiq, almost unhorsing the younger rider. Another opportunity would present itself; he and Pamir would be ready.

Instantly Rafiq was set upon and lost the calf. A Gulbahar player passed it to a Hazara on a glossy black. 'He'll be caught,' the Baghlan chief surmised, judging from the crowd of horsemen ringing the tenacious little man. Seconds later a big chestnut ploughed into the scuffle and the black with Sayyid arched over his withers spurted free to reverse the course.

High on the ridge the Baghlan fans saw it: Kanji surrounded, Rafiq unable to hold the calf and the little man on a black horse dashing in a southerly direction. Ali Mohammed was furious; spitefully he threw rocks at the red bearded hulk on the great white horse below. He had watched Ikandar cross the shallow southern bend and wondered why he had reined up. An armful of rocks had been spent, trying to hit him. But Ali's throws landed short, and neither horse nor rider took notice.

Within minutes the black stallion, galloping the length of the valley, had gained half a furlong on its closest rival. Shortly Sayyid would be on the east bank, heading north, and once he reached the half way point there would be nothing to prevent him from rounding the flag and re-crossing the river. To catch him half the pack swerved into the deep water of the middle bend but hooves failed to touch bottom and horses rolled, throwing their riders into the lazy current.

The land before the southern gorge was flat. Without breaking stride the black horse splashed across to be followed by a geyser of legs.

Merrily twirling his whip, Sayyid guided Zeus around the southern pole and turned north through boulders and cul-de-sacs. Though either could be used to his advantage more seconds were spent avoiding them and shortly his forward progress slowed. He gripped the lash between his teeth, leaving his hands free to tug the reins, but instinctively Zeus cut in the right direction.

A few Baghlan riders made it across the middle bend, climbed the bank and headed south while a handful of Gulbahari rode to block them off.

Sayyid yanked to the left and Zeus responded by dodging a boulder. Slanting right on his own, the black rushed two Baghlan riders converging desperately close. Dashing upon them, Sayyid shouted and Zeus swerved, countering with greater speed and slipped between them.

The black horse seemed to enjoy each trend of the game, adding tricks of his own: pivoting, rearing, bucking, stopping, biting and racing with expediency beyond Sayyid's wildest dreams.

Suddenly Ikander re-appeared. He shot out of the rocks aimed at three horsemen blocking Sayyid's path. Ali Mohammed screamed but none of the players could hear.

Caucasius drove the closest into the others, leaving a tangle of harness, horses and men.

In the confusion Zeus was free to gallop toward the north end. The only horseman to prevent him from completing the circuit was the giant on the tall grey.

Kanji waited. It made more sense to let Sayyid carry the carcass around the pole. He'd catch him on the way back. There was still the river to re-cross before the little man attained the circle of justice.

Sayyid ran into Kanji on the bank. With barely enough footing Zeus swung his rear and skidded. There was a snap, he saw the Baghlan's face and water boiling over the rocks below. Free of the saddle he was falling.

Grasping the carcass in his big hands Kanji stared down the embankment. Pamir had ploughed into the smaller mount as it finished the turn. There had been a collision, so stiff the Baghlan rider tottered. To his surprise Sayyid had let go. Kanji felt some misfortune had happened, but didn't have time to investigate.

Cantering along the west bank, Dari and Ikander saw the calf change hands, Sayyid's fall and Zeus, standing without a saddle. Kanji and the grey horse had vanished behind a labyrinth of rocks. With a nod they parted. The leader intent on catching the Baghlan chief turned Caucasius to the north while Dari looked for his friend beside the river.

CHAPTER FORTY-SIX

Sayyid was spotted, lying on the shore partly in the current. Leaving big Herk at the top of the bank, Dari struggled to find a less steep slope to the water's edge and when he finally came upon the Hazara, his friend was unconscious. But his chest heaved with breath. Dari knelt beside the silent form. Cupping his hands in the flow, he poured their contents over Sayyid's bare head repeatedly until the Hazara began to rouse. "Praise be to the most Beneficent and Merciful," He whispered and discovered a broken jaw and missing teeth.

Sayyid sat up and attempted to ask what had happened but couldn't speak. Holding his face he tried again, garbling the words.

"How should I know?" Dari replied, "You fell off your horse." He turned away to inspect the height from which Sayyid had fallen. Zeus' saddle, lying at the foot of the steep incline caught his eye and he went for it.

Sayyid struggled to his feet, supporting the side of his face. His head ached and he felt his skull would burst.

When Dari returned the Hazara was retching bile; a concussion crossed his mind and he began to worry; his friend could have serious brain damage.

After throwing up Sayyid staggered to the river. More cold water improved his sensibility. He recalled the Baghlan's face inches from his, and a fiendish grin. "I must get back in the game." he slurred.

"You're not going anywhere." Dari held out the saddle. "The cinch is torn."

"Or cut," Sayyid reacted angrily. The swine must have had a knife, he yanked the saddle away to examined it. No, it wasn't cut, the leather was old and dry. He threw it at the bank and stared at Mahmud.

Dari shrugged. Fate had dealt Sayyid a rotten blow and there might be something more hapless in store. The Hazara needed rest and monitoring. If there was bleeding inside the cranium or damage to brain tissue it would show up in time to correct it. "Forget the game," he advised. "You gave it all you had."

No. I'm stupid, Sayyid thought. Why had he not checked his gear? Then he remembered Dari had offered him Zeus and he'd jumped at the chance. This dreadful accident might not have happened if he had stuck to the original plan. Possibly Mahmud would be here by the river nursing his head.

Dari was thinking the same thing. He'd not checked his gear either. Ghubar was becoming more preoccupied and less thorough. He looked up at the bank. Directly overhead Zeus was hoofing the ground; Herk was standing further downstream where his rider had left him, casually cropping grass.

Sayyid also saw the chestnut stallion, and recalled the rule, 'A player could exchange his mount for a riderless horse.' He left Dari and scrambled up the slope. His jaw throbbed and he had a terrible headache but the pain served to urge him on.

Stumbling behind, unsure of his friend's intentions, Dari called for him to wait but Sayyid appeared not to listen. He called again and again until he was close to where he had descended the bank. When he saw the Hazara reach for Herk's reins he knew.

"Don't do it," he shouted helplessly. "You'll kill yourself."

Hercules treated Sayyid like a lost friend and turned his powerful neck to nudge the horseman's arm. The Hazara appeared not to notice; he was busy unstrapping Dari's special boot. Disregarding the warning, he tossed the boot to the edge of the bank where Dari would easily find it. Then he circled the big horse, mounted the left side and pulled himself into the saddle. If Allah willed, he would die whether or not he went back to the Buzkashi.

The game was still in progress, the second round had begun. Maybe the third. Sayyid couldn't tell; his memory was hazy. Most of the horses were floundering a furlong downstream, their riders deep in water. In a swirl of activity closer to the west bank Gulbahar's chief chapandaz was trying to wrest the wet calf from Kanji.

He yanked big Herk to the right and skidded down the steep slope. The river bottom was smooth and the chestnut had no difficulty with footing until near midstream when they began to float. Rather than topple Sayyid rolled off and for a few yards clung to big Herk's tail. Closer to the west bank the stallion's hooves struck ground and he bounded upward; the Hazara hastily remounting.

Ikander and Kanji were locked in a personal duel, tugging at the disintegrating calf, inching closer to the circle. Pamir had his teeth clamped to Caucasius' bridle, diverging their rears. Riding full out,

Sayyid came from behind, directing big Herk at the opening, screaming into his ear.

Ali Mohammed could climb no higher. He saw many horsemen but three stood out: Kanji, the man on the white stallion and an unknown, riding a big chestnut. The little man was not the same Gulbahar rider he had seen earlier. Before he could be certain, the Hazara was out of the stirrups balanced on the chestnut's mane. Ali saw the charge, big Herk splay the grey from the white, spilling their riders and the Hazara tackle the carcass. The rest was a dusty haze. Determined not to let go of their share of the prize the riders clung desperately to the remains, each possessing an end while the little man, hugging the body to his horse's neck gained the circle of justice.

Sayyid knew he'd won. Neither Kanji nor Ikander were in their saddles. They skipped beside him, tugging at crossed purposes, bound to steal the glory.

Young Hamid from his father's shoulders saw the conclusion of the round and threw a handful of munchy nuts and raisins at his older brother. "Ayub," he shouted, trying to make himself heard above the cheering crowd. "Sayyid has turned the game upside down. It's no longer Buzkashi! The carcass is dragging a man and not one but two!"

When Kanji and Ikander let go Sayyid raised what was left of the fated calf and pumped it high above his shoulders. Basking in the winner's circle, he barely felt the bursting pain in his skull. Gradually the noon light began to pale as if a black cloud were blocking the sun. He shook his head violently to bring back his sight but the motion made his misery worse and a tremendous roaring filled his ears. He stopped and grasped his rigid neck. For a moment he sat blind, deaf and stiff. Then he fell.

"Who won?" Dari asked the nearest Gulbahar rider.
    "Us" the man replied. "It is 1 to 0 with two tries left."
    In the middle of the circle Big Herk had set himself over Sayyid's unconscious body, sheltering the little man between his legs. Only when the chestnut sensed it was Dari who lifted the dangling reins did he permit himself to be led away.

Do Unto Others

Sayyid was lying on his right side. His breathing was stertorous and the left upper extremity was jerking convulsively.

Dari knelt beside his best friend and called him by name. After removing his wet jerkin he wrung it out letting the moisture drip over Sayyid's forehead. There was no reaction. A blink did not occur when he touched his sleeve to the right cornea and the pupil remained constricted in spite of his shading it from the bright sun. He palpated Sayyid's temple; a rapid thready pulse beat beneath his fingertips.

Turning to Khushal who had quietly joined him, Dari said, "He's alive but not for long if the pressure in his skull is not relieved. We must get him to a surgeon fast."

A few days ago Dari had been in Beirut, anxious to be home in time for Malikar's birthday and the Buzkashi. The whole family, looking forward to a joyous week of celebration were at the airport to greet him. His internship had ended. Roxane was to become his wife and the two of them would fly to America the end of June. Now as he sat motionless in the back of Malikar's plane, bracing his best friend's broken head on his knee, there was no joy in his heart.

Sayyid's condition was much the same as it had been when Dari first examined him by the river. He was unconscious, the right pupil constricted and muscles constantly twitched in his left arm. His breathing was becoming increasingly irregular.

Dari listened in fear as the sounds became less audible, wondering if they would cease altogether. "Khushal," he called, "Can't you get more speed out of this machine? If we don't get there soon he'll die."

"Keep your tartar cap on, little brother," Khushal replied. "We'll be on the ground in five minutes."

The operating room was not prepared to receive Sayyid. Dari had called while his friend was being packed into the plane. It was Sunday, the S.E.R.V.E. Medico team had quit work and left. This information had been gathered from Amir Kash who had also said he would arrange for an ambulance to be at the Kabul airport. So far so good, Dari thought, sitting in back with the patient. Amir had kept his word, but when they pulled into the hospital there was no one other than the Afghan surgeon present.

"I suspect he has a space occupying lesion." The young doctor remarked as the chief surgeon was examining the patient.

"Probably due to a collection of blood. He must have hit his head on a rock."

"It could also be due to a tumour," said Amir, thinking aloud, "or a stroke."

"Be reasonable," Dari argued. "He's never had any symptoms which makes 'tumour' an unlikely diagnosis and he is too young for a stroke."

"Not for a berry Aneurysm."

Mahmud was growing impatient. "The chances are he has bleeding inside his head whether it is due to a fracture of the bone, rupture of the middle meningeal artery or bleeding into the brain tissue directly from laceration or contusion. Amir, my bet is it's due to arterial trauma and there is a haematoma. We've got to do him right away."

The chief surgeon frowned. He was not about to be coerced into an operation, not foremost in his repertoire. He noticed Rabia the nurse-in-charge of the O.R., who had come while Dari had been goading him and nodded recognition.

"What size burr will you need?" she asked, assuming the nod meant Amir agreed to proceed.

"It seems I'm about to operate," he remarked, "whether I wish to or not. I'm uncertain of the diagnosis and what to expect." Kash paused, exhaling deeply and added, "Okay. Pick out a sharp three quarter inch one, and don't forget the brace."

When Sayyid was placed on the table his condition had deteriorated further. Respiration was extremely irregular. The inspiratory sounds became weaker until they all but disappeared. At one time they actually did for about thirty seconds. Just before Dari was about to start mouth to mouth resuscitation, breathing returned faster and deeper but stopped again a few moments later. Again there was a period of apnoea followed by tachycardia and again and again, recurring at cyclic intervals. Cheyne-Stokes syndrome he realized, a sign the brain was crowding the foramen magnum, a large hole at the base of the skull, allowing just enough room for the spinal cord to escape. He knew it was only a matter of time until the vital reflex centres in the brain stem would be irreversibly damaged, eliminating any reflexive rhythmic beating of the heart and lungs. Then it would be all over.

No anaesthesia was necessary. The surgeon, noting the jaw had been fractured, cautiously passed a tube into the windpipe through the patient's throat to ensure against suffocation if there was vomiting, also that plenty of oxygen would perfuse the tissues. As Amir told Dari at the scrub sink, "Every traumatologist knows anoxic patients with brain damage don't do well."

The table had been lowered and Sayyid was supine in a semi sitting position. Rabia had shaved the right half of his scalp and was preparing the skin with a coating of iodine when Amir asked for a towel.

"The bleeding may be within or without the dura," he said. "Let us hope it is not a laceration of the brain itself."

Once his patient was prepared, Amir made an elliptical cut convex upward between the outer crease of the right eye and the front of the ear. It was deepened down to the skull while Dari stemmed the bleeding with haemostats and retracted the skin flap.

Before accepting the burr from Rabia, Amir explored the surface of the bone with a gloved finger. "No fracture," he commented. "Feel for yourself."

Dari still had doubts although he concurred with the surgeon's findings. It was possible to have a linear crack, not seen on x-rays. If one were present and in the path of the drill the outcome could be catastrophic.

Amir began to work the brace, twisting the burr slowly through the outer layer of bone, then down through the thin marrow cavity. When he had barely penetrated the inner table dark blood arose from the hole. "You were right!" he exclaimed. "Extradural haemorrhage! Now we have to find the source."

The drill was put aside and a bone nibbler used to enlarge the opening. As it was expanded more coagulated blood exuded from the extradural space.

"Rabia," Amir demanded, "Get the suction and some anticoagulant."

"There is no suction Doktar," she answered. "The pump is broken."

"Then get us a bulbous syringe and saline. We must wash out the clot to discover the source of the bleeding and stop it. Get bone wax. There's some in the instrument cupboard."

The surgeon was able to find the bleeding point and plugged the marrow as well. Another twenty minutes passed trying to re-expand the dura, aided by Rabia's throttling the patient to increase the CSF pressure. Whether the brain resumed its normal shape, the surgeon couldn't tell.

"He should be all right now," said Kash, checking Sayyid's temporal pulse. "The Cheyne Stokes phenomena has lessened."

"When do you expect him to wake up?" Dari asked.

"Anytime. Maybe in a day or two but certainly within two weeks. There is nothing to do now but finish the closure and wait."

"What about the paralysis?"

"I expect he'll have a complete recovery."

Dari was quiet. "You sound encouraging," he said, "What do you base your conclusions on?"

Amir grinned behind his mask. "Hope," he answered, having nothing scientific to establish his prognosis.

CHAPTER FORTY-SEVEN

"Vee expect to be unza grond at 15:15 hours Eastern Standard Time," the Lufthanza Captain declared. "Fifty-Vun minutes from now."

Roxane smiled, and kept her voice low, "Praise Allah," and squeezed Dari's arm. From Frankfort the bumpy crossing had already taken longer than expected. "You told me jet planes are smoother, something about flying above the weather." She shook her head, swirling her blue-black hair and added, "You lied to me, Darius Mahmud."

"Ah ma cheri," he explained in a deep baritone. "All part of a ploy to entice you along."

"Too bad everyone couldn't come," she said wistfully, "I miss them already."

They had foregone the traditional three day wedding in favour of combining the engagement party, the signing of the contract and the marriage ceremony into one glittering night at Amir Abdur Rahman Khan's Moon Palace, restored to its nineteenth century grandeur. Malikar invited five hundred guests, including the king. After His Majesty accepted another two hundred were added - wherever the king went so did his court.

Roxane would have chosen a western style dress complete with veil and train, not inappropriate - she had been obliged to wear white since the death of grandfather Zor - but she bowed to her mother's wish and wore the same red velvet gown Soroya had worn when wedded to Rishtya. It had to be altered; Soroya had been pregnant five times before she married her dead sister's husband. The end product was terrific and a match for Roxane's beauty. Dari wore a tuxedo, indistinguishable from most of the other males at the party.

Their first socially acceptable night together moved to the palatial bedroom as the carousing below continued to noon of the following day. Until they left Afghanistan, well wishers were still arriving with a ton of presents; others barely made the departure gate.

Roxane pressed her face against Dari's shoulder and he put his arm around her. "Who could you possibly miss more than me?" he asked.

"I've never missed anyone more disturbingly than you. I was lonely when you were in Beirut. But I do miss my sisters and my mother. Oh how they would enjoy this trip." She looked up and smiled. "And," she hesitated, "your brother Khushal."

"Khushal! That scoundrel!"

"He's been very kind and thoughtful." Roxane teased.

"Sounds interesting, do go on."

"Dari if I didn't know you better I'd say you were jealous."

"A tinge."

"He was always a gentleman," she turned to look out the plane window adding, "and very dashing."

Dari gestured indifferently. In a moment she refaced him and asked, "Doesn't Khushal look like the king?"

"Yes! He does have the same oblong face, creases in his cheeks, and a long straight nose. If Khushal shaved the top of his head and grew a moustache he could pass for the king." Why not, Dari thought. His father was distantly related to the monarch. Both could trace their lineage back to Sultan Mohammed of Peshawar, Zulfikar's great grandfather, the only difference being the King's heritage was legitimate. Zulfikar's father had been the result of a union between Yahya Khan, a direct descendent of the Peshawar Mohammadzai and a Qisilbash concubine, meaning the present King Zahir Shaw and Khushal had the same paternal great grandfather. Also Dari himself was genetically related to the King. Unlike his brothers Dari had Ferangi blood. Malikar had told him, 'Your mother, Nicole was a Frenchwoman and left for France when you were very young. It is rumoured she didn't stay long in Europe and proceeded to Canada.'

"What are you thinking about?" Roxane asked, observing her husband had become quite still.

"My mother."

"You never had a mother."

"Everyone has a mother," Dari smiled. "You think I was born in a roghan-i-dumbah."

Roxane laughed, "What about her?"

"She might be living in Canada somewhere. Wouldn't it be strange to meet her."

"Highly unlikely. There must be over twenty-five million people living there. Besides we're not going to Canada. We'll be in the United States."

"We'll get to Canada sometime," Dari assured. "Rochester isn't far from the border."

"When I was young I heard Zor tell my mother about a woman Malikar had brought back from France but I never connected her with you. In fact I've never connected you with anyone but me.

I'm thankful you don't have a mother for my sake. It cuts the competition in half."

"Too bad Zor's dead," said Dari, thinking he might have learned more of Nicole from the old man - he could still ask Malikar.

"Yes," Roxane agreed. "It is a pity he did not live long enough to see us married. And Tahmina. I was fond of your grandmother. Remember the trip we made to Nuristan? I think I was ten years old."

"How can I forget?" Dari murmured. "You saved my life."

"Save a person's life and you are beholden to him for the rest of his days," Roxane laughed. "I read that somewhere." She paused, then asked. "Do you have such feelings for Sayyid?"

"Next to you, yes."

Dari's affection for the fearless Hazara had always been greater than his love for anyone of his own blood; Sayyid was like a dearest brother. Favours solicited or not had been an essence of their existence.

"I tried to warn him," he continued. "If he had listened he wouldn't be paralyzed."

"The paralysis will wear off Dari. Dr. Kash is confident it will and you've said so yourself."

"I did say that, but I don't know. I've had little experience with head injuries. I'm going by what I've read. Sayyid was moving his arms and legs when I last saw him but with little control. Anyhow there's nothing more to be done."

"Maybe there is nothing more any human can do," Roxane remarked. "But Allah might help. You should pray more, Dari. He might listen to you."

The conversation had taken a sombre turn and Roxane changed its course. "How long will we be in New York City?" she asked.

"As long as it takes to get through customs and transfer from Kennedy Airport to LaGuardia."

"Can't we stay a day or two? I'd like to see all the touristy places." She poked him playfully in the ribs. "I've heard there is an Afghan restaurant; probably your last chance to get a decent meal."

"So you're not going to cook for me?"

"I want you around a while," she laughed.

"We'll find a cook."

"Do you think so?"

"Why not. There are plenty of poor people in America too."

"But they're free."

"Next week they celebrate their freedom. Tuesday is July 4th, Independence Day."

"Let's stay in New York awhile. I've heard they have fireworks, second to none."

"That's almost a week away. I imagine we'll see the same in Rochester."

"Rochester doesn't have the Statue of Liberty and the Empire State Building." Roxane paused. "Can you picture us trying to find an apartment when the whole town is celebrating. They'll not expect you till after the holiday. Let's stay. Besides I've promised to send a story to the news media and this looks like a good break for a story."

CHAPTER FORTY-EIGHT

It was the Cunningham's fiftieth wedding anniversary. Fully enjoying themselves in spite of the sultry evening they were seated at opposite ends of a reserved table in the glassed-in porch of the Inn. Their entire family was spread between them like a string of paper dolls. Across the river Fort Niagara was visible through the haze and in the long twilight, straggling golfers edged toward the nineteenth hole in the club house across the road.

Jim listened to his nephew's account of how he managed a hole-in-one when a waitress, crisp in black and white muslin, tapped him on the shoulder.

"There's a call for you, Dr. Lindsay," she said. "You can take it at the reception desk."

Merri saw him leave and turned to her dad. "I do hope it's not urgent," she said. "This is the first time we've all been together since I can remember."

"I can," ventured Doc Cunningham. "It was at Kathy's christening."

"That's right," Margaret agreed. "It was before you moved to the country. You put us all up in Jim's office." She laughed. "There weren't enough beds and our Mary Ann slept on his examining table."

Dave Bagley answered Jim's "Lindsay here."
"Sorry to disturb you, but Crooky's wife has broken her hip."
"How did it happen?"
"I didn't ask her."
"Where is she?"
"In the E.R. at St. Mary's."
"And Crooky?"
"With her, pulling on her leg. He won't let go and asked me to call you."

Jim let out a long breath. It was just like Crooky, leaning backward at the foot of the cot, hands grasped around Celeste's ankle, trying to maintain a steady traction along the length of her leg to make her more comfortable; Crooky knew the various types of hip fractures and Jim sensed Celeste had an intracapsular, notorious for cutting off blood supply to the femoral head. Crooky was doing all in his power to avoid further blood vessel damage. "God bless him," Jim smiled.

"That's why he didn't call you himself," Dave added. "He's sure she'll need a pin."

"Tell him I'll be there soon. Have them type and cross match a couple of pints and alert the O.R."

"How long do you think you'll be?"

"A half hour, plus or minus five."

"Better add on another ten," Dave suggested. "There's a lot of traffic downtown. Centennial celebrations!"

Jim could see the lift bridge over the canal. It was down, and he decided to chance a crossing and reach St. Mary's by the shortest route. He made the bridge, beating a 'Laker' by a quarter of a mile, and swung off the main road onto Canal Street to avoid any congestion. His way was blocked by people watching a fireworks display at the East-side Park and he had to double back to the service road of the main highway. Bagley was right, he thought, as he checked the car clock, pulling into St. Mary's. It had taken a full three quarters of an hour. He slammed the car door and bolted for the Emergency Entrance.

Bagley met him in the hall.

"I guess you'll need an assistant," he said. "I'd like to help. The old boy has done a lot for me in the past; it's a way of partially paying him back."

"Sure, why not! Where is she?"

Dave nodded, indicating for him to follow and they entered the small Recovery Room."

Crooky was doing exactly as Jim had imagined. "Let me relieve you," he said, grasping his colleague by the elbow. "Your arms must be weary."

"No," the little chief coughed. "I'm all right. Though I'd appreciate your sticking an elastoplast on her. She'll need skin traction until you get her to the O.R. Larson's up there waiting for you."

Nurse Pennington had everything ready and it took but a few minutes to apply the tape and hang a weight over the foot of the bed. When he had finished Jim turned to Celeste and asked her to explain.

"There's a damn tree root in front of the house next door. The city should have done something about it. It's raised the side-walk three inches and while walking Digger I tripped over it."

"You didn't faint and fall?" Jim asked.

"Heavens no."

"She's been ill a lot," Crooky imparted. "Neurasthenia, Atwater says. Her haemoglobin's not bad and an electrocardiogram is normal. Any other information you need is in her previous admissions. Her record's at the desk."

The total anaesthetic time had been twenty-eight minutes. Jim had completed the operation, skin to skin, in under a quarter of an hour. Celeste had coughed up the endotracheal tube and was regaining consciousness as she left the O.R. A three stitching on the outside of her upper left thigh was all she had to show.

"The new gadget sure saves time," Larsen remarked.

Jim had to agree. Pinning a hip with the 'C' arm and Image Intensifier made the procedure a lot easier. He was able to secure the two fragments with a pin directed obliquely from the outer aspect of her femur through the neck smack into the centre of the head. He'd seen every move on a TV screen. All the technician had to do was slide the semi-circular arm through its stationary base and the x-ray tube could be positioned anywhere within an angle of ninety degrees. No x-ray films were taken until the operation was completed.

"It takes a lot of skill away from the surgeon," he commented.

"You mean guess work", Bagley grinned.

"Not necessarily," Jim argued. "There were lots of hip pinnings carried out on the Albee-Compare table. The operator was limited to two stationary views but it worked well if the surgeon knew his anatomy and had a well coordinated eye."

"What are her chances?" Bagley asked.

"If you mean a normal hip, they're less than fifty percent."

"Why so low?"

"There are three possible complications: non-union, avascular necrosis and post-traumatic degenerative arthritis. The first is unlikely we've a good reduction and fixation. The second depends on whether the blood supply to the head of her femur was damaged. Crooky, bless him, did everything in his power to minimize any further injury. The last shows up much later and might be due to the second complication or some abuse occurring to the joint surface when her hip was injured." Jim laughed. "This patient, being a doctor's wife, will probably get all three. Anyhow", he added. "We can deal with the problems as they arise. Too bad the fracture occurred inside the joint space. If it had been a bit lower down none of these complications would arise.

"As her chances are only fifty-fifty," Bagley reasoned, "then why didn't you put in a prosthesis right off? Might save her another operation."

"I would've if she were elderly," Jim explained. "But she's only 58 and a healed normal head is far better than any of the metal balls they've come up with. The balls only increase in diameter by an eighth of an inch so it would be unusual to get a perfect fit.

"She's fine Crooky. Out of the anaesthesia and talking a blue streak," Jim smiled.

"Really," Andy's eyes widened, holding the wetness about to overflow. Slowly he shook his head. "How can I ever thank you?"

Jim's smile widened, "You don't have to. You've done the same for me."

Crooky knew it was a fact. It was an honour to be asked to consult on a colleague or a member of a colleague's family. A doctor could have no greater compliment. "About the party," he apologized. "Please convey my regrets to Merri. She's no doubt disappointed about your being called away."

"Sure," said Jim, "but she understands. She asked me to convey her love and sympathy. Besides you're one of her kissing cousins. Tonight is a family affair so why don't you come back to the party with me?"

"Any other time, I'd accept your invitation but not now. I'm sure you appreciate my feelings."

"Certainly. By the way, I've been meaning to talk to you for over a month but our paths haven't crossed. I'd hoped we could get together this week-end but with the folks arriving I haven't had a chance. It's about Best."

"So," Dr. Cruikshank frowned, "what's he done now?"

"Nothing in particular."

"Oh I thought you were going to tell me he'd broken the Golden Rule of Surgery again, give me some more ammunition."

"Sorry Crooky! It's not easy. I don't like him any more than you but I've had trouble trying to decide whether his bungling is justified, particularly regarding personal issues and I've come to believe we must do something positive about him or he'll trouble us forever," Jim paused, "and who needs it?"

It's too bad circumstances gummed up things, the tornado and the euphoria it created," Crooky growled. "But that damn Peer Review Meeting will be held whether or not Paolone and Alligood agree. Even if we have to set up a temporary orthopaedic department."

"Now who's sounding autocratic?" Jim teased.

CHAPTER FORTY-NINE

Dr. Lindsay brooded over the scrub sink.

There was Cohen's writ. George Bartlett had spoken to his young friend, advising him to drop the case. Cohen went a step further and referred the client to Marvin Husselman, a fellow member of the Bar, currently being investigated for embezzling old folk's money. Husselman without hesitation took on the Ireson case and dashed off a copy of Cohen's writ on his own stationery. After receiving two legal notices of the Iresons' complaints Dr. Lindsay called the Canadian Medical Protective Association. The doctor to whom he spoke was sympathetic and non committal but did say the Society would be in touch regarding protocol. A week ago, two months after talking to the CMPA, an appointment was sent via registered mail to see McNutt of Lowenstein and McNutt, a Toronto law firm. Finding the nurses' notes was important; they'd prove Jim's innocence and were the most meaningful part of the child's record.

In addition to his law suit, he was doing a new procedure. The patient was an old man with degenerative arthritis of the hip. Although Jim was confident, having been out of town to observe and assist a few times, the O.R. staff at St. Mary's was not familiar with the operation. To augment his concern it was the day before a national holiday and there would be a lack of concentration among those assigned to help. While he prayed nothing would go wrong Mrs. Burwin burst into the scrub room to say, "Shocker dropped your instruments on the floor. We'll have to re-sterilize the whole lot."

An hour later the operation was under way. Ron Byers had referred the case and was assisting. The patient was positioned on his back with a sand bag under the affected side and Larson administered the anaesthetic. Jim readily opened the hip and placed three reciprocally curved retractors around the socket to improve the exposure.

The Simpson case had altered Ron's thinking and he had no intention of revealing his feelings. He was disenchanted with a close colleague. It was not part of his personality to castigate others but the Simpson case had left him probing Beecher's judgment. When the golfer had asked specifically to be referred to Dr. Lindsay he had complied. Ordinarily he might have tried to persuade the man otherwise. It would not have been difficult. He was on a first name basis with most of his patients.

"He's a nice old guy," said Ron. "I'd often see him Saturday morning at the club. He has a handicap of 15 and scores five points higher than his age. Once I played with him in a tournament; he shot a 32 on the front nine."

"Well," Jim drawled, "I doubt if this procedure will help his golf but it should lessen the pain."

"If you'll excuse my impertinence, Dr. Byers," Larson asked from behind a cordoning sheet, "where's your friend Duggan? He usually gives your anesthetics."

Ron Byers felt his face flush. Larson was opening an old wound, 'G.P. anesthetists should be available afternoons.' The anesthesiologist's beef was with Duggan, not himself. All Ron did was to throw a little business Duggan's way and why not? They were both supporting a clinic faced with bills. It was none of Larson's business. Actually Duggan's behaviour was harder on his partners. His choice to give anesthetics only in the morning and do general practice in the afternoons meant Byers and Clayton had to cover Duggan's morning house calls and the amount of money they made was not worth it. "Huh," Ron grunted, thinking Larson was more likely jealous of Duggan. In limiting himself to anesthetics Larson had restricted his income. G.P. anesthetists could make more by working afternoons in the office. Anyway you cut it, Ron thought, it boiled down to bucks. His answer to Larson was a nondescript fact, revealing nothing of his agitation. "He's at the General."

"He usually is," the anesthesiologist replied. "I suppose this case was to go there but preferred St. Mary's."

"Not so," Jim intervened. "Mr. Hollingshead had no preference at all. It was my suggestion."

"Which means," Larson argued, "if Dr. Byers insisted Mr. Hollingshead be admitted to the General the patient wouldn't have minded either. Seems to me you're running contrary to the rule Ron."

"What rule are you talking about? If you must know," Byers added, "the patient asked me to send him to Dr. Lindsay so I did."

Larson had been up all night and was in an ornery mood. "Best must have been out of town," he pursued continuing to bait the G.P. "Otherwise you'd have sent the patient to him."

Actually there were grounds for Larson's comments. Byers had been sending all his bone cases to Best but so had Clayton and Duggan and their new partner Gloria Knightingale, another family doctor. There were reasons. All of them except Gloria had been in the same class in med school and their clinic was close to the General where Best preferred to work.

"If you guys don't mind," said Jim. "I'd prefer less talk and more heed. Those virulent bugs you've been storing in your upper respiratory tract might land in this wound. The old guy won't take kindly to an infection, especially if he has to sell his clubs. I've removed the capsule," he added. "Now Ron, if you will gently flex the knee and roll it outward we'll dislocate the joint."

There was a slurp like a rubber boot being pulled out of the mud.

"The head is out of the socket," Dr. Lindsay announced. "Hold it right there while I cut the neck. Mrs. Schocker, may I have the saw?"

Jim took the pistol grip, angled the blade in line with the trochanters and squeezed the trigger. The instrument was air powered and a fine mist of blood and bone sprayed from the wound.

"Careful," he said as Byers leaned closer. "You don't want this stuff in your eyes."

A slight twist and the head and neck of the femur came away in Jim's hand. He passed it to Byers commenting, "could be the cause of his pain. The cartilaginous surface has been completely eroded. He's literally been walking on bone."

"Why do you say 'could be the cause of his pain'." Ron asked, adding sarcastically, "It looks awfully painful to me."

"Bone tissue has no pain fibres. Pain must come from the periosteum, the fibrous tissue surrounding it. That's why it hurts like the deuce when you get kicked in the shin."

"The incongruity of the size of the head compared to the socket accounts for the stiffness?" Byers queried.

"Right but some stiffness is due to pain and muscle spasm."

"What do you think caused this mess?"

"There you've got me. Probably a lot of factors: an old injury, growth disturbance in childhood, an earlier inflammatory joint disease. The theorists have a field day. The explanation puzzling me is 'a constitutional predisposition'. Whatever that means."

"Byers snickered. "You might as well ask an astrologist."

"Now the reamer, Schocker," Jim ordered. "We have to widen the marrow cavity to fit the stem."

So far the hip replacement operation was similar to inserting a prothesis, a procedure applicable to broken hips and familiar to

Janet Schocker. She anticipated the surgeon and had the long raspy instrument waiting for him.

When the femoral component had been fitted to his liking Jim fixed a large burr into a brace and began to bore out the socket. When a plastic cup fit snugly he took a half inch bit and began to drill more bone.

"What are you doing?" Byers asked.

"Putting a hole in each of the bones making up the socket to anchor the prosthesis with cement." Turning to Schocker he instructed. "Now you can prepare the acrylic. I want two batches, one for each component. Wait till I ask you to mix the second."

It didn't take long to stir the fluid into the powder and stuff a metallic syringe with the whitish paste-like result. Handing the syringe to Dr. Lindsay, she questioned, "I've filled it, what about the stuff left over?"

Jim sucked in his breath. "You mixed it all?" he shouted. "I distinctly told you I wanted it prepared in two batches."

There was only one thing to do; apply the acrylic as fast as possible. Jim grabbed the syringe from Schocker and stuffed the nozzle into the neck of the femur, remembering to run a narrow polyethylene tube down first, to allow trapped air to escape. Forcing as much cement as the neck could hold, he rammed home the stem of the femoral component and handed the femoral impactor to Dr. Byers.

"Here, press this firmly against the head and hold it snugly until I tell you to let up."

He grabbed the rest of the acrylic from Schocker. It felt reasonably soft but he knew moments later it would be unworkable. Quickly, he fashioned a paddy, while literally running to Schocker's table, where he picked up the acetabular impactor. He kneaded the stiffening paddy into the holes in the bone before placing the impactor in the cup and positioning it in the socket. Leaning his full body weight against the impactor, Jim held his breath.

"Phew!" he blew aloud when the cement had set. "Let's not do that again. I don't know what we'd have done if the cement had hardened before the components were in place. It was the only packet we had."

"The General could have sent us some," Schocker suggested.

"What makes you think the General has any?" Jim asked. "I don't think a Charnley-Mueller hip replacement has ever been done there."

"Bee, er, Dr. Best is doing one this morning," she stuttered.

Mrs. Burwin regarded Janet shrewdly. Every nurse in her department had been thoroughly investigated and Schocker's relationship with Dr. Best had not escaped her. "I suppose you know all about it," she asserted.

"He mentioned earlier this week he had a case. The General also has a new electric drill for reaming out the acetabulum," she added.

"They're dangerous," warned Larson. "One stray spark can set off an explosion. It's happened. I read of a case in the Journal of Anaesthesia. A patient had his lungs blown up."

Jim barked, "Okay folks, back to work. Let's put this old fellow together." Nodding to Dr. Byers he asked, "pull down on the thigh and roll it back to neutral."

With a slight amount of leverage the femoral component slid easily into its counterpart. Satisfied with the stability of the new hip joint and the position of the entire extremity Dr. Lindsay began the closure.

Janet passed the sutures automatically, her mind drifting.

She would have to be more careful. Mrs. Burwin knew something but what? Nobody had seen her with Beecher. They'd been careful for his sake. 'I don't want to hurt anyone,' he'd say. The last time was Sunday on the way home from a week-end in the 'big apple'. It was then she realized Lil headed the list, his milk-toast wife for whom he had respect but little accord and less intercourse, sexual or otherwise. On the way to New York he'd ground out his tale of discontent. Then during their stay he'd become increasingly remorseful, determined to end their relationship, anxious to get home and make amends. On the way back she'd struck him, angrily shouting, 'I'm just your whore. When you've had enough you want to run away, as if I were unclean. To hell with you Beecher Best!'

They hadn't spoken after that and he dropped her at a taxi stand near her house. Then two nights ago they were in her Capri parked behind the barn next to his country property. All he had to do was ask and she was his for as long as he wanted her. She'd listened again to the same old complaint about a negative wife with skin as cold as a marble floor. He didn't want to hurt anyone. What a lot of bull!

Now to complicate matters lily-livered Peter had to show up. Peter unilaterally had decided to give their marriage another try. The last thing she'd wanted but went along, not because she agreed with him but to see what she could get out of the marriage counsellor, an old acquaintance. But the jerk couldn't place her.

'Kids need both a mother and father,' Peter said. 'They have,' she argued. 'You and me, but not us.' He persisted and sounded sincere. Taking him back hadn't worked and never would. Compared to Beecher, Peter was a Nerd, a nobody with nothing, working as a guard at the city jail. The few bucks he'd accumulated would never grow, not under his direction and he didn't trust her to handle them. Sexually he was a flop compared to other men in her life, including Beecher, endowed with less but knew how to use it.

Granted the good Dr. Best was a bit strange in his approach to many things, particularly religion, but livelier and more considerate than her husband. He would listen to her and offer moral support when needed. Lately he had even given her money and he could certainly afford it. The nearness of him turned her on. She had reacted the same way to a number of men, even Peter at first.

Now with her life on an upswing she had agreed to let her estranged mate crawl back. If she didn't look out she'd have another kid on her hands. Hell, what did it matter. Beecher was still married. If he was free she knew he'd marry her. The problem was how to go about setting him free. It would have to be up to his wife. Perhaps, Janet thought, I'll give her a bit of assistance.

CHAPTER FIFTY

Gloria Knightingale was built like an olympic wrestler. Dr. Best asked her to rotate Mrs. Bataglia's knee outward to identify the socket of a congenital dislocation of the hip. When she tackled the patient's leg, nothing happened.

"You'll have to push harder," He demanded.

There was a loud crack and the patient's thigh swung like a gate. Everyone in the O.R. heard it. Chalmers had her back to the scene, giving instructions to Tallmadge on how to open packages of acrylic cement. She spun around, suspicious something had gone wrong.

"What was that?" Gloria asked, knotting her pencilled brow.

No one ventured a reply.

Beecher had been excising fibrous tissue from the outer wall of the pelvis and was still holding the scalpel. He put it down and in the stunning silence moved from the patient's side to the foot of the operating table to test the limb.

"The femoral shaft is broken," he stated categorically. "I'll fix it later."

"Shall I call X-ray?" Chalmers asked.

"That won't be necessary," Beecher winked at her.

The assistant supervisor rolled her eyes and bit her lip. She despised Beecher and his casual attitude. The crack sounded ominous. Any other surgeon would have welcomed her suggestion. The devil with him, she thought, and left the room to seek advice.

At the Nursing Station, Tanya Harrington was on the phone with Dr. Bagley and there was a slight delay before Chalmers got through to Mrs. Burwin at St. Mary's.

"Is Dr. Lindsay there?" she asked.

"I'm not sure. He's probably still dressing. Hold on."

There was a further wait while Burwin spoke into the intercom. "Just a minute," she added, "I'll have you transferred to the surgeons' lounge."

When Chalmers recognized Jim's soft "Hello" she did not know exactly how to word what she wanted to say. She began, "I know you're busy and aren't scheduled in our O.R. this morning but I think you should come and have a look at a case Dr. Best is doing."

There was a pause before Jim replied. He wanted nothing to do with Beecher, not since the Ireson case.

"Are you asking because of a problem or is Dr. Best doing something worth my seeing?"

"I think the patient's in trouble."

"How's that?"

"He's broken her femur accidentally while trying to dislocate the hip."

"I've heard it happens sometimes."

"But he refuses to get an x-ray, says he'll look after it when he's finished doing the replacement."

"What's her diagnosis?"

"Congenital Dislocation of the Hip."

"How old is she?"

"Mid fifties."

"I don't understand!" Jim exclaimed. "I thought you said he was trying to dislocate her hip. Now you tell me her hip is already dislocated."

Betty Chalmers was impatient. She had a feeling Dr. Best didn't know what he was doing and she wanted no part of the case. "Please Dr. Lindsay. I'd feel much better if you come and give your opinion."

"Have you asked Fortier?"

"He's not around."

Jim sighed and reluctantly agreed. "Okay, tell him you've called me and I'll be there in fifteen minutes. Have him take AP and lateral x-rays of the entire femur."

After he hung up and all the way to the General he tried to equate the diagnosis with the procedure. To make a hip socket for a patient without one would be a monumental task. Either he was about to learn something valuable or be a witness to another of Beecher's blunders.

When Betty Chalmers returned to O.R.3., she loosened the outer wrappings of an acetabular reamer and dropped its packaged contents on Tallmadge's instrument table.

Dr. Best was still trying to find a probable fracture of Mrs. Bataglia's upper femur."I've just spoken to Dr. Lindsay," Chalmers informed him. "He'll be here shortly."

"What for?" Beecher sounded indignant.

"I think you need help. His assistance won't hurt. He suggests the patient have an x-ray before he arrives."

"I don't think it'll prove anything I don't already know." Beecher shrugged and stretched for the reamer. "It'll take time and that's not good for the patient."

"I've called for a technician." Chalmers knew she'd overstepped her bounds but the fact had to be known.

Beecher ignored her and jammed the instrument against the outside wall of the pelvis, about where he reckoned a socket should be. When he turned on the motor the reamer caught on the fragmented femur and jumped forward through the iliac crest, shredding a swath of soft tissue. Before he stopped a large nerve had wound around the reamer.

"What's that?" Gloria asked, as he tried to disentangle the rope like remains.

"No problem," he remarked, ignoring Gloria's question. Turning to Tallmadge he demanded, "Hand me some five 0 dexon. I'll suture this."

He was still trying to locate the end of the nerve which had disappeared into the groin when Dr. Lindsay's face appeared over his shoulder.

"What are you looking for?" Jim asked.

"Just a piece of muscle," Beecher lied. He'd placed a retaining stitch in the end of the nerve he'd unwound from the reamer and while Dr. Lindsay was looking on decided to abandon his attempt at repairing it. Perhaps it wouldn't be noticed.

"What muscle's that?"

"The ah, ah," Beecher stammered. "If you must know." - there was no recourse but to blame his predicament on something - "the reamer slipped."

"Yes I see," and to Beecher's chagrin Jim added, "It's cut the femoral nerve as well." Good God, he thought, Best has magnified the poor woman's initial problem with two serious complications. Bewildered he backed off, trying to think of a solution. His maltreatment of the nerve would make walking difficult - if not impossible - and the damage to her ilium would negate reconstructing her hip.

"How much walking did she do?" he asked.

"None." Dr. Knightingale volunteered. "She uses a wheel chair. The purpose of this operation is to get her on her feet."

"Was she having any pain?"

"She never complained to me."

"Well she did to me," Beecher lied. "That's the main reason I decided to operate."

"Personally I can't see the point in doing anything else," Jim stated. "You've converted her from a wheelchair to a bedridden invalid, at least until her fractured femur heals. Now it's a matter of survival and she'll stand a better chance if you close her up and put her leg in traction." Jim shook his head. There really was nothing else he could suggest. Caustically, he appended his remarks, "I'm sure she'll be grateful for all you've done Beecher."

CHAPTER FIFTY-ONE

On Thursday evening, July 13th, ten doctors affiliated with the surgical departments of Shipton's two major hospitals were in camera with Dr. Best, locked in the Sisters' dining room at St. Mary's. Eight others were either on vacation or excused from the meeting. Family physicians had begged off as they felt because of the technological nature of the review they were not qualified to give an opinion. Finny was down with the flu and the Gynecologists, Ophthalmolgists and Ear Nose and Throat specialists had their own departments and didn't want to attend.

The investigation had been unofficially called by Dr. Cruikshank, acting as chairman. He was flanked by Drs. Lindsay and Alligood. Beecher sat at the far end of the table behind a pile of charts. The remainder were scattered, leaving Beecher plenty of room.

"Now, is it correct you were advised by Drs. Paolone and Alligood to get more consultations on your operative cases?" Andy stated.

Best blinked and when he did not immediately answer Paolone spoke. "To jog your memory Beecher, Alligood and I talked to you the morning of grand rounds about ten days after the tornado." Joe paused and looked at the ceiling. "Saturday, June 3rd, I believe."

"I don't recall anything about consultations." Beecher ran both hands through his dark curly hair and leaned his chair backwards. "I can't remember anything specific about the conversation."

"We were sitting in the snack bar at the General," Joe prodded.

"Sure I remember the incident," Beecher smiled. "I still remember a few of your jokes."

"Wait a minute," John Alligood interrupted and addressed the head of the table. "Mr. Chairman I have notes I made before and after the meeting." Alligood did not submit any reasons as to why he kept a record. He had found the task embarrassing and had not wanted to discuss Beecher's shortcomings at all, let alone face to face. Consequently he had been meticulously careful in wording what he, as chief of surgery at St. Mary's, was obliged to say. Opening a file he began to read. "10.30, Saturday morning, June 3rd. At the request of Dr. Cruikshank, spokesman for the orthopaedic surgeons, I've been asked to advise that your work is under question and the general feeling is you should seek opinions on your major surgical cases and have assistance in the operating room."

"Is that exactly what you said to him?" Andy asked.

"Yes."

"And what was his reaction?"

"He made no comment. He was too busy listening to Paolone congratulate him on the marvellous job he'd done in the E. R. during the tornado. I sent him a signed copy of the statement by registered mail. Someone at his office signed for it, so I assume he got it."

Alligood passed a copy of his letter and the registered receipt to the chairman who looked pleased at this unexpected disclosure. "Now that's cleared up," said Andy. "I'd like Dr. Best to tell us about the Bataglia case."

Beecher turned pale.

"Please Dr. Best," Dr. Cruikshank insisted. "Why did you do a total hip replacement on this 58 year old woman?"

Beecher shuffled through his files.

"If you can't find her chart," Crooky suggested, "You can use my copy. I've made copies for everyone," he added, and gave them to Jim to pass around.

"What was it you wanted to know?" Beecher asked, "She's still in hospital."

"Your indications."

"She had severe pain in both hips and has been confined to a wheelchair for the past two years."

"The nurses' notes show and I quote. 'On July 4th,1967, at 14.30 hours Mrs. Bataglia entered the ward on a stretcher, scheduled for a total hip replacement July 5th,1967. Claims she has been confined to a wheel chair for several years. Pain medication refused. Patient states she didn't need any. Drs. Knightingale and Best notified.' "Seems to me", Andy paused, glancing around the long table, "The nurse who wrote this - I can't make out her signature - had different information."

"Well Gina told me otherwise," Beecher disagreed.

"Gina?"

"Mrs. Bataglia."

"I guess you're the only one who knew about the pain then," Andy pursued. "Dr. Knightingale, in her brief history of the patient, doesn't mention it."

Dr. Best chose not to comment. Andy adjusted his glasses and went on. "Okay, we see at the end of your admission note her diagnosis was 'bilateral congenital dislocation of the hip'". Sliding his spectacles to the tip of his nose he glared at Beecher and asked, "Could we look at her x-rays?"

"I don't have them with me."

"Why not?"

"There's no point. You've already seen them."

"That's true." Andy stuck out his petulant lower lip. "In the letter you must have received, otherwise you wouldn't be here, you were asked specifically to bring along all of the x-rays taken of the patients we wished to discuss. I believe there were 13 on the list."

"I've brought most of them," Beecher sounded annoyed.

"And I've got Mrs. Bataglia's," commented Andy, looking rather satisfied. "They go back to when she was a child. She was born in the General and has been seen by almost every specialist in Toronto." He placed the films on a view box, conveniently sitting on the server behind him. "As you all can see the patient has rudimentary sockets and the heads of her femurs are small and riding high above where her sockets normally are." He turned to re-address Beecher.

"Why did you want to do a total hip replacement in lieu of another procedure?"

"There wasn't any other choice."

"What about an osteotomy, or a simple resection of the femoral head, or a fusion of the joint? Aren't these operations for pain?" Andy asked. "Indeed you did record she had pain. Why not choose one of them instead of a THR? The simplest thing to do would've been to resect the head of her femur. Girdlestone used to do the operation for TB of the hip."

"It wouldn't have given her stability," Beecher argued.

"So you wanted to play God and build her a socket so she could walk again. If it didn't work you'd take her or her relatives to the Chapel and pray for her salvation, like the Bennett case. We'll get around to that one later."

Crooky needn't have made the remark. It was personal and slanted. The chief's animosity was bubbling like a hot spring. In the charged atmosphere, Jim coughed and bent forward, diverting attention from the chairman's growing agitation. "Tell me Dr. Best," he asked. "How did you go about building the socket?"

"By reaming the pelvis."

"But the wall of the pelvis wasn't thick enough, was it? Judging from these x-rays it appears your reamer went through the ilium. Is that how you caught the femoral nerve?"

"The reamer jumped."

"And how did you fracture the femur?"

"I didn't."

"Then how did it happen?"

"It was Dr. Knightingale. She twisted the leg too far."

"But wasn't she under your instructions?"

There was no reply from Dr. Best and Jim turned to the x-rays again, observing the patient's bone looked considerably washed out in keeping with prolonged inactivity. "She has a lot of osteoporosis," he remarked. "Her femur wouldn't have taken much force to break." Returning to her record, he asked. "How many times has she been back to the O.R. since your first operation?"

"Once."

"But I notice she's had four anaesthetics during this admission. Could you please explain?"

"After the first operation the replacement dislocated twice which I reduced by manipulation in the E.R. The fourth was a re-exploration."

"A re-exploration," Jim echoed. "What did you discover? I can't find a copy of your notes."

"It was done yesterday. The dictation's still in medical records." Beecher looked annoyed.

"So what did you discover?" Jim reiterated.

"The acetabular component was loose. In fact it had moved out of place."

"Yes," Jim agreed. "From the looks of these films taken, let's see - he held a large x-ray to the overhead light - taken on the 11th, your cup had moved inside her pelvis."

"Let me have a look at the damn thing," Dr. Shorter demanded. "Christ it could be in her bladder."

"Well it wasn't," Beecher smiled. "Anyway I've removed it."

"Without it," Gord chuckled, peering at the x-ray, "there's no need for the femoral component either, other than an intramedullary fixator to treat her fracture."

Ramamurti, full of curiosity, took the film from the urologist. He could see the break quite clearly in the upper third of the femoral shaft. Its spiral outline crossed the stem of the prosthesis. "But it's not fixing the fracture securely," he observed. "Already a slight angulation has occurred."

"Good grief!" Andy burst out, as though Mehendra's observation was of great significance and the former chief had just realized it. "Bloody awful in fact! You've put this woman through misery and left her with a broken thigh, an extremely large hole in her pelvis and a paralyzed knee. My God man, how can you justify what you've done? It's outrageous! How would you like to be in her shoes?"

Gord Shorter grinned. "A rather irrelevant question," he said, "in view of her not having the need."

"Need for what?" Eldridge asked.

"Shoes." Gord shook his St. Bernard jowls. Barnofsky had turned to Dave Bagley and whispered. "From the size of the fucking hole Beecher drilled Gina will have no trouble making a little money on the side." The two of them were sniggering into their hands when Fortier asked, "What's so funny?" and leaned across the table to hear for himself.

"Call this meeting to order, Mr. Chairman," Dr. Paolone shouted. "Come on guys, simmer down. Mr. Chairman, please," Joe hollered. "There are thirteen cases and it's taken half an hour to get through the first. We'll be here all night."

It was past mid-night when Beecher got home. Lil was relieved to see him. The phone had rung three times and each time she had heard heavy breathing. The caller, whoever it was, hung up without saying a word.

"Boy am I glad you're home," she said. "I'm scared stiff."

"Oh," he replied carelessly. "How do you think I feel? I've been through a medieval inquisition; the only thing missing was the rack."

Lillian wasn't sure how Beecher felt. He showed a steady indifference toward her until she did something to annoy him. Then he'd shout at her. She put aside her own fears and tried to humour him. "How did it go?" she asked.

"It's a conspiracy. Cruikshank and Lindsay are out to get me."

"It can't be true Beech. I'm sure they're trying to help. They're older and more experienced. Listen to them."

"You weren't at the meeting."

"What happened?"

"They had thirteen cases lined up, going back over three and a half years." He took off his shoes and lay down beside her outside the covers fully clothed.

"Aren't you coming to bed?"

"I'm too worked up."

"Tell me about them?" she asked. If Beecher had problems regarding patients, surely they'd be minor. How could they be anything else.

"The first criticism came from Lindsay. He said I was too aggressive. In '64 I had a patient with calcification of the heel cord. I excised the deposit and three weeks later the heel cord ruptured. He said I'd shown poor judgement and had made a weakened tendon worse. I should have treated the patient with a heel lift. If that didn't work, to lengthen the tendon, an easier operation than the reconstruction I was forced to do later when the tendon ruptured on its own."

"That sounds like inexperience. I'm sure you'd handle it differently now."

"There wasn't anything wrong with the way I handled it then," Beecher snapped. "Can I be blamed for the guy refusing to give up tennis? He did it by lunging for a ball. Lindsay's method sounds more aggressive than mine."

"He also disagreed with my plating and grafting a broken tibia. I tried to prevent the patient from getting a non union. Then he really raked me over the coals on three back operations, even when I said I wasn't doing any more. On Ramamurti's advice I send my back cases out of town."

"Is that what Mehendra told you? To send your patients out of town?"

"Not exactly. He told me I was under surveillance and I'd be wise to get a consultation on back operations and have someone experienced in spine surgery assist me. Selfish advice - I've heard he's not busy and needs extra work. I haven't done any since because the neurosurgeon in Toronto never sends them back. I've scrubbed with him a few times and learned a better technique."

"So what's wrong with that?"

"Dammit Lil, the whole scene was " - The phone began to ring and Beecher stopped in mid sentence.

Lillian sat bolt upright. "If that's another harassing call I'm going to the police."

Beecher answered it.

The voice on the other end was Janet's and she whispered.

"I'm sorry I can't hear you. Speak up?"

"No," he barely heard her say, "I don't want to wake Peter. How about meeting me in fifteen minutes?"

There was a pause while Beecher calculated the odds Lillian could hear. He rolled into a sitting position and said, "Car accident two patients at the General. Okay, tell them I'll be there soon." Schocker had clicked off before he added, "Thank you."

"Who was that? Lil asked.

"The answering service."

"Thank goodness it wasn't my mysterious mute." Lillian fell back on the pillow.

"What about these phone calls?" Beecher asked.

"I've been getting them for two weeks. At first I thought it was one of the boys' friends, too shy to ask for them. Our cleaning lady has also answered the calls."

"Why notify the police? How can they catch the person?"

"Tap the line," Lil suggested.

"How's that going to help?" He argued. "They'd have to trace the incoming call and do it before the person hung up. We'd need two lines."

Beecher found his shoes and as he was re-tying them, continued to tell of the meeting.

"Cruikshank's the one I must look out for. He's got a file an inch thick - keeps a record of everything I do."

"Why?"

"Ever since I pinned the wrong hi - " The word 'Hip' was on the tip of his tongue until he remembered Lillian had been given a distorted version.

"You didn't tell me about it."

"What?"

"Pinning the wrong hip. That's what you were going to say wasn't it? You said Clayton had done it, you were assisting."

"I didn't say that Lil."

"You did. You were about to say Dr. Cruikshank is blaming you for it."

Beecher went on evasively. "It was unjust. The case was a combination of errors. No one person was at fault. But the old busy body holds me responsible."

"So you did pin the wrong hip!" Lillian felt nauseated and tried to shake it off. "Beecher," she groaned, "how could you do such a thing and then deliberately deceive me?"

"No harm was done. The patient is perfectly fine. She had both hips done for the price of one." His ensuing smile disappeared as he read the disgust on his wife's face.

"Think of the unnecessary pain you caused, for goodness sake. Didn't it bother you?"

"I went to the chapel with her daughter every morning for a week."

"You didn't answer my question," she called after him as he left for the bathroom.

When he returned she was still sitting up in bed, looking even more morose, taut with the act of catching him in a lie. "Honestly Beecher." Her normally shrill voice had reached its zenith. "When are you going to grow up? People aren't out to get you. The meeting was called for your benefit. What else did they have to say?"

"I'm not any more accountable to you than to them."

Lillian's disappointment turned to shock. "Beecher, be more humble," she whimpered. "You're putting yourself above everyone."

"Except God. He's the only one I atone to."

"He also says you must love your neighbour as yourself." Tears were gathering in Lillian's eyes and she fiddled for a tissue. Before she could find one they began to stream.

"That damn Lindsay, if you must know everything, has a law suit on his hands because he interfered with the treatment of one of my patients, the Ireson boy. Talk about self righteousness, he's the epitome, implying my error caused Volkmann's ischemic contracture."

The only word in Beecher's outburst Lil heard was 'Ireson' and as the name sunk in she remembered coming across it before. Yes, it was the name of the patient on the nurses' record she had photocopied. "Ireson," she mumbled. The notes had indicated Beecher was not available when he should have been.

"Where were you when they tried all night to get you?"

"What are you talking about?"

"You know."

"I haven't a clue," he shouted.

"Yes you do. Think about it."

"For God's sake Lil, I can't stand here playing guessing games with you I've got work to do."

Lillian looked up through her swollen eyes. She'd gone one step too far. It was a secret she'd withheld from him and she could be accused of being as close-mouthed as he was. "You go now," she muttered. "Somebody out there needs you more."

Puzzled he whirled away, slamming the bedroom door, and seconds later she heard the car rumble out of the garage. She switched off the light but was unable to sleep, tossing and turning with her thoughts.

The confrontation with Beecher replayed and frightened her. She felt the first stone in her foundation had been loosened and it was a matter of time until her whole world crumbled.

Then the phone rang. She was reluctant to answer. The last thing she needed was another crank call. It was the answering service again, asking if her husband had left for the General. Odd she thought, it was a strange voice. They must have hired a new girl.

CHAPTER FIFTY-TWO

On the way to the rendezvous Beecher's ego began to shrivel. Feeling insecure and remorseful he struck the side of his head with an open hand as if the blow would re-set his troubled mind. No matter how clearly he argued his cases not one of the surgeons openly supported him and he had left the meeting apprehensive of his future. Then Lil had broken into her customary tears when he revealed how one of his cases had two operations to fix a broken hip. He casually passed it off and she became reproachful. And what was all that drivel concerning where he was the night the paediatric ward was trying to locate him?

Her concern struck him like a precordial pain. "Oh my God," he shuddered, "The Ireson case!" She must have gone through my jacket. That was it; it had to be the only way she could have found out.

But why the silence? She'd held back for some reason. He had to find out and impulsively slammed on the brakes, looking for a place to turn around. If she'd found out about Schocker it could mean the end of his relationship with both and he was reluctant to give up either. He could hear Lillian's ultimatum years ago, after finding out about a fling he had in med school. "Chose Beecher, it's me or her." He'd not really cared for the girl. Janet was different, exactly opposite. There was nothing melancholy about her. When he was up she raised him higher and when he was down her wantonness rekindled his spirit.

After making a U turn there was an alarming hiss and the Toyota slackened and swerved to the curb. More frustrated than ever he cursed, "God dammit, what next!"

It had been the right front tire and while changing it he decided to keep the assignation. Shocker should be told of his present feelings. At least he'd make sure she got home okay.

Janet was sitting behind the wheel of her Capri, backed in beside the barn, out of range of passing headlights but with a view of any car approaching from town. She had thrown a blanket over a bed of straw in one of the abandoned stalls.

Beecher drove over the dirt track and stopped abreast of her driver's side. Before he turned off the Toyota's lights she greeted him with a delightful smile.

"Well, big boy," she said provocatively, "What kept you so long?"

"I had a flat."

"Come on Beech, don't hand me that." She was still smiling. "What's her name?"

He regarded her blankly through their open windows and sighed. "We have to go."

"Why?"

"Because I've a lot on my mind."

Janet got out of her car and poked her head into his. "Come see the little nest I've made and tell me all about it?"

"I'm afraid you'll have to take a rain check."

"Why?"

He evaded her eyes. "I told you."

"Look at me Beech," she demanded, grasping his chin in an effort to turn his face. "So!" she said and ran her fingers through the front of his shirt. "Come on Beechie, fifteen minutes, that's all I ask."

"Nope."

"Hang on," she implored and withdrew, groping around the Toyota to end up in the passenger seat beside him. In the pale light of the stars her eyes sparkled and she began to tug at his zipper."

"I said no, not tonight Janet."

Beecher forcefully removed her hand and she looked at him in disbelief. "Why the hell did you come?" she cried. "Why are you treating me this way. It's your damn wife, isn't it. You've gone soft on her again?"

He could feel the fine spray of her spittle on his cheek and eased away. Her wild look was no longer a cute annoyance and he contemplated tossing her out before she attacked him. "Please, he said. "I only came by to make sure you got home all right."

Janet didn't wait for him to finish; she flew out of the car and into her own. "Screw you, Dr. Best," she hissed, turning the key.

The engine started immediately, the rear wheels churned the dust and she raced for the main road.

Beecher did not waste any time and reversed along the farm lane with the accelerator flush on the floor. Gauging from its receding tail-lights he reckoned the Capri was doing well over his seventy and he let it go. Going by her house he saw her car parked in the driveway.

It had been a demoralizing night. His reputation had blown. Even Paolone avoided him after the meeting. Paolone whom he'd thought was one of his promoters had listened quietly to each presentation till the very end and suggested, "everyone should sleep on the matter and reserve their opinions for the next scheduled meeting where they can be aired and a unified decision reached. Recommendations will be made to the interested parties." Joe felt it was best for all if Beecher were not there. No one objected.

Then there was Lillian's repressed knowledge of the Ireson case. How much she knew was a mystery. Perhaps there would be a chance to talk to her on the week end. For the moment he did not have the courage, nor did he know how to introduce the subject.

And Janet! Why did he bother with her? "God in Heaven. What am I going to do?" he shouted. He had got himself into this mess and if he were God he'd fucking well suggest he get himself out. He slapped the steering wheel, and a second and third time with his clenched fist. The more he thought about his predicament the more distraught he became.

Lillian was feigning sleep when Beecher crawled into bed. The phone rang and she sat up with a start. Beecher answered it. "You bastard," he heard Janet say and hung up.

"Who was it?" Lillian asked.

"Another crank call I guess. I'm leaving the line open."

"That settles it. First thing tomorrow morning I'm going to the police."

He moved over and cradled her face on his shoulder.

"Why don't we take off this week-end," he whispered. "Just us. Mum will look after the kids."

"We can't."

"Why not?"

"We have to take Robby to camp Saturday. Sunday's your mother's birthday and I've invited her for dinner."

Beecher sighed and turned on his face.

"Don't I get a kiss?"

"Sure," he said raising his head to give her a peck.

Sunday was beautiful, one of those summer intervals following a rain when a stationary high favoured the land with fresh clear air. Looking out from the limestone ridge, Beecher and Janet felt on top of the world. They had met on a country road, overgrown with bushes, grass and weeds and found a path, leading to the escarpment trail. Beeches, ash and oak tangled in greenery overhead. It was cool and profoundly silent.

They stood quietly admiring the tailored landscape spread below - as far as they could see - until Janet shivered. She was wearing a knee length pale green dress with an elasticised bodice around her firm round bust.

"I'm cold Beechie boy," she complained. "Do something about it."

"Let's get back in the sun."

"Not yet. I haven't finished with this gorgeous view. Pointing to the right she said, "It's so clear you can see the mist over the Falls."

Beecher was standing behind her and pulled her against him, cupping her breasts in his hands. She could feel him rising and deliberately pressed backwards. Her arm dropped and he could feel her fingers close on the front of his khaki shorts.

"That's like the old peachy Beechy," she purred and twisted to kiss him, full mouthed, her little tongue flicking like a snake's.

"Come on, let's go down below," he said breaking away. "It's warmer there."

"Things are getting warmer right here," she smirked.

"Where shall we do it? On the moss covered rock or up against one of those trees. Take your pick. There are several varieties. Maple? Oak? Ash?" How about it?" he queried. "Or would you prefer Fir?"

Janet laughed nervously. "Let's try one of those meadows with the tall cool grass."

"Anything you say," he replied and followed as she skipped over the crevices and tree roots until the trail swerved down a cut in the limestone face. He went first to help her. At the bottom the land fell away less steeply and he let go of her hand. The sight of her hoisting her skirt to her hips set him off. She was bare underneath.

"What would you do if you were in an accident?" he asked, "And you were examined in the E.R. with no underpants?"

"Throw my legs around the doctor," she laughed.

Beecher shook his head and led on. Their course bordered the stony bottom of a brook and angled to avoid a waterfall reduced to a summer trickle. The damp earth exhaled a cool sweetness and now and again the trees opened up and they saw blue sky and heard birds, crying excitedly, disturbed by their presence. As they reached the meadow a squirrel ran out of the high grass and darted for a stand of evergreens. Beneath a magnificent pine were clumps of wild flowers: yellow, blue and white, in patches of sunlight.

"I can't make it to the grass, Beech. I'm wetter than a dugong. You're going to have to take me right here."

With the last drop of lust spent Janet and Beecher lay on their backs on their fir needle bed, gazing up through tangled boughs at a speckled sun.

Janet rolled on her side, bracing her head with an arm and lazily began to rub her thigh across Beecher's.

"Where did you get such an unusual name?" she asked.

"It was my mother's," he replied, still facing the treetops. "Jessica Ann Beecher. Which reminds me - I left the house to pick her up. If I don't get back soon Lil's going to start phoning around. Come on, we've got to go," he urged, jumping to his feet.

"Ah shit," Janet exploded. "Why does it always have to be like this? We have a good time and then you have to run off to your wife."

"What about you? Peter must wonder where you've gone."

"Peter! That nitwit! "He took the kids to his parents after lunch. Tell me," she added, pulling herself up in front of him. "Would you have married me if I'd got to you first?"

Beecher stretched his arms skyward and arched his back to relieve the stiffness. "Sure," he grinned, "You're the greatest."

"I wish you had."

Janet was thinking of the country house Beecher was building when he suddenly took her by the hand and started back along the trail. As they walked he talked as he habitually did and reviewed the main arguments presented during his meeting with the surgeons.

"Cruikshank started it all," he said. He's been out to get me since I operated on Agnes Bennet over three years ago."

Janet knew the case well. She'd scrubbed for it "But it wasn't your fault, pinning the wrong hip," she said comfortingly. "How can you be blamed for the technician mixing up the x-rays?"

"That's not the point Janet. I'd have pinned both of her hips anyway. She had so much osteoporosis the other hip was going to break sooner or later."

Unbelievable, she thought, after examining the expression in his eyes. He has rationalized this error so many times he actually believes it himself. She said nothing but shrugged and plodded silently beside him, listening to his excuses for the other blunders.

Back at their cars before parting Beecher was smiling as if nothing mattered.

"I can't see how any of them can cast stones," he said. "They've all made mistakes."

"You haven't made any mistakes, Beech. It's bad luck. Things will get better."

Janet sounded warm and agreeable. But as she drove away she decided maybe she was better off not married to him. Someday he might do something horrific, affecting everyone close to him. But it would be great in the meantime to take in some of his cash.

At the monthly surgical meeting Gord Shorter spluttered, "After wasting another four hours of my time on this son-of-a-bitch Best I'm for canning him." The urologist was bored with the whole business. First there was the Peer Review lasting past midnight and now they had rehashed Beecher's behaviour again, case by case, without getting into any other business. There had been a few items he had intended to bring up.

"It's not that easy," said Joe. "When it comes up before the Board of Governors at the General they'll want well documented evidence Beecher has been given an equitable chance."

Secretary of the Surgical Department, Phil Barnofsky, was tired. He'd been taking notes all evening. When Joe had finished, Phil caught the eye of Lloyd Alligood and waved a potential final draft.

"Go ahead," Lloyd nodded.

Barnofsky exhaled and smiled, "Thank you Mr. Chairman. So we're all in agreement." Phil considered his statement a fact and did not pause to confirm. "To summarize, we recommend" - he began to read aloud the motion collectively worded by the other members - "1. Dr. Best is not allowed to do back surgery, involving the decompression of nerve roots but is encouraged to assist and take further training in such surgery. 2. He takes no case to the operating room without an orthopaedic consultation in writing prior to booking the said case. Emergencies are not excluded. 3. He will comply with these rules for one year. 4. At the end of each three month period the orthopaedic surgeons will meet with the chiefs of Surgery of both hospitals to discuss any problems arising in these matters."

Paolone looked about the board room. "This is basically my motion and my name will go on record. Perhaps someone other than a chief and chairman should move it." He paused before demanding, "The result must be unanimous."

Crooky started to laugh. "What are you afraid of Joe? If you want a seconder I'll back you up."

"Just a minute," Dr. Lindsay spoke up. "Personally, I'm not in favour of points 2. and 4. Why should I get out of bed and trundle down to the E.R. to cover this idiot for the rest of you and then report back like a school teacher to the principal. Give us a separate orthopaedic department and we'll deal with Dr. Best as we see fit."

Breaking the ensuing silence Marcel Fortier suggested, "I'd like to move the department of surgery recommend through the MAC, the Governing Boards of both hospitals establish autonomous Orthopaedic Departments.

"They can't do that Mr. Chairman," Barnofsky interrupted. "There's already a motion."

"Then scrap it and deal with Dr. Fortier's," Jim insisted.

"Why should you have a separate department," Joe asked. "There's only three of you."

"Four," Jim corrected. "We'll make Crooky our first chairman."

"He's no orthopod," Paolone argued.

"He may not be certified but his war experience and common sense account for a lot more."

Crooky's normally striking colour turned to beet red and he put aside the panatella he'd been smoking. "After such a fine compliment," he coughed. "I'd be most honoured and pleased to accept."

"Huh! said Joe. "You're fragmenting the department."

"Don't be ridiculous," Jim reasoned. "At the moment you have one vote on the MAC for sixteen members. There's no way we as orthopaedic surgeons can isolate ourselves from any of the rest of you. We'll still be affiliated. So when it comes to the surgeons versus the other departments represented on the MAC you'll have two votes in place of one." Jim smiled. "It might be good to split off all the other surgical sub-specialties."

Paolone looked disgruntled with this last suggestion. He enjoyed being the god-father and the more soldiers he had under him the better. "I'm against Fortier's motion," he grumbled.

"Anyone else have anything to say?" Alligood asked.

When no one spoke he turned to Barnofsky. "Please read out the motion again."

"Which one?" Phil asked. He was the only plastic surgeon in the area and Dr. Lindsay's scenario of complete subdivision of the department appealed to him. Why not? There was only one ear specialist and he was on his own. The idea of taking his concerns directly to the Medical Advisory Committee would be much more expedient than passing a request through Paolone or Alligood. "The first or the second?" he added. "As I see it there's no point in voting on the first until Fortier's is out of the way."

"Okay, okay," Joe growled, "We vote on number two. Let's have it. All in favour?"

The result was not unanimous but firm enough, Joe's protest vote did not matter and he kept his hand down. "So," he scowled, "Lindsay's crew can look after Dr. Best. If it's any use to you our first motion can go as a recommendation as to how you go about it."

CHAPTER FIFTY-THREE

The morning after the Department of Surgery meeting Beecher was called from the shower to answer the phone. It was Joe Paolone and he insisted he did not have time to wait. The recently elected Chairman of the MAC was atypically succinct.

"We expect you at 1.30 pm. in the Board room at the General and don't be late."

"Who's we?"

"Dr. Alligood and myself."

"Can't you make it later. I have a dental appointment."

There was a pause while Joe mentally debated whether it was worth missing his Friday afternoon tennis. He decided, "No. It won't take long. Delay your appointment." Before another word was uttered the line went dead.

"What was that all about?" Lillian asked.

Dismissing her question Beecher went back to his toilet.

Lloyd Alligood seated at the Board Room table reading a journal noted Best arrived fifteen minutes earlier than expected. "Joe's on his way," he remarked, rising to his penitent height and with a furtive glance while replacing the magazine in a rack by the door, added, "If you'll pardon me I've a few things to do."

Dr. Paolone's route must have led him halfway across the Province, Beecher surmised cynically as the diminutive Chief of Surgery barged in well after the scheduled time.

Offering nary an excuse nor an apology, Joe snapped, "Where's Alligood?"

Beecher picked up the house phone. Before he could dial, the doctor in question materialized as if he had walked through the wall.

Joe settled into the padded armchair at the head of the table. "Okay," he said, indicating the other two should sit. "We're here not to discuss what went on at the surgical meeting but the outcome." Addressing Beecher, seated on his left he continued in a matter of fact tone. "There was a motion consisting of four points two of which were duly seconded and passed. You're prohibited from operating on any more backs but you can assist in this type of surgery and are encouraged to upgrade yourself along these lines. The other point is these restrictions are to be obeyed for one year."

"You mean on any part of the back?" Beecher asked.

"I don't understand?" Joe growled.

"What about superficial lesions, lipomas, cysts?"

"I think it's only fair to tell you," Dr. Alligood stated, "The other two parts of the motion will affect you more severely."

Paolone looked annoyed. "That's got nothing to do with us Lloyd," he groused. "If the orthopods have anything to say to Best they can speak for themselves."

"How's that?" Beecher protested.

"They're forming their own department. I figure as a certified specialist in orthopaedics you'll no doubt be included. Give him a copy of our motion Lloyd."

Standing abruptly and banging his chair into the panelled wall, Joe declared. "Now that everything is clear I must run along."

Office bound, Beecher mulled over the last fifteen minutes. He would never have been able to keep his two o'clock dental appointment and realized he had done the best thing in cancelling. Paolone sure had audacity, keeping him and Alligood waiting so long. Had the shoe been on the other foot the bastard would have screamed bloody murder. After the little 'wop' had left Alligood had not been long in following, though much less ostentatiously. Lloyd had simply evaded any further questions, advised him to get in touch with Dr. Cruikshank who would likely head up the new department and slipped away, leaving him confused and apprehensive. The thought of dealing directly with Cruikshank tendered little hope. Beecher shook his head. The bonds would tighten. It was becoming more obvious everyone was lining up against him. Even Fortier and the soft spoken Ramamurti with his helpful approach had been harsh in their criticism, as if they would be happy to be rid of him. The best thing to do, he concluded, was to get in touch with Robb. Perhaps the Toronto surgeon had a solution.

Lil was rooted under the chestnut tree in the backyard reading 'Black Beauty' to the boys and did not budge as the Toyota drove in. While his father was getting out of the car Michael ran to him and tackled a leg.

"I want a horse," the child demanded.

Beecher picked up his youngest and threw him in the air. "You shall have one," he said, catching Michael by the waist. "After we move to the country."

"When?" the boy pouted.

"Pretty soon."

Tousling the youngster's damp curly hair Beecher directed, "Go get the ball and we'll play catch." He ignored his wife who had hesitantly joined him, leaving Robby in the wheel chair to read on his own.

"Beecher, I must talk to you."

He frowned at her worried expression and answered gruffly, "Can't it wait?"

"No."

"Lil, we've got the rest of the afternoon. Let me toss the ball with Mike awhile. We can talk later."

He walked over to a rose bush and began examining for aphids.

She followed. "I've just had a call," she remarked. What she had to tell him was a delicate matter, extremely upsetting, and she did not know how he was going to react.

Squatting and directing his, "Not another," at a blighted leaf he sounded unconcerned and inaccessible. "I thought you were going to the police."

"It wasn't one of those." Lil paused to take a deep breath. Her voice quavered as she continued. "It was from a nurse at St. Mary's."

"Who?"

"She didn't say."

Lil tried to keep from weeping but failed.

Beecher looked up sharply.

Her face was now running with tears. "Let's go inside," she sobbed. "I don't want the children to hear any part of this."

"It can't be that bad," he sneered.

"You were out with Mrs. Schocker on Sunday, weren't you?"

"Who told you that nonsense?"

Michael had reappeared and was holding a soft ball and two gloves. Curious, he approached his mother who turned away, covering her face with her hands. Then, thinking no more of her, tried his dad. "I'm ready," he said.

"Our game will have to wait, Michael. Go play with Robby."

"But he can't catch."

"Sure he can as long as you throw the ball right at him."

"Ah nuts!" the boy exclaimed and wandered to the side of the house where he began to bounce the ball off the neighbour's wooden fence.

Reaching to touch his wife, Beecher's hand was trembling as much as her body. Finally he placed it on the back of her shoulder.

"Look! It's not so," he lied. "Someone's trying to cause trouble."

"Who and why?" Lil cried, still unable to face him. "Why should anyone want to be so cruel? Even if it's the truth."

Her husband's vagueness told her nothing.

"Possibly the same person is making the other calls," he proposed. "What exactly did she say?"

"I'm not sure now." Lil removed tissue, shrivelled with use, from inside her dress. Carefully she unravelled it and began to wipe her face and eyes. "The person said I hadn't met her, the wife was always the last to know and she had seen you on the escarpment trail with Mrs. Schocker Sunday afternoon."

She paused, awaiting his denial and when it didn't come asked, "Tell me Beecher, who is Mrs. Schocker?"

"Just a nurse who works in the operating room."

"What is she to you?"

"Nothing," he replied.

The offices of Lowenstein and McNutt occupied the twenty second floor of a skyscraper in downtown Toronto. Finding the building was easy. Seen from across the lake it stood out like a wart on a witch's nose.

Finding a place to park was another matter. After a few unsuccessful turns, thwarted by one way streets leading in the wrong direction, Jim miraculously discovered the entrance to an underground garage.

The receptionist was an attractive woman. Streamlined by a grey pin-striped suit she charmed him through a maze of corridors lined with dark wood panels into a second waiting area and introduced him to the lawyers' private secretary, to Jim's surprise a male.

"Have a seat Dr. Lindsay." He smiled from behind a noisy Underwood. "Mr. McNutt is expecting you. He'll be with you in a moment."

The man was right. A door leading into a hive of cubicles soon opened and a tall slim young man with fair hair, prematurely thin on top, asked. "Dr. Lindsay?"

"Yes," Jim replied, wondering who else the man thought he was.

"I'm Jamie McNutt nice to meet you," he oozed confidently. His fingers were long and sinewy like a pianist's, his smile pretentious. "Would you step into my office?" He asked, grasping Jim's hand.

The space was half the size of Dr. Lindsay's consultation room but its vacantness and the corner windows made it appear bigger.

McNutt directed his client to a straight back chair, facing the only impressive piece of furniture in the room, a hand carved Jacobean desk. Placed diagonally across the floor he squeezed behind it and hummed, "well now," lifted a folder from the tray marked 'in' followed by, "Let me see," as he donned a pair of dark rimmed glasses.

The sole piece of paper in the folder was a letter from the Canadian Medical Protective Association.

Finished reading it, McNutt asked, "May I see your file?"

"What file?"

The only records Jim had on the Ireson child were of the boy's visits to his office three years ago, now covered with dust in his basement.

"Your file on the child, Dr. Lindsay."

"I don't have one."

"You did receive my letter?"

"Yes."

"You read it?"

"Yes."

"Then you are aware they are needed."

"You don't understand. I do not have anything pertinent to this ridiculous charge, either in my office or at the hospital."

"Well." McNutt took a deep breath and started to run his tongue around his teeth. It wasn't the first time he'd seen a client for the CMPA who failed to keep records.

"Let me explain," said Jim. "It's really not a complicated story. This child, the plaintiff, as you lawyers call him, was being treated by someone else. That someone was unavailable and the nurses asked me to see him."

McNutt interrupted. "Who's this someone?"

"An orthopaedic surgeon named Best, Beecher F. N. Best." Jim paused while the lawyer made a note of the name before continuing. "The child was seen at St. Mary's Hospital in Shipton late in the morning of March the 18th this year. He was in a bad way. Dr. Best had operated on him the day before."

"How bad?"

"There was no circulation in his foot. So I split the cast."

"That's all you did."

"I spread it a little when there was no immediate improvement."

"Can you prove it?"

"The sister was with me."

"What I'm getting at" - McNutt clenched his jaw - "I need documentation!"

"There is. I described what I'd done in a progress note. The nurses' notes are missing."

"So you were playing the role of the Good Samaritan?"

"As a matter of fact that's a very good analogy. He stopped to help someone who was beaten up."

"That's all in the past, Dr. Lindsay. In this day and age doctors don't stop to help anyone. Too many of them have been sued - and they didn't keep any records either." There was a short pause before McNutt inquired, "What's happened to the boy since?"

"I'm not sure and can offer only rumours. Best sent the boy to the Paediatric Hospital to see Geoffrey Robb whom I believe did another operation, one to improve the circulation. I've heard it has helped but the long range outlook is not good. Maybe you should contact him."

"We can and it would also be helpful if you could arrange to have photocopies of the boy's admission to St. Mary's sent to us."

McNutt stood abruptly. The interview apparently had ended. He didn't say a word, not even 'That will be all', but moved to the door and opened it, waiting for his client to exit.

With no reassurance nor hope of a successful defence Jim felt let down. The man's impoliteness grated. He stood slowly, opened his tobacco pouch, loaded his briar and lit up. When opposite McNutt he stalled commenting, "For some reason, I suppose it's because of your name being on the letterhead, I thought you would've been more senior."

McNutt smiled before answering. "You're talking about my father O.J. I'm B.J."

Jim grinned. "That accounts for your present ambience and not being from the old school," Jim blew out a puff of smoke, "Your poor manners as well. Good day Mr. McNutt."

The traffic on the Trans-Canada Highway out of Toronto, at the best of times, was heavy but between 4 and 6 pm. it was impossible. Someday Jim mused, while the Pontiac bucked along bumper to bumper, jerkily stopping and starting like a road runner doing the 'Tennessee Bird Walk', there will be a final jam and the freedom of western civilization I've known will come to a grinding halt. It was still fairly solid as he drew near Shipton and took the curved exit onto the service road.

At the end of the lane Jim pulled a copy of the Shipton Shield from the mailbox and rolled up the hill. He passed through the kitchen, gave his wife a gentle newspaper-spank and strolled into the family room.

"Hi!" he said to the kids, engrossed in a television program.

Nobody moved. Fine, he thought, and settled with the paper. There was not much on the front page so he opened it and started down the obituary columns. Invariably there would be someone on the list he knew, usually people who had been to see him. Sure enough a familiar name grabbed his attention.

Eckheusen, he read, Mrs. Nicole, formerly of White Horse Corners died suddenly after a prolonged illness. Mrs. Eckheusen nee Leframboise migrated to Canada from France shortly after the war. Her husband, Hans, predeceased her in 1964. She is survived by a sister Oudette. A Funeral Service will be held at 2.00 pm, Friday.

On page five there was a longer write up entitled 'Suicide', and Jim scanned it before calling Merri.

"I can't hear you," she shouted back from the kitchen.

She was forking a frying pan full of spluttering meat when he entered.

"No wonder!" Jim raised his voice. "There's enough racket in here to drown the kitchen sink." There being nothing either of them could do to lessen the interfering noise he went on shouting, "Another calamity in the saga of the patient I treated a few years back. Strange how we've been plugged into the media each time. Listen to this."

"Afternoon visitors to the Seafarer's Hospital were horrified yesterday to see Mrs. Hans Eckheusen plunge to her death. How she found her way to the roof of the building remains a mystery. Narrowly missing a window cleaner on the floor beneath, her body landed on the sidewalk beside the car park."

"The man, Mr. A. C. Chevaux, was so overwrought seeing her crumpled in a pool of blood, he fainted and would have fallen had it not been for his safety belt."

"Ambulance attendants, stationed at the hospital, rushed her to the Emergency where she died from multiple injuries a short time later. Mrs. Eckheusen's physician, Dr. Conrad Reich, was unavailable for comment. However a spokesman for the hospital revealed she had been repeatedly admitted for severe depression, most recently three days ago and was under heavy sedation."

"Mrs. Eckheusen, nee Nicole Leframboise, has had more than her share of anguish. After the war she married Hans, formerly an S.S. sergeant attached to the Wehrmacht. In 1964, having difficulty rehabilitating, he became gradually demented and committed suicide by jumping into the Niagara river above the Falls. His tragic death was sensationally filmed by a tourist and shown on global TV. Mrs. Eckheusen's common law husband, Mr. Emil Larocque, also had a spectacular ending when his car stalled at a level crossing. The west bound express dragged it a quarter of a mile. The incident occurred in May of this year. Mrs. Eckheusen, who was with him, escaped injury and has been living alone since. She had no children of her own and has devoted a large part of her life caring for others, particularly orphans and underprivileged." Jim omitted reading the visitation hours and funeral announcement. The write up was accompanied by a very old photograph.

"There's more!" Merri exclaimed, "It's uncanny like a voice from the grave."

She wiped her hands on her apron and went to the dining room where she'd left the mail.

Jim followed to be handed a large envelope with Government of Canada splashed across a corner.

"Sorry to have opened your mail," she said, "But I thought this was our long lost tax refund."

Do Unto Others 473

Inside was a note from the Postal Department, explaining the smaller envelope it contained. 'This letter was found in a box that hasn't been collected for years. We're very sorry for any inconvenience you may have experienced. Please accept the postmaster's apology. Under the circumstances you are not being charged for insufficient postage.'

"Everybody wants to be a comedian," Jim shook his head in disbelief. "Huh," he grunted. "No word as to how the letter was found. I guess that's a story in itself."

"Wait till you see what's inside the smaller envelope." Merri could barely keep a straight face. "There are some days, Jim dear, when you can't win."

He fingered it pensively and withdrew a Personal Savings check. It was made out to him, dated Jan. 5th 1964, signed by Nicole Eckheusen in payment of his bill. How strange he thought. The whole woeful tale had been a chain of bizarre coincidences so novel they appeared to be contrived and he wondered if there was not an alien hand guiding them. He tried to visualize Eckheusen. The photograph of Nicole struck no familiar cord either. After a while he laughed.

"Two hundred bucks! In a check too old to cash and not a soul alive to rewrite it! I guess I wasn't meant to get paid for this one."

Jim was about to tear it up, then paused. "We have a great bunch in Ottawa. They do you out of a couple of hundred and imply you're one of their preferred customers when they let you off the hook for ten cents."

"Let me have it." Merri suggested. "Maybe she left an estate. You might still get something."

"Nah it's not worth the trouble."

"Then I'll put it in my scrap book along with the news article. The story alone is worth a couple of hundred. You should send it to Reader's Digest."

"But who'd ever believe it?"

After supper when the dishes had been put away and Merri had joined her husband in the living room, Jim detailed his interview with McNutt.

"What's he going to do about it?" she asked.

Jim shrugged. "He didn't say. In fact he gave me the impression I was a crank."

"How's that?"

"By his attitude and tone of voice when he discovered I had no records, and his rudeness, particularly on my way out of his office."

"I forgot to tell you," Merri said, changing the subject. "That young friend of yours from Afghanistan called this afternoon and left a number. You've spoken so highly of him I've invited him and his wife for a week-end in August. I hope it's okay."

"Why not?" Jim smiled. "It will be great to see Dari again."

CHAPTER FIFTY-FOUR

Barely a quorum was present at the August meeting of the General's Medical Advisory Committee, held during lunch hour on the third Thursday of the month. Joe Paolone was in the chair, pontificating as usual. The Surgical Department had dwindled in size since he became the elected Chief of Staff. No matter, he was now Lord of all.

Not everyone was pleased with the 'bombastic little bugger's' elevation, Ed Atwater head of the department of Internal Medicine for one. "For Christ sake Joe," he entreated. "Shut up so we can get back to our offices. It's already ten past two."

Paolone had reviewed at great length the two previous surgical meetings.

"Basically, you're asking us to ratify the motion of the new Department of Orthopaedics." Ed added. "Personally I'm for them and I'm sure everyone is ready for the vote. So let's get on with it."

Joe stroked his awesome nose and said he was not quite finished. Before the MAC Chief could proceed Crooky demanded to be heard, speaking forcefully, cigar ashes dribbling down the front of his dark blue suit. "Mr. Chairman if you'll allow me!"

It had been Dr. Cruikshank's task to report the details of Best's cases. Paolone's monopolization of the meeting had not allowed time for it. "Please Mr. Chairman." Andy reiterated. "You have done a stellar job in presenting the main concerns" - Andy was going to say 'dragging out' but refrained, sensing it would infuriate Paolone. A little diplomacy might get Joe to contain himself. "If you'll allow me, Sir," he continued. "All that is needed is a motion, majority approval and the minutes of the first meeting of the Department of Orthopaedics will be history. I so move. Do I hear a second?"

Asking for a seconder was Joe's job as chairman. Cruikshank had violated his rights. "Hold on," he glared. "What about Best? Alligood and I told him about the restrictions placed on back surgery. Has anyone notified him concerning the obligatory consultations required on all of his surgical cases?"

"As chief of the new department I intend to tell him right after this meeting."

"How?"

"Not verbally," Crooky scowled, "You tried talking to him already. I have a letter typed by the secretary on hospital stationery. I'll mail it to him. Now will someone please speak up?"

"Certainly Andy," Atwater replied and raised his hand. "You can have my proxy as well. I'm leaving."

Paolone disapproved and showed it if his screwed up face was an indication. He made no comments after counting raised hands other than to relay the motion had passed.

Best would long remember the mixture of triumph and pity on Dr. Cruikshank's face as the letter passed between them. He had been sitting in the snack bar with Clayton, quietly absorbing a run down on what had transpired during the meeting, when Crooky approached them. The new Chief of Orthopaedics simply presented the letter and walked away. Clayton, knowing what it contained, also took off, leaving Beecher alone to become increasingly angered as he read and re-read the imposing limitations. Finally he threw the notification into a plastic bin.

Still smarting from humiliation, Beecher entered his office through the back door, avoiding a full room and the new girl, Lil's partial replacement. He hurried up the back stairs to the living quarters. Lillian was in tears again.

"For God's sake," he hissed, "What the shit's wrong now?"

"I'm going out of my mind," she cried. "That interfering nurse called to say you'd been out with Mrs. Schocker again."

"Hell Lil!" Beecher was seething but fearful the patients might hear kept his voice down, "It's just not true." For once he was telling the truth. He'd not seen Janet for two weeks. She had taken her kids to their grandparents in Gananogue. "When?" he asked.

"Ten minutes ago. She wanted to know what I was doing about it and hung up."

Beecher had never seen his wife look so wretched. Her face was pale and puffy, and wisps of hair adhered to her pasty cheeks.

She stared back at him. "I can't believe it," she said and meant it. From the first warning call Beecher had spent most of his leisure at home. They had been to the movies twice; after work each day he had driven her to their country plot to check the house. His activities were accountable. She had almost forgotten the informer and there had been no crank calls. Now her doubt flooded back with renewed impetus and she closed her eyes tightly.

It was late afternoon at the Lindsays. In swim suits Jenny and Brad were playing tennis while Julia, her friend Richard, Heather and Kathy cheered from their perch on the stone wall beside the house.

"You've had the court for over an hour," Heather hollered. "How about giving us a chance?"

"We're almost finished." Jenny grunted as she lunged for Brad's slamming return, missed and lost a tie-breaker seven to six. In her struggle to hit the ball she dove from the clay surface and landed in the grass at the spectators' feet.

Julia in adoration rapped her sister on the head with a racquet and exclaimed, "nice try!"

Jenny was too busy searching for a tear in her Bikini to appreciate the compliment. No harm apparently done other than a slight abrasion on her knee, she smiled effortlessly, and turned to Julia's friend suggesting, "You take him on, Richard."

"No way. I'm a novice at this game."

"Come on," Brad shouted beckoning to Heather from across the court. "We'll play doubles. You and I against Julie and Dick."

"I thought you'd had enough," Jenny teased as she swiped at her perspiring face with the crook of an elbow.

"Are you kidding? I've just warmed up. You okay?"

"Yeah," she answered lightheartedly. "How nice of you to ask."

Before the foursome were ready Kitty became entwined in the net, playfully rolling, clawing and biting at the cords. While Kathy went to her rescue a beige Plymouth with New York plates rounded the traffic circle and stopped in front of the house.

"This has to be Dad's friend," Jenny declared and dashed off to find her parents.

The others held back in a curious group while the Mahmuds got out of their car.

Heather was all eyes and gushed. "Neato! Boy is he good looking!"

"It's definitely Dari," Julia whispered. "I recognize him from Dad's slides."

Tugging at Julie's arm Kathy followed suit, "How come he's not wearimg his proper clothes?"

Julia frowned, briefly puzzled by the question, then giggled commenting, "You mean his baggy pants and turned up shoes?"

"Yeah! And that silly hat."

Suddenly conscious their gawking was rude, Julia pushed her younger sister playfully aside. "We must go welcome our guests," she said, adding, "after a while you can ask him."

The Mahmuds' suitcase was placed in Jenny's room, temporarily vacated as she had arranged to move in with Heather. When their visitors had time to freshen up, the Lindsays upon Roxane's request, showed them around the house.

She recognized the bronze bust Dari's father had given to Jim. It had been placed on the cadenza near the baby grand.

"Who plays?" she asked, less fluent in English than her husband.

It was a natural question posed many times by other visitors and one which Merri had modestly allowed her husband to answer. For the moment he was lost in a nimbus of bobbed blue black hair with sparkling dark eyes. A stiff nudge by an elbow in the side prompted him.

"Oh yes, the girls," he explained, "Merri too! She teaches them."

Roxane pointed at him then back to the piano. "You play?"

Jim laughed. "No, but I'm a good listener."

After a barbecued dinner of New York cut sirloin with a baked potato, roasted corn and tossed green salad the girls volunteered to clear the table, leaving the adults free to socialize and stroll about the grounds. They ended up at the edge of the bank, overlooking the pond where Jim had set out a handful of lawn-chairs.

Merri picked a chair to the right of Roxane and when they were comfortably seated turned to the younger woman commenting, "Jim tells me in your country women are not allowed to join the men at meal time or in casual talk, such as we're having now."

It was Roxane's favourite topic. Eagerly she replied, "That is changing. In grandmother's day, yes, not now. My mama is very liberal and he has allowed it. My husband," - she leaned to her left, grasping Dari's shirt sleeve in her two small hands - "is very understanding. Aren't you Dari-jan?"

Dari grinned and put an arm behind his wife's lawn-chair.

Merri was puzzled by Roxane's use of pronouns. She was sure her visitor had said 'mama', and referred to 'mama' as 'he'. "Is your mama as pretty as you?" she asked.

Dari chuckled. "Her mama is her stepfather."

Now Merri was really mixed up. She had heard there were a lot of sexual hang-ups in Afghanistan. But for the life of her she couldn't figure out how Roxane's father was her mama.

Dari let her fluster momentarily then with a touch of humour, explained, "You are confused," pronouncing the 'ed' in confused exactly as Jim had first heard him three years ago. 'Mama' is our word for maternal uncle. Roxane's 'mama' was married before and to her mother's dead sister."

"Please tell me, Dari," Merri smiled. "I'm very curious about your blondness. How do you come by it?"

Mahmud sobered slowly before replying, "It is probably because I'm part Nuristani." He paused, wondering whether to go on. His mother was little more than a vague curiosity. "My mother Nicole was also blonde," he said finally. "She was French and couldn't take the harshness of Afghanistan nor the household competition. I have no memory of her but I've heard she lives here somewhere. Possibly my father has more information, her maiden name perhaps, though it is likely she remarried and the name would mean nothing. I will write and ask him. It would be interesting to meet her."

They talked of many things: people they knew in common, places they'd been, his new job, interesting cases, Rochester and lake Canandaigua until it was evening and time to go inside. Across the pond an uncommonly brazen sun, rebellious to bed down was throwing a tantrum of rays.

Before going to sleep Merri reflected on why Dari had been reticent to speak of his mother and how she herself might feel in his shoes. She had always had a mother who cared, one she cherished and likely would for a while, having her live with them permanently after Brahms died, which could happen any day.

In the morning she was still thinking of Dari's situation. 'Nicole,' he had said. His mother's name was Nicole and she was French. Would it not be a weird coincidence if the Eckheusen woman who committed suicide two weeks ago was the same one. She was about to wake Jim and tell him about her strong premonition. "Ah, it couldn't be," she muttered and rolled over to catch more Sunday morning shut-eye.

Brunch was served on a table in the screened-in porch and shortly after one the Mahmuds were on their way back to Rochester. Later Merri prepared soup and a sandwich and the whole family, plus Richard and Brad, were again seated in the airy screened in porch.

"A nice young couple," Merri remarked.

"I really liked them," said Julie.

Heather agreed with a roll of her eyes, sighing, "He's gorgeous. What a hunk! They acted as if they were still on their honeymoon."

"So they should," said Jenny. "They were married only six weeks ago."

Jim chuckled and added nothing. If a couple were lucky they could have a honeymoon the rest of their lives, but off and on and less conspicuously, like he and Merri.

"Did you see Dari's butterfly?" Brad exclaimed.

"Yeah!" replied Jenny and immediately upbraided her friend. "He was on his third lap before you completed your second."

Brad's "Excuse me" was cut short as she launched into her father asking, "How come he has no foot Dad?" as if she believed Jim had the answer to all the wrongs in the world.

"He had an amputation."

"Why?"

"I really don't know. He told me once he was born with a club foot deformity. Why it was amputated he didn't say."

"Anyway," Jenny conceded, "even if you doctors couldn't fix it, he sure can swim!"

Jim was thinking of the fateful day on Sher Darwaza and how bashful Mahmud had been in discussing his disability when the telephone rang.

It was Geoffrey Robb. "Sorry to disturb you on a week-end, but I have to talk to you about our friend Beecher."

"Oh," replied Jim, surprised to have the Toronto surgeon return his call on a Sunday afternoon and by the intimation Beecher was his friend. The only connection he had with Robb was the Ireson case through the Medical Protective Association.

"He came to see me last week with a list of problems."

Jim wanted to know if Robb had heard anything from B. J. McNutt but the eminent surgeon was not to be interrupted.

"How would you feel about our back specialist taking Beecher under his wing?" he asked. "The chap obviously needs further training."

There was a slight delay before Jim answered, "Fine," thinking as long as he was not involved he had no objections.

"He's quite shaken," Robb continued. "He's confessed his mistakes and wants to make amends. Even wishes he'd listened to advice in the first place." Robb didn't say whose. "Best will benefit most by future counselling with me or someone not so closely involved. Perhaps it's a communication problem. He claims he has no rapport with you people." He cleared his throat. "Take the Ireson case for example, a real tragedy, the result of poor judgment. The operation should never have been done."

Jim had heard enough and cut him off. "Would you swear to that in a court of law?"

The Toronto specialist hedged, "Not if it meant getting the man in trouble."

"The man in this case is me and I need it to get me out of trouble."

"How's that?"

"Haven't you been contacted by McNutt?"

"Who's he?"

"A lawyer designated by the Medical Protective Association."

"Never heard of him, nor from him."

"When you do and he asks for your written operative findings, I'd appreciate a copy."

"I'll see what I can do," said Robb hesitantly and with a curt, "Good-bye," went off the line.

CHAPTER FIFTY-FIVE

Autumn arrives earlier in Rochester than on the Koh Daman Plain, Mahmud thought. He shivered, drawing his cotton lab coat closer around him and stepped up his awkward pace. It was late September and already the foliage was changing colour. Two blocks from the old frame house where he and Roxane had found a small apartment he traversed Genesee Boulevard under an arbour of dark green maples, piquant with patches of red, and turned south, toward the General Hospital.

    Although the General was old it functioned well and he'd come to appreciate the hospital as a lesser problem than some of the staff doctors. Still it was only a temporary post and after three more months he would return to the University for the remainder of his training.

    Most of the Staff surgeons were more interested in providing a service to their patients than they were in teaching, which irritated him. One of them in particular, Phil Barlow, would rush in to do an appendectomy, snub the intern, partially acknowledge his assistant and complete the operation in under fifteen minutes. Often he'd be back in his Stingray, wheeling wherever: his treadmill office, home, or the golf course, before he could be asked if there were any post op. orders. If his help was lucky to catch him in time he would shout 'Routine' and be gone without a word of thanks.

    The previous night Dari had been on call and was required to assist Dr. Barlow several times. As a result he had little sleep. At home during lunch Roxane had insisted he lie down for a while, but his rest was terminated by a telephone message from the nurse-in-charge of the urological ward. Dr. Hogg had admitted a patient for a suprapubic prostatectomy the next day and needed a work up. Miss Dewar related the intern was sick and if there was blood to be typed and cross matched the lab should be alerted before 3.30 pm.

    Now as he trudged into the hospital via the E.R. Dari was pleased he'd soon be transferred back to the University. He'd be even happier when his general surgical year was over. Then they could exchange him for another 'wallah.'

Mr. P. Leslie was lying on his side, both knees drawn up, when Dr. Mahmud poked a rubber shod finger up the man's rectum. The prostate gland felt enlarged and above it there was a peculiar pulsation. Dari looked puzzled and repeated his 'palpation' to the patient's mortification.

"Sorry Sir," he said, frowning. "I had to double check something."

"Nothing serious Doc?"

Dr. Mahmud said nothing but spoke to the nurse standing across from Mr. Leslie and asked if she would call Dr. Quinn. In the many times he performed a rectal examination Mahmud had never encountered anything like this and needed the chief surgical resident to corroborate his findings.

"What if he's busy?" she remarked.

"He can't be. I passed him downstairs, having coffee with the E.R. staff."

"If you say so," she commented icily and picked up the examination tray.

"Better leave that here," he advised. "I haven't finished yet."

The woman did as she was told and wandered off, allowing him to proceed with his clinical appraisal of the patient undisturbed.

When the chief surgical resident appeared Mahmud had completed his examination and was prodding the patient's belly. "I found something odd on rectal," he whispered, "a pulsation high up on the left. I'd like your opinion."

Dr. Quinn, darkly handsome and fit as a jogger should be, rolled on a fresh finger cot and after a minute with his digit in the man's rectum nodded his agreement. Quietly he hitched his head toward the door; Dari followed him into the hall.

"What are the possibilities?" Quinn asked, testing Mahmud's clinical acumen.

"There's only one thing it can be. An aortic aneurysm and a big one, involving the common iliac arteries. I'm surprised this man doesn't have any arterial insufficiency to his legs."

Tony Quinn was preparing for his 'Boards' and in all his reading had only come across one article, claiming an aortic aneurysm could be diagnosed by rectal examination. "Anything else?" he asked.

"I can't think of anything. How about you?"

Quinn answered the question with one of his own. "What about his belly?"

"I thought I could feel a pulsation there as well, a faint one, low down, just left of the mid-line."

Tony went back into Mr. Leslie's room and put his strong hand on the suspicious area. After a moment he motioned for Mahmud to accompany him into the hall a second time.

"I agree," he said. "He probably does have an aneurysm but we must not tip him off. I doubt if Dr. Hogg knows and this info must be conveyed to him first. Let Hogg deal with it. The question is what's causing the man's symptoms - the enlarged prostate or this incidental discovery? According to your notes," he went on, "the patient complains of difficulty voiding and when he's finished he feels his bladder is still full. These symptoms could be due to either. I"ll get hold of Dr. Hogg this evening and hear what he has to say. I'd sure hate to run into a dissecting aneurysm in the process of reaming out this guy's prostate. In the meantime, go ahead with your write up and include both with your provisional diagnoses." Tony smiled. "Whichever you put first is up to you."

Dr. Hogg was not the sort of man many admired because of his gruffness and a tuft of grey hair issuing from a wart on his left cheek. He was routing in his locker, looking for a set of special filigree catheters and grunted at the chief resident as if it were Tony's fault he couldn't find them. "Where are those damn tubes?"

"Try your lab coat pocket Sir," Quinn replied, noting a peculiar outline as the urologist bent over.

"Christ who put the god damn things there?" Hogg smiled with a faint movement of his mouth.

Quinn shrugged and changed into a scrub suit. As he was leaving the surgeon's dressing room he commented, "I've assigned Mahmud to scrub on this one, Sir. He worked up the patient and asked if he could assist."

"That Asian?"

"Yes Sir. Have you read his note?"

Hogg rarely read anything a first year resident wrote on his patients' charts. Most of it was trivia and bored the piss out of him. He lowered his head and cocked a bushy eyebrow. "Should I have?"

Tony Quinn frowned, holding his senior's insolent stare. The night before he had contacted Hogg at home and describe a pulsation that shouldn't have been where it was. The urologist had scoffed and minimized the finding. 'At the risk of appearing impertinent Sir,' he retorted, 'I think you should have a feel for yourself.'

The bladder had been exposed through a lengthy cut below the umbilicus. Hogg had his hand in the incision, trying to isolate it. His intention once inside was to open the organ and ream out the prostate but he had trouble mobilizing it and began to mutter in frustration. "There's something very firm stuck to the deep surface. Probably prostatic carcinoma. Turning to Quinn he commented. "Nothing much we can do for the poor bastard. I'll take a piece of tissue and send it to the lab for confirmation."

Quinn was not satisfied. Sure it was possible the patient had cancer but it had to be fairly well advanced to have spread outside the prostate gland itself and the patient did not look ill. His blood count was normal as were the biochemical tests, routinely ordered upon admission to the urological ward, in particular the acid phosphatase. "May I have a feel?" he asked.

Hogg had a number 21 blade between his fingers about to slice. "Make it snappy," he snarled.

Ignoring the surgeon's irascible remark, Tony took his time, feeling very carefully. "I think you should consider other possibilities."

"Like what?"

"An aneurysm."

"You guys have got fairies in your head."

Hogg tried to sink the knife into the suspected mass. "Christ it's tough!" he declared, adding as a piece of it broke away "and there's another layer underneath - probably calcium."

"That's enough for a biopsy, Sir." It was the only remark Dari made during the operation. When the surgeon paused to inspect the rent more closely Dr. Mahmud grew bolder. "It looks like the wall of an aneurysm to me," checking himself from adding, 'if you persist it will rupture.'

The urologist looked as wary as a wart-hog backed into its hole, his pebbly eyes alternating between Quinn and Mahmud. Suppose the sassy buggers were right? They could be, he thought. Delicately he pried the mass with the handle of his knife. Wouldn't that be a bummer! He shoved away from the table. "Close him up Tony," he ordered. "We'll wait for the pathology report."

The following morning at Grand Rounds, Mr. Leslie was first on the list. Kevin Hogg was seated beside the chief of Vascular Surgery, Professor Sheffield.

"I'm referring this one to you Miles. He has an operable aortic aneurysm. Confirmed by a frozen section yesterday afternoon."

Sheffield's brow rinkled. "Biopsied?" He'd never heard of anyone going to such lengths. The diagnosis was usually made on clinical and x-ray investigation. The procedure was dangerous. The vessel could have burst and the patient died on the table. He waited with British forbearance while the case history was recited and the patient's x-rays displayed on a row of view boxes. All were taken from front to back he noticed, routine shots to study the passage of dye through the kidneys into the bladder. He moved closer to examine them in more detail and discovered a suspicious calcific shadow.

"Is there a lateral view?" he asked.

Quinn searched the folder and couldn't find one.

"Never mind old boy. It's here in front of us." Once he had traced an outline of the pathology it became clear to everyone. "I'm amazed the radiologist didn't pick this up. Kevin I agree, it is operable, well below the kidneys, but I'll have to wait for your incision to heal which will take a week or two. Let us pray," he added with amusement, "it doesn't rupture from your intrusion."

CHAPTER FIFTY-SIX

Outside the Boardroom Sister McCarthy was having a last minute word with her Chief of Staff. Though she felt uneasy regarding her role in the present hearing there was no way Dr. Patrick Nealy could tell from her round face, so full of zest it glowed like a full moon. In his twenty five year association with Amy McCarthy it seemed nothing ever dulled the sparkle in her bright blue eyes. If it weren't for the black coif no one would believe she was a nun. Her old habits had been discarded in favour of a chic medium blue suit and sometimes the coif as well. 'Frankly' Pat had said to his wife, 'Why she has remained in the order sure beats me.'

"It's my understanding, Dr. Nealy," said Amy, picking a piece of lint from his dark green blazer, "We must decide whether we of the Sister's Governing Board and Council should approve or disapprove the recommendations of your committee, specifically to restrict Dr. Best's privileges." She paused and bit her lip. "I feel like Robespierre at a French tribunal, sentencing someone to the guillotine. In my heart I believe he's guilty but I don't know if I can handle reprimanding him. You're sure this is what the doctors want?" Her accompanying smile was shamefully affectionate.

The Chairman of the Medical Advisory nodded comfortingly. Amy was fishing for attention before moving to centre stage. As Chairman of the hearing she would get a bucket full. He knew her well or thought he did. She had often been accused by various levels of staff, including one or two of the other nuns, of being too forward and irresponsible. But when it came to people she loved them all, especially the men on her Lay and Medical Advisory Boards. Pat Nealy took Amy's hands in his and looked directly into her radiant face.

"Don't worry about a thing, Sister," he said in a polished Anglo-Irish accent. "Mr. Carney will advise you on matters pertaining to the law. Mr. Jorgenson, the doctors' lawyer, will take care of the opposition. All you have to do is direct traffic. You're not a tribunal; there are four of you. So please let us not have a hung jury."

A number of rectangular tables from the cafeteria had been arranged in a U and spread with St. Marys' finest cloth. Amy sat near the centre with the hospital's Legal Advisor Mr. Braydon Carney. Sister Bernadette flanked him, leaving a seat between them. On the

Chairman's right were the other two presiding members, Sisters Magdalene and Mulhaney.

Amy opened the proceedings with an explanation of what it was all about and acquainted the various representatives with each other. She had thought of using the phrase 'memorable occasion' in her official welcome but had scrapped it upon Sister Bernadette's insistence. How many Nuns on the Council had faced this sort of situation? None as far as she knew. Not a soul to give her advice, other than pompous old Carney who she suspected had no previous experience in trying a doctor for negligence and incompetence either.

Best heard his name and mirrored the Sister's innocent smile. "Next to Dr. Best," she went on, "Is Ms. Stacey Turnbull, legal assistant to-" Amy hesitated and placed a magnifying glass over her notes," Dr. Best's representative"- there was another thespian pause -" Mr. Marvin Husselman Q.C., seated beside her." During this introduction Beecher's lawyer puckered his mouth and strummed diamond studded fingers on the Irish linen. He dipped a disproportionately large head in acknowledgment and turned to leer, first at his legal assistant, then at the doctors gathered at the far end of the table. One by one they bowed to his glowering and diverted their curiosity to doodling on scratch pads, provided by the hospital's secretary. But not Jim Lindsay.

He stared across the void like a man bent on murder. This son-of-a-bitch had to be the same Husselman who had sent him the writ concerning the Ireson case. How many Husselmans could there be with the first name, 'Marvin'? No doubt such a good friend of Best's he probably had been recommended to the Iresons by Beecher himself. His resentment shifted to the younger orthopaedic surgeon who seemed to be enjoying the hearing as much as Amy.

Jim's hostility cooled when he heard the sister say to Linus Jorgenson. "You may proceed now Mr. Counsellor."

Linus was an inch taller than Jim and had also played Varsity basketball. In a deep baritone voice he called the Chief of Staff to read out the recommendations of the MAC.

Before Nealy could react, Husselman was on his dumpy legs protesting.

"Madam chairman," he rasped, "This is undemocratic. My client Dr. Best" - he pointed to Beecher with the sharp end of his pencil - "has been unfairly treated by a group of doctors jealously guarding their incomes."

"Objection!" Linus rose, towering over his litter of plaintiffs like a meerkat looking for snakes. "Madame Chairman this man's innuendos are abrasive and out of order."

Amy looked delighted. Perhaps this was her big moment. She leaned close to Carney while the two men frowned litigiously. In an uncertain tone she whispered, "How do I deal with this?"

"Voice your prerogative Sister," he answered.

"How? she repeated louder as if she neither heard nor understood him.

"Give 'em the gavel!"

Which is exactly what Amy did, slamming it solidly on an upturned ashtray and stated, "If anyone is to rule on impropriety during this hearing, Mr. Jorgenson, it is I." Then addressing Husselman, she added, "We of the Sisters Board and Council will ignore your remark Mr. Counsellor. You will have plenty of time to argue Dr. Best's case in a gentlemanly manner, according to our agenda - case after case."

There was an instant huddle with Hussleman in the middle, mumbling to his sexy looking legal assistant and Beecher hovering over them. After a moment Mr. Hussleman hailed the bench again.

"Madam Chairman we request the Sisters Governing Board and Council appoint a Committee of Independent Orthopaedic Surgeons to advise the Board and Council on all surgical questions in conjunction with all cases discussed at the Peer Review meeting, July 13th, 1967, and the recommendations ratified by the MAC when it met a week later."

Amy's answer was emphatic. "No! Request denied. To suggest such a proposal is deplorable, Mr. Husselman." His name was pronounced clearly and with incense. "You're intimating none of us know what we're doing. The surgeons on our staff are capable of deciding for themselves. In the past we've put our trust in them, second to the Lord; we do now and likely will in the future. We don't need outsiders to tell us how to run our hospital."

Another deliberation followed in which Hussleman's eyes moved up and down between the ceiling and his scruffy shoes before he threw up his hands and said, "Well! There is really no point in our being here. Indisputably you run an autocratic institution my dear Sister." He paused then asked, "Would you consider a second request.

The hearing be adjourned until Dr. Best is prepared to call his own witnesses, qualified to render independent professional opinions?"

Again Amy conferred with Carney before answering very simply. "I've been advised by our attorney to deny this as well." Turning to Beecher, she slowly shook her head. "I'm sorry Dr. Best. You were notified of this hearing two months ago, ample time in which to prepare. If you have anyone to back you, arrangements could have been made to have them here this evening."

Husselman's eyes narrowed as he regarded Carney, then swung back to Amy McCarthy.

He said as a matter of course, "Thank you Sister. As I stated a moment ago there really is no reason for our being here. With your permission we'll take our leave."

She was going to thank them for coming but refrained and sat quietly, watching the three of them pick up their papers and exit into the hall. "Now what, Mr. Carney?" she asked.

"Get on with the hearing."

"Do we have to?"

"Certainly. You still have to decide whether you'll accept your MAC's recommendations or not."

Sister McCarthy laughed. "Why can't we endorse the doctor's advice and call it a night."

"It's not that easy. If Dr. Best chooses to sue you for cutting his privileges you'll need documented proof you examined all the evidence."

"Can he do that?"

"Knowing the idiosyncrasies of Marvin Husselman he very well might."

Amy shrugged. "Well, we'd better get on with it. Mr. Nealy can we go back to you?"

"At your pleasure Sister." Patrick opened his presentation with a quick look at his pocket watch. Tucking it back in his vest he carried on. "At your last Board meeting you approved the minutes of the Medical Advisory Committee meeting of August 22nd and the setting up of a separate Department of Orthopaedic Surgery. The General Hospital has done the same. As all of the members of this new department are on the active staffs of both hospitals, including Dr. Best, I'll let them proceed with their complaints against him. But before I turn the meeting over to Dr. Cruikshank I'd like to mention although only 6 of the 13 cases involve this hospital, all of them will be presented as evidence Dr. Best has a serious problem in judgment. The orthopods have been lenient and have gone out of their way to help him. In spite of the imposition of obligatory consultations - more of an imposition on themselves than on Dr. Best as they have been forced to take time to supervise him - he has either argued against their opinions unreasonably or ignored them."

"How could he ignore them?" Sister McCarthy interjected. "He's been informed of the rules."

"Yes, but in emergency situations Best has gone ahead with an operation and called the orthopod scheduled to supervise after the fact. Two cases have developed complications which might not have happened had they been handled differently."

Nealy stopped talking to light a cigarette and continued. "In his last report to my committee Dr. Cruikshank indicated a third of Best's proposed operations have been turned down by all members of his department and it has been noted Best no longer asks to do specific procedures. Instead he suggests two or three alternative operations and leaves the choice to the consulting surgeon. The orthopaedic surgeons would rather have nothing to do with him. It's a case of being damned if they do and damned if they don't. I think the modern expression is a 'Catch 22' situation. The best thing Dr. Best will ever do for this hospital is to leave and the sooner the better. As he has no intention of doing it on his own we'll have to get rid of him. Otherwise someday we'll all get blamed for his shortcomings."

Jorgenson laughed. "Tell me Pat. How much Sicilian blood do you have flowing through your veins?"

"It's Irish!" Crooky corrected, "IRA. Transfusing North America."

Nealy stroked his dappled grey moustache. "Now you've spoken up my friend I suggest you proceed with the denigrating facts." Then facing the Sisters, he bowed his head politely. "With your leave ladies I must go. You have my verbal opinion and the report of the MAC has been sworn and filed. The rest is up to you." At the door he turned and smiled. "Good hunting boys."

The hearing broke up shortly before eleven and the sisters were to reach a verdict. In his summary Crooky had suggested there was no hurry. He did mention the end of the month would be fine. His idea of a joke Carney surmised, as they were barely over twenty four hours away from the first of October.

Sister McCarthy was an angel floating on the clouds. She'd never chaired a more exciting meeting and likely never would again.

Her 'well' was exhaled noisily. She beamed at the hospital's solicitor who had been asked to stay and advise them. "What do you think?"

Braydon Carney was tired. He pushed his black hair piece in place and looked pleased. "I'd say we've shot the works."

"So we vote sisters," Amy said. "I move the recommendations of the MAC be accepted."

When Sister Mulhaney held up a hand to second the motion Bernadette's cheeks drained slightly as the nun decided to speak. "I'm not wholly in favour."

Amy's smile expanded. Good, she thought, we can discuss it some more. The scandal she had heard over the last three hours was more exciting than sneaking off to the 'john' with a tabloid magazine. "Why?" she asked.

"I feel sorry for the doctors. Crooky's retired and shouldn't have to baby-sit the man. Besides he has problems at home. Celeste needs his attention and poor Dr. Lindsay! He's just too busy."

"So what do you propose?"

"Dr. Best should not be allowed to use our hospital at all."

Braydon hunched forward, resting on his elbows. "That will stir things up," he said. "You don't have to go so far. Once you limit his privileges it has to be reported to the College. If that happens he'll have to account to them and they jolly well might suspend or revoke his licence. Without a license he wouldn't qualify for your staff. Discharging him would be automatic."

"There's one question I have to ask." said Sister Mulhaney. She was the thinnest of the four nuns and wore a constant worried expression. "How can we manage a law suit if he decides to sue. It could be costly and what if we lost. We'd have to let him use our facilities enduring a terrible enmity."

"I don't think he'll sue," said Braydon. "He'll need expert witnesses to back up his blunders. Even with my scanty knowledge of medicine I can't imagine any doctors agreeing with what he's done."

Mr. Carney scratched the side of his face thoughtfully. "The Ireson case could give us trouble. I can't understand how the nurses' notes disappeared. Without them we're vulnerable. Jim Lindsay is being sued over it. Husselman has the case and could involve us. If the case ever goes to court with no factual evidence it could be decided by who makes the best impression. The hospital would get a lot of bad publicity."

"You did say you didn't trust Husselman. He can't do anything without Dr. Best's instructions can he?" Mulhaney asked.

Braydon laughed. "Those two have been bosom buddies for as far back as I can remember. After the war Marvin took over George Best's store. He later sold it and studied law. He always was a bit seedy but since starting up his activities have become more sophisticated. The rumour going around is he's embezzling elderly clients' savings through estate management."

"About those nurses' notes," Sister Magdalene commented. "I think Dr. Best has them or he's destroyed them. He was with Mrs. Starling when the Ireson boy was sent to Toronto and walked off with them under his arm. I watched the Iresons get into their car and Dr. Best hand them an envelope. But the envelope contained only copies. The original was returned to the ward. I took it from there to Medical Records and it was complete at that time." Mary Magdalene slowly shook her big handsome head and frowned. "I plain don't know."

"Possibly whoever saw the child in Toronto still has the copies," Braydon suggested. Get me his name Sister and I'll call him first thing Monday morning."

Three days after the hearing Lillian took Jessie and the children to the annual Grape Festival parade. Beecher had told her he wanted to make rounds before the streets were cordoned off and plugged with people if not he'd be stuck at one of the hospitals until it was over. She suggested he join them on the corner of York and Brock at eleven o'clock but he piled on excuses: the new house required inspection, the grading had been completed and the landscaper needed instructions on where to plant the shrubs, also the decorators should have finished varnishing his study. Why he couldn't wait until later when they all might go bothered her. He added something about Marvin Husselman, and an appointment to revise their strategy. After returning home the night before, earlier than expected, Beecher felt an appeal to a federal court was the course to follow. When Lil hinted he should have taken a more humble approach he became angry and refused to discuss the subject any further.

Now as the Regimental Band broke into 'Colonel Bogey' she wondered if he was up to something else. The annoying calls persisted but had become less frequent. She had phoned the police and was told nothing could be done. Maybe the calls had been from the same nurse who had withheld her name. The mere thought of the anonymous caller sent a shiver through Lil's body.

"Are you feeling all right?" Jessie asked.

Despite her quilted jacket Lil felt suddenly cold and frightened. What if Beecher was now with that Schocker woman? She had to know and turned to her mother-in-law.

"I have to go. Look after the kids for a while. Stay here so I can find you later."

Before she could ask where, her daughter-in-law disappeared into the crowd.

Lil needed to be alone to look somewhere, anywhere. She gunned the Volkswagen and headed west across the bridge. Husselman's office was in the shopping plaza on the far side but there was no sign of Beecher's Toyota. From there she turned south, taking a different route through a suburban area. The road wound past the reservoir above the escarpment. A few bends later generally up and down a range of low hills brought her onto a highway. Three minutes later she was at the farm.

The new house looked almost liveable and the thought of moving soon was a slight comfort. There was no sign of his car. The landscaper had been around. A row of young cedars marked the property line and to one side of the graded earth was a heap of fresh sod waiting to be rolled. She drove on, wondering where to look next and swung right, thinking she should return to the boys. The tarmac lead to a cut in the escarpment and she was on the brow starting down when she saw Beecher's Toyota. It was parked off the shoulder behind a green Capri.

They came out of the woods so playful in talk they didn't notice the Volkswagon until nearly upon it.

Beecher's normally sallow complexion turned lighter as Lil stepped out of her car and passed him. Before Schocker had a chance to defend herself Lillian struck. The blow, rendered with an open fist, landed solidly on Janet's eye and might have caused serious damage if Lillian had not pushed so hard with her left at the same time. When Lil was about to pummel her, Beecher interfered. He grabbed his wife by the wrist and while she was sobbing with rage he caught the other hand.

"You, you, Beecher, how could you?" she screamed and aimed a knee at his groin. He backed away, hauling her with him and continued to hang on until she had exhausted herself.

Once released Lil was down the hill and out of sight in the length of time it took Beecher to examine Janet's face.

"You'll be all right," he said, and started his Toyota. Glancing at her bent over the Capri he called, "You're going to have a shiner. Go home and put an ice-pack on it."

When Lillian returned to the corner of York and Brock the tail of the parade had passed and Jessie was feeding taffy apples to the kids.

"'bout time you showed up," the senior Mrs. Best commented. "I thought we'd have to walk home."

Lil said nothing. She felt numb and guided them to the VW. While folding the wheelchair into the back seat she noticed a pain in her hand which increased as she was driving home.

Beecher's Toyota was in the garage. He greeted them at the back door.

"Did you have lots of fun?" he asked, grinning as if the incident had never occurred.

"Yeah Dad. Lots of clowns and horses!" Michael exclaimed.

Before he could blather on Lillian told him to take Robby outside to play while she prepared lunch.

After they'd disappeared and Jessie had gone into the makeshift living room to relax with a Time magazine she confronted Beecher who'd been self-consciously following her around.

"I think I've broken my hand."

"Oh!" he said nervously, holding her fingers in his palm. There was tenderness and swelling over the knuckle of the fifth finger. "You've got a boxer's fracture," he smiled and added. "That was quite a punch"! He felt proud of the way she had delivered it. "I'll take you to the E.R. for an x-ray. You'll need a plaster."

"Not until we've straightened out a few other things." Lillian's troubled green eyes constricted as her anger returned but her voice was imbued with pity. "You've really let yourself down. What's the matter Beech? First your behaviour at the hospital, now this nonsensical business and with such a tramp! Can't you find anything better? You're destroying everything we've worked for."

"I'm sorry," he said sounding remorseful. "It won't happen again."

"Beecher, it's been happening again and again for some time. I want you to be honest with me."

"It hasn't been long," he lied.

"Then how long? You didn't suddenly pick up Mrs. Schocker this morning and ask her along for a hike on the escarpment. You must think I'm awfully naive."

"No."

"When did this affair begin? It must be over six weeks since I've been getting these strange phone calls."

"Well I did take her for a walk awhile ago."

"Why Beecher, why? You're lying through your teeth."

"I'm not lying!" he shouted.

Lil shook her head. Of course he was. The nurses' notes were not enough. What did they tell her other than he wasn't around to take his call. Better for her if he confessed. Or was it? What to do? It wasn't the time to confront him. She'd wait until a better opportunity arose.

CHAPTER FIFTY-SEVEN

Hearing the moving van roar up the drive, Beecher and Michael rushed into the pelting rain. Everything they owned was on the truck except a few precious items previously transported by car: Lillian's silver, china and souvenirs from Afghanistan.

A stout middle aged man rolled down the window on the passenger's side. "Nice place you got here Doc!" he said, noting the attractive integration of redwood and Credit Valley stone.

"It'll do," Beecher, replied spontaneously. He would've lingered to relish more compliments but standing beside the cab, he was rapidly getting wet.

"Where do you want this stuff?" the driver asked.

"Better take it through the front," Beecher waved toward a wide porch on their right.

The house was a large split-level, backing on a ravine. Double doors opened into a central foyer, lined with vestibule closets. A hallway connected a comfortably sized living room to the dining area and kitchen.

"Don't mind my asking, Doc," said the huge fat man driving the cab. "How much did this place set you back?"

"About one hundred and seventy-five thousand," Beecher exaggerated, plus the extras we'll add in the next year.

"Phew! You guys are sure hauling it in. My place ain't anywhere near this big. Where the hell do you get all the money?"

His passenger butted in, "If you can't figure it out Wilbur, I ought to tell you. From all us poor sick folk, that's where!" He'd been groping around for a slicker and couldn't forego the opportunity of getting in his licks.

The bloody doctors were making too god damn much money in his opinion. Every year since the war Statistics Canada had put them on top of the heap and he'd read it in the paper.

He finally found his raincoat and climbed down from the cab. Turning on the driver like an elephant tamer, he snapped, "Get your lard-ass out from behind that wheel and open the back."

The fat man wasn't quite ready to slug furniture and walked around the outside of the house looking for a place to relieve himself. Behind an indigenous bush, broad enough to screen anyone snooping from a bedroom window, he added his trickle to the rain and the brook traversing the bottom of the ravine. By the time he returned his boss and Beecher were off-loading the dining room table.

"You docs covered by compensation?" he asked.

Beecher grinned, "Are you kidding!"

"If you ain't, you better let me have it."

"You can't carry it all by yourself. It's too cumbersome."

"Says you, Doc. Just help me under the damn thing."

Wilbur had the woolly hair of a Bantu and a thick neck. He balanced the table on his leather cap and charged the doors like a hang glider running at the edge of a cliff. Lil had to duck into the vestibule closet to let him by.

"Where do you want it lady?" he puffed.

"To your right," she replied, frowning with curiosity.

There was a muffled thump followed by another and Wilber oozed from under the table.

"What a place you got here Mam. Stairs going everywhere."

Lillian laughed. "No, just up and down."

The staircase was at the back of the house and open, revealing the passage to the bedrooms upstairs separated from the living room by a balcony railing.

Wilbur whistled. "Real sexy! Like in the movies. I can see Errol Flynn, leaping around with a sword in his hand." He spied the lower stairs. "Where do they go?"

"To the garage." She didn't mention the glassed-in section with a sliding door, opening onto an outdoor patio and pool.

The rain eventually quit.

When the boys had been put to bed Lillian and Beecher were lounging on a scruffy sofa in front of a fire. After the movers had left it took them the rest of the day to arrange what little furniture they had and tidy up the floors. Zapped but happy, Lillian was smiling.

"I'll get a grate for the fireplace," Beecher said, mesmerized by the licking yellow green and blue flames. "But the fire's not doing badly. Must be because the chimney draws so well."

"There are a lot of things we need, Beech. A new chesterfield suite for one." Lillian shifted her bottom and a spring twanged to prove her point. "Also rugs and wall to wall carpet to cover the plywood."

"In due time."

"Plus a new bedroom suite, kitchen furniture, lamps, piano, grandfather's clock."

"Grandfather's clock?"

"Yes." said Lil lazily. "Ever since I was a kid I've wanted one. Maybe because I once lived with a family who had one. Never kept me awake; I liked its tick-tock."

Just like the puppies his mother raised, Beecher thought. Jessie had put an alarm clock in their basket.

"When I did wake," Lillian continued, "I never knew where I was until I heard the clock. No wonder, having lived in so many places."

Beecher's beeper started its high pitched hum. "Shit," he muttered into a lapel pocket; after a moment's fumbling a voice told him to call his answering service.

Lil sighed with exasperation. "I was hoping they'd leave you alone tonight. Promise me you won't go. Let them get someone else."

"I'll have to go out to answer the page. Our phone isn't hooked up."

"When do you suppose they'll get around to that?"

"Maybe tomorrow, assuming they work Saturdays. I know they do in emergencies; we could be considered an emergency. People need to get in touch." Beecher pursed his lips adding, "It probably won't be till Monday."

"Great!" Lil smiled, "A week-end without interruptions. It's a shame you can't answer back on your pager and tell them to get lost."

'Get lost' had been the words Lillian had screamed this morning at the heavy breather.

"Surely we're not going to keep the same number?" she asked.

Beecher hesitated, knowing what his wife was thinking. "We don't have to," he replied. "If we do change, it'll be a lot of trouble. I'll have to inform the hospitals and our friends."

"I'd really like a new number, an unlisted one," she insisted. "Anyone wanting to get in touch can call the office or the answering service. Make those girls on the switchboard earn their money."

"I guess," Beecher placidly agreed. A lot of people took their time answering messages just as he was doing. "I'd better pick up this one," he added, gathering himself together. "It might be some news from Husselman. Maybe one of our witnesses has cancelled and he wants to postpone the hearing."

"When is it?" The meeting was scheduled for the next day and Lillian corrected herself. "I mean what time tomorrow?"

"Ten o'clock."

"The General's Administrator is assuming a lot, arranging the hearing on a Saturday morning. Who wants to give up half a weekend to sit in a Board Room. He probably won't have a quorum."

"So much the better," Beecher replied and went to the closet to find his leather jacket. "We have our own experts," he commented, stepping back into the living room, "who'll have put themselves to a lot of trouble to get here. The Board will be remiss not to listen to them."

Lillian wasn't sure. A Board apparently could do as it wished if St. Mary's was any example. "How many witnesses do you have?"

"Four. Robb's driving over from Toronto with John Koslinski, the guy I've been sending my backs to, and Mel Cardigan from the Deaconess."

"All the way from Detroit?" Lil sounded surprised and exhilarated.

"Yes and McCoy. He's a hip specialist from Toronto."

Lil bubbling with delight spun around to face him. "Where's Dr. Cardigan staying? Will he be here long. Oh it will be nice to see him again. It's been four years. Do you know that Beech? Four years since we've been back to the Deaconess."

"I don't know where he's staying," Beecher answered casually. "He did mention something about visiting friends in Buffalo." To Beecher where Cardigan stayed was immaterial. The important thing was the American surgeon had agreed to come and speak in his defense. They'd meet outside the Board Room an hour before the hearing.

"Well Lil," Beecher added, "I hope this isn't the usual Friday night alcohol-induced accident." He opened the front door, retraced his steps and hugged his wife, kissing her tenderly on the mouth. "Be back in a flash," he smiled.

Janet Schocker had manipulated another free evening. One kid had been coaxed into sleeping over at a friend's, the other had gone up north to a neighbour's cottage and Peter was playing hockey. The customary Friday night pick-up series had started and if the event turned out like last season's she could count on him having a few beers with the boys. Rarely was he home before two. Soaking in a warm tub she murmured, "Christ do I have the hots."

Before running the water she had called Best's office and left a message with the answering service. He'd be able to pinpoint her number; he'd damn well better and ring her back. Suppose he didn't get the message or paid no heed to it. Then what? She could do something constructive like the ironing. Shit! Or study the reading material for the night course she was taking at the University. What I really need is a back-up man.

There was a randy old Prof, pressuring her lately. Several times he'd asked her out for coffee. Taking him would be too easy. From his looks hardly worth the effort but you can't tell a book by its cover, nor a stud by his intentions. No, she decided. He'd have to wait. She needed something harder to get, with risk involved, Best for instance and he was worth it. Oh how to get her mitts on some of his money. How to pry peachy Beechie away from monotonous Lil? She no longer had his number, a crying shame for it meant an end to bugging his wife. A strange woman that Lillian. Let her know her husband is fooling around and she does nothing about it.'

The message was distorted. 'A Mrs. Janoshacha had called about a pain in her groin.' The operator repeated the name twice but the number was Janet's. He called the answering service from his office but decided to return hers from a pay phone outside the corner store in the next block. It would be his luck to have Lil barge in on the pretence of having left something in one of the rooms upstairs. She had been doing a lot of checking lately, unexpectedly showing up in the oddest places, or calling the E.R. to have a nurse tell him she needed him right away.

It started to rain again.

"Where are you?" Janet asked.

"In a phone booth."

"Well jump into your superman outfit and fly over."

In a receptive mood, listening to her laughter could excite him. Now was one of those times, the lilt of it plucked at him as if he were a harp trapped between her thighs. He snickered. "If I talk any longer, I'll be up up and away."

Janet was a terrific mimic and took off on the 'Amos and Andy Show'. "Well now Honey-chile yo dun drag yo beeg steeck over hyar right-ah-way un see wha' mamma's got waitin' fo yo."

"I can't."

"Nun of dat' nunsense Amos. Yo hyar me now. Or I'll dun hav' yo panz down and tampa wid ya."

She sounded very funny and though he tried to remain resolute his snickering grew louder. "No, not tonight," he said.

"Rally peachy baby? Ain't yo all dun hav' da time fo yo lil ole Sapphire? Not even fo one lil ole kiss?"

"Well," he paused indecisively and his genitals impounded his brain. "Maybe one."

"A quickie!"

She was like a Siren and he was fresh out of ear plugs. The hell with it. Here I go again. "Okay see you in five."

Winding home through the country, Beecher felt utterly hopeless.
The rain, the dark, and a cold north east wind added to his depression. He'd not intended to see Janet. Not tonight of all nights. His move into a new house did not include her. It was a family affair, a symbol of oneness, success, independence, a chance at a fresh start, a chance to right a few wrongs. Even the pending hearing seemed unimportant. He'd left Lil in good spirits. They would have gone to bed and made love, a rare occasion. He felt as if a flaming torch had been extended and he lacked the courage to grab it. Now there was nothing but darkness and the night. Why? Why had he done it? Janet was a first class slut and he had actually told her he loved her. My God!

CHAPTER FIFTY-EIGHT

Jim Lindsay gazed at the grey bars of dawn and began to run. Though the rain had stopped the slope behind the house was wet and slippery. He managed it gingerly, ground through a hazardous lowland and chugged up the far side. For the first quarter of a mile his feet felt like they would break in half. He turned south, passed a neighbour's property and across the hog's back to an adjoining farm.

Thanksgiving had come and gone and if the fog lifted the woods would be radiant with autumn colour.

Increasing his pace he ran down a lane between two rows of scrawny peach trees. As his metabolism began to race so did his mind.

He was not keen on the hearing. Why the examining body of the Royal College did not take responsibility for its Fellows was beyond him.

Crooky had written to the Royal College explaining Best's inadequacies and asked what sort of backing the local authorities could expect if they curtailed Dr. Best's privileges. When they referred him to the Licensing Board of the Ontario College he wrote a second time. Three weeks later he had an answer. Curtailment of privileges was up to the Hospital Board and must be reported to the Ontario College.

'We're back where we started,' deplored Crooky. 'It's all or nothing at all. If Best can't practise as a specialist he has no place in medicine. There's simply no one to fight our battle.'

'What's wrong with me?' Linus Jorgenson had asked when the orthopaedic department invited him to lunch.

'Nothing personal.' Crooky answered. 'It appears everyone looks after his own interests first and nobody wants to take charge.' The chief's right, Jim thought, particularly after Ramamurti indicated how he relished the present situation. If anything it had increased his referral practice. Mehendra based his impression on the growing number of second opinions he'd been asked to give.

'Your profiteering will pass.' Linus added. "After Best has moved on life will revert to business as usual.'

Perhaps, Jim thought, approaching Lake View Cemetery, the far end of his run. Through the mist he could make out the stone, marking

Jason's grave beside the venerable Tamarack. "Business as usual maybe," he muttered, "but never the same."

Bosco Harrington started the hearing on time. The Board Room, packed to capacity, seated two thirds of the forty Governors, a court recorder, ten staff doctors, six out of town witnesses - four for Best - two invited by Dr. Cruikshank - three lawyers and their assistants, paid hospital office staff, Beecher and other interested parties.

Ramamurti sauntered in late and received a reproving look from the Chairman who was elucidating the purpose of the hearing. Mehendra stood in the doorway, facing the board, until he located a vacant seat to his left, apparently the Orthopaedic Department's place as his colleagues motioned for him to join them.

He scrunched in between Fortier and Wyndom, the Hospital's Liability Insurer, his roving eyes encompassing the panelled oak walls, stopping periodically at the portraits of past chairmen.

There was the grey-bearded founder, Jonas Clark, painted from a very old photograph. Captain Markham in his khaki uniform, killed in the First World War and space for a few more.

Mehendra wondered how Bosco might pose for his portrait, or if in the years to come there would be an Asian among these distinguished Anglo-Saxons."Now I will turn the hearing over to the hospital solicitor," he heard the chairman say.

George Bartlett, a serious man in his late-fifties, was so accustomed to courtroom drama while speaking he was unable to produce the slightest trace of a smile. He droned through a string of documents which included the outcome of other meetings mailed or delivered to Dr. Beecher F. N. Best and the files and x-rays of the thirteen patients considered by the MAC. Each item was submitted as sworn evidence by the Hospital Administrator, Bert Smith, as sonorous and drab as the solicitor himself.

"Sounds like we're in for a boring time, Mehendra," Marcel whispered.

There was no response from Ramamurti; he was comparing the present sobriety with the jubilant atmosphere felt at St. Mary's where even Best had appeared rather cavalier. As his dark eyes took in the defendant he wondered if the word 'defendant' was too mild for Beecher looked more like a docked prisoner awaiting the death sentence.

Then Paolone began to speak, wielding a surplus of words to make it clear the contentious issues were between Best and the new Orthopaedic Department. He, as the chief of the MAC, had an impartial view. Joe went to the top of the list and started to read out the MAC's criticism of the Bataglia case.

At this point Crooky began to cough so unmanageably he chose to leave the room. Allowing his colleague to pass, Jim was suddenly struck with the frailness of the smaller man. The hand, covering Crooky's mouth, was as ashen as his face and trembled so much Jim contemplated going to his aid. Dr. Cruikshank made it to the door and returned in time to listen to Best's expert witness, Dr. Mc Coy, being questioned by Marvin Husselman.

"Doctor, you have told us total hip replacement is your method of treating older patients with congenital dislocation of the hip. Correct?"

Bruce McCoy's handsome wavy white hair did not fit his cadaverous profile. He smiled broadly, exuding not a trace of uncertainty. "Yes," he answered.

"Have you had a chance to examine Mrs. Bataglia."

"Yes."

"Before her operation?"

"Yes."

"When was the last time?"

McCoy fished into a coat pocket for his horn-rimmed glasses and holding them out from his eyes read from a file. "Two years ago, October 21st, 1965. He paused before commenting further, "That's exactly two years ago."

"And what did you find?" Husselman asked.

McCoy turned over the pages of his file. "I've been seeing this lass for years. She was originally a patient of my former partner, Clancy Yates. I inherited her after Clancy died. I found she indeed had dislocated hips and because the balls remained out of the sockets for so long, the sockets had never developed."

"At that time did you recommend she have a total hip replacement?"

"Partly."

"What do you mean?"

"I told her the technology was improving at a fantastic rate and if she waited a few years I might be able to promise a better result."

"How many times have you performed a total hip replacement for this kind of condition?"

"Twice."

"Over how long a period?"

"Twice in the past six months."

Husselman hesitated. He had made his point; the operation was an acceptable procedure. The local orthopaedic surgeons had indicated none of them would have operated and Best had used poor judgment in attempting it. "That will be all," he said. "Thank you doctor." Then, turning to the Board's lawyer acknowledged, "Your witness."

Bartlett could not think of a single question and asked if Jorgenson had anything to add.

"Plenty!" Linus replied. "Dr. McCoy. Did you meet Dr. Best before the events leading up to this hearing?"

"Yes."

"Could you please tell us under what circumstances?"

"I taught him in Medical School."

"I see. What kind of a student was he?"

Dr. McCoy smiled. "That was more than ten years ago. I can't remember. There were over a hundred students in the class. If I answer what difference does it make? He passed his Licentiate Examinations and since then has completed his Fellowship in Orthopaedics. In both instances I had nothing to do with examining him."

Linus nodded and leaned his huge hands on the table as he stated his next question.

"What do you think Dr. Best's chances were of successfully replacing Mrs. Bataglia's hip?"

"How do you mean?"

"The way he went about it."

The doctor hedged, "in my limited experience the acetabulum is a problem."

"By acetabulum you mean the socket."

"Correct."

"What sort of problems would concern you?"

"There actually isn't an acetabulum in these long-standing congenital dislocations or if so, it is shallow and has to be established to anchor the acetabular component."

The court recorder Pemberton held up his hand and asked if the witness would speak slowly and spell out 'acetabular component' or any other technical terms in the future.

Linus continued his questioning. "Is that difficult?"

"Tricky. In my manifold series," McCoy smiled and shook his head, realizing how silly it was to appear as an expert witness with only two cases under his belt. "I've staged the operations," he explained. "In the first stage I take down the upper half of the iliac crest and roll it outward to form a buttress." Seeing a dumbfounded look on Pemberton's face the surgeon put his hand on the outside of his own hip to demonstrate. "I wait a few months until the upper half has stuck to the lower and go back in and ream out a socket."

"I understand Dr. Best did not do this reinforcing operation. You could call it a reinforcing operation, Dr. McCoy?"

"Call it that if you wish. The whole point is to provide a layer of bone strong and deep enough to support the prosthesis."

"The prosthesis?"

"That's p r o s t h e s i s," McCoy spelled the word for Pemberton's benefit, "A plastic cup".

"Suppose you did not do this 'buttressing'?"

"I'd hate to think! Either the hip would dislocate because the angle of the prosthesis would be too steep or the reamer would plunge through the innominate bone into the pelvic cavity."

Before Pemberton asked again McCoy explained the 'innominate' as a large irregular shaped bone forming half the pelvic basin which in turn contains a number of important organs such as the bowel and bladder.

"It wouldn't surprise you if that's what happened in Mrs. Bataglia's case. Dr. Best drove a reamer through the innominate and tore up the femoral nerve."

Dr. McCoy looked annoyed. Best had not told him about the nerve. There was a long pause before he answered quietly, "Not in the least."

After an eleven thirty coffee break with two cases out of the way John Koslinski was in the 'hot spot' where the witnesses stood to address the Board. Bert Smith asked him to swear on a Bible before Bartlett started his routine quiz on professional qualifications. Once it was established the doctor was overqualified and had read law at Harvard he listed the condemnations on the three back cases.

Husselman had been nibbling the end of a pencil stuck in his mouth, waiting for Bartlett to finish. He withdrew it to scratch his head.

"The first patient Mr. Wolenski had back pain for three weeks before his operation and the MAC claims he should have had more conservative treatment. Tell me Sir how long after a patient starts to complain of a back ache do you wait before operating?"

"That depends." Koslinski, lean and straight, looked much younger than his fifty-four years.

"Please explain."

"It depends on the reasons. I've operated on a back as early as twenty-four hours after the onset of symptoms."

Husselman made a note and went on to his next question.

"Do you routinely do a myelogram on your back patients?"

"If they haven't had one before I see them - often."

"Finally. If a hole is inadvertently placed in the dura, which I understand forms a sac containing fluid around the nerve roots, is it a serious problem?"

"Not if it's recognized early and adequately treated at the time."

Husselman reshuffled his papers. "As for the second back case, Mr. Overton."

"Now hang on a minute." Jorgenson was on his feet. "Mr. Chairman," he pleaded. "Before we proceed to the next patient I'd like to ask Dr. Koslinski to clarify a few points. My friend Mr. Husselman had the good doctor make a couple of general statements which likely will not apply in Mr. Wolenski's situation, once the details are known."

Bosco had quiet words with Bartlett, fondling his moustache simultaneously. His worry was the action might dawdle forever. When the hospital's lawyer emphasized the local doctors had been extremely meticulous in preparing their argument he gave in.

Jorgenson smiled. "Dr. Koslinski, I infer from what you've said you would operate on any backache. Personally my back has been sore many times and I sure wouldn't want an operation. I'm afraid of them."

"I think you've misjudged me Sir." Beads of sweat appeared on the doctor's upper lip.

"I sure hope so!"

"In the case of Mr. Wolenski I likely would not have."

"I see. Why not?"

"He is a compensation patient and they often have neurotic tendencies. It's hard to know if they're honest."

"You'd have sent him to a psychiatrist."

"Possibly. Certainly before I considered surgery."

"Did Dr. Best do this?"

"I was not led to believe he did."

"I see. About the myelogram. Would you have done one on Mr. Wolenski?"

"A myelogram is an investigative procedure to determine nerve root compression. In the absence of certain clinical findings it wouldn't be necessary."

"What sort of findings?"

"Pain in the leg on straight leg raising, numbness, tingling, muscle weakness, reflex changes."

"Did Mr. Wolenski elicit any of these findings?"

"I don't know."

"I thought you had examined the patient."

"I did."

"When?"

"After his second operation. But I didn't see him before."

"When you saw him after Dr. Best's second operation did you discover anything positively wrong with him?"

"Yes."

"Could you please describe your findings to the Board."

"He had a drop foot - he couldn't raise his forefoot off the floor - and the sole of his foot was numb. There was also numbness in the saddle area, the region around his anus and inner thighs, and he had no control over his bowel and bladder. The fusion of his lower back appeared solid. I understand it was done under Dr. Ramamurti's supervision."

"Where is the patient now?"

"In Toronto at the WCB hospital, attending the pain clinic. He's had a third operation to destroy part of his spinal cord, that part which conveys pain impulses to his brain."

"And it all started with a sore back." Jorgenson shook his head grimly and asked. "How do you think he ended up in such a sorry state, Doctor?"

"There are several possibilities but essentially something has damaged his peripheral nerves."

"Or someone," Jorgenson growled. "Dr. Best's admission work up prior to his first operation manifests nothing about pain, numbness or weakness in either lower extremity just a backache. But it was all there afterward when Dr. Ramamurti examined the patient. From what I understand the second operation was a re-exploration and fusion. During its performance the nerve roots were found to be severely scarred. Do you have any comment to make, regarding that observation?" Before Koslinski could answer, Jorgenson asked, "What about the hole in the dura?"

John Koslinski's jaw muscles were rippling. "I don't like to judge fellow doctors; I'd rather not say."

The lunch hour came and went and not one of the Governors asked to be excused. Duggan was quickly sworn as the MAC's witness and Jorgenson proceeded with the questioning.

"How long have you known Dr. Best?"

"Since High School. We went through Medicine together."

"I understand you usually give his patient's anesthetics."

"Yes, a fair number."

"Do you recall a Mrs. Anna Gillies?"

Duggan would never forget the Saturday night he'd spent pumping blood and bagging oxygen into the unfortunate woman. At the time it seemed like a bad dream. "Yes," he replied.

"You gave her an anesthetic the night of April 24th, 1965."

"I believe so."

"She was admitted with severe injuries after a head-on collision." Jorgenson paused until Duggan nodded confirmation. "She had many fractures: her pelvis, ribs and both thigh bones. I believe she was in shock. Could I ask you to explain to the Board of Governors what shock is."

Duggan let out a deep breath and rocked his head negatively. "That's very difficult. Even the researchers don't have all the answers. There are various causes. In Mrs. Gillies' case it was from collapse of the vascular system due to blood loss."

"Is it a dangerous condition?"

"If it isn't treated immediately and adequately with blood replacement the victim can die."

"Can you operate on patients in shock?"

"Yes. Sometimes we have to. In a case of internal bleeding from a ruptured spleen the patient will bleed to death if it isn't stopped."

"Did Mrs. Gillies have any sign of internal bleeding?"

"Yes. There was bleeding into the chest cavity as a result of broken ribs. This type of haemorrhage doesn't require surgical intervention but certainly impedes a patient's breathing if it's not drained with a chest tube."

"Did Mrs. Gillies require a chest tube?"

"It was done in the E.R. by Dr. Eldridge shortly after she'd been x-rayed."

Linus regarded the sandy haired G.P. for a moment, liking what he saw. Dick Duggan was a calm soft spoken man with sharp reflexes and able to think on the spot. "Dr. Duggan," he asked, "if shock can kill you must have means of monitoring the patient? How can you tell if it's getting worse or improving?"

"Mainly by taking the blood pressure but the pulse and respiratory rates are indicative."

"Did you monitor Mrs. Gillies at any time?"

"Yes throughout her entire operation."

"Operation for what?"

"To fix her broken femurs."

"How long did it take?"

"Seven hours."

"And you recorded her blood pressure throughout the entire period?"

"Yes, every fifteen minutes."

"What did you find?"

"It never rose above 90/70. Most of the time it hovered around 80/60, even though I gave her three pints of blood and two bottles of saline until she was returned to the recovery room. It gradually returned to 130/90 which is apparently normal for her."

"Then you really kept her alive during the operation?" When Duggan said nothing and looked embarrassed Jorgenson added. "I must commend you doctor. You obviously know your job."

As Husselman had nothing to ask Duggan, Jorgenson discharged his witness and called upon Dr. Henry James, an orthopaedic surgeon.

Dr. James was a refined man of seventy-three, retired from practice, immaculate in a Donegal tweed jacket. His hair and neatly trimmed moustache were snow-white.

"How many fractured femurs have you treated Sir?" Jorgenson asked.

"In my lifetime?" Henry hesitated before replying, "God only knows but I'd say a fair number."

"Have you ever treated them by double plating?"

"Once a few years ago."

"Once out of many, many cases?"

"Yes."

"How do you usually treat them?"

"In traction."

"Could you please tell the Board of Governors what the word 'traction' means."

Henry rolled up a heavy worsted trouser leg and pointed to a bony prominence below his knee cap. "A pin is driven sideways through the tibial tuberosity," he said. "The protruding ends of it are attached to a bow that keeps the pin taught and provides a point where a weight can be tied and slung from the end of a bed." He smiled. "Traction is the safest way to treat a fractured femur. Most people are in too much of a hurry. They won't stay in bed long enough for it to heal."

"You said you performed a double plating on one occasion Sir," Jorgenson interrupted, afraid Dr. James would get away from the main point. "Can you tell us why?"

"The patient was a soldier wounded by a grenade. There were three inches missing from the shaft of his thigh bone. When the wound had healed - fortunately without infection - he needed a graft to replace the missing bone and the only way to fix it was with two plates along the length of the bone."

"So you wouldn't advise a double plating as routine treatment."

"Not at all. It's unnecessary."

"What do you think of the overall treatment of Mrs. Gillies?"

"Very laudable in view of the result. Dr. Duggan deserves a tremendous amount of credit." Dr. James paused and looked at Beecher. "You took a lot of unnecessary risks young man. You should have put her in traction till she was out of shock, then opened her femurs and fixed them but not with two plates! She's lucky to be alive!"

During the afternoon coffee break Beecher sat alone with Dr. Cardigan.

"I wish you'd given me more information," the Detroit orthopaedic surgeon said. "It will be difficult to say anything on your behalf."

Beecher glumly sipped away, partly hidden behind a water cooler. He had purposely omitted sending his mentor incriminating details, hoping he could be defended on general principles. It was too late now. He regarded Dr. Cardigan anxiously, feeling the affect of the surgeon's frosty stare, certainly different from the warmth exhibited during their reunion earlier.

After the hearing had resumed Geoffrey Robb was called to the stand. He was slightly built with a gentle intelligent face and a full head of brown hair.

His imposing credentials were repeated by Husselman who stated, "Your specialty, or rather sub-specialty, is Paediatric Orthopaedics."

"Correct," Dr. Robb nodded, "I do a lot of reconstruction of congenital anomalies."

"You've just heard my friend Mr. Jorgenson present the opinions of the MAC basically those of the Orthopaedic Department, criticizing how Dr. Best handled the Lucas baby."

"Yes."

"The main point was that Dr. Best was too aggressive in his management of this three month old infant. He performed an adductor tenotomy under local anaesthetic and placed her in a plaster cast. According to Dr. Best's notes the muscles on the inside of the thigh were tight and needed to be released by cutting tendons in the groin. Local doctors believe he should have stretched the tight muscles by some type of splint which would keep the hips spread apart. In your vast experience Sir, how would you have handled this problem?"

"I can't fault Beecher with his management of the patient. I've treated infants similarly without any untoward results. The procedure is quite innocuous. It's far more important to prevent the deformity from developing into a complete dislocation requiring more difficult and perilous surgery later."

Husselman looked very stuffy and turned to Jorgenson, allowing the doctor's lawyer a chance to cross examine. Linus declined. "I've a few questions to ask Dr. Robb, regarding the Ireson child, next on the list."

Jim Lindsay had been waiting for this. It could be a preview of what would happen if the Ireson case reached a Civil Court. His eyes strayed in Beecher's direction, but Best was at the door through which Dr. Cardigan had made a hasty exit.

Fifty yards down the corridor Beecher caught up to his mentor. "Where are you going? I think you're next."

"There's nothing I can say, without making fools of both of us."

"But!"

"No 'buts' about it, Beecher. I can't say anything to benefit you. I agree with every criticism levelled against you. Where you fit in the scheme of things is a mystery."

Cardigan did not break stride until he reached the doctor's cloak room. Nor did he turn to see if he were followed until getting into his car. Beecher's being nowhere in sight came as no surprise.

Pemberton had filled thirty dictaphone belts and another five after the summations of the lawyers had been recorded. At 11 pm. all but the Board members entitled to vote were asked to leave the room.

Bosco Harrington studied the twenty-seven Governors all present when the meeting had convened fourteen hours ago. Horncastle in his eighties sat as rigid as Rodin's 'Thinker' and the Chairman wondered if the man had turned to stone.

"What do you say," Bosco asked. "We have a seconded motion to uphold the minutes of the MAC. Any further discussion? I hope not for it's almost twelve"

"One thing I'd like to know Mr. Chairman." The inquiry came from Bob Smyllie boss of the local UAW CIO. "Why do we have to go along with the docs?"

"If you disagree you don't have to vote in favour."

"I'll reword the question. Can we forbid Dr. Best access to the hospital altogether? He sounds like a hopeless case, a menace. He should be cut off completely."

Ernie Freeman, President of the Shipton Rotary Club, started to laugh. "If you had your way Smyllie you'd have all the doctors kicked off staff and then where would we be?" He turned to the Chairman. "It's been a long day, suppose we ratify these minutes, where do we go from there?"

Bosco's reply was succinct, "To the Disciplinary Committee of the Ontario College." He added a personal note. "I fear for Dr. Best's family. They've moved into a new house but won't be there long unless he comes up with a way to pay for it."

The vote was carried with one dissension and when the meeting adjourned at half past midnight George Bartlett informed Marvin Husselman of the outcome.

CHAPTER FIFTY-NINE

There'd been a heavy frost and yesterday's lawn had crystallized to shards of glazed grass. Time to winterize the pump before I have a split pipe on my hands, Jim thought and slid down the crunchy white embankment to find a thin layer of ice along the edge of the pond. A strip of rushes hissed in a skittish southerly breeze. Likely the wind would hold and the air would grow warmer but one could never be sure of mid-November weather. He climbed back up to the garage and exchanged his suit coat for an anorak and hip waders. A few minutes later he reached the intake pipe, drained it and was on his way to St. Mary's.

He took the middle road through farmland pierced by early sun, past mist shrouded orchards and vineyards peppered with anthracitic clusters of unpicked grapes. A wasted succulence, he mused, and turned east into the city.

Ed Atwater arrived about the same time. As there was hardly space to turn around in the small cloak room Jim let the internist go first.

"Say", said Ed, keeping his voice down. "Last night I admitted Crooky. He's on the third floor."

"Anything serious?"

"Either a small stroke or he has metastases, terminal I'm afraid."

Jim had not seen the Chief of Orthopaedics since the hearing; Crooky had called a few days after, with word the General's Administrator had reported Best's curtailed privileges to the Ontario College and to thank him for his participation. 'I guess we showed those SOB's from out-of-town,' he'd said. 'What beats me Jim is how unprepared they were.'

Crooky may have been right. The expert witnesses weren't prepared or hadn't armed themselves to counter the criticisms aimed at Best. Jim reasoned it may have been purposely planned. Accepting Dr. Best's invitation to speak on his behalf, did not necessarily mean they agreed with everything he'd done.

"I would bet on metastases," said Atwater gloomily. "Lung cancer commonly spreads to the brain. If so it's only a matter of days."

"Is he conscious?"

"Oh yes. He's quite lucid at times. You'd think there was nothing wrong with him. Then suddenly he twitches and appears to sleep. His lungs are riddled. From the last chest x-ray you'd wonder how he gets any oxygen through them, and the lesions in his spine have spread." Ed Atwater had stopped shaving and a stubble of grey hair filled the hollows of his cheeks. It was the first time he'd let hair grow on his face and was stroking it as most bearded men do. "I'm going to miss the little bugger," he said. "For the size of him he sure has a lot of guts and a lot of feeling. I've never known a more courageous and gentle person."

"I guess it depends who's side he's on." The corner of Jim's mouth drew backward slightly as he clenched his jaw. "I doubt if Beecher Best thinks he's gentle."

"The stupid ass had it coming."

"You think it's a matter of stupidity?"

"Not really," Ed submitted. "He's got a personality problem which interferes with his judgment - some type of neurosis. I doubt if it's worth a psychiatrist's time to sort out."

In Medical Records Jim ran into two long-standing friends, Charlie McGiven and Keith Johnston, both orthopaedic surgeons on a fact finding team, recruited by the College. "How's it going?" he asked.

Charlie smiled and tipped his head. "We've been over most of Best's charts and there's a definite pattern. His work-ups are skimpy, almost the same for each patient: Head and Neck - negative; Chest - clear to percussion and auscultation; Abdomen - soft, etcetera. Then he writes: admitted for exploration of such and such, with no diagnosis. He's either lazy or isn't sure himself. No matter he's determined to find out by operating. Frankly I don't think he's lazy from the length of his operative notes. He goes into monstrous detail like a medical student describing an anatomical dissection."

"We'll finish this afternoon," Keith announced, "but next week we'll be back to do the General. I imagine the College will be ready to try this guy sometime next month."

Jim's bunionectomies were scheduled for ten, leaving him time to see his patients. He started on the third floor and after rounding on the other private rooms went to see Crooky.

Andy was sitting in a chair, a dressing robe over his hospital pyjamas, his voice loud and rattling. "Ah a friendly face," he cried. "For God's sake get me out of here!"

"Where to?"

"Home. I want to go home."

The childlike expression and verging tears brought a lump to Jim's throat and he was unable to speak.

"Jim please." Crooky sounded very pathetic. "I'm dying and I'd rather do it at home."

Why not, Jim thought, When my time comes I'd probably want the same.

"Hang on a sec Andy. I'll get a wheel chair." His words were barely out when Celeste, on the arm of her eldest son, strolled into the room.

"Celeste!" She caught Jim by surprise. "It's good to see you." He would have reached for her hand but it held a cane. "I was about to pack him up and take him home."

Mrs. Cruikshank was over six feet tall. Her cold grey eyes looked straight into Jim's. "He's staying right here," she sounded determined. "In my state I can't possibly look after him."

It was over four months since her hip pinning and Jim knew bony union was progressing satisfactorily. For almost two weeks Celeste had been swimming daily. She could walk without a cane. The night of her operation Andy had stuck to her like a faithful dog, trying his damnedest to prevent any further damage by tugging on her leg. Crooky had treated his wife the way he wanted to be treated himself. Now she had a chance to return the favour. Jim took her by the arm and led her outside. "Celeste," he sighed, "How would you like to be left alone to die?"

"He's not going to die!"

"You say that because you don't wish to think anything different. After he's gone he can't look after you."

Celeste interrupted, "I have my children."

"They could have problems of their own." Jim's remark had been involuntary. It involved the future and wasn't predictable. Whether or not her children looked after her had nothing to do with the present circumstance. "Please," he added, "as a last kindness to him. You owe it."

"Dr. Lindsay. It's our affair and I'd appreciate if you'd let us handle it our way." She had drawn herself erect and stubbornness rang like a freedom bell.

Jim was the first to break eye contact. In fear of disclosing his anger, he turned and walked away.

Taking the back stairs two at a time, Dr. Lindsay's was still thinking of the Cruikshanks. Surely Celeste could afford to hire help. Her excuse, 'In my state' didn't hold water. No doubt there were other reasons, probably related to family affairs. When his time came he knew Merri would not treat him with such dispassion.

On the fifth floor he opened the O.R.'s Emergency door as Janet Schocker charged out and almost fell into him.

"Whoops!" she said, hurrying past, "sorry Dr. Lindsay," and mounted the top flight of stairs.

Before entering the small kitchen Janet checked to find the Conference Room was empty and none of the O.R. girls were in the 'john'. She pulled a piece of paper from her smock and memorized the figures on it. 'Getting Beecher's unlisted number had been easy. She knew he would have to give it to Sister Bernadette who would pass it on to her secretary. All the doctors' phone numbers were under the clear plastic sheet, covering the secretary's desk. It was simply a matter of popping in for a chat and peering over dear Hazel's shoulder.

Inside the kitchen there was a telephone with a cord long enough to drag it into the hall. She peeked out the door and checked the elevator indicator. As it was going down she dialled Best's number.

After three rings Lillian answered. Schocker recognized the voice and began her heavy breathing routine. She called successfully again at noon but on a third try later the new number was engaged.

Following the second call Lillian had left the line open but forgot to do so after she phoned in the afternoon. Ten minutes later it was ringing again. This time it was Beecher.

"I'm so glad it's you," she said. "That 'Air Hole's' bugging me again."

"I don't understand."

"My friend without a voice."

Beecher paused. Schocker was up to her old tricks. She had to be the caller. How did she get his new number? "I'm at Husselman's office. Have 'Builders Supplies' brought the cement." He was planning on pouring the patio foundation over the week-end. "You did order it?"

"Yes, and it's arrived, all thirty bags piled out back with a load of sand."

"Fine. If they hadn't I was going to stop on the way home." His 'see you soon' was followed by a click and this time Lil left the phone out of its cradle.

Marvin Husselman was seated at a large chrome trimmed desk, supporting his head with his stubby fingers. He gestured to a letter on the slate surface in front of him as Beecher hung up.

"This arrived today from Lowenstein and McNutt with a copy of a letter they received from Robb. Actually it's the same one Robb sent me." Marvin lit a cigar so thick Beecher wondered how the lawyer got his stingy mouth around it.

"He's written several pages," Husselman continued, "dealing mainly with his operation and the prognosis, not a word regarding the cause. Really Beech, he's not much help to us. Nor is he to Lindsay."

The last comment did little to bolster Beecher's morale. The last time he had spoken to Marvin the day after the hearing he was advised the Iresons would likely include him in the litigation.

As he sat, avoiding an engulfing cloud of smoke, Beecher wanted to turn back the clock. He should never have sent the Iresons to Marvin. They had come to him when Harrison Bartlett and Samuels turned them down. He thought by helping the boy's parents find a lawyer they would bypass him and lay the blame on Lindsay. Now they wanted to sue everybody from Shipton to Timbuktu and Beecher suspected Marvin had a hand in it. The more defendants Marvin could line up the better the chances of hanging the blame on someone. When the Iresons asked if Beecher's operation had anything to do with the boy's misfortune his buddy should have dropped the case. Not Marvin. He stood to make money regardless. "So what's your next move?" Beecher asked.

Marvin tapped the ashes of his enormous cigar into the open mouth of a frog, a souvenir from the Caribbean. He smiled as though he had three aces showing and had just been dealt a wild card. "I was going to ask you the same question Beech."

Lillian was on the sofa, seated in her favourite hollow, glancing through 'Better Homes and Gardens'. She hadn't heard Beecher come in but turned when he entered the living room. Disregarding her "Hi!" he began to pace in front of her grumbling.

"I'm finished with Husselman, Lil. He's not the friend I thought he was."

This revelation was welcomed. She'd never liked Marvin Husselman; to her he was a lewd, foul mouthed leech. He had a strange twisted smile as if her innermost thoughts were plastered on a billboard, attended by such base remarks, she found him positively disgusting. They could manage without him.

Lillian had saved her inheritance from Beecher's father, now worth close to seventy thousand. It was her nest egg, mad money or down-payment on things needed for the house. Beecher seemed to have forgotten about it and she had no intention of reminding him. She'd continue to use it as a safeguard as she'd been doing for years. He and her two children were her only family. If Beecher had chucked out Husselman so much the better. Without Marvin life would be more pleasant. "How did you arrive at that conclusion," she asked.

"I don't like the way he's handling the Ireson case. He's included me on the list of defendants. That's gratitude!"

There were still so many particulars requiring an airing of the infamous week-end back in March Lillian didn't know where to start. She took a deep breath, fearful of what she might be getting into.

"Beecher, I won't discuss it unless you level with me. Exactly where were you that Friday night? You weren't anywhere near Husselman's, were you?"

He did not answer so she went on. "I checked with Marvin, using his pool table as an excuse." Lil laughed, "Looking back he must have thought I was loony. I asked him where he bought it. His response was an obscene titter as he asked if I wanted to come over and play with his balls. I told him I wanted to get you one for Christmas. When he said he didn't have one your alibi was blown." Lillian shook her head and entreated, "You weren't anywhere near Marvins the week-end I was in Toronto were you? Why not tell me the truth?"

He looked muddled and defeated, so many lies had been told he was disgusted. To improve his image he turned on Marvin. "If Husselman had done a proper job my restrictions wouldn't have been rescinded. Damn the creep!" he cursed suddenly recalling another stab in the back. He'd paid Marvin for the lost bet he could screw Schocker twenty times on a week-end. What the hell did Marvin or anyone else care about him! Lil's pleading eyes were wet and shiny. Things couldn't get any worse. He had nothing to lose and replied dully, "I wasn't anywhere near his place."

"Then where were you?"

"At Janet Schocker's."

"All night?"

"Yes and half the following day."

"What you were doing is unimportant. I want to know she's out of our lives."

"Yes." He answered, hardly above a whisper.

"What do you mean, yes?"

"Yes. She's out of our lives."

"That's really the truth?"

He nodded and she produced a Bible. Handing it to him she asked, "You'll swear on this?"

"Why not?" His voice was barely audible. "I swear I'll have nothing to do with her except on a professional basis."

"I can accept that," Lil smiled, "As long as she doesn't change her profession and become a hooker. For the record," she asked, "When did you last see her unprofessionally?"

"Our first night here."

"Beecher," Lil trembled. "How could you?"

"I don't know. I really don't know. God knows I didn't want to."

"How did she get our unlisted number? I've had two calls from her today."

He had immediately thought of Janet when he called from Husselman's office and Lil had told him about her mysterious 'Airhole'. He thought it unlikely because he'd given no one other than the Administrator their new number. "Why should it be her?" he asked reflectively.

"Who else wants to keep us in constant discord? Who has access to our number?" Lil answered her own question spontaneously. "Both hospitals. Anyone working at St. Mary's could get it."

"So you're asking me to have it changed again and give it to no one, not even the hospitals?"

"No Beech. Tell Mrs. Schocker you love your wife and want nothing more to do with her." Lil's green eyes glinted with determination. "And mean it," she added.

What Lil was demanding was impossible. He had tried it a dozen times. Shunning Schocker altogether was the only chance he had. "It's best I ignore her entirely," he said.

"Suppose she doesn't want to ignore you? Then what?"

Beecher exhaled loudly. "I don't know." He was bored talking about Schocker and his thoughts returned to the Ireson case. "I'm being sued," he said.

The declaration came as no surprise to Lil. All his misadventures, surfacing during the hearing, were bound to incite legal action. "By whom?" she asked.

"The Iresons. Thanks to good old affable Marvin! They're going after everyone and it'll be hard to pin the blame on anyone because part of the chart is missing."

"What part?"

"The nurses' notes."

So we're back to them, Lil thought. She could have brought up the nurses' notes earlier in the conversation when she mentioned how she'd checked out his alibi using Husselman's Pool Table as an excuse. "You know something about them don't you Beech?" Lil regarded his confused expression and decided to free her own conscience. "I know," she said, "They were in your jacket pocket. They fell out while I was getting it ready for the cleaners and I read them! Why were you carrying them around and what have you done with them?"

"I destroyed them."

"Beecher. That's against the law." Lil remembered how her copy had been made from a photocopy. She still had hers. "Every page?" she asked, "including the originals?"

"Yes."

"It's too bad Beecher," Lil sympathized. Her husband had brought the whole thing upon himself. If he hadn't gone to that woman it wouldn't have happened. But she was not about to bring Schocker back into the conversation. The affair hadn't finished; not until the harassment stopped. For a change Beecher probably told the truth. Lillian decided against telling him of her copy of the nurses' notes. He had admitted what she suspected and there was no need to show them to him. The copy could have been used as evidence in a divorce but now she knew she could never go through with it, not even a legal separation. Perhaps St. Marys would like to have them. In the morning she would take them to the Administrator.

Her second singular action took less courage to divulge. "I've made an appointment for us to see a marriage counsellor. You know him - Garwood Trussell. He'll meet us in his office to-night after supper."

Beecher seemed surprised though not in a negative way. "If you want I'll go along," he said, thinking of the prospect of getting back into the mission field. Reverend Trussell could enlighten him on that as well. Conditions in Afghanistan may have been primitive but it was a place without law suits and interfering doctors.

CHAPTER SIXTY

"You two marvellous young Christians can't be having hopeless marital troubles. You've just strayed a little." There was an ageing timbre in the resonant voice but Garwood Trussell's baggy eyes had lost none of their sparkle. He adjusted a pair of dark rimmed reading glasses and flipped through the worn pages of the large leather bound Bible, given to him by his father years ago. A white fringe of hair, encircling his pale head, glistened like a silver halo beneath the swag lamp above his desk. Stopping at the book of Acts, he said. "I suggest, you, Beecher read this tonight. It's concerned with Peter and his transformation after receiving the Holy Ghost." Garwood's closed-mouth smile broadened his square face. "You are sanguineous by nature and could modify your traits as he did, once instilled with the Spirit of the Lord. You mean well Beecher, but your most serious problem is a weakness of will. You lie under pressure rather than face shame or penalty and get entangled in all sorts of webs. You've behaved like many adulterers, lying and deceiving to the point of contradicting yourself. Confronted with your sins you become so guilt ridden you break down and weep as you have this evening."

"Lil and I know you're sorry for your actions but repentance is not enough. You must embrace the Holy Spirit! Without it you cannot trust yourself."

Garwood paused and turned to the Old Testament. "Read Genesis and Hebrews. You're indecisive, fearful and self-protective. Abraham behaved like this. He was a fearful man until he learned more of God and trusted him. Genesis 15:1 'Fear not Abraham: I am thy shield and thy exceedingly great reward'. "The evolution of Abraham made him one of the greatest men who ever lived."

"And both of you," he added, "must continually request replenishment of the Holy Spirit, and to help you I suggest Ephesians and Galatians."

Garwood put the book away. "As you know, Beecher, I'm a member of the Board of Governors at the General Hospital. I was present during the hearing. Also I cast the one dissenting vote. You definitely have problems and certainly need more training and experience. But you don't deserve to lose your licence to practise which could happen. You did a fine job as a medical missionary in Afghanistan and we'd like to have you serve again. But not if they take your licence away. You should pray as I will myself that God may open the hearts and broaden the minds of the decision makers."

Beecher, still slightly red eyed and remorseful, spoke after a long silence. "One reason I came tonight was to ask if there was any chance I might return to the mission and you've answered my question." He was going to lie and say I guess the Lord has answered my prayers but he'd made no such request. He smiled and quietly thanked God for helping him contain his compulsiveness.

"You were advised to restrain yourself Beech, especially your restlessness. So put your nose in a book. I'll take mother home."

Jessie puffed into her full length muskrat coat.

"That didn't take long," she remarked. "What did the Minister have to say?"

Neither of them had told the senior Mrs. Best the real purpose of their visit to Reverend Trussell. They had implied it was to join him in a friendly talk, a custom he'd started sometime ago. When they didn't answer right away she inquired. "How many were there?"

Lillian countered with, "How were the kids?"

Jessie's flat eyes brightened. "Oh real good. We read and played parchesi until eight and they went to bed, good as gold."

After they'd gone Beecher found the stillness difficult. He wanted to be with people, tell the whole world of his re-infusion with the Holy Spirit and gain a few disciples. Lillian's Bible was lying where she had left it. He turned to Galatians and started to read but the exaltation surging through his body left no room for concentration. Religion was an emotion to be shared not a scholarly translation of an ancient book. He replaced it and tried Newsweek, then Time, followed by a spin of the TV stations.

The phone rang and he jumped like a stallion at the gate, joyful with the prospect of some action.

"Peachy Baby are you alone?" It was Janet's voice. He didn't answer. "Ah shucks honey ah knows yo thar awl by yo lil' ol' sef. Ah jus saw Lillikins on da way inna town wid dat beeg grannie strapped beside her. How 'bout a roll in da hay?"

"I'm busy."

"Thet neva stop yo befo'."

"No. I've got a few urgent things to take care of."

"Nuthin' mo urgin dan me, honey. Peter's out stoppin' pucks. Da keeds ar stayin wid dare friens und ah's as free as da breeze."

Beecher was still infused with Trussell's Holy Spirit. He felt cleansed, rejuvenated. The whole world was waiting for him to save it from sin. He hung up.

She called back. "I guess we were cut off." The Minstrel Show accent had disappeared.

"No we weren't Janet. You don't understand. You're the devil incarnate," he bellowed and hung up for a second time.

The phone did not ring again.

Lillian was gone much longer than expected. She burst into the living room to find Beecher flaked out on the sofa, his euphoria passed.

He barely recognized her. Her fine hair, at the best of times unmanageable, looked as if it had been set by a whirling dervish. Her cheeks were on fire and green rage poured from her eyes.

"That does it!" she snarled. "That damn girl friend of yours chased me all over town."

"Whoa down." Beecher suddenly sat up. He had never seen Lil in such a state.

"That evil woman," she screamed. "One more trick. Just one more, I tell you I'll kill her!"

"Okay I believe you," Beecher said, reassuringly. "Now calm down and tell me all about it."

Lillian, still agitated but in control of herself took off her coat and threw it at the back of a chair. "After I dropped off your mum I crossed the old canal bridge and a car behind me flashed its brights in my rear view mirror, two or three times. When I turned left at the intersection on Western road I was so confused I almost ran head-on into a truck. She stayed on my tail no matter how fast I went. Then down the road where the big maple is, where the road makes a sharp bend, I swerved onto the shoulder to let her pass. She was going awfully fast."

Lil was talking a mile a minute.

"Wait a sec," Beecher pleaded, "How do you know it was a woman?"

"I spotted her in my headlights, plain as I'm sitting here. It was that Schocker woman driving her green Capri. So I lit out after her. It took a good fifteen minutes to overtake her. I chased her all over the country. Finally caught up when she stopped for traffic at an intersection."

"What did you do to her?"

"Nothing except get her licence number."

Lil began to shake and sat down on the sofa beside him. "Really crazy!"

The next morning Lillian drove her Volkswagen into town. She had two stops to make. The first was at the police station.

Sergeant Robinson offered her a chair in his noisy office. "So! You're the lady who's getting all the annoying phone calls."

"That's right."

Sergeant Robinson's interest went a little deeper than the sceptical look on his wrinkled face. "Do you have any idea who?"

"Yes, She's having an affair with my husband."

"You want to get even?" the Sergeant interrupted.

"That's not it, I want her to leave me alone. Tap her phone and you'll catch her making the calls. I get at least three a day. She's a nurse at St.Mary's."

"Why are you so sure she's the one?"

"I've caught them together and I believe they see each other often. My husband's a doctor."

"Do you love him?"

"What do you think?"

"I'm just curious."

"Would I come here if I didn't?"

The Sergeant smiled, "No! But I need a number."

Lil stood, searched her purse and wrote on a slip of paper. "It's under Schocker, Peter on Park Avenue," she said. "I've taken all I can handle and if you don't do something about it, then maybe I'll- Oh forget I ever came," she sighed and turned to leave.

Robinson watched her slalom through the maze of office desks. In his experience, harassing phone calls invariably involved an extramarital affair. Out of curiosity he'd investigate Schocker. Maybe he'd order a line-tap.

At St. Mary's Lillian had intended to hand in the nurses' notes and leave without having to explain. However because it was Saturday morning the Administration Office was closed. She was standing outside the door, looking confused, when Sister Bernadette emerged from the Chapel across the hall.

"Is there something I can do for you?" the sister asked.

Lil felt like running. "I'm not sure," she answered. "I have a letter for the Administrator."

Sister Bernadette smiled, "It so happens, I'm that person and will be happy to receive it."

"Oh, fine, Tha' That's fine," Lil stammered. She had no choice but to hand over the envelope."

It was marked 'Administrator, St. Mary's Hospital' on the front. "May I ask who it's from?"

Lil was incapable of lying. "From me."

Sister Bernadette had never met Lil. Her face glowed beneath her coif. "And who are you?"

"Oh, I'm sorry," Lil still felt very apprehensive. "I work for Dr. Best. I, I'm his wife."

"I see." Sister Bernadette's smile broadened.

CHAPTER SIXTY-ONE

At the eleventh hour on the eleventh day of the eleventh month while the Commanding Officer of his former regiment was placing a wreath on the Cenotaph Captain Andrew Robert Cruikshank died in his sleep. Shortly after Sister Magdalene notified the Administrator who called his wife.

Celeste took the news calmly, shed a few tears and asked her son Christopher to make the necessary arrangements.

Crooky's remains were cremated on the following Monday and a Memorial was scheduled for Wednesday at 2 pm. in the Chapel of Radcliffe's Funeral Home.

"Beecher, you're asking me to lie on a stack of Bibles."

"Not really Janet. All I want you to do is show up and support me at the Inquiry in Toronto." They were parked at the Community College where Janet took a night class every Tuesday.

"But you weren't anywhere near St. Mary's the night of March 17th," she argued.

"No one but you knows I lied. All you need to say, after I tell them I saw the kid early in the morning, is I spoke to you on the phone. We did a lot of talking that night, among other things."

Janet had a trigger spot on the inside of her thigh just above the knee which set off all sorts of erotic behaviour. Beecher began to stroke it.

"Yo all cut dat out honey chile," she said, sliding closer and crossing a leg over his. They were sitting in her Capri in the parking lot. "If I don't get in there soon," she added, "they'll look for me. It's my turn to do the seminar."

His hand was level with her crotch. Through the softness of her panties he could feel her stomach muscles tighten. "You were on second call," he whispered, "I phoned, alerting you I might have to take the Ireson boy back to the O.R. That's all you have to say."

Beecher was quiet a moment, studying her eyes.

"I've told a lot of whoppers Beechie but I've never lied with a hand on the good book. I'd be afraid God would strike me dead."

"You won't have your hand on a Bible."

"Not at that moment but I'd be sworn, to tell the truth, the whole truth, and nothing but the truth, so help me God."

She suddenly pulled herself together. "How about we talk about this later."

"Okay," he said, opening the passenger door, "same place an hour from now. I'll be waiting."

Outside the funeral home after a service attended by most of the medical community, the Lindsays were waiting in line to offer sympathy to the grieving family when Sister Bernadette approached. She expressed her admiration of Ed Atwater's eulogy and brought up another matter.

"This may not be the place to discuss it," she said, apologetically, "But I thought you'd like to know a copy of the missing nurses' notes on the Ireson boy has turned up. As it isn't the original, Braydon Carney says it possibly won't be admissible in court, but we'll see."

"Where did you find it?" Jim asked.

"Saturday morning Mrs. Best gave me an envelope. I didn't open it till later. Even though Crooky's death had been expected there was much to do." She hesitated, recalling the shock and her voice became tremulous. "As you know he was our very first Chief of Staff. He did a lot of good for our hospital."

"He was a dear friend," Merri interjected. "Once he popped in looking for Jim just to see how we were doing, called us his kissing cousins. I was feeding Julie at the time and he took over so I could start supper. He was a super chap. We'll really miss him too."

Jim put a comforting hand on Bernadette's shoulder. "About Lillian Best -"

"So that's her name," The sister interrupted and smiled. "She didn't wait for me to ask, timid little soul."

"It's odd," Jim commented, "How she came to have a copy and decided to return it. Did you have a chance to find out?"

Bernadette shook her head and explained, "I've tried unsuccessfully to contact her. Either her line has been busy or there's no answer."

"Could I please see it?" Jim asked.

"Certainly, I'll have Hazel run off a copy this afternoon."

"Maybe I'll call Mrs. Best and see if she knows what happened to the originals."

Bernadette shrugged. She knew Dr. Lindsay had as much at stake in the Ireson case as the hospital and could see no harm. "That's good of you," she said. "By all means."

Early Thursday morning the front door chimes startled Lil and she accidentally pinched her son's tummy in the zipper of his blue jeans. "Sorry my lovely," she said. "It's only the doorbell."

Any ringing noise jarred her. Three times the day before she had calls and notified the sergeant at Police Headquarters. She hoped he'd catch whoever it was soon.

To her great surprise the visitor was Dr. Lindsay. "Good morning," he smiled. "I don't make a habit of barging in on people but last evening I tried several times to reach you by phone and - It seems I've caught you at a bad time."

"Not really. We were just getting ready for our morning jaunt to the Children's Clinic. Please come in."

"Thank's but no. I'm in a hurry," Jim apologized. "I have to be in Toronto by ten." If he wanted information he'd ask regardless of the fluster his approach might cause. It usually worked, provided he asked in private; he wondered how Lillian would react. He was a good foot taller and her large green eyes peering up at him, conveyed nothing more than surprise.

"Where are the original nurses' notes on the Ireson boy," he asked.

Lil blinked. "I don't know."

"How did you come to have a photocopy?"

"I made it from another copy."

"I see, and where is the other copy?"

"I don't know."

"You lost it?"

"No. I returned it to a pocket, exactly where I found it."

Jim frowned. Many wives were guilty of rummaging their husband's pockets but he'd never heard of making a photocopy of anything they discovered. "Why did you do that?"

"I had my reasons."

"I see."

"I haven't seen the nurses' notes since. I imagine they've been destroyed; likely so have the originals." Sadness tugged at the corners of her mouth. "I wish I could help, Dr. Lindsay but I can't and I'm sorry."

"Well," Jim sighed, "I thought it was worth a try."

"You're off to the Inquiry now?"

"Yes."

"Beecher left an hour ago."

"Perhaps I should have given myself more time but I hate the early traffic into Toronto. It usually clears up by nine thirty. I'll make it by ten. He won't be much ahead of me."

"You remind me of the Hare and the Tortoise," Lil chuckled then sobered quickly. "I don't mean you're slow," she said. "You're a lot more thorough."

Jim laughed. "I suppose that's meant to be a compliment."

Lillian might appear shy, he thought, but she doesn't lack a sense of humour. He liked her openness and felt she was honest. If she had the originals she would have returned them too.

The phone rang. He thanked her for her time and started down the steps.

Before 7.00 am. Janet Schocker had lied to three people. First to Peter when he left for work at 6.30 am. "I'm going to Hog-town to do some Christmas shopping. Probably take in a movie. Don't expect me home for supper." She repeated this story to her baby sitter who arrived shortly after Peter left. Then she called Mrs. Burwin and begged off sick. "I've been up all night with vomiting and diarrhoea. There's no way I can make it in today." Burwin had not asked any questions, merely said, "Okay, see you tomorrow." That was it. Easy as pie. Her big act was yet to come.

As she swept through her closet, trying to choose something to wear, her favourite mini skirt leapt at her and her mind raced back to when she'd last worn it.

Lillian had chased her all over the place. It had been the same night Beecher had supplied that religious nonsense. Next he was sniffing around as if nothing had happened. Between then and now she had seen him twice. Monday he came to the O.R. and apologized for his behaviour; and Tuesday evening he'd asked her to lie for him. Otherwise, he'd been busy with his new house, sticking close to dish-pan Lil. But some things had improved. Now his wife was out of the office they had been able to sneak in for a bit of nooky on the examining table.

Peter probably suspected what she was doing but it made no difference. She had taken him back on a trial basis. Some trial, she kicked him out of bed on his first attempt. Afterward he'd asked for an arrangement. 'Okay,' she'd agreed. 'you in the spare bedroom and I in mine.' He'd gone along for the sake of the kids. 'With such a selfish slut for a mother they lack decency in their lives.'

Decency really, she thought, what decent things has he ever done for me? I've paid for all my own clothes. Take this pleated skirt and the dark brown velvet jacket for instance, bought with my own money. Think I'll wear it today. Probably the most appropriate rag I have for a court room.

She laid her clothes out on the bed, stripped for a quick shower and tripped over the phone wire. "Damn," she muttered, then smiled, "One for the road, Lil dear, to make sure you're home where you belong."

Lillian picked it up on the eighth ring.

"Now kids be good for Mrs. Wilson," said Janet, in time with her spiked heels, clicking down the hall. At the landing she called, "Bye-bye," and wiggled into a light tan trench-coat. She turned the door-nob to go out just as a uniformed man appeared in the side-door window.

After, identifying her by name, he introduced himself as McDonough.

"Constable O'Reilly, my partner,"- he motioned to the man in the cruiser parked in the driveway - "and I, would like you to come to the station to answer a few questions."

Janet stared, aghast. "May I ask why?"

"It's about telephone calls you're making."

"There must be some mistake," she blurted.

"Nope."

"I can't possibly go now. I'm on my way to Toronto to give evidence at an Inquiry."

This ploy, McDonough hadn't heard before. He smiled as if he'd heard the punch line to a Newfie joke. "Then I assume you have a subpoena?" he asked.

Janet looked confused, so he explained. "If your presence at this Inquiry is essential you must have a court order to appear. If not, then lady you have no alternative but to come along with us."

"Okay big boy," she said. "But let's be quick about it."

The constable laughed. "They're probably going to lock you up and throw away the key."

Do Unto Others 535

It seemed proceedings related to Best's inadequacy were too frequent, unavoidable and offensive. Jim was sick of them. Seated at one end of the oval table with Mr. Lloyd-Davis, legal counsel for the five member Complaints Committee, he calculated the present one was the sixth in six months. He silently chastised the good Lord for taking Crooky away before the nasty business had finished.

He had been introduced to Best's new lawyer, Kenneth Barstow and to Geoffrey Robb who said amicably, "I'm well acquainted with Jim Lindsay." An exaggeration full of ambiguous interpretation, Jim thought, wondering why Robb was present. Undoubtedly Beecher had the right to call witnesses, but why Robb? The man had no first hand knowledge, except the Ireson boy, of any of the patients Beecher had been accused of mismanaging.

The Committee had allotted two days for the Inquiry and Dr. Lindsay wondered if it would be enough. "We'll never get through this stuff," he confided to John Lloyd-Davis.

Best was expanding his rationale, interrupted occasionally by a member of the Committee with meticulously thought-out questions, often beside the point. Lloyd-Davis half raised his hand for Jim's silence, listening carefully to what the participants were saying.

When there was a lull he confided. "We don't have to go through the entire thirteen cases, one convincing instance is all that's required to convict him of professional misconduct. When the Committee has heard enough it can signify an end to the proceedings. They've probably made up their minds already. The report of the fact finding delegation has been circulated among them and they've received copies of letters from the Shipton hospitals, outlining the reasons for reducing his privileges. The big decision as to whether or not he's guilty has probably been reached. It's a matter of settling his penalty which may be influenced by how Best presents himself, his attitude, that sort of thing."

"Finding him guilty in a few instances won't show the pattern." Jim argued. "He has a personality problem and shouldn't be allowed to do surgery. The only way to bring this out is to sift the whole lot."

"Doesn't matter. We need to find him guilty of negligence and misconduct in one instance. That's enough! Then we have the right to lift his license and that's why we're here?"

As Mr. Lloyd-Davis was beginning to sound annoyed Jim remained silent.

During the first half of the morning's session only the Lucas baby's problem had been discussed. It had proven educational. Geoffrey Robb gave a dissertation on the adverse effects on the ball of the hip when young thighs were spread wide apart for prolonged periods of time. "What he's done," Robb said in summary "is exactly what I'd have done! Reduce the forces compressing the joint and allow earlier movement." Whether the child ever had a dislocation and needed any kind of surgical treatment was completely glossed over.

While they broke for coffee Beecher looked about the parking lot for Janet's green Capri and returned to the Chambers muttering, "Where the hell is she?"

When he returned to the chambers the chairman spoke, "Dr. Best, we're waiting for you to tell us about the Ireson case."

Beecher felt cold, gloomy and pitifully alone.

"When did you first examine this child?" John Lloyd-Davis asked.

Unable to find the information immediately Beecher replied, "Around the middle of March."

"This year?"

"Yes."

"You'd never seen the child before?"

"No Sir."

Lloyd-Davis turned to the Chairman. "Sir," he said, "Before Dr. Best continues with this presentation I'd like Dr. Lindsay's account of the child's Past History to go on record."

"Proceed counselor. The Committee acknowledges Dr. Lindsay had treated the child previously. There is a copy of his office records on file."

Jim stood, smiled and began to speak slowly, "I must beg your pardon for the state they're in. Seems my notes have picked up a few stains. I was treating this child from birth until three months of age. He had a mild club foot deformity. The forefoot was turned in more than normal. I thought it was due to cramping in the womb."

"An intrauterine positional problem," Committeeman Fedorchuk, an obstetrician inserted.

"Correct. I treated it with casts, about five altogether. It wasn't quite normal when the mother took the infant elsewhere."

"To whom?" the Chairman asked.

"I'm not sure. I suggested she go to the Paediatric Hospital in Toronto. I didn't refer her to anyone in particular. I didn't see the child again until after Dr. Best had operated on him."

Geoffrey Robb had his hand up, drawing the chairman's attention. "I've logged a note, dating back to December 2nd '63. The child was placed in a Denis Browne splint. I saw him regularly until he started walking when I up-graded him to special shoes."

Beecher frowned. Robb's evidence was a revelation. He was still befuddled when the Chairman asked him if he would carry on with his part of the story.

"Mrs. Ireson was unhappy about the boy's left foot turning in more than the right." Beecher paused, seeing Jim Lindsay nudge Lloyd-Davis and awaited an inevitable question.

"Both feet were turning in?" the lawyer asked.

"Yes. But the left was worse."

"Is in-toeing an uncommon finding in children of this age?"

As Beecher failed to reply immediately Lloyd-Davis commented. "Dr. Lindsay tells me it's not uncommon. What is your opinion Dr. Robb?"

Geoffrey Robb shrugged, then sited various causes of in-toeing from malalignments of the hip to the toes themselves, waffling around Lloyd-Davis' question.

"So, Dr. Best," the Chairman recapped. "You felt the problem was severe and operated. What did you do?"

Beecher read his lengthy report of the surgical procedure and ended with the application of a cast, allowing Lloyd-Davis plenty of time to arm himself with more questions.

"You cut the lower shinbone above the ankle?"

"Yes."

"Then you twisted the lower half outward ninety degrees?'

"Yes. To correct the toeing-in one has to overcorrect to keep it from recurring as the child grows."

Lindsay and Robb exchange frowns and Robb addressed the chairman.

"It is a well documented fact, rotational malalignments do not revert to normal with bone growth and development. We have observed this in children with neglected fractures." Turning to Best he added. "Had you studied my text you'd have known this."

Lloyd-Davis had more points to clear up. "You kept the lower end of the bone rotated outward by placing a pin through each half and incorporating them in a cast?"

"Yes."

"Much like wringing out a dishcloth I'd imagine. You must have been worried about wringing the blood out of the leg."

"The circulation was fine after the operation and when I re-checked it during the night. It became impaired after the cast was split the next day."

Jim had doubted Beecher's audacity but here it was, an implication because Jim had split the cast he was responsible for the boy's circulatory problem. Jim shook his head solemnly. He'd not wanted to reveal the nurses' notes at this Inquiry. They were to be used in a Civil Court if the Iresons pushed him that far. To Lloyd-Davis he said, "I didn't think he'd make such an indefensible allegation. You can present those notes now if you wish."

"Mr. Chairman I have here a copy of the nursing record made at the time of the Ireson boy's sojourn in St. Mary's Hospital in Shipton."

"Where did you get that?" Beecher shouted.

"From Dr. Lindsay during the coffee break."

"I'm not at liberty to say more," Jim stated, "than it came from the hospital."

Barstow was on his feet. "Surely you can't accept the document as evidence, Mr.Chairman. It's a copy!"

"With an affidavit," Lloyd-Davis appended, "by all the nurses who'd signed their names on Ireson's chart during his admission between March 16th and 18th of this year. Now," he continued slowly for Dr. Best's benefit, "It boils down to your word against your honourable sisters in the nursing profession. Your version, there was no problem, or their's, he was screaming with pain, and they were unable to contact you."

Jim turned down Geoffrey Robb's invitation to join Beecher and him for lunch. He wondered how a hangman would feel under similar circumstances, watching the condemned choke on his last mouthful. Instead he accepted John Lloyd-Davis' offer to take him to the Manatee for seafood.

Over a smoked salmon salad John said, "We can have this thing wrapped up by Friday noon. I doubt if there's a member on the committee who wouldn't charge him with misconduct on the last case. And negligence," he added emphatically. "One out of two cases tried with eleven to go."

"How about this afternoon?" Jim asked.

"Possibly for you. There'll be summing up, not likely until tomorrow. But it depends. The members are practising docs and don't give up any more of their time than they have to."

"Fine, said Jim, "Then let's hit them with the back cases this afternoon." He suddenly remembered an appointment he had with McNutt. "Actual it doesn't matter; I have to come back to Toronto tomorrow anyway.

CHAPTER SIXTY-TWO

At Old Luigi's Restaurant Beecher was listening to Geoffrey Robb reminisce on his African experience. He wasn't hungry and marvelled how a man of Geoffrey's size could stash away so much food and stay so thin.

"It was primitive in those days. Half a week from Salisbury to Cape Town by train then another eleven days by steamer to Southampton, or one could travel through Mozambique to Beira and sail up the coast of Kenya. The airplane has sure made a difference."

"How long were you there?"

"Twelve years, throughout the war and then some."

"I remember the talk you gave back in '52. I was a second year medical student. A lot has happened since."

"True, the Federation has come and gone. Half of Rhodesia is now Zambia."

"Would you go back if you had the chance?"

"I don't think so. There's going to be big trouble I'm afraid. Smith declared unilateral independence two years ago, UDI they call it. The blacks want to run the country. Fighting's spotty but it'll spread."

"What about somewhere else?"

"Possibly. In fact, I've been thinking about it lately. The socialism in Canada is getting to me. If I'm to be a slave to the profession I'd like to chose my own master."

"Where would you go?"

"Asia most likely." Robb smiled. "However the kids have us tied down. When they're off to university we'll do something about it. In the meantime we dream."

"I'd like to go back," Beecher said.

"To Afghanistan?"

"Or somewhere similar."

"Does the church still have a mission there?"

"I don't know. If they'd take me I'd leave tomorrow."

Robb regarded Beecher critically. "As a start you've got to haul yourself out of this chaos, my friend. And what about your wife? Would she go back?"

Lil's feelings had never been of great concern to Beecher. He'd taken her for granted so long the idea of her having a mind of her own was completely foreign. He stared at his half eaten lasagna. He'd have to ask her and the thought pricked him.

"Beecher, you'll be lucky to come through this Inquiry with your licence intact. If you do, you'll have to take stock and protect what's left. Let me give you a bit of brotherly advice. Your wife started with nothing. She's sacrificed many times, before you entered her life, with you and after you. If you're foolish and drive her away, she'll do it again and again because it's her nature. Losing your licence would be nothing to losing her. If I'm any judge of Christians she's full of the Holy Spirit." Robb laughed, "She turns the other cheek so often she reminds me of an agitator in a dish washer. Might sound funny but it's applicable in your case because someone's always cleaning up after you. Lose her and you'll be left with nothing." Robb paused then added. "I know your personal life is your own business but I've heard rumours you're lusting after some chick who's not worthy of you. Drop her like a bag of shit!"

It was dark when Beecher got home. The afternoon session had been as bad as the morning's. The Committee had spent the earlier half on the Wolenski case, regarding Dr. Best as someone to be put in his place and avoided. The other back cases and the 'hanging hip' disaster had taken the rest of the day. He was asked to return at 9 am. the following morning.

Lillian was framed in the doorway leading into the house. She was wearing the broadest grin he had ever seen and looked anything but her pusillanimous self. She had even been to a hair dresser.

"Guess what?" she cried.

Beecher was bewildered.

"I nailed her good. That's what. She'll never call me again."

"I don't get it?"

"Your girlfriend Schocker was caught calling me this morning and the police pulled her in. They told me afterward how apologetic they were about not getting her sooner. It's a criminal offence. They'd have kept her in jail but agreed to let her go because she has a responsible job and two kids. Provided she doesn't leave town and shows up for a sentencing - probably after Christmas - her penalty could range from a fine to doing community service. How about that!"

"I wish my day had gone so well."

They ate a late supper in a shiny new room, on a decadent table with a pair of lighted candles. Having no table cloth she laid out woven maroon place mats from Bamiyan.

"Haven't seen those for a while," Beecher noted. "In fact, I had lunch with Dr. Robb today and Afghanistan came up in our conversation."

"Would you really like to go back there?"

"Depends on how you feel."

Lillian gaped in surprise. "Do you really care how I feel, Beech?" she asked.

He was slow to reply, "I'm beginning to."

"That's a concession I don't believe. But it does help. Now, tell me about all the terrible things that happened today."

His elbows were resting on the table. Setting his face in his hands he resembled a basset hound with harassed eyes. "I'll be lucky to keep my licence. The Ireson case killed me. Lindsay showed up with a copy of the nurses' notes and the members of the Complaints Committee put more stock in them than in me."

Lil was thinking to have another's trust one had to earn it and Beecher hadn't even the right to apply. Still she stuck to her premise in the long run he'd improve. His behaviour couldn't get any worse. It was as good a time as any for an umpteenth beginning. Before reconstruction all of the old walls had to come down and the facts bared. "I gave him the copy," she announced.

Beecher's jaw retracted, impeding his speech, and he choked.

"Indirectly," Lil revealed, "Through Sister Bernadette. Call it disloyalty if you wish but you've been unfaithful to me so many times I've lost count. Even after our talk with Reverend Trussell."

His lips barely moved. "How did you get it?"

"I made a copy of a copy." She smiled. "Of the one I found in your pocket."

"Why?"

"I was thinking of divorce." Her voice tailed off, "I couldn't go through with it." She looked at his hapless face, the dark curly hair she'd fondled so long and spoke warmly, the candlelight brightening her green eyes. "Sure Beech, I'd go to Afghanistan. I'd go anywhere with you but you've got to change."

Janet Schocker had spent a large part of her day answering questions at the police station. If she had told the truth in the beginning it wouldn't have taken so long. The officers had been lenient, permitting her to follow in her car but had confiscated her keys upon arrival. At noon she was served a ham and cheese sandwich and while waiting there were magazines to read. Finally they had her sign a confession. Pending a sentence, she was to take cognizance of her travel rights and stay within fifty miles of town.

Released and frightened by the thought of how to resolve her problem she drove her Capri, neither caring nor worrying where she was going, subconsciously heading east to her parents in Gananoque. Not until the wretched vehicle was gasping from gas hunger near Kingston did her environment come into focus, a gravel shoulder and a road sign motionless in the high beams. The question of what to do next was solved by the appearance of a flashing red light in her rear-view mirror. Expectantly she rolled down the window.

"Are you in trouble Miss?" The patrolman asked.

Janet's hands were quivering on the wheel. My God she thought, I'm not supposed to be here. There was nothing she could say.

"May I have your driver's licence and the car registration please?"

The officer held a flashlight aimed at her purse. She made no effort to open it. When he sniffed inside and asked if she'd been drinking she could only shrug.

"You do have some credentials?"

There was still no verbal response.

"Look here Miss I'm talking to you!"

Janet felt paralysed and held her breath. He shook her shoulder. "Are you okay?" he asked.

"Wheeew." She let it all out and exhausted, replied, "Yes, I've just run out of gas."

"There's a service centre two miles further along. If you'd like I'll take you there. Sorry to have frightened you," he added, misinterpreting her reaction.

"That's all right," she smiled. "Will they have to tow this old clunker in?"

"Not likely. They'll come back with enough gas to get you into the station where you can fill up."

It was late when Janet returned to Shipton. The house was in complete darkness. Fumbling to get her key in the lock she noticed a white envelope plastered to the window. Her name was scrawled on it, readable with the aid of the street lamp. She chucked the envelope into her purse and tried the lock again. Her key didn't fit. She banged on the door. Uncertain of her next move she got back in the Capri, turned on the dome light and ripped open the envelope. Inside was a note from Peter! 'Go find your own place,' she read. 'I know all there is to know, thanks to George McDonough. It's unfortunate they didn't bring you over to the city jail, so I could've looked after you personally.'

The proceedings had resumed and the Bataglia case was under discussion. Jim had difficulty staying interested. Beecher was wound in knots. While Barstow was trying to untangle him with leading questions, John Lloyd-Davis said for Jim's ears alone. "This'll wrap it up. There's no point in going any farther. We've got him on five counts of incompetence and two for negligence. I will suggest to the Committee during the mid morning break they call a halt. There's still a summation and the sentencing but we won't need you for that. Possibly his lawyer will make a plea for leniency through Dr. Robb. Even if there's some sort of compromise it won't interfere with removing him from the Staff of your Orthopaedic Department. With restrictions on his licence no one can order you to take him back."

Jim did not seem pleased. Another stressful situation had arisen. During the night Brahms had been admitted to the Westdale Hospital in Toronto.

Martha had called to say it wasn't urgent and there was no need to rush over, but Merri had a premonition. She insisted Jim meet her in the lobby at three. She would collect the younger girls and they could visit Boppa together.

After Dr. Lindsay's departure the Committee met in private and agreed unanimously upon the charges. Beecher was brought in and his licence would've been revoked had it not been for Geoffrey Robb's professional stature and power of persuasion. He convinced the five members of the Discipline Committee the young orthopaedist's problem was more a lack of proper training than bad judgement. "He needs a year or two in a good teaching centre with someone to put him straight. No one in Shipton is qualified to do this nor is there anyone interested in offering constructive criticism. This has led to a communication gap, the main reason for his getting into trouble. I can secure a grant for him at the Cancer Research Institute for six months, then take him on as my assistant."

    A few brows rose at Dr Robb's generosity, but more in doubt of his succeeding. The members agreed to a two year probational period in which Beecher would have to report his activities to the Committee on a quarterly basis. When it had terminated his case would be reviewed.

"It's the best you could have hoped for my friend," said Robb later. "Two years from now the Committee will have changed membership. If anyone remains, he'll either have forgotten the details of this Inquiry or not be inclined to sift through them again. Everything depends on an improvement in your behaviour. Suppose you start by communing with our Lord."

McNutt was absent from his office. Jim had not expected to see him because his appointment had been for later in the day. The purpose of the visit was to convey the nurses' affidavit accompanied by a copy of their notes on the Ireson boy. He cancelled and left the data with the lawyer's secretary.

    Leaving his car in the underground parking he ambled around downtown. It was unseasonably balmy, out of keeping with the Christmas decorations. The scene did remind him there was nothing like being prepared. With time to kill he dropped into the Woolen Shop and purchased a cashmere sweater set for Merri followed by a romp through Eaton's furniture department. A Stiffel lamp took his fancy so he bought it too, paused momentarily in the Toy Department and before walking back onto the street had two pairs of soft leather moccasin slippers tucked under his arm, thinking Heather and Kathy would really enjoy their beaded motif and furry lining.

After an overdue lunch alone he reached Westdale Hospital ten minutes early. Heather and Kathy, to his amusement, were practising gymnastics on the front lawn. Julie greeted him.

    "Mum has gone to see Boppa by herself," she said. "He's in a coma and the doctor said it's better we wait. Can you sneak us in?"

    Jim smiled and put an arm around her. "This isn't St. Mary's Julie. Here, I'm just another customer." He gave her shoulders a squeeze. "But I'll try."

It was an old place with high ceilings and tall airy windows. Burl Cunningham had been admitted to a room over the main entrance. His eyes were closed and a blanket had been drawn to his chin. On the far side Martha knelt on the floor, leaning against the bed, her tear-stained cheeks resting in the bend of an elbow. Jim felt Merri's hand close on his own as he looked down at the pale yellow oval once radiant with strength, now sunken on a pillow. After a moment his gaze shifted from the old man, beyond his mother-in-law, and the misty pane to where their genes spun cartwheels on the lawn outside.

Part Four

Monday, March 1, 1971
to
Monday, December 13, 1971

Dr. Lindsay & Dr. Mahmud

CHAPTER SIXTY-THREE

"Thompson's Disease! What the hell is that?" Joel Callahan's eyes narrowed, listening to the chief resident's provisional diagnosis. The condition had deserted him.

"It's spelled without a 'p', and ends in 'en'. Thomsen's Disease," Mahmud corrected, "or myotonia congenita, was first described by a Dane."

The attending shook his head slowly. "You sure?"

"No. I've never seen a case before but from her exaggerated tendon jerks it would be my first choice."

The two were standing in an outpatient cubicle beside a three year old girl, seated on the edge of the examining table. Dari pocketed his reflex hammer, lifted the child by the waist and transferred her to a nearby chair. "Now Missy," he smiled, pushing the curtain aside, "run down the hall."

A request readily accepted for the girl viewed the opening as a means of escape. White coated doctors frightened her. She bounded off the seat and one spastic step later fell flat on her face.

Dari picked her off the floor and put her back on the table. "Okay," he said with assurance, "Do it again but not so fast."

At a slower pace her gait improved and within the time it took to reach the waiting room she was walking normally.

Allowing her to rest a few minutes, the test was repeated with the same results.

"Well!" Joel's brow wrinkled with curiosity. "Very interesting," he remarked. "What do we do about it?"

"Get a paediatric consultation." Dari shrugged. "I'm not even sure this is a case of Thomsen's Disease. If it is, maybe there's a specific drug for it, an antispasmodic perhaps. She's certainly not a candidate for orthopaedic appliances, nor an operation. Physiotherapy possibly."

Callahan turned to the plain-faced, plump young woman who had brought the child for examination. "How long has she been this way, mother?"

"I'm not her mother. I'm from Social Services."

"I see." The attending regarded her contemptible look, wondering if it was worth while asking anything more. She hadn't answered his first question.

"What do you know about her?" Dari pursued.

"Nothing. The administrator at the orphanage suggested someone should see her because she wasn't walking properly. I made an appointment with your department."

"Has she been to any other doctors?" Callahan asked.

"Just a child psychiatrist," she submitted, sarcastically.

"They're doctors too," Mahmud smirked, adding, "although you may think otherwise." While he was scribbling a note to the Paediatric Clinic he paused to ask the child's name.

"I know her only as Penny."

"Okay. I'll put her down as Penny Farthing. How's that?"

"Not so funny," Callahan smiled.

Dari handed the slip of paper to the social worker and told her where to take it. "Too bad, that negates investigating the family which could prove interesting; it's an inheritable condition."

Dr. Joel Callahan was impressed. "You really are a clever bugger Mahmud. How come you know so much about it?"

"Reading. Since I've been researching muscle pedicle grafts anything about muscle attracts me."

"How's the project going?"

Dari's answer lacked enthusiasm. "I'm not keen on it."

"How's that?"

"The experiment is like re-inventing the wheel."

A group of medical students had been looking on throughout Mahmud's demonstration. One of them interrupted to ask. "What's a muscle pedicle graft?"

"A transplant of bone with its blood supply intact," Dari answered. "It includes a major muscle attachment. Most of the blood supply to bone comes through its muscular connections, either its origins or insertions. The purpose of our experiment is to prove it works better than using conventional bone chips which are necessarily stripped of muscle tissue. So far the results are promising. We're doing a comparative study in the lab. It would be a better method of filling gaps, reconstructing bone and fusing joints, the hip for instance."

After the clinic Mahmud went to the dog-lab to check the animals he had worked on during the morning. Their food trays were untouched. None of them appeared hungry although they would have chewed the dressings off their hind legs given the chance. To prevent this from

Do Unto Others 551

happening they had been outfitted with Elizabethan collars, made from plastic pails, and kept in special wire mesh kennels.

While Dari squatted, bent forward peering into a cage, hands in the pockets of his lab coat, the keeper asked, "How many more to go Doc?"

"That depends on Durnford, Buck."

The project relied upon another grant from the Westmoreland Foundation and Sandy Durnford, head of orthopaedics, had run out of funds.

To Dari the experiment was like a whirl on a merry-go-round; essentially he was refining another investigator's work. 'Duplication and re-duplication is the name of the game, proof beyond a shadow of doubt', Durnford had exclaimed! If Dari accepted the job he had the option of staying a fifth year, to either finish or continue the research. After a few months he had begun to wonder if the project wasn't to ensure Durnford's publishing a yearly paper for the University. 'Won't do you any harm to have your name in a scientific journal as well,' his chief suggested and as usual had his way.

In the beginning he had marvelled at the equipment; the University was well endowed. Each department had the latest state of the art devices. There wasn't an electron microscope in the whole of Afghanistan, not that it matter, there were more vital things his country had to do without. As time passed the work had become tedious.

In addition Dari still had the chief resident's responsibilities with no one to back him.

Buck was a hirsute, scrawny man. With a long nose and undercut chin, he blended well with the specimens under his care. He loved dogs and they loved him. He had worked for the SPCA where unwanted animals had to be destroyed. 'Culling the canine crowd' was the phrase his employer had used. No one had suggested doing transplants on them. If Buck had his way he would have bought a forsaken island, one of the thousand in the upper St. Lawrence, and let them fend for themselves. Not a bad idea! Wasn't there a band of ponies, living on a sandy spit off Nova Scotia? An impractical wish to which he clung, killing with compassion, until the thought occurred if they had to die why not for something worthwhile, for the good rather than the meanness of their masters. Medicine seemed like a fine place to start. Everyone had heard of Banting and his quest for insulin but how many knew the names of the sacrificed dogs, indeed if the pitiful creatures had any identification other than numbers? Rearing them for research did prolong their start, and he had taken the job at the animal lab with a commitment to look after them. To him they were unsung heroes and should have statues erected to them. He misread Dari's concrete silence.

"You feel sorry for them doc?"

"In a way," Dari replied. He had no intention of discussing his aversion to an experiment which he felt was a waste of money, time and dogs. It stood to reason, transplanted bone with its blood supply intact had to fare better than the customary bloodless chips. What was the point of proving it?

On the private ward Mahmud went to see Paul Wurtmann's patient, scheduled for a meniscectomy the following morning.

"What's your complaint?" He asked the tall well proportioned young woman, reading beside the window. She had large protruding blue eyes, focused on him in a belligerent stare. Slowly the book was lowered to her lap and she studied him cagily.

Her smile was forced. "To whom must I answer?"

"Mahmud, Dr. Darius Abdullah Mahmud." Dari frowned as he glanced over the patient's chart. "You're Debra Hathaway. Am I correct?"

She nodded, insensitive to his handsome features and superior physique. "To save you any more questions," she condescended, "I'm a gymnast, a Phys Ed major in perfect health. Wurtmann is to remove a torn cartilage from my left knee."

Sufficient information allotted, Ms. Hathaway returned to her reading. But Dari wasn't through. Her crustiness did not deter him; he'd come to do a History and Physical. She had a problem and he needed experience. If she did not wish to let him examine her that was her privilege and there was nothing he could do about it. Nevertheless he would give it a try. "That's great," he said mechanically. "The doctor expects me to write you up. May I have a look?"

Wurtmann had not told her what to expect and she was not in favour of being pawed by a trainee. "You're Dr. Paul's intern?" She asked.

"No." Mahmud paused, "Jonathon, the intern, should have seen you earlier."

"Then what - I mean - who are you?"

"A research fellow, relieving while the chief orthopaedic resident is on holiday."

From the twitching of her facial muscles, he had trouble differentiating between a temporary muddling of her cerebrum and a thyroid storm. She poked a leg through the front of her kimono and grumbled, "Be my guest."

"On your back in bed with your knees straight," he demanded.

Miss Hathaway did as she was told. "Now what?" she sneered.

Dari stressed the ligaments when the knee was extended. Content there was no medial or lateral instability he checked the cruciates by flexing the knee and drawing the leg forward and backward. After detecting an abnormal amount of motion he studied the supposedly normal knee and frowned.

Her, "What's the matter?", was ignored while Dari proceeded with the rest of the examination, producing a definite clunk in the affected knee when he rotated the flexed leg outward on the thigh.

"I agree," he said, "You probably have torn your cartilage, in addition to the anterior cruciate ligament."

The latter finding had not been mentioned by Dr. Wurtmann and Ms. Hathaway bit her clenched fist. "What's the anterior cruciate ligament?" she asked, sounding more polemic than puzzled.

"It's a tough fibrous cord within your knee which stabilizes the joint."

"Is it a serious problem?"

Looking cold and impenetrable, Dari answered. "Depends how much stress you put on your leg."

"I plan on setting up a Gymnastics School when I graduate this spring."

"You should reconsider. Overuse will aggravate it. Taking out your cartilage will get rid of the temporary locking but won't prevent your knee from giving way. There are means of bracing it, either by building up your muscle strength, or surgically reconstructing the ligament. Taking everything into account any excess strain on the joint afterwards could put you right back where you are."

While he had been advising Ms. Hathaway, she drew herself up in bed, disbelieving whatever he said.

Before leaving he frowned. "Sorry about that!"

A fresh topping of snow dismayed Mahmud. By the end of February Rochester had endured a hundred inches and the glittering stuff was no patron of amputees.

In the warmth of the medical school's lounge a disc jockey humoured a million marooned listeners with the latest ski reports. 'There's more of the soft slumberous stuff to come folks. So haul yourself out of hibernation and break a leg with the rest of the nation, on 'Bristol Hills'.

Without 4-wheel drive who can reach the slopes? Mahmud smiled. He had not driven in weeks. There were flashing blue lights everywhere as snow trucks rumbled through the long nights: ploughing, salting, sanding, moving one pile to another and raising banks to lamppost height.

Dari stepped into slush and trudged for home, thinking to meet a yeti on the road would come as no surprise.

"My peg has blistered again," he surmised by the stickiness of his stump-sock.

Roxane helped him out of his parka and he dropped uncomfortably into a Lazy-Boy. She knelt, tenderly raised his sodden trouser cuffs and removed his boots. Blood seeped through an elastoplast dressing; she detached it and set his leg in a basin of warm water.

A hot supper gradually restored him. She knew Dari too well not to detect he was troubled. During the meal she avoided comment, and later as they sat together on the sofa, busied herself sewing.

"I hate to complain Roxane, and I hate to worry you. I've kept hoping at some later date my feelings would improve and still might. Maybe when I'm on my own, when I have control over my practice, I'll feel better. Now I'm discouraged."

These statements were new, a side of Dari never before exposed. Her reaction was to listen intently.

"You must remember how keen I was to come here. I raved about the chance to learn orthopaedics, the best specialty, and to be admitted to such a fine institution."

She nodded in agreement.

"I was deluding myself. It's not an institution. It's a market place and I've been treated no better than a baccha."

Roxane looked surprised then concerned, waiting for him to elaborate.

"Most patients have insurance and are treated by their own doctors." Mahmud's speech quickened. "There are a few free ward cases at the County Hospital, mainly geriatric patients and most have fractured hips. Staff men at the university don't mind us residents pinning them but do they let us operate on any of their paying customers? No Sir! I feel I'm being used."

"This morning Wurtmann sent me to his office across the street to pick up x-rays of a patient he was about to open. He wanted them right away. I ran into Stowe, his associate, who complained about my wet boots, saying they did not appreciate assistants messing their carpets. When I returned to the O.R. Wurtmann, without a word of thanks growls, 'put them on the view box,' and wraps his first assistant Ted Mason on the knuckles for letting up on the retractors. 'Get in here and give me a hand he shouts.' I tell you, Roxane, I feel like quitting. He's more high and mighty than a camel's ass."

Dari paused and was about to rant on when the phone rang. Roxane managed a sympathetic glance and went to answer it. In a moment she returned. "It's Dr. Wurtmann."

"Damn it all! What does he want now?"

"He didn't say," she smiled and continued in a whisper. "Maybe he's called to apologize."

"Not on your life!" Dari squeezed the base of his nose and rubbed his eyes, pulling himself off the chesterfield.

He returned more livid than ever. "I've just had a blast of vehemence from that bastard!"

"I'm terribly sorry Dari jan." Whatever had been said to upset him she knew he didn't deserve.

"All I did was offer practical advice to one of his patients and he tells me I had no business talking to her. She's in her late twenties and wants to be a gymnastic teacher. She asked me for my opinion and I told her. Her knee has had it. He knows himself but says she shouldn't lose hope. After I'd spoken to her she called him, distressed and in tears. When it comes to shekels Wurtmann is as shady as the Arab traders who've been deceiving us for centuries. He knows her anterior cruciate ligament is torn so why not fix it when he removes her meniscus. Why? because he can make a little extra with a second operation. Dari hesitated to catch his breath before barrelling on. "I think it's for his convenience, not the patient's."

He was becoming carried away and Roxane brought him back to reality.

"What exactly did he say?"

"Oh what does it matter. By sucking around him I might get more to do but that's not my style. I knew he'd be bothered by my advising his patient and subliminally I did it to annoy him."

"Is he a good surgeon?"

"The best in Rochester! From watching him I've learned a lot. But as far as his allowing me any responsibility I might as well have stayed home. Afghanistan is loaded with pathology. I came here for operating experience, and I'm not being given a chance."

Roxane remained silent while he quietly brooded.

Probably it was time they went home, she thought, half way through her first pregnancy. If they didn't move soon it would be inadvisable. They had talked about the possibility of becoming permanent residents but neither was keen on staying. They had not met another Afghan since they arrived in '67. They were a true minority! Why did blacks and Mexicans complain? There were many more of them.'

She went to the kitchen and brought him a cup of coffee.

"How would you like to try Canada? he asked.

"Why?"

"I think the training might be better. They've got a form of socialized medicine that pays for doctors' services. The more work the docs do, the more they get paid. I would imagine they'd be only too happy to have someone come along and make a bit extra for them. They could pay me a locum tenens salary, pocket the rest, and I'd get some experience. Doctor Lindsay's overworked. I'm sure he'd be happy to have me. He's also a very good teacher. In Afghanistan he wasn't afraid to let Amir Kash operate on his elbow, provided he could instruct. He had confidence in their combined skill. It would be no different than my performing on some of his cases. Maybe he'd let me solo once I'd proven myself."

Roxane had no view on this assumption but was anxious about shunting themselves north of the border. "Suppose Dr. Lindsay honoured your intentions. How long would we stay?"

"At least until autumn when I could take the Fellowship examination and add an F.R.S.C.(C) to my name." He smiled wryly. "Who knows, we might like Canada. It's also a multicultural country.

Likely it has an Afghan ghetto. We're stuck here until the end of June unless I can finish the experiments earlier, or Durnford gets somebody else to take them on. I'll call Lindsay tomorrow. How would you like to run over and see his family again?"

"I'd love to, Dari jan. But not in this weather!"

That night as they lay close he became aware of a stirring beside him. Awake he felt it again, poking his flank. The first movements of the child within Roxane. His child. He held himself taut, enjoying an enchanting feeling. Damn! he mouthed an instant later. Afghanistan was their home and the child ought to be born in the warmth of the zunana.

In May Mahmud made the trip to Shipton alone. A week earlier on a lilac scented evening he had returned from New York where with a prolonged hug and a promise to write regularly he saw Roxane off at Kennedy Airport. Now as he drove the seventy odd miles to the Canadian border his loneliness was almost overwhelming.

Their companionship had always been a meaningful part of his life. He'd miss their secrets, their triumphs and despair, their inseparable silences and her buoyant vitality in answer to his jubilant call whenever he entered the apartment. All of which he realized was so casually accepted.

Other than her picture and the few articles of clothing remaining he was left with her intangible love and a pledge to take care of herself. The apartment was as dull as a suite of rooms in a second rate hotel without room service; to compensate most of his meals were taken in a eatery around the corner. He hated to go home and sought diversion in his research. With luck it would be completed soon.

CHAPTER SIXTY-FOUR

Dari met Dr. Lindsay at ten to eight in the foyer of St. Mary's Hospital. A young man, five years his junior, was introduced as Rich Mosley.

"Rich is a local boy soon to finish a year of General Surgery in the 'Queens' program," Jim explained. "Thinks he'd like to become an orthopaedic surgeon."

Mahmud's smile concealed his disinterest as he politely shook the stranger's hand and turned to ask. "You mentioned you are doing two knee replacements this morning - what implant are you using?"

"Gunsten's," replied Jim, checking his watch. "The first has been scheduled for eight. Then we'll go to the General and do the second."

Two months earlier Mahmud had written to Dr. Lindsay indicating he was interested in coming to Canada. In a corner of the crowded elevator he thought of the orthopaedist's reply, urging him to contact the Provincial and Federal Colleges. He did and learned that his credentials permitted him to practise under supervision until he passed the Fellowship examination. He received a favourable reply from the Federal College enabling him to attempt the Fellowship in the fall. If he associated with a recognized hospital he could start work any time, provided he had passed the ECFMG examination. He called Lindsay to share the encouraging news and was invited to Shipton for the day. The only question was whether the Canadian government would issue an Immigrant Visa. For the time-being he bridged the mighty Niagara as a visitor and was happy to have Jim's invitation.

"What sort of prosthesis are they implanting in Rochester?" Dr. Lindsay asked.

"Animetric non-constrained," Mahmud sighed, adding, "not for general use yet."

"Tell me about the components," Jim asked.

"There are only two, not four as in the prosthesis you are about to insert, which makes it less complicated. Still the Animetric Total condylar replacement is an exacting procedure and should not be undertaken by an inexperienced surgeon. The materials used are the same, metal femoral runners to articulate with plastic implanted into the tibia. Both halves are cemented into position. So far

Wurtmann has been using three sizes of each and has been replacing the surface of the knee cap with a small polyethylene pad."

"How many have you done yourself?"

Mahmud looked embarrassed. "I've pleaded to operate on one of the County patients but have been refused. 'The fewer variables the better', Wurtmann claims, which means one operator. No need to tell you who. The company will probably name it after him."

The discourse ended in the Doctors' Lounge of the O.R. where Jim was trapped by Joe Paolone. The General Hospital's retiring Chief of Staff was waving an application.

"Hey! Lindsayello," he sung, "Put your John Henry on this sheet of paper and enter the Archives of the College as one of the three prestigious surgeons who proposed for Fellowship the most brilliant operator of all times - me."

Sensing it was a personal matter, Dari did not wait for an introduction and went with Mosley to look for a scrub suit.

Jim grabbed the document. He had not attended the Annual Meeting of the College but did receive a copy of the minutes, the main issue being how doctors possessing a Specialist Certificate could be admitted as Fellows. All it took was the signatures of three bona fide Fellows, practising in the area. Noting the blank spaces on the application form Jim decided to tease Paolone.

"I find it difficult to understand why you can't get anyone else to sign."

"I'd thought your attitude might be different than the others."

"By 'others', you mean Atwater, Alligood and Bagley? They've all passed the Fellowship exam."

When Dr. Paolone didn't answer, Jim assumed that Joe had already asked them. He smiled facetiously. "What good is one 'aye' against two abstentions."

"I haven't talked to them yet. I thought you might be more sympathetic, having taken a dislike to a certain examiner for making you repeat your oral and for the lack of support given to us by the Royal College during the Best hearings.

"My attitude toward the College has nothing to do with signing your paper." Jim chuckled. "But it might be a way of getting revenge - foisting you upon them."

"Don't hand me that crap Lindsayello. We go back a long way. I was one of the guys who supplied you with a reference to join the Medical Staff at the General remember! I got you a job in the E.R. when you first came to town so you could put a little food on the table remember! Sure I haven't sent you many cases - I don't see a lot of orthopaedic problems. But in good faith and because I think you're the greatest bone setter around, I asked you to look after Angela. Though you don't know it I supported you after the Best fiasco when half the docs were cutting you up behind your back, claiming you had a vendetta, being sued by a patient of his. I told them they couldn't see between their own two feet, that the cause of the kid's problem was Best's own doing and you had done the bunch of them and the town a big favour by getting rid of him." All of this Joe managed in one breath then ended abruptly, "So you'll sign it?"

"I didn't say I would, nor did I refuse," Jim affirmed, looking down at a pair of flat inflamed eyes.

Paolone was no scholar - In '47 when the College devised a lower examination Joe hadn't been required to write it either and became certified through the grandfather clause. But he was a clever technician, smart enough to stay out of trouble.

Jim grinned devilishly. "I will! Mainly because years ago you predicted this would happen. 'Someday,' you said, 'they're going to do away with that damned examination.'" Jim turned to the wall to support his pen and autographed the form. "There," he added, "Join the club."

Rich Mosley was an errant gossip, so galling during his visits to the Lindsays, Merri would remove herself from the living room, leaving Jim alone to listen to the young man's rubbish. Physically he was as solid as a truck and kept his motor idling with interspersed 'ah ums' when he had nothing to say. Passing through the scrub room, Jim overheard him telling Dari how much the Kingston doctors were making.

"How do you know?" Mahmud asked. Never in Rochester had an 'attending' leaked such classified information. Certainly there was speculation among the house staff, especially over Wurtmann's earnings.

"I've seen their books."

"In fact!"

"Yes. We had a course in office procedures. A lot were logging over a thousand a day. That's over two hundred thousand a year. One G.P., a sports medicine expert, told us he grosses over four hundred thousand but has a heavy overhead: three clinics and five physiotherapists. Now that the Province has joined the National Health scheme he'll be able to bill for their help. He's lucky! Since the program started only hospitals can hire physios."

"Isn't that an infringement on free enterprise?" Mahmud sounded sceptical, adding, "How does one tap this cornucopia?"

"Easy. You just have to sign up. You're given a number and a stack of cards. Fill in one for each patient and send it to a central office. At the end of the month the bills are processed and 'voila' a check by return mail a month later. How's that for service?"

The door suddenly swung open as Dr. Lindsay re-entered and Rich reverted to his 'ah ums'.

"When you finish scrubbing, Dari, it'll save time if you prep the patient." Jim moved into the spot vacated by Rich and wet his hands. "I've positioned him and applied the tourniquet. We'll inflate it later after he's been draped. Rich, Mrs. Schocker will help you gown and glove. Stand well back until we get under way. And do the patient and me a big favour by not talking."

Rich Mosley had a benign appearance, more innocuous than friendly. His droopy outer lids lent him a woeful expression. Where Mahmud's eyelashes were long and dark Rich's were lighter but of matching length. They fluttered in annoyance behind a pair of minimizing lenses. Eyes were all Jim could see, the rest of his assistants were covered in green paper throw away gear.

Rich followed Mahmud into the theatre and Jim began his aseptic toilet, pondering as he automatically ran the brush over his fingers, how quickly his profession was changing. If Wurtmann was successful in developing a new knee prosthesis, the operation they were about to start was already obsolete. Momentarily he contemplated cancelling. In the few patients who underwent the Gunsten knee replacement the immediate results were promising. To cancel now would be a setback to the patient. Waiting for general acceptance were the arthroscope and computerized axial tomography or CAT scan - investigative techniques to alter orthopaedics.

Jim smiled to himself, because of these advances we have acronyms such as 'THR' and 'TKR' for total hip and total knee replacement, bandied about by instrument 'sales reps' like the old patent medicine pedlars.

The business of Paolone's application was another example of a powerful medical body's attempt to catch up. The Royal College founded by an elite group of scholars forty years ago was sadly out of date. How could an individual hope to learn the vast amount of knowledge accumulating on any medical subject? Small wonder increasingly more doctors were specializing and it was a credit to the collective intelligence of the College to incorporate them.

A 'Right Wing Crank', Gloria Knightingale had called Jim, for refusing to join the Ontario Health Insurance Plan. The G.P. was part of a new breed and could not understand his motives so he let the comment pass. She came from a school that believed in problem oriented teaching and tackled each patient in the same geometric fashion. The system riled him, a system where donkeys were to be prodded by carrots not sticks. Few of his classmates had learned by their own initiative, most had to be beaten into it. With Gloria it had been the carrot, an attractive government assured payment, almost a guaranteed minimum wage. "Mediocrity!," Jim exclaimed and raising his dripping hands strode into the O.R.

The operation went smoothly. Mahmud was permitted to expose the joint and close it after the four components were aligned and cemented in position.

On the way to the General Dari commented, "At the University of Rochester Hospital Sandy Durnford wants to refurbish the orthopaedic O.R. with laminar air flow, a system instituted in England for its beneficial effect on wound contamination."

"Sounds ideal for managing hips and knees," Jim added, "but how do they operate on the neck and upper extremities?"

Mahmud laughed. "I don't think that's been worked out yet. The whole patient and anaesthetist would have to be included. I'd hate to give an anaesthetic, encumbered by all that gear."

"Larson, whom you'll meet soon, could handle it." Remembering how Reif had intubated a patient upside-down, put a smile on Jim's face. "But he's getting set in his ways."

"Then I'm sorry for him." said Mahmud seriously. "One must accept new challenges or be dropped along the way."

Rich Mosley's parents lived midway between the auto factory and the General Hospital. As they approached their corner he tapped Dr. Lindsay on the shoulder and asked to be let out.

"You're welcome to come along," said Jim.

Do Unto Others 563

Rich grunted, "To watch another total knee!" His head wagged negatively. "Ah um, not me. You see one, you've seen 'em all."

Jim gave him an indifferent nod. "How about this afternoon?" he invited. "I've scheduled a discotomy."

Halfway out of the back seat Dr. Mosley trained his droopy eyes on the back of Jim's neck. His lower lip closed momentarily then he licked it, uncovering a protuberance of upper teeth. "Ah um," he said, "Backs don't turn me on," adding, "count me out," and was gone.

Mahmud turned to Jim with a questioning frown. It's hard to believe. "He told me he wants to be an orthopaedic surgeon."

The second case went as well as the first, with Keefer passing instruments, Jim mainly assisting and Mahmud performing most of the operation. The Afghan handled the soft tissues with the gentleness of an expert and only drew upon Jim's experience in placing the jig and positioning the templates. His cuts were done with accuracy; the components fitted and cemented. As soon as the methylmethacrylate had set the knee joint fell back into perfect alignment. "See one, do one," Jim beamed. "Now you can go back to the university and teach one."

More interested in the young surgeon's physical attributes than his manual dexterity, Tanya Harrington had pretended to watch the operation. He had to be at least fifteen years younger but who could tell? Nature had been kind, her skin was as smooth as silk, greyness was managed with a bottle of hair dye and she didn't look a day over thirty.

While the patient was being splinted she stepped up her familiarity. "What part of Afghanistan are you from?"

He answered with another question. "Have you ever been there?"

"No, but my stepfather has and I've read about it. Bamiyan, 'cross-road of the world' is said to be BE-U-tiful," she affected. "A veritable Shangrila!"

"That is true." His back was to her but Keefer saw his face light up as he added, "My wife is from there."

Tanya never drew a man into idle conversation without an ulterior motive. "Where is she now?"

Mahmud was used to inquisitive North Americans asking personal questions, a part of their culture and relatively harmless. "She is now in Gulbahar with my family, soon to expect our first born."

Jim was surprised. Nothing had been said about Roxane's pregnancy. "Merri will be delighted with this news. She's expecting us for lunch and will want to hear all about her."

Behind her mask Tanya drooled. The wife was no problem. "Do you come to Shipton often?" she asked.

"This is my first time but I might in future if I can find a job."

"Well," she crooned lasciviously. "You must come around for a meal sometime. My father-in-law has been to Afghanistan and would be delighted to meet you."

Dari failed to notice the glow in her amber eyes. "Your courteous invitation is gratefully accepted," he smiled. "At present I'm very busy and must refuse."

Merri served a tureen of Jim's favourite shrimp, celery and barley soup followed by super hamburgers. Hearing of Roxane's pregnancy, she had greeted Mahmud more excitedly than on previous visits. She too had important news to tell but wasn't sure how to go about it. There was a spinster, living in the burgh of Abbey, who could be Dari's aunt. After lunch she joined the men in the screened-in-porch and facing them supported a paper bag on her lap.

They were discussing Mahmud's move to Canada.

"I'd be pleased to have you come in with me," said Jim. "I haven't had a close association with anyone in the twenty years I've been here."

"It wouldn't be permanent," Mahmud stated. "I'd like to take the exam this fall. Afterward I'm not sure where I'd prefer to settle."

Jim guessed at the younger man's undeclared reasons, thinking they were the same as his; a working relationship should have a trial run. It might not be compatible. "That's fine!" he agreed. "Suppose we give it six months plus or minus, say till the end of the year. You'll have a better idea where you're going. You might want to return to the States."

Dari smiled, "Maybe. I was thinking I'm needed in my own country."

Merri could hold her secret no longer. "But I do have some news which may be apropos to what you're discussing. If Dr. Mahmud wishes to immigrate, having a relative in Canada could be a big advantage."

Both Dari and Jim turned with open mouths.

"You remember the Eckheusens Jim?" He motioned for her to proceed. "I saved the newspaper article and the obituary. I've meant to follow up a hunch but kept putting it off. This morning I decided to look into it and found Nicole's sister Oudette. She's teaching in a country school and took me across the road to her home. We've had an interesting talk." Merri began to remove the contents of the bag. "She has lent me this photograph of her sister's wedding. It took place in France a year before the war. According to Oudette the husband was an Afghan fur-trader named Malikar."

Dari accepted the picture and for a long time stared at it thoughtfully. "The groom does resemble my father," he admitted. "The woman? I was a babe when she left." He canted his head sadly. "I must meet Oudette."

The discectomy took less time than Mahmud had expected. In Rochester the operation was done by neurosurgeons. Rotating through the neurosurgical service, he'd no chance to perform any part of the procedure. One of the neurosurgeons couldn't do it in less than three hours.

He thanked Jim profusely for the demonstrations, begged to return and said he'd be in touch soon.

Aimed west and using Merri's sketchy road map, Dari found his way to Abbey and an unheard-of aunt. Oudette Leframboise greeted him curiously and offered him a rocking chair so he could look out at her modest garden.

Forsythia, Lilac and Crab formed a frame of vivid colour. Between sips of coffee and nibbling hot buttered blueberry muffins he learned of the woman who had deserted him long ago.

"Your father met Nicole on a trip to Paris. She was pretty and wildly excited his urbane tastes. They fell in love. As our father favoured the young man they were married. But Nicole was spoiled, naive, flighty and unsuited to a change of culture. Later she wrote from Afghanistan of her discontent, not with Malikar as much as the strange ruthless women of the zunana who shared him. She wanted out and to take her child but the child was refused. If she had her way," Oudette smiled, "You would've led a different life. Don't judge her too harshly. It cost her dearly. I didn't see her until after the war when she'd married Eckheusen."

During the long shadows of summer twilight Dari headed toward the border and his lonely rooms, thinking of a mother whom he barely knew and had missed a reunion by a handful of years. Had Malikar learned of her? He wondered. Surely not or he would have told him.

CHAPTER SIXTY-FIVE

Jenny and Brad Coleman graduated in medicine during the first week of June. It was a beautiful sunny day in London, and while the orchestra played Brahm's Academic Festival Overture the most recent alumni of the University of Western Ontario spilled out on the dandelion infested lawn, a naughty breeze raising mortar boards, gowns and skirts promiscuously. Jenny and Brad looked great: vigorous, bright and smiling, set to catch the world by the tail. Neither had definitive plans, having put off major decisions until they completed their internship. A promising beginning, Jim thought, scanning the roses, diplomas and happy faces.

They were standing outside Alumni Hall, snapping photos, when Jim commented to Brad's father. "The ceremony was simpler in my day. There was a war on. Fewer graduates, the whole bunch and their relatives crowded into a Quonset hut for the reception."

Stuart Coleman was thick-necked with a bull-horn voice three years Jim's senior and equally fit at fifty-five. His BA in languages from the U. of T. was obtained in the veterans' rush for higher education and helped secure a job on the Shipton newspaper.

"That's right," he replied. "Now degrees are a dime a dozen and not much help in getting a job. I believe we've lived through the best of times, more opportunities and a looser rein. So much red tape to get approval for an associate, ridiculous!" A smile rippled one side of his broad face. "You've taken on such expensive help I suppose I'll have to foot the dinner to-night."

"Not a bad idea," Jim grinned, more content with the freedom gained in having Mahmud's assistance than Stu's offer of a treat.

In the General's Emergency Dari was preparing to reduce a dislocated hip. The day had gone well. He had been operating with Marcel Fortier. Together they had performed surgery on six patients: three bilateral bunionectomies, two meniscectomies, and an L5-S1 discectomy. His proctor had congratulated him after the last case, a tricky torn lateral knee cartilage. "You have now completed twelve procedures under supervision and are on your own, faster than when I was starting up." Marcel winked, adding. "Good luck on the hip."

In the second cast room Louis Desjardins lay on his back on the floor as Mahmud had ordered. "Christ Doc," he moaned, "Can't you put me to sleep. My God-damn hip is killing me!"

"If you'll relax a minute we can fix it without an anaesthetic." Dari was kneeling beside the patient, slowly injecting 50 mgms. of demerol into a cubital vein. When the syringe was empty he stood and straddled the affected side. The man's left thigh was flexed, shortened and crossed over the right; any effort to straighten it was fraught with pain and muscle spasm.

"I've heard you're a truck driver and you've been in an accident," Mahmud commented. "Were you wearing a seat belt?"

"What difference does it make, for Chrissake. Do something about this fucking pain!"

"It makes plenty of difference." Both of Dari's arms were wrapped around the flexed left knee and he was gradually tugging the man's thigh toward the ceiling, simultaneously adducting and rotating the knee inward. He asked the orderly to press downward with all his weight on the patient's pelvis. "More force please, Andrey, but keep his pelvis on the floor. Seat belts will be mandatory soon," he grunted. "Keep you from smashing into the dash." Then to distract the patient further and slacken his taut muscles he added, "I guess you're too stupid to figure that out."

If the orderly had not been sitting on the truck driver's belly, Mahmud would have had a nose full of fist. The diversion worked, the orderly caught the blow on his back and the head of the femur found it's socket. "Now," Dari challenged, "Tell me your belt was cinched tight and I'll re-dislocate your hip and let you put it back yourself." Smilingly he asked, "are you okay Andrey?"

"Yeah I'm fine," the orderly laughed. "Such a cowardly thing to do - strike a man in the back."

The flabby fellow let out a deep sigh, his discomfort relieved. "Christ, that was a bugger," he bellowed. "You're a miserable bastard Doc! But I love you!"

It took another ten minutes to lift the patient onto a bed and apply skin traction. Mahmud clearly stated the 'iffy' complications, offered a guarded prognosis and hustled off to the office.

Speculating Dr. Lindsay was out of town, a number of his regular patients had called to cancel. Her workload lessened, Betsy was in fine spirits. She was bent over the counter, talking to a man who had come to pay a bill, unaware of Mahmud's slipping through the side door. Her posterior protruded and she jumped reflexively as he brushed passed. The last person to have come in so quietly was Rick Mosely and he had pinched her.

"Not many left," she murmured. "A couple down the hall, one in each examining room and Mrs. Harrington." Betsy's voice was even more quiet as she indicated with a slant of her head at the waiting room. "Apparently her foot's giving her trouble. She insisted on seeing you today."

"I see," said Dari. "Send her to the consulting room. I'll deal with the others first."

Betsy relayed his instructions while he checked the appointment book for openings in the following week. Both of them heard a pair of high heeled shoes scud along the carpet and Betsy's muffled exclamation, "Good God, no wonder!"

As Mahmud appeared not to understand she explained. "Did you see those blinking shoes? There isn't anything to them but a slab and three inches of heel. She sashayed by like a Shetland pony."

"Was she limping?" Dari asked.

"Not that I could see."

The patients in the two examining rooms were dispatched with injections of hydrocortisone for their tendinitis: one in the elbow, the other in the shoulder.

Tanya, sitting saucily with her knees crossed, smiled sweetly when Mahmud opened the examining room door.

"That was a beautiful piece of surgery you did this morning. I once saw Dr. Best struggle for two hours, trying to excise a lateral meniscus. Even then I don't think he got it all."

"Oh," It took a moment for Dari to react. His jaw sagged as if he had bitten on a sensitive tooth. "Who did you say?"

"Best, Dr. Beecher Best. The surgeons ran him out of town some time ago. Man he was a wild one!"

"I see."

"A non conformist. Had his own way of handling everything, usually with calamitous results. It's a wonder he didn't kill somebody."

A creepy feeling grasped the base of Mahmud's neck and his mouth became a tight cruel line. "Where is he now?"

"Don't ask me!"

She paused and tried to read the strange look steeling his sapphire eyes. "I'm sorry," she finally offered. "I didn't come to gossip. I'd like you to look at my foot. The toes feel numb."

"Has your back ever bothered you?"

"Occasionally. I have pain low down in the hollow."

Hastily Mahmud said, "Go into the next room and put on a gown. I'll be along in a minute."

So, he thought, the Butcher of Bamiyan has left his mark here as well. He had almost forgotten Best. It had been a long time since he had contemplated revenge and what he would actually do if he ever met the man. Allah had guided him and if it were his fate to meet Best again he would think about it when the occasion arose. Strange how time changes one's mind. I've learned of my mother's tragic end and met an aunt whom I've come to admire and respect. He would take her to dinner over the week-end.

Allowing his patient to prepare herself, Mahmud deliberated where to entertain Oudette. With the question still unresolved he wandered into the examining room.

Tanya was perched, legs crossed and naked on the table. Every stitch she wore was lying on the floor as if she couldn't get her clothes off fast enough.

Dari handed her a gown. "Put this on please," he said and ignoring her state of undress added, "Where's a good place to eat?"

Tanya's mouth opened in surprise. Not another one, she thought. This guy's as sexless as Noel. As asked, she put on the gown and tied the straps behind her.

"I've an aunt who lives in Abbey," Dari explained. "I've promised to wine and dine her."

"No problem. Try the L'Auberge. Excellent French cuisine. It's on the Niagara Parkway near the mouth of the river. You'll have no trouble finding it."

Dari nodded his appreciation. "Now where's your trouble?"

"The third and fourth toes of my right foot are numb." Sitting on the edge of the examining table, she demonstrated, by bringing her affected foot to rest on the opposite knee and pried her toes apart.

He leaned close and caught a whiff of sweet perfume. It had been generously applied.

Her circulation and peripheral nerves checked out normal. He had her stand and bend in all directions, tapped her reflexes, ran the joints of her lower extremities through a full range of motion and returned to the site of her complaint. When he squeezed the web space she winced.

"You have a Morton's neuroma."

This announcement caused no outward reaction. Tanya was familiar with the condition.

"Will you cut it out?" she asked.

"It's not really a tumour as the word implies, just a thickening of the nerve caused by pressure due to abnormal posturing. Why don't you wear more sensible shoes? In time it will improve."

"I'd rather have the operation."

"I'll give you a prescription. Take it to a cobbler. He can attach a metatarsal bar to your nursing shoes or a suitable equivalent with a low heel. Wear them for a while."

"How long?"

"Six weeks. If it's no better I'll remove it."

Tanya jumped off the examining table, thanked him with a friendly kiss on the cheek and before he left the room began to dress.

Throughout the intimacy of the examination she had been absolutely stunned by his total abstraction. To add him to her list of idolizers she would have to try another approach.

"I'm having a small group for lunch, the Saturday of Canada Day week-end, why don't you drop around?" When he didn't reply she added, "Think about it and give me a call. I'll tell you how to find us."

A withered man in a white jacket answered his ring and led him inside. The house took Mahmud's breath away. He had never seen anything so luxurious: the wide teak-wood hall, the pink and silver living room, glass panelled cabinets loaded with antique Chinese ivory, Eskimo soap stone carvings, marble pedestals with busts of the Old Masters and a drawing room, containing a harp and full sized Baldwin grand.

Tanya found him in the sitting room. She entered, wearing a terri-cloth bathrobe and skipped across the deep-piled, cream coloured carpet to plant a welcome kiss on each cheek. "The others are out by the pool," she remarked. "Would you like to join them?"

"In a minute," said Dari. The house was so quiet he could not imagine anyone else's presence. "I've never been in such an elegant place," he smiled. "Would you mind showing me around?"

"Not at all," she replied and looped her arm in his, her amber eyes and open smile fixed on him. This action made him feel right at home. It was also Roxane's habit to lead him in the same way from the front door of their apartment into the kitchen to let him sniff what she had been preparing for the evening meal. He regarded his hostess more closely. She was not the piece of anatomy he had studied the previous afternoon. Perhaps the environment was responsible. There is nothing more sterile and unimaginative than an examining room. She had fine bones, narrow wrists and her hands were delicately small. Her whole figure reminded him of Roxane, flexible and exquisitely moulded. In her dark, beautifully-waved hair, a few steel-grey strands were an added attraction.

"Who plays the piano?" he asked.

"Mother. She's an old trooper, used to sing in the San Francisco Opera. She and my step-father have retired to the Bahamas."

Dari paused, intrigued by a skin hanging on a wall in the drawing room. "Where did you get the Snow Leopard?"

She grinned. "My father-in-law, also my step-father, which may be difficult for you to grasp, has been to Afghanistan. He shot it. There are more trophies, stuffed Ibex, Markhor heads, fox-belly blankets. If you'd like I'll show you."

Dari was not insistent, "Some other time. Maybe later if your husband wishes to oblige me."

They passed on to a library with shelves of old leather bound books on any topic one might choose.

Upstairs she led him into a large bright bedroom with a balcony where they could look over the Niagara river. "When my husband sails I see him off from here."

"I assume that's his yacht," said Dari, awed by the sleekness of the twelve meter racing sloop.

"We have our own slip. There! You can see it," she said, pointing at a cut in the bank. "He'll likely take you out this afternoon. That's if you want to. Do you like sailing?"

"I don't know. I've never been."

As they walked back through the bedroom he noticed the whole ceiling was a sheet of mirrors.

"Come," she said, "we must go join the others."

Three people clustered under a sun umbrella on the patio: two middle aged men and a maid servant. Both of the men in bathing suits lounged in deck chairs like a couple of off-duty lifeguards. The invitation had been for 11 am. It was now past noon and Dari asked, "Where is everyone?"

"I only invited you," Tanya smiled.

"But you said you were having a small group for lunch."

She giggled, "We are. You must come and meet the others."

Both of the men rose to accept Dari's hand as Tanya introduced them, "My husband Noel, and Gary Fast." She turned to the maid, standing a few yards away, "and this is Mimi."

The domestique took Dari's order for plain tonic water and headed for the house.

Mahmud thought he recognized the middle-aged man in the cherry red trunks, having seen him in the E.R., though they had never been formally introduced. "Dr. Gerhardt Fast?" he assumed.

"The same."

"I think I've seen you at the General."

"Probably." Gary's pale eyes swept Dari like a metal detector. "I believe you're the new orthopod."

"That's right. Working with Dr. Lindsay. Been here about a month."

"Where are you staying?"

"Bachelor apartment in the north end."

"So I take it you're not married." Gary smiled at Tanya as if he had caught her with a hand in the cookie jar.

"I am! Roxane, my wife, has gone home to have our baby."

Gary chuckled in a profane way. "That makes it less sporting doesn't it, Tanya my sweet."

Tanya ignored him and removed her robe while three pairs of masculine eyes lasciviously attacked her. "A swim before lunch anyone?" she said, pulling up the bottom half of her white bikini. She was perfectly tanned, the colour of a fawn and just as graceful.

Gary gave a low whistle. "So we're into Act One, Scene One!" he exclaimed.

Tanya knew exactly what he meant. What Gary didn't know was she had rewritten the script. "Wait till I get to the 'denouement'," she smiled, mispronouncing the theatrical word.

"Please keep me posted, sweetie"

"That's up to you!"

Suspecting the pair shared some secret joke, Dari turned to her husband. "You have a magnificent home."

Noel had downed three rye and gingers in the past half hour. His speech had begun to betray him. "Tha's very kind. "Bah ish not ar 'ouse. B'longs old man."

"Time to eat." Tanya intervened, changing her mind about the swim. If Noel didn't put something in his stomach soon, he would make a complete ass of himself.

"Na s'fass," her husband objected. "Our new frien' 'asn't wet his whisssel."

"If you'll excuse me, I'll check on our dinner and speed things up." She glanced at Gary and shook her head.

Before Tanya reached the house, Mimi passed her. She set Dari's tonic water in front of him, apologized for having run out of lemons and picked up Noel's near empty glass.

Gary gently clasped her wrist and retrieved the drink. "There's enough in it to toast our new friend," he said, handing the glass to Noel and raising his own. "To your good health, Dr. Mahmud."

"Cheers," Dari replied to Noel's sck'sckol!"

"Now Harrington, my good friend," Gary smiled, "that's all you get till next time."

CHAPTER SIXTY-SIX

By mid afternoon the breeze and Noel were becoming cantankerous. The 'Halena', skimming along on a half reach, beating for the middle of the lake, had cleared the river's mouth and its deceptive churning. Soft broken clouds offered little shade and without the cold spray and lashing wind the merciless sun would have been insufferable. Not the best weather for a postprandial headache inflicted on a dehydrated drunk - if Noel's language were representative. He could not say a two syllable word without inserting 'fucken' in the middle.

Conversely, Mahmud was really enjoying himself. The wind catching the sail, the sudden lurch and heeling caused his blood to surge with excitement. He was stripped, save for a pair of worn jeans, rolled to the knee. His prosthesis had been discarded and he stomped around the deck like "Long John Silver," as Gary exclaimed. "Except that old bastard had a patch on his eye."

"Avast ye God'amn D.P.," Noel hollered from the shallow hold. "Take care and tighten your sheet. The winds blowing up your ass."

"What's a D.P.?" Dari asked.

Gary smiled to assuage his partner's goading remark, and drew upon the first words that came to mind. "Disabled Person!"

This was enough to infuriate their handicapped guest and Gary quickly sensed his faux pas. "As the cliche goes - out of the frying pan into the fire. Sorry old chap!"

"Like fucken hell you are!" Noel slurred. "He's another disfuckenplaced person come over here to milk us dry. My family built this country and thanks to our multifuckencultural government the money's disappearing like shit."

"My dear Noel," said Gary in a placating tone. He'd been cooling off Noel for a long time. "I do wish you'd curb your speech."

Noel glared at his friend, puffing momentarily and abruptly grinned, his animosity dispersing as rapidly as it had appeared. "If I didn't know you better Gary, I'd say you were a bit loose-wristed."

His hosts split with laughter and Dari waited until they'd settled before asking, "I take it, Mr. Harrington, you're a native born Canadian?"

"You're damn right!"

"That's strange! I don't see any" - Dari paused long enough for effect - "feathers in your hair."

Noel shook his head in disgust. "Bloody, blooming hilarious! Hasn't done a god damn thing for my headache. Time to crack open another quart." Stretching up to Mahmud sitting on the edge of the cockpit, hauling on the jib sheet, he offered, "Want some rye, buddy?"

"No thanks."

"You're the first guy we've had out here who doesn't like Crown Royal. But that's okay, we've got a locker full of scotch, rum, gin, vodka."

"I don't drink alcoholic beverages."

Noel's beefy face turned purple with wheezing; he started to choke and spluttered, "Hey! Gary check this guy. He doesn't drink." When he'd finally controlled himself, he asked, "You some kind of Jesus freak?"

It was Mahmud's turn to laugh. "No, I'm Muslim!"

Noel took a swig from the bottle. "Halla-blooming-luya Gary! We got a bloody Paki on board."

"I'm not from Pakistan." Dari wanted to tell his host if he hadn't been so incoherent over lunch he'd have learned otherwise, when from the helm Gary shouted into the wind. "If he doesn't want a drink he needn't have one, but I will. Hand me the bottle."

"Not on your life boy." Noel poured three fingers into a copper mug and held it out. "Here my Paki friend, take it to him and be careful not to spill any on yourself. It'll burn a hole." He snorted and took another swig.

Pleased with himself Noel ducked under the foredeck and collapsed on a bunk, eyeing the bottle as if it were a priceless commodity.

Mahmud squinted at Gary, an amorphous blur against the refulgence of the sun, and headed aft. The shimmering water was blinding. Shading his eyes with a free hand he offered the mug.

"Don't let him get to you," Gary advised. "He's meaner sober than drunk." His eyes were on the bow and a pair of telltales, fluttering from the stays. "Wanna take over?"

"If you show me what to do."

"It's easy. We're steering broadside to the wind. You calculate the angle from those ribbons attached to the stays. As you turn into or 'upwind' the ribbons will swing back toward us. See," he said, pointing, at the same time putting the helm down so the nose of the sloop swung left into the wind. The jib began to flutter and the mainsail developed a ripple along its leading edge. "Now we're losing wind and should pull in the sheets. Go forward and crank in the jib a bit and the fluttering will cease."

Dari did as suggested while Gary hauled in the main before continuing his discourse. "Instead of sailing at ninety degrees we've turned upwind to about forty-five which is about as far as this sloop will go. It's known as 'tacking' and because the wind is coming from the left it's called a port tack. Notice how much stronger the wind seems, blowing into our faces. If we go more directly into it we'll stall or luff. If the bow swings further left the wind will come on to our starboard side. This manoeuvre is called 'coming about' and is the way to travel upwind or against the wind by shifting from one tack to the other. Okay! so now we'll swing downwind." The helm was pulled up so the bow swung hard right and Dari could hear an instantaneous rippling of the wake."The wind is now abaft the beam. Notice how much quieter it is as we run with it and how I've let the mainsail out so the boom is over the side." Gazing behind them Gary commented further. "I'd say from the trail of foam we're doing about five knots."

"What happens if we turn even more right?"

Gary had removed a straight stemmed briar from his pocket and was scraping the bowl. He chuckled. "A very dangerous thing to do, known as jibbing. If the wind catches the sail improperly the boom will swing back across the cockpit and over the other side. Anyone standing up would get a good crack on the noggin or be dumped overboard. Caught off guard I've done it unintentionally many times. The wind's a bit temperamental today. I think we're in for a change in the weather."

The sloop was brought back on its previous course. "Here, you take over. I'm going to stretch out on deck."

Mahmud played with the helm and mainsail until he'd got the hang of sailing. "How much does a boat like this cost?" he asked when his tutor rejoined him.

Fast removed his pipe and spat over the side, "Upward of thirty thousand. It was second hand when the old man bought it. Picked it up down in the States. Newport News I believe."

"I understand Harrington has retired?"

"Old Bosco? Yes! He was smart. Moved most of his assets out. Invested elsewhere. He considers he's doing the country a big service. His money was made in Canada and he feels Canadians have the first option to borrow it. He maintains until people come to their senses and recognize free enterprise as the means of developing our country he'll hold their loan in abeyance, preserving Canadian capital. When things open up he'll bring it back and bail the country out but not while the government throws his tax dollars away which it seems bent on doing. I think he has a point. If old Bob Scofield lives long enough he might become the greatest patriot of all time and not an absconding rogue as the socialists would have us believe."

"Does he still own this yacht?"
Gary smiled. "I'm not sure," and broke off the conversation. He propped himself against the shrouds and pretended to read.

Bosco's political views were common knowledge and Gary didn't mind discussing them. Disclosing the Harringtons' private affairs was different, and not to be talked over with anyone. He didn't like answering questions, worse being quoted.

The yacht like the house had been transferred to Tanya when the elder Harrington took her mother off to live in Nassau. Old Bosco mistrusted his son because of his incurable drinking and came to hate him, an emotion shared with his daughter-in-law, although for different reasons. The impotence accompanying his chronic alcoholism was more detestable to her.

If Bosco had known his daughter-in-law was an incurable nymphomaniac he might not have been so generous.

Gary had taken her on for two reasons. The challenge of satisfying her carnal pleasure and the conviction he was doing Noel a favour. A good screwing might take the bitch out of her.

Her voice was infused with sensuality and her sylph-like appearance attracted him. Few women were as impassioned and skilful, so avid to perform and so difficult to satisfy. For someone so boring socially, she knew plenty of tricks to provide a limitless amount of pleasure in bed.

When Gary found out she had been jumping others, Paolone for one, his ego had blown and he tossed her out, feeling humiliated and as inadequate as his life-long friend. That was three years ago.

She had been allowed a last visit and arrived trim and chic in a sheer dress of black silk, snugly cinched around her slim waist by a soft leather belt. He had listened to her for all of five minutes, protesting as usual. When she got on to Noel's inferiority her complaining finally seized him and without a warning his hands lashed out, grabbing her by the shoulders. Before either of them knew how far he'd go, she was screaming obscenities and calling him names.

Two weeks later Tanya met someone else. Gary had seen them accidentally as he was scanning the horizon with his telescope, walking hand in hand along the edge of the golf course, overlooking the lake. How long the intrigue lasted he couldn't guess; he had little doubt there were others. Likely Mahmud was the latest to cross her sights. He figured both Noel and he had come through the ordeal reasonably well. They were back to their sporting activities, free of any commitments to Tanya. She had actually brought them closer together, Noel needing his guidance and instruction, and he the idolatry and appreciation.

Presently the three of them were co-existing, rather affably to the casual observer, and all the time Tanya was planning how to get her hands on the rest of the family money.

Gary knew all about them. He knew much about a lot of people and things, where money could be found when needed. Presently he had invested in a large piece of property south-east of the city. The town planning board had decided to include a pumping station nearby which meant a new subdivision with a mall and all the benefits. He might relocate his office. But why change, he thought, I'm better off where I am.

The outing had begun on a fair day with a favourable south-westerly breeze; drenching spray and white caps were all about. In the late afternoon, as a declining sun choked convulsively on the rim of a towering cumulus, air ceased to move, and slapping low rollers gave way to silence and a surface as sleek as glass. Earlier Mahmud had found the cruise exhilarating, now it had become dreadfully dull.

The mast stood straight, the sails hung limp and no pressure was felt on the helm. There was nothing to do but sit or pace the deck, like a prisoner confined to a cell.

"Not unusual for this time of day," Gary muttered. "It'll freshen soon and come at us from off-shore." He waved at the peninsula five miles away adding, "from the south."

"Is it all right for me to swim?"

"There are no sea monsters about and we're not apt to sail away if that's what's stopping you."

Dr. Fast who had taken to baby-sit the dozy helm, snickered at his own joke.

The water was ominous, deep green, impossible to gauge its murky depth. Dari decided on a shallow dive, hit the cold surface and swam out a few yards. Doubling back he ducked under the hull, briefly examined the weighted keel and emerged on the opposite side. The sloop had at least his height of freeboard. Gary casually threw him a line. With his strong arms Mahmud hauled himself aboard, content to be back in the warm air.

"Look over there," Gary pointed. "It's already started."

Mahmud was not sure of the reference. "What?" he asked.

"The wind. See how the surface has ruffled. You'll feel it soon."

Noel came out of the hold uncertain of his haunts, rising like a misplaced apparition. He looked awful, bloated and ungainly, standing beside the cockpit. "Fer Chrissake," he called, "we've run out of bejesus juice."

"What do you mean?" Gary questioned calmly. "The locker was full when we put out."

"There's sno more fuggen rye."

"Then try something else."

"Ssskid's stuff, not fit for a tea party. Piss on it." Noel's face was so puffy his slitted eyes were almost imperceptible. He grasped the larboard stay, steadied himself, fumbling with his zipper. "Tha's a good idea! Piss on it," he repeated and commenced to relieve himself."

Gary chuckled, watching him sway back and forth. "Make sure it goes into the lake or your wife will rub your nose in it."

The wind struck, not violently, but at the right angle and the loosely sheeted main whipped across the deck dragging the boom with it, swinging with the strength of a power hitter. Noel, a sacrificial bunt, was batted into the lake, falling heavily downward.

"Get him!" Gary shouted. "He can't swim!"

Mahmud was already poised on the gunwale and this time he dove deep, aimed at the spot where Noel had disappeared. He found him in the darkening depths, fighting for his life like a hooked fish, every ounce of reserve strength clawing frantically at a medium unable to support him. Mahmud sank deeper, trying to get under Noel's body and buoy him up. A hand clawed his face. He grasped it and spun, trying to force Noel over a shoulder, but a desperate arm wrapped around Dari's neck and pulled him further down.

He was terrified, near panic. If he didn't wriggle free soon his own oxygen would be depleted. He tried an elbow, levelled at the solar plexus but the water was too dense to permit enough force. Kicking had less effect. He reached for the scrotum and squeezed. It worked! Noel was still conscious enough to cringe, and Mahmud was free. He floated upward. The line he'd used to pull himself on board had not moved.

He broke surface, sucked in air and went under again, dragging the line with him. Noel was within range, twenty feet away, limp and drifting deeper. Dari descended into the cold, pressure building in his head but he managed to get a loop around the unconscious form and tighten it under the arms before coming up fast, aching for breath.

Gary was adjusting the sea anchor when Mahmud gasped, "Grab the line and haul him in."

Out of the water Noel weighed a ton. It took a concerted effort to pull him on board. He was apnoeic and unconscious, though his heart beat strongly.

On Dari's advice they rolled him to the edge of the cockpit and onto his stomach, lowering his head and trunk inside the hull. While Gary straddled the back of Noel's legs, Dari lifted the flail arms, bringing the trunk upwards. Down and up, in and out of the cockpit Noel was swung, and on each downswing froth bubbled from his mouth. After a few minutes he began to moan.

"By God he's coming around," Gary was ecstatic.

"Don't get too optimistic," Mahmud warned. "He might have brain damage. It's too early to tell."

"He's a tough old bird. He'll make it."

"We don't know how long he went without oxygen," Dari commented. "He's not breathing on his own yet."

"I'll fix that," Gary smiled. "We'll tie him to the yard arm and let him dangle upside down until he does. Seriously," he added. "We've got oxygen on board."

"Mouth to mouth will work better," Mahmud contended. "You haven't an objection to alcohol so I'll let you do it."

Noel came around, but in a state of shock he required blankets and oxygen. They left him on a bunk bed in the hold.

Over a steaming cup of coffee Mahmud suggested, "How about we get under way. I've got plenty to do."

"Shortly." Gary looked like he had something to confide. "You've already done us a great favour, putting it mildly," he said. "I'd like to ask another."

Mahmud regarded him curiously. He had just rescued the man's best friend. What more does he want?

"We'd be most grateful if you forget about this."

"What's in it for me?" asked Dari, having no intention of saying a word to anyone.

Gary smiled. "Who knows? Someday you may need a favour from us."

CHAPTER SIXTY-SEVEN

During July, Mahmud accepted more inviations to the Harringtons, taking flowers, chocolates or a bottle of wine.

On each occasion Gary was there. Never was the near drowning incident discussed. Noel had simply come down with the flu and was forced to lie low for a few days. The lung congestion was a mild complication.

Mahmud had the impression Noel was not sure what had happened, which meant either Gary hadn't told him or all three were keeping quiet about it.

Surely Noel must have wondered enough to ask questions. Even in his drunken state at the time he could have remembered losing his balance and falling overboard. The coldness of the water alone would stir the senses of anyone. His continuing rudeness bothered Dari to the point he himself had developed a stress induced paranoia. He had too much to worry about: Roxane expecting, the pressure of preparing for an examination, covering Dr. Lindsay's practice. At times he felt like Atlas with the world on his shoulders.

Dari had considered telling Noel the truth. It might alter his attitude, make him a little more respectful, he certainly was a miserable character; but Mahmud remembered Gary's comment, 'he's meaner sober than drunk'. If this were true, Noel's lack of appreciation had more to do with his current total abstinence than any personal reasons. Dari shrugged off his feelings, nothing had changed.

His visits had been most enjoyable. He learned a lot about sailing and could bring the big sloop, single-handed, up river and dock it. Tanya maintained his interests through her singing and enthusiastic conversation. In return he rendered advice on tennis elbow, carpal tunnel syndrome and other common musculoskeletal ailments, in particular low back pain which plagued her from time to time. On one occasion he had Gary and Tanya lie on their backs beside him, on the cream coloured rug, rocking their pelvi, an exercise devised to lessen the hollow in the lumbar region and take strain off the ligaments while Noel looked on, making porn of it all.

The visits offset his loneliness and gave him a break from his studies. He never stayed long, arriving on time and leaving before 9 pm.

One Saturday Gary took him for a spin in his 'Piper Cub'. It was a clear, windless afternoon and their view from a few thousand feet encompassed the whole peninsula. They flew through the mist above the Falls, traced the mighty Niagara, weaving through its gorge, over orchards and pencilled vineyards, stretching from the river to Hamilton. As they approached the blinding surface of the 'Twenty Mile Pond' Noel appeared in his 'Chipmunk', buzzing them head-on, pulling up at the last minute into a steep spiralling loop to dive from behind, narrowly missing a wing tip. As his prop wash buffeted them, Gary's sole comment, "It's a damn good thing he's not flying a jet or we'd be in real trouble," convinced Dari that Noel Harrington was more of a reckless fool than his friend, Sayyid, and would be lucky to end up with only a fractured skull.

Over Sunday dinner, a few weeks before the Lindsays left for a canoe trip in Algonquin park, the girls tried to coax him into accompanying them. Kathy was on the verge of sexual maturity and very coy, much easier to handle than Heather who made a big fuss over him. "Impossible!" he maintained. "Who's going to cover your dad's practice?"

"You can baby sit the house," Jim suggested. Dari also refused his offer. "It's best I stay where I am, close to your office, the hospitals and my books. If I don't, I won't get any studying done."

Late July was oppressively humid with temperatures in the nineties, twice topping a hundred. There had been very little rain and lawns were as dun and dry as midsummer in the Bamiyan Valley. August brought no relief and Mahmud found it extremely difficult to concentrate on reading. There was so much material his head swam.

When he turned down Tanya's supper invitations, she would drop by his apartment, always in the evening, bringing sweets, sympathetically offering assistance. At first he found her to be a time saver, getting his meals and brewing coffee. Visits became more frequent and she would drag on about Noel's incompatibility while his mind was on the differential diagnoses of the limping child or destructive bone lesions. She would turn on the TV, cuddle up beside him and suggest they watch a show. Once he had her listen to his regurgitation of memorized data and found her a hindrance. He remained patient until the evening she arrived with an overnight bag. "I'm sorry Tanya," he said, acting very polite. "There's just too much

Do Unto Others

work to cover. Nobody can learn this stuff for me. Go away and leave me alone."

She left with an apologetic smile to show up a few days later in his office. "If this is the only way I'm permitted to see you, then that's the way it is," she grinned. "I want you to operate on my foot."

It was the first time she'd mentioned her numb toes since he prescribed the shoe correction six weeks earlier.

Her case was booked and within a week she was admitted to St. Mary's.

It definitely was a Morton's neuroma and was excised with aplomb. After the operation, while Wigmore was cleaning up, Mahmud laid it out on a gauze square and described the pathology to her. The errant nerve was exactly what he had predicted and so thickened it would take a long time to subside with conservative treatment.

"I thought this condition was more commonly found in older women?" Wigmore remarked.

Mahmud gestured palms up. "There's no reason a thirty year old can't develop it."

Mrs. Burwin overheard him and jerked to attention. "If she's thirty I'm my own mother. She was three years ahead of me in the Bachelor course."

"Check her chart." Dari suggested. He had no idea how old Tanya was.

Burwin showed him the front sheet.

"Date of Birth," he read aloud, "May 22nd, 1925. "Well I'll be a - how do you say it - a monkey's uncle!" he snickered. "You're right! She is lying."

"Through her teeth," Reif Larson chuckled. While extracting the endotracheal tube, he had a look inside Tanya's mouth. "From the nuggets in here she's been panhandling since the Klondike. I'd say her front sheet is fifteen years behind." Then he picked at her hair like a baboon searching its mate for fleas, and added. "Asparagus hair!"

Burwin giggled. "What's that mean?"

"Faded at the roots."

Wigmore clicked her tongue reprovingly. "Ah, come on Reif, you can do better than that."

Dari went to discharge Tanya the next morning, Miss Finan accompanying him. When they entered her private room she was sitting up in bed.

"Darling," Tanya gushed. "You look so tired. Have they been working you too hard?"

Mahmud blushed and as he stood, bewildered beside her, she threw both her arms around his neck and dragged him down for a kiss. Though planned for his mouth he turned away at the last second and it landed rather sloppily on a cheek. He twisted his face away, and hoped she would release him. Still Tanya clung. "I'm so grateful," she cooed. "Already I feel so much better."

Hugging the patients' charts, Moira Finan took in the scene, unable to move. The doctor was literally swept off his feet. His prosthetic limb, trapped between his good leg and the bed, offered no sense of balance. Grinning with delight, Tanya took her time to release him.

When he had regained his stability Dari told her everything had gone as expected. The physiotherapist would be in to fit her with crutches and she could increase the weight on her foot as the discomfort subsided. She was to see him in ten days to have her sutures out but to call for an appointment first.

"Won't you come to Niagara and take them out?"

Mahmud addressed her formally, sounding flat but emphatic. "Mrs. Harrington, you must appreciate I'm too busy to make house calls. If you have problems let me know but I'm sure you'll be fine. Good bye."

Tanya's frowning eyes followed him to the door and like a school girl she whimpered. "Please," but he did not look back.

In the hall Finan exhaled loudly, "Whew! How can you resist her?"

Mahmud smiled and answered wryly. "She's too old for me."

Dari was in the office early the day Tanya was to have her sutures removed.

He was leaning over Betsy's shoulder, perusing the list of patients when she whispered, "Check the change; Mrs. Harrington's wearing sensible shoes."

"Oh" Mahmud paused and stole a casual look.

Sporting the prescribed brown nursing oxfords, dressed in a beige poplin suit with a mink neck piece, Tanya sat in front of the mantle like an old auntie in a sepia photograph. She had brought Mimi along. Her butler, who also dubbed as a chauffeur, was strolling around the empty waiting room, admiring Merri's oil paintings.

Mahmud noted the absence of crutches and from the way she sprang to her feet when he called her name, she did not need them. He conducted her into the nearest examining room and asked her to remove her shoe and stocking. He excused himself and went to collect scissors and thumb-forceps from the autoclave.

Again she was completely naked, cross-legged on the table, just as she had been two months ago. He bowed his head, ran both hands through his hair and clasped the back of his neck. Cooped up in an apartment, studying ferociously, Roxane's absence, exposed every day to a working environment crawling with attractive nurses - how much frustration could he take? Now, here was this gorgeous woman, taunting him with her salaciousness. He wanted to ravish her on the spot.

As he bent cautiously clipping each stitch to avoid hurting her, he felt her fingers kneed the flesh of his shoulder, then up to an ear gently teasing. He removed the last one and she sighed with passion and murmured, "I want you to make love to me."

Her aggressiveness caused him to move away and she followed, glancing off the edge of the table to stand before him. He was excited. She sensed it and whispered. "I want you right now; please make love to me."

It wasn't love she wanted; it was unadulterated sex. The office with her servants and Betsy within earshot was not the place, better her bedroom with the mirrored ceiling. He was about to tell her to go home when she wrapped her arms around his neck and covered his mouth with hers. As she pinned him, helpless as a butterfly on a board, he flattened his hands against the wall and chanced to feel the doorknob and button beside it. He had a choice, push the button and buzz for Betsy or twist the lock on the nob. He wedged his arms inside of hers and broke her grip.

"This is not the time nor the place, Mrs. Harrington," he tried to reason in his ambivalent state.

She beamed. "Then come tonight. There'll be no one around to make you nervous. Noel has flown north to fish."

Dari thought he should agree, anything to appease her; she might leave. Instead he blurted more rationalization. "You have a husband and I don't intend to interfere with that relationship. I would turn you into an adulteress. In my country you could be stoned."

"In your country a woman must remain loyal to one man but a man can have many wives. You're in North America. Women are not restricted by such archaic customs. Why should you mind? Nothing will happen to me."

Tanya was in the corner next to the door. "There," she added twisting the nob lock. "No one can disturb us."

"Tonight," he agreed, saying anything to put her off.

"That'll be twice in one day. Marvellous," she smiled and began to loosen his belt.

Her determination was irritating. It had become more contentious by the moment and had the effect of a cold shower. He broke free, pressed the buzzer and picked up a gown from the back of a chair.

"When Betsy arrives," he said flinging it at her. "I want you covered."

Spurned like a fishmonger, the bastard. She glared at him briefly and before he could stop her she turned to her heap of clothing and began to rip.

The door was still locked preventing Betsy from entering. "What do you want?" she called.

Tanya was first to reach the knob and unlocked the door. Pulling it open she barricaded herself in a corner and began to sob hysterically. "This man tried to rape me! Look," she cried, holding up her shredded panty-hose, "he tore my clothes off!"

Mahmud was disgusted and strode from the room. In a moment he was seated behind Dr. Lindsay's desk, holding his head in his hands.

Betsy appeared in the doorway. "Mind if I come in?" she asked.

"Are you sure you want to? I might jump you."

She smiled. "I'm not afraid of you. I don't believe a word she said."

"What was that?"

"First of all she held up her torn panty-hose, the sum of her underclothes, throws them at her maid and tells the three of us you tried to rape her. After you'd taken out her stitches you locked her in the room and ordered her to undress. You were like an animal and while you were tugging at her panty-hose she saw her chance, jumped off the table and pushed the buzzer. What an act! Her maid was in tears."

"It was nothing like that at all."

"I'm sure it wasn't." Betsy waited but Dari withheld his side of the story. He looked down at the desk and blew a loud breath. "Well," he said, "Now, maybe she'll leave me alone."

Tanya had lied about Noel being away fishing. He was at home reading the newspaper, cold sober, a glass of soda water on the table beside him.

He hadn't had a drink since the Halena affair. Gary had given him hell and told him he damn near drowned. If he didn't get off the rye soon he'd kill himself. He'd taken the advice. In a while he began to feel better physically and his outlook improved. Moreover, when Tanya came in late one night and clawed at his body like a lioness in heat. He'd been able to sustain an erection long enough for her to reach a climax; his self image soared.

Mrs. Harrington placed a tray of smoked salmon, lentils and buttered slices of brown bread in front of her husband and while he ate repeated her story, garnishing it with more lies. Noel suggested calling his lawyer; no fucken D.P. was going to insult his wife!

"Sit down," she ordered, "There's more to it. He's been after me for weeks." Tanya paused to make her story sound convincing before proceeding in an assertive voice. "He stayed over on my invitation. We sat up till after midnight watching blue movies on the TV. I was highly excited and he took advantage of me."

Noel frowned, confused. "How may I ask?"

"You know what I'm saying without switching to your vulgar way of speaking."

"I see. And then?"

"He left the next morning." Tanya thought a moment. She hung her head shamefully. "It was partly my fault. Though you have to admit you've been unconcerned for some time. He was attentive - sent me flowers with a note telling me how wonderful I was. I fell in love with him. We've had intercourse at least a dozen times."

Noel was confused. Nothing fit. "If you've been so in love with this guy how come today he had to force himself on you?"

"Before I went in for surgery I told him we were through. He wouldn't take no for an answer and begged me to leave you."

"You don't understand. Why your change of heart?" Noel's puffy eyes narrowed.

"He lacks maturity. He's like a child in many ways - still going to school." Tanya paused. "To be honest I need a man like you, a man I can depend on, someone who makes me feel like a woman."

"You've been playing around behind my back with a snivelling kid? A toy boy!" His voice rose.

"Not really Noel." Tanya looked contrite, her tone full of remorse. "I'd never run out on you. I've always been here to look after you. For the last month you've been different, like the Noel I first met. Then you only drank cappuccinos, remember?" She giggled, knowing they had been laced with rum. She had mixed them herself.

Tanya spoke so sweetly he wanted to believe her. He suspected that she had slept around before he married her but he figured she'd eventually get things straight. At no time had their marriage been a happy one. Things still didn't fit.

"Cut the crap Tanya and tell the truth." he shouted. "You're not interested in me."

The tears began to flow.

"I love you Noel," she whimpered. "I swear I'll be true to you from now on. You can have the yacht to do as you please. Sell it and I won't ask for a penny."

"What about the house?"

"You can have half."

Half was fair enough, she would get that much if he divorced her. He began to regard her more generously.'

"Let's fly down to the Bahamas and visit the old folks." She didn't answer. The present affair had to be cleaned up. "Someone has to teach that damned Muslim a lesson," she hissed, "He can't go on stealing other men's wives."

Facing Noel she went to her knees and regarded him with mixed feelings, thinking how easy it was to manipulate him. The yacht and house would have to wait. She had no mind to give up either. That damn surgeon! The first man to ever refuse her was going to pay.

At 9 pm. the phone rang. Dari answered it.

"Noel Harrington here," said the gruff voice at the other end.

Dari was deep in Boyd's Surgical Pathology. "Yes," he answered.

"You've been playing around with my wife!"

Dumbfounded, Mahmud remained silent.

"That's right, you heard me," Noel repeated, "You've been screwing my wife!"

"I haven't got the faintest idea what you're talking about."

"You know fucken well what I'm talking about. Alienation of Affection, that's what! You've been seducing her for weeks. Right under my nose! Show you a bit of hospitality and you take advantage of it."

"Let me try to understand. You say I've been having sex with Tanya."

"You got it Buster!"

"I say that's a pile of rubbish. Who ever told you that is a liar."

"Never mind. You're lucky I don't come over and beat the shit out of you."

"Listen to me." Dari was still trying to be reasonable. "It is not true. The closest I've ever been to your wife was her third and fourth toes, right foot. You can bloody well go to hell."

Mahmud slammed the phone back on its cradle.

A few seconds later it rang again. Noel was fuming this time. "You'll be hearing from our lawyer."

Dari had not quite re-slotted Boyd's in his mind when the door chimes sounded, then resounded over and over as a relentless finger pressed until he was able to reach the intercom.

"Robinson, Detective Sergeant Shipton Police," returned a voice from the lobby downstairs. "If you don't let me come up I have a warrant to enter anyway."

The sergeant was just short of six feet, thickset, in his forties. Looking very fit in his undershirt Dari was an inch taller. The apartment was sweltering.

Robinson began to sweat more noticeably as he realized he would never be able to take the younger man if he should refuse to submit peacefully. He smiled amiably and asked, "Dr. Mahmud?"

Dari acknowledged him with a faint nod.

The policeman continued, "There's been a complaint registered against you. Mrs. Noel Harrington came to the station and signed a statement. Apparently this afternoon you tried to rape her in your office." He paused, waiting for a denial. When it failed to appear he advised, "You have the right to make a statement as well. To do so you must accompany me. The sergeant's brow smoothed as he felt the reassuring holster against the side of his chest. "If you don't cooperate," he smiled, "I can take you in and lock you up. Assault is a Statutory Offence. If we go that route you'll have to get a lawyer with a lot of money for bail. Understand?"

Dari put his hands in his pockets and stretched backward. He scowled, about to ask if the matter could wait till morning, then calculated the chances were better if he cooperated. "If you'll wait a second I'll get dressed," he submitted.

To ensure his man didn't try to escape Robinson followed into the small bedroom. Books were scattered all over the place. "I'm studying for an exam and this isn't helping," Dari grumbled.

"You live alone?"

"Temporarily. My wife has gone home to have a baby. It's due any day now."

Maybe the Harrington woman was telling the truth. "What kind of doctor are you?" he asked.

"Orthopaedic. I've been working with Dr. Lindsay."

Robinson's countenance brightened. With less apprehension he exclaimed. "Jim Lindsay! Sure, I know him. He fixed my ankle when I smashed up my car. Nice guy! Never have any trouble with it."

At the station Mahmud asked to see Tanya's statement but was not permitted until after he'd made out his own.

The staff were helpful. They instructed him on how to write his narrative and showed him where to sign. He was not asked any questions other than his full name, address and telephone number. He received a copy of his narrative and was handed hers which read almost verbatim with what Betsy had told him, plus embellishments, how he had grabbed her vagina before she broke free.

As he was about to leave a young woman standing patiently in the background approached him. She was wearing a gauzy pale blue summer dress and had a writing pad and pencil in her hand. Quietly she asked him for an interview. "What for?" He answered astounded.

"I'm Linda Schwartz from the Shield. "Did you really assault 'the' Mrs. Harrington?"

Mahmud's lips pulled back, baring his teeth as if he were about to chew her apart. How did she get this information? What business was it of hers? "I have just given a statement to the police," he said. "Other than that, I have nothing to say." He found his way to the waiting cruiser and Sergeant Robinson. She followed to the door.

"If you'll pardon me, Miss Schwartz," he objected. "I can't spare the time."

CHAPTER SIXTY-EIGHT

Saturday morning followed a hectic night. Mahmud, unable to sleep or resume his studies, showered but unshaven, left at dawn and drove around the peninsula. What in hell was he going to do? It was all a pack of lies. Tanya must be crazy? He'd been a benefactor, saved her husband's life and cured her foot. Why did she punish him?

    Periodically, he would stop, once at a Lake Erie beach where he'd skipped flat stones across the water until his arm ached. He covered five miles of the Escarpment Trail, the last two on an agonizing stump. By noon he dragged back to his apartment, praying Allah would rid him of torment and grant him sleep. Too tired to climb the six flights of stairs he took the elevator. A ringing phone greeted him while he was inserting his key.

There was a bleep followed by a short silence before the voice of an operator inquired, "Dr. Darius Abdullah Mahmud please."

    "Here," he cried. It had to be from home. No one else would call him by his full name.

    "Dari?"

    "Yes!"

    "Dari. It's Khushal."

    "I know, I know! I recognize your voice. How's Roxane?"

    "Very well indeed! She had a girl!"

    "I want to speak to her!"

    "I'm sorry you can't. She's in Bamiyan."

    "The child was born in Bamiyan?"

    "Yes. She's with her mother and Rishtya."

    "Praise Allah." Dari choked. He was tearing, almost sobbing.

    "What good tidings shall I convey from you?"

    Taking a few short gasps Dari braced himself and replied, "I'm fine. Everything's fine. Give her my love Khushal, and to yourself and father. May Allah bless you with his beneficence. Thank you, thanks for calling Khushal. I'll be home in October as soon as the exams are over."

    He hung up enlivened. An hour later he was back at the books his concentration totally restored.

The Lindsays arrived home, brown as berries and a few pounds lighter. Shortly afterward, Jim took to his Lazy Boy with a heap of mail, mollified by a glass of scotch. He'd not been opening it long when Julie brought him the paper, declaring his name was on the front page.

"How's that?" he sighed, sounding only mildly interested. The drive from Algonquin had been tedious and he was tired.

"You better read it." Julie jabbed at an article headed 'DENIES CHARGES'.

He recognized the photograph of Dari instantly. It was the same picture he'd given to the Shield a few weeks ago, announcing their association. After reading the article twice he sprang out of his chair to look for his wife. She was downstairs, dumping a number of indescribably dirty items into the washer. "I can't believe this!"

Merri laid the newspaper over the dryer and read aloud. "'The police are investigating allegations brought by Mrs. Tanya Harrington against Dr. Darius Abdullah Mahmud. The claimant states yesterday afternoon she went to the office of Dr. C. James Lindsay of 244 James St., Shipton for a scheduled appointment. According to Mrs. Harrington who released her story to Shield reporter Linda Schwartz, Dr. Mahmud tried to assault her sexually. As she resisted her clothes were torn and she received bruises to her upper arms and body. She escaped by attracting the attention of Dr. Lindsay's secretary Ms. Betsy Cramer. Dr. Mahmud's story conflicted'" - Merri continued reading in silence until she reached the bottom lines. "'When asked what she intended to do about it, Mrs. Harrington said, Plenty, of course, including all in my power to ensure this man will never lay hands on another patient.'" "This is awful!" Turning to Jim with dismay and doubt in her eyes, she asked, "Can she really do this?"

Jim's jaw muscles quivered and through clenched teeth he replied, "I've got to talk to Mahmud."

"While you're at it why don't you call Stu Coleman and find out how such scurrilous material gets published."

Dari offered to come immediately. He had not seen the paper and was horrified. Apologizing for the embarrassment caused, he maintained his innocence and promised to clear up everything when he got there.

Jim was on the phone talking to Stu Coleman when the Afghan arrived. Kathy and Heather greeted him merrily, perched on the arms of the old soft leather chair where they seated him. They told him the highlight of the canoe trip; Merri's hat blowing off in the middle of a squall and how they turned around to retrieve it. "We were lucky we didn't all drown," Kathy cried excitedly. Though the girls were unwilling they left when their father insisted he must speak to Dr. Mahmud alone.

Jim asked what it was all about; and Dari told him the sequence of events from Tanya's first visit to the office until her sutures were removed. After reading the news article he frowned. "I thought any statement given to the police is held in confidence. What right have they got to betray it?"

"I've just spoken to Stu Coleman, editor of the Shield, and asked him that very question. The police aren't supposed to disclose privileged information unless it's for the general welfare of the public. They may use their own discretion. If you said nothing to the reporter she's found out through someone at the station who either allowed her to read your statement or told her what it contained. Stu saw the write up before it went to press and suggests you'll see any reference to your story is prefaced with either, 'it is said that' or 'from reliable sources'. None of it's a direct quote." Jim paused and glumly continued. "Mrs. Harrington's father-in-law Bosco owns a controlling interest in the paper. If Stu objects to the handling of the story he'll be putting his job on the line. But he's nobody's fool. I've a feeling he'll take this case straight to the old man."

"What about the so-called beating," Dari asked. "The bruises. Wouldn't the police check it out?"

Jim was quiet for a moment. "That's a point. They'd have to send her to their own surgeon Hastings. They'd be remiss not to."

"What if she refused to be examined?"

"Then it would be on her record."

Dari's hope began to flicker. He smiled. "She loses because I didn't touch her."

"It's possible Tanya might have self-inflicted bruises. From what I've heard she's crazy enough to do it or she might have none as you suspect and lied about them."

Dari sighed. "I don't have a chance."

"We'll see." Jim made a mental note to call Hastings the following Monday. He grinned unexpectedly as if the whole situation had become so futile it was ridiculous. "What else has happened?" he asked.

Dari had almost forgotten. "Roxane had a girl!"

"Terrific!" Jim, sounding very pleased shouted, "Hey, Merri come in here. The Mahmuds had a girl."

Merri was equally excited. "How wonderful!" she exclaimed. "What are you going to call her?"

"Soroya after Roxane's mother. We are breaking tradition. She should have a name of her own. I guess the Western way has rubbed off on us."

"You must be dying to get home to see her."

"Yes! In October as soon as I finish the 'writtens'."

"Jim wants to go back to Afghanistan," she poked her husband teasingly. "Don't you darling? You did mention it up north."

"Only if you'll join me."

"Okay," she agreed. " Now you better write to that outfit in Washington - what's it called - S.E.R.V.E.? And sign up."

A week after the alleged attack Dunc Hastings ran into Jim at St. Mary's. "In answer to your inquiry, Lindsay," the police surgeon bellowed, "Mrs. Harrington showed up this morning with a small bruise over her left deltoid."

"What about her torso?"

Dunc grinned. "Oh she showed me that alright. What a body!"

"Was it marked?"

Dunc started to cackle. "I can't remember."

"What do you mean you can't remember?"

"I couldn't see for looking."

"Nothing then?"

"There may have been a slight purple area on a buttock but certainly not the yellow tissue staining I would have expected. Her alleged beating was some time ago." He hesitated a moment. "I'm not at liberty to send you my report but trusting you won't say anything I can tell you the chief has read it and there won't be any further investigation. Clearly her story was grossly exaggerated."

The office was packed as usual. Normally it would have been a perturbing sight but Jim passed through the waiting room humming. He asked Betsy to send Dari back to his inner sanctum and calmly waited behind his big desk for his associate to appear.

Mahmud entered looking depressed and his facial expression did not budge when Jim provided Hasting's uplifting message.

"What's the trouble?" Jim asked.

"I got this in the mail today," the young doctor replied, drawing a crumpled letter from his pocket. "It's a writ from Harrington's lawyer. I'm being sued for Alienation of Affection. Now what do I do?"

"Good question." It was an unusual charge. Jim wondered if his insurance would cover it. He had been paying premiums for years, only drawing on the association's expertise once. "I suppose we could get in touch with the C.M.P.A.," he suggested, then paused thoughtfully, "I'd get Linus Jorgenson. He's smart, full of common sense and has a commanding presence in court. A good guy to have on your side, or rather our side since I'll be stuck with the bills."

"No. No, you won't," said Dari forcefully. "I'll pay."

Jim dismissed this with, "We'll see. You'll have to put this entire fiasco out of your mind. Get back to your studying. Jorgenson can stall the Harringtons. So my friend, as of now you're off the hook! Need any advice or consoling, a laugh, a nourishing meal, anything, just give us a call."

Before closing for the Labour Day weekend the Shipton Shield printed a retraction on the last page of the Entertainment Section. The word 'apology' was never used nor were any reasons given. There was a statement, 'the police are no longer investigating the allegations against Dr. Darius Abdullah Mahmud.' As Dr. Lindsay read on he wondered why good news always came at the end, in a spot where it could easily be missed and at a time when few people would be around to read it. Aspersions had been cast upon an innocent man that would dwell not only in his memory, but in the minds of others.

CHAPTER SIXTY-NINE

It took several years to raise enough money to improve the Bamiyan mission. Inside the mud walls of the caravanserai brick buildings had supplanted a section of the earthen maze surrounding the central common. The clinic or hospital located on the northern perimeter had grown from cottage to rural proportions. Whereas before space provided room for both medical and surgical patients there were now four wards: two surgical, one with more beds for males than females and two medical. Also included were an outpatient area, a small laboratory and a larger operating theatre.

The O.R. had been gutted and renovated. The lower six feet of its walls were tiled with Istalif blue, terrazzo replaced the concrete floor and lighting was better. Beecher's door slab had succumbed to a used operating table, complemented by stainless steel instrument and wash basin stands, improved anaesthetic equipment and a portable X-ray machine. Other than a new roof and a fresh coat of plaster the recovery room remained the same.

Additional living quarters had been constructed to house an increased staff. Tom Bereskin had two teachers responsible to him and there were half a dozen other missionaries employed on the medical side. Dr. Ivor Silversmith was an internist; Olie Bradigan, a retired engineer from Manitoba, ran the lab and x-ray machine; and the Clark sisters, Betty and Maureen, both RN's from New York, managed patients wherever they were sent. The men were married and their wives helped when they were needed, which was most of the time. Accompanying this new team to lend his undaunted enthusiasm came Dr. Beecher F. N. Best with endurable Lil and their boys.

The years spent with Dr. Robb had been stimulating, but in limbo at the Cancer Research Institution was hard to take. Beecher had no concept of what his superior was trying to do, and was inept on the job. He had broken more test tubes than his salary was worth.

The surgeons at the Paediatric Hospital hadn't been kind either, nor had ageing. A permanent furrow knotted his brow, his hair was thinner and a paunch forced him into blousey shirts. He hated the work at the hospital. None of the attendings would allow him to touch a patient without their being present. He had asked a horde of questions - too many according to one surgeon - and was told to look up the answers in a text. When Beecher complained to Robb he was told he was exceedingly argumentative. 'Stop acting like a smart ass, Beecher,' his mentor said. 'You're here to learn, not to tell everybody what to do.'

    Gradually he withdrew, putting in time until his case came up for review. Surprisingly it passed quite smoothly. As Robb had predicted, there had been a turnover of disciplinarians. Dr. Geoffrey Robb BSc., MD., FRCS(C), FRCS(E), FAAOS, etc., told the panel Beecher's work had been acceptable and he personally would have no qualms to take him into his office as an associate. He didn't tell the Committee Dr. Best had been rehired by the church as a medical missionary or that he'd arranged for his protege to spend six months in a General Surgery rotation to prepare him for overseas' work. Beecher was simply released, bursting with enthusiasm and goodwill.

    Dr. Robb and a number of elders had shown up at the airport to wish the team 'bon voyage'. His remarks concerned his envy and how he wanted to go along.

Robb was rarely out of Beecher's mind. He was thinking of his champion as he closed an incision at the base of the throat. Throughout the case, an open reduction of a dislocated clavicle, he had been remembering Robb's advice to the residents. A houseman had operated to reduce and hold the broken shaft of a collar bone with a Steinman pin. An x-ray revealed all was well and the patient was discharged. Robb didn't think so and gave the resident hell. Never put a pin of any sort in a kid's clavicle. It'll migrate, possibly out of the bone, and you'll be lucky to find it. Six weeks post op., Beecher saw the child in the outpatient clinic. The pin hadn't migrated at all, and by x-ray the break had united. It was easily removed. The pin was plain, not threaded like the one he had just inserted.

    My pin shouldn't move either, Beecher thought, Besides the pathology is different. This boy has a dislocation of the proximal end of the collar bone, not a mid-shaft fracture. Drilling it was easy. He re-examined the joint, happy with the stability and dressed the wound.

    "What about a sling?" Ms. Clark asked.

    "He won't need one, Maureen. But if you must, put one on; it won't do him any harm."

Lillian turned off the oxygen. Beecher had not learned the language, so she asked, "What shall I tell his father?"

"Back in a week for stitch removal."
"Any precautions?"
"Nope!"

The patient's father waited patiently, his swarthy features taut with worry. Lillian tucked the boy's chart under an arm, courteously shook the man's hand then excused herself to read the history.

Bereskin, the only other person at the mission fluent in both Farsi and Pashto, had interviewed the father when his son was brought for treatment a week ago. He was thorough and had written in Pashto. According to Bereskin the father was a Maldar, leader of the semi nomadic Shinwari tribe, wandering from their winter quarters near Jalalabad to greener pastures in a mountainous valley east of Bamiyan.

The teenager had fallen, climbing a rocky cliff. As the incident occurred in a remote area, several days had elapsed before the Maldar arrived at the mission. By then the front of the throat and upper chest were swollen but the boy was in reasonable shape.

Lillian stopped reading momentarily as she recalled the discussion preceding surgery. Controversy had arisen over Beecher's proposed treatment and she assumed it hadn't been relayed to the father. Argument stemmed from Dr. Silversmith's suggestion of leaving the injury alone. 'Does it matter if he's left with a lump at the base of his throat! The pain will go away and I doubt if he'll have any problems.' However Beecher had his way, contending an open reduction besides diminishing the bump would prevent post traumatic arthritis.

The Maldar didn't understand the surgeon's words; he could see the obvious lump. The swelling should be reduced. What escaped him, was putting it right would not be as big a problem as holding it. His son, Abdul, should've stayed at the hospital until it was safe to discharge him, but the Maldar was anxious to leave. Now Lil was faced with having to interpret the importance of the pin in Pashto.

She struggled through an explanation, using a bobby pin. Uncertain he had understood, she reiterated Beecher's message of the necessity of remaining. The Maldar shook his head unconvinced. Tossing the tail of his turban over a shoulder, he claimed. "It is October and time to leave before the snows begin." Motioning toward the back of his truck, he said, "The trek has already started."

The box was packed with black goat skin tents and nondescript baggage. Three crones, their leathery faces shaded against the morning sun, were perched in their black shawls amidst an assortment of small domestic animals. The rest of his band had started the migration on foot and by now should have traversed the Unai pass. He would wait for them in Kabul where he and Abdul would go to Begrami on the King's birthday to watch the Buzkashi.

You leave at your own risk, Lillian advised, worried with her translation and wondering whether she had used the correct pashto word for 'risk'.

As the plane fizzled to a stop in front of the air terminal Jim restated how much smoother, quieter and faster the jet flight had been than on his first visit to Afghanistan. "I flew in a D.C.6 then," he said, leaning forward to face Dari who was seated next to the aisle. "Remember that old crate? You couldn't wait to get off."

"Yes," Mahmud nodded thoughtfully, "I had many worries, but not this time."

"Darling," Merri smiled and patted Jim on the thigh. "Please can the comparison. I'd like to discover this place gradually and not be told a dozen times how it was or what to expect."

Jim grinned. "I won't say another word." Difficult for him because he was more excited than before, knowing what was in store.

Outside the Kabul airport his wife pointed at a figure completely covered in a red silk shroud carrying two caged birds on her head. "I know she's wearing a chadri but what are they?"

"What's what?"

"The birds! What species are they?"

Jim feigned indifference. "I'm not telling. You'll have to find out for yourself."

"That's because you don't know," Merri chortled.

"Oh I know! You'd never believe me and as soon as you find a bird book you'll look it up to prove I'm a liar."

"Try me."

"Okay," he agreed. "They're caged crested double breasted sugar tits."

After the Lindsays were assured of transportation Mahmud left with a promise to contact them soon and found his way to the Landrover where he joined Taraki, the new driver. Allah had not blessed this motorwan with Ghubar's height and bearing but he made up for it in effusiveness. By the time Dari arrived at Gulbahar he had heard all the latest household gossip.

In the courtyard his father and Khushal greeted him joyously, alternately kissing, hugging and holding hands. They congratulated him on the baby and Khushal promised to fly him to Bamiyan.

"It has been a long time my son," Malikar barely managed, his cheeks wet with tears.

"Too long father! Much too long," Dari agreed as he gripped the frail old man in his arms, thinking a strong wind would knock him down.

Malikar's wit was mercurial. "Tell us all about the U.S. of A.," he croaked, "Are the people as snoopy as the volunteers sent to help us?"

"Sort of. They attack their own paragons through the media. Nothing is sacred. They are just as aggressive and intolerant at home as they are here. Canadians are much the same except they tend to stagnate. Neither appear to have any manners."

When they were seated in front of the walk-in fireplace in the large room off the main hall Dari resumed where he'd left off. "Lately I've had some adverse publicity, an insinuation mainly. A woman accused me of attempting to rape her."

Khushal smirked. "My virtuous little brother! You?"

Dari continued, "The charges have been altered. Her husband claims I wilfully wooed her away. Alienation of Affection it's called. I doubt if it warrants a jail sentence but it could be expensive and worse - I could lose my temporary licence to practise."

"Did you?" Khushal found it fascinatingly funny. He could not imagine Dari stealing another man's wife. Nor did he understand the charges. If anyone carried off one of his wives he would be grateful. Stealing horses was something else.

"No I didn't. Although the opportunity was there."

"How's that?"

"I was alone with her many times."

"And nothing happened?"

"I swear as I'm standing here!"

"Then she must have been a hag?"

"No she's extremely good looking."

The facts seemed out of line. Khushal shook his head. "You sure you didn't do anything risque?"

"I'm sure for the last time!"

The sardonic grin on Khushal's tanned face dwindled as his mind revolted. "Then you really are a fool little brother!"

A hush fell. Dari ignored the remark and his eyes swept the magnificent room. The glass cabinet containing Malikar's artifacts still adorned the end wall. Before him, above the heavy oak mantle was the majestic urial head, preserved and postured like the Markhor he'd seen in Niagara. "Harrington," he murmured.

Khushal scarcely heard him. "Who's that?"

Dari didn't answer but turned to his father. "Did you ever meet a Canadian hunter by the name of Bosco Harrington - Bob Scofield Harrington or possibly Robert S. Harrington."

A blank stare accompanied Malikar's negative reply. "If I did I can't recall. I haven't met many foreign hunters. How long ago was he here?"

"During the fifties. He'd be about your age."

When it appeared Malikar had no recollection, Dari referred to the cabinet. "I see you still have your collection."

His father sighed, "I was going to donate it to the Kabul Museum. We do have a building now." He paused. "But I've changed my mind. I'd hate to have them destroyed or vandalized. Better if they were buried where they were found."

Fair enough, Dari thought. Antiques had never been one of his pursuits. He smiled and speaking slowly said, "I also have dug up something of interest." Then he told them of Nicole. How he'd learned of her demise, the deaths leading up to it and an unknown aunt who had befriended him. Malikar was skeptical until his son produced a photograph taken at his father's third wedding reception thirty-four years ago. The old man drew a monocle from his vest pocket and studied the faces. The group was gathered around a table in a French cafe. "Ah, Nicole, yes I recognize her, and Oudette; she was taller, a brunette, more subservient than Nicole. I should have married her."

"She also sent you this," said Dari, producing another print smaller and richly coloured. It was a photograph of Nicole and Oudette standing before Niagara Falls, a squat surly looking man between them. Dari laid a finger tip on the picture. "He was Nicole's second husband, a German. He climbed the fence behind them and jumped into the current." Other photos of the Falls and environs materialized, then snaps Dari and Roxane had taken over the last four years, until the box was empty.

Outside the light was beginning to fade. Replacing the pictures Dari decided it was time to listen. But Khushal seemed reluctant to talk.

With prodding his stepbrother finally related he was tired of the present government, blaming most of the problems on the King who was trafficking drugs, and speculating the ruler himself was a junky. University graduates and those trained abroad were having difficulty procuring government posts and were joining the leftists. Khushal muttered if there weren't drastic changes soon there'd be a nasty civil war.

CHAPTER SEVENTY

Early next morning Khushal and Dari took off for Bamiyan in Malikar's Cessna. They flew west over brown and yellow autumn fields, into the Ghorband valley. At seventeen thousand feet, breathing in the pressurized cabin was as easy as in the American jet but how much more enjoyable was the scenery. Dari wanted to reach out and touch the snow.

The small plane waggled a wing at a massive peak and with altitude to spare, cleared the Shibar pass. Soon it began to descend, gradually angling away from a steep soft purple bluff to come in low, skimming an encampment of conical yurts, clustered on a bank of the Bamiyan Rud. Kushal made it look so simple, landing them on a gravel airstrip near the hotel.

A short time later Rishtya and his driver rolled up in four wheel drive and after a further round of happy greetings the trio climbed into his range rover and headed west.

Five miles past the Valley of Foladi, the Rover mounted a low foothill and upon reaching a pistachio grove at the summit, passed through a gate into Rishtya's fortress residence. They stepped out into glorious sunshine and were immediately encircled by Roxane's family.

Dari took his wife in his arms, sweeping her off her feet. "I thought I'd never get here," he smiled, spinning her around. "Let me look at you Roxane. You're as beautiful as ever."

"I've just fed little Soroya and put her down but as you've come so far, I'll let you have a peek," she teased.

The baby's eyes were open when her parents entered the nursery. She was staring at a mobile, dangling above the bassinet; hearing her mother's voice she instinctively turned her head.

Roxane placed a tender hand on Dari's shoulder. "See how you attract women, my love."

He reciprocated with an arm around her waist and smiled, thinking you don't know the half of it.

Holding each other as if their life together had just begun, they stole the short distance to the cradle and stood, gazing down at their precious little gift.

Roxane picked up the infant, cradled Soroya in one arm and reached into the crib for a blanket. The swaddled bundle was lovingly presented and Dari drew Soroya to his chest. Gently he supported her tiny head as it bobbed backward, striving to focus on this stranger. She was dark and delicate like her mother, soft against his cheek. Then he held her away from him, regarding her more objectively. "You're sure she's all right?" he asked.

"Why not," Roxane declared. "She's a Mahmud."

"Exactly why I'm worried. How are her feet?"

"Fine! They're like mine - dancer's toes."

Dari put the baby back in the bassinet and removed her night shirt and nappy. As Roxane watched, little Soroya was rolled around, until she became unsettled and began to cry.

"You're right," Dari announced. "No club foot, no hip problems, nor has she anything wrong with her back."

His wife wrinkled her brow as if subjected to a minor insult. "You certainly are rough! I've a mind to change doctors."

In the middle of the night Roxane got up to feed little Soroya and her shuffling about awakened him. While waiting for her to return Dari lay, thinking of something she had said.

Shortly after his arrival she told him about the delivery. 'She had an epidural block at the Mission Hospital across the valley. No pain at all, and guess who gave the anaesthetic? Lillian Best!'

Now fully alert Dari shuddered. Best himself had to be in Afghanistan. But so much good has come my way, he thought, revenge doesn't make sense. What good is it? The incident is best forgotten.

When Roxane returned to bed he told her about his move to Canada: the new apartment, his ordeal with the written part of the Fellowship, the pleasant association he had with Dr. Lindsay and his family, and a serendipitous aunt. But he put off the Harrington affair because he didn't know how to approach it.

He wondered why. Was it a tinge of guilt? It was easy to rationalize his innocence, he had done no wrong and was no longer tempted by her. What if she had taken a less aggressive approach? Would she have broken his resistance? The answers, praise Allah, did not matter. Roxane was soaring as a result of having a baby and they had a phenomenal daughter. He prayed to Allah and thanked him for being so bountiful.

The next morning he lay beside his wife, still talking as if half their world had slipped by, pouring out their hearts. It was like old times, a cherished custom from America when he was not on call to sleep or lie in bed, discussing the order of the day and to plan the future.

Finally he brought up Tanya, and how she had come to him for treatment, her hospitality, her irascible husband and how he had saved the man's life, her visits to his apartment and her odd behaviour following the surgery. "How did I let myself in for such treatment? It seemed like a nightmare!"

She soothed him. "It all happened so fast you were almost carried away." Roxane paused, a jealous notion traversing her mind. "She must have something special."

Dari laughed. He felt stronger, having aired a possible transgression and pulled her towards him. Mrs. Harrington hadn't got away with a thing. If she had been wilfully trying to wreck his marriage it hadn't worked.

Kabul was not the delight Jim had described. Although Merri found the sights and sounds compelling, the smell was repulsive. She had been complaining to the Smiths during breakfast.

"You need to get upwind of it," Walt was explaining. "We plan on doing that this morning. Yar Zamir is dropping us off at the Bala Hissar. From there we'll follow the Kabul wall over Sher Darwaza. Why don't you come with us?"

Betty Ann Smith, five feet tall in pumps, was a 'little general,' as her six foot husband Walter, a gynaecologist from Elgin, Nebraska, called her. "I don't know if there's room in the car," she whined. "Can't they provide a larger one?"

The vehicle available for volunteers was a five passenger Ford. The only one, it had to be shared. The new Country Director for S.E.R.V.E. Medicare, Carl Spence, had brought all of them plus their baggage from the airport. Jim mentioned how roomy it was, but remembering a promise to Merri, he didn't compare it to the much smaller Fiat, provided for volunteers on his last visit.

He was not keen on Betty Ann; she was too talkative. Sick to death of her, he would've declined Walt's offer but as her husband had said, 'There's lots of room in the Ford,' Jim felt obliged to go along.

From the moment they had been dropped at the annex Betty Ann had parked on the Lindsay's doorstep, whirring on about everything. Her father had died, leaving her an 'immense' fortune and she had plans of how it could be used to improve the Third World, mainly the emancipation of women. She and Walter were on a round the world tour and to please 'Stinky Finger', as she called him, had agreed to two weeks in Afghanistan. "The way these Afghans treat their women," she declared, "they should be strung up by the you know what!"

Last night at supper Betty Ann made it clear Dr. and Mrs. Smith were staying only two weeks, in spite of Walter's argument, 'It'll take longer just to find my way around the hospital.'

Merri, not to miss a chance of seeing something different, especially a hike along the wall, accepted the offer. "Sounds great Walt. When are we leaving?"

"Yar says he'll be out front at eight thirty."

The Smiths were already occupying the back seat when Jim and Merri found them. Behind the wheel Yar Zamir was reading the Karwan Daily. Walt moved to the middle to let Merri have a window seat and Jim folded into the front.

"You haven't grown much!" The orthopaedist said, directing his remark at the driver.

There was a delay while Yar put down his newspaper to identify the man who addressed him. Then his smile broadened. "Ah it is the tall ferangi with the camera," he cried. "Forgive'd me, your name elud'es me."

"Lindsay," Jim smiled. "This time I brought my wife in place of the camera."

The little Afghan still a study in brown clapped his hands and held them as if in prayer. "After so long'ed!"

"Huh!" Betty Ann was indignant. "You didn't tell us you'd been here before."

Twisting, Jim replied, "You never asked."

"I am happy this time you drive to Bala Hissar," said Yar, starting up the car. "The wall is too dangerous!"

"We're taking the wall too." asserted Jim. "Let us out on the gravel road, bordering the moat where you met me last time. We'll walk back. It's not far, nor is it far from the end of the wall to the Staff House. We won't need you afterwards."

"Why? asked Betty Ann.

"Sorry," said Jim. "I assumed you didn't have other plans for the day or that you might need the car."

"You don't understand." Betty Ann's indignation was growing. Lindsay was being uppity and mulish, not about to share anything. "Tell me why is the wall dangerous?" Neither Yar nor Jim answered, instead they talked of the transformations in Kabul. She persevered until Jim finally told her.

"It isn't really. You'll be alright as long as you've got a good pair of sneakers and don't go close to the edge." He did not mention the encounter he had on his last trip.

Their ascent began at the cemetery below the ragged towers of the Bala Hissar. Merri started off and when Jim overtook her, said, "I can't stand that woman. Why don't we light out ahead?"

"I agree," he replied and began to jog.

Glancing back, Merri saw the gap had widened, "Thank goodness her legs are shorter than her tongue."

"Madam! How unkind!"

They cut north-west and climbed a hill, connecting the eastern end of the wall to the Citadel. The downtown section of the city extended below them.

"Is that an observatory?" Merri asked and pointed at a structure off to their right.

"No. I think it's King Nadir Shaw's tomb. Beyond it - see that elevation - that's Bemaru, a height Babur controlled long ago. It was from there he ordered his troops to attack the city."

"Who was Babur?"

"I'm not sure but I think he was from India. I'm glad you're along. It was boring the first time, no one to ask questions or share this beauty and history." He put his arm around her shoulders and kissed her forehead. "Not just anybody."

Recalling he was not entirely alone on his last trip over this mysterious mountain, Merri asked, "You sure there's no danger here? What about the crazy man who attacked you. You don't suppose he's lurking around?"

"I doubt it." Jim spoke as if he didn't give the idea a second thought.

They walked for some time along the north side of the wall. Near the summit it veered more west. The rampart had widened a bit and was lower than it had been in the beginning.

"That must be the observatory!" Merri exclaimed, indicating a building farther to the north west, similar to the Mausoleum of Nadir Shaw.

"Wrong again," said Jim, squinting from the bright sun now halfway to its zenith. Although the structure looked the same, beside its semi-spherical blue dome stood a tall minaret. "That's Masjid-i-Sherpur, the Sherpur Mosque. Just beyond it is the cantonment where the British troops encamped back in the second Anglo" - Jim stopped in mid sentence and exclaimed, "It was right here! Where I was attacked."

"How can you tell?"

"This view of the mosque and the bench. See!"

At the base of a buttress was a rectangular projection. His gaze travelled to a cleft in the wall. He looked through into an enclosure. "I cut across the rampart at this point. It was a warm day. I took off my tie and jacket and sat about here."

A narrow strip of level ground lay between them and the brink where the land dropped off steeply. "Hashim fell and landed about" - again Jim halted. Thirty feet below was a mound of rubble dissimilar to the general terrain, more like the unevenness of the ground inside the rectangular enclosure behind him - or a Muslim grave - "there," he concluded, studying it curiously. A gleaming substance, smoother and whiter, projected from the heap of rock.

If it was a grave there was only one way to find out. He backed over the edge and scrambled down the slope.

From the edge of the drop she watched him remove several large stones and pull away a fragment of cloth and something resembling a bone. Waving his findings he started back up.

Without a rope, he soon ran into difficulty. The steepness and crumbling shale forced him to traverse the slope lower down in order to attain the path. Jim reached his wife about the same time as the Smiths.

"What you got there?" Walt asked.

"A souvenir," Jim grinned. "I've discovered the Ratbils' burying grounds."

Back at the annex Jim described his investigation to Merri. "The body had decomposed. All that remained was the skeleton and bits of cotton cloth. The cloth was part of Hashim's clothing," he smiled, "But most Afghans wear the same dirty shade of grey. The skull was intact, fallen away from the vertebra and the face was unrecognizable. His neck came apart in my hand, probably because it had been broken. The fall must have caused his death." Jim paused reflectively. "It has to be Hashim. What I don't understand is why Mahmud lied. I can't remember his exact words but I believed Hashim had gone. 'Nothing but rocks on the side of the mountain,' he said."

Merri smiled. "Could fit. Dari wasn't specific. The man's spirit had left. He didn't mention the body."

CHAPTER SEVENTY-ONE

The first half of October passed unbelievably fast. While Jim operated Merri took a tour each day, beginning at Pushtunistan Square in front of the Khyber restaurant. According to the Afghan tour guide, in the past year there had been two thousand Canadians and six times as many Americans, with an increasing number arriving each year. There were so many others to share a common interest she was relieved when Betty Ann elected to take a taxi instead of accompanying her. "It won't work anyway," the little general declared. "I'm due at the Zahishqah Women's Hospital in an hour. Walter's lined up an appointment for me to talk to the matron. I want to set up a nursing scholarship in memory of my Pa."

  In the evening they swapped experiences; Jim excited about challenging operations and Merri awed by everything else. "You will never guess what I saw today darling," she said, after the first tour. "Gardens! Babur's and the those at Chilsitoon Palace, incredibly colourful. Mausoleums! The Kabul Museum. I saw coins like your friend gave you."

  Thursday she was more enthusiastic, especially after Carl Spence asked if the Lindsays would like to drive to Bost for the week end; he had equipment to deliver to the hospital. The Smiths could have the five passenger Ford, Merri thought, all to themselves plus poor old Yar Zamir.

  "I think you'll enjoy the Medicare facilities, better than at the Avicenna. It's a beautiful building, cleanliness throughout, particularly in the operating suite. And," the Director grinned, "we'll do some sight-seeing along the way."

  "You're on!" said Jim. "How can we refuse?"

Leaving at dawn on the Muslim sabbath, they rolled into their first stop, breakfast at Ghazni and saw the ancient towers, built of sun-baked brick and inscribed with Kufic characters. They visited the bazaar where smithies sold guns, copper samovars and silver bracelets.

  "Interesting, how they group together," Jim noted as he bartered for a dyed sheepskin coat for Julie. There were a dozen stalls in a row, all selling posteens, gorgeously embroidered and of vivid colours. He refused the first's price and by the time he reached the end of the line, refusing one man after another, the cost had split in half. While he was negotiating with the last, the first who had been trailing along, lowering his price competitively, was rudely ousted by Spence.

"What did you tell him?" Merri asked as the Afghan slunk away.

Carl smiled, "Roughly translated I called him the son of a snake. I was a practitioner of black magic and would have his appendages removed."

After detouring north for a look at the Helmand Valley Project's dam on the Arghandab river, they arrived in the strategic city of Kandahar, stronghold of patriots. At Chihil Zina, he took them to another landmark, the Forty Steps, carved into a vertical rocky outcrop. "Go ahead," he recommended. "Climb to the top, if your legs are strong enough, and gain a spectacular view."

An hour's ride west near Girishk, they pulled off the main road to inspect an intake head of the Boghra Canal system. By a wider dispersion of water it was turning acres of barren land green and fertile.

"The canal hasn't been particularly successful. The locals still dig for water," Carl said, braking beside a well of sorts.

Two men were unravelling a heavy rope from a reel, lowering a third into a hole. Before the one to be interred disappeared Merri asked, "Why does he have a bucket slung from his shoulder?"

"To clean out a plug in the primitive irrigation system or qanat," Carl explained. "It's been in existence for years. The underground water table, covering the root of the mountain, forms a tunnel under the desert. It branches and rebranches at varying depths usually deeper toward the base of the mountain. Holes are dug to the tunnel and hence to the underground stream. The team is performing a highly dangerous operation."

To confirm what Carl had said, the rope began to joggle and the two men beside the hole strained at the winch. The sweeper, minus his bucket, was hauled up choking and spitting, his baggy clothes covered in mud.

"It's important those chaps get along with each other," Carl commented seriously, once the Land Rover was in motion again.

Jim couldn't help commenting. "Not only are you fluent in the language," he smiled, "you've adopted their sense of humour."

With all the delays it was well after dark when they stopped in front of the rest house in Bost, equivalent to a four star hotel in North America.

Saturday morning, after Jim tried unsuccessfully to reduce a couple of old fractures, they went off again, this time to the ancient city, partially engulfed by desert. Scorched sand was all that remained of the effluence of the Helmand river. They took pictures, one of the famous arch of Qala Bist. As they parked beside the soaring brick span Carl indicated, "Framed by the arch is a mountain and the remains of a castle. In the heat of summer, seen from the desert it floats like a mirage."

The second week was also unforgettable with a trip to Paghman on Wednesday, and an invitation from Malikar to spend their third weekend at his Gulbahar qala. "For as long as 'Dari's friends' wish."

"You call this work, Jim Lindsay," Merri tittered. "With two Sabbaths the work week is cut in half."

Jim grinned. "Wait till multiculturalism takes over back home. With all the holidays added there won't be a workday left."

They were picked up by Malikar's driver, and after arriving at the qala, were treated to a light meal. A spectacular aerial survey of the Hindu Kush followed, including a hedge hopping flight over the Salang pass. Khushal would have taken a short-cut through the tunnel if Merri had not objected strenuously. He laughed recklessly, but apologized for the fright he had given her.

At supper they talked of many things, on many subjects, though none of Malikar's Farsi speaking wives joined in. When Merri reverted to the use of her hands and produced more laughs than nods she gave up and chatted with the men.

After the meal the head of the house paraded them through his antique collection, and Khushal with his stepbrothers, Kamal and Ahmad, entertained them musically; in the morning their down bed was difficult to leave. The following day Malikar proudly displayed his stables and showed them through his textile plant where he presented Merri with cotton sheets and pillow cases.

At the union of the Ghorband and Panjshir rivers they explored the ruins of Kapisa. "This is where I discovered many of my antiques," he stated. "There's not much to be found today but the site offers a stirring view of an Alexandrian fort."

The absence of Roxane and Dari was disappointing, but relieved by Dari's late arrival with an invitation from Rishtya to have them visit his qala in Bamiyan some time before they left.

"What I've really come to ask, is for you to come with me tomorrow to the Buzkashi in Kabul. Every year the game is played on the King's birthday."

It was the highlight of the month, according to Jim. They were seated under a striped black and yellow tent in Ghazi Stadium when Merri refuted him openly. "It's not a game; it's organized mayhem."

After seeing a black stallion slam into a lesser horse, her husband was inclined to agree. "No worse than ice hockey," he said.

"Why do players try to kill each other instead of getting on with the game?"

Listening to her, Dari explained, "It is essential; how else can a chapandaz keep the calf away from an opponent if he doesn't use force?"

Merri was captivated by the pageantry. The King occupied a crimson armchair in the central section. Two teams in brilliant chapans of scarlet and green, black and gold, colours of the Afghan flag, opposed each other, and the fans with such a variety of faces and dress created so much rumpus by the end of the game she was breathless and could barely reply when Dari introduced, "The star performer, my best friend, Sayyid from Baghlan."

The man was short but his body was as stout as the trunk of an oak. In halting English and with a glint in his almond eyes, he acknowledged the guests. A brief smile twisted the livelier half of his round flat face, and his speech was slow like a boxer's.

"Vedi khoob," he said and returned to the Circle of Justice to accept the coveted King's banner on behalf of the winning team.

"I'll tell you more about him someday," said Dari. "He was a brilliant student of agriculture once. Almost died during a game. Now Buzkashi is all he remembers."

On their late afternoon return to Karti Char, relaxed in Mahmud's Land Rover, thinking of the past seventy-two hours, the Lindsays couldn't remember having had a more exciting time. When Dari let them out in front of the Annex in the chilly October air, they thanked him and asked that he convey their elated feelings and gratitude to his father.

Do Unto Others 617

"Yes, I will" he answered, "but you must not forget to favour me by coming to Bamiyan. Roxane will never forgive me if I fail to get your - His remark was cut off by a messenger.

The man had run up behind them, labouring heavily. "Dr. Lindsay, you go to hospital. A truck come," he began to stammer counting on his fingers. "Fu fu fuhty five minutes ago."

"I'll take you," Dari offered.

"Just a minute," said Jim and turned to the messenger."What's the problem?"

The man was not sure, nor did he know enough English to converse. He gestured indifferently.

Dari finally got through in Farsi but all he could learn was a teenage patient had been admitted with severe chest pain.

"Sounds like a case for an internist," said Jim.

Dari nodded and asked a few more questions. "He says it was Dr. Kash who asked for you."

"Okay," I guess we'd better find out what this is all about." "You sure you don't mind dropping me?"

"I have nothing important to do. I'll give you a hand."

Merri was standing at the annex gate as her husband raced away in Mahmud's landrover. She shook her head, thinking. Here I am halfway round the world with lots of things to talk about and no one to listen.

The boy was dead when Drs. Lindsay and Mahmud arrived at the Avicenna Emergency.

Trying to bag breath into the lungs, Amir had given up and was disconnecting the respirator. "No use!" he exclaimed, dejectedly. "He no breathe on his own. No heart sounds. Massage not possible." The resident surgeon looked sadly at Lindsay and continued, "When he brought in, I here. Then he conscious but in shock. Low BP. I do cut down and pump six bags of blood vedi quickly, no response. No BP. I put tube in bladder. No urine comes. I give him oxygen, no use I stop. See for self," he added lifting an eyelid. "Pupils no constrict."

"What do you think caused it?" Jim asked.

"No time to talk to father. Too busy try fix him."

Jim had a superficial look at the body and noticed swelling and discoloration at the base of the neck. It appeared to have been cut and sutured, according to the cross markings on the skin - a surgical incision. "What's that all about?" he asked.

"No chance to find out."

Mahmud had seen the scar and while Amir and Jim were talking, slipped into the hall to question the father.

In a moment he was joined by the others.

"What's he saying?" Jim asked, growing impatient.

"Two weeks ago the boy had an operation at the Ferangi hospital in Bamiyan. When he awoke his father took him away - the father is a Maldar of the Shinwari tribe from Jalalabad and removed the stitches himself two days ago. Everything was fine until the boy collapsed at the stadium. His father brought him here by truck."

"I would like to see what was done," said Jim, thinking aloud and led Dari away from the father. "How much have you told him?"

"Sir, I haven't said anything. He does not know his son is dead."

Jim smiled cynically. "You are very good at hiding the truth my friend. You told a white lie in '64 and got away with it. Maybe you can tell another. I'd like an autopsy. Can you persuade the father it would be in Allah's best interests to allow it?"

Dari ran his fingers through his hair. "So! you found out about the madman?"

"Yes. I killed him and you buried the evidence."

"Half right," Mahmud smiled, his sparkling blue eyes teasingly benevolent. "Yes, I buried the body," he admitted. "You didn't kill him. Call it an accident."

Dari paused, "I think I might be able to stretch the truth again. But why go so far? Get an x-ray first?"

Jim considered the suggestion momentarily, then asked Amir, "Can you arrange it?"

Dr. Kash shuddered at the idea of doing anything further. The boy was dead. No treatment would bring him back. He should be given to his father for burial. "Why?" he asked.

"It's the next best thing to an autopsy."

"No portable. Body must be taken to X-ray Department."

Realizing his approach would not carry any weight with this visiting surgeon and was only keeping him at the hospital longer than required, Amir frowned and went to find a porter.

Dari covered the boy with a blanket and returned to the father. "Lala-jan, he said, "your son is in a coma and might die. We need an x-ray. If you will forbear and wait here we'll be able to give you news soon."

The films did not disclose what Jim had expected to find. The collar bone was not broken but had been dislocated from the breast-bone. A threaded Steinman pin was not in the joint but lay in the soft tissue.

"It must have pierced the heart or Aorta," Jim commented. "Now that we have the modus operandi we should produce the weapon. I still think we should try for an autopsy."

Mahmud grasped the film. "I will see what I can do. You must stay here. I wish to talk to the father alone."

Jim read success in Mahmud's expression when he came back a few minutes later, though the Afghan sounded grave. "He agreed on the condition we give him the pin when it is removed."

"How did you get him to agree?"

"I told him his son was dead and it was urgent we remove the pin. I showed him the x-ray and explained the pin might have caused his son's death by penetrating the heart. He looked frightened but for a different reason. If the boy is to be admitted to paradise he must be pure," Mahmud explained. "No foreign bodies should be admitted with him. I told the Maldar there'd be no problem if we removed it.

CHAPTER SEVENTY-TWO

"You've got a telegram Dr. Lindsay," said Betsy. "It's on your desk."

Jim opened the envelope, wondering if Mahmud had received his communique. Before he and Merri had left Bamiyan Jim promised to forward news from the Royal College regarding the results of the Fellowship Examination. Learning Dari had passed the 'writtens' he had kept his word. That was over a week ago and if his associate didn't return soon he'd miss the practical and orals due to begin the following week.

Mahmud's message was succinct: 'arriving BA 092 Toronto International at 5.40 pm. Nov. 6th.' Great! Jim thought I'll be there to meet him.

Betsy brought him coffee. Before opening the rest of his mail he savoured it, thinking how rapid air travel had become. The world was shrinking. It had taken only two days for Merri and him to reach home from almost halfway around the world. One week ago Dari had seen them off at the Kabul airport.

The trip to Bamiyan had been terrific, ending their Afghan tour. Khushal had flown them from the Kabul airport to the extraordinary valley. They had grown fond of Dari's devil-may-care brother. 'More considerate of us than his wives,' Merri objected, 'keeping them cooped up in his compound the way he does.'

Rishtya's qala was not as extravagant as Malikar's. The residence was dark and Germanic. Fortunately they had been allotted a pleasant room on the second floor with a western exposure and could look over the eight foot wall encircling them. On the clear sunny days they could see from the pistachio grove as far as the caravanserai, embracing the mission.

Jim was unaware Beecher had returned until he went with Rishtya to satisfy his curiosity.

Bereskin kindly showed him around. At tea when it was revealed his visitor was from Canada, precisely Shipton, he had exclaimed, 'Then surely you must know our Beecher Best!' Jim was surprised. There had been no feedback from the Ontario College and he had lost track of Best since the hearing. Keeping abreast of Beecher's activities was not his concern; he had more important things on his mind, mollified by Beecher's elimination.

So it dawned the mission was where Best started his career. There being no other Christian centres in Afghanistan it also had to be where the Shinwari lad had been treated. If Beecher had performed the operation his two year's of supervision had not done him any good. When Jim asked about the boy, Bereskin didn't know. Beecher had taken his family to Herat and was not around to answer questions. But the mission's other doctor, Ivor Silverstein, had filled in the details. Appalled by the outcome he was also very sorry. 'In fact,' he'd said, 'I advised him to leave it alone. Maybe I should have taken a stronger stand.'

Consoling Silverstein, Jim had commented, 'If you'd written a textbook on the subject it wouldn't have meant a hill of beans. Beecher never listens to anybody.' Jim backed up his remark with more devastating slurs all of which were gossip as far as Silverstein was concerned. After telling of the trouble Beecher had caused in Shipton Jim had ended his tirade with, 'He's finally killed someone. What more can he do? The idiot must know better than to stick an unthreaded pin so close to the heart.'

For Jim's unsolicited bluntness Silverstein had rebuked him, 'In the words of our Lord, let he who is without sin cast the first stone.'

Jim remembered Rishtya's remarks made on the way back to the qala. 'It is with our self-imposed restraint Christians are allowed to stay. Long ago they erected their cross, which we have made them take down. If it wasn't for the valuable service they provide, we'd force them to leave.'

Valuable service be damned! Jim thought. Service of a sort, certainly not for the purist. How could any doctor practise scientific medicine in such an intellectual vacuum? Was it better they had no service at all? Fatalists, putting their trust in Allah. As for the missionaries, was their spiritual satisfaction more important, an overall sedative, covering a multitude of sins?

He had brought up Best in a private conversation with Dari on a jaunt to Band-i-Amir Lakes. There was such a nakedness about the barren hills and pure blue water, as if earth held no secrets. After reciting the trouble Beecher had got into while he was in Shipton, Jim listened for the first time to Dari's dismal affair, of how vain he'd been to have his foot fixed, Best's promise to correct the deformity, how dry gangrene had resulted from damaged blood vessels and the subsequent amputation by another surgeon.

Dari had spoken of his desire for revenge. 'It doesn't matter to me any more,' he concluded. 'I'm content with my lot. He'll get what's coming to him someday.'

But Mahmud's 'lot' might be on a downswing, Jim thought as he opened two important looking letters. One was from the Ontario College, asking for a reply to a complaint they'd received from Tanya Harrington, concerning Dari's indecent behaviour towards her. The other requested Dari to appear at an Examination for Discovery regarding charges laid by the woman's husband.

On Wednesday the 22nd on November, Dari set off for Toronto alone. Now as the time of his final examination neared a calmness settled over him. All his labour, restlessness and periodic desire to chuck the whole thing seemed to have happened to someone else. His brain was dormant - as it had been when he approached the writtens in September - waiting for the right question to awaken it. Questions he asked himself had no answers.

The written part of the examination for Fellowship had been held in several centres throughout the country. Dari had chosen London because he'd never been there and wanted to see another part of the Province. But he saw very little outside his small room, his books spread around him. The only other familiar object was a photograph of Roxane with Soroyo on her lap, propped on a night table.

Between papers he'd lived in a daze, now and again taking an hour off to go out for fresh air. It had been a writing marathon, continuously for three hours on three consecutive days, until his fingers had become numb and his head reeled. He had no idea of how he had done, just a typed notice he had passed the 'writtens' and was entitled to take the 'orals'.

For the vocal section there was no choice; he had to appear in Toronto. On Dr. Lindsay's suggestion he'd taken a room in a motor hotel on Jarvis Street. The place was not cheap but he stayed because it was quiet, had a good restaurant and he would need his rest and energy. Nothing seemed to worry him.

The practical at the Toronto Hospital went very well. He had allowed himself the full allotted time to work up the case, an old woman on the surgical ward; and had been there since she was crippled in a motor vehicle accident years ago. One by one the trainees had a go at her, straightening her bones and replacing her joints. To complicate matters the woman had a severe case of osteoporosis. As he knew the condition intimately, having seen it often among the swaddled women of the zunana, he thought he had written a good report. It was anything but a straight forward problem and consisted of a dozen pages.

Asked to bring her x-rays along for comment he was standing in the hall holding them when Dr. Geoffrey Robb came out of a small conference room. Robb extended a welcoming hand and after hearing Dari's accent, asked where he was from.

Robb's familiarity became embarrassing when he turned to the other two examiners, Briggs and Salmon, and loudly proclaimed, "this man is from Afghanistan." Returning to Mahmud he asked, "You must know Dr. Beecher Best? He's there with the Christian Medical Mission."

"Yes, I know him," Dari scowled.

Neither Briggs nor Salmon had been favourably impressed with Robb's white haired boy. Their smiles broadened when Dari sprung his reply. "My footless extremity has the distinction of being the result of his first orthopaedic blunder.

There was an abrupt hush. To Dari's surprise nothing was asked regarding Mrs. Vivian Beadle, the patient whom he'd been responsible for working up. Nor were his examiners curious about her interesting x-rays. Thirty minutes later, after covering a number of orthopaedic topics he was dismissed by the Toronto group with instructions to report at 2 pm. when he would be interrogated by three men from other centres.

Vivian Beadle's case proved more interesting to the out-of-towners who left not a stone unturned. The eleven major fractures Vivian had sustained were discussed. Mahmud was asked to diagnose, comment on various choices of treatment and prognosticate.

All went well until the matter of the patient's long-standing osteoporosis arose. "Because of this complication," Dari told his examiners, "I would not recommend an operation."

"What do you know about osteoporosis?" Parker had asked.

"It's a serious weakening of bone, leading to fractures and deformity," Dari replied. "It's a loss of connective tissue, Sir."

"I see. Would you please define connective tissue?"

"It is the whole body between two layers of single cells, one lining the gut, the other forming the superficial skin."

"What makes up this connective tissue?"

"Matrix and cells."

"And the matrix?"

"It consists of water, minerals and protein fibres. There are hard and soft matrix, depending on the ratio of these integral substances. Bone and cartilage of course belong to the former.

"In osteoporosis are all substances lost?"

"Not necessarily. Primarily there is a loss of protein fibre or collagen, but as some of the minerals such as calcium and phosphorus are bound to the collagen they too are lost. But it's mainly the loss of protein that causes the problem. Without protein the mineral has nothing on which to adhere and floats around in body fluids."

"What do you know about amino acids Dr. Mahmud?" Wakefield asked.

"Protein differs from the other two organic chemical substances, carbohydrate and fat, in that it contains nitrogen. When proteins are broken down into smaller and smaller units amino acids eventually result. In reality they are acids of ammonium salts - the ammonium being made up of hydrogen and nitrogen."

Gibbons was anxiously awaiting his turn. "Essential amino acids, Dr. Mahmud. Tells us about them?"

"The nitty gritty," he replied, "is they are the amino acids found in nature and can not be synthesized in the body, but they are still essential to life. Various investigators differ on how many there are, reportedly between eight and twenty."

Mahmud paused dramatically and repeated the words "they exist", then continued. "Like the first two letters of the word amino acid itself 'am' - I am, or I exist. It's remarkable," he added, "how many times those two little letters 'am' are involved in reference to existence. Amon, the supreme Egyptian deity, the God of Life itself, was such a powerful human even the Egyptian kings suffixed his name to their own, such as Tutankhamon or Tutenkhamen - no matter, it's all phonetic spelling anyway - which leads us to 'amen' a Christian utterance, to acknowledge the word or existence of their Lord at the end of a prayer."

Dari spread his hands like a Mullah and shrugged. "Life! Existence! Coming back to the amino acids, they are derived from ammonium which occurs naturally in Lybia, close to the temple of Ammon or Jupiter as the Romans called their supreme God. Interestingly, the substance ammonia found so many centuries ago was named in honour of Ammon, the God of Life, because of its property of reviving consciousness, the smelling salts commonly used. In the old days without a scientific explanation the substance was thought to have the property of returning life."

Dari paused again, smiled broadly and said, "Getting back to the problem of Vivian Beadle, she's running out of existence. I would never operate on her."

There was a silence during which Mahmud studied the reaction of his examiners. No one returned his gaze. Had he told them something they hadn't considered, or had he failed?

"Dr. Mahmud," said Parker. "You've a very conservative outlook. One might gather you don't believe in surgery at all and wonder why you've spent so much time studying it. Tell me one thing. How do you look upon the Specialty or the Medical Profession as a whole?"

When Dari said nothing, trying to form an answer, Parker rephrased his question. "What do you think is important in contemplating any form of treatment?"

"To do no harm."

In the following silence, Dari realized the oral was over. Parker and Wakefield were observing him with peculiar expressions. Gibbons was smiling. Finally Parker turned to the other two and said, "If there are no further questions I think we can let this man go." Gibbons promptly rose and opened the door.

The same evening, with forty other hopefuls, Dari received a slip of paper, informing him he had passed. There was no one there to congratulate him. Feeling so elated he couldn't keep from running, he reached the motor hotel and a phone.

Expecting Dari's call, Jim answered on the third ring.

"I made it!" the Afghan announced. "I didn't think it was in me."

Jim laughed, "What do you mean? Congratulations! Well done!"

Dari smiled. "All the hard work hasn't been for nought. Now I must wire Roxane as soon as I can find a telegraph office. Tomorrow it's work as usual. See you in the morning, chief."

CHAPTER SEVENTY-THREE

The developers of the Parkway Mall encircled Gerhardt Fast's dining room. Heavy maroon draperies over the tall windows at the back and sides of the antique mansion shut out any prying eyes and the cold night air. For additional security his position at the head of the massive mahogany table provided Gary with a guarded view of the traffic circle out front, allowing sufficient warning should an unexpected visitor drive in. Gary was not antisocial; he was shy and reclusive. Having someone arrive unannounced was contrary to everyone's best interests, especial town planner Fred Arsenault and Mike Herzog, MPP for Niagara West. Their presence, in the midst of such a high powered enterprising company, could be misconstrued as crooked, when all they intended was to benefit the community at large with an irrelevant supplement to their incomes. A difficult situation to explain to a community-minded individual.

Both men were presently seated with Issac Honsberger on Gary's left, Noel and Marvin Husselman to his right. In the grate behind the chairman a fire had died to smouldering ashes.

Marvin rose and began to fill his brief case.

"Noel and I want you to remain for a while," said Gary, placing a hand on the lawyer's arm. "We've some personal things we'd like arranged. The rest of you are free to go."

"Isaac Honsberger spoke up. "I'd like some confirmation my bills will get paid. Construction is on schedule because I've doubled the shifts, and my unionized crews are demanding time and a half. If I'm to meet their pay at the end of the month I'll need another hundred thousand, or the brick layers will go on strike. With cold weather coming completion of the framework could be delayed till spring.

"Make him out a check, Noel." Gary ordered. "Another thing Mike, telling us the ramp is in the works isn't enough. You've got to get it legislated soon. Traffic should be rolling off the parkway before the Mall opens, not months later. Think of the money we'll lose."

Gary sounded like a military commander as he fired more orders. "You might see if the Province can float a loan to the township, eh Fred, to finance the sewage and water supply you've planned?"

Then he shot them a parting grin. "While you guys are doing your duty Noel and I will keep signing lessees. We've over eighty, and next week I hope to land Eatons who want fifty thousand square feet."

When Honsberger, Arsenault and Herzog had left by the rear entrance Gary turned to Husselman.

"Noel and I are in up to our eyeballs. Between us we can swing it without selling shares on the market. The rest are in for a percentage, to be negotiated when the project's completed."

"That'll be around ten," Noel suggested, nodding in Gary's direction, any figure to keep Husselman coming and silent.

Gary missed the gleam in Noel's eyes and looked annoyed. His friend had no idea what the final tab was going to be and giving their money away was damn stupid. Success was not guaranteed.

"My final fee will be worth more than that," Husselman complained.

Gary frowned. "You'll be lucky if you, Honsberger, Arsenault and Herzog receive that much collectively. Besides Marv, you're making plenty off us already. We could drop you and hire somebody else cheaper. Lawyers are dispensable, a dime a dozen. So be a good chap and do as you're asked, draw up the lease contracts."

Marvin had no chance to reply, as Gary swung into the chief reason for his being detained. "We want codicils to our wills. We're leaving everything to each other in case something happens."

Noel laughed. "It's a policy, Marvin, to ensure everything works out and you'll get your share. What do you think of that?"

Marvin rolled his head from side to side. "I'll go a step better and have your wills completely rewritten. It really makes no difference."

Actually it did matter to Gary; he didn't trust Tanya Harrington. In case the worst transpired, he wanted her out of it.

Gary regarded his life-long friend. Noel looked healthier than he had in years and Gary told him so.

"I haven't had a drink since you saved my life," Noel replied adding, "And Tanya's been treating me super."

Gary grunted, well acquainted with Tanya's peculiarities. "Nevertheless, Marv," he insisted, we want codicils. Just be a good chap and draw them up right away.

The Examination for Discovery was the seventh of December at the James Street offices of the Court Recorder D. B. Pemberton. Dari had provided councillor Jorgenson with every available scrap of information, but nothing of the alleged illicit relationship with Mrs. Harrington could be disproved. The only documented evidence, relating him to her, was the office and hospital records which were useless other than to confirm the plaintiff had been a patient.

Tanya had shown up with her husband and Marvin Husselman whom Linus despised. For a long time Husselman had been suspected of illicit behaviour but no one would accuse him.

"It's your move my friend," said Linus, recalling the last time they'd opposed each other some three ago. "This time," he added, "I represent the defendant."

Marvin smiled at the Harringtons and popped a peppermint in his mouth. He rolled it around his tongue as he addressed Pemberton. Discovering he was on tape, he spat it into his podgy hand and proceeded to read aloud from his notes. "From the 3rd day of July till the 26th of August inclusive Dr. Darius Abdullah Mahmud did wilfully act to cause an estrangement between my client, Mr. Noel Molyneaux Harrington, and his legal wife Tanya, nee Chernofsky. Mr. and Mrs. Harrington befriended Dr. Mahmud during the aforesaid period of time and he took advantage of this friendship and his professional relationship with the wife Tanya to alienate her loyalty, sympathy and admiration for her husband Noel. The defendants action through the aforesaid interval was immoral, disgusting and unbecoming of a man in his professional capacity."

"Okay okay," Linus interrupted. "We admit after Dr. Mahmud arrived in Shipton the Harringtons were kind to him and this relationship did begin on the 3rd of July. Prior to that date, though he'd never met Mr. Harrington he had occasion to meet his wife professionally as a co-worker at the General Hospital and as a patient two days before he appeared at their house."

Linus slid a sheet of paper across the table to Husselman. "This is a list of dates supplied by my client, outlining as clearly as he can remember, when he actually visited the Harrington's home and the evenings Mrs. Harrington showed up at his apartment, uninvited. Mr. Counsellor, I might add, it's up to you to prove my client is worthy of the charges you are bringing against him. If you have no evidence you have no case!"

"For starters he gave gifts," Noel blurted.

Husselman was on his feet instantly, "Now just a second, Noel. I'll handle this."

"Says who?" Noel retorted. "I'm paying your way whether you talk or not, so sit down and shut up."

"What sort of gifts," Linus asked.

"Wine, chocolates, flowers!"

"When?"

"Each time he came for a visit."

"That's all?"

"That's enough!" Noel glared. "He made a big fuss about it, hugging and kissing her."

"Nothing more personal?"

"Perfume," Tanya interjected. Prying open her purse she drew out a tiny leather pouch and extracted a bottle of Este Lauder.

"I see," said Linus. "You could have purchased it yourself."

Tanya denied this vehemently and turned to Husselman. "Am I to sit here and listen to this bull...these lies?" she corrected herself.

"There's more to it," Husselman remarked. "I believe the Dutch used similar items in the purchase of Manhattan Island from the Indians." Linus thought for a lawyer getting paid for saying nothing, Husselman was wasting a lot of imagery.

"These trinkets," Marvin continued, "were to sweeten the enticement and they worked. My client's wife felt obliged. She reciprocated and took gifts to Dr. Mahmud at his apartment."

Linus began to chuckle. His big fingers were spread out on the table. He brought them together prayerfully. Looking straight into Tanya's amber eyes, he asked, "Who is seducing who?"

"You misunderstand," said Husselman. "My client's wife took food to Dr. Mahmud. He played on her sympathy, her maternal instincts, pretending to be cooped up in his apartment studying for exams." Then Marvin got off on another tack. "My client had not been well. I have a letter from his family physician, Dr. Gerhardt Fast, indicating he was suffering from a liver ailment which cut down on his libido. It culminated in a bout of pneumonia, following Dr. Mahmud's first visit to the Harringtons."

"Wasn't it the result of his near drowning?" Linus asked.

Tanya regarded Husselman, then Noel. This was news to her. Noel neither admitted nor denied it.

Linus continued. "My client, at great risk to his own safety, went overboard to rescue him."

"A God damned blooming lie," Noel shouted. "That stupid Paki with his bloody peg-leg probably can't swim a stroke."

"I must warn you," Pemberton advised, "everything you're saying is on tape." The court recorder's face cracked as he added, "including libellous statements."

"Also," Marvin smirked, "there's the sex. Because of my client's loss of libido, Mrs. Harrington had to go elsewhere. According to her, Dr. Mahmud had been most obliging. He started treating her on the second visit. She was complaining of pain in her lower back. In front of her husband, he had her lie in a supine position on the floor, flex her hips and knees, then with one hand behind her buttocks and the other in her crotch, raised her pelvis. He did this manoeuvre several times until she was able to carry on doing the exercise herself - pelvic rocking he called it. She found it helped for a while but because she had previous advice from a gynaecologist who said her low back pain was caused by a retroverted uterus, she asked Dr. Mahmud whether she should go back to the 'gynie man'. Mahmud had said what you need is more sex, a male organ, thrashing around inside, will do you a world of good." At this point Husselman smiled pruriently, adding, "Dr. Mahmud did a pelvic examination on Mrs. Harrington and confirmed the gynaecologist's findings. Afterward he continued to treat her sexually until her husband began to feel better."

"Mr. Harrington quit drinking, his libido returned and he needed her himself. Mrs. Harrington went to Dr. Mahmud and told him their relationship was finished. That same day, he tried to rape her. As evidence of this heinous act I will submit one torn pair of panty hose, endorsed as belonging to her, by her maid and witnessed by her chauffeur. Both of them accompanied her to Dr. Mahmud's office on the fateful day."

Standing outside Pemberton's office, Mahmud could not believe the charges. "Tell me, Mr. Jorgenson," he asked. "How do they arrive at fifty thousand dollars? If all Harrington was missing was a bit of sex and had to buy it, the cost would be no where near that amount."

Jorgenson laughed. "Depends on where you shop." His facetiousness tapered as he continued, "They haven't got enough evidence. No one saw you and her in a compromising position. It's her word against yours. If we offer them a cent we're admitting guilt which is what marvellous Marvin is trying to get."

"I've told you several times," Mahmud sighed. "I did not fornicate with her. It is true I taught her those pelvic exercises in front of her husband. He made a lewd joke about it then. The rest of her story is confabulation."

"Well," said Linus, tilting his head sympathetically, "Today's investigation is nothing compared to what we face. I hope your medical peers at the College will see through her."

CHAPTER SEVENTY-FOUR

Early Monday, the 13th of December, Linus Jorgenson picked up Dari at his apartment and left for Toronto, planning to arrive at the Ontario College's chambers in plenty of time for the scheduled 9.30 am. inquiry.

Twenty minutes later Marvin Husselman saw Mrs. Harrington into his Chrysler New Yorker and packed himself behind the wheel. As he steered onto the main highway he asked, "Where's Noel?"

Tanya sighed audibly. She had to think. "I heard him talking to Gary last night. They're flying over for a meeting."

"Toronto?"

"Yes, I believe so, something about a client."

"Too bad!"

"How's that?"

"We could have flown with them."

"I doubt if there'd be room. They're each taking a passenger."

"You mean they're taking two planes?"

"Yes they usually do. They're like a couple of kids trying to outmanoeuvre each other." Tanya checked her watch. "They won't be leaving till later." She opened the front of her mink coat and adjusted the skirt of her suit. "Let's not be exactly on time, but no later than ten minutes," she added, thinking she must not appear too eager. She had designed her entrance to attract attention and would play the role of a woman disgraced, though reluctant to point a finger. She had to sound convincing. That bastard Mahmud! Holier than thou Asian! She'd fix his hash. By the end of the day he'd never practise again.

The Chairman of the five member Discipline Committee opened the meeting ten minutes after the appointed time, bowing to Tanya's implored forgiveness for being late. The Notice of Inquiry was then read out, charging Dr. Darius Abdullah Mahmud with professional misconduct for:

(a) engaging in sexual impropriety with a patient.
(b) engaging in conduct or an act relevant to the practice of medicine that having regard to all the circumstances would reasonably be

regarded by members of the profession as disgraceful, dishonourable and unprofessional.

While the particulars of the alleged misconduct charge were being read Dari looked about the room, wondering what it was used for otherwise. Opposite himself and Linus sat the complainant and her lawyer. The advocate for the College, Mr. John Lloyd-Davis was on their right. He heard his name mentioned.

"I'm sorry Mr. Chairman," he said, "could you repeat that."

"How do you plead Dr. Mahmud?"

Dari's voice was firm and of medium volume. "Not guilty!"

John Lloyd-Davis took over and in his opening remarks submitted the crux of the case involved an assessment of the credibility of the protagonists. As the College's lawyer said he would be taking evidence from the complainant. Dari whispered to Linus, "Isn't that Husselman's job?"

Keeping his volume on a level with Dari's, Linus replied. "The College's lawyer acts for both sides."

"In other words I'm guilty as far as the college is concerned until we can prove otherwise."

When Lloyd-Davis finished his opening remarks with a reiteration of the Complainant's allegation that her treatment had included sexual intercourse with the defendant, Linus was on his feet immediately denying it and stated Dr. Mahmud's relationship to Mrs. Harrington was strictly the management of an ailment which he treated surgically.

Tanya then testified that on June 29th she went to see the doctor with pain between the third and fourth toes of the left foot. He advised her to wear flat shoes for six weeks which she did. It did not improve and Dr. Mahmud scheduled her for surgery August 12th. She was discharged from the hospital the next day and had her sutures removed two weeks later.

"I have not come because of my foot ," Tanya, acknowledged righteously. "It doesn't bother me now. It's because of his behavior. The first time I went to his office I invited him home for dinner. I felt sorry for him. On his first visit he met my husband and a family friend, Dr. Gerhardt Fast. My husband and Gary took him sailing in the afternoon. Noel took sick on board and when they returned the doctors put him to bed. Dr. Mahmud stayed quite late. Eventually I left him lying on the couch and went to bed. He was gone at 9 am. when we came down for breakfast."

"He came back every Saturday until the middle of August. The sexual encounters began gradually. On the 17th of July, I was having low back pain and he offered to fix it. He had me lie on the floor with my knees bent. 'You must tense your buttocks and lift your hips toward the ceiling,' he said. My husband can verify this. I don't think Noel liked the way Mahmud was handling me with one hand under my rump and the other between my thighs right on my crotch, lifting upward."

Tanya groped in her handbag for a kleenex tissue and sniffled into it. After a moment she continued. "The following Saturday I told him about my 'retroverted' uterus, a diagnosis made by my Gynaecologist.

"Dr. Mahmud said he never took anyone else's word and if I agreed he'd do a pelvic examination. Of course I agreed."

"He had me lie on the bedroom floor and start the pelvic exercises. This time he placed two fingers in my vagina while I was lifting up my pelvis. He said his fingers were keeping my uterus in place and he made me continue until I had an orgasm."

John Lloyd-Davis interrupted Tanya's testimony. "Where was your husband all this time?"

"Out at the boat slip. I could see him from the bed."

"I thought you said you were lying on the floor."

"Well," Tanya threw up her hands, "the bed, the floor. Does it matter. I knew Noel was out at the boat."

"When did the sexual intercourse begin?" Lloyd-Davis shook his head. A faint smile crossed his mouth. He found it hard to believe her. There had been a lot of weird stories told within the sacred walls of the College but this had to be one of the most novel excuses for introducing sex he had ever heard.

"A week later I took food to his apartment. He was studying for an examination. He had been very thoughtful, bringing flowers, candy or wine whenever he came to call, so I thought it proper to pay him back."

"I see. And the intercourse?"

"He asked if I needed another treatment."

"Before or after you told him your back was bothering you?"

The table suddenly jerked as Linus rose from his chair. "Mr. Chairman," he declared. "I object. My learned friend, you have just asked the complainant a leading question."

"I'm allowed to do that Mr. Jorgenson. You may proceed Mrs. Harrington.

Tanya resumed her narrative. "I returned to Dr. Mahmud's apartment several times and each time we had sex, often more than once."

"During his illness Noel quit drinking. He began to regain his strength and libido and treated me like a human being. I felt guilty, particularly after Noel made love to me. I refused Dr. Mahmud and he came to our house begging me to leave my husband. He just wouldn't take no for an answer."

Tanya ended her testimony by repeating her version of the alleged rape following the surgery on her foot.

"One thing I don't understand Mrs. Harrington," Lloyd-Davis asked. "Why did you have the operation?"

Tanya pulled herself up in her chair. "Because I needed it."

"Well," said Lloyd-Davis, pausing to shake his heavy jowls. After a moment, thinking Tanya's story was so neatly put together nothing made sense, he asked, "How could you trust him?"

"I've never been afraid of him; not until he tried to force himself on me."

Jorgenson waived cross examining the complainant until Dari had been given a chance to testify. He introduced the defendant and quickly established Dr. Darius Abdullah Mahmud was a well qualified orthopaedist, pointing out he had only a temporary licence and was under the supervision of Dr. C. J. Lindsay.

Dari refuted the sexual allegations in a cold off-handed manner. In his opinion the woman was a liar and his anger radiated like a spiked collar on a bulldog. He did admit teaching Mrs. Harrington the pelvic exercises but the rest of her evidence was confabulation. He stressed the near drowning of her husband and how he saved the man's life. "Dr. Fast can testify I'm telling the truth," he stated, sorry Gary had not been subpoenaed to attend.

Linus raised his greying eyebrows and stood. "I have one question to ask Mrs. Harrington." Turning to study the faces of the doctors around the table, he smiled. "I believe it is important before making a diagnosis to get a thorough history, including a list of the patient's Past Illnesses," he commented. Delaying long enough to assure himself of their attention he went on. "In this case, Past Behaviour, is a more appropriate term."

There were one or two agreeable nods which encouraged him to proceed. Looking at the complainant, he asked. "Tell me, Mrs. Harrington, how many men during your marriage to Mr. Harrington, have you seduced?"

When Lloyd-Davis objected to the word 'seduced', Linus rephrased his question. "With how many men other than your husband have you had sexual intercourse?"

Tanya opened her chic yellow jacket and pulled a fresh Kleenex from a modestly revealing satin blouse. "None", she sobbed and covered her face.

"If you expect me to believe that," Linus affirmed, "I would have to include Dr. Mahmud among them."

The principals were excused while the committee members remained to examine the evidence.

Seated in the antechamber Dari asked, "How long do you think it'll take?"

"Hard to tell," Linus replied. "The longer they're out the worse for us because they'll be placing credibility on her testimony. There's nothing we can do now. Relax my friend, we'll just have to wait and find out."

Close to noon, unexpectedly the street door to the antechamber was flung open and Gerhardt Fast appeared, so rumpled it looked as if he'd been up all night. His faint blue eyes picked out Tanya right away and he blurted, "Noel's dead! He damn near got me, the reckless fool! I don't know what happened. I heard his engine and a bang as his landing gear struck my plane. I was too busy controlling the Cub to look for him. I think he went down in the lake. Herzog was with him."

There was not a trace of emotion in Tanya's bearing. Just a pretty face with a body dressed in a canary yellow suit. She could have graced the cover of a fashion magazine. Husselman who had sat as if he were part of the furniture throughout the Inquiry clasped her by the elbow. "Let's get out of here. I'll take you home."

"No," she asserted. "This business isn't finished."

Gary watched her from a few feet away. Not a sign of remorse. She's like a big cat after a kill, waiting to gorge herself. A one track mind - money. Poor Noel. Gary picked a chair placed against the wall and slumped into it. Christ, she's not even curious about how I got here. Look at her. Who the hell is she smiling at? Or is she smiling at anyone. He hated her.

After Fast's appearance they didn't have long to wait. It had been difficult for Mahmud to sit in the anteroom, staring at Mrs. Harrington and her lawyer friend. He felt like killing her. The heavy silence, particularly after Gary had burst in, was unnerving. So Noel was dead, a finality awaiting attention. The verdict Dari awaited was a living issue and it throbbed with his racing pulse.

Finally they were invited to return to the chamber. Gary found a vacant seat and slouched similar to the way he sat in the antechamber, his head inclined against the panelled wall. In a moment the Chairman read out the Committee's decision.

"After considering all the evidence and having duly deliberated the seriousness of the charges, we find the allegations against Dr. Darius Abdullah Mahmud to be proved and find him guilty of professional misconduct. On the issue of the penalty the committee has decided his temporary licence to practice be revoked."

Gary swore under his breath and stood, scraping his chair abrasively against the wall.

"Just a minute Mr. Chairman," he shouted. "I wasn't here during the testimonies so I don't know what so-called evidence led you to arrive at your decision, and not having sat through your deliberation do I know what member of your committee coerced you into such ridiculousness."

The Chairman who had been caught off base by this intrusion suddenly found his voice. Staring at the dishevelled figure glaring back at him with equal intensity he demanded, "And who are you?"

"Mr. and Mrs. Harrington's personal physician. Fast's the name. I've known this woman for over ten years. Whatever she's told you is a pack of lies. She's a confirmed nymphomaniac and she only married Noel for his money. She'll go after anything in male pants." Gary began to laugh hysterically but suddenly stopped. "Sorry about that Mahmud," he added pointing at Dari, "this guy saved her husband's life some five months ago. What more does she want? Noel was my best friend and he's dead."

Gary dropped back into his chair, holding his head in his hands. His breath came in gasps but not a sound crossed his lips.

Jorgenson had seen and heard enough. Addressing the chairman, he asked. "In view of what we've learned in the last few minutes I'd like you to either reconsider your decision or-"

"We can't do that, Mr. Jorgenson," the chairman interrupted, sounding mildly impatient. "It was based on the evidence heard today. But you can appeal it and ask for a new trial."

"If we have no other recourse, fine. That's exactly what we'll do. But I think it would be extremely improper for you to publish this man's name in the College's Annual Report or anywhere else." Jorgenson couldn't get over the whole incredible scene. "Some time ago, you tried a man in this same room for incompetence, negligence and professional misconduct. His name was Best, Beecher F. N. Best. You found him guilty on all counts but let him go with a reprimand and a proctor to mother him awhile. His judgment hasn't changed and it has come to my attention recently, through an error of commission, he is responsible for a death. You'd likely never hear about it if I hadn't told you because it happened in a far off land. Today through some medieval notion you're going to deprive this man Mahmud of his livelihood." Linus paused to draw in a short breath. "But far more important you're denying excellent surgical care to your fellow human beings. What kind of justice are you dishing out?"

Epilogue

1972 - Nawruz

Dr. Mahmud & Dr. Best

MID 1972

Bereskin nervously rumpled his baseball cap. "How good of you to come, how very kind!" He said, jamming the cap on his head.

Once his baldness was hidden he reached out eagerly for Mahmud's hand. They were standing on the edge of the airstrip beside a DeHavilland, smiling.

While a few remaining passengers were disembarking Dari was first to let go and stepped back to study the Mission Chief. As he remembered Bereskin was an inch taller; he seemed to have shrunk. Loose flesh hung from his forearms and the cherubic face, Dari remembered, was crimped and haggard as if a malignancy were stealing his weight. "Nice to see you again Pak."

"It sure has been a few years!" Tom's rusty baritone clogged, "Thirteen I reckon!"

Taking the doctor's brief case he straightened, inhaling the summer air and turned to admire the background. "Another Bamiyan day," he declared, wrinkling his tanned brow. "Look at those frosty peaks, clear as a bell." Bereskin's smile broadened as he re-faced Dari. "It sure has been a long time; lots of snow has fallen since but it seems to have missed your dome."

"In light of my problems," Dari replied, "it is remarkable, Pak; but that's another story. Tell me yours first."

"When we're under way," said the Mission Chief. Suddenly remembering the urgency of his trip, Tom bolted for the Wagoneer, speaking louder, "It's good of you to come Dari. We didn't know what else to do, or who to call. I'm afraid it's gangrene. Yes, yes," he repeated, adjusting his seat belt. "How good of you to come!"

Old Tom was resounding like a cowbell and Dari was beginning to wonder if his past teacher wasn't a bit doddery.

Bereskin blushed as if he'd read the young man's thoughts. In fact he was glowing, having had his distress call answered so quickly. For the moment he could think of nothing else to say.

Nor was Dari in a talkative mood. A possibility had been presented which until recently seemed so remote he had all but forgotten. A chance to even the score. As it neared he had no idea how to handle it. In the past, many times, he had fantasized to meet his enemy head on, sword in hand, and lop off his foot, burn it off or dip it in boiling oil. He was young then, overcome with hate and bent on punishment.

In his telegram the Mission Chief had communicated, 'Dr. Best has a compound fracture of the leg, horribly infected. Please come.'

This stupefying news had caught Dari unprepared. He could not believe it. "What an opportunity!" he said, thinking how 'ironic' it was, repeating the word over each time it came to mind. A chance only Allah himself could've arranged. Dr. Best had to see him. Dari shook his head in disbelief. Best's need was urgent; it was no longer a case of vengeance, it was one of necessity.

Seated in the vehicle next to Tom, he closed his eyes, concentrating on the communique collected the day before. No details had been supplied, just twenty words handed over the counter at the telegraph office. He could have refused the call and would have, if it weren't for his feelings. Following acceptance his hands were tied; he had a duty to perform and he must do it to the best of his ability. Facing the instigator of his misery meant nothing.

How considerate of Allah to supply a reason - wet gangrene. An amputation might do Best a favour.

Tom swung the Wagoneer off the plateau and headed south-west across a valley. Turning to his preoccupied passenger, he asked, "How long have you been back?"

Dari mumbled, sounding disinterested, "I don't know, perhaps three to four months", and closed his eyes again. Leaning against the head rest, he gave the impression he didn't wish to be disturbed.

Bereskin concentrated on the dusty track ahead. In the streaky morning light he headed down a straight passage lined by tall poplars, quivering in a light breeze. Now and again he glanced at Dari, noting even the stroboscopic effect of the passing shadows did little to liven his handsome features.

They turned west at a T-junction, passed a bazaar and around the base of a cliff.

Beyond the valley Bereskin took the south fork away from the road to Band-i-Amir lakes. With all four wheels engaged he fastened his eyes on the uneven terrain ahead. His previous tire marks were easily followed across rolling foothills, weaving between dips and boulders, through a gravel wadi and across a narrow stream to re-appear on the far side.

While the Mission Chief picked the way Mahmud continued to meditate. His imminent meeting with Best was temporarily pushed aside by a more important decision, where to live and set up an orthopaedic practice.

Canada was no longer out of the question as he had feared following the first Inquiry. He had a letter from Linus Jorgenson and learned of their successful appeal. It arrived by courier with a bundle of documents and apologies from the Divisional Court and the Discipline Committee of the Ontario College after re-trying the Alienation of Affection charge. The appeal was accepted in view of Dr. Fast's evidence; Tanya Harrington had not appeared to refute it. So Dari was clear. On the basis of his passing the Fellowship examination he had been given a licence to practise in any hospital anywhere in Canada, provided he had the Hospital Board's approval. If he passed up this opportunity he could re-apply.

The United States was another choice and there was Roxane to consider. With a small baby her preference was to remain in Afghanistan but neither of them wanted him to end up at the Avicenna. He smiled, thinking life is more complicated than making a diagnosis and choosing a method of treatment.

Bereskin had been driving for sometime, up and down, climbing again, before Dari opened his eyes. They were nearing the caravanserai; the top of its crenellated walls could be seen from the crest of each rise.

Tom waved his arm through the window, pointing toward a shallow valley to the north. A Kuchi encampment was taking shape and as they approached he spotted the battered green box of a lorrie. The chief nomad hunkered alongside, directing the unloading of its contents.

"They weren't here when I left earlier!" Tom noted, "Let's have a look."

The Maldar's name was Mustafi. He had come ahead of his Shinwari Kuchi to drop off the tents. Most of the others were strung out somewhere between the Mission and the Foladi valley. There being an abundance of fresh spring grass, Mustafi expected the animals would be satisfied and move along quickly, reaching the present site by late afternoon.

"Don't I know you?" Tom asked in Pashto.

The man's heavy moustaches rocked negatively and he fastened a look on the Mission Chief to discourage further inquiry.

"I know you," Dari joined in. "You're the Maldar I met in Kabul. I spoke to you at the Avicenna. You lost your son Abdul."

Mustafi's expression remained cold, haughty and malicious. He was going to lie to his interrogators but hesitated.

"Yes, I remember. You were here last October," said Tom. "If I'm not mistaken, I interpreted for you. Your son fell, while climbing the rocky Hajigak pass. You brought him here for treatment."

The Maldar's dark eyes compressed to flint and the rest of his swarthy features puckered with bitterness. He said nothing and turned from the Mission Chief to the Doktar.

Dari reverted to English, addressing Tom. "That is the truth. The boy died in Kabul of a ruptured aorta."

"Yes I heard, very sad. An orthopaedic surgeon from Canada came for a visit last year and told Dr. Silversmith about it."

"That would have been Jim Lindsay," Dari guessed. "He was very angry."

While they were having this private conversation the Maldar backed toward his truck, muttering an unintelligible phrase and Bereskin curiously asked what he'd said.

"He has cursed us," Mahmud translated, then straightened himself." Personally I don't believe in curses. Revenge is something a man must do for himself."

Bereskin felt a tug on his elbow as the Wagoneer reached an incline before the main entrance to the Caravanserai.

"Wait," said Dari, "I'd like to walk the rest of the way."

The Mission Chief considered the request unusual but braked and idled the engine.

"It's been many years since I climbed this hill," Mahmud continued, nostalgically. "When I was a child I bounded up and down like a gazelle. Even on my club foot I could scramble up as fast as Anisa, Sayyid and the others. Remember those summers so long ago Pak? We chose to come here rather than to the village Mullah. You taught us to speak English, and I'll be forever grateful. You taught us many things; more meaningful, you taught us with kindness, and kindness begets kindness regardless of religious belief. We played football on the common. Often the ball would roll out the gate and down this hill. We'd tumble after it, rolling, wrestling and laughing."

Dari paused, frowning, and his speech was almost indistinct. "The last time I came down I wasn't laughing, nor was I rolling and tumbling. I was so weak I could barely sit. They took me to Kabul. A week later my foot was removed by a visiting surgeon. It was gangrenous, 'the dry type' he said and would rot off. What a choice!"

"Three months before I was full of hope, full of the prospect of going to university. I'd thought very little of my deformity; my foot was ugly but it held me up. Then came the temptation, the promise and the disaster. He said he could straighten it and by the time classes started it would be healed, not perfect but so similar to the other no one could tell the difference. I was proud. At most things I was better than the rest, perhaps I tried harder. I became aware of the difference and it grew into an obsession, so urgent I had to have it fixed and consented to the operation."

Bereskin had heard nothing of Dari's ordeal before. His face softened as he listened intently.

"As an undergraduate while I was studying philosophy I came across an interesting passage from Nietzsche - he was neither Muslim nor Christian." Dari smiled. "If you choose to discuss his views Pak, we'll be on neutral ground. In those days like most students in search of truth I was more broad-minded. Nietzsche was an atheist and argued an individual's will to power resides within himself. Man does not need a supreme being. As I mature I disagree more and more with him. There has to be a divine power to interpret for us. If there's truth in anything it's not totally comprehensible to the human mind and someone has to point it out." Dari continued to smile as he went on. "So in my ignorance I am content to let Allah sort out the fine points; I even want to believe in miracles along with most Muslims."

"Be that as it may, Nietzsche's thoughts on Redemption through his prophet Zarathustra still fascinate me. 'If one takes the hump from the hunchback, one takes away his spirit; if one gives eyes to the blind man, he sees too many bad things on earth so he curses the one who cured him; but he who makes a lame man walk, does him the greatest harm, for no sooner can he walk than his vices run away with him.'"

"As I practise orthopaedics these thoughts haunt me. Every time I operate to improve some ailment, I wonder if a successful result will really benefit my patient. In my case, I suspect Dr. Best did me a favour because he made me into a greater cripple than I was. I became filled with more determination and lofty ambition than I'd ever had. Perhaps Nietzsche was right."

Throughout this monologue Dari had been staring at the hill in front of them. Finally he turned to Bereskin and with a trace of a smile added, "But the bracemaker has interfered and fitted me with this vicarious foot and ankle. Wearing it I'm no longer a superman, but just another artificial human being." Dari laughed, swung open the door and backed out of the Wagoneer.

Balanced on the ground he spoke louder. "Race you to the top Pak."

Bereskin watched for some time, noticing as the grade steepened Dari's progress slowed and the artificial foot rotated outwards. Like a skier ascending an icy slope, he turned sideways and inched upward. It was a heart-rending sight to old Tom. But his admiration of the man and his accomplishments, the pride of having tutored him in his early years and the pleasure he was now feeling overcame any pitiful emotion. In the twenty-five years Ruth and he had been teaching in this ancient part of the world Dari had been their greatest hope, their most brilliant pupil and he hadn't disappointed them. Ruth had never conceived. Without children of their own, they had temporarily adopted every young person who dared to come near the mission. Their 'borrowed children' sustained them. Neither the affluence nor security of western civilization offered as much peace of mind and they had no desire to leave. Retirement was never a consideration. The Bereskins were happy to carry on teaching until the encumbrance of age overtook them.

Certain Mahmud would make it to the top and the southern wall, Bereskin shifted to low gear and crawled up the hill. The vehicle was new, larger, enclosed and comfortably air conditioned, more substantial than the previous Jeeps. After succumbing in succession, they were blocked outside the main gate of the caravanserai, twelve years and forty feet apart. Like couchant lions they were a monument, testifying to the tenacity of his pedagogical implantations. He stopped the wagoneer midway between them and waited for Dari to catch up. "Come on, hop in," he ordered. "We still have a few hundred yards to go."

The climb had been taxing; Dari readily accepted and asked, "Now where?"

"Same old place, but new buildings." Steering in the direction of the northern battlements the Mission Chief stated, "Beecher's on the surgical ward."

"Tell me about it Pak, starting with what happened."

Before Dari could receive any information a score of fat-tailed sheep sprang from the ground and darted helter-skelter in front of them. Reflexively Tom braked and the engine stalled. He shook his head at the skittish beasts and turned solemnly to Mahmud.

"It's a terrible situation," he said, restarting the motor. "Beecher was hiking west of here with his two sons. Mike's okay but Robby has cerebral palsy. He's in his teens now and doesn't fare badly."

Beecher fell into a karez. The boys saw him climb a hillock and disappear. It's fortunate they were watching because the opening was only a few feet wide and partly obscured by shrubs. Robby waited while Michael went for help. That was a week ago. Beecher was semiconscious when I got to him."

Tom digressed, "There have been a number of changes." He pointed out new buildings as they drove by the school, heading for the clinic. "We have a couple of extra cars as well," he added, "owned by our engineer and Dr. Silversmith."

"Getting back to Beecher. I could hear him moaning and spotted him with a flashlight about twenty feet down. To get him out I drove up to the hole and lowered myself on the winch. I was cramped for space, especially when I reached the bottom and needed room to tie a rope around his chest. Before hauling him up I had to free myself. Not easy! Rested a lot, braced against the well wall. Once Beecher was up the boys helped and we laid him on the ground. He was pale and sweaty, plenty of abrasions and his right leg was twisted badly. We couldn't get an x-ray until Bradigan returned because he'd taken the keys to the new machine. We cleaned Beecher and splinted his leg. The bone was sticking out about two inches. Silversmith tried to set it the next day but he's no expert. We'd have sent him to Kabul but Beecher was in no shape to travel."

Dari recognized nothing. According to Bereskin, the whole place had been revised. Instead of one ward there were now four, male and female patients being admitted separately to medical and surgical wards. The small room where he had been confined following his operation had succumbed to the main entrance.

Lillian met them in the male surgical ward. To Mahmud she appeared thinner and smaller than when last seen; her mousy hair, more grey than brown, was untidy and her deeply-lined face bore dark shadows under the eyes. She put out her hand limply.

"How are you Mrs. Best?" Dari asked, accepting it.

She didn't answer his question directly. "Very kind of you to come, Dari. He needs help badly. Oh! I'm fine!," she exclaimed and added. "We haven't seen you in years, not since Beecher operated on your foot." His eyes were as blue as ever, still the colour of the Band-i-Amir lakes. Fascinated she remarked, "You're looking very fit Dari."

"Thank you," he replied and put his hand on her shoulder. "I see you've improved the place."

"There are a lot of things we still need. More bed space for instance." She motioned toward several patients lying on the floor and led Mahmud into a private room.

Beecher was resting on a hospital cot, his casted right leg raised by pillows. Dari recognized him although he was heavier and his hair was sparse on top. He also detected a putrid smell.

Dr. Best lowered his head and sweat streamed down his pasty face. "I'm glad you're here Mahmud," he managed with effort.

An interesting comment, Dari thought, wondering how Best had known to call him. "Why?" he asked.

Beecher gasped, "You're the only orthopaedic surgeon in the country, and I need help."

"I see! Just how did you find out about me?"

"We get reports. Shipton is our home. Your picture was in the paper last year - remember? People sent it to us." A coarse grin doubled Beecher's chin. "We know all about you."

Mahmud's face reddened. "So!" He exploded angrily. "You know all about me. Well, I'll tell you something you don't know because I think you should!" Dari stumbled over his words. The hesitation was momentary and he plunged recklessly ahead. "I lost my foot because of your incompetence. You were definitely the cause, cutting off the blood supply, performing an operation for the first time. Perhaps you'd never even seen it done before."

Beecher laughed deliriously. "Now you've come to cut off mine, giving you not an eye for an eye but a foot for a foot."

As his laughter became convulsive Dari wondered if Best had lost his mind. Either that or he had a toxic reaction to the infection. The situation needed rethinking. He had to gain control. Forcing a smile he said calmly. "May Allah's will be done!"

"Allah's will! my foot, my foot! Ha!" Beecher became hysterical, throwing himself about, hyperventilating.

Mahmud pinned him down.

In awhile Best became calm and regarded the Afghan forlornly. "How did you get here?"

Dari chose his words, careful not to trigger another outburst. "There are daily flights from Kabul and I had no trouble getting a seat on the plane. Feeling a bit better?" he asked.

"Still painful." Beecher whimpered.

The rotten stench emanated from the cast. Mahmud bent to inspect it and found a dressing soaked in pus.

"It's infected," said Beecher, "strange how fate has reversed our roles. The last time we talked you were in the bed and I was examining your leg."

Mahmud did not comment. An x-ray folder stuck out from under the mattress and he removed the films.

While he studied them against a window he heard Beecher say, "Not a pretty sight. The midshafts of both the tibia and fibula are broken transversely and the fragments are markedly displaced."

"Can you move your toes?" Dari asked.

Beecher, with effort, demonstrated he could move them down but not up.

"Have they been like this for long?"

"No," Beecher groaned. "Just since last night but I can feel them all right."

A temperature chart hanging above the bed indicated fever, at times slightly above one hundred and four degrees. A rise as expected had occurred over the first three days following the injury. After dropping to normal it started to rise again.

"According to what I've heard," Mahmud remarked, feeling Best's forehead. "Your injury was a week ago. Have wound cultures been taken?"

"Silversmith has plated three separate swabs," Lillian interjected. "Nothing has grown."

"That's because you've probably given him an antibiotic."

"Penicillin," said Lillian. "Silversmith put him on it."

"Do you have chloramphenicol?"

"Plenty, but it causes aplastic anemia. Our internist doesn't like to use it."

"It is still the best antibiotic for intestinal bacteria," Mahmud argued. "All dead muscle must be removed; anaerobic bacteria like the gas bacillus thrive on dead muscle. The wound has to be opened widely and left open to the air, otherwise it'll take forever to heal." He rolled his head impatiently. "The quicker we start the better."

Beecher whined. "Or I'll die!"

"Not likely," Dari consoled. "There's even a chance of saving your leg" - whatever prompted me to say that, he thought. For years I've plotted to remove it as painfully as imaginable. He clicked his tongue and added. "As you said, you owe me a foot. I'm anxious to collect but -"

"- then take the damn thing," Beecher shouted.

"- maybe not! I can't tell until I open your leg and have a look." Mahmud hesitated. Thinking aloud, he deliberated, "An x-ray out of plaster could be helpful."

"How's a bloody x-ray going to make any difference?" Beecher grimaced. "Get on with it. Take off my leg."

"Hmm," Mahmud droned brewing an idea. Sure he could do an amputation and save Best's life, but preserving the leg was better. "A good film," he explained, "might tell us the extent of the gangrene. Gas bubbles should show up. The infection spreads up and down along the muscle bundles, not across them. If only one compartment is involved, it's possible to eradicate the disease without amputating."

"Look," said Beecher, sweat pouring from his forehead. "Don't mess around. If your experiment doesn't work I'll die from toxicity."

Mahmud decided to pacify him. When it came time to make decisions Beecher'd be asleep on the table. "Okay, have it your own way," he said and turning to Lillian asked, "when can we start?"

"Immediately. He hasn't had anything to eat since midnight."

Dari looked around for Tom Bereskin but the Mission Chief had disappeared. Thinking Lillian could help just as well, he asked. "Would you get my brief case from the Jeep? It contains equipment I intend to use."

In the morning Mahmud found Beecher, sitting up in bed eating breakfast. After inspecting the external fixation device and tubes he'd inserted into the leg he noticed his patient's temperature had dropped but was not normal. "I think you're improving," he said. "How do you feel?"

"This time not so painful. What did you find?"

"Your anterior compartment was shot. I had to cut away most of the muscle. You won't be able to dorsiflex your ankle, but a spring-loaded brace ought to take care of that" - and a lot easier to manage than my prosthesis, he thought. "Of course the brace is a long way off; it will still take a few months for the bone to heal."

"How do you know you got out all the infected muscle?"

"We'll have to wait and see. The stuff left behind looked viable. In five days we'll be able to tell. Your friends have agreed to nurse you round the clock. They'll have to regulate the rate of flow through the tubes. There's also a profusion of oxygen bathing the wound. I don't know if it will help but it's worth a try."

"Where did you get the external fixator?"

"From Canada. It's holding the bone fragments solidly. You might even be able to walk on it; the device will take quite a pounding." Dari paused and smiled. "Bereskin very kindly drove me over to Rishtya's yesterday and I've borrowed a vehicle. I'll come by, same time tomorrow."

The Kuchis were now fully encamped in the valley. It was a large band. As Dari drove by he counted five black goat skin tents and seventy camels. Earlier the Maldar was seen on his white horse, riding in an easterly direction.

On the third post operative day Beecher's temperature was not quite normal but he felt well.

"When are you going to let my friends get some sleep?" he asked.

"Now's the time to be extra careful," Dari warned. "It's possible a secondary infection might have been introduced at the time of your operation. If your temperature stays down and there are signs of healthy repair tissue I'll stop the irrigation. I don't want anything disturbed, which means someone should keep a close eye on it." He added, "You're a long way from being cured. There's skin to replace and possibly bone grafting. You'll have to be patient. During the later stages you'll probably want to go back to Canada. I know I would."

Their conversation was terminated by a message from Sister Clark. Tom Bereskin wanted a word with Dari.

The Mission Chief was seated behind his office desk in the Administration block. "Is it possible," he asked, "we send our orthopaedic cases to you in Kabul? Beecher will be out of commission for some time."

"It would be better if you discuss your problem with Amir Kash, the Chief of Surgery at the Avicenna. I won't be around for more than a few weeks."

Bereskin looked disappointed. "Where are you going?"

"I'm not sure. Perhaps the Wazir Akbar Khan or back to Canada." Dari grinned. "Life is better overseas, more choices. If I succeed there will be even more, like the geometric progression you taught us long ago." Dari beamed, "I want an academic career, do some teaching."

"What about your own people?"

"They can't be taught much now. The illiteracy rate is too high and they don't care. They're happy to go on living in the same way, free to do as they please. Take the Kuchi band camped in the valley. They'll stay a few days and move on."

"That Maldar we talked to was here around midnight, asking for medicine. Claims some of his followers have dysentery. The man worries me. So far nothing has been stolen."

"How do you know?"

"We've checked everything in the male surgical ward where he was seen. Mrs. Bradigan took the eleven to seven shift last night and was attending Beecher's tubes. The chap just walked right in."

"Where was the ward nurse?"

"Sitting behind her desk where she's supposed to be. Apparently he passed her, unseen."

As Mahmud drove back and forth between the Mission Clinic and Rishtya's qala he forgot the incident of the Kuchi Chief and was barely aware of the Shinwari encampment, his mind absorbed with future plans. On the fifth postoperative day he noticed the Kuchis were still around. Strange, he thought, they usually don't stay so long in one place.

After he'd looked at the wound Beecher was in greater spirits. Due to Mahmud's interference healthy granulation tissue covered the incision, now extending from below the knee almost to the ankle. Turning to the doctor he exclaimed, "It smells good!"

Dari chuckled. "You mean there's no smell at all. The way it should be."

A cast was applied, incorporating the external fixation pins and everyone was instructed to leave it alone. "You can all go home and rest now," the surgeon declared.

Beecher agreed. "Maybe I can sleep myself; having them poke around all night isn't very conducive."

An Afghan nurse on midnight rounds shone a torch in Beecher's room and saw him outstretched in bed his eyes fixed on the ceiling. She called from the doorway but he continued to stare as if a jagged crack held some compelling fascination. Not until she turned on the light and approached the side of his cot did she notice the pool of semi-clotted blood and the deep slash across the base of his throat.

She threw a blanket over the body and very quietly reported her discovery to Dr. Silversmith.

Printed in the United States
1278100002BB/1-12